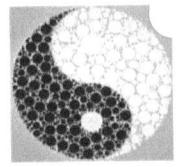

AMNION

(When Eternal Life is in Our Grasp)

a novel by Mark Fraz

~Available as an eBook or hardcopy at Amazon-Kindle~

Acknowledgements:

Patrick Cauchi – for the initial confidence and encouragement to write fiction
Anthony (Andy) Frascinella – for reading early chapters and providing constructive criticism

Civilization is a hideously fragile affair - there's not much between us and the horrors underneath, …..just a thin coat of varnish.
~ C.P.Snow

CHAPTER 1
Paved with good intentions

In this near future story, unprincipled men have redefined self-actualization through science, pitting unbridled entitlement against the defenseless.

****

In the late afternoon, the engineer calmly stood and swayed idly behind the smoked glass of his second floor office window at Lifespan Corporation in New Jersey. He was watching the melee at the corporation's front gate some 50 yards distant. *Just raising more dust for all that matters*, he mused.

Mike Santino stood relaxed with his hands in his pockets. He was used to years of demonstrations at Lifespan. There were always some small groups sporadically picketing for or against Decoupling - fetal cadaver reclamation. Usually they were kept outside the security chainlink fence down the block. Nobody really paid much attention anymore. The world had moved on, but today's spectacle was another story.

Santino's Director level entitled him to a window view that was one perk of being a higher-level manager. With the distant chaos, he felt grateful at this moment, that he only had the Facilities and Instrumentation Engineering Departments reporting to him.

While staring out the window, Mike immediately envisioned the dictatorial president of Lifespan. For sure, he figured, old 'Mad Max' was going to have a shit fit. This time his network of informers did not warn of the demonstration below. Moreover, his 'retired consultants' at the police department did not head it off like usual either.

Mike shook his head and laughed to himself, *Max, you're just going to solve this problem like you solve everything else. Spread more money around.*

Then his attention was drawn back outside to the main security shack. He could make out the gate sergeant at the back window with a phone to his ear. Mike assumed that about now, the guard was speaking with the squirming executives in the Lifespan high-rise office tower far behind his own building.

He ruminated sarcastically *They probably would gas 'em, if they thought they could get away with it.*

****

From inside his guard shack at the front gate, literally under siege, security sergeant Harry Sullivan peered up at the smoked glass windows on the fifth floor of the remote corporate offices. With his finger in one ear, he had to yell into the phone receiver to be heard above the din of demonstrator noise outside, "No! No! We can't just chase these people down a public street," he implored. "They're still outside our gates. Let's wait for the police!"

His boss, Jane Savage, shot right back, "Max wants them off the block and the police are tied up with that racial incident in Newark. They can't respond for at least another hour. And, there's word a TV camera crew coming!"

As an ex-police lieutenant, Harry knew better and plaintively warned, "We could provoke some violence here, there's women and little children in that crowd... infants!"

The answer came back without hesitation, "Are you listening to me? We want them out of here before the TV people arrive. You've got your orders. Get out there and do it!"

Harry hung up and cursed the phone, looking up and glaring one more time at the cold smoked glass edifice of the corporate building in the distance. He exhaled a deep breath as he turned to his men. "We do this my way. Nice and easy. No rough stuff. Leave side arms in the shack, no clubs."

His small crew of men stood ready to obey, each fearing the uncertainty involved in mob control.

"We'll use a company car," Harry directed, "and just nudge them back a bit."

As the chain link entrance gate was opened, the car crept slowly forward followed by guards on foot. The crowd immediately converged on it and the yelling reached a crescendo. Someone jeered, "Running out of babies for spare parts?"

Harry's men stayed close to the car. Forward progress was limited to only a few inches at a time. With dozens of provoked demonstrators surrounding them, any chance of crowd control was soon hopeless. His men began to feel hemmed in... And a bit scared now.

In the chaos, a woman at the front of the car became trapped between the press of the crowd and the front bumper. She started screaming hysterically that she was being run over. The other demonstrators reacted instantly. They pounded the car with placards and fists. The terrified driver stopped, he couldn't see anything through the windows anymore, just

4

flailing arms, and shouting faces pressed against the glass. All he knew was that he wanted out. With his rear view blocked by a human wall, in near panic, he put the gear in Park, and forced open the door to escape back to the guard shack with the other retreating guards. By now, back in the Lifespan offices, all work in the nearby buildings had ceased. Everyone was at the windows observing the debacle below.

Eventually, the demonstrators retreated from the car and migrated along the chainlink security fence, Mike Santino could not help but smile with satisfaction from his own office perch. He was witnessing the results of another stupid corporate decision made at the top. And at the same time, grateful not to be part of this evolving mess.

Mike folded his arms and breathe a sigh of relief. However, from his second floor perch, he noticed two demonstrators maneuvering something along the chainlink fence some distance from the main gate. That something turned out to be an aluminum ladder. They shoved it over the 6 foot high chainlink fence, sliding it between the horizontal razor wire strands at the top of the fence.

It caught Mike's attention right away, narrowing his gaze, and unfolding his arms. He and leaned forward on the windowsill for a keener view.

After the ladder slid over and landed upright on the Lifespan property side, a young woman joined them with what looked like a camera dangling from her neck. They hoisted the woman on their shoulders and unsteadily lifted her to the top of the fence. They used the melee at the front gate to distract any onlookers from their activity.

Watching the woman's tottering figure at the top of the fence, all Mike could think was, *Oh Christ! No. Concertina wire!* The hair rose up on the back of his neck. He asked himself if those young people grasped the danger of the coiled barbs. Mike understood. They used that stuff at the Army bases for security installations back in the Middle East

The two men struggled to steady the young woman's shaky ascent over the wire. Mike became increasingly uneasy as the young girl gingerly tried to step over the wires to the top rung of the unstable ladder on the other side. She turned her attention to the side as someone farther back along the fence shouted, "Here comes the TV people!" Distracted and impatient, the woman attempted to hop over the intimidating coiled wires. Instead, the ladder slipped sideways when she put her full weight on it. As it fell away, she plunged down into the wires, momentarily straddling the top. The two men underneath tried to grasp one foot, and came away with only her sneaker. She pitched forward onto the Lifespan property side as the wire twisted itself around her legs, the razored barbs instantly slashed at her legs in a dozen places. It showered blood onto the men below. During her descent, the tangled wire pulled tight like a jumbled knot around her ankles

5

and calves, stopping her fall, just before her head could hit the ground.

Mike's shoulders cringed and his face winced in empathy, moaning, "Owww," as he watched her dangling form contort in anguish, her screams silenced by the thick thermo pane window glass between them.

Even from this distance Mike could see the blood spattered on her legs, her blouse, and on the demonstrators helplessly trying to reach her from the other side of the fence.

Mike could only think in revulsion, *Jeez, she's hung out there like a butchered animal! Damn! Enough of this circus!*

Mike pivoted into action, running out of his office and down the hall to the stairs. He bounded down the steps, two at a time, almost splaying himself out at the bottom from the momentum on his legs. Crossing through his first floor instrumentation repair shop, he shouted, "Phil! Emergency! Get the heavy wire cutters!"

Phil instantly locked onto Mike's eyes, as his boss sped by, slamming through the shop doors. Phil knew this was serious, already aware of the demonstration outside. He just knew something would get out of hand. His technician swung open the metal tool locker door, grabbed the heavy cutter, and threw it across the workbench into Phil's waiting grasp.

Once outside, Mike hit full stride across the manicured lawn. Even at 50 years old, Mike was physically trim from 25 years of jogging. Normally he could cover the 50-yard distance easily, but the added excitement and stress made him struggle for breath. The resistance of the grass beneath his feet felt like it was grabbing at each shoe. At 10 yards, he could see her body was now limp; legs tightly wound, arms held out to the side. He puffed gobs of air. Visible were thin rivulets of blood like bright red strings coursing down her pants, blouse, and arms. *Like she's crucified upside down*, he grimaced.

Mike arrived exhausted, expecting the worst, and saw it. Her calf muscle was almost split halfway across its entire width. It reminded him of pictures he'd seen of a shark attack.

At the fence it was absolute chaos and noise. Demonstrators from the other side of the fence were trying desperately to reach over the fence to untie the woman's legs. They would reach up, only to cut their fingers on the stiff and unforgiving razor wire. Everyone was shouting to do something different. Two Lifespan security guards had now arrived and lifted the woman from under the shoulders to take tension off the wire looped around her legs, and still didn't have the where-with-all to free her.

While the guards supported the woman by her shoulders, a panting Mike tore off his white dress shirt and tie, his Lifespan five-year service tie clip falling to the blood soaked turf below. It was immediately crushed under someone's foot and disappeared into the dark crimson mud below, like a metaphor of things to come.

With the shredded shirt sleeves he fashioned a tourniquet around each of the woman's thighs.

"Has anybody called 911 yet?" Mike called out as he took charge.

A guard replied, "Yeah, we got it covered. Yeah, somebody called."

Mike bellowed, "Somebody's not good enough. You get a name, confirmation it was done!"

Phil, Mike's assistant finally arrived with the wire cutters, and intuitively knew what was needed He stretched onto his toes and reached up with the cutters, gingerly snipping at the wires one by one. It seemed to take an eternity. The bystanders, on both sides of the fence, finally calmed down, stupefied by the wounded woman's comatose body.

"Careful", Mike cautioned, "leave that section of wire embedded in the calf alone, there might be a blade inside that we can't see. We could sever an artery trying to pull it out."

With the last wire finally cut, the full weight of the young woman fell on the security guards, and Mike and Phil guided her mangled legs to the side. The four men lowered the unconscious form gently to the ground, and Mike began delivering more orders. "Phil get some shipping blankets from the warehouse." Turning to one of the guards he ordered, "Get two bags of ice from the cafeteria."

Another arriving security guard removed his jacket and placed it over the victim's chest to keep her warm. Mike bent down on his hands and knees, leaned over, and opened an eyelid to peer into the woman's blood soaked eyes. They were totally dilated. His fingers could still palpate a faint heartbeat along her neck. I was apparent that she was already going into shock, and based on the loss of blood, he was most concerned with how much life was still left in her. He wasn't looking forward to facing that point without paramedics around.

"Where are the medics?" he groaned in utter frustration.

As if answering a prayer, he heard a woman's voice among the muffled sobs and murmuring of the crowd on the other side of the fence. A feeling of relief came over him. "Let me through. Move aside. I need to get closer." The woman shouted.

He anticipated a female medic, never occurring to him that there had not been any sirens announcing that arrival. From his kneeling position, he looked upward through the nearby chainlink fence into the crowd on the other side. A well-dressed woman approached, vaguely familiar, in full makeup, with a microphone raised to her lips.

"Patty Marshall, bringing you 'news breaker' coverage of today's tragedy at Lifespan headquarters!" the woman announced to a video camera man at her side.

An astonished Mike just said, "What the fff..."

Oblivious to everyone, she launched into her interview. "What's the lady's name? How come, with all that blood, none of you has taken proper precautions against Covid or AIDS? Can you remove that jacket so we can get a better pictures of her injuries?"

She pointed the microphone back through a hole in the chain fence. The video cameraman was standing right behind, pointing over her shoulder. For a second no one moved - they all just stared silently in disbelief.

Mike looked down and mumbled to himself, "Another heartless bitch!" Then he looked up and erupted, "Get the hell outta here!"

She withdrew the microphone and indignantly made her reply facing towards the video cameraman, "I'm on public property. We are trying to bring this important story to the public. Haven't you heard of freedom of press?"

She stuck the microphone back through the fence again like a fat finger pointed at him, demanding her answer.

That was it for Mike. He exploded with rage. He grabbed the cable cutter, and with lightning speed slashed at the microphone with a blow so powerful that the microphone shattered in mid-air, plastic and metal shards flying in all directions. All that was left visible was the frazzled end of the coax cable dangling through the fence.

"Hey, my audio, you can't do that!" Patty cried. "Who the hell do you think you are? My viewers have a right to see this... you....you asshole!"

This woman's arrogant, privileged attitude had finally collided with the wrong man. Mike clenched his teeth so hard the muscles of his jaws seemed to ripple on his cheeks. From his crouched position, legs straining, he sprang like a mountain lion in the reporter's direction, smashing his face and shoulder into the chain link with a loud clang. The impact sent a clanking shock wave up and down the metal fence, some 30 feet in both directions.

On the other side of the fence, startled by his sudden advance, the newswoman stumbled backward into her cameraman and slide down with her skirt sliding up.

Mike looked down through the fence at the newswoman lying on her back. He grinned, telling the cameraman, "Shoot that, her viewers are probably interested in seeing that too!"

For a brief moment the sarcasm restored his composure... and made a few people giggle.

Guard Harry Sullivan came up behind Mike, grabbed Mike's shoulder, and spoke softly in his ear, "Easy does it, Mikey. That's a media person. Corporate likes us to stroke'em not poke'm."

Patty was helped up by her grinning cameraman and retreated into the crowd grunting as she looked back, "That coverage might have gotten me an Emmy." Looking down over her shoulder, she lifted her calf to reveal a giant run in her stocking. "Oh shit-damn! Look what he did! That idiot's got as much class as a junkyard dog."

As Mike calmly watched her retreat, a guard hollered from behind, "Mikey, this lady don't look good!"

They all quickly forgot the news reporter and turned their attention back on the critically injured woman. Mike knelt down next to the woman again, and noticed her eyes starting to blink slowly open through the clotting blood. Her limpid gaze turned to Mike. Her strength seemed to give out and she faded unconscious again. He got an unmistakable, sinking feeling that without help soon, this lady would be one her way out.

Mike looked around wishing those paramedics were here right now.

As he studied her face, the dried blood stains gave it an odd appearance. The rivulets ran up her pale white face from her hanging inverted on the fence, exhibiting a surreal look. A firm hand clasped Mike's shoulder, interrupting his meditation, "Son, I'm Father Thomas."

Mike looked up, a bit astonished, as the old Catholic priest knelt down next to him on one knee. *How the hell did he get in?* Was all Mike could think, then, remembered this was right-to-life demonstration. Mike regarded the kindly looking gray-haired priest and answered. "Father, this lady is about to check out. I think she could arrest any time now."

"Oh Lord," the priest said as he regarded the tragedy at his feet. "Well, let us pray not." He tried to act reassuring and added, "I'm going to give her Last Rites ...you know... but just as a precaution," he answered reassuringly.

Mike said, 'I dunno. Guess she looks Catholic", and struggled up from the ground on his stiff back and knees. The kneeling clergyman put some kind of purple scarf around his neck, and softly spoke the ritual prayers of departure in Latin. Mike looked over towards the corporate building to see Jane Savage, Director of Corporate Security, and Harry's boss, stomping across the grass straight towards him. Mike let out an "Uh-oh," thinking, *Here comes the Amazon.*

Jane was upset, and she was always frustrated, especially by undisciplined men like Mike. She had spent ten years as an Army MP, and considered herself one tough cookie - any man's equal.

"OK Mister Santino," she demanded with eyebrows knitted together in mean face. "What the hell do you think you're doing here?"

With a measure of his usual sarcasm, he answered, "Ah, Janie. How 'bout we can the formality. Why don't you call me by my first name? After all, darlin', we've known each other four years now."

She ignored his quaint patronizing and barked, "Look, we have a serious security situation with people that have been harassing our company from the beginning. Your meddling can cost us litigation over this woman's suicide stunt."

Mike approached her more closely, to be face to face, and looked down, "I saw how it happened. It was an accident."

Jane did not like his close proximity, fingering her sidearm. She did not like it when men were not intimidated by her job title - were not deferential enough. Most men would not stand up to her bluff nowadays. They had surrendered their male dominance to the women's movement decades ago.

He obviously missed the boat, she smugly concluded to herself.

Jane carefully measured his demeanor. She could never tell what an undomesticated male might do. She inadvertently retreated two steps and explained. "This woman is part of a group of Right-to-Life nuts, trying to get publicity for herself and destroy our company."

"It's a mighty painful way to get attention, Janie... if you're correct."

"Who's side are you on, anyway Santino?" she retorted with her hands now on her slender waist and curved hips. "And its Miz Savage to you."

The posture pulled her blouse tightly back against her breasts. Mike could not help being instinctively distracted by her seductive figure and thought to himself, *Geez that's a good lookin' babe. What a waste on a personality like hers. I wonder what kind of jelly-bellies she dates?*

An impatient Jane snarled, "Well?"

Mike re-focused his easily distracted male brain to the conversation. "Well, Janie .... well right now, I'm on the side of a human being that needs a little help. I'll sort out the legal imperative crap later."

Jane realized that there was no sense in continuing this line of discussion, so she pointed down at the kneeling priest. "Who authorized him to enter company grounds?"

Mike looked down and stepped back to touch the praying cleric's shoulder, then glanced back up and folded his arms defiantly saying, "I invited him."

"Where's his visitors badge? You know company policy on this?" she demanded.

Again he replied sarcastically, pointing to the injured woman, "This lady doesn't have a visitors badge either. Let's throw her back over the fence too!"

Impatient, Jane barked, "Don't get smart ass with me buster! We can't undo what happened to her. You should show a better appreciation for company policy." She pointed at the priest, "Get him the hell outta here!"

Mike was surprisingly cool in his response, walking up nose to nose with Jane again and placing his bloody index finger on her security badge. He spoke slowly and forcefully through clenched teeth. "I take full responsibility for him." Then, Mike glanced around at the other guards,

"Anybody who wants to touch him has to go through me first."

Jane swiped his hand away, but the guards stood paralyzed, not wanting to openly oppose their boss...and not wanting to tangle with a bobcat like Mike. The silent priest stayed in the background observing the spectacle with amused interest.

Jane sensed a loosing battle developing. Her security people now had their arms folded too, still pissed at what they had to do at the guard shack earlier. If she were a male, she would have to force the situation or loose face. As a woman, there was no pressure to prove anything. She was expert at playing these gender things both ways.

So, she backed off using her woman's prerogative, replying with a corporate correct response. "OK, then that's the way it will be in my formal incident report!"

In the midst of the conversation, Mike heard the distant sirens getting louder, meaning help was not far away. Then he stooped down to retrieve a blood stained razor wire from the grass, and chided Jane with it. "When you write your lousy report, don't forget to ask who insisted on this stupid concertina wire on top of the fence…and use red ink!"

Jane ignored the statement, turned, and stomped off to the main gate wondering how a guy like Santino ever became a Director.

As she retreated, Mike muttered to himself, "Thin lipped bitch."

Behind him, the Father Tom became alarmed by the sudden change in the woman's condition. Mike knelt down over her. She weakly reached up with a bloody hand, straining to gently touch his forearm. Her dried lips parted. Mike leaned over to get closer, hear better. With widening eyes and blank stare, she asked quizzically, "Grandpa... you've come for me?" Her eyes rolled up in their sockets, and her lids slowly closed. Her pained face became relaxed and took on a peaceful countenance.

Mike tried to stay emotionally detached from her, but a cool late afternoon breeze blew gently across them both, and accentuated the illusion of a spirit moving away from its abode. The noise and turmoil of the surrounding crowd drifted away, as he noticed the gentle breeze toss the woman's twisted hair strands slowly back and forth as if she were floating underwater. Mike's skin crawled with the goose bumps of impending death.

... Then her pulse was gone.

EMT sirens were on the company grounds now. Mike knew they were out of time. He looked up and blurted out, "She's going cyanotic!" Now his worst fears about this woman had come true. He shifted on his knees and began to excitedly shout, "We're gonna do CPR! Yeah, we're gonna do it right now!" Looking up he ordered, "Phil, you get ready to massage the heart. We do it in rhythm with the beat of *Stayin' Alive'* by the Bee Gees. We'll alternate between compressions and breathing. I'll do the mouth to mouth."

The prostrate lifeless woman was surrounded by anxious and apprehensive men and women, each doing whatever they could to help. Father Tom handled a tourniquet on one leg, while Harry the guard kept tension on the other. The intense little group began CPR in rapid sequences of breaths and chest compressions. In a course voice, Mike kept whispering, "Stayin alive, stayin alive....." Periodically checking for some sign of a heartbeat or a breath, then stood up to look for the EMT's. The guards took turns at the chest compressions. Minutes seemed to pass like hours. The woman's body jerked under the stimulation, but her face remained pallid, body inert.

Now closing in, the blaring sirens and flashing lights of the rescue van and fire engines brought a rush of relief to Mike. As the rescue ambulance bounced towards them across the rough grass, his responsibility for the injured woman was now almost over. He just had to keep going.

At last, the EMTs hurried over and quickly evaluated the situation, placing a ventilating bag on the women's face, and high voltage paddles on her chest. Mike was roughly brushed away by one of them, and fell backwards on his rear end. He stood up, brushed of the wet grass, and huddled in the background with the other security people that had pitched in to help. All of them hushed and suddenly feeling kind of useless at this point.

Yelling, "Clear!" each time, the medics gave her three successive shocks to restart her heart. Everyone waited in muted silence between each jolt. With each sharp snap of the pads. Life? Or death? Mike whispered uder his breath, *stayin alive, stayin alive.....*

When the EMTs finally announced a pulse and placed and oxygen mask over her face, everyone breathe a collective sigh of relief. Then, the EMTs moved quickly to start dextrose and saline IV's in each arm as color returned to her face. The make-shift ice packs on the legs were retained, and she was immediately placed on a stretcher.

Peering over the backs of the paramedics, Mike felt a huge weight lifted from him. Somehow, this young lady was going to make it. One of the guards threw a security jacket over his shoulders, and a relieved Mike gladly accepted it, commenting, "Yeah, that's enough excitement for one day. Huh guys?"

With the injured woman's departure in the ambulance, the tired old priest came over to Mike, head bowed slightly. "I guess we're both in deep trouble."

Mike was puzzled. "How so Father?"

"My Archbishop is against decoupling and this fetal cadaver reclamation business. He doesn't like his priests embroiled in any violent protests that get in the papers. Makes the Church look bad."

"Really?" Mike said, "I don't remember Jesus worrying about public reaction in the Temple."

"Yes, I know," he regretfully continued. "The Church is afraid they will alienate a lot of women by actively opposing decoupling. We know that even Catholic women have made these terrible choices already."

Mike responded in his usual blunt manner, "You've been pounding away at this issue for a long time now. You think those women are listening anymore?"

The kindly priest shrugged, "It doesn't matter. We'll keep on repeating God's natural truth until they do listen."

Mike interrupted the flow of conversation by asking for the priest's parish.

"Infant Jesus over in Newark," Father Tom answered, pointing north.

In his awkward and clumsy way, Mike extended his hand and belatedly introduced himself, "I'm Mike Santino from Lifespan Corporation."

The old cleric took his hand and gently grasped Mike's shoulder, asking, "You work here. Do you ever think about fetal life?"

Mike was taken aback a bit by such a direct question. It was something he never particularly thought about...or for that matter, let himself dwell on.

He quickly replied defensively, while pointing to one of the Lifespan buildings, "All I know Father, is whatever we process is castoff biologics – waste recovery."

"Yes my son, I know what your company does," Father Tom said with regret. "But, do you understand how that, using finger quotation marks, "biologics' becomes lifeless to begin with?"

The somber priest focused on Mike's eyes as a mirror to his soul, awaiting a reply. Mike's delayed silence and weary face conveyed a good heart. Father Tom gave a tolerant smile, and said perceptively, "I think I see you have your doubts too."

Mike tried to ease out of the question and replied awkwardly, "We're licensed by the government. They seem to think it's OK."

The cleric countered, "When did the government ever become a good model of morality?"

Mike was embarrassed by his quick answer. It sounded stupid right after he said it.

The gentle priest was not contentious in tone though, and continued. "Try to spend sometime thinking about it, my son. I think you are a Christian. And, as you so succinctly pointed out earlier, ask yourself; What would Jesus think? What would He do about all this?"

Mike was not about to field that prickly question and put his palms up in acquiescence, his energy to debate, much less carry on a philosophical

13

conversation all but gone. He had high regard for missionaries and priests like the good Father. Mike always reserved his admiration for the people in the trenches, on the front line of things. Finally, he answered, "I'm sorry Father. I really try not to spend a lot of time thinking about things I can't change."

"That's alright my son," he gently patted Mike on the back, "You go home and rest. Your good work here is done. I'll pray for you... and that poor young woman."

Mike shrugged his shoulders, and shook the empathetic Father's hand saying, facetiously "Thanks, I can always use help from the big guy upstairs," then added, "And I hope you don't take too much heat for being here today either."

They waved goodbye to each other, each assuming this would be their only fleeting contact - neither realizing that their destinies were already perilously intertwined.

Mike headed back along the fence, stopping a the guard shack to drop off the blood soaked guard's jacket, glad that he didn't have to defend his employment at Lifespan to some priest anymore. Fortunately, his car keys were in his pants pocket. As he continued walking across the grass to the parking lot, his body felt cold. It was the aftershock of fatigue and emotional stress. The ambulance and fire engines were already gone, and the demonstrators dispersed. In the distance, he observed Jane Savage from Security and Eve West, Community Relations Director, at the entrance gate in a heated discussion with Patty the news lady.

He joked sarcastically to himself; *Janie must be telling her what a wonderful employee I really am.*

What Mike did not guess, is that they were rewriting the day's events to fit the objectives of Lifespan Corporation and the media.

Mike thought about the office, but it was heading towards sunset. He knew Phil and his Admin would lock things up. Besides, he was physically and emotionally drained. His clothes were soiled with mud, grass stains, and the salty metallic smell of dried blood. His sweaty T-shirt now chilled him in the breeze. The vision of a hot shower, a sandwich and a cold beer at home was compelling and gave impetus to his fatigued legs.

Before getting into his car, he opened the trunk and got out an old blanket to prevent staining the recently restored bucket seats with blood. He climbed into the driver's seat, and sat back for a moment. He felt a lot like that old car, a '68 Mustang GT - still capable of remarkable performance, but painted in gray primer and so out-of-date

Mike sat there, sullen - the sky pale with muted tones of a cloudy sunset. He should be feeling elated to have had a hand in saving that woman's life. He knew the executives at Lifespan did not appreciate his kind of decisiveness.

14

He recalled a Director's planning meeting three years ago when the subject of plant security was discussed. He objected to the lunacy of using military grade razor wire on top of a chain link fence that was already 6 feet high. Corporate was almost paranoid on having it, and Mike didn't make any political points by questioning Lifespan corporate judgment. Worse yet, Mike quipped that the planned facility was going to look like 'Stalag 17', an obvious reference to an old Nazi prisoner of war camp movie starring William Holden. He recommended using drones instead.

Even the other managers distanced themselves from him during the meeting, although privately, they confided that they agreed with him.

Puppets on a string, Mike liked to call his management coworkers.

He had a strong sense of Euro-Christian values from his father; family, country, honest devotion to the task at hand. It gave him the strength to endure tremendous amounts of both physical and psychological strain. In years past, those same values gave him the ability to fight as a Navy pilot in the confused skies over the Middle East.

This supreme confidence gave him what appeared to be a rather cavalier attitude about business problems. It made other executives uncomfortable. He did not see the problems as so intimidating: not after facing the life and death in the perils of warfare.

Lastly, he did not convey any fear of his superiors. He wouldn't grovel at their feet. Any corporation, especially Lifespan, could not function without fear. To the other pompous managers, Mike's behavior meant an automatic career plateau - not useful to their pretensions of promotion to the executive ranks.

Mike knew they admired his tenacity and sharp wit in solving technical problems with them, except they all drew the line at friendship. In a sense his attitude made him something of an organizational leper, a rebel without a rebellion.

These last thoughts made him realize how really alone he was. The loneliness made him pull out his wallet and look at an old wrinkled photograph inside – his deceased wife Laura. It was one of many reminders he kept tucked away. This one from his college days some 25 years earlier. Mike and Laura surfing at the beach.

Mike sadly reflected, *We thought our lives would last forever..*

His vision blurred as tears formed in his eyes. Old wounds eventually heal, except the scars, the scars, they last forever. Mike wasn't sure why he was getting all filled up with emotion. Was it for almost losing that young woman on the fence, as he lost his wife, Laura, five years ago? Or himself? Maybe what he needed was a friend, somebody to confide his doubts and misgivings with.

He still had half a lifetime to go, and really needed the support of a compassionate woman again - like Laura. Someone devoted, always ready to take his side. Then he could handle everything life throws at him.

Regaining his composure, Mike realized that the employee parking lot wasn't any place for consolation, and he still had two sons at home to take care of. He yanked the heavy car door closed, wiped his eyes with his fingers, and turned the engine over. The familiar, deep rumble of his rebuilt 4-barrel 289 V8 was welcome, and brought his attention back to his love of driving. As he clutched and throttled back out of his parking spot he thought, *save your tears for tomorrow buddy, when corporate calls you on the carpet.*

Mike sighed to himself in resignation. He had been a marked man before. At least, he did have the rest of the evening to prepare his defense. That's more lead time then he usually got from corporate, anyway.

As he drove home, an old song of the Walker Brothers came on the radio, 'The Sun Ain't Gonna Shine Anymore'.

'Loneliness is a cloak you wear,
A deep shade of blue is always there...'

CHAPTER 2
A glimpse into our future

Earlier that same day in the quiet dawn , across the Hudson on Long Island, Phylis Daye entered the empty hospital elevator at University Hospital and pressed the second floor button. The slim, dark haired Lifespan Corporation representative slumped against the back wall and stared up, feeling tired, and, well, a bit apprehensive too - the consequence of a restless night in bed.

Above the door, little round lights sequentially blinked, passively indicating her ascension from the lower level to the Administration floor. Little did she know how today's mundane events would somehow come full circle and change her life forever.

The confines of this bland stainless steel chamber provided a brief moment of isolation from the working world. It allowed more personal memories to creep forward - of past times. Before the career woman. Back to earlier, less hectic years at home —as a wife, a mother - children. Glancing at her watch, she began to reminisce about what she would've been doing back then, about this time in the morning.

She wistfully recalled, *Kissing her husband off to work, and packing the kids off to school. Then, finally, peacefully, nursing a warm cup of coffee in the kitchen while watching Good Morning America.*

Suddenly, the daydream of bygone days evaporated with the intruding ding of the elevator floor bell. Annoyed by the rude interruption, sighing with resignation she murmured, *How things change.* And then it was back to the day's work.

An uneasy feeling churned within her about today's decoupling procedure. Normally the acquisition job was not so difficult when arranged over the Web - almost routine. However, today's client had one of those emotionally soft personalities, and would surely have to be guided the whole way in person. Moreover, the specimen release form had not been authorized yet. The company had already invested a lot of money into testing this woman, and there was no time for a last minute change of heart. Experience as a Lifespan Corporation procurement specialist had taught her that it was so much simpler to deal with women when they are not emotionally involved. When feelings got involved, guilt and doubt were never too far behind.

The elevator doors eventually slid open on the second floor, and Phylis' mind abruptly snapped into the business persona. It was as if a little switch in her brain could turn on or turn off the true feminine identity inside – no doubt a result of the intense training seminars at Lifespan. They taught her how to suppress personal feelings. Focus on closing deals. Always think in the third person.

Phylis stepped into the hall on a route she had taken so many times before. Familiar hospital personnel passed, exchanging the usual mundane pleasantries until she reached Ambulatory Admissions. Walking into the nicely appointed office, a young Neal Katz was settled at his expensive solid oak desk. As Phylis approached, he noticed, smiled, and picked up the desk telephone, starting to dial. This was his usual 'Mister Important Administrator Act', and it always annoyed her. Reaching his desk, she impatiently leaned over, plucked the receiver from his ear, and firmly placed it down onto the receptacle with a clunk.

Phylis reproached him, "I don't have time for your usual nonsense, Neal! Have you got the release paper work-up for Maria Alvarez?!"

Her blazer opened slightly, and at the same moment Neil sneaked a glimpse at the cleavage beneath her lacey bra and sheer blouse. "Keep your shirt on," he said with a smirk.

Phylis noticed his tactless stare, and her green eyes glinted as she impatiently answered back, "Neal, I don't like rushing these things. It's not like we're doing hernias here. This is a big ticket item."

Neal sat back and smugly answered, "She's still in pre-op room 410 and not scheduled for decoupling for another hour."

When Phylis reached for the case file, Neal childishly teased her with the manila folder. "Come on Neal," she demanded, "Her IV needs to get started," and deftly grabbed the folder from him. She turned, and began to walk away. Behind her, she vaguely heard Neal sniveling something that sounded like "bee-ah-ch".

Phylis quickly made her way back to an unoccupied elevator, stepped in and hesitated, still slightly incensed by Neil's moronic behavior. With her EDC (Embryonic Decoupling Curettage) caseload so hectic now, it did not take much of a distraction to forget which hospital she was in, or what floor to go to. After a moment, she pushed the fourth floor button and the elevator lurched, and then slowly climbed - and so did the anxiety of closing the deal.

The bell clanged as the doors opened on the fourth floor, and Phylis inwardly reacted to the sound like a prize fighter, by quietly whispering, "OK. Opening bell for the last round".

Gliding down the hallway, briefcase in hand, dressed in a skirt and blazer, hair in a short flip, she looked and felt like today's professional woman. Her attentive eyes rapidly scanned the descending room numbers, ticking them off in her mind like a countdown to liftoff.

Just before reaching Pre-op Surgery, Phylis paused and leaned her back against the hallway wall just outside the room to collect her thoughts. It was time for her mind to focus on one thing. *Your on stage now honey*, she thought emphatically. *Forget everything else. Get the specimen*! Then pivoting off the wall on one shoulder, the confident Lifespan agent entered Pre-Surg, observing the patient's beds lined up against the wall with privacy curtains separating them. She found Maria's bed, and what greeted her eyes was not encouraging.

Inside, the client, Maria Alvarez, was sitting up in bed with a light, baby-blue surgical gown on. Her hands were loosely clasped with fingers slowly contorted together - a box of Kleenex nearby. A drooping head concealed reddened eyes, swelling with fluid. A loose strand of hair, dangling over one eyebrow, seemingly conveyed her inner confusion. This was exactly what Lifespan had been so fearful about happening.

Recalling her initial screening report, it indicated that although Maria's specimen extraction potential was outstanding, but she did have this serious drawback on her psychological profile. The data scan indicated a client that was too religious, too sensitive, already involved with child rearing - not the typical career-orientated client of today. She might not follow through on the decoupling. Phylis surmised that the most likely aspect that kept Maria in this program was her Hispanic surname. Lifespan probably needed her to make their month's EOC (Equal Opportunity Client) quota. Maria, soft personality and all, was probably this month's answer.

Phylis approached the distraught client with a sympathetic smile, and gingerly sat down on the bedside. She gently reached for the woman's hand and said reassuringly, "Good morning dear."

The subdued Maria looked up and appeared grateful to see a familiar face, while obviously struggling with her own inner turmoil. Phylis had seen this vacillating behavior before, and with her procurement specialist expertise, knew just how to cope with it.

Phylis thoughtfully sat up, and rearranged Maria's disheveled dark hair back behind her ear. Then, started right in, using a well rehearsed presentation. "Maria, remember you have two wonderful children. Remember how we discussed this situation with you and your husband weeks ago. And, how the money from this decoupling would finally allow your family to get a little ahead. Remember that you weren't doing this for yourself, you were doing it for them."

She paused for a moment to measure her still wavering client, then continued. "You know, by law I cannot advise you on what to do. Lifespan didn't solicit you. You told your doctor that you couldn't afford more children, and at your age, just didn't have the same level of energy to raise another child. You authorized the doctor to contact us, and we spent a whole lot of time and money screening you and setting up this procedure in the hospital."

Maria's eyes lifted. She spoke hesitantly, "I know. I know. I don't mean to be ungrateful. I have this funny feeling deep inside my heart. I don't know. Maybe it's the money part of all this." She wiped her eyes and looked down at her contorting hands again, adding in a low voice. "It's just...well, maybe I'm deciding something not meant to be decided."

Phylis, still anxious to retain this case, responded quickly, "Maria I have a folder full of forms from the Hospital, the City, the State, the Federal Government." She patted her brief case for emphasis and added, "All these smart, educated people condone this procedure, right up to the Supreme Court. You didn't see a line of doctors or police stopping you from coming in here. EDC decoupling is perfectly legal in our State... and ethical too!"

Maria's mind seemed to be drifting off in some other direction, and Phylis gently patted her hand to regain her attention. "Remember, thousands of women have had decouplings for the past 5 years without the slightest misgivings. Fortunately, our company came along and found a useful purpose for all that wasted tissue."

Finally, Phylis concluded matter-of-factly, "You're just getting rid of some formless tissue...like an appendix. So you...."

Then, Phylis hesitated for a second. She halted midway in her argument. For a fleeting moment, in the zeal of delivering her sales pitch, her own words seemed to hit some subconscious limit of credibility.

During Phylis' awkward silence, Maria delicately wiped her eyes, one at a time, and blew her nose before speaking indecisively. In a quivering voice she sought more reassurance. "Phylis, you've done this for years with many other women. Am I over reacting? Are they all as certain as you say?"

Maria's surgical gown was now drooping down from her shoulder, and Phylis thoughtfully lifted it back in place before answering. Regaining her train of thought, Phylis continued. "You're not overreacting, dear. But you do have to get past the present. What you're donating today is going to save countless lives in the future. Think of it. Years from now. Some woman will be contributing a specimen that may save your child, or your husband, or your father. Wouldn't you want that woman to help?"

Maria's head lifted and her anxiety began to ebb somewhat. "Maybe you're right. I'm thinking about myself too much. Maybe I needed to know that what I'm doing is helping other people. What could be wrong with that? "

"Absolutely," Phylis added emphatically, sensing that her verbal barrage was working, "and you'll join thousands of other women donors who made the same legitimate choice to save lives."

Maria's eyes began to clear and her attitude changed. She resigned herself to the seeming inevitability of her situation, and was now too embarrassed at this point to acknowledge her nurturing instinct which would stop all this. She sniffled and cleared her throat, "I'm so glad you came down here to help me through this."

"Of course, of course, Maria," Phylis said confidently, as she sat back down on the bedside, feeling the worst was over. Now it seemed appropriate to shift the focus of the conversation. So she exclaimed, "I love what you did with your hair."

Maria brightened slightly and touched her hair, almost welcoming the change in topic. "Oh, you like it?"

"Yes, very much," Phylis said, as she rose from the bed.

"I wanted to look different after this is over," Maria added, "Sort of un-pregnant."

Just then the pre-op nurse entered, smiled, and greeted them with a cheery "Good morning ladies, time for the local block by the Anesthesiologist."

"Wait a minute!" Phylis suddenly interrupted. With all the distracting conversation, she'd almost forgotten the specimen release form. Rummaging through her briefcase quickly produced a pen and paper. Both were judiciously placed in the lap of the indecisive client. Maria's puffy eyes scanned the form in slight confusion, and signed it hurriedly, too quickly to have really read it.

Phylis finally could relax. All the anxiety and stress instantly abated - she had earned another commission.

Strangely, this time she felt no joy or satisfaction from making the money. Maybe it was the personal, up close, hard sell involved here. In reality, buried deep inside, feminine sensitivities still dwelled in Phylis. They lurked beneath the hardened layers of so many years in business, yet were never totally obliterated. The feelings that Lifespan training had taught her not to feel. Soon, those unwelcome sensations left her, sort of...

well, sort of empty about how this particular specimen extraction was going today.

The pre-op nurse moved methodically to maintain schedule and, presumably, prevent any change of heart. She said softly but dryly, "Maria, I am going to give you a mild sedative to relax your muscles prior to decoupling. You will feel a little groggy, so just lay back and go with it."

Maria slid down to recline on her pillow, while Phylis routinely packed the signed release form into her briefcase. As Phylis got up and turned away to leave, the drowsy Maria suddenly grasped her wrist. The woman's suppressed inner soul was struggling to be heard. With her eyelids half closed and facing the ceiling, Maria whispered almost imperceptibly, "Take care of my lamb".

"What?" Phylis said as she swiveled around back towards the rapidly fading woman. She had not quite heard exactly what she said. Leaning closer to Maria's face with her hand softly touching Maria's shoulder, she queried, "What did you want to tell me, dear? What?"

Maria turned her head sideways, her uncooperative lips struggling against the debilitating effect of the anesthesia. Again she struggled to murmur in a low voice, "Take...slur...m.. lamb." Then her eyes rolled up and she faded off.

"Strange...," Phylis muttered, her face contorted in mild confusion. She glanced at the pre-op nurse across the bed, "Did you hear what she said? Why tell us to do what's already been decided?"

The nurse shrugged her shoulders, indifferent to the patient's mumbling, and continued prepping the blankets and rolling bed.

Maria's last attempt to speak left Phylis even more unsettled. They did say at the company training school that these cases could be tough if too much personal contact was involved.

Still, business was business and this case was closed, she forced herself to conclude, and retreated to the doorway. At the threshold the Lifespan agent turned and looked back one last time at a poor gentle woman that she'd never see again. Phylis asked herself, *Still, I wonder what she was trying to tell me?*

Back in the busy corridors outside, this very personal interlude was promptly supplanted by the scurry of daily hospital routine. The troubling thoughts dissolved in the commotion, and Phylis decided to pass the hour in the hospital cafeteria waiting for the procedure to be finished. Thereafter, she could pick up the specimen, and take it back to Lifespan headquarters for processing.

At the cafeteria counter, Phylis grabbed a salad and ice tea, and glanced around the room. With tray in hand she maneuvered around the tables until she found one unoccupied by the windows. She sat and stared out into the parking lot with a vacant gaze on the activity below.

Then Maria's parting words emerged again, somehow tangled in the web of her conscience. Phylis wondered why the usual excitement and satisfaction of a job successfully completed and commissioned earned, was strangely diminished this time. This time, the conclusion felt strangely ambiguous, like she was getting bogged down between the opposing worlds of people's feelings and Lifespan's business. She found her thoughts starting to dwell on repressed memories of the past - memories of her own decoupling.

Her introspection was interrupted by a man's voice nearby, "Hi Phylis, mind if I join you". She looked up to see sociopath Peter Kullic, General Surgeon, and ardent ladies hit man. Divorced, he was always on the make, and Phylis was in no mood for any repartee today.

"You look a bit troubled Phyl", he presumed, as he lowered his tray to the table, assuming his importance as a surgeon automatically allowed the intrusion.

Choosing to keep it formal, Phylis responded in a curt tone, "Doctor Kullic, I'm not good company today - my mind is with a client."

Familiar with Phylis' line of work he asked, "Got a no-show?"

"It's nothing like that. I really just don't want to talk about it."

Doctor Kullic was one of those people she'd learned never to share ones true feelings with. Phylis remembered how the operating nurses were loath to spend any time assisting on his surgical cases. He liked to discuss his personal investments and advertise his sordid affairs to anybody in earshot- even while operating. Sometimes, they noticed that his operating caseload would increase right after he mentioned some personal financial investment disaster.

Privately, the nurses believed that many of these cases were unnecessary. One nurse even went as far as registering a formal complaint with the hospital director. At Kullic's Hospital Board hearing, his defense was to take the offense, threatening to take his practice elsewhere. He argued that nurses were not certified to make diagnostic conclusions, asserting that the tissues removed were diseased anyway. It was simply a matter of judgment as to how soon they had to be excised. In the end, when administration looked at how much revenue he was bringing in, they backed off. The offending surgical nurse was eventually transferred to Emergency Room duties.

Phylis was vexed by the seeming inability of his colleagues to contain the excesses of a person like him. It bothered her and that the inaction of the good surgeons, ultimately, allowed the bad ones to undermine public respect for the whole profession.

Dr. Kullic, oblivious to Phylis' personal feelings finished his tuna salad and had to rush off to his next case. "Hey, maybe another time Phyl," he said.

Phylis giggled inside to herself, *Yeah, around the time of the next Ice Age, you jerk!*

Regaining control, she just gave a polite smile, and a goodbye wave of the fingertips.

With a half hour still to wait for Maria's specimen, Phylis wandered down the hallway to the waiting lounge area. An upholstered chair by the window looked comfortable and had a cocktail table in front. It would be a perfect spot for getting some paperwork done.

As she gazed out the window across the parking lot, the looming construction of the new Rejuvenation Center below caught her attention. University Hospital was building a huge new free-standing rejuvenation center, and Phylis could relate instantly to what this structure meant. She and Lifespan Corporation were at the beginning of a chain of fantastic events, producing the medicinal treatments which made that building and all it represented possible. Lifespan had already introduced specimen extracts to reverse the effects of debilitating diseases like Alzheimer's, Parkinson's, rheumatoid arthritis, osteoporosis, diabetes, and arteriosclerosis. Even bone marrow transplants were being done with stem and precursor fetal cells to finally beat leukemia. It was no surprise, that the FDA issued an Emergency Use Authorization for Lifespan's drugs.

The drugs had to be administered every month, or more, to maintain their remedial effects. Of extraordinary interest, was a rumor she had heard that some fetal extracts, if taken even more frequently, could reverse the aging process. There was nothing official about it, but if it had that kind of result, it was no small wonder that the demand was increasing astronomically. Even if it wasn't so, the treated patients were living much longer lives now. So that each extended life drove the demand for specimens even higher. It made Phylis' procurement job feel all the more significant.

From what she had heard, the treatments averaged several thousand dollars each, and the treatments were needed to be continued every week. Still intentionally classified as experimental treatments, they were not covered by health insurance. This limited the treatments to the dominion of only the wealthiest people in the world. Lifespan diffused the initial negative publicity of this fact, by advertising that the cost would eventually come down so everyone would benefit.

She also knew there were more new drug treatments in development at the company's R&D labs for other diseases, like cartilage repair, restored eyesight, and re-growth of amputated limbs and organs. The possibilities seemed endless - the cutting edge of biotechnology. It lent a certain prestige to her procurement department. It was becoming a huge multi-billion dollar business.

For an instant, she felt a combination of pride and individual importance, thinking of all those elderly people, who will be given a second chance at a healthy life. In a way, her job seemed almost virtuous, maybe even noble. A pleasant smile came to her lips.

After a second of self-indulgence, Phylis reached into her brief case and pulled out the client's file folder on her tablet. For a change, she welcomed the casework work as a distraction from any further deliberation about this morning's disturbing decoupling with Maria. Still, there was this haunting, subconscious need to justify the day's events. In the months that followed, she would know why.

Running down the list of electronic documents it seemed like every agency in the government was involved in the decoupling business now. Even the EPA squeezed in with tissue handling and disposal procedures. Everybody in the specimen procurement chain collected a fee, a tax, a tariff or some consideration. Likewise, Phylis had a commission arrangement with Lifespan.. Reflecting on decoupling history, objections to fetal cadaver reclamation, by mostly right wing religious zealots or something caused all kinds of problems – something about a slippery slope. With the last Supreme Court decision, it was now up to individual State governments to regulate decoupled specimens. New Jersey formulated 'special organ donor' regulations for Lifespan's decoupling operations. The human fetus was now defined as a female organ and a women's health issue. New York, New Jersey, and California were early adopters of this strategy. However, some regulations were followed more than others were. Lifespan Corporation's exclusive license prohibited directly soliciting or directly paying women for fetal cadaver specimens to prevent encouraging unnecessary decouplings. Lifespan easily circumvented that provision by using a loophole provision in the law allowing reasonable payment for the removal, processing, disposal, preservation, quality control, storage, transplantation, or implantation of embryonic or cadaveric fetal tissue. They used the hospitals as an intermediary firewall between them and the donor women, advancing the hospital $35,000 per cadaver in a 'fetal research program'. Of that amount, the hospital gave the 'special organ donors' women $25,000 for the pain and discomfort from the "experimental" decoupling procedure. For a finder's fee, doctors screened pregnant women for possible donors, then contacted Phylis' department.

However, after the proven success of Lifespan's therapeutics, no one was really prohibiting anything anymore. She could not recall any oversight done on all these operations – no one ever questioned any of her submissions.

Phylis set aside the preliminary work-up from the Lifespan lab tests. All to insure harvesting of only the very best embryonic tissue. As it turned out, the data showed Phylis what an outstanding find Maria's specimen really was, and why Lifespan wanted it.

Phylis finally finished her review and packed her tablet into her briefcase. She fidgeted in her seat, checking her watch from time to time for the scheduled extraction, anxious to be on her way to corporate headquarters. In a way, closing the briefcase with all the monotonous forms figuratively brought this specimen extraction case to a conclusion - and helped bury any more troubling thoughts about Maria.

CHAPTER 3
Whatever you do… don't look

While Phylis waited downstairs, Mari Alvarez was in the Operating Room under conscious sedation. The decoupling procedure was similar to early routine abortion techniques, but nobody used the term 'Abortion' anymore because of its negative connotation. Today, political correctness dictated that you had either a 'Termination' or a 'Decoupling'.

Vaginal suction of the specimen, although still appropriate for normal terminations, would not be used for this procedure. Suction shredded the specimen into pieces, essentially destroying it. Lifespan needed the fetal organs intact, free from contamination, and separate from the mother's relatively valueless blood. They learned that there were psychological advantages to keeping an intact advanced specimen from the eyes of operating personnel. Lifespan's decoupling procedure had been designed to preclude that uncomfortable psychological problem when considering taking the specimen whole, as an entire human being.

Lifespan developed a unique tool and procedure to preserve fetal tissue in an undamaged condition. The tool was a specially designed plastic 'egg' extractor gently inserted through the cervix after expansion. The surgeon then inserts a hysteroscope that includes a light, a camera , and CO_2 gas line. With the uterus inflated, it provided working space for other surgical tools and visualization of the fetus. The whole affair fed the uterus images to a TV monitor suspended above the operating table.

Maria was fortunate. Her decoupling would leave virtually no scaring memory to remind her of this day's events.

Obstetrician, Dr. Andre Petersen was perfect for this operation. At 37 years of age, already an expert in microsurgery... and an agnostic. Cool, organized, self-centered - and to some, arrogantly so. In fact, today's decoupling operation was to be video taped. The doctor would use it to instruct other surgeons in the delicate idiosyncrasies of a new placenta abruption technique, and in a subtle way, show off his skills too.

25

Squinting at the TV monitor above, under high magnification, the fetus and decoupling tool were clearly visible. Earlier sonograms had located the specimen's attachment inside the uterus to the upper left surface.

As he worked, Petersen couldn't help reflecting on all the hundreds of previous decouplings he'd done, and wondered what circumstances dictated this woman's choice. Was it money? He turned to his PA to query, "What are these women getting now, 20 maybe 30 grand now?"

The PA shrugged his shoulders, and timidly turned his head sideways. He busied himself adjusting the monitor, deeming that kind of monetary discussion inappropriate to the operating room. Watching the monitor screen, the surgeon observed the specimen, its entire body enclosed and cushioned in its usual transparent, yellow tinted amniotic fluid sac.

At about 14 weeks, a human fetus is about the size of an adult's pinky and weighs approximately 3 ounces. A well-formed head and spinal column are formed, and through the translucent skin, a tiny, two chambered heart can be seen functioning. The arms, hands, legs, and feet are also formed at this point. Even the fingers have finger prints and toes are clearly discernible. With its eye sockets having recently moved forward, it truly looks like a distinct, tiny human. There still was the disproportionate development of the cranial and chest cavity, compared to the region below the waist - an imbalance in proportion that would take a childhood to rectify - an existence this specimen was not meant to have.

Dr. Petersen always felt a certain excitement each time he intruded into this private world. It was like observing a miniature alien in its special purpose space vehicle – like the ending scene of *2001 A Space Odyssey*. There was this still forming face that had an elusive expression, reminding Petersen of the fixed, curved smile of a bottle-nosed dolphin.

The specimen just sat there peacefully functioning in the soft, dark pink of its inner world. No stress, no noise, just the whooshing pulsation of the mother's blood flowing around it, and the furious flutter of its own heart - a little being, going about its own singular purpose, totally oblivious to the business demands and politics of the outside world.

It had good reason to look preoccupied. After all, it was figuratively 'reading' the book of life. With its head hunched over, it reminded Petersen of a little old monk, pouring over a set of incredibly detailed organic chemical formulas and schematics. A complex manual of information, carefully passed on and rewritten from generation to generation. An unbroken chain, stretching back over the course of a billion years. It was a text so intricate in detail that conscious man, in all his modern computerized genome brilliance, had still not created from scratch.

In a way it had made an incredible journey to this point. In microscopic terms, it had figuratively traveled hundreds of miles, undergone billions of cell divisions, and made it past the critical 8 week threshold. All without a misread of DNA instruction or any genetic damage that would cause it to spontaneously abort.

Returning his concentration to the decoupling, Dr. Petersen began examining the specimen for general physical condition, focusing on the cranial and chest cavities. At times like this he could almost feel how a dispassionate God might feel at the moment of creation. He would decide a life's fate with a simple snip of his suture. That is, if he believed in a God.

"Nice healthy specimen", he remarked aloud. "Internal organ development is well along - should yield some outstanding extracts."

For a moment the doctor remembered some old archaic scientific theories of fetal maturation. Back then, it was taught that the human fetus 'evolved' through the stages of animal evolution as it grew in the womb. First, it had 'gill slits' like a fish. Then, after a while it grew a 'tail' like a monkey. He grinned beneath his mask at those primitive concepts. He imagined that a good portion of the general population still wants to retain some of that obsolete visualization.

With the advent of newer internal observation technology in the 1980's, the medical community was able to determine that the 'gills' are actually the starting points for bones that separate two weeks later, developing into the middle ear, the jaw, and tongue bottom. The 'tail' is actually the end of a rapidly developing spinal cord. The body cavity and legs eventually growing along it to catch up to the end of the cord as its rapid development continues.

Quickly, the surgeon regained his concentration again and returned to the subject at hand. Normally, in order to separate the specimen from the uterus, he would insert a micro-scalpel, puncture the sac, then tie off and sever the life-giving umbilical cord. However, new extraction instructions, just received from Lifespan Corporation, required keeping the cord, placenta and specimen intact as an integral unit.

As is the case in a normal procedure, a synthetic hormone, similar to mifepristone followed by misoprostol, was done earlier to begin loosening the placenta. Next, it was necessary to remove the whole combination from the womb without trauma. This is usually not much of a challenge, as the specimen is already immobilized by the Demerol sedative administered to the mother during pre-op. Normally, within a few minutes of severing the umbilical cord, the primitive heart gives up its struggle and motion ceases.

That would not be the case today. With the placenta and its own blood supply still attached, a surprise was in store for this operating team.

The special tool developed by Lifespan engineers to withdraw the expired specimen acted much like an ice cream scoop. The two plastic half shells of the egg were normally sitting one inside the other. Once specimen was captured into one half, the other half rotated around to close the top and the whole tool was withdrawn vaginally. Once outside, the container looked like a light blue eggshell - just as Lifespan planned. And that was all the operating team needed to see.

Petersen inserted the extraction tool, but this time the procedure turned out to be more difficult than it had been in the literature. The combination of fetus and placenta masses was now bigger than anticipated, and still contained in its slippery amniotic sack. Complicating matters further, the specimen was still alive! With the placenta still intact, the isolated fetal blood supply allowed life to continue much longer than usual. In distress, the tiny organism was now arching and squirming within the amniotic sac. Its small head jerked in irritated defiance. Tiny legs flailed and minuscule fingers and toes clenched, then drew up to its face in a protective gesture. The sack broke. Under high magnification, its desperate struggle was even visible to the operating team on the video monitor above.

At the same time the abruption of the placenta only partially detached, allowed blood vessels in the uteral wall to begin filling the organ itself.

Dr. Petersen was visibly anxious and agitated. Now he had a hemorrhaging patient and a moving specimen. Beads of sweat appeared on his forehead. He began to move the hysteroscope around for better leverage while uncomfortably twisting his head to watch the video monitor above. The specimen was still obscured somewhere beneath the pool of its mother's blood.

The operating team began to react to the developing problem, as Dr. Petersen bellowed, "Suction!" Then quickly ordered, "PA, over here! Endometrial ablation! Cauterize the bleeder! I'll stay with the fiberoptics and locate the specimen!"

A nurse wiped sweat from the surgeon's brow.

With operating team proficiency, the blood was drained and the hemorrhage finally repaired. A few more tense moments of suctioning later, the errant specimen was located next to the extraction tool.

An impatient Petersen spoke. "Damn it, you bugger! We need a bigger extractor!" Petersen's voice started to rise in frustration. He turned from the video scope, now more concerned about his image before the operating staff. "Nurse, get ready with 20cc's of sodium chloride for direct injection!"

The assisting nurses began nervously glancing at each other and the video monitor. Their eyes darted back and forth over their surgical masks. When the procedure went smoothly there was no time for conversation or dwelling on what they were doing. It was just a routine day's work. However, this was different. They understood that Dr. Petersen's direction meant actively killing this still living entity right before their eyes. The younger nurse in training, Jennifer, was not prepared for it, not this way. What she was witnessing came across as some new, bizarre category of murder. Feeling queasy in the stomach, she grabbed the cold steel edge of the operating table.

Senior nurse, Ozzie Smith, noticed her distress and stared intensely at Jennifer to hold her attention and support her through this ordeal by sheer will. With her eyes locked to Jennifer's eyes, she replied to the doctor, "20cc sodium chloride ready doctor."

The overwrought PA intervened, saying, "The new protocol won't allow contamination!"

Petersen responded, "Never mind... the bugger finally gave up. The little girl fetus gave up the fight.

Whew! How long did that take? Must've been a good 10 minutes." He paused to glance at his PA, "Well, whoever that little guy was, he would've been some fighter." The rest of the operating team avoided his stare and ignored his uncouth comment. Everybody busied themselves with their own operating responsibilities, looking down to avoid even each other's gaze.

The surgeon finally snared the specimen and attached placenta, loading them into the extraction tool. A local injection of a prostaglandin hormone derivative induced the cervix to dilate. He closed the cover-half securely over the specimen, and removed the 'egg' vaginally. The CO2 gas hissed around the tool as the cervix closed tight again.

Petersen activated the tool release mechanism, and for a moment, he held what had been simple human life in the palm of his gloved hand. Without a trace of compassion, he handed the closed 'egg' to nurse Ozzie. In his dry clinical manner he noted, "For all future procedures of this type, double the pre-op dosage of Demerol. Next time, I want that specimen out cold."

Ozzie wiped the residual sweat from his forehead as he turned to his Physician's Assistant, "Suture up her uterus... and check the vagina if it needs a stitch or two. I'm going to call Strauss at Lifespan. We're going to need a bigger extraction tools if this is going to go like clockwork."

The 'egg' was given to Ozzie for interior and exterior cleaning with sterile saline solution. Petersen left the operating room. The nurses completed their post-operative duties as the CO2 pressure was vented. Jennifer packed the vaginal area with sterilized gauze, making sure the urinary catheter was in place.

Checking that Maria's vital signs were normal, the PA left the nurses to take care of her and the specimen.

With his departure Nurse Jennifer finally released her pent up emotions and tore off her surgical mask. "Who does that jackass Petersen think he is? He acted like he was playing a video game!" she fumed.

Ozzie replied in her easy Jamaican accent, "Easy honey," she said, "Petersen is the hospital expert on this procedure, and administration says this operation is going to be our bread and butter in the future." For emphasis, she pointed over her shoulder, "You see that Rejuvenation construction out front? They've got a three and a half year backlog of cases on a waiting list to get in there. They need these specimens to support that caseload."

Jennifer's exasperation turned to disgust. "Well, I don't want to be a part of it if it's going to be like this!"

Ozzie continued in a condescending tone, "Sweetpea, this isn't the 2020's. With all this A.I. Nurses are a dime a dozen now. You need this job more than you know. And you're not gonna find it easy gettin' another position on the day shift. This kind of operation is the wave of the future. Then added , "Besides don't we do D&Cs all the time?"

Ozzie stopped speaking as the two nurses lowered Maria's legs from the stirrups, then added, "Mind your own business and you'll survive."

"How can you be so callous and unfeeling," the young nurse accused.

Ozzie said resentfully, "Experience!", and pointed down at Maria's unconscious form. "This lady made her decision, right or wrong. The law says that's her choice to make, so it's none of our business anymore."

Jennifer retorted, "Maybe this lady didn't know how we actually do this stuff when she decided. Besides, I still think Petersen's behavior was egotistical and unprofessional. He reminded me of my six year old playing a video game through a VR headset. Administration should know that."

The elder nurse was now clearly running short on patience and words flowed smoothly in her Caribbean accent. "Look, I've been working here 8 years. You start an inquiry and I'll tell you what happens to the doctor. Nuthin'! They'll investigate you and me and all the nursing staff, until they find one lousy slip up in our procedures… anywhere. Then the investigation will focus on that and us."

Ozzie began to relent and added, "If you still can't handle it, go see your priest, or maybe, honeychild, bend your husband's ear tonight in bed."

Nurse Jennifer tried to interrupt but Ozzie waved her to silence. "Petersen can operate in the nude if he wants to. You just make sure you don't mention this incident again, to me or any other nurses. Or, you'll be working the Emergency Room graveyard shift next week." Ozzie then motioned to Jennifer to help her put Maria on the gurney. "You take the patient to recovery. I'll take care of the specimen."

The elder nurse failed to mention one very important piece of information about her personal stake in all of this. The 5-year waiting list for Lifespan treatments at the hospital was filled by the most famous rich people in the country: Hollywood entertainers, sports stars, business tycoons, political figures. A small concession to diversity resulted in a few dozen senior hospital minority staff being on the list. Luckily, Ozzie was one of those minority people on that list with a genetic pre-disposition for rheumatoid arthritis.

Alone now, the senior nurse turned her attention back to the plastic 'egg', wondering if she had come on too strong with Jennifer. Looking at its smooth oval shape she pondered if this one's tissues would ultimately be used in the future to treat her condition.

The last stage in finishing this task was to place the 'egg' into the low temperature transport case. It was specially designed by the engineers at Lifespan to keep fetal tissues at a low enough temperature to preserve the integrity of the blood and proto-organs. Too low a temperature, near 32°F, would cause destructive crystallization tearing apart the cell membranes. Conversely, the high temperature limit was 45°F, in order to limit the potential for growth of harmful bacteria or resumption of metabolic activity. These were lessons learned from hibernating mammal research studies.

Besides the thermal transport issue, there was the possibility of physical damage of the specimen by either dropping or a vehicular accident on its way to the lab.

To solve those problems a carbon-fiber box was designed which was about the size of a professional carpenter's toolbox. It came with a top hinged cover and handle, plus a shoulder strap anchored at each side. In addition, a groove was molded around its sides to allow a car seat belt to hold it firmly during transportation. Inside was a one and a half inch thick styrofoam sleeve that functioned as a shock insulator, and then filled with a cold proprietary preservative solution, and a reusable 'blue ice' pack clipped inside to maintain the low temperature. Suspended in the middle was a perforated plastic tray with a molded center section to secure the 'egg'. A temperature probe was attached to the tray near its center, and an insulated hinged lid finished the job of holding everything in place when its latch is closed.

For some impulsive reason, curiosity caught Nurse Ozzie today. Maybe it was the fight this specimen put up during the decoupling. She used the extraction tool to re-open the plastic egg, peeking inside to examine the fragile contents. She could clearly discern the genital tubercle directed inferior indicating female, not male as Petersen mistook in his haste. In the frenzy of the extraction no one really noticed, or for that matter, cared. Then the realization that this could have been a live little girl gave a cold morbid feeling that chilled her spirits. Suddenly Ozzie noticed her image with the egg was still in view of the video camera. With a shudder, she quickly moved out of view, and closed the egg, placing it back in the transport container, and dropped the lid. She murmured to herself, "Girl, don't never do that again!" and nervously snapped the two metal cover latches closed.

Following Lifespan procedure, she pressed the blue temperature check button on the side and it read 38°F on the cover LED display. Coincidentally, the same body temperature of a hibernating woodchuck.

Next, she pressed the yellow battery charge check button and an 'OK' was displayed for the integral Lithium battery pack. With everything in order, Ozzie picked up the case and put the strap on her shoulder.

Exiting the operating room helped her put the unsettling events and sights of the morning behind her. Proceeding down the busy hallway, she forced herself to focus on the afternoon case where she was scheduled to assist on an intubation of a 24 week-gestation, premature baby in the neonatal ICU.

The hospital was a study in contradictions to her. Upstairs, wretched scenes of parents and babies struggling to survive for each other, one day at a time. Nurses, like herself, having to be cheerleaders in a game where the odds are never better than 50-50. Doctors and medical equipment that can either simply prolong the agony, or conversely, preserve the gift of life. Recollections of some of those victories she had a role in, made her smile for a moment.

Downstairs, they ended life. Ozzie concluded to herself, *No discussion. No heroics. Just routine.* She had always been torn between the two worlds of giving life and taking it away - a place where convictions can easily get muddled.

However, her dander could still be raised. Like the hospital department administrator complaining last month that on top of delivery charges, it was costing an average of $150,000 in medical expenses to save one premature fetus. The big managed care insurance companies were pressuring the medical staff to abort them during the delivery, rather then try to save them later. After all, it was a lot cheaper, and they were not classified legally as human beings anyway. Moreover, there would not be those years of medical services during infancy for inevitably sick babies. So, she always thought it strange that when someone wants them to save a 24-week-old life, it is called an infant – a baby, and cost is no object. Conversely, when they want to abort it, at 24 weeks it is called a fetus, and its human value is nil. Ozzie began to realize that if she dwelled on this issue any longer, it would drive her out of her mind. It was not a revelation to know that nurses were always the ones caught in the middle of things anyway.

At the service elevator, the senior nurse entered the elevator and pressed the second floor button for the administration, where dopey admin Neil Katz would be waiting.

As usual, this morning's events would be buried in the back recesses of her mind - hauntingly, like the floating dust of their cremated remains.

* * * * * * *

Phylis returned to the Administration floor a second time, not understanding what could be taking so long. At 1:30 PM anxiety was already building as she thought about the commuter traffic to Lifespan labs in New Jersey. She arrived at Neil's office anticipating Maria's specimen, transport box, and release form would be waiting. Today's experience with Maria made her uneasy enough to want to just put this day behind her just a little bit sooner. So, when Phylis arrived at Neil's office, he wasn't there. "Now where the heck is the twit!" she grumbled.

As she turned to start searching for him, Neil came smiling through the door, transport case. "Sorry honey. The specimen just came down from OR. There was some kind of delay, a screw up with anesthesia. I don't know why. It just took longer than usual."

"First of all, I'm not your 'honey," His familiar tone grated on Phylis, "Neil, you should work at a supermarket checkout counter. Then, you could screw up the lives of 100 women a day!"

"Listen kid," he whined, "sometimes shit happens. I'm taking a late lunch because of this screw up. Try taking the chip off your shoulder for five minutes and I'll have you outta here." Neil hunched down at his desk and flashed the barcode reader on the specimen transport case. He mumbled something about a phone call from Lifespan Corporation, but his admin that had taken the message was on lunch break.

Phylis was annoyed and defused by the events of the day, and didn't feel argumentative at this point. It could be worse. She could be arguing with the service manager at her car dealership.

She leaned over his desk sensing he was going to need some help completing the data file entry. Neil looked up and asked, "What's the Lifespan case number for this one?"

"UH 0744," she competently replied. All Lifespan specimens received an alpha numeric code which essentially identifies the Hospital where it originates and the ascending sequence number of specimen from that location.

On the descriptive line of the file form Neil was completing, she leaned over to notice him typing, '**Embryulcia / Abruption of Placenta**'.

Her brow furrowed. "Neil, what's this placenta business?"

"You don't know?" he smiled, now amused that she didn't know. "We received an Email from Lifespan just last week that all future specimens must be obtained with the placenta intact".

"Why is that?"

"Apparently," he smugly answered, "it enhances the extract potential and captures more of the specimen superblood".

33

Being caught off guard and fatigued, Phylis just sighed a perfunctory, "Uh-huh."

She did asked herself why she wasn't told about this in advance. None of the other procurement agents at Lifespan were informed as far as she knew. She made a note to herself to question her boss about this later. It probably was just another bureaucratic snafu for Lifespan, she surmised.

Neil completed his database entry. Phylis let him flash the QR code on her cell phone as acceptance for Lifespan.

Several minutes later, Neil found the message that came in earlier for Phylis from Lifespan Corporation. He read the note to himself, which alluded to something about a back-up plan 'Bravo'. A strange message of no consequence, he concluded - she'll find out when she gets to Lifespan,

It was now 2:00 PM and Phylis would never make it to the office and back home before the rush hour. She'd have to call the kids after school and tell them to eat dinner without her tonight. Rushing to the parking lot, the transport case was feeling a lot heavier than 10 pounds, and Phylis was thankful for the shoulder strap.

Her thoughts were interrupted by a swirl of dust enveloping her on the sidewalk. A layer of clay and dirt had flowed across the hospital driveway during yesterday's thunderstorm, and was now dried and caked on the road. Each passing car stirred the fine dust particles into twin swirls that blew it in Phylis' path. She complained, "Just what I need with a black dress and black shoes."

In a futile gesture to escape the dust, Phylis broke into a halting trot. It was the best the woman could do, limited by a tight skirt and pumps, and 10 pounds of specimen transport. Her hips swayed in rhythm, and her tight skirt clung alternatively to each shapely thigh in turn. A light breeze blew her blazer lapels apart, revealing her silk blouse and the contour of gently bouncing breasts that kept time with each rhythmic step. This seemingly innocuous sight did not go unnoticed, and brought cheers of encouragement from some construction workers on coffee break across the street at the Rejuvenation building. From the girder work they cheered so loudly you would have thought she was OJ Simpson running from the police.

Phylis thought, *Men...If these guys were in a crippled airliner about to go down, and the pilot said bend over and assume the crash position. The last thing they would do is look up the skirt of any woman behind them.*

One part of her, the working professional, resented this kind of chauvinistic attention. The funny thing though, was that the other part of her, the feminine side, enjoyed the flirtation. It was nice to think that all those sweaty aerobics classes had kept her body tight and supple - that men still looked at her with desire... even at 47. Distracted and already behind schedule she never checked to see that her company supplied SatCom 5 phone was off.

At last, she reached her car, put her hand into her purse, and unlocked the car with a squawk from the key fob. She opened the back door, and carefully strapped the transport box onto a special net cradle in the back seat. Lifespan directives dictated that it be secured in the back seat in the event of an accident. Never the front seat or the trunk. Yet nowhere in the directive did it discuss protecting the procuring agent who was driving the transport case to begin with!

She imagined being in a car wreck one day with the Lifespan emergency crew dispatched to the scene, while she's pinned in the wreckage with a steering wheel wrapped around her neck. Of course, her rescue would have to wait until the specimen was saved.

Still smiling from her thoughts, Phylis backed out of her space and exited the lot, smiling and waving to the construction workers still eyeing her from the girders above. Deciding on the Belt Parkway to the Verrazano Bridge as the best route to New Jersey, her trip to Lifespan Headquarters started.

Driving alone back to Lifespan was always the time best for getting her thoughts organized. It was fortunate that the company car had an eight speaker stereo and a secure Satcom satellite link as standard equipment. So, she had a choice of rock, country, and easy listening stations depending on her mood. Today it would be soft music.

Cruising in the slower right lane, her thoughts turned to her precious cargo in the back seat. Although Lifespan did not discuss exact figures, various coworkers guessed a specimens value at between 500 and 800 thousand dollars worth of cultured drug treatments. In spite of the high value she wasn't nervous driving with that responsibility. Phylis had been doing this for a long time now, close to a hundred decouplings. It was all just routine.

Routine meant 3 years experience working as a procuring specialist for Lifespan. It was exciting in the beginning, and recollections of that past entered her consciousness. Back then, it was quite a stressful time too. Divorce and a late life pregnancy leading to restarting her own career. Having to stifle her obsolete homemaker instincts to adapt to the cold world of business.

Phylis remembered when her simple home life was turned upside down and inside out. A twenty year marriage that seemed to run out of gas just when it should have been coasting. An unwanted pregnancy that would have prevented any hope of a restarting her life. A successful husband who used that success to indulge in self-gratification on every level; fancy foreign cars, club memberships, extended business trips and, worst of all, other businesswomen. And, finally, the prospect of trying to re-start her career with a 20 year old Liberal Arts degree. With her only experience as a homemaker, her resume would have only had three lines;

35

Raised two kids that were never late to school.
Cared for a husband who never had to wear dirty underwear.
Kept a clean house for them to mess up on a daily basis.

Phylis could feel the pressure in her head and chest as these thoughts could still provoke latent animosity and disappointment. Two decades wasted with the wrong man.

Lifespan Corporation was a Godsend at that point in her life. She had enthusiastically volunteered her specimen, as one of the first women to do so. The money they gave her was the springboard she needed to get back to school and into a career on her own two feet again. Her cooperation and interest so impressed the Lifespan people that they offered her a job! To think, 20 years ago a dependent homemaker. Now an independent professional pulling $250,000 a year in income.

Not too shabby, she thought.

Her deliberations turned to her own two children, Mark and Kristy. They would be entering college soon and be on their own in six years. Then the sporadic child support will stop, and Phylis would really be on her own. She was 47 years old now, in 3 years, 50! The good news was that she was confident she could maintain her financial well-being and afford to send the kids to college - thanks to Lifespan.

However, there was a down side. After the kids leave, with no man to lean on, it would be a lonely finish to her life. She was not hardened into a single life style like many of those other career women. The money wasn't enough. Other women's loveless sob stories only seem to compound her inner frustrations. She needed to be held in a man's arms. Love. Emotional security. Someone to care about... and not just a dog or cat!

And her new found freedom and independence? That translated into quite a different life than all those media people portrayed. It meant working full-time at what was becoming a job for survival. And, still working essentially a second job at home raising her children. One day blending into the next. Weeks becoming months...then years. Life just drifting by like billowing cumulus clouds in the sky.

Her reward for all this? A dysfunctional family, and, living and sleeping alone.

If the bottom-line of this restructured society was supposed to be happiness, it was becoming increasingly elusive to Phylis. If anything, she found herself becoming more hardened and progressively more cynical and bitter about how life turned out. *As if slowly being chiseled into some kind of stone cold icon of a feminist*, Phylis could only conclude.

And the future? She tried not to think too much about it.

Traffic slowed to a crawl at the usual construction sites. Phylis switched the radio to 1010 WINS for traffic reports and to distract her from these recurring frustrations.

A strenuous hour later, Phylis exited the Garden State Parkway in New Jersey about one mile from the industrial park where Lifespan headquarters was located. Continuing to her destination on secondary roads, she noticed ominous flashing lights and sirens among the low silhouette of the industrial park ahead. She was thankful that this wasn't happening later during the rush hour, or the roadways would be jammed.

Getting closer to her street, she was also getting closer to the source of the noise. At the turn onto Technology Drive, Phylis slowed down at the intersection and pulled over to the curb about 100 yards away from the main entrance of Lifespan, observing the distant crowd of demonstrators through her windshield. A large number of demonstrators, wielding placards, were chanting some indistinct slogans in unison, Two EMT vehicles were on company grounds, flashing red and blue strobe lights. That meant there were physical injuries, and it was obvious that Lifespan security had their hands full.

"Oh shoot," Phylis exclaimed. Then, she remembered to turn on her SatCom5 link. It beeped continuously, with a 'RED ALERT' text message, "Execute Plan Bravo."

Phylis began to rant out aloud in her car, "Why does this have to happen today. I'm already late?"

Of course, Phylis was unaware of the message left with Neil Katz back at University Hospital. In a couple of seconds Phylis regained her composure, and realized that eventually this street would soon be crawling with more police She remembered that Lifespan Corporation emergency procedure Plan Bravo dictated not to approach the facility during any kind of demonstration. With a quick glance to her rearview mirrors, she made an abrupt U-turn, and headed in the opposite direction. The emergency procedure also specified the nearby and innocuous *Atlas Meat Distributors* as a temporary drop-off point under these conditions. They have leased refrigerated storage lockers ideal for holding the specimens for a day or two.

During the short 3-block trip, Phylis pondered the motivations of those outrageous demonstrators and wondered in rapid succession, *where do these loonies come from in the middle of the day? Don't they have real jobs to work - like me? Why don't they pester the whale hunters? Save the sea otters,... or close some nuclear power plant? Where are the police?*

Then she parked in front at the tranquil *Atlas* facility, and entered the main entrance with the transport case. The receptionist greeted her with, "Let me guess," pointing her barcode reader at the transport box. " Lifespan. Right?"

Placing the case on the counter, Phylis asked, "How'd you know?"

The girl laughed, "Well.you're not carrying a side of beef, and your not the first one here today either."

Katie O'Connell, another Lifespan procuring agent waltzed over returning from the lobby Ladies room to explain, "Some fun, huh? I just dropped off my specimen from Queens General. More agents were here earlier. Are you gonna try going back to the office?"

Phylis replied softly, in a beleaguered tone, "No. I've had enough excitement for one day. And the rush hour has already started. I can't even get home."

"How about joining me at the gym club, we'll work off some stress?" Katie enthusiastically asked, "And then down to Applebees for a light salad?"

Phylis said, "OK, but just let me make a call."

Katie smirked and said, "Tell'em to take out a frozen pizza."

Phylis felt a bit defensive about her maternal responsibilities. It was supposed to be the age of child neglect without guilt. She changed direction and added, "I'll call my parents. Mom and dad can warm up a leftover cooked meal from my fridge instead."

****

Much later that evening, Phylis finally made it home after dinner, and behind the rush hour traffic. Her effervescent daughter, Kristy, met her expectantly on the driveway, hardly waiting for Phylis to park before greeting her. She always thought her mother looked beautiful dressed for work.

Delighted with mom's arrival, she launched into a barrage of questions. "Hi mommy, I saw your company on the six o'clock news! Did you see the demonstration? Did you know the lady that got hurt? Did they arrest her?"

Phylis, exhausted, trudged up the driveway to the front door of her three-bedroom Cape. "No honey, I didn't. I stayed far away from it."

"Aw mom, you missed it? All of it?"

She stopped to kiss her daughter's cheek, and in a low, exhausted whisper said, "Honey, I'm pooped. Just let me get into the house, get my robe on, and get these heels off. Then we'll talk some more."

Concerned about their eating, she added, "Did you both have the dinner I prepared this morning?"

"Yes mom," she replied, adding, "And grandma and grandpa came over with even more food."

Phylis didn't remember seeing her parent's car out in the street and asked as she entered the house, "Where are they?"

"They had to leave early for grandpa's dentist appointment." Then added proudly, "Grandma did the pots, I did the dishes myself."

Phylis wandered alone down the hallway to her bedroom, asking herself with amusement, why this same helpful daughter seemed to disappear when she needed help doing the dishes.

After changing into her silk pajamas, and filling a dish of mint chocolate-chip ice cream from the freezer, it was over to the family room to unwind. She snuggled deeply into her favorite chair, turned on her home laptop and checked her email. After a few relaxing moments she called out, "Kristy, where's your brother, where's Mark?"

"He's next door at John's.....doing homework."

"All accounted for," she sighed.

Mark was more likely playing video games with John rather than studying. Overall, the kids handled the working mother situation pretty well. Only at eighteen, Mark was getting more demonstrative and independent, and tougher to control.

Phylis paused to reflect on her son's behavior lately, feeling that it would sure help to have a 'father figure' around to ride herd on him. Someone, if need be, would draw a line in the sand that he wouldn't dare to cross.

Unfortunately, working full time left her with little time or ambition to start playing the dating game again in search of a mate. Life already seemed complicated enough just earning a living. And, divorce had somehow left her with an innate fear of failure in new relationships.

As a divergence from her troubling thoughts, she grabbed the remote and clicked on the TV to the seven o'clock news. Highlights came on with coverage of the Lifespan demonstration, and it immediately drew her attention.

Phylis and the viewers were going to, unknowingly, get Lifespan's distorted version of today's story, courtesy of newswoman Patty and Jane Savage from Lifespan Security. She looked at the violent images and was glad she missed it. Then Patty Marshall's face filled the screen.

Her report started with, "It was another day of conflict at Lifespan headquarters, as Right-to-Life advocates turned violent, wrecking a security vehicle, and causing severe injuries to one woman bystander."

The video panned the faces of angry demonstrators, and the injured woman carried into the ambulance on a stretcher.

"We're sorry that there's no audio with this coverage. We had equipment damaged by protesters during our filming." (courtesy of Mike)

Watching the injured woman being loaded into the ambulance, Phylis was vexed.

These protesters don't care who they hurt, she thought. *The country and courts have moved on.*

Patty continued, putting her own 'spin' on the video. "This woman was fortunate that quick action by the Lifespan security staff may have saved her life. I asked a spokeswoman for the company, Jane Savage, why this woman was at the demonstration."

A close up of Jane appeared, commenting, "We're working on the theory the she may have been an industrial spy, since a witness saw her carrying a camera shortly before the incident."

The coverage continued with pictures of the damaged car. Patty proceeded with her voice-over dialogue, "Lifespan officials, while shocked at the blatant disregard for human life shown by the demonstrators, vowed to continue producing their life saving treatments. And, they say that today's disturbance will have no effect on pharmaceutical production."

What followed was a series of videos of pitiful children cured of debilitating diseases from Lifespan extracts. The report closed with the camera panning the sign on the corner with the corporate logo and slogan '*The pursuit of healthy longevity*'. The logo was composed of a 'yin and yang' circle with a modernistic embryo inside that looked like a backwards numeral nine

How appropriate, Phylis thought, as Kristy entered the room at the tail end of the story. Up until now, the young girl only knew that her mother worker for a drug company. For some reason Phylis never felt the compulsion to reveal exactly how they made those wonderful drugs.

"Mommy, why do those people keep giving your company such a hard time?" her daughter asked sympathetically.

"They just don't understand the importance of what my company does. We help people. We don't hurt them. We make sick people well again."

Phylis shifted her argument, "Those protesters think that women don't have the right to decide things for themselves."

"Decide what things?" Kristy asked in a puzzled tone.

Phylis was not in the mood for an ethical discussion, answering anyway, "Whether to have babies or not."

Kristy found the choice incongruous. She always enjoyed being around the babies in her neighbor's home, so she innocently replied, "Why wouldn't you want to have your own baby?"

"It's not always easy to understand," her mother reluctantly explained. "When you get older, things get more complicated, you have your own life to think about first. Babies take a lot of care and time. They prevent you from doing other things." Phylis looked up at the ceiling, "Lord, don't I know."

Kristy wasn't accepting this too well, and queried, "What does all this have to do with your company, Mom?"

Phylis was afraid that question was coming and answered in a more perturbed tone, "Look Kristy, when women are pregnant at inconvenient times, they end it. Then my company decouples the specimen and cultures the tissues. We reclaim certain fluids and organic material, and process and

40

purify them into drugs. Sick people receive injections of these medicines to help them to fight their disease. It's that simple."

Kristy frowned as her simplistic adolescent perspective of the discussion became obvious. "Yuck! You make babies into something that sounds like chicken soup."

"Enough!" Phylis exclaimed. Her daughter obviously touched a sore nerve. "You're being ridiculous. They're not babies yet - fetuses. It's just dead tissue. There's no human life there! Don't they teach you anything in school?"

Kristy resented her mother's tone, and said indignantly. "Then why do mothers call the fetuses in their tummy's babies?

"End of discussion!" Phylis exclaimed, "You're beginning to sound like those demonstrators on TV. All this life stuff was thoroughly investigated for 90 some odd years by all these scientific people and the courts. There's no question about it. Nothing is human until it's born. …Period!"

Kristy recognized she'd reached her mother's limit, and decided to drop the dialogue. Still she had seen so many pregnant relatives have babies. They seemed to enjoy interacting with their babies in their stomachs. Kristy wondered to herself, *If they weren't humans in there, then what the heck were they?* Then she concluded, *Besides, the only inhuman person I know is my brother!*

Although unsatisfied with the explanation, Kristy retreated into the kitchen to do her schoolwork on the table. She knew the limitations of her mother's patience and didn't want to upset her any further.

Phylis, still unsettled, sat down to think about tomorrow. She wanted to speak to her boss, Jerry, about why this placenta business was added to the normal extraction. It crossed her mind that she failed to keep her Sat COM 5 phone charged and might have missed an update. So, she placed it on the charging block. Phylis imagined that the office would be buzzing tomorrow about the demonstration, and she was anxious to get caught up on that and all the latest Lifespan gossip.

Finally relaxed, her attention returned to her laptop, casually browsing the new emails. Finding one email advertised as a free week on a middle-aged dating website called **Middle Earth**. Feeling adventurous, she clicked on the link. She registered and filled out the profile for herself and her potential match.

I need a laugh, she conceded, as an excuse to begin scanning the potential matches.

Everybody likes 'quiet walks on the beach', 'watching sunsets together', 'intimate dinners and music'. Most were so repetitious. Some of the presumptuous people appeared to be totally caught up in writing a detailed specification for a perfect mate, as if they were the catch of the year.

Then Phylis started to feel a bit cruel to belittle their desperate attempts at middle-aged companionship. She wondered if there were still real men out there that could be honest with a woman, and take responsibility for a lasting relationship. Reaching the last match she saw something odd - out of place. It caught her eye and, smiling, she called out to her daughter in the next room, "Kristy, listen to this guys pitch."

Phylis read aloud:

~USED MALE~

Euro-American with brown top and blue headlights.
Body in excellent condition with minor dings and scratches from normal wear and tear.
Dependable daily rider, never failed to start in 50 years.
Documented track record of professional successes in business and athletics.
All parts and personality are genuine and original.
Classic values and emotions in storage for 5 years,
BUT, with very feminine TLC can run with the big boys again.
How about a test spin?
Sorry, licensed drivers over 40 only. Current PIC below

Match # 105
~ Mike"

His picture reminded her a bit of Mel Gibson - a bit rugged, with sincere looking eyes. He also looked faintly familiar, but she couldn't place him. And the name, - just Mike - Mike who?

Kristy and Phylis laughed out loud together. Kristy got up from the kitchen table and said, "Let me read that guy's pitch again."

Phylis sat back to reflect, her polished fingernail resting on her lower lip, while Kris read it again.

Giggling, Kristy offered, "Hey Mommy, why don't you answer him! He sounds cool."

"Wait a minute little girl, what do I know about him?"

"He's funny!"

"If I wanted to meet comedians, I'd date some of the executives at Lifespan."

"Come on maaa...."

"How do I know who this person is? Five years in storage? He might have been in jail! Or worse, just released from an insane asylum! Maybe he was cryogenically frozen and just thawed out!" Phylis was already starting to laugh at her own commentary, continuing with a chuckle, "For all I know it took him 5 years to scribble that ad." She set her laptop aside.

Kristy chastised her saying, "Mom, get real!"

Just then, Mark came home through the back door, "Hey, what's so funny?" He walked over to Phylis, leaned over, kissed his mother's forehead, and expressed his tender feelings. "Yo, ma."

Phylis looked up and returned his affections with a question, "The laces on your sneakers aren't tied."

"I know ma."

"Then why don't you tie them?'

" 'cause I'm taking them off now."

Phylis decided to abandon such a demanding line of reasoning and shifted to, "Did you finish your homework?"

"Sure."

"Then let me see it."

She looked at his Calculus and Physics assignments without the foggiest idea of what she was looking at, but knew Mark always needed prodding to get through school. Phylis couldn't shake this feeling deep down inside, that she was short changing her kids. That she didn't spend enough time with them growing up. That she wasn't following their educations close enough. She daydreamed about her own formative years. How much time her mother spent at home making it cozy, secure... and policing the homework. How she benefited from having both a mother and a father.

Then sighed to herself in resignation, *At least they will never know what they missed.*

Meanwhile, Kristy showed the website to Mark. He read it and said, "Coolo-mundo, this guy is probably rich and drives a Corvette! You should check him out, Mom."

Phylis looked up sternly and responded, "You kids have got to understand that I can't take chances bringing strange men into our lives. I'm responsible for our safety first."

Mark was quick to answer protectively, "Mom, if he hassles you I'll kick his butt."

Phylis quipped back in amusement, "But first you'll have to learn to tie your shoelaces."

They all laughed together, and Phylis handed Mark his homework back.

Mark knew his mother didn't really fathom all the equations and formulas, but he played along, figuring it made her happy doing her concerned parent thing.

Undistracted, Kristy diligently dragged her kitchen chair into the family room and set herself up next to Phylis' recliner. She took her mother's laptop and said very deliberately, "OK, answer this guy."

Phylis continued to back peddle, "He'll probably get dozens of responses. How do I know he'll even respond to me? Suppose I meet him and it doesn't click."

"Ask him for a 30 day warranty," Kristy retorted.

"Maybe I'll write tomorrow."

Kristy persisted, "Mom if you don't do it tonight, you'll never do it."

"OK, OK," Phylis relented and sat quietly for a while, outlining a response in her mind. She decided to use the same tack he used, and not go into to much physical detail or requirements. The hardest part was finding a recent, flattering photo of herself.

Dear Used Male,

I never leave my car out in the street.
 It's always garaged, safe and sound with me every night.
My last ride lasted 20 years before it quit on me.
Since then, I've been looking for a classic replacement,
preferably of investment quality to keep forever.
TLC waiting for the right deal.
PIC enclosed.
Match# 333
Call my answering machine at (201) 296-5015, after 9 AM.
PS. My PIC is recent. Is yours?
                                      Phylis"

Phylis, although still interested, was cautious in responding, giving her office telephone number and little else. This made her feel comfortably in control. She could quit at anytime along the way.

Phylis admired the wild abandon of her young romantic daughter. She was more excited about all this than her mother. Still, there was something about this guy's eyes and straight forward line that made her want to find out more. He also looked so familiar. It almost seemed as though a fresh relationship might only be a phone call away. Her reverie allowed for that dormant little girl dream to return after so many years - of meeting that one man who would dramatically change her life for the better, and they'd live happily ever after.

Phylis smiled at Kris, put her arm around her with a kiss to the cheek, and parodied the soap operas, saying, "Will divorced, suburban career woman find true happiness? Tune in tomorrow!"

CHAPTER 4
The best defense is offense

The next morning, a weary Mike approached the main gate at Lifespan in his car, driving past the damaged security car from the day before.

Passing the guard shack, he waved to security Sergeant Harry, who grinned and gave a mock-salute in return. After parking his car, it was still 7:30 AM, early enough for Mike to spend some quiet time in his empty office upstairs. When he arrived at his desk, the voice mail message light blinked away on his desk phone. Mike listened to an invitation from his boss, VP Al Greene, to an 8 AM meeting. Next, Mike sat down behind his desk and logged onto his desktop terminal, sticking a memory stick into the 'forbidden' USB port – forbidden because company policy forbid output ports. Mike had one because he was in charge of Facilities. Hence, he and never reported it. He casually browsed through some old file folders going back several years. After a few minutes, he found the 'ammunition' for his defense and began copying the internal Emails that covered the corporate planning meetings surrounding the installation of the razor wire fence. Some other Emails embarrassing to the company were added. Thereafter, he printed out his own version of what really happened at yesterday's incident, along with other pertinent documentation.

Satisfied with his collection of information, he sat back and pondered his fate. In a few minutes he'd find out if this exercise was worth staying up late all night to prepare. At 8:05 AM Mike reluctantly left his office, manila folder in hand, just as everyone else in his department was arriving. For sure, his demeanor revealed a hint of dread of the verbal tongue lashing his boss had waiting for him. His subordinates, aware of the fence incident, timidly looked at him in silence. They regarded him as if he was a prisoner on his way to death row, figuring these were his last moments as an employee. Privately, they admired his actions at the security fence. Mike thought of the heavy set Al Greene, whose large girth and obese appearance disguised a sharp intellect and a demanding supervisor. Normally when Al was leaning on Mike it was no picnic, and Mike really didn't mind.

He respected Al. His boss leaned on all his managers equally hard, and was technically competent to boot. Today, Mike would have to approach this like any other business crisis - let Al explode, gasp for air, and wait for him to finally cool down.

Mike grabbed a cup of coffee from the canteen and walked down the hall to Al's office. Inside, Al's hulk was hunched over his keyboard, typing and mouse clicking something on his desktop terminal. With his pudgy hands, he almost looked like a sumo wrestler smothering a real mouse.

Pausing briefly at the office entrance, Mike rapped on the door frame. The moment ended abruptly as Al failed to answer, or even look away from his monitor, motioning only with his hand for Mike to take a chair opposite his desk.

Mike put his folder on his lap, and tried opening with a neutral, "Good Morning", and it was evident that Al was in no mood for cordiality.

His boss finally slid the mouse away and focused on him with a squinting eye, "Damn it Mike, you're doing it again," he railed, pointing with his gold Cross pen. "How many times have I explained it to you?"

Mike didn't respond, simply staring down into his coffee cup, observing the concentric swirls of cream spiraling on the surface. It seemed like an appropriate metaphor for his career lately. He held his tongue.

Al continued, "We've known each other for what, 5 years now? And, how many times have I had to save your ass from corporate?"

Al stood up and walked over to his office door, slamming it shut with a bang. "Let me put it in plain words again. There are only two groups of people in this corporation, <u>Them</u> and <u>Us</u>. You will never be part of <u>Us</u>, unless you stick to the party line. Play with the team!" Al returned to his desk and continued, "If you tried a little harder you wouldn't be considered such a pariah!"

Mike leaned forward, cradling the coffee cup in his hands between his knees. It was time to interrupt his boss's monologue. "Whoa, Al! How 'bout telling me what crime I committed this time?"

Al held up a hard copy of a fresh Email from Jane Savage, in corporate Security. He was clearly irritated that the memo was directed over his head to his superiors. "Here's what you did. This memo was E-mailed straight to Max Brewster, Chairman of the Board!" Al slapped the page with the back of his fingers each time as he ticked off another charge, "Assisting a Right-to-Life organization; interfering with security personnel; allowing unauthorized visitors on company premises; and worst of all insulting the News Media!"

Exasperated, Al let his huge girth fall back into his leather chair, "You gave corporate the gun and the bullets." With palms pointed skyward, he concluded, "I can't save your bacon anymore."

Mike took a moment to shrewdly scan the top of Al's desk, and immediately felt his job was safe. There were no severance check envelopes, no COBRA medical insurance extension forms, and no company property checklists. Mike knew full well what the routine was for terminating employees. Feeling more secure now, Mike figured it was his turn to be agitated, and responded in a firm voice, "Al, I can tell you right now, I'm not apologizing for anything I did yesterday. You know me long enough to understand how my mind works. I still have a conscience."

Al answered condescendingly, pointing his pen at Mike. "What makes <u>you</u> so Goddamn special... so conscience bound?"

Mike replied sharply, "I just do what other people know they should do, but don't do.

Irritated by that last remark, Al took it personally, and reacted with his flushed rotund face. "You know Mike, you think and sound like your God's gift to Lifespan." Finally, he sighed, "Santino, I think you just enjoy being beat up. This time, don't expect me to take a lickin' with you."

Mike paused, leaned forward in his chair, and crossed his legs. He glanced at his worn shoe soles, feeling more and more like an old war-horse. So, the time seemed right to introduce his little write-up, and said, "Well Al, maybe this time you don't have to take a lickin' for me."

Al dismissed him straightaway, "It doesn't matter, I have to give you a formal written reprimand for the personnel files, and, possibly, for immediate company dismissal."

Mike picked up the folder on his lap, pulling four pages from his folder, Mike decided to get right down to the point saying, "Here's my written recollections of the events leading up to that disaster on the fence. It also lists all the other Lifespan employees who witnessed the events and what they did. Then there are the relevant meetings, Emails, and attendees at earlier security meetings that added the military grade razor wire to the top of the fence. I also have copies of the old purchase orders which state specifically to <u>buy mil-spec, anti-personnel grade, razor wire.</u>" My brother-in-law is an attorney and he has a copy of all this.

Al winced at that last phrase, knowing full well the embarrassing legal ramifications if that 'military razor wire' phrase became public. In the public arena it would sound as bad as placing land mines on the front lawn.

Mike continued, "I don't have to remind you what company policy states that; 'The employee may respond in writing to any formal reprimand in his personnel folder'. If the company wants to make a formal issue out of this, then into the file all this goes too. If they still want to play hardball, then this write-up goes to the lawyer of the lady lacerated on the fence."

Al reached out a pudgy hand for the write-up and folder, and reflected to himself, *Totally in character for him. Thorough. Like a good engineer.*

Tacitly acknowledging Mike's point, Al's reply was less argumentative, more advisory in tone. "I know, Mike. You may think that's a clever move, but you saw the news reports last night. The people upstairs always control the conversation. They are tough and vindictive - totally without mercy. You're going to be labeled disloyal, even if you survive this."

Quickly Mike answered, "Loyalty is a two way street, Al. They don't want loyalty. They want a conspiracy of silence from witless slaves."

Al felt like he was listening to corporate heresy, and stood up, lest he be stained by the words falling on him. It was no wonder Mike hadn't any friends at Lifespan. However, he responded in a conciliatory tone, and signaled the end of debate. "OK Mike, enough of this horseshit already. I'll pass your version upstairs today and get back to you later. In the meantime, don't discuss this with anyone else."

Confidently, Mike stood up and gulped down the last of his coffee. "Just remember Al, I'm still personally loyal to you."

After his departure, Al sat back down and leaned back in his leather chair, clasped his hands behind his head and to strategize. *If I lose Santino, I might lose the entire instrument engineering group with him. This folder might be the vehicle to make it all work. The threat of legal involvements and public scrutiny are the only things I know that can put corporate on edge. I'll just drop this write-up at the meeting, and act as a neutral go-between. Then see which way the wind blows. Either way, I come out clean.* Al knew he needed Santino. The bulk of his technical staff were molecular biologists, chemists and quantum computer scientists. Santino's group was the only practical electrical and mechanical engineering people he had. What they couldn't build, they'd buy off-the-shelf. What they couldn't find cheaply, they'd copy. Their model shop was also able to fabricate all the oddball fixtures his biochemists could dream up.

Al was convinced that he needed Mike's expertise to support the peripheral edges of his technical pyramid. Mike was a walking catalog of sources of hardware and software with the insights to select just the right instrumentation for the job. He also was a quick study who often gave ideas to his other scientists with common sense observations and suggestions. All the specimen transport cases, tooling, production processing equipment, and screening instrumentation had Mike's mark on them somewhere.

Al shuddered at the potential loss of Mike, and perhaps some of his subordinates. They could be replaced. But at what cost... and how long would it take? Production had to double every quarter to keep up with drug treatment demand. Plus, there was another treatment clinic being built in the Hamptons, and two new plants in Pasadena in some old NASA buildings.

* * * * * * *

Mike wandered down the plush carpeted hallway until he passed a double door and transitioned from plush carpeting to the regular tile floor, a subtle signal about "Us and Them." His mind was relieved that the episode with Al Greene was over for now. The chips will fall where they may. *Isn't it odd*, he reflected, *in all our company discussions, that badly injured woman on the fence was never mentioned.*

On his trip down the hallway he dawdled at the company bulletin board, observing the posted announcements and activities. Lifespan seemed like such a great company to work for. The bowling team won their league championship, the physical fitness club was getting four new Nautilus

48

machines, and Daycare added two more teaching staff.

Regardless, Mike knew how corporations work. Hire good, dedicated, genuine people, then drain the company's profits off with perks for top management. Sell it before the lack of reinvestment cripples the organization. . Blame the economy for the company's failure.

Mike sensed that he was beginning to wallow in pointless frustration and thought, *Enough Mikey-boy. You're becoming a real middle-aged cynic.*

Before he turned from the bulletin board, the Company Spring Dance announcement caught his eye. Apparently, they were arranging to charter two Circle Line boats to sail around Manhattan Island for an evening of dinner and dancing. Mike read it, then continued down the hallway, his mind drifting further from work. He imagined how much fun it would be if his wife, Laura were still here to enjoy it, recalling how she loved to dance - how light she felt in his embrace. On the dance floor, Laura never mentioned what he actually looked like on the dance floor - she was too gracious for that.

Five years had past since Laura's untimely death, except he could recall only general fragments – as if it was almost a past life, instead of this one. Memories alone were not enough. He needed help now to get through the remaining days of life on earth. Mike sighed sadly, "*Well, at least I had it all once.*"

He reached his office and shook off the daydreams of better times. Slipping down into his office chair, he changed his mind set by signing time cards left over from the prior day. As he mechanically thumbed through them, a personal thought came to mind anyway. Maybe it was triggered by his lonely thoughts at the bulletin board.

Mike slapped his forehead and muttered, "Oh, crap. My 'Used Male' posting on the *Middle Earth* website. I never looked for it." He had been so busy preparing and writing his defense that he completely forgot about it. He wondered if any women had seen it, not sure how the posting would go over, since he wasn't too specific about himself or what he was looking for.

Then he made a mental note to check the website and Emails when he arrived home tonight.

Just then, Nancy, Mike's department administrator, peered through his office door way leaning an arm against the jamb and interrupted his thoughts, "Morning' Mike. How are you feeling? Then she smiled," We took care of closing up shop."

"Good job. I appreciate that, and yeah, I'm OK, I guess," And pointed to his E-mail screen on the monitor, "Got some catching up to do."

Nancy lingered, indecisively a bit at the doorway, speaking somewhat sheepishly, I, uh, well, actually we...., the department, just wanted you to know we think you did the right thing helping that woman on the fence."

Mike stopped sifting through E-mail and looked up with those bright blue eyes of his. "You tell everyone I appreciate that. I really do."

"And," she continued, "no matter how the company portrayed it. Or, even if she was a Pro-lifer or whatever."

She stepped out, hesitated a moment and stepped back in, adding in a muted tone, "Just don't tell anybody I said that, Mike. Please."

"Sure, Nancy," Mike acknowledged and waved his hand, "Sure. I understand." Then Nancy looked down and quickly returned to her desk outside.

Mike could sense the caution in her tone. He was a pariah in the company now. His department's sympathy was touching, but he knew if push came to shove, no one would make an active move to help him. Realistically, what could they do at their level in Lifespan? They had their jobs and families to think of first.

Mike was used to putting his career on the line. In the real world, it always means doing it alone, and paying the price alone.

He turned his attention to his Email In-Box, sorting and dumping the endless pile of technical junk mail that arrived every day. At the end of the pile was a strange Email.

Mike was puzzled, *Another requisition for blood from the downtown blood bank? That's 24 more units this month for the R&D department? Maybe old Doc Strauss really is a vampire from Transylvania?"* He comically guessed.

Mike never trusted Strauss from the first time they met. The guy was downright sinister looking, with bushy eyebrows, beady eyes and a long pointed nose. And the little ferret was the company president's buddy. That was enough for guilt by association in Mike's book.

Mike signed off the requisition and sent it on its way, digging further into his in-box. There was a memorandum with an attached purchase order copy from Dr. Joel Rosen, Director of Specimen Extract Production. Normally, he ran the fetal cell dissection &extracting stations, culturing vats, and medicinal purification equipment. This time, the request was for Mike's department to perform incoming inspection and test of twelve portable dialysis machines.

He questioned himself, *What the hell are we going to do with a dozen more renal dialysis machines, and blood respirators?* Facetiously continuing, *Probably, old Max, the president, is on life support?*

Mike glanced at the attached purchase order copy for $600,000, signed by Max, Strauss and the dopey charm-boy, CFO Lombardo - all the big guns. Flipping back to the memo, he wrote a message in the top margin to his supervisor Phil, to dig out the written manuals and specs from the

50

vendor in advance of shipment, so they would be ready ahead of time.

Mike recollected that several months ago, the people at R&D had requested a half dozen or so dialysis machines and respirators. When he asked around the company, it was explained that they were evaluating using it as a filtering technique to purify compounds from the specimen extractions. Mike flipped back to the Purchase Order to check the deliveries' internal destination at Lifespan.

Oddly enough, they weren't going to Joel's Extraction Production Department, where all biochemical drug production is accomplished. The dialysis units were going to Doctor Strauss' R&D department. It didn't make any sense.

Mike decided to call Joel Rosen himself. Then he figured that his boss, Al Greene, may know something. He could ask him later, after his pow-wow with corporate...that is if he's still working for Lifespan.

Mike decided to call Joel directly anyway. They'd worked with each other for five years now, and Mike developed a good, working rapport with him. They even played on the company softball team together, and were known as the two 'old farts' of the club. A lab tech answered and indicated Joel was out on the lab floor. After a short delay Joel was on the line and spoke chidingly, "I expected your call, Mike. You probably want to borrow a clean shirt after yesterday's excitement."

Mike picked up on the banter, "You hump, you're lucky you're in the other building, or I'd throw you another bean ball."

Joel laughed as he recalled that play. "OK, OK, so what's on your mind anyway?"

"I've got this requisition copy for some dialysis units with your John Hancock on it. You guys need to separate all that piss and vinegar you generate over there?"

Mike expected another rank-out in return, except Joel became strangely quiet. "Hey Joel buddy, you using the bad ear again," Mike continued in jest, after some hesitation, Joel stammered more seriously, "Uh, well, I'm in the middle of a procedure in the lab. Can't talk anymore."

Mike wasn't sure if he offended him or what, and noticed a distinct shift in tone. "Look, maybe I should come over there and we can talk."

"No. No! That's not necessary." Joel continued to falter, and finally offered, "Why don't we have lunch on Monday next week? We can talk more then."

Mike immediately answered in the affirmative, adding, "I'll pick you up over there, lefty?"

Joel said, "Yeah. See ya then," and quickly hung up.

Mike was a bit perplexed. *What did he say wrong?*

Joel and he had a good team relationship at work and on the softball field. Maybe the word was out that Mike had corporate leprosy again. It left

51

an uneasy feeling, that an associate that he considered a friend, might have turned on him. That and the purchase order mystery would bother Mike until they met the next week.

* * * * * * *

Later that morning Phylis arrived at her Lifespan office. In spite of yesterday's hassles, she felt in good spirits. On the car radio this morning she heard the old Carly Simon song '*I Believe in Love*'.

> *...So if you're willing to play the game*
> *Love will be comin' around again...*

It made Phylis wonder about the chances of finding real love at middle age. She pondered, *Did I waste all my opportunities of meeting "mister right" in the first half of my life?*

That 'Used Male' guy played on her mind, adding a combination of excitement and expectation to her dull repetitive routine. She had looked at the website on her smartphone and her response again over breakfast, and tucked it in her purse before leaving for work. Carrying that concealed liaison of words, seemed to heighten the air of mystery surrounding it.

What Phylis could not foresee, was that life could be infinitely more complex and frightening than the monotonous life she trudged through today. And, having someone come into her life at this stage, and change everything, involve a lot of risk.

Little did she know that in the near future, Phylis' single-minded devotion, would test the limits of a woman's ability to love a doggedly principled man.

Unaware of such consequences, Phylis breezed into her cubicle where her desk was covered in sticky notes, and her answering machine was blinking with more voice-mail.

First things first, she thought, turning on her desktop terminal. After boot-up, she plugged in her memory stick, and clicked her mouse on her own database application icon. She called up the company database file on her client cases and added Maria Alvarez to the list along with the date, hospital and specimen code, UH0744, and updated commission status as due. Phylis kept her own database records to insure that her quarterly commission check jived with her delivered specimens on the company network.

The commission record was also tied to another relational database she created, which listed information on new client's status with record fields for address, cell phone numbers, screening test date, test results, referring physician, and hospital extraction date.

Phylis gave up many Saturdays to learn this database application business during computer classes at Hofstra University. Overcoming her computer illiteracy was just another part of catching up for time spent at home raising a family. In the long run, it turned out to be a handy tool, since she could keep all her procurement activity on a single memory stick. She could update it at the office, or at her home laptop. The other agents were always relying on the Lifespan's cloud database for accurate accounting.

Anyway, she thought, *"It was their financial system, and she wouldn't trust corporate accounting with her money. The Lifespan Finance Department was as incompetent as the 'bozo', John Lombardo, who ran it."*

For some odd reason, Lifespan did not keep any historical records on the specimens after the commissions were paid at year-end - wiped clean. It always seemed unusual to Phylis that she had the only permanent record of three and a half years of specimen extractions handled by her and other associates.

Before she could be distracted, Phylis modified the database to add this new placenta business as a new record field, and exited the program with a beep.

Phylis turned her attention to the first message on her answering machine. It was Heather Vanderbeck, due in for her procedure on Monday. Phylis decided to call her back immediately.

"Hello, Heather, this is Phylis at Lifespan, returning your call."

"OH.... Uh.....Hi, this is Heather."

There was a moment of silence as Phylis expected Heather to continue speaking, but she didn't, so Phylis continued, "Heather you called me yesterday. Remember? Is there a problem? Are you ill?"

"No, No. Nothing like that," she stumbled. "You see, I was contacted by another company that wants to buy my specimen, and their offering more money than you people."

Caught off guard, Phylis could only respond with, "Oh, really, what company would that be?"

"It's named Cal Extentech, and their willing to fly me on a free round trip to Pasadena for the decoupling." Phylis' worry wheels began to turn, and stopped speaking, so Heather felt obliged to keep going. "I just thought I'd let you people know... in case, you know... you wanted to do something."

Phylis was upset, and asked herself, *'What the heck was this Cal Extentech doing in New York? How did they get her client's name?'* Something smelled fishy. She had believed Lifespan exclusively had the decoupling business to themselves. Her mind continued to question Heather's motives. The woman was making a damn auction out of this thing. In a way it wasn't surprising. Not after Phylis had visited her estate in

Eatons Neck.

A 21 year old long legged blond married to a 65 year old stockbroker husband - a gold digger! After meeting her, Phylis even had doubts that her husband was the specimen's father. She remembered leaving that appointment wondering, what the hell this woman needed with more money? She could have just have a quick procedure and be done with the inconvenience.

Phylis had to act quickly and spoke courteously into the phone, "Heather, what I'd like to do is call you back in about an hour after I speak to my supervisor"

Heather's tone was almost casual, "It'll have to be quick, because I have to make travel arrangements."

"OK, catch you later."

Phylis hung up the phone, rolled her mouse to flip off the screen saver, and clicked on her database icon. She entered a search command for Heather Vanderbeck's record and isolated her test screening results.

Just what I thought, AB Negative!

Heather had a very rare blood type that was important in treating some of the unique patients needing Lifespan's extracts. It was no wonder that they'd come all the way to the East Coast to get her.

Phylis decided to check for her referring physician, figuring he might give her some insight into Heather's motivation.

Odd, she thought, *there's no entry in the physician field.*

Now she wondered how Heather got into the Lifespan system. Federal regulations prohibited direct procurement from a client. Phylis was perplexed, and didn't stop to dwell on the peculiarity of it all.

Phylis pivoted around in her chair and headed for her boss, Klein's office. Jerry was recruited five years ago from big pharma Huffnam-Burke, where he was Eastern Regional Sales Manager for Gynecological Pharmaceuticals. After 20 years in that business, he seemed like he knew every gynecologist and hospital director in the Metropolitan area. Jerry ran the Lifespan Procurement Department like a true sales organization. There were weekly pep talks, monthly specimen quotas, and daily department meetings to divide up the doctor referrals that came into his office. In fact, he spent just about the entire day on the phone.

Phylis tapped on Jerry's open door, and, as expected, he had the desk telephone in his ear. Jerry looked up and held up his index finger, signaling her to wait. She stood dutifully at the doorway since this was important, and let her mind wander a bit. Phylis knew that Jerry was on some kind of lucrative cash incentive plan that gave him a commission on what each procurement agent brought in. Jerry would have been a dynamo anyway, that was just his achievement-orientated personality.

Although her boss showed little interest in the science behind

Lifespan's products, he was a real people person. His department was well motivated and the rivalry you'd expect between so many female agents was held to a minimum. Phylis often wondered as a senior procurement specialist in her department, if she could do his job as well. The thought of promotion and the extra money crossed her mind many times, particularly now, as the frenetic pace of her work on the road every day was starting to wear her down. Her accumulated case mileage for last year turned out to be a phenomenal 35,000 miles.

Still, she wasn't even sure she wanted her boss's job.

"OK, Phyl, come on in," Jerry suddenly announced.

Phylis snapped out of her daydream, and entered his office. "Good mornin' Jer," she returned. "I've got a problem that can't wait."

"You already missed some excitement here yesterday, a real carnival," Jerry replied.

Phylis answered quickly, "Yes, I saw it on the evening news."

Jerry continued, "Naw, they didn't show you the half of it. I didn't get to see it all myself, because it was in back of the other building, but I heard some of it through the grapevine. Did you know that a woman was almost killed on our perimeter fence?"

A distracted Phylis answered, "No, not really."

"Well, she was actually hung by her legs in the barbed wire, like a plucked chicken in a meat market."

Phylis winced, but wanted to get to the Vanderbeck issue. "Jerry I need…"

He interrupted and persisted with his story. "It seems one of our managers ran out here, and tore off his shirt to make tourniquets - saved the woman's life." Jerry leaned forward. " Now get this. This guy locks horns with Jane Savage and then the big time TV reporter, Patty Marshall. He must have been out of his mind. They could've strung the guy up on that fence right next to that lady!"

Phylis listened inattentively, wanting get back to Heather, but felt puzzled by this story. "I don't understand. I don't remember hearing any of this mentioned on the news report last night. In fact, I don't recall anything about a fence either. There was just a damaged car, and some people injured by the rioters."

"Yeah, yeah. Media snow job. Corporate's got big pull with the major networks. Everybody knows that big conglomerate, Trans National Communications, has its president on our Board of Directors at Lifespan."

Phylis found herself even more bewildered, and now miffed at his insensitivity. Biting her tongue, she decided to return to her original dilemma.

"Jerry, I have some decoupling things to talk about, but one of them is very urgent."

55

Finally, sitting back Jerry relented and said, "Let's hear it. Shoot."

"One of my cases is a Heather Vanderbeck. She's been screened with AB negative blood."

Jerry interrupted, "Hey, rare stuff. That's a great find!"

"Hold on, I'm not finished," she said. "It seems she's been offered a better deal for her specimen from a company called Cal Extentech."

Jerry's demeanor turned serious. He leaned forward, picked up his pencil and began to take notes.

"Apparently they offered her more money and tickets to California to have the procedure done there."

Jerry frowned, "How much more?"

"I don't know. I didn't want to get into any monetary discussions with her until we talked about it face to face."

"Good move," he replied,"I heard a little bit about this company from our marketing people. They are a start-up operation backed by some big-time Hollywood capital. They might have found a way around some of our patents and have lots of political clout in California and Washington."

Phylis questioned, "I thought we had exclusive licensing from the FDA - Food and Drug Administration?"

"Yeah, we do, except our agreement expires in another year."

"OK, so why are they here now? On whose authority?"

Jerry shrugged his shoulders. "I don't know either, but the boys upstairs are going to be interested in this. I'll call Bob Fisher, our marketing VP, and see him right away."

Phylis interjected, "Are you kidding? Corporate couldn't react in less than a month. I have to get back to Vanderbeck in a half-hour, and she's scheduled for extraction on Monday."

Jerry turned to the phone to start the ball rolling. Phylis didn't have the chance to broach the new placenta extraction mystery. The timing just didn't seem right. So she left to make her appointment with Heather.

As she reached the doorway, Jerry called out, "Oh, by the way, you did well yesterday getting your specimen in safely to Atlas." He gave a 'thumbs up' sign and added, "Well done! Now, don't let this one get away either!"

Phylis gave him a reluctant smile, and a patronizing 'thumbs up' in reply.

CHAPTER 5
Hell hath no fury

Later in the day, Mike's boss, Al Greene, decided to walk between Lifespan buildings to his 11 AM meeting with Human Resources. With his girth it would be a slow walk. It was a clear, cool spring day with light green foliage blooming everywhere, birds and squirrels actively scrounging for food. The air fresh with the beginnings of new life. So nice a day, that it seemed almost inappropriate to decide Santino's fate with the company. Al casually scanned his gaze around at the company grounds. He never could fathom the logic of three separate buildings. *Realistically*, he surmised, *it could all fit in one large building*.

Nevertheless, the plant layout was decided long before he arrived. The two story buildings on each side of the main corporate building were set up to house the operating departments. On one side, Al's building contained the model shop, along with equipment engineering and facilities. On the other side, the building contained procurement, production extraction, drug culture lab, and the R&D lab. A lot of duplication of equipment from Al's perspective.

As he passed between buildings, he briskly walked up the main driveway to Corporate Center. It was a five-story building of modern smoked glass design, set back from the other buildings, except all the metal work was done in gold anodize - a bit gaudy, like Donald Trump would design.

His eyes scanned around while he walked, and he noticed the cinderblock, windowless back walls of the two side buildings. He remembered asking his boss, Peter Strauss, why that was. The reply was that all three buildings had windowless north walls as an energy conservation design. In fact, rows of arborvitae evergreens and poplars were planted on that side to act as a windbreak in the winter. Al complimented him on their energy consciousness.

Of course, that was before one day, he mentioned it to Mike. When Al related that explanation to Mike, he remembered his terse response; "Oh, bullshit, the specimen waste stream ends at the crematorium back there. They just don't want anyone to see the back end of the business."

Al thought this was another vindictive Santino criticism until Mike added, "Since when are three free standing buildings more energy efficient than a single large building? Besides, why would you put an arborvitae windbreak 70 yards behind a building? Where it can't have any effect? Nah, it's there to hide the crematorium from the street and us."

Al needed little convincing by that last argument. He had first hand experience on windbreak effectiveness while walking between buildings in January. The bitter cold gusts from the north whistled along totally unaffected by the windbreak. Anyway, he reasoned that it made good sense not to view the place where the specimen remnants were reduced to ash.

Al had a political conscience of convenience. It had a way of overlooking or minimizing corporate inconsistencies. It also insured his longevity in the corporation. The main thing was to carry the party line, no matter how ridiculous the position.

A now huffing and puffing Al, was on the circular driveway in front of the corporate building, where carefully manicured shrubs and colorful flowers were beginning to bloom. Looking up five stories as he entered, he felt a little perturbed at not having his office here with the other senior executives. He was not part of the "inner circle" of top executives, which consisted of Max Brewster, Strauss, John Lombardo, and Eve West.

He mentioned this concern on several occasions to his boss, Dr. Strauss. In reply, Strauss' opinion was that as the VP of Technical Operations, he should be located in the engineering buildings themselves, near his people. Al was more convinced that his overweight appearance had more to do with it than anything else.

It was also odd to have all Lifespan's technical personnel reporting to Al except R&D. It was the only department his boss, Strauss, insisted on personally supervising himself. In fact, R&D was so remote from the internal organization that it was primarily staffed by outside consultant researchers and government NIH, FDA, and CDC people. The 'party line' for this curious arrangement was something about taking the workload off other Lifespan technical staff.

Still, it was peculiar to Al that some of these 'temporary consultants' had been working there for more than three years. Al resigned himself to the quirkiness of Strauss and the fact that Strauss had Max Brewster's ear. There was one advantage to all this; R&D kept his boss preoccupied enough to leave Al pretty free hand with his own departments. Al finally dismissed the thoughts and, instead, admired the impressive surroundings he'd finally reached.

The front lobby of corporate was done with a beautiful five story atrium, with exquisite furniture, carpeting, draperies and exotic plants. An inside elevator had one side of clear glass open to the atrium - very impressive...and intimidating. Al judged the five-floor high-rise as reflecting the corporate pecking order of the departments. The first floor housed personnel and security. On the second was data systems, third floor was finance, fourth was legal and fifth, executive row.

Well, he thought of this extravagance, *They're not burning up my money. I still pull $390,000 a year out of here.*

Al was glad the meeting was called by the new Human Recourses VP, Dean Reynolds. That meant he was not going to face Max in person on this Santino issue.

Showing his security badge to the receptionist, he proceeded down the hall to the elevator and Executive Conference Room. Al was last to arrive. Seated at the walnut Board Table were: Dean Reynolds, VP Human Resources; Jane Savage, Corporate Security; Norm Stark, Chief Legal Counsel; and the striking image of Eve West, Community Relations Director. Of all the people in the room, Eve was the one that scared him the most. He nervously deliberated, *what the hell is the 'Tiger Lady' doing here?*

Eve was Max's main squeeze, and everybody knew it. It gave her status and clout, as if she was 'Queen Consort' to the 'Prince of Wales in England. Before joining Lifespan, Eve was Deputy Assistant Under Secretary at Health, Education and Welfare (HEW) in Washington. At 40, she was divorced, and childless by choice. A good looker, tall and curvaceous, who came to work everyday dressed to kill. Some people said she lived at a cosmetic surgeon's office in Manhattan. She had a penchant for wearing full make up everyday, including foundation, which always gave her the look of a movie actress ready to go on stage. Her most noticeable feature was her bright red lipstick set against a smooth, pearl-white face and auburn hair. To Al, her red-lipped mouth formed a reptilian-like opening from which you could envision a darting forked tongue protruding when disturbed.

Al sheepishly sat down, and Dean Reynolds opened the discussions, "I thought we should discuss this Santino problem together before we take disciplinary action. Being new with the company, I really don't know this character, but understandably, he did assist people that are against this corporation's very existence. Not the kind of example we need as a mid-level manager at Lifespan."

Reynolds paused to measure everyone's tacit agreement. "In light of his past transgressions, I know some of you would like to have given Mister Santino his termination notice at the front gate this morning." He smiled at Jane and continued, "However, we should examine any potential downside of our actions beforehand."

Turning to Al, Dean gestured, "You're his direct supervisor, what are your comments and recommendations?"

Al was not prepared to discuss anything as drastic as Mike's dismissal. It was all coming too fast at him. The stiff, formal air in the room made him feel like they were in a 'kangaroo' jury room ready to take the final vote to deliver a previously decided death sentence. In that atmosphere Al was definitely not going to stick his neck out and say anything in Mike's defense, so he placed Mike's four page write up on the table and said, "He gave me this earlier. I think it should be reviewed before any decision is made."

Norm Stark, Chief Counsel, asked to see it, and Al gladly slid it across the table to him. There was silence in the room, as the highly respected, portly, and gray haired attorney leaned back in his chair and flipped the pages one by one. Al kept focused on Norm, avoiding eye contact with anyone else, especially Eve.

Norm's gray bushy eyebrows lifted, as he regretfully concluded, "This guy's done his homework alright. If he brings a wrongful dismissal suit against us, there's enough damaging issues here that even a mediocre lawyer could give us a hard time in court."

"Let me see it please," Dean Reynolds requested, "I'd like to see if I can find anything from the personnel perspective."

Eve was becoming fidgety in her chair as she shifted her focus from Norm to Dean and back to Norm. Suddenly she stood up, slammed her tablet on the desk, and exclaimed, "I want Santino's head on a silver platter."

The outburst was of biblical proportions. Al Greene thought he saw her breath condense in mid air from the frigid delivery.

Young Dean Reynolds was speechless. He was new at Lifespan. In fact, he was the third Human Resources VP in 5 years, and now he knew why. This was real first-hand training on Lifespan politics, and who really runs things.

Jane enjoyed Eve's assertive display, grinned and nodded approvingly.

Then Eve hunched over onto the table placing both hands on the table for support. Her long perfectly manicured nails spread out like glistening crimson talons. Staring down and sweeping the table with her stern glance, her neck seemed to hang down on her shoulders like a vulture staring at a carcass. "Max and I have decided that this kind of insubordination and disloyalty will not be tolerated in my company. You people are here to enforce that policy. So let's get it over with!"

They all looked at each other nervously as Eve slithered back into her chair, satisfied that she made her point.

Then silence. No one dared to be first to speak.

Norm Stark leaned back and retained his relaxed demeanor, twirling his pen between his fingers. He was not the least bit intimidated by Eve, and broke the silence. "Look Eve, even a decapitated head without a body still has teeth that can bite your beautiful...er...I mean bite our collective asses."

Norm was a sharp, innovative attorney with his own successful, private practice. As a historically close advisor to Max Brewster, he could speak freely and with authority. "Let's suppose we take this drastic action and Santino sues us for wrongful dismissal, with or without a meritorious case. He'll file his case in New York, meaning we'll have to hire attorneys over there to support the pre-trial motions. They'll probably be six months of those. Then there's the pre-trial discovery phase. From this documentation here, he could have access to all our internal security procedures and files, purchasing records, hiring and firing practices, client lists, and safety records, at a minimum. If they find anything relevant, they can make a motion to the pre-trial judge to subpoena access to other Lifespan records."

Eve responded, "What are a bunch of paralegals going to understand about our records. Why don't we simply show them only what we want them to see - burn the rest. Then who cares where they look."

"Well", Norm calmly added, "If Santino participates in the search, and he has every right to, I would anticipate that he's technically sharp enough to understand everything about this company. He is a manager here, and this write-up is obvious evidence of in-depth knowledge of our operations. If we get caught withholding or destroying evidence, our defense would be demolished even before we entered a courtroom."

Eve retorted, "Norm, you've got a staff of 15 lawyers and 25 paralegals downstairs. What are we paying them for?"

Norm was now becoming clearly vexed. Now she was trampling on his turf. "Look, Eve, my job is prevention, and to keep the Lifespan executives and partners out of trouble, out of the public eye, and out of prison! You don't accomplish that by going into a State Supreme Courtroom for destroying evidence." Norm leaned forward, looking directly at Eve, adding, "Would you like to give a personal deposition, under oath and in writing, to probing questions posed by his attorney?"

Norm looked around the table and waved his hand up in the air, "Furthermore, the lady injured on the fence is sure as hell going to sue us. We'd drive Santino right into her attorney's lap. Force us to fight two related cases at once, an overlapping litigation nightmare!"

Dean Reynolds saw an opportunity to make points with Eve and jumped in. "It makes some sense to keep Santino on where we have some control. So, I agree with Eve that we need to punish his insubordinate behavior. It would set an example for other Lifespan employees." Dean made sure he read Eve's face for an implied approval before continuing. Eve nodded, so he proceeded.

"At some point in the near future we'll create a staff reorganization. Since Santino is on overhead, we can lay him off with everyone else at that time. It'll be part of an organization downsizing at that point. He won't be able to sue us or anything. The only thing he'll be able to do is sign up for unemployment. All we have to do is be patient." Dean cautiously measured Eve' demeanor. "For now, why not demote him?" Turning to Al Greene, Dean said, "What do you think, Al?"

Al hesitated for a moment, knowing he still needed Santino in the equipment engineering role. "Well, uh." Al had to think quickly now, and offered a compromise. "I'll relieve him of responsibility for the Facilities Department. That will diminish his authority right away, and his Director salary. Still, I need to keep him as Engineering Department head. He's working on production fixtures for that new process I hear is coming out of the R&D group."

Dean and Norm agreed to the suggestion.

However, Eve interjected, "Don't post it on the bulletin board. Let people keep calling him on facilities problems. It'll be embarrassing for him to explain his reduced management role everyday, for weeks on end."

Al nodded agreement, thankful the meeting was over, and anxious to return to the perceived safety of his own building.

Norm grabbed Mike's write-up folder and left the meeting with his arm around Eve's shoulder, explaining how they would get together with Max later to discuss their decision. When they were further down the hall, away from everyone else, Eve leaned over to Norm and smiled saying, "Scared the piss out of 'em, didn't I!" They laughed together as they disappeared into the elevator.

Al decided to have lunch alone to figure out how to tell Mike of their decision. Difficult as it was, Al was glad about one thing today - he didn't bring Mike to the meeting. Al chuckled to himself imagining Mike and Eve going at it. God knows what they would've done to each other in person. Mike did not take crap from anybody, and Eve does not know a man she could not subjugate. They would have to move the meeting to Madison Square Garden. Al grinned and thought, *Could've billed the event as, 'Gladiator Mike' versus 'The Tigerlady'.*

* * * * * *

Phylis grabbed her pocketbook, and left her office to head for her car and the meeting with Heather Vanderbeck. Fellow agent Katie grabbed her as she went by, and begged for a lift on the way to Manhasset where her car was in the dealer for repair.

"No problem Katie... but we have to leave right now!" Phylis replied with urgency.

As they drove towards Long Island, Katie filled her in on the latest gossip, Katie was Phylis' good friend, although 10 years her junior. She was also divorced with no house and no children to tie her down. Two points that made Phylis feel a tad envious at times. And, Katie was a lot of fun too, and they surprisingly had a lot in common, in spite of the age difference.

On occasion, they double-dated for support, and always seemed to wind up dumping their dates during those episodes. Katie was a free spirit, and attractive enough to rarely spend a Saturday night alone. Phylis doubted that her younger friend would ever marry again, especially with the jerks that were available. Katie's opinion was that men were either totally pre-occupied with themselves, or sufficiently intimidated by women to spend the night patronizing their female companions with politically correct clichés. All for a chance at a one night stand in her underwear.

Katie was an endless source of hilarious stories about her dating misadventures. Phylis decide to confide in her about the 'Used Male' website posting she answered.

She pulled her cell phone out of her purse, thumbed to the dating website, and turned to Katie, "Hey, read this. What do you think?"

Katie began to smile as she read the clipping and finished exclaiming, "Honk if you're horny!" They laughed hysterically together, as Phylis honked the car horn and exited the expressway.

"Seriously though," Phylis continued, "What do you think?"

"He's original, and handsome that's for sure," Katie answered while sensing Phylis' interest, and chose her words carefully so as not to offend. "Did you really answer this?"

"Yes, I did," she answered, now a little embarrassed. "And I told him less than he told me."

"Well then, what the hell. If you don't hit it off, maybe I'll take a shot at 'em," Katie chuckled.

They looked at each other and giggled some more, as the car pulled up to Katie's car dealer.

"Gotta go kiddo," Katie announced, "Good luck with Heather, and keep me informed on your mystery man!"

Phylis smiled and waved thinking, *She's a dear*.

****

Continuing to drive east and north, the congested track-built middle class homes receded behind, leading to the winding roads and remote heavily wooded estates in Etons Neck. Finding a house up there isn't easy when the houses were setback so far from the road. It was intentionally so. She was grateful for her GPS and that it was not dark yet.

Fortunately this time, the familiar, wrought iron gate with the big gold double " V's " was there, and she proceeded up the long, maroon gravel driveway to Heather's house. It was an imposing structure, modeled after the plantation homes of the South. The front facade was replete with six massive columns that supported the second story portico. A veranda ran the entire length of the second floor.

Phylis exited the car with a parody of 'Gone with the Wind'. She placed the back of her palm to her forehead and said, "Oh Tara, I've missed you." Then, looking up at the veranda she continued," Rhett. Rhett Butler, you're not here to welcome me?"

She'd heard that the real estate agents here don't actually sell these things by size or number of rooms, but by the number of front columns. Phylis could only conclude to herself, *Doesn't wealth put a value on the right things*.

Approaching the double door entrance, Phylis noticed the neglect and peeling paint around the windows and door trim moldings. It was typical rich people. The place was meant to impress from a distance.

However, when you get up close, there's no substance. Just like the tarnished doorbell button in front of her. Her fingertip depressed it. From its overall neglected appearance, it was surprising that the bell worked at all.

An older black woman greeted her, and led her to a dark study off the marble entrance foyer with its 8 foot wide curved staircase. Heather was seated, gently stroking some kind of Persian pussycat. The ladies exchanged pleasantries, and Heather offered refreshments by way of Jasmine, the maid. Phylis declined, preferring to get down to business.

With the departure of Jasmine, there was a brief interlude of uncomfortable silence with neither of them sure on how to start the conversation. Phylis decided to use her usual routine for reluctant clients, slowly pacing around the seated target.

"Heather, we, that is Lifespan, has made a considerable investment in your specimen already. There's been doctor examinations, screening tests, and hospital appointments already made. This is a heck of a time to bring that other company into this."

Phylis stopped and stood in front of Heather, and stared down, "You mentioned that they made you a better deal?"

Heather tried to avoid direct eye contact, and gazed instead at the cat she held up and in front of her face. Unexpectedly, she turned and whispered, "Can you keep a secret?"

Phylis was startled, drew closer, and said lightheartedly, "Sure... as long as you didn't kill anybody or something."

Heather put the cat down, sat back in her chair and turned her head left to stare out the window, quietly explaining, "Before I married my husband, Vernon, I signed a pre-nuptial agreement not to have any children. He already had two children, and didn't see the sense in diluting his estate with more heirs. If I deliver a child, I lose my share of the inheritance."

Phylis sat down a bit flustered, and found herself feeling almost sorry for her. "We'll why don't you just have a plain procedure, or isn't it his child?"

"Oh, it's his all right," Heather was quick to reply. "In fact, he surreptitiously wanted me to get pregnant."

Phylis was getting confused, "I thought you said he didn't want children?"

"He doesn't....He just wants the fetus."

Phylis looked around at the dark cherry wood walls whose swirling dark grain took on a sinister appearance. Just like the bewildering conversation she was having. She really was at a loss for words, and sat down side-saddle on a chair opposite Heather.

"Phylis, before I carry on, I don't want you to think I'm an unfeeling person. I only agreed to this under duress. You see, my weekly allowance is only $1200 a week, just about what a lousy secretary makes. That's all I have to live on. And my husband cut off my credit cards,"

Phylis wasn't particularly sympathetic to her money problem anymore, knowing this woman had essentially free room and board. At the same time she did not want to risk alienating a client and said, "Yes, but I still don't know why you need the money from this specimen extraction."

"It's very expensive to look the part of a successful executive's wife," Heather rebutted as she paced behind Phylis."

So, you need the Lifespan money to cover more. Right."

"Well, yeah."

"At this point Phylis was too agitated to remain seated, and got up to walk around her chair, feeling like a prosecuting attorney unraveling a defense witness in court. Leaning forward with her hands on the chair back, she queried, "I still don't understand why your husband wants the baby."

"He doesn't want a baby," Heather insisted. "I told you before, he just wants the fetus." Then she rose from the chair to gaze out the window and said hestitatingly,"You see, uh. Vernon is on the waiting list at North Harbor Hospital for one of your company's drug treatments for clogged arteries or something. He's way down on the waiting list because of his rare blood type."

"That's right! The specimen blood type is AB negative."

Heather smiled and nodded appreciatively , "Uh huh. And Vernon is AB negative. Sooo, he made a deal with somebody over in your company to jump the waiting list if he managed to find a fetal specimen. Vernon said after that, he could get 12 months of therapy, starting in a month."

Phylis could not believe what she was hearing. She thought to herself, "These two people have cooked up a deal to both make out at the price of the same specimen. Equally confusing was that for Vanderbeck's condition, the specimen would only be good for a year. Then what?"

She surmised to herself, *I guess there's a lot of people nowadays that would consider these two egocentrics clever.*

Phylis suppressed her revulsion by falling back on the idea that, 'this is just business'. It felt like this business seemed to be getting nastier every day.

She continued the conversation, "Sounds like you have it all neatly tied up. Why then, did you bring this other company, Cal Extentech, into it? "

Heather's mood turned vindictive. "Because I found out that bastard, Vernon, was fooling around with some slut at the office. While I'm suffering morning sickness! If I give this thing to the other company, I get my 35,000 and he gets nothin'. Besides, if he gets the treatments, he'll live another 30, maybe 40 years. I'll be 65 before he croaks, and I see any inheritance!"

Phylis felt only more disdain for this woman, and a chilling clamminess ran over her skin. She started to feel like escaping from the increasingly stale atmosphere of this mansion and its occupants. Her mind was in turmoil as she considered this mess. She had to get control, and avoid all the personal aspects with this client. Focus on, and stay with the specimen. A solution to this quagmire was needed - and fast.

Heather sensed something wrong with Phylis, and asked if she wanted something cold to drink. Phylis shook her head positively, and asked for a diet coke, trying not to convey her inner feelings of disgust.

Heather left to find the maid, Jasmine. *Good, I need time to pull myself together*, Phylis sighed.

She found herself biting her fingernail, and walked over to the welcome light of the window as a figurative deliverance from the gloom of the place. Phylis had to think down at Heather's level. *Think selfish! Lie. That's the strategy,*" she finally surmised. Phylis didn't have the authority to offer more money.

Heather returned, and inquired, "Are you OK, you look better now."

Phylis thanked her and started her argument. "Heather, if I were you, and had some evidence on Vernon's affair, I'd get a good private detective and lawyer and take him to the cleaners. Then you won't have to wait 30 years for your inheritance! Why don't you use our $5000 advance for a legal retainer to get that started?" Phylis swallowed a sip from her Coke for emphasis.

"Gee, I never thought of that," Heather said enthusiastically.

Phylis continued, knowing she was about to lie. "I also don't know who your husband contacted at Lifespan, but I can assure you that your specimen would, at best, only give him 1 month of therapy. Hardly worth the fuss, one way or the other."

"Vernon seemed awful sure he was getting one year of treatment out of this arrangement," Heather reiterated.

Phylis realized she needed something extra to swing Heather around, but couldn't match $35,000 Extentech offer.

Heather sat back down in her chair. "I'd like to speak to my mother in Florida about this."

"No kidding," Phylis said, adding,"And we could pay for a week's vacation down there after your decoupling. Get away from that husband of yours."

Heather said appreciatively. "You've really been helpful and supportive Phylis."

"And remember Heather, I've been here, with Lifespan, for you, since the beginning of your pregnancy. And I'll be at your bedside for the procedure." Phylis couldn't resist laying on some apprehension, "God forbid something develops during the procedure, a damaged specimen is worthless, and you could wind up with zero compensation. You really should stick with experienced people you know and trust."

Heather added, "I am definitely not going to go through all this suffering for nothing. You've always been honest with me."

Phylis walked up to her and extended her hand to symbolically seal the arrangement. While continuing to shake Heather's hand, "Then, I'll see you at the hospital on Monday morning."

"I'm glad you came, Phylis," an overjoyed Heather exclaimed, and proceeded to walk Phylis to the front door. Heather was satisfied that she had squeezed every last advantage out of her predicament. They exchanged more pleasantries as Phylis anxiously entered her car and left.

Phylis grasped the steering wheel firmly, throttled the accelerator, and happily watched the Vanderbeck estate disappear in her rear view mirror. Loosening her top blouse button, and opening a window, she took a deep breath to ventilate the pent-up anxiety and revulsion she had been keeping inside.

What an episode that was. Those two clowns really deserve each other. Suddenly, my single life doesn't seem so screwed up after all!

Farther down the road, she made a mental note to remember to ask her boss, Jerry, just who at Lifespan is scalping positions on the hospital waiting lists. She recalled her database record search earlier in the day, and wondered how Heather got into the extraction system without a referring doctor. Someone was bending the rules at Lifespan.

Driving home, Phylis was anxious to be home with her children. For the first time she seriously dwelled about what ethical compromises she might be making at work to support her family. And just what her career revolved around. Living things being converted into dollars and cents – commodity items. The early fun and enthusiasm working for Lifespan was definitely eroding, turning more and more into a mere pretense to get the next specimen, the next paycheck. She never imagined that she would be 'horse trading' airline tickets for fetuses.

Then she thought of the Lifespan Corporation motto, 'The Pursuit of Healthy Longevity.'

It made her question just who really was deciding which people received this 'gift'. And, was it really worth it? Keeping the Vanderbecks of the world around even a single second longer.

It was a lonely feeling, not having anyone around to truly confide in about these concerns, or someone to share her doubts with. She wouldn't dare reveal her skepticism and feelings to her associates at work, not even Katie. That would be a real career killer...and on her single income position, economic suicide.

CHAPTER 6
An odd surrogate

In the midst of a peaceful dark tranquility, the growing, 8-inch long UH0744 lay hidden, silent, and warm. At about 15 weeks, she is 4.0 ounces and about the size of an orange in her totality. A mind preoccupied with orchestrating the development of all the flesh and blood that would allow her to survive in a very different world. For now, lungs 'breathing' amniotic fluid in a steady whooshing rhythm, like a whale's song echoing in a dark blue sea. An uncluttered place where just the chance of existence was a miracle of nature in itself. At specimen UH0744's epicenter, a tiny heart pumping to move 24 quarters a day moving through her. It fluttered in a steady frantic rhythm, driven toward a life, yet, unknown - the only vibration discernible.

A developing mind drifting within the seamless, soft nebulous world of the in-between, neither conscious nor unconscious -no distant past to regret, no future to anticipate. Her knowledge base consisting of only the simple instincts and the human DNA program to strive and survive. A creature not meant to be distracted from its purposefully designed goal. A hidden human, still unrevealed, as a seed within a flower, waiting for her chance to bloom and show her beauty.

* * * * * * *

The clicking vibration of a hatch and flash of brilliant light startled her. The fine layer of peach fuzz lanugo hair covering her body immediately raised itself into stiff bristles. She jerked her legs at the hip and made a symbolic gesture with her fists to shield her eye buds from the light's intensity. Her face took on a frown, and even without eyelids, she would squint. In spite of an undeveloped mind, the daily intrusions into her world, taught her nervous system to instinctively anticipate that light would become the prelude to systematic pain.

She was not old enough to scream, but even if she could, who would hear her cry? Even if she were heard, who would care anyway? Specimen 0744 was now...legally...the property of Lifespan Corporation. She continued to jerk and shudder as the probe pierced the tissue thin skin of her abdomen cavity at the dark spot where the umbilical cord joined to her liver. She tried to curl up into a tighter ball. It proved ineffectual, as a small quantity of blood was drawn away from her spleen, with the gradual weakening of her metabolism.

With the snapping noise of the closing hatch, the torment would disappear as suddenly as it came upon her. Specimen 0744's reaction to the attack was immediate. Antibodies and platelets were rushed to the scene of the damage site to plug the wound and rapidly begin the necessary repairs. Unfortunately, nothing in nature or heaven prepared her for so many of these regular intrusions so early in her life. A now overworked liver struggled to produce the inordinate supply of replacement red corpuscles. She was fighting a slow, loosing battle - slowly dying without even knowing it.

The return of darkness meant return brought a soothing peace that enveloped her little world again. With no memory yet, it was as if nothing ever happened. It meant she could settle down again and suck her thumb. The assault was over. It was time to return to that innocent pleasure of isolation, and the singular destiny she was created for - of trying to grow into a complete girl.

In spite of the daily torment, she continued to survive, having no perception of being out of her mother's real womb, or any sense that this torturous existence was inside an artificial womb. No memory of being extracted 2 weeks ago, chilled and transported to an unnamed world that was just...well...just somewhere else. No idea that her mother had been replaced by the complex revival machinery of a Lifespan Corporation artificial womb.

Biochemically, the artificial womb was a good match of the real thing, sustaining Specimen 0744's inconsequential life for some time now. Below her was a silicone gel-like substance that gently supported her tiny mass from below. A warm clear synthetic amniotic solution floated on the surface of the gel, enveloping her and completely filling the chamber above. She swallowed the urine-tinged fluid to assist kidney development and absorb waste. An umbilical cord randomly meandered to the growing placenta located somewhere above her head. The placenta, in turn, was attached to a special pure cellulose mucous membrane at the end of the immersion tube. On the other side of this cotton-like membrane was a chamber of a continuously flowing bath of oxygenated and dialyzable blood. In this way, fetal wastes were transferred out, and oxygen and nutrients brought in. Glucose, carbohydrates, fats, vitamins, electrolytes, and minerals were added to the blood supply, providing nourishment to both the placenta and fetus.

Except for the periodic, life threatening interruptions from outside her sphere, development strove to proceed as planned. She just kept running an instinctive higher level DNA program making the right connections to control the involuntary functions of biologically surviving moment to moment.

Besides, there was no sense having a cognitive brain at this point if the circulatory and digestive systems were not in proper working order first. So, things are kept simple. Some occasional jerking of limbs is conducted to test and coordinate muscle development with bone and cartilage. Even wastes were passed from the bladder and rectum into the amino solution, and then re-swallowed to return to the placenta for outside cleaning.

Somehow, though, Specimen 0744 managed to keep this most complex machine in creation all working together towards the singular goal of leaving a stable inner liquid realm for the unstable external reaches of an air-filled world.

Of course, she could not know that her plight was now totally out of her control. The biological mother normally provided by nature was somewhere else. A mother totally unaware that a part of her was not dead, that her progeny was living a very different life - and, a tortuous one at that. Specimen UH0744 was also not aware that her remaining life would be measured in weeks, not decades. All because Lifespan Corporation had redefined her measure of worth into pharmaceutical sales and profits. Her contribution to humanity would be measured in milliliters of superblood extract, not by athletic or intellectual accomplishments in the outer world. Her epitaph would be a case number quickly scratched in a lab notebook, a dollar entry in an accountant's ledger - just another nameless life never lived.

Ultimately, gray dust in an incinerator.

Still in her brief existence, she was luckier than most fetal specimens in this new Lifespan environment. Those specimen's contribution to the grand business plan would involve considerably more pain and destruction of tissue before they expired. Those weak ones were the lucky ones - they perished quickly.

And so, Specimen 0744 curled up snugly, thumb in her mouth, in the perceived peace of her private inner space. In a dreamlike state, unaware, naturally secure in the entwined helical strength of her DNA helix. There was no reason to doubt that her human DNA would not guide her to her destiny. Consistently, as it had done billions of times for other humans before her... from the time of creation.

Specimen UH0744 would ultimately survive long enough to be rescued and by an enigmatic engineer with hairbrained schemes. He would name her Amnion.

CHAPTER 7
The "big cheese"

Max Brewster, the plump President and CEO of Lifespan Corporation was seated at his executive desk, and leaned forward to squint at the faint numbers on the computer print out. "God Damn it, Lombardo! Why the hell do I have to strain my eyeballs every time I read one of these financial reports?"

"Sorry, Max," John stuttered. "Uh, nobody changed the toner cartridge on the laser printer. Everybody wants to use the high capacity one.

With all the monthly closing reports, it takes a beating at the end of every month."

"John, you're the fucking CEO. Solve it."

John Lombardo was appointed to the Chief Financial Officer slot by Max five years ago. It was a favor to John's father, a major investment partner of Maxes. John's obedience and reverence for Max was how he kept the job, not competence in financial matters. He was only a bookeeping clerk before his appointment at Lifespan - no managerial experience either.

Max was not sympathetic or satisfied with the excuse John gave, and shot him a piercing stare above the rim of his glasses, and smoldering cigar.
John timidly looked away surveying Max's executive suite. The room had the air of a formal living room with plush carpets, table lamps, loveseats, wet bar, and cocktail tables - all the trappings of success. To give it an erudite polish, Max even had a wall of bookshelves custom installed and filled with classic novels he never read. On the walls were expensive lithographs of the works of famous painters.

"Well John boy," Max interrupted. "Are we going to get on wth the month's figures?"

John's meandering thoughts returned to the meeting and he resumed his briefing. "These are the April closing financials," he said, John cleared his throat, "Max. We've got to address accumulated Engineering R&D and Legal expenses. We can't keep postponing writing it off."

His annoyed boss hunched over his desk, seemingly crushing the edges of his print out copy with both hands like he was about to wrestle it to the floor. Max continued to gripe, "Every month you bring it up, and every month I tell you we'll take care of it, a piece at a time."

"That's okay Max, and I agree if we expense as we incur," John answered. "Except if you look, we still have R&D and Legal department inventory of $24 million that haven't expensed against cost of sales. I can't carry this forever Max. Some of these R&D work orders are almost four years old now and still not written off."

The unscrupulous Max was agitated as he flipped pages forward to review the details. For some unexplained reason, he wanted the books to look as rosy as possible. He was not about to let John know the real reason why – the company was for sale. There were also bigger deals in jeopardy in sunny California. So, he continued his tirade. "You bean counters just don't understand business. That R&D investment built this business. Our huge Legal department scares off any competitors."

"Max," John whined, "I just finished dancing around the auditors from Arthur Andersen, when we closed the books for last year. I keep telling 'em what you and Strauss tell me about all the new products that are about to be introduced. I think they're running out of patience and if we

71

don't come up with something by year end, they're not going to certify our books."

"Screw 'em! We'll hire another auditing firm that will!"
Then Max grinned and gave John another dig of sarcasm. "Give 'em one of these crummy faded printout copies to audit... except, print it in tiny font."

John remained serious, "It's not that easy. If we're dirty, word gets around in the financial markets. Any new auditing firm is going to be suspicious, after you dump the one you've been using for five years. Besides, how do we explain it in our annual report?"

There was a moment of silence as Max sulked, "What the hell do I tell the Board of Directors? All of a sudden, I got fiduciary religion, meshugana? How do I attract new investors?"

A 'now educated' John put his printout copy down on the cocktail table, sat back on the couch, and remained uncomfortably silent. He was a lightweight that Max could bully. John tried an uninvited cost cutting suggestion. "Why don't we trim our generous employee bonus pool?

Max leaned forward again for emphasis, his balding head reflecting the ceiling light. "Those five and six figure bonuses buys employee loyalty. Did you notice that for 5 years there have been no leaks coming out of this company? That's a necessary cost of doing business,"

Exasperated with explanations, an impatient Max reduced the discussion to human self-interest. "John, if we do what you say, you can kiss your year end bonus good bye."

John got burned on that one. He was done suggesting anything else. John was still perplexed though. This was not your normal, rudimentary accounting procedure discussion. Meanwhile, Max continued to dominate the meeting, and returned to his leather chair, and looking up at the ceiling deep in thought. Only his attorney, Norm Stark, knew what he was pondering.

John used the lull in conversation to ask, "While you're on a roll of good ideas, Max, maybe you can give me some advice on how to handle the auditors on the R&D write-off issue."

Max sat up with his head erect in a pose like a bust of Benito Mussolini. Tell them... Hmm.... Tell them we're going ahead with a monthly write-down plan. Yeah! Then, write off $50,000 right now so you're not lying. Right?"

"Good, OK," John replied with relief. Max was finally acting responsibly... so he thought.

Max looked down and added, "After they certify, we don't take any more write downs this year."

John was totally confused again. "I think next year they won't forget what we committed to and ignored," he said nervously.

Max was obviously determined and amused, "We'll worry about

that next year...when they won't be our auditors."

John sensed that Max had something up his sleeve, and capitulated to his wishes with, a simple, "You're our CEO, you know best."

The meeting seemed to be over as Norm and Eve knocked and poked their heads in the office door. Max stood up and motioned the duo to come in and they exchanged casual 'hellos'. There was a moment of awkward silence as they all stared at John still seated without a clue. After a pause, John realized his presence was no longer appreciated, and quietly excused himself.

John's behavior always amused Norm. John backed himself towards the door, half stooping over, with his hands full of computer printouts. It almost appeared as if he was bowing in front of royalty as he exited. Norm thought it ludicrous that any executive could act that way. Eve sat down gracefully on a loveseat, while Norm plopped casually in a Queen Ann Chair.

Max walked back around to his desk chair and questioned Eve, "So how'd you make out with this Santini guy?"

Norm interjected, "I believe the correct pronunciation of his name is Santino."

"Santino, schmamtino, what-the-hell! Who cares," Max grunted, loose tobacco leave fragments stuck onto his lips.

Eve began to explain. "Apparently, this character is building some important new processing equipment for us that will ramp up the new extraction program from R&D to full production in three months."

Norm chimed in. "He also submitted this written defense of his actions at the security fence incident," then stood up and walked over to toss the copy on Max's desk. He continued the briefing as Max read. "We're demoting him for now, and anticipate dumping him in six months."

Max sat back with a grimace, clamped down hard on the end of his cigar, as he listened to Norm, thinking, *In six months I'll be in California!*. He stood up, withdrew the cigar, and spit the tobacco shreds at the wastebasket on the floor. He missed his target, and the brown tobacco shreds landed on the carpet beside his desk. The site caused Eve to roll her eyes, staring at the ceiling to avoid his repulsive display. Norm stooped over to offer Max another garbage can nearby.

"Goddamn engineers!" Max erupted as he waved away Norm's offer. "They aren't worth the gunpowder to blow'em to hell!" Then he slapped Mike's written reply on the desk. "Where's this guy's loyalty to the company?"

Max paced the floor with Santino's write-up clutched in his hand. "He's no company man. I paid his bonuses, sick time, vacation pay, medical insurance for five years. Why doesn't he appreciate it like everyone else?" Looking at Mike's write-up again, "Yeah, logical, organized... covering his own ass!"

Norm lamented, "I know how you feel Max. These engineering people always seem to know too much, always too curious about things that don't concern them. Questions, endless questions."

"No, that's not what frustrates me" Max retorted. "Naw, that's not it. You know what really burns my ass? What bugs me? That I can never tell when those technical people are bull shitting me. All that engineering claptrap. Like from Strauss over in Research. You give them a work order budget to invent something, they build it, and it doesn't work. Then they come back with another line of technical horseshit, and want double the amount of budget to fix what they screwed up in the first place. No sense of profitability and schedules. No business orientation."

Norm chuckled. "Ha, maybe they're just more educated shysters than we are."

Max smiled. He would only accept that kind of self-parody from Norm. Max adjusted his tie and extended his chin. "Maybe, but they're still small potatoes compared to us." He handed the write-up back to Norm with the curt instruction, "Do what you want with this shmuck."

Eve piped up, "Wait, if we let him go in six months, it'll be November. Lets' hold him a little longer and terminate him right before Christmas."

Norm's eyebrows raised. "I'm glad you're on my side, Eve. You sure know how to drive in the stake."

Max walked back to his desk chair, and seemed pre-occupied with something. Looking down at the floor he changed subjects and said, "Eve, I have a personal problem to discuss with Norm. Could you excuse us for a while?"

Eve was vexed a bit. She wanted to be privy to everything going on at Lifespan. She prided herself on being able to manipulate men with influence, especially the ones molded into gender wimps. To save face she looked at her watch, and made up a story saying, "That's alright, I have to chair a public relations meeting in five minutes, anyway." Then, she departed in a huff.

When she closed the outer door, Max gestured for Norm to sit closer. He returned to his calming 'Slink toy'. Speaking in a lower tone, he lifted the coils from palm to palm, listening to the soothing clink of each coil. Now relaxed he asked, "Who have we got for buyers, so far?"

"Well," Norm said, "We've definitely got the Japs interested. The French want to tour our operation before they'll open up to making a serious offer. Then there's the British and Germans, they're more cautious then we'd hoped."

"How much are they offering? Did any of 'em discuss any figures?"

"Not yet, I gave them a hint that the asking price is $50 billion plus and nobody flinched so far."

Max was delighted. Even at $50 billion, he and his partners on the Board of Directors would get a 1000 % return on their investment in Lifespan - all in just five years. He cautioned Norm, "Did you tell them, how important it was to maintain the secrecy of these discussions?"

"Of course. In fact, I stressed that any publicity would bring in more uninvited bidders, like the Chinks, and just drive up the price to them."

"Okay, okay, Norm. You're doing fine. Just make sure any plant tours or visits by these people are made after 6 PM when we don't have lots of employees hanging around. Cover any possible Wall Street rumors of the sale with the 'unofficial' story that we're looking to license our technology to some overseas companies. That'll smokescreen this for several months."

"Not a bad idea," Norm said, "It's tough to do this kind of maneuvering without raising some suspicions and something leaking out." Norm stood up assuming the discussion was nearing an end.

"Wait, wait," Max waved his hands to Norm to sit down. "One more thing," he added. "Our marketing department reported some competition coming in from a California competitor named Cal Extentech."

Norm chuckled. "That's what happens when you're burning both sides of the candle."

"I know, I know," Max said with a sly grin. "I want you to get a message through to Extentech by the usual intermediaries. They are to back off the metropolitan area until I specifically give the OK? And not any sooner before we sell. Let's not panic the new owners, in the middle of this deal."

Norm found Max to be the consummate entrepreneur. Here he is, president of one company, and, at the same time, majority partner of his chief future competitor, Cal Extentech. By the time anyone finds out he's on both sides, he will have dumped his Lifespan stock, and become the CEO of the west coast competitor. What's more, no one ever noticed that Extentech was the only future competitor that Lifespan did not file a nuisance patent infringement suit.

Norm could not resist teasing Max. "Geez, I guess you never did finish the company ethics training course."

They laughed out loud together.

Max pontificated, "Ethics is the cross of the poor. That's why they'll always stay poor... and why we just keep making more money." He walked around his desk to escort Norm to the door. Putting his hand on his shoulder, he smiled. "I couldn't operate without you and your 'legal-shpegal' system."

Norm responded sarcastically, "Oh, It's really not that hard when the lawyers get to write the laws too."

"See you next week."

"Have a good weekend," a jovial Norm answered, as he headed for the elevator.

The afternoon was getting late and Max was tired from a busy day of wheeling and dealing. He took out his favorite method of relaxation from his desk draw. It was a metal Slinky toy, about 3 inches in diameter. He listened to the metal clinking as he bounced it from palm to palm. So peaceful. So soothing. After a few moments he put it back in his desk draw, lit a cigar, and gravitated to the picture windows facing the east.

From his fifth floor perch, there was a clear view of lower Manhattan with its unique 9-11 Freedom Tower monument. Farther to the south, the tiny Statue of Liberty and the giant stretch of the Verrazano Bridge. The sunset bathed the city towers in oranges and golds. Windows sparkled in the fading light. To Max the image was as beautiful and inspiring as the spires in Monument Valley. In the lower Manhattan canyons between buildings, was Wall Street. All the country's wealth and resources up for grabs, every day. All value defined by paper, no substance. It was his kind of place, as a veritable pioneer of industry. Starting with almost nothing and here today on the threshold of actual immortality.

Max daydreamed about his plans for the future, now closer than ever. The secret R&D project 'Greenhouse' was showing early signs of success, and would be his ticket to Shangri-La.

He looked down at the world five floors below, remembering what the Pharaohs of Egypt did to insure their place in eternity. *Fools*, he thought, *all that pyramid building just to store their dead bodies like dried prunes for 3000 years. And all those kings of Europe drying out in cathedrals. All their priests and mystics never stopped the grim reaper.*

He had a monument infinitely more practical...the immortality of a corporation! Something to keep him alive forever, and more over, forever wealthy! Looking down at the Cuban cigar in his hand and thought, *I'll be smoking these cigars for the next 3000 years. You Idiots!* he snorted to himself.

The first stars began to twinkle in the eastern sky, and Max regarded them as the cold and distant witnesses to the ages. It never occurred to his predecessors that the secret of eternal life was always there with them from the beginning of time. Now, it was so obvious, that the secret would be in a woman's womb.

Max felt tingly all over, folding his arms together, seemingly hugging his large frame with immortality. Then he glanced skyward with a leering grin, "*Who needs another Jesus or a Messiah when you can never die!*"

Max eagerly thought, *If I can just pull off one more deal...*

The peaceful scene of industry winding down from the day made him think of his childhood years visiting his father's garment factory on the lower east side of Manhattan. It was staffed by illegal immigrants and their children. As far as his father was concerned, everybody made out. The kid's immigrant parents made more money as a family, and his father had a higher profit margin. The workers could stay in the U.S, and h e could keep his business in New York

The scheme worked for years until he was at the factory late, with a night shift crew of workers. Around 6 pm, he stumbled out of his office onto the factory floor grimacing in pain and clutching his left shoulder. As he knelt to the floor, he screamed for someone to call the police."

Max cleared his throat, constricting with emotion. "Well, the immigrants didn't understand much English, but they sure understood the word 'police'. They all took off, and left my father alone, unconscious on the floor. It's when I learned, that a good deal never lasts forever, and a good deal maker always knows when it's time to bailout.

Of course, little could his father dream the huge deals his little son, Max, would eventually pull off...and precipitously pull out of.

Max admired his father back then. He seemed to know everything. Although, as the years went by, he saw less and less of him. Father was also religious, and at times it seemed to Max that those beliefs placed an upper limit on what he could accomplish in business. As Max matured, his father insisted that he attend formal religious instruction. It had little impact on young Max.

Max rolled his leather chair over to the office window, kicked off his shoes and rested his tired feet on the windowsill. He turned around and used his remote to shut off the ceiling lights behind him to eliminate their reflections off the windows. He sighed, "Ah, that's better, now I can enjoy the city's lights... like diamonds in a jewelry store."

Below, commuter car lights snaked in red and white silent dotted chains on roads and bridges out of the city. The image heightened his feeling of superiority, not having to be part of that daily commuter schlep.

He remembered going home from work on occasions with his father to Cedarhurst, on Long Island. Max's eyes scanned the dim horizon, now fading in purple darkness, as searching for obscure memories some miles distant.

For some reason his thoughts went back to his teenage years in high school, and the disappointment of quitting football after only the second day of tryouts. He just couldn't take the punishment. He was envious of the guys that made the team, they got the prettiest girls.

At those times when Max was down, his father was a real boost. He introduced him to tennis at the club. He hired a professional player to give him a whole summer of personal instruction. The next school year, Max was the star of the school tennis team. Sadly, that did not last either. There will always be more talented, smarter people to compete with. No amount of practice or desire can offset a genetic advantage in any human endeavor. Open competition was a fool's game, Max concluded. That's why putting in the 'fix' was invented.

His father insisted he get a college education and the only school willing to take him with such poor grades was the University of Bridgeport. *They'd take anybody*, he laughed to himself. College was a turning point for Max. He made friends with the son of a horse trainer from Belmont race track. As the course work proved difficult, he changed majors from Political Science to Business Administration to Finance to the easiest General Studies. By his sophomore year, he arranged to get his tuition money transferred to a bank account in Bridgeport and used it to finance his racetrack wagering. With tips on horse from his school friend, he not only paid his tuition, and he could buy a new car too. Making money could not have been simpler.

Max's daydreaming was interrupted by a knock on the door.

A fatigued Eve let herself in and greeted Max, "What a day. It's a good thing you have me out there on the front lines, looking after this company. All our people want to do is spend the company's money." She strolled over to the wet bar to pour herself a white wine. "How about you Max," holding her glass in the air and swirling the liquor inside, "Cocktail time?"

Max turned his head and said, "Sure, why not? Stick with the white wine," and returned to staring out the window.

Eve prepared his drink. She kicked off her high-heels and walked over to Max across the soft plush carpet. It felt soothing to her tired, stocking feet. Handing the wine glass to Max, she leaned her hip on the windowsill to face him, her tall svelte figure looking delectable in the dim light. She assumed he was in a good mood and was curious about what earlier conversation had transpired between Max and Norm.

"A penny for your thoughts," she said.

"Oh, I was just thinking about my childhood... my father."

Eve was disappointed. His answer wasn't a good lead-in to further prying about the business. So, she sipped more wine and asked, "Tell me about him."

"He died while I was in college," and Max looked down at his glass for a moment.

"Sorry to hear that, Max. I'll bet you miss him a lot."

Max held his wine glass up to the light, as though peering into it would give him the answer. "I dunno," was his indifferent answer, "We became distant before I really got to know him better."

"How'd he die?"

Max looked up at Eve with a blank stare. "It's along story. He died overnight alone in his garment factory, when his immigrant employees abandoned him. I only know what my mother told me. Max cleared his throat and took a sip of wine. "Apparently he would have lived if someone had called 911. Max peered down again into his glass. "His body was discovered the next morning by the regular day-shift workers."

Eve was moved to remark, "What a terrible tragedy. How could those immigrant people just leave him like that?"

Leaving the question unanswered, Max swirled the remains of his drink in his glass. "I learned one other important lesson from my father's experiences."

"Really? What lesson was that?"

"If your gonna take advantage of someone or some group, make sure they can't fight back."

Eve smirked as she sipped her drink and added, "I guess that means I'm safe, huh?"

Max just smiled politely back, and gulped down the last of the wine. He gave no hint that, in his mind, her days with Lifespan were numbered too.

As night darkened his view, Max stared at his gloomy reflection in the blackness of the window, and started to reminisce again.

"Yeah, my dad left an estate of around $2 million, plus the business. He even set up a $1 million trust for me."

Eve left the windowsill and sat on the desk edge behind Max. Big money was an irresistible magnet to her. She spoke to his reflection in the black glass window, and said facetiously, "I assume that's where my Max Brewster got his start on the road to the rich and infamous of Wall Street."

Staring at Eve's reflection behind him, "Actually, no. My mother was trustee of the estate and wouldn't release my half unless I agreed to run my father's garment business. Besides, I still had this deal going at the trotters, and she thought I'd gamble away my share."

"Geez what could you do?"

"What else? I got a lawyer, and fought it out in court. I was introduced to this lawyer's father at Sunday school. His son was a bright, young lawyer and willing to work *pro bono* without an up-front fee. He just wanted a percentage of the settlement... if we won."

The conversation finally was getting interesting to Eve. She was always titillated by Max's ruthlessness. "So you sued your mother?" She stood up behind him and messaged his shoulders again with her long manicured fingers. "Yeah! And I beat her in court!" Max was effervescent and seemed to enjoy bathing in the memories of that victory again. He ignored Eve's touch. "In fact, my lawyer even accepted my share in the rag factory as payment for his fee, something about needing a tax shelter. So, I got to keep the whole million in cash! When word got out that I had that kind of loot, the stockbrokers began to call. But first, I tried to go to back to Belmont to really cash in on the tips from the mob. Unfortunately, it was too late. By then everybody knew the fix was in. You couldn't get odds anymore on the horse selected to win. Even the fans were able to tell the races were fixed, and started booing and throwing beer cans on the track. The Feds stepped in and that was the end of that."

Eve, hands still draped around Max, whispered in his ear, "Then what happened."

"Well, I needed another angle and got interested in Wall Street through my new lawyer and my father's broker."

"That's a big difference from the race track game," Eve added.

"Not really. If you have serious money and you know the right people in the brokerages you can get some pretty good insider tips. Like double your money in a week or two."

"Sounds pretty impressive Max," Eve smirked, "And probably illegal."

"Sweet cakes, you don't know the half of it. They used to call me 'Mister Find Gold' down on Wall Street."

"And why was that?"

Max got a devilish look, "Because I always made quick money for me and my partners, seeing opportunities where no one else did. Maybe, someday, I'll tell you a story of those days."

He interrupted himself and looked down at his watch. It was 7:30 P.M. "How about dinner?" Italian?"

"Sure," Eve replied in delight, turning to look for her high heels.

As they walked to the door Eve asked, "One last question Max... Who was you're lawyer back then when you sued your mom?"

Max grinned, "It was Norm Stark. He's been my attorney ever since. That's over 30 years!"

Now Eve understood why the two of them were so tight. She still wanted to know about Max's earlier private conversation with Norm. She decided to probe the subject later after dinner, drinks, and some bedtime play. That was the one time she would have all the leverage.

CHAPTER 8
A strange encounter

A l Greene was called out of town on business and never had his meeting with Mike to inform him of corporate's decision to demote him. Mike merely took the delay as a sign that nothing spectacular was going to happen, and assumed Al probably didn't want to ruin his own weekend with an uncomfortable clash beforehand.

By now it was Saturday morning, and Mike was standing in his garage with his sons, Brian and Matthew. Mike had decided, after his wife Laura died, to start some car projects to keep them together and distract them from their grief and old memories of their mom.

The boys were busy restoring a 1967 Corvette coupe. It was the last model year for the original Stingray, and Mike felt it was the best year of that classic body style. The car was cheap, meaning it needed a complete restoration, inside and out. The doors, trunk lid, and hood were removed and carefully stored in the house. Seats and tires leaned against the garage walls. Tools were everywhere. The front and rear windows where also popped out and under someone's bed.

Matt was inside the car skeleton, less the bucket seats moaning, "Ouch! Shit! These spring clips are a pain in my ass."

Mike poked his head in to observe the new headliner wrapped around Matt's head. "Careful with your mouth buddy, or I'll stretch your ears with one of those bow rods."

"Well, come in dad, you try to do this by yourself."

"Uh-uh, pal." Mike replied unsympathetically, "This is your project car. I gave my blood on the Mustang project - and be careful when you use that contact cement. Open the garage door, or you'll go to la-la land."

Brian interrupted, "Hey dad, could you give some help with the engine hoist. I want to see if the flywheel will line up with the tranny."

Mike and Brian maneuvered the rebuilt 327 V8 over the hollow engine compartment, and slowly lowered the engine. Suspended by the hoist chain, Mike directed, "Easy and slow."

Brian lowered the motor passed all the electrical harnesses and lines tied back to the fender and firewall. Then he slipped under the car to guide the rear flywheel to the torque converter.

"Holy shit! Is this a tight fit or what?" Brian quipped.

"OK, OK. But there's not much room for me to work down here."

"Now you know why I insisted on the small block." Mike reminded him.

Brian finished the alignment check. Then, Mike helped him hoist the engine block back up and out. "It'll mate fine, dad."

"Good. Finish the build-up on the engine stand and we'll drop it back in tomorrow."

In the meantime, Matt continued the car interior detail work. The division of labor was appropriate. Brian was the older one. Physically stronger and more aggressive, somewhat like his father. Matthew had a leaner build with a flair for art and science - like his mother, Mike would say. The boy also had the patience and precise skill with his hands for the meticulous work.

81

The difference in physical size somehow never stopped the boys from arguing and fighting. Mike never sanctioned these wrestling matches between his sons, but they did it anyway. Fortunately, neither did any serious damage to the other. Absent a mother to break them up, even Mike would occasionally get into the horseplay.

At least restoring the old cars was a project the boys could do together with a minimum of hostility. At their age, the only other real common denominator was probably girls.

Mike felt they could continue in the garage safely alone, so he announced, "I'm going inside to clean the downstairs toilet," and retreated to the kitchen door. As he opened it, 12 year old 'Zoot' was waiting. He was a seventy pound mutt that resembled an Irish Wolf Hound, and loved cars too. Mike leaned down to pat the dogs head, and whispered the magic words in his gray tipped floppy ear, "Go bye-bye in car!"

Without hesitation, old Zoot launched into the garage and lumbered aboard the doorless Corvette. Mike closed the kitchen door behind, as Matthew screamed, "Get him outta here!. Matthew bellowed. "Get him off me! Who let him out?"

Mike envisioned Zoot's wagging tail slapping Matt around in the close confines of the car. His smelly, urine-tinged tongue licking the tip of Matthew's nose.

Lunch found Mike strolling through a house that had become a warehouse since Laura died. It was, as they say, 'men behaving badly'. The dining room was filled with boxes of assorted engine parts. The living room's soft carpet was home to the fiberglass exterior body panels from the 'Vette. Surfboards were under everybody's bed. The family room was decorated with posters of racecars, surfers and World War II fighter planes - no rock-star morons with earrings and gold chains. Curiously, though, nothing bothered him about his own, rather unconventional, decor.

Mike wound up cleaning the bathrooms. Fortunately, the bathrooms were too small to store anything.

Down the hall, the house phone rang and Brian picked it up in the kitchen, where he was devouring lunch.

"Hey, Dad!" Brian yelled. "It's for you."

"Who is it?"

"Dunno," was the reply.

Mike grit his teeth saying, "After 15 years they still can't answer a phone properly." He called out, "I'm busy. Take a message."

"He says it's urgent," Brian shouted again.

Mike reluctantly returned to the kitchen, impatiently yanking the receiver from his son.

"Michael Santino?" said the caller.

"Yeah, who am I speaking to?"

"Shawn O'Reilly," was the reply. Mike searched his memory, but the name didn't ring a bell. The pause was ended by the caller. "You saved by sister, Mary Lou, last week, over at the Lifespan compound."

"Oh...Oh yeah. How's she doing?"

"Fine now. Out of Intensive Care... she'd really like to see you, and thank you personally."

"It's really not necessary," Mike offered, "We did what anybody would do in that situation. A lot of people were there helping her besides me. They all deserve credit."

Even so, Shawn persisted, "Mary Lou said she wants to see you in particular. I don't really understand this, and she said she has a message to give you."

Mike was perplexed. He was not graceful about accepting gratitude, so he delayed giving an answer. He also didn't know if this Right-to-Life lady was a religious fanatic or a 'born again' whatever. The possibility of listening to a litany of scripture quotes wasn't his idea of conversation either.

Shawn continued, "Maybe you feel awkward about this. I had some difficulty calling you - as a stranger to you myself. I understood you stuck your neck out with your company to help her. And I saw how they white-washed it on TV. I can understand how you might want to put all this behind you. Except, my sister has been a little depressed by her injuries and all that trauma. Not quite sure why. She said your arrival would cheer her up."

Mike paused on his end of the line, and felt himself softening. "OK. What hospital? Visiting hours?"

"University Hospital, tomorrow afternoon from twelve noon on. Can I tell Mary Lou you'll be there?"

"Uh, yes," he sighed, "probably early afternoon."

They exchanged goodbyes and Mike wondered what message this woman had for him.

Thereafter, sitting down in the kitchen with a pastrami on rye sandwich, he turned on his tablet to check the *Middle Earth* website and his 'Used Male' posting. Surprised, he stopped chewing his sandwich. He actually received some responses, opening them with little optimism. One woman, responding to the car angle, went on about sitting on his stick shift.

File that in the one-night-stand bin, he decided.

Another requested photo and resume by mail to her executive office address. It contained several stipulations about personal habits and hygiene, and reading more like a purchase order for companionship.

Career executives make lousy lovers, male or female, he promptly concluded, as he resumed chewing his sandwich.

Only one really caught his interest. It was brief and didn't specify any pre-conditions. This woman had a sense of humor too. He liked that.

Brief and clever. adventurous but cautious, he surmised.

He would start his foray into relationships with someone named Phylis. Mike looked at the phone number and was intrigued by the area code. He muttered, "Strange. There was something familiar about the phone number too."

He dialed the number, not intending to speak, and heard the click of the answering machine.

"Hello, you have reached Phylis, Lifespan Procurement Associate. I'm not available at the moment, but I know how important your inquiry is. If you leave your name and number at the tone, we'll contact you as soon as possible... Thank you."

Mike stopped chewing and hung on listening to that a pleasant voice. – Flustered, he let the time ran out on the recorder before he could collect himself. It automatically disconnected.

So, this was his mystery lady.

For a next step, Mike's mind began to churn to find an amusing way to approach her. An idea finally came to him and he decided to wait until work on Monday to carry it out.

She'll either find me entertaining or a total jerk, he surmised.

* * * * * * *

Mike and the unenthusiastic boys returned from Church on Sunday morning. Laura made him promise to take them every Sunday, even if she wasn't around. He reluctantly honored her request, more as a chore than strong faith. His deep conviction in a merciful God eroded with her passing.

Upon mentioning his intention to visit Mary Lou O'Reilly at the Hospital later, the boys surprisingly asked to tag along. Presumably, because she was a one-day celebrity on the TV news. Mike agreed to their company, and they finished lunch and headed for the hospital.

* * * * * * *

Mike cautiously entered Mary Lou's room and really couldn't recognize the woman as the one on the fence. The last time they'd met, her face was swollen and covered in blood. She was a pleasant looking unremarkable kind of girl, just an innocent look.

Mike walked over to her bedside and started, "Hi, are you Mary Lou O'Reilly ?"

"Yes, and you're Michael Santino I bet," she smiled.

84

"Uh, these are my two sons, Matt and Brian".

"Hello Ma'am," they managed in unison.

There was a moment of awkward silence. Mike observed her bandaged calves and feet, and the intravenous line taped into her arm. Looking at her face, he guessed she was maybe twenty-five years old. Younger then she looked at the fence. There was no wedding ring on her finger, so he concluded she was single. Mike was sufficiently discomforted by his shyness to break the ice with a mundane comment. "Well, you sure look better than you did the last time I saw you."

"And you're fully dressed," she kidded, referring to the shirt he shredded at the fence. "Come here I want to thank you," the young woman added, and reached out one hand to draw him forward. Mike took it and leaned over. She kissed his cheek, and an embarrassed Mike awkwardly tried to retreat. Reaching for his other hand, Mary Lou held him fast, and continued, "I talked to the EMT people that brought me to the hospital. They said your tourniquets on my thighs probably kept me alive. And my legs, those ice packs you used, preserved by muscle and nerve endings. I had great surgeons - still got all my feet and toes. After some rehab, they say I'll be able to walk again!"

Mary Lou looked down at her legs, "And that wire you left in my leg was a smart move. I could have had enough artery damage to have bled to death."

Mike interrupted, "I have to be honest," he said withdrawing his hand and holding them up, trying to be modest about it. "I had help from a lot of good men...the guards, the EMTs. We were all pulling together for you." Then he engineeringly added, "Besides, when you were hanging upside down, you couldn't bleed to death because most of your blood was down in your chest and arms."

Mary Lou wouldn't accept his humility. "I know I owe a debt to all of them. You're the one who didn't have to get involved. You're the one who got chewed out for it."

Mike questioned, "How'd you know that."

Mary Lou laughed, "You'd be surprised what you hear and remember when you're outside your body!"

He managed a condescending smile and started to feel a little weird with where this was going. In his usual blunt manner he asked, "So why did ya do it?"

Mary Lou was taken back by his directness and somewhat embarrassed, She responded anyway, "Well, I didn't plan on being cut to shreds by that razor wire," pointing down to her legs. "I just wanted to get near the Lifespan buildings, maybe get some pictures of what's going on in there. Get media attention focused on this decoupling business that they do. Worst case, be arrested for trespassing."

"Turned into a mighty costly statement," Mike observed.

Mary Lou looked down and clasped her hands together. "This is probably going to sound stupid, but I feel it was worth it."

Why?" Mike replied. "It didn't accomplish anything. You got one day's TV news coverage, that's all! In today's media you're already yesterday's news."

An undeterred Mary Lou looked up at Mike with her head bowed slightly forward. "About five years ago I had a procedure at 8 weeks gestation. At the time it didn't faze me. I wasn't married and had a year to go to finish my college degree."

She looked up at Mike and continued, "Now, you're not going to understand this next part. You're a man, and I think only a woman could appreciate it." She took a deep breath and was starting to have difficulty keeping her composure, her moist eyes welling with feminine emotion.

Mike tried to head her off. He was always more comfortable with technical exchanges. "You don't have to tell me any of this personal stuff. It's none of my business. It's only going to upset you more to discuss it."

Now t was too late. Mary Lou reached out and held his fingertips, as a tear formed in her eye. "There isn't a month that goes by that I don't remember that baby....wondering who it might have been....how my life would've been different - wondering if God will punish me in the end."

"Guilt is a tough feeling to handle," Mike noted, thinking of how he dealt with it when his wife died.

"Oh, it's not like I've taken sole ownership to that tragedy. Nobody told me what my other options were back then. I had this vague idea that it was just a mass of protoplasm. All the advice I received was just to quickly get rid of it, and get on with my own life. At the time, it didn't seem wrong, or even questionable. I mean, the government pretty much let you do whatever you wanted to do. In fact, it seemed like they actually encouraged it. Even my boyfriend, the father, was ambivalent. It was his child too."

Mike was moved by her story, and as a male, even felt a little defensive. "I can't argue with you about how we guys handle these things." Mike gave a nervous smile, "If its outta site, its outta mind."

Mary Lou's tears slowly dripped down her still swollen cheeks as she sniffled. "I joined *Operation Rescue* because I thought about termination and my conscience won't let me do it again. I just want other women to know more about it than I did. Know it is not a single, casual decision, like having a tooth pulled. There's more at stake. Some future person losses their destiny - along with your own. It's a decision you question over and over again the rest of your life... if you really let yourself think about it."

"Well you sure made your point on that last week," Mike added. He did find himself feeling empathetic for her internal struggle. It didn't affect his ambivalent viewpoint on the decoupling issue. His boys remained unusually quiet behind him.

Mike was glad they came. He reasoned that maybe, when they run around with the girls, they will understand the sometimes cruel consequences to a girl from a casual roll in the hay.

Mary Lou wiped her eyes with a tissue and seemed to feel more composed and continued her conversation with less hesitation. "After this little episode, you'll find it hard to believe I've got a positive attitude towards life again. The way I see it, if God wanted to judge me for what I'd done, he had the opportunity to pass judgment when I was strung up on that fence."

Sarcastically, Mike said, "You think Mike Santino was directed by God to save you?"

"No. I don't think it works quite that way. But I do think he depends on people like you, Michael, to step forward and do the right thing at the right time, regardless of the consequences."

Mike felt sorry about his last remark. "I didn't mean to sound like I was making fun of you, Mary Lou."

"No offense taken, Michael," and she held his hand again, reassuringly, just peacefully staring at him.

As a male, Mike was still a bit uncomfortable with all this interpersonal stuff, and this moment of silence was his opening to end the visit. "Well...uh... me and the boys have to get home for dinner."

"Wait. Wait, I have something else to tell you...personal." Mary Lou glanced around Mike and added, "Uh, maybe the boys can wait outside for a few minutes".

Mike motioned to them to stay in the hall and turned back to Mary Lou.

She invited Mike to sit down on her bedside, her gaze more intense. She spoke in a slow, deliberate tone. "When I was unconscious at the fence I had this experience. Some people might call it 'near death'. I don't know. There was this bright white circular cone of light. Sort of circles of light that decreased in size as the distance increased. I felt myself floating on the fringe of that tunnel. Just kind of suspended. Not going forward, not going backward. It's hard to describe it physically - in words. It's more like feelings. Anticipation. Like standing on the threshold of forever. The excitement of preparing to receive all the answers to all the questions in the universe."

With widening eyes, she shifted forward in her bed to face Mike. "About that moment an all encompassing sensation in every part of my being made me feel like I had some kind of choice to make that wasn't clear at the time. I began feeling very fatigued, and had this option of kind of relaxing and going with the flow. Or, I could fight to remain in the game.

And, there was no moral judgment to either decision."

Her face took on a resolute look, "I remember choosing to fight."

Mike felt some kinship with her since he had been in the jaws of death himself on at least three occasions in his own life. Only, not quite that close. He shifted on his feet, looking for an excuse to break away.

Mary Lou remained intent on telling her story. "The next thing that happened was that a small translucent oval shape appeared deep at the middle of those distant circles of light. It began to move rapidly towards me. As it approached, my tranquility turned to fear. I could see a crouched creature inside that object, encased in a translucent oval glass-like egg." Mary Lou's visage took on a far away look as she continued. "It glided directly toward me. At the same time I could feel its intent to reach me. Getting larger and larger, until I thought it would crash into my face. I cringed and then, suddenly, the bright white light around me turned a soft amber. Then, I realized why the light had dimmed...."

In a hushed voice she paused... "Somehow, I was inside that 'egg'."

Mike shifted in his seat thinking how bizarre this conversation was becoming, but avoided interrupting.

Mary Lou continued in an almost whispering tone, her eyes cast downward at her abdomen, her mind still focused somewhere in the distance. "That figure inside was a fetus, still not a completely formed human being. I was drawn through the amber fluid as if I was in miniature and that being inside was a giant, until I was close up, face to face with the creature. So close that its face took up my whole field of vision. I remember the smooth coating of peach fuzz-like hair on its face. It slowly turned its head so that one partially developed eye looked directly at me. Then my mind heard this pleasant voice, like a 3 or 4 year old child. And it spoke with the precise diction of a scholar."

Mary Lou paused from relating the rest of the story saying, "Wait a minute." She pointed her index finger upward. "I want to get this right." After a brief moment she smiled saying, "I remember now. It said to me,

'Behold the son of creation.
See the twilight of the past,
....the dawn of the future'.'

Mary Lou looked into Mike's eyes with obvious elation. "I felt my fear slowly subside as it reached out a developing palm to caress my cheek. The touch was smooth like silk and the warm fluid around me moved gentle as the evening breeze. I could feel little eddy currents sort of slowly swirl and wrap around me - caressing me. Kind of an ethereal bond between me and that child."

She moved closer to Mike, paused again to collect her thoughts and said, "Then this tiny and strangely familiar voice said softly,

'The Father has sent me to his beloved daughter so that you will know this;
All these creatures serve my purpose, else they not be created.
Even the simplest of my children are dear to me."

Mary Lou stopped and swallowed, the emotional memory constricting her throat. "Ok let me see." She caught her breath and continued. Err, it was something like this:

'Lest you error and hinder my purpose,
know what is created and what is destroyed.
Take this truth to your heart, and then...
Go in peace my child.'

Mike tried to keep a compassionate face, not knowing where this was going.

Mary Lou continued with a far off look. "The slit of the mouth curled into what I thought was a smile. Then, I felt freer...freer than I ever felt. No pain, no guilt, no fear, no care whatsoever. There was an enveloping tenderness in that touch and in that voice that I can't find words for. Maybe unconditional love is the best expression I can think of."

Engineer Mike interrupted with a typical careless remark, "Yeah, I know. The kind you get from an autistic kid."

Mary Lou gave Mike an annoyed look, "Are you making fun of me?"

"No, not at all," Mike, shrugged. "Honestly, that's the only analogy that I could think of what you're describing. It just came out crude... I'm sorry."

"Well, I felt forgiven at that point."

"For what? By who?"

"For my own termination!" Mary Lou exclaimed.

Then she stared straight into Mike's wide eyes, hesitated again, and added, "I actually think I met my own baby!"

Mike thought sardonically, *Geez, this lady has some vivid imagination, or somebody over-medicated her!*

He felt increasingly uncomfortable being draw into this very personal situation and said, "You don't have to tell me anymore if you don't want to." He stood up from the bed to get ready to leave.

Unexpectedly Mary Lou seemed to change topics and asked Mike, "Do you swim a lot?"

Mike was puzzled. "Occasionally. Surfing. Yeah. What does that have to do with anything?"

Mary Lou cleared her throat, and appeared hesitant. "Wait a minute," she said, as she started her story again. "The end of this encounter experience came as I felt myself being pulled backward out of the glowing egg.

"Once outside, I saw my decreased Grandfather, which filled me with a great joy. He seemed to embrace me from behind me, over and under me."

"He looked up and I followed his gaze to see a dazzling bright blue rippled surface above us. There was a human form floating above. It was man in distress. He looked like he was drowning. My grandfather reached up and somehow forced him to the surface. I saw this struggling man's face. I didn't recognize him at first."

She paused to swallow. "It was <u>you</u> Mike, I saw you in trouble."

Mike was disbelieving at first, so in his usual careless fashion he said, "Well, that's the end of surfing at the beach."

Mary Lou remained dead serious, "Michael, you weren't there so you don't know how real it all was. I hope to God that it was just a figurative dream - not prophetic. It's not my intent to frighten you or anything. I only know what I saw. So, I thought if you knew this, you might, somehow, be able to avoid something disastrous."

Mary Lou pulled him down toward her, and kissed his forehead. "I'm sorry. God will protect you, Michael. I just know it."

Mike did not know what to think. He was perplexed and just said flippantly, "Thanks Mary Lou O'Reilly, I'll just have to keep my eyes peeled, and wear a 'May West' under my shirt," and then turned to leave. Unexpectedly, it crossed his mind about his own troubles with Lifespan. He stopped halfway to the door and asked, "One last thing," he said, "are you going to sue Lifespan?"

Mary Lou thought it was an odd question at this time, and answered anyway. "Their lawyers have already been talking to my brother Shawn. I'm really not interested in pursuing a court case. It makes what happened to me seem theatrical and contrived, and it won't undo what happened. Instead, I'm going to use the time off to try and write my experience in an article for a magazine or something, and share it with everyone. Shawn knows some publishing people that are interested.

"I think Lifespan has offered to cover my hospital expenses, and rehabilitation, and $100,000 for psychological distress."

Mike started to get an unsure feeling. The thought occurred to him that Lifespan might come after him if there is no threat from her. He had to ask the question. "This might seem like I'm rudely intruding, but are you going to settle out of court?"

"Yes. Probably. Why?"

Mike looked down at the floor, and swiped the tile with the tip of one foot. "Well, now it may sound a bit paranoid on my part....and selfish too." His gaze returned to her and added sheepishly, "You already know my job is kind of shaky at Lifespan. My supervisor gave me the impression that the company would like to fire me."

"I'm sorry to hear that. Is there anything that I can do to help you?"

"Well this is purely speculation on my part, but I think they won't go after me as long as you're a litigation threat."

Mary Lou briefly weighed his answer and concluded, "Oh, so as long as I keep the Lifespan lawyers busy talking, then you're OK?"

"More or less. If you stretch out the settlement discussions a few months, it would give me time to find another job." Mike felt relieved to get his reservations out on the table.

Mary Lou's reaction was spontaneous. "Michael, there isn't anything I wouldn't do for you. I mean, I owe you my life. I'll talk to Shawn and the lawyers. We'll figure a way to drag it out."

Mike was thankful and inquired, "What about money. How will you live?"

"I think Lifespan is already picking up the medical bills, and I'll be on disability for a few months. It won't be a burden, and I'm in no rush for their money."

"It's kind of you Mary Lou. If you need any financial help, let me know."

Mary Lou gestured for Mike to return to her bedside. She pulled him down to kiss him goodbye once more on the cheek. Her hand held him gently behind his head to look him straight in the eye "God works through people," she said, "Good only conquers evil when someone is willing to dedicate their life in that cause. It's the amount of sacrifice that measures the size of the victory. And, a human life is the ultimate measure."

Once released Mike back peddled for the door again, Mary Lou added, "You're a good man Michael, I'll pray for you. Sooner or later, your purpose will be revealed. Then, Jesus will be there to keep the wolves at bay."

Mike was mystified, and stopped to look back at her, admiring her spirit and strong faith. "Well, whatever comes at me, let Him know that all I usually need is a good head start."

He leaned on the doorjamb and said, "Thanks again Mary Lou, you're probably gonna taken some Lifespan heat off of me. So, let's call us even in the gratitude department."

Mary Lou got misty eyed and gave a simple wave from her palm resting on her chest. She whispered, "Peace be with you."

Mike joined the boys in the hallway.

"Hey dad you look like you've seen a ghost. What did she tell you?"

Mike felt foolish trying to repeat her story. He told the boys, "It was nothing, just some other personal problems she had."

Mike changed the subject to the Corvette restoration project as they drove home together.

Throughout the rest of the day, Mike tried to shake the haunting images from his hospital visit, and that whole spiritual mumbo-jumbo.

Surely, if God was looking for a champion, Mike had to be at the bottom of that batting order.

Later in the day Mike's focus returned to more secular problems, and thought more and more about his lunch appointment this coming week with Dr. Joel Rosen of extraction production. Mike could not figure it out. *Maybe it was the tone of his voice. Something was definitely off with Joel. Maybe he had marital problems? Or, it could be some dirty politics at Lifespan,* was all Mike could speculate at this point.

CHAPTER 9
So many secrets

Monday morning always came too soon for Phylis. If the week days passed like a runny nose, the weekends were a sneeze. Between food shopping, cleaning the house, catching up on laundry, chauffeuring the kids and her own personal grooming, there didn't seem like there was much time left for anything else. Phylis would often wonder why, if life was supposed to get easier when you get older, hers only became more difficult, more hectic.

Today, Phylis was headed for a specimen pickup at North Harbor Hospital. If all went according to plan, she'd meet Heather Vanderbeck, take care of business, and be at her Lifespan office by twelve noon.

Phylis stopped at the travel agency to pick up Heather's airline tickets and timed her arrival at the hospital so that her contact with Heather would be at the bare minimum. At the hospital she picked up the release paperwork and made her way to Heather's pre-op room. When she arrived, Heather was sitting up in her bed happily chatting away to two interns and a nurse Heather was telling her audience some 'cock and bull' story about how sorry she was that she couldn't afford to keep the baby.

That lying little bimbo. Why doesn't she tell 'em about her 'horse trading' dealings, Phylis thought. She had to bite her tongue as she grumbled, *Thank God this is the last time I see this ditz.*

Phylis walked over to the group and said with a forced smile, "Good morning, how are we all today?"

They exchanged pleasantries, even the hospital staff could sense a certain coldness in her tone, and they used the interruption as an excuse to get away from Heather. Phyllis feigned a smile and gave Heather the releases to sign.

Heather also seemed disappointed that Phylis wasn't as friendly as usual and inquired, "Phylis, is everything alright? You're not your bubbly self."

Phylis picked up the signed forms trying not to look her in the eye and betray her true feelings, and curtly replied, "Oh, I just had a trying weekend with the kids."

She reached into her purse, withdrew the airline tickets, and handed them to Heather. "This concludes our deal as promised. Have a safe trip. I'm sure you'll have a good time in Florida."

Before Heather could engage her in further conversation, Phylis began walking to the door. "Sorry, I have another appointment, Heather." Sarcastically adding, "Call me when you want to do this again."

As Phylis exited the house, Heather felt a bit slighted and sensed that Phylis might not actually approve of her. She surmised to herself, *who gives a damn anyway*. In another few days, she would be the one on the beach in Palm Springs. Phylis will still be stuck with her kids in New York. Heather was used to people being jealous of her. She had her wealth, her good looks, and her jet set life style. Those are the things that really count.

* * * * * * *

Phylis arrived late in the day at Lifespan Headquarters with specimen NH0633 compliments of Heather Vanderbeck. She delivered it to the Specimen Receiving Department, got her receipt, and went to her office.

Sitting down in her cubicle, she put the whole Heather affair behind her and turned on her desktop terminal. She checked her voice-mail, and wondered if one of the recorded messages might be from the guy on the Middle Earth website.

With a few clicks of her computer mouse, her calendar software opened, and an appointment display for the next two weeks appeared on the screen. Then she played back the phone messages, answered tem, and filled in the screen days as appropriate. It took about an hour to finish. She felt disappointed when she reached the end of the voice-mail and softly sighed, "No message from Mister Used Male."

Just then her boss, Jerry, came over to drop off her monthly commission check, and proceeded to distribute them to the other procurement agents present in the department. Phylis kissed the envelope playfully saying, "If it wasn't for you every month, I'd pack this whole business in once and for all."

She removed the check from the envelope, then opened the company database application, searching for the commission file, "COMM.$$$". The display came up, and immediately she knew something was wrong. It showed five specimens actually brought in. Unexpectedly, the company commission check worked out to four specimens last month - short changed by one again!

The check stub listed the specimen numbers, so she crossed off each one that was on the screen until there was only the remaining specimen,

UH0744.

I'll be damned! she thought. *That was the Maria Alvarez case I dropped off at that Atlas Meat Company. I'll bet they never did the receiving paperwork over there.*

She rummaged through her desk draw to retrieve the receipt she obtained from Atlas.

Katie walked nearby and Phylis called to her to join her in her cubicle. "Katie, did you get a commission on your specimen delivery last week to Atlas?"

Katie looked perplexed. "Nah. Did you?"

"Nope. Somebody must have screwed up the paperwork. Those were premium specimens with an extra bonus commission."

Katie shrugged her shoulders, "Too bad, but I'm sure Jerry can get it straightened out." She excused herself, and hurried to keep an appointment with another specimen candidate on Long Island.

Phylis was perturbed for a moment, then decided to call the Payroll Department herself. After being bounced through two bookkeepers she talked to a payroll supervisor. Phylis was told that they had a receiver on it and no acceptance code from the Extraction Department. Without an acceptance code from the Extraction Department they can't clear a commission.

So, she called Vicki in Extraction Department Receiving. Vicki was pleasantly cooperative, having known Phylis for the last three years at Lifespan.

"Let me check it out, Honey. That was UH0744, right ? Hang on a minute."

"Oh, Yeah, here it is. I've got it logged in from Atlas last week".

Phylis felt relieved and said, "Good! Now how come the Payroll Department doesn't have an acceptance code?" Phylis waited patiently, gratified that the specimen didn't get lost in some "Black Hole" at Lifespan.

"Uh, Phylis, I, uh, hate to tell you this. It was never accepted."

Phylis's calm turned to agitation. "How can that be? It had one of the best extraction potential workups I've seen. Are you sure?"

Vicki replied sympathetically, "I'm sorry Phylis. I don't know why it wasn't coded as OK, but that's the story."

Phylis thanked her and hung up. She went through a lot of anxiety with Maria over this case. She stopped thinking about the commission and thought about the specimen, discarded like an old sneaker without shoelaces.

She grumbled, *I'm gonna see Jerry on this one. I can't accept that after all I went through to get it, that now it's totally useless. That specimen had the best DNA markers I'd ever seen.*

Phylis marched into her boss' office. She filled him in on the little investigation she'd already done. Jerry called Dr. Joel Rosen. Rosen indicated that if it were a specimen with an attached placenta, those would be forwarded directly to Dr. Strauss's R&D Lab. He did not seem to know which specimen numbers or procedures were followed after that.

Jerry thanked the doctor and dialed Strauss's Lab. He was unavailable, so Jerry told Phylis that he'd get back to her later on the matter.

Phylis left Jerry's office with some measure of satisfaction, since she knew where the specimen went and that it must have been used. At the same time she wondered why placenta specimens went to R&D and why no procedure was in place to record their acceptability. She thought, *Lifespan has always been a stickler for written procedures. Why did they not just give Vicki in the Receiving Department the acceptance code, same as Dr. Rosen's Department?*

* * * * * * *

Mike arrived at his office earlier to see a note from his boss, Greene. He took a deep breath and left for Al's office. Mike knocked on the open door jamb to Al's office and entered with a 'Good Morning' greeting.

Al looked up in a serious mood and just acknowledge with an, "Uh-Huh."

Mike thought to himself, *OK, no jokes, no sarcasm today. Al has his 'I'm the serious Boss' face on.*

Al cleared his throat and started right in. "I hope you had a good weekend. I waited to give you the results of our corporate level meeting, figuring you could enjoy one more weekend."

Mike answered, "I appreciate that consideration Al. I hope you enjoyed your weekend too." Then he grinned, "And not having to worry about what I might do."

Al didn't quite know how to take Mike's remark, and decided to continue with his slanted summary of the meeting. He was careful to avoid the appearance of being a messenger boy from corporate and fabricated a story.

"I fought hard for you last week. Really hung my ass out with corporate and Eve, trying to save you job here at Lifespan. You know you don't have any friends here. I mean your standing alone around here... except for me. If I didn't do such a good job defending you, you might not be here today."

Mike wasn't buying it. He'd seen Al kiss-up to corporate too many times to believe him. "Thanks for the 'head's up' Al, and I already know where I stand here. Let's cut to the bottom-line, OK."

Al was irritated that Mike had cut short his buildup to the decision made on the meeting.

"Well, look at it this way. Anything is an improvement over being fired. You could work your way back into Corporate's good graces if you cooperate for a change, and carry the 'party line'.

Mike was his usual direct and un-endearing self. "Al, don't pontificate, just get to the point. I'm too old and scarred for a guidance counselor at this point in my career."

Al was pissed. Then he thought, *He is actually making this easy for me.* He told him flat out, "Mike you've been demoted from Director to Department Head. I'm assuming control of Facilities until further notice."

The pragmatic Mike was amused more than anything else. It could have be a lot worse if they canned him right now. Mike decided to feign disappointment. "Geez, Al, I've had Facilities since I started with the company."

"I know how terrible you feel Mike, but that's what happens when you anger the God's."

At this point Mike was concerned about only one thing. "What about my salary, Al."

"Well, there's, uh, good news and, uh, bad news."

Mike hunched forward in his chair, "Well let's hear it big guy."

Al leaned back, paused and said, "The good news is your salary will only be cut by 15Gs – and I wouldn't anticipate any raise next year. But, the really bad news is that you're out of the Executive incentive bonus plan."

To Mike it was a relief to know he still had a living salary, but the bonus plan added $50,000 a year to his income. Those bonuses were being used for his boy's college fund savings. It was too bad, he thought. Usually, it's just him suffering the consequences. Now his kids were indirectly affected too.

Mike had done what most people would not do. He pushed up against the 'big boys' enough to make his family suffer the consequences too. He comforted himself with the thought that if his boys are as tough as him and Laura, they'll survive this too.

Mike sat back, and carefully kept his feelings to himself, telling Al, "Boy, I'm gonna miss that income."

"Sorry Mike, you made your bed. Now you have to sleep in it."

Mike looked down at the floor. Al used the pause in conversation to shift to his last point. "Mike, they'll be no posted announcement of your demotion. I'll leave it up to you to inform your people of the new order of things." Al was fulfilling Eve's mean-spirited direction to have Mike experience the embarrassment of explaining his demotion to everybody.

Mike lifted his head and said, "OK. I guess that's it then," and stood up to leave, trying to look as dejected as expected. While heading for the door, Al requested a progress report on the fabrication of the new R&D

extraction fixtures he was designing and building in his test department.

"Oh by the way, Mike. I need you keys to all the Facilities."

"I'll have the report and keys it for you tomorrow morning, Al. But, I still need my office keys."

With a wave of the hands he answered, "Whatever."

As soon as he turned the corner and out of sight, he smiled. He already knew his days were numbered. He knew how to handle this demotion, and he had time to plan his way out of Lifespan's grasp. He reached his Admin and stopped to give her some instructions.

"Nancy, I'm not handling Facilities problems any more. Screen my incoming calls for any matter related to it and direct them to Al Green's office. I don't want to talk to anybody about anything further regarding the Facility Department. The boss thinks I've got too much on my plate already."

He figured he'd let Al explain things, since it was corporate's reorganization idea anyway. Mike did not realize it. He had easily defused the embarrassment that Eve intended. Mike took a positive attitude about his predicament. For one thing, he had half the problems and responsibilities he had before. That would make his daily work load lighter, and give him time to maybe land a better job. Another positive was that his reduced salary was still substantial.

Later in the day, after his Test Department people went home, Mike went downstairs to the secure equipment locker where the building keys were kept. He worked the combination, opened it, and removed the key sets for all three Lifespan buildings including Corporate. He located the master key for the R&D floor. Mike felt a bit giddy, like a kid breaking into the school principal's office. When they demoted Mike, it never occurred to Management that he still had access to Facility's security keys.

Mike was amused with the idea that he could still have free admittance to the entire Lifespan compound, with the exception of the corporate executive offices themselves. Mike thought, *this little detail wouldn't occur to those corporate boobs, since they had no idea of how the company actually runs anyway.* He also knew that Al Greene was to busy to really dig into the details of running Facilities himself.

Later, Mike took his Facility keys to Home Depot and copied some of them before turning them in. Now he had a master key for each building.

Mike spent the next morning getting updated status from his technicians on the R&D fixture project for Al. He visited Al Greene's office, but Al was not there. He left the keys and the requested report with Al's Admin.

With his extra time now, Mike returned to his office, thinking about how he would approach this Phylis Daye person, who answered his 'Used Male' web posting. Then, an idea came to him on his desktop monitor as he reviewed the capital equipment lists that he would no longer be responsible for. He typed in her name and found an outlawed desktop terminal assigned to her.

Hmm, he thought, *This could be my opening. Give her a little tweak. See who she really is when I annoy her.*

* * * * * * *

Phylis spent the afternoon in her cubicle to begin answering her text messages and Emails, then scheduling her calendar. She was content to believe that the commission error on her paycheck was going to be resolved.

Shortly, down the hall, she heard some animated conversations, and her curiosity was aroused. She peeked over her wall divider, and noticed a smiling shaggy-haired, middle-aged guy with a clipboard. The other procurement associates seemed to be engaged by him, and she strained to hear. He was dressed in a brushed brown leather jacket, white shirt and a blue tie with little animals on it. It reminded her more of the casual look of some of the younger technicians around Lifespan. He seemed familiar, probably the Lifespan manager that she had seen in some corporate computer training meetings. Phylis, half sitting, tried to keep one eye on him and another on her monitor screen.

Suddenly, he finished the conversation, and turned towards her. Phylis quickly slid down behind her cubicle wall and pretended not to notice him.

In another moment, Mike peeked in. A friendly sounding voice announced, "Hi, I'm Mike Santino from Engineering and Facilities. How ya doin?" Mikes loss of Facilities was not widely known yet.

Phylis acted busy and shuffled some papers. She stood up and extended her hand in a business fashion, and mimicked Mike' lingo. "And how are ya doin?"

While looking at him, the first thing she noticed was his blue eyes, deep set and clear. Not the handsomest face, but engaging - trim build, intelligent, somewhat sincere looking.

Mike shook her hand and held it, staring a second longer than necessary, which Phylis thought was a bit odd. She added, "Phylis Daye."

Phylis broke contact, remaining coy, and with a pretty smile said, "Well, Mike Santino, did your wife pick out that tie?"

He answered, glancing down, "Oh, the Penguins... Uh no... No wife. He fingered the tie. I think Penguins are funny." Looking back up, he was transfixed by her pretty face and dimpled smile for a moment, loosing control of the conversation.

Phylis broke the silence again, saying in a friendly, professional tone, "Well, what can we do for you today?"

A nervous Mike remembered some Internet advice about meeting new women; *step 1; Start with a compliment.* "Well, uh, you have a very neat, clean cubicle."

Phylis let out an audible sigh, thinking, *Nice come on. Just the thing every woman is waiting to here.* Still, she found his boyish awkwardness in presentation appealing. And, his eyes, they were different. He had beautiful long eyelashes, unusual for a middle-aged male.

Mike recalled 'step 2' for meeting women: *find something in common.* Mike finally spoke up. "We both have the same Lifespan capital equipment, pointing to her computer terminal."

Phylis frowned suspiciously with a drawn out, "Annnd?"

"Well, except, it's… Uh, yours is non-standard - unsecured USB output port."

Phylis face flushed, now feeling defensive. "What of it? What's the problem?" She reached down to the terminal on her desk, unplugged the memory stick from the USB socket, and threw it in an open draw.

Mike enjoyed her spirit in defending her turf and smiled, but instead of charming her, he was making her angry. Mike remembered another tip not from the Internet; *do not piss the woman off.* "Easy, easy, Miz Daye." Mike said, and formed his palms into a 'T', saying, "Time out – reset button. If you knew me better, you would understand my view on company policies. You see, if you have terminal output ports, the company is worried that you could access new restricted areas of the network, and copy all Lifespan's super-duper secrets."

With hands on hips, an exasperated Phylis countered his remark. "All I know is my boss, Mister Klein, approved it and I've used it for three years with no security issues... that is, until you came along."

Mike's explanation did not pacify the concern that Phylis felt about her handy computer terminal and she sarcastically demanded, "So, what happens next Mister Penguin?"

Mike gave a wide grin. "Oh well…maybe nothing," Then, casually, he leaned behind the cubicle divider wall, looked down, wrote something on his clipboard, and reappeared. Pointing to it, he showed her the names and computer serial numbers. Phylis leaned forward to look – her computer terminal was checked as compliant."

Phylis stepped back, a crooked smile of satisfaction on her face. "Mister Santino, this wouldn't be your crude way of bribing a woman for a date? Would it?…because it's not working."

"Au contaire ma cherie, this is my way of appearing both charming and magnanimous."

"So far you're neither, mister Frenchie," she came back with, now starting to enjoy the repartee again.

OK," he said," so I'm not French either. Anyway, let me make it up to you over lunch."

Phylis looked at him dubiously, and Mike felt he needed to do more of a selling job. Lacking any better ideas, he said, "Well, hey, do you like classic cars? I can take you to lunch in one."

At that moment, his reply piqued Phylis's curiosity again, thinking of the 'Used Male' posting – Mike –classic. She gave him a critical stare. Mike just stood there, looking at the ceiling - the look of a naughty boy after his hand in the cookie jar.

Phylis cocked her head sideways slightly. "Well, Monsieur Penguin, do you know something you're not telling me?"

Mike was wily in his response, "The only way you'll find out, is to go to lunch with me.....and I'll even buy."

Phylis was thinking to herself, *of course you'll buy, you idiot.* But was still intrigued enough to give in and accept.

"OK. Since you're buying." she replied. Then added, "And you'll promise, right now, to answer all my questions honestly over lunch?"

Mike's rolled eyes towards heaven, with two fingers together. "Yes, boyscout's honor." Then he turned to walk away. Phylis called over the cubicle wall, "What day?"

Mike pivoted, as he walked down the corridor and gave the traditional hand signal of thumb and pinky fingers by his ear. "I'll call you." Still looking back, he tripped over some boxes temporarily piled in the hallway, stumbling against the wall.

Phylis smiled and thought to herself, *Cool move 'classic' Santino.*

As she sat down at her desk, an idea came to her that might help her to double check exactly who this character might be. She walked down the aisle to the front outside window overlooking the parking lot. Staring through the tinted glass, she waited for Mike to exit the building and appear below. Her boss, Jerry, happen to stroll by and asked her what she was looking at. Pointing down to the man walking to his old Mustang in gray primer, Phylis answered, "Do you know that man, Jer?"

"Oh yeah," Jerry said as he leaned towards the glass, adding," Getting into to that old car?" Her boss pointed to the security fence in the distance. "I finally found out that he's the guy that got involved with the woman that hung herself on our fence last week.

"You know Harry, the security sergeant who works the guardhouse? He was there. Filled me in. Says Santino went up against corporate security. He said that guy took over the whole scene, and probably saved that woman's life. It was nothing like what they showed on TV. "

Jerry grinned and shook his head in dismay, saying, "I'm surprised he's still an employee." He turned to face Phylis and inquired, "Why do you ask?" Phylis looked down and was careful to hide her interest, trying to act casual in responding. "Oh, nothing. He was around here earlier doing an inventory of our computer equipment or something."

Jerry sensed that her mind was something else, shrugged and said, "Well, anyway, he's a 'persona non grata' around here now. Demoted. No longer supervises Facilities. Finished...kaput."

She resented the belittling comments for an unsung hero, finding herself feeling defensive for Santino, most probably the *Used Male*

"By the way," Jerry added, "I talked to Payroll. They'll automatically accept a placenta specimen as soon a received and routes it directly to R&D. Job 901. No Receiving acceptance required. So you'll get your commission immediately without anymore hassles."

"A bit unusual to bypass inspection and acceptance," Phylis remarked with astonishment.

"Yeah, I guess," he shrugged. "Must want it real bad." Then he turned and walked away.

Phylis returned to the window and placed her fingers tips against the glass between her and Mike's departing car, pondering this stranger. He disappeared in the other building. From the look of his Mustang in gray primer and Jerry's comments, she felt her suspicions reinforced that he was the beat up 'Used Male" from the website. As she turned away from the glass, she realized, she was beginning to care about him. *Strange*, she thought, *demoted, but still using that Facilities department angle to chat her up.*

* * * * * *

When Mike returned to his office, it was late in the afternoon. Waiting inside was Carlos Rivera, his trusted supervisor from the evening maintenance crew. The aging Carlos was there to find out what his situation was with his new boss, Al Greene, now that he had assumed Mike's Facilities Department responsibilities.

Mike greeted the small rotund man and sat down behind his desk opposite Carlos. The two had worked amicably together for three years. Mike never displayed a condescending manner towards him, as others in the company did, just because Carlos was a maintenance man. In spite of his age, the man was conscientious about cleaning the facility, and didn't see it as demeaning. Carlos was a person who took pride in shiny waxed floors, clear windows, vacuumed carpeting, replacing dead light bulbs. Uneducated but dedicated. The kind of person they just don't make anymore.

Mike said, "Cheer up; this reorganization thing won't effect you or your routine."

Carlos seemed disturbed and nervous, and rubbed the few stubbles of gray hair left on his beard. He still spoke with a thick Hispanic accent, "Mikey, I don't like what dey do to you. You a good man. You don'a deserve dis."

Mike put on a cheerful facade. "Thanks pal. It's OK. They just made my job easier."

Carlos looked down and shook his head slowly from side to side saying, "It's a no good, no fair. I'm a quit dis place."

Mike was surprised that his demotion would effect someone as distant from him as Carlos. Mike couldn't remember anybody ever quitting their job because of someone else's misadventures and responded, "Hold on buddy. I appreciate the gesture. Except, your leaving won't change anything. I have time to find another job, so it's no big tragedy."

Still Carlos seemed distraught, stood up and walked around the desk to be nearer Mike. "If dey don't needa good man lika you, den I don't wan to work with dem."

"Look Carlos, a lot of things can change over time. Who knows, a few years from now someone else might own this company. You just keep doing your job satisfactorily and things will get better."

Carlos nodded his head in resignation, and retreated to sit nervously in his seat. "Dere is one more thing , Mikey. I dunno if I should bring it up to you now or not."

Mike leaned back in his chair and crossed his legs to appear more casual and relaxed towards Carlos. "You may as well tell me now. If it's something I can't help you with, I'll forget you told me, or, if you wish, Mister Greene can handle it."

Carlos' wrinkled face distorted, and he leaned forward to exclaim, "Oh no. I won't tell dis to mista Greene. It must be kept a secret. You don't hear dis from me. Si! "

Mike nodded approvingly, so Carlos continued. "You know in my home town, Guadalajara, when you see something bad...illegal, you keep you mouth shut."

"Yeah, I know," Mike interrupted, "so things never change down there because nobody can fight back."

Carlos was annoyed at Mike's quick judgment, and stood up to lean across the desk. "Oh, you say dat because you never lived there like that. A place where the whole town is run by crooks, murderers. They run your life. They can make you family disappear without a trace." Carlos snapped his fingers, "Just like dat!"

Mike began to sense the fear in Carlos' voice. He stood up with a grin, and patted the back of Carlos's hand on the desk. "You don't have to worry about that kind of thing here in the good ol' U.S.of A."

Carlos' eyes fixed on Mike's movement around the office to the window. Mike stared out through the blinds as employees scurried to their cars to get home. He couldn't fathom what was making Carlos so jittery.

They were interrupted by his Admin, Nancy, as she popped in to say goodnight. They both stared at her, expressionless. She recognized it as that peculiar look engineers usually have when they're deep in thought on some technical problem or another. So, she just turned and left.

Then, Carlos began again, "Mikey, you swear on your children to keep what I tell you between us?"

"Sure pal"

Carlos began. "You know how every night I burn dose boxes. I write down the date, the serial numba, and den throw it in the furnace."

"Yeah , Yeah, go on."

Carlos swallowed hard, "Well, some boxes come from the room, the lab were da scientist work, in the other building."

"I know, you mean R&D."

"Uh-huh, that's it," Carlos continued. "Well, I never go in dat room 'cause it's always locked. Ezepta, every coupla days they put out a big box of little, sealed boxes. So, I write down the numbers and burn them with everything else."

"That's not so unusual, Carlos. R&D does experiments on some specimens too. They're developing new extracts that may be useful in the future."

"Entiendio," he replied. Then looked down at his hands as if measuring something in mid air, "But in with the small boxes are a the bigga ones. I helda one in my hand. It was heavy, maybe a pound, pound and a half."

"What's the point?" Mike queried. "Maybe they collected a whole bunch of specimen debris and put it in one big box."

"That's what I thought. Until one night, I cut open the sealing tape and found it." Carlo's tired baggy eyes were beginning to swell as he hesitated. "I shouldn't tell this. I shouldn't have done it."

Mike sensed his distress, and urged him to continue.

Carlos sat down and persevered, "This box didn't have a serial number like the small ones. I was curious why." Carlos looked up with sad eyes, as though seeking forgiveness. "It was a baby, a tiny baby, Mikey. As big as my palm." He wiped his eyes with his sleeve. "It had hands, fingers, feet , toes...eyes." Carlos's throat constricted as he seemed to choke on his words. "The head was opened.. the head, it had no brainas left inside."

Carlos leaned his head onto the wall, and rubbed his forehead.

Mike was initially appalled by what he heard, and searched for a reasonable explanation. "Carlos you must be mistaken. We don't take specimens beyond about 14 weeks gestation, the end of the first tri-mester. I mean, we could be off by two or three weeks. Except, what you're describing sounds like 20 weeks plus."

Carlos stood up in a confrontational pose, "No, no," he persisted.

"This was a baby! You know. It had eyelashes...hair,...

103

fingernails,.. a face."

Mike was alarmed by Carlos' story, and sought to rationalize exactly what might be going on, and tried his answer on Carlos.

"You know what? It probably was a second trimester spontaneous miscarriage that was donated for scientific study. We might be doing some R&D on those, once in a while."

Carlos listened carefully to Mike's explanation, anxious to be relieved of his anxiety. His bushy eyebrows frowned and he asked, "I hear what you say, Mikey, about scientific tings once in a while. So, how come I see one of these heavy boxes now every day?"

Mike was surprised by the frequency. "Are you sure? Once a day ...for how long?"

"Two , maybe three month," he replied.

Mike ran his hand over his evening beard bristles. He was less sure of his first solution to this paradox, and felt he had to dig some more. Carlos wiped his eyes again, thanked Mike for listening, and indicated he had to start his collection rounds for the incinerator.

He stopped at the office door and turned to say, "One last thing. Dis baby had the twisted rope and this umbrella like thing attached to it."

Mike added, "You mean the umbilical cord."

"Yeah dats it, the cord."

Mike got up from his desk to speak to Carlos more intently. "Did you actually see any others in this condition?"

"What, are you kidding, Mikey? You see this once and you don't sleep for a week! I don't look in the bigga box anymore."

"Tell you what, Carlos. Next time you get one of those big, heavier boxes, don't destroy it put it aside in the refrigeration unit in my Test Department downstairs."

Carlos was concerned by the request. "I could get in bigga trouble for not burning it."

Mike tried to act reassuring and confident about it and replied, "As far as you're concerned, I took it out of the disposal tray before you got there."

Carlos reluctantly agreed, and felt somewhat relieved that this burden he had been carrying was being addressed by someone else. He trusted Mike, and left for his usual rounds.

Mike remained in his office staring at the now, almost empty parking lot below, and then over to where Mary Lou was hung on the security fence several days ago. He was bothered not so much by what Carlos saw. More so, by the number of these larger specimens, and the umbilical cords and placentas still attached. Even with still births, they were always cut and discarded the chord... as far as he knew.

He wanted to have one of these specimens examined by his friend,

Joel Rosen. Get an expert opinion on what Carlos had seen. Mike made a note to call him first thing in the morning for lunch.

CHAPTER 10
A mystery deepens

At noontime, Mike left work in his old '68 Mustang, first stopping at the Lifespan processing building to pick up Joel. They'd go to lunch and discuss whatever mystery was on his good friend's mind.

Dr. Rosen was a story in himself, hired personally by Strauss because of his unique experience. Joel started his medical internship as an obstetrician, but found his dry, clinical bedside manner a limiting factor with women patients. He made a dramatic change by switching to pathology, and completing his residency in that specialty. Thereafter, his diseased and deceased patients never seem to complain about his lack of bedside manner.

It turned out that he excelled at analyzing morbid tissue with both surgical and observational skills. By age 36 and with some luck, he became Chief of Pathology at Downstate Medical Hospital. A few years working in New York City gave him a caseload of cadavers and experience that would normally take others a lifetime to achieve. In particular he examined a large number of dead pregnant women and their doomed fetuses. The drugs they took kept the gutters of New York filled with an endless supply of victims, and many required autopsy.

It didn't take Joel long to become immune to this trail of broken lives and despair. In fact, it strengthened his conviction that termination and decoupling was a necessary part of combating this chain of wasted lives. There was no sense in producing more people in a society that doesn't care that some people sleep in the garbage. And, there were so many important people who deserved longer, better lives.

This all led Dr. Rosen to publish a series of articles in the '*Journal of American Medicine*', on the effects of hazardous chemicals on fetal development. He'd dissected morbid fetuses at every point in the gestation cycle, matrixed with numerous debilitating drugs, alcohol, and poisons ingested by the deceased mothers. These articles were read with interest by Dr. Strauss, while still a researcher at the National Institute of Health. Impressed, he contacted Dr. Rosen on several occasions with biomedical related questions. When Lifespan was started, Strauss knew exactly who he wanted to head the Extraction Production Department.

Strauss could not have found a better candidate. His combination of fetal anatomy training and pathological experience was a perfect fit. With a personality hardened by exposure to human tragedy, he could provide the leadership necessary to train technicians to work with efficient detachment. Lifespan needed those traits to conduct the precise dissections required to remove fetal precursor and stem cells for culturing on a large-scale basis.

* * * * * * *

Joel was waiting at the curb in front of the Processing building, as Mike pulled up. He leaned into the open passenger side window of Mike's Mustang, and greeted Mike with a slight, nervous, smile. As he eased himself into the car, Mike asked him casually how the wife and kids were.

Joel seemed distracted as he glanced around the Lifespan parking lot, "Oh, fine...fine," then quickly added, "Let's eat somewhere where we won't be seen together."

Mike originally thought they'd eat lunch at their usual watering hole, the *Black Whale*, so he hesitated while thinking about both an alternate eating spot, and to wonder why Joel didn't want to be seen at their usual place. Finally, Mike spoke up, "Hey Doctor J. How about *Finnegan's Rainbow* 'over by the airport?"

Joel answered as he turned to glance out the back window and said sarcastically, "Yeah and if somebody spots us, we can leave the country."

Mike smiled, still not aware of Joel's serious concerns.

They continued their drive to the airport, although not much was said. Joel just gazed out the window. Apparently, his thoughts were somewhere else. Arriving at *Finnegan's*, they parked, entered the dimly lit bar, and picked a table in the back. The waitress came and they ordered some drinks and sandwiches. Mike was anxious to start his questions and waited until the drinks came and the waitress' departure afforded more privacy.

Mike raised his glass to toast. "To old softball players. They never die, they just get thrown out at first." As he sipped his beer, Mike glanced over his glass at Joel's eyes. They looked tired and drawn like the weight of the world was on Joel's shoulders.

"You've been working a lot of overtime at the lab, pal?"

Joel put down his glass, cupped his hands over the bridge of his nose as he wiped his eyes. It made his face look even thinner. Leaning forward he started. "Mike. Mike, I want to share some suspicions I have about what Dr. Strauss is doing at Lifespan." Joel looked down and grasped a cocktail stirring stick with one hand, bending and folding it between his fingers until it looked like an accordion. "If I didn't trust you implicitly, I wouldn't be telling you this."

Mike grew more attentive, uncrossing his legs and sat upright, his eyes fixed on Joel's and conveying an unspoken comradely. In his usual flippant style he said, "I get it! Strauss was banging Eve in your Lab storage closet."

Joel didn't appreciate Mike's careless attempt at humor, "I'm afraid it's more than that, Mike. If you're not going to take this more seriously then I'm talking to the wrong guy."

Mike finally sensed that this was more that just the usual corporate adultery and held up the two fingers of his right hand. "Sorry, cub scouts honor, Joel, no more fooling around."

The waitress interrupted and deposited their meals with a forced smile, then scurried off. Mike grabbed a french fry from his dish and settled back as Joel began his story.

"Remember that corporate R&D meeting last December? The one where they leaned hard on us to come up with new ideas to get more competitive."

Mike interrupted, "Yeah, I remember. That's the meeting where I suggested selling the corporate Gulfstream VII Jet. Save a quarter million dollars a year on installment payments, and another half million cash on insurance, maintenance and travel expenses. They only used it for weekends in Vegas anyway."

"You know, you really pissed our CEO off with that suggestion. I thought Brewster would can you for that, for sure. The other managers didn't even know the company had one."

Joel chided him, "I was a great revelation Mike, but kinda dumb comment with that crowd."

Joel looked at his watch nervously "Let me get back to the issue at hand before we run out of time," and continued, "If you recall, Brewster announced that our 5 year grace period to do this whole specimen extraction business in New Jersey was expiring in one more year. Then, the government, I mean the State and FDA, was going to open up our business to competition. And that translated into more competition for specimens."

Mike interjected, "Yeah, I remember. And the government has been getting political pressure that the cost for extracts is already out of sight. Insurance companies won't cover the procedures, and now only the rich can afford our fountain of youth."

Mike hesitated and then added sarcastically, "Brewster's convinced that we pay these women donors two much for their specimens, but in reality most of our costs are in R&D overhead."

Joel agreed."The direct costs in the extraction department are only 10% of what we charge for the pharmaceuticals."

Joel returned to his story. "After that R&D meeting, Brewster leaned hard on Strauss to cut the costs of extraction, even though it only represented a small fraction of the costs, and threatened to cut Strauss's R&D budget in half. So, about a month latter Strauss called in all his bioengineers and technical staff to announce a new R&D program."

Mike interrupted again. "Don't tell me. We're going to use orangutan fetuses. Use monkey brain extracts for all the politicians suffering from Alhzeimers! No one will notice the difference!" Mike sat back with his hands behind his head, satisfied with his little pun.

Joel hissed back, "God damn it Mike! There's no humor in what I'm talking about. I know you don't give a bull's balls about your career. This is serious shit now, and I really need your help. You're the only one I know who won't sell me out to Lifespan, and you know your way around those buildings... being in Facilities and all that."

"Sorry, Joel, sarcasm is just how I survive this life, the ups and downs. And lately, it's been mostly downs, and I lost Facilities"

Joel gave Mike a critical eye and said, "Really?"

"Demoted."

Joel accepted the answer without question, after the fence incident.

"Well Mike, to continue, Dr. Strauss announced a new R&D program. We were going to try to grow the extracted live fetal material *in vitro*. You know, grow them just like the cells in a culture medium. That way we could take the usual few grams of specimen tissue and multiply it ten fold...maybe a thousand times. We could produce more extracts without more fetal donor specimen's being necessary."

Mike added, "They're gonna disappoint a lot of women who were counting on making some nice bucks."

Joel answered, "Well I could care less about that, at this point. This whole decoupling business has become just that, another commodity business."

"Anyway," Joel continued after sipping his coke, "Strauss walks up to me one day about three months ago with 1500 milliliters of fetal blood. He says, "Assay it for purity and quality. It's the first batch of *in vitro* culture."

Mike was impressed and quipped, "Sounds like a real break through. Time to buy Lifespan stock, I guess."

"Yeah, not so quick, Mike," Joel replied. "You see, under the microscope that blood sample had all the components of blood; platelets, fats, hemoglobin, red cells, white cells, antigens, electrolytes. And, it was highly oxygenated "

"So?" Mike interjected.

"So, how did they culture every blood component together?" You can culture red cells by themselves or white cells singularly, but how could you reproduce the non-biological products. The electrolytes, the fats and carbohydrate components ? That's all complex chemistry."

"Good question" Mike added, now as perplexed as Joel.

"I asked Strauss about that, and he gave me a rather vague answer about 'company proprietary'. He said that they were using packed red cell blood as the growing medium. That is where the other blood components are coming from. Mike, I'll tell you this, he's already producing about 10% of my production blood extract from just his R&D lab. And, all the electrolytes and other constituents are always in the right proportion!"

Mike's memory was jogged and he interrupted, "Jeez, you know, this story is crazy. Why have I been ordering 30 units a month of packed red blood plasma, and PRCBs for those guys in R&D."

"No shit?" Joel answered as he rubbed the stubble on his chin. He was intrigued by Mike's statement, and hesitated as he digested Mike's account. Then he replied, "No good. If they were using adult donor plasma the ratio of red corpuscles and lymphocytes would be higher, because you would be adding more cells to the same amount of pre-existing electrolytes. No this was fetal superblood."

Mike responded. "All I know is that they been using that blood plasma for three months now, using more every month. They could be doing something real clever that you haven't thought of."

"Well, wait. There's more," Joel explained. "About two weeks ago, Strauss comes over to my department with a small crushed bone and fragment about a centimeter long. He told me they just succeeded in growing it *in vitro* also. He wanted me to assess the bone marrow content."

"What struck me as peculiar, was how well formed it was. The marrow had grown on the inside bone structure just like in it would be *in vivo*. Even one end showed a curved flaring out as if it could form a terminal end cap for a joint."

The engineer side of Mike's mind was intrigued and he asked, "So, where are you headed with all this, Joel?"

"Before I answer, there's one more piece of data. I didn't crush the bone specimen right away. Instead I examined it under a microscope."

Joel's face seemed to light up. "You already know about my forensic background, he continued, "so, I examined the surface structure of the bone near the flared end under about 100 times magnification. I observed tiny striations and lines on both ends in addition to some pitting."

"Mike asked, "So, Doctor J, what's the bottom line on these mysterious bone marks?"

"The marks are ligament and tendon attachments. From my analysis the bone came from the femur of a 20 week-old fetus. Not some *in vitro* breakthrough!"

With that statement, Mike instantly recalled his meeting last week with his plant custodian, Carlos Rivera, about the incinerator, and the more mature human fetuses coming out of the lab.

Mike concluded, "I guess Strauss is trying to fool Brewster into thinking his R&D people made a real find. Instead, he's just substituting body parts from older experimental specimens."

Joel shook his head in the negative. "Naw, I think it's more than that, Mike. There's just too much live organic product coming out of the R&D lab now. Too much to originate from a few older experimental specimens. And there's no evidence of morbidity in the tissue I've been getting."

Mike was intrigued by all this information. It wasn't all tied together in his mind yet. It had the distinct odor of corporate expediency. Mike learned forward and asked, "So, what do you propose to do next?"

"I don't know, Mike. I'm out of my element. I would like to know a lot more, so I can sleep at night. My wife says I've been tossing around in bed during the night. Every morning I wake up to see that I've pulled the bottom sheet out of our bed."

"I don't understand," Mike said with a slight smile, "you're acting like your Lifespan dissection work is getting to you."

Joel held his palm forward, and shook his head side to side. "No. Uh-uh. I haven't changed by views on anything. I'm a forensic pathologist by training. I only work on dead tissue. If a woman makes her choice to donate a fetus, it's her business, not mine. Her conscience not mine

Mike reached across the table and patted Joel's wrist. "Easy paranoid boy! I'm not questioning your ethics. It's just that I haven't seen you this excitable in a long time. Why all the emotion over just another Lifespan ruse?'

Joel sat back in his chair. He took a deep breath and then continued. "There's one last thing. I received a call a couple of days ago, from some woman, uh, Phylis… in procurement. They were trying to trace a specimen with an attached placenta. Lifespan is changing procedures for these things. Specimens are coming into R&D with no paper work trail."

Joel leaned forward across the table, as his voice became a hushed, "Mike I think I know what's going on in R&D, and I'm sure not telling anybody what I think until I know for sure myself. I'll tell you this. I took an oath in medical school just like the doctors in that R&D lab. If it is what I guess it is, then their not honoring that oath." Joel pointed his finger down at the table adding, "And, I'll destroy whoever is behind it at Lifespan."

Mike lifted his eyebrows. "Pretty strong stuff, Joel. You gonna use automatic weapons or flame throwers?" he parodied.

"It's not funny anymore, Mike." Joel was vexed. "If you can't take this seriously, then there's nobody else to trust at Lifespan."

Mike acted reassuring, sat back, and looked up. "I've got an idea, if you're game for it."

"Like what ?"

"How about we visit Dr. Strauss's R&D lab?" Mike said with a grin. "See what magic these Sci-Fi boys are up to. Find out what's on the up 'n up."

Joel asked nervously, "And how do you propose we do that? Ask Strauss for a personal tour?"

"Too conventional," Mike chided. "Besides, I happen to have master key copies for all of the Lab and office buildings when I ran the Facilities Department." Mike's face took on that 'bad-boy grin' and said, "Pick a night and we'll work some overtime at R&D."

Joel was increasingly uncomfortable. He was a professional medical type that chose to avoid confrontation and politics. He had a good income, and a good family life. He responded. "Isn't that illegal, like breaking and entering?"

Mike laughed, "How can you break into a place where you're hired to work? I'll figure out a cover story. Anyway, aren't you the guy that was going to destroy all monsters a little while ago? In the meantime, you think about what to bring with us."

They left the restaurant and discussed the layout of the R&D lab. Joel thought Sunday, after midnight, would be the best night to stage their visit. Not too many 'dedicated' researchers put in overtime on that night.

Back at Lifespan, Mike dropped off Joel at his building, and parked in his own building lot.

Thinking about the coming escapade, Mike savored the opportunity to perhaps embarrass the corporation over some trumped-up research breakthrough. In his mind this caper was another game between him and the rich boys, between him and the bureaucrats.

"Probably just trying to drive up the price of Lifespan stock", he muttered to himself. His experience in management always proved that when corporate launches into some hush-hush program on their own, it usually ends in disaster. They never learn that it is their own workers and managers who understand what makes their business tick, not them.

Mike returned to his office and finished his paperwork when he remembered that he hadn't called Phylis for that luncheon date. He looked at his watch and thought, *Oh crap, its 3:00 PM already. She might be on her way home.*

His hand clasped the office telephone receiver. He hesitated, with the thought of his deceased wife, Laura. *What would she think of this? Me going out with another woman.* He loved Laura for 25 years. Unfortunately, he could still live another 50 years alone and unloved. *What am I supposed to do? It feels likes I'm cheating on her.*

The phone rang under his hand as if to answer his doubts, and startled him from his deliberations. He answered with a perfunctory, "Oh,.. er, hello"

"Hi mister Penguin. This is Phylis Daye over in Procurement."

A surprised Mike was momentarily confused thinking, *Penguin?*...

Oh yeah, that old tie. He stumbled out his words "Yeah, I mean yes, I was just going to call you."

Phylis chuckled, "Uh-Huh. Come on mister, you can do better than that old line."

Mike gathered his composure and replied more decisively, "How about lunch tomorrow? I'll pick you up in front of your building."

Phylis remained silent for a few seconds, then said, "Just let me check my business calendar for a moment. Uh... yeah. It's clear. Consider it a date."

She hung up leaving a flustered Mike wondering how the phone call started in the first place. He looked up at the ceiling and said, while shrugging his shoulders, "OK, Laura, does this coincidence mean its OK with you, too."

* * * * * *

Mike went downstairs to one of the equipment cabinets in his Test department. The last thing to check was to make sure the high definition digital camera was fully charged in the Test Lab'. Mike was not sure what they would find in they R&D lab and wanted to be prepared for low lighting or anything they might discover. Mike opened the steel storage cabinet on the opposite wall and took the camera off its shelf. He peered through the viewfinder and mimicked a German accent saying, "Schmile, Ductor Frankunshteen, oon vee take your schtick pooblic."

* * * * * * *

Mike left work in the evening, and stopped at Avis to reserve the rental of a nondescript sedan for the night of his break-in. His old Mustang would surely be noted by Lifespan security people in the company parking lot late on a Friday night. A plain sedan wouldn't be remembered if Mike and Joel's visit was discovered in the future. There was a constant flow of rental cars for researchers visiting from Virginia and North Carolina. It wasn't unusual to see cars in the lot at all hours.

When he arrived home, he telephoned Joel to confirm Friday night's rendezvous, and explain the precautions he was taking to insure their success. It was a relief to here that Joel was still gung-ho about visiting the lab together. Joel even arranged to get his wife to drop him off at Lifespan on Friday morning so his car would not be there at night either.

Mike was more accustomed to people backing out when push really came to shove. Instead, Joel volunteered to bring some sterile test tubes in case they wanted a sample of any chemicals in the R&D lab.

For the remainder of the night, Mike sat alone in his living room, and thought about CCTV surveillance cameras were and other security measures. Him being in Facilities overlapped with the Security Department, so he remembered where they were installed. This whole idea was still an exciting amusement. Doing things right under Lifespan Security's nose was a reward in itself.

Later on, Mike lay down in bed and turned out the light on the nightstand. Staring into the darkness, he reflected on what events would unfold tomorrow night.... and wondered if Lifespan's big secret would turn out to be a big nothing after all. He felt confident in his ability to plan. More confident as he covered more contingencies for the unexpected.

CHAPTER 11
A necessary evil

Mike arrived at work early the next day, his mind still pre-occupied with planning his nocturnal break-in of Strauss's lab. The whole idea had this childish fascination of doing mischief, more as a prank than anything else - another vehicle to antagonize the petty executives at Lifespan.

Later, sitting in his office, he tried to re-focus on other things, and found that thinking about his future lunch date with Phylis was a good distraction. In fact, he couldn't decide which was going to be more stimulating; his date with Phylis, or his date with the R&D Lab.

At lunch break, Mike drove his Mustang to the other building to pick up Phylis, and arrived at its front entrance. It was a crowded scene with women scurrying to the parking lot to run some lunchtime errands. Leaning slightly over the dashboard, he scanned each woman through squinted eyes for his date. His vision wasn't what it was 10 years ago.

Disappointed, he leaned back and began thinking, *Did she forget? Or, maybe found out about my demotion?*

Phylis was waiting in the lobby observing Mike's car pull up. She didn't want to appear to be too anxious by waiting for him, so she delayed her appearance outside until about the time it looked like Mike was about to get out of his car. Then, she glided outside to the curb by his car.

"Hi Santino." She said innocently as she approached. "Were you waiting long?"

By this time, Mike was out his door, one foot inside and his arm leaning on the car roof. He tried to look casual and said with a grin, "Naw, Miss Daye. Patience is my middle name. And call me Mike."

When he walked around the car to open the door for her, she said with a smile, "And you can call me Phylis."

Seated inside, she was surprised how clean and new the vinyl interior looked compared to the gray primer exterior. "What year is this car?" she asked.

"It's a '68. I had one as a kid. I restore these old things with my kids now - sort of a bonding hobby."

Phylis used the comment to pry a little. "So, what does your wife think of that?"

He became subdued, and answered curtly, "Lost her 5 years ago…accident."

"Sorry. I didn't know."

"Anway …." he said, and his conversation drifted off.

Mike jumped into his black vinyl bucket seat, engaged the clutch and pulled away, exiting the Lifespan parking lot. Phylis was waiting for the quiet Mike to ask where she would like to go for lunch, except he never asked. They made some small talk about the old Mustang, until Mike pulled into the parking lot of a luncheon bar named 'The Blarney Stone'.

Mike's friendly demeanor returned, and announced, "Well, here we are!"

Phylis had passed this place many times, but never had the desire to enter because it looked seedy from the outside. Parked motorcycles out front always looked menacing. She had some reservations about going in, as Mike came around to open her door. After a few seconds delay, thought, *Oh, what the heck!*

Mike sensed her trepidation, and gently took her hand smiling, "Don't worry, it's much nicer inside than out."

He opened the bar room door for her, and she was met by a cacophony of noisy voices. The couple pressed through the crowded entrance to a table in the corner. There were two huge TVs hanging at both ends of the room. The smell of beer permeated the air, and apparently the brains and clothes of many patrons who were speaking at the limits of their vocal cords. Numerous barmaids hurriedly squeezed between laughing patrons, standing compressed around the bar. Some waitresses nodded a smile of recognition in their direction, which Mike returned with a nod and a grin. This annoyed Phylis somewhat, and she remarked to him, "I suppose you come here often?"

"Not really, they're just a friendly crew. I always leave a good tip and a joke, so I guess they remember me for that."

When seated, Mike swung his chair around to sit closer to hers. Phylis was startled by his sudden advance. Mike noticed and explained, "Sorry. Background noise. I think we want to converse. No?"

"Quite a place, "She shouted above the din, "they must have put a lot of effort into replicating an Irish pub."

Mike beamed enthusiastically and said, "It is an Irish pub!"

Phylis gave a skeptical glare.

"No kidding," Mike continued, "They really brought this one over to America piece by piece, and re-assembled it here."

Pointing to the ceiling, he added, "See that glass rack. It's authentic and so are the crystal mugs hanging there. And those leaded glass cabinet doors. It's all the real McCoy. Straight from Dublin!"

Phylis eventually began to feel comfortable in the bar and Mike proved to be entertaining company. They ordered pot roast sandwiches, a Modelo beer, and a rosé wine for her Mike told some amusing stories about his boss and other executives at Lifespan, and Phylis countered with some hilarious stories Katie had disclosed about some men she dated from the company. Carefully, they avoided talking about themselves throughout their conversation - not yet trusting enough to share really personal information. Neither did they discuss the incident of the woman injured on the Lifespan fence.

Mike's demeanor intrigued Phylis. He was not your stereotype engineer. For that matter, he was not a starchy department head type either. For a fifty-something year old guy, he had an engagingly, mischievous spirit. There was an honest openness in his conversation, and he projected self-confidence without the usual vanity of most guys she has met. He had a way of keeping her off balance, and was unpredictable. Sometimes she could not tell if he was really serious or just kidding around. What they did share was a common disrespect for management.

On the drive back to Lifespan, Mike asked her to join him Sunday for a trip into the Auto Show in Manhattan. She thought it an odd place for a first date, but so was the bar where they just had lunch. She did feel comfortable with him though, like she's known him for a while. It was enjoyable just being in his company, so it really didn't matter where they were going, she surmised. Dinner date things really tended to be a bore anyway, sitting around, strained conversation, and bloating up on food. Besides, she didn't really find out anything personal about him yet. That would take more digging, and the car ride into the city would be an opportunity to talk. There was still the issue of whether he was the 'Used Male' she had responded to. Phylis accepted the invitation as they arrived back at Lifespan.

Mike lightly skipped around the back of the car to open her door. As she stepped out she confronted him with a sly grin and a question. "You're the *'Used Male'* on the *'Middle Earth'* website aren't you Michael?"

He blushed, as she stared directly into his eyes. "Well, uh...what can I say? You got me," was his reply, while trying to subdue a devilish grin. "Would you believe it took me a week to come up with that thing, and a month to get up the courage to put it on the website?"

Phylis giggled, "So now we have 'bashful used male'?"

Mike stood closer to her as he leaned on the open car door, and stopped smiling. "About some things...not about other things."

Phylis felt him closing in. It was an awkward moment, as the mood turned more serious romantically. Of course, standing in front of the office building in everybody's sight did not add ambiance to his flirtations either. She blocked his advance by gently placing a palm on his chest and glancing down at her watch, "Well Michael, it's time for work again!"

Mike retreated, Phylis ducked under his arm, and headed for the building entrance. She turned at the outer door and called back to him, "I'll E-mail my address."

Mike waved his hand and shouted, "I'll pick you up on Sunday, 9 AM."

He returned to the driver's side of the car and stopped in the partially opened door, his chin resting on his arm on the car roof. Wistfully, he watched her compact figure disappear into the building and stood there for a moment at the curb. He realized that he missed her company already, and he knew what that meant – she was worth pursuing.

Glancing at his iphone, it was time to shift gears and drive over to Avis to pick up the rental sedan, and then return to work.

In the building lobby, Phylis heard the short chirp of his tires as his Mustang pulled away. It was reminiscent of the behavior of the wilder boyfriends from her college days, some 25 years earlier.

* * * * * *

Mike left the Lifespan compound, and returned to work later with the rental car, parking it in front of the R&D building and walked back to his office. He already mounted the out-of-state plates he bought years ago from a junk yard in Newark. Once inside he answered, he checked some texts that came in while he was out to lunch with Phylis. One message was from Joel Rosen, and Mike, wondered out loud, "Geez, I hope he's not getting cold feet."

Mike checked with Carlos to see where the maintenance cleaning crew would be in that night, and found that they would not be in the R&D Lab until late Saturday morning. Then, he called Joel back to confirm their meeting for 8 PM, when darkness was assured.

* * * * * *

At day's end, Mike watched his people quickly file out between 4:30 and 5:00 PM. With no Friday night overtime to hold anybody, except for the usual scattering of cars. He was soon quietly alone in the building, except for the low whooshing sound of the heating ventilators. Mike went down to the empty test lab and loaded a rolling cart with a large back up battery, an oscilloscope on top, and placed the digital camera in a box on the shelf underneath. He grabbed two red filtered flashlights, a notebook and his duplicate set of keys. While doing this, he tried to review in his mind all the possible things that could go wrong, and all the alibis to cover those possibilities. The feeling of anticipation was strangely similar to his pre-flight briefings before flying sorties over the Middle East.

He rolled the cart outside and down the dimly lit cement walkway to Joel's Extraction Department building. Mike knew the side entrance was not covered by CCTV. He waited for a distant security guard to get inside his patrol car and leave. With his passkeys, he entered the building, and took his cart down the hall to collect Joel in his Extract Production Department. Then, they took the service elevator to the second floor.

They followed a corridor past vacant cubicles leading to the R&D Lab. Neither spoke, as Joel went ahead, scanning the offices along the way for any lingering employees. The building was quiet except for the sound of a wiggly wheel on the instrumentation cart. Joel stopped and turned around to Mike, and said in an aggravated hush, "Why bother whispering if I can here your cart down the hall?"

Mike leaned over to look down at the troublesome wheel and squirted it with stinky WD40 lubricant, saying in a singsong, "*No more squeaky on the wheel.*"

Joel shook his head, and gave a nervous nod as they reached the outer door to R&D. Both slipped on their latex gloves.

Mike fumbled with the keys, not sure which would fit. Joel impatiently whispered, "Hey, what if someone's still in there?"

Mike was hunched over, concentrating on fitting the keys. "We're just delivery boys tonight, Joel. That is why the oscilloscope is here on the cart. It's our cover story." The door finally opened and Mike said excitedly, "Me first!"

The lights were still on in the inner R&D office cubicles, and Mike waltzed around as if he owned the place. He poked his head into the cubicles one by one, finding them all unoccupied. There was no internal CCTV due to strong privacy objections by the consultant scientists.

He whispered to his comrade, "OK, to the Lab!"

Joel rolled in the cart and they proceeded to the research laboratory itself. Mike fumbled with the keys again. Joel looked nervously around, and rasped, "I thought you had all this figured out!"

"There she goes", Mike exclaimed, as he turned the key in the lock. He gestured to Joel with the sweep of his hand, "Entré-vous, Dr. Who."

The entering light revealed only a tile floor as it split the room into two darkened halves, ending at the smoked glass windows of the outside wall. Mike pushed in his equipment cart behind Joel, and closed the door behind them, plunging them into darkness. Both their heartbeats raise a notch from the sudden darkness, and the eerie steady whir of small pumps and rhythmic whooshing noises surrounding them. Shinning out of the blackness were dozens of red power indicator lights and green numerical LED displays. You could tell that this wet lab was loaded with the latest in digital electronic equipment.

Joel and Mike debated whether to turn on the lights, and decided against it, since the light would be visible through the outside windows to the parking lot below. Mike clicked on his red filtered flashlight.

Sweeping his lamp around the room Mike found them surrounded by over a dozen equipment carts. Each cart had a portable dialysis machine, a blood plasma bag, a micro cardio-pulmonary bypass machine, and a microprocessor control box. There was a tangle of tubes and wires into an unfamiliar 4 inch diameter PVC pipe, about 1 foot long on top of each cart. An oximeter, and dialysate tube, and oxygen tank hung on one side. Heating coils were underneath the tubes.

Mike immediately recognized some of the apparatus on the tray beneath the tube.

"Hey Joel! he hissed as he knelt, "Underneath. These are the lash-ups I designed and built for Strauss for the 'in vitro' research. Calibration stickers and all!" Mike stood up and asked, "What are these plastic PVC tubes on top?"

Joel placed his red filtered flashlight on one tube and carefully studied the exterior equipment and interconnections. He leaned over to closely examine the blood oxygenator, and dialysis machine hookups. "Holy shit," He said incredulously. "I can't believe they did it."

"Did what?" Mike asked.

Joel rose and fiddled with a curved access hatch on top on the tube's centerline. He opened it and peered in with his flashlight. His face took on a spooky visage as the light reflection formed inverted shadows on his face from below. "Look Mike," he said in a kind of bitter satisfaction, "This is the amazing part... just what I suspected."

Mike came over and added his flashlights' glow into the open tube. Below them, was a human fetus, seemingly suspended in clear fluid. It appeared fully formed, squirming in irritation, heart furiously beating, hands shielding its eye buds from the glare. The protective amniotic sack was gone, nevertheless, it still kept its feet and arms naturally curled up.

Joel explained, "Looks like 16, maybe 18 weeks gestation. Certainly beyond 12 weeks development limit." Then, he pointed to the inside far end of the tube, "See, look. They have a separate PRCBs plasma chamber. See, they have the placenta attached to some kind of a cellulose membrane. And this yellow liquid must be a synthetic amniotic fluid – amazing." Turning to face Mike he added, "Those sons of a bitches! - an artificial womb!"

"I'll be damned," Mike said as he looked at Joel's face inches from his own. Mike had never been this close to the actual entity that Lifespan Corporations's business revolved around.

After a few seconds Joel asked, "So Mike, let's hear one of those wisecracks of yours now."

Mike's usual witty humor had vanished, and replaced by the look of revulsion. An expression Joel had not seen since he'd known Mike.

Mike stepped back to let the darkness envelop him. Then clicked off his flashlight, and slowly leaned his back against a cabinet. For a moment, there was only Mike and the feeling of spirits of the unborn around him. The stillness being interrupted only by the steady purring of pumps and the silent sentinels of red and green LED displays. "God have mercy on my soul," he whispered.

"What?" Joel asked.

"I designed and built some of this stuff on the shelf below, Joel. I'm a part of this house of horrors."

"Easy Mike," Joel cautioned, "You couldn't know what these R&D people were going to do with it. None of us knew. I'm sure Strauss and Corporate knew, but nobody else."

An anguished Mike did not move. A cascade of conclusions finally hit him, "How did I miss all the clues?" Mike wondered to himself, *Ordering all those dialysis units. The packed blood red plasma. I even had first hand evidence from Carlos's fetal discoveries at the incinerator.*

Joel handled the situation more clinically. He was a pathologist. He had seen human beings in the worst possible conditions. So, things tended to appear less hideous to him.

Mike moaned, "Joel, this maybe easy to take for you. You're a doctor. You see this slimy stuff every day. You trained for it. I'm a nuts and bolts hardware engineer, there's no blood and guts in a piece of lab equipment. This is first year medical school for me."

Joel sensed Mike's weakness and took charge. "Look Mike," he cautioned," We can't stay here long. We can either start collecting evidence or we can leave and forget we ever came here. So just follow my directions and I'll get you through this. Try to look at this as an experiment, and block out any deeper meaning or significance to what you see until we're out of here."

He offered Mike a hand. "Let's get to work."

Mike accepted his grasp and pushed himself forward. His feeling of remorse and revulsion finally turned into outrage. "OK Joel, let's get the goods on these research bastards."

Joel took over instructing Mike to take photos of the contents of each revival tube and copying down reference data on each fetus specimen. Joel busied himself at the workbenches and desks along the walls, looking for records and engineering notes describing how this 'breakthrough science' works.

Mike was not as cool as usual, nervously fumbling with the camera in the dark. He had this queer anxiety and he remarked to Joel in the darkness across the room, "I feel like I'm trapped in some alien spaceship on its way to hell!"

Joel continued rifling through files with his flashlight, and in a shushing whisper said, "Mike just get pictures, get evidence, and then we'll get the hell out of here! We'll sort out what it all means later."

Mike went from revival tube to revival tube. He grimaced as he observed several fetus's with some missing limbs. One floated motionless in a smelly murky cloud of brownish red fluid obscuring its features. He kept murmuring to himself, "Jesus Christ have mercy," with each specimen visited. Several specimens had their skulls dotted with a white puffy material, like tiny cotton balls, hanging on the outside. Mike wondered aloud what they were.

While Joel ok photos of the cart's operating instructions, he answered from across the Lab, "Those are brain cell extractions - it's frontal lobe brain tissue fragments."

"For what?"

"For treating Alzheimer and Parkinson disease. It's the transplant tissue they use for culturalization. You know, I think they even use it to cure felons with drug induced schizophrenia."

"Oh great," Mike grunted, "Another triumph for the 'Great Society'. Now we're saving drug pushers?"

Mike continued talking as he worked. It helped to take his mind off what he was seeing. "I thought they could use dead fetal brain tissue for that treatment?"

"Yeah, the effectiveness of grown fetal brain cells is 10 percent after patient implantation. With live brain fresh tissue survival rate jumps to 95%."

"So, the profits jump 950% for Lifespan too," Mike interjected. Then added, "Wait a minute. There's only a thimbles worth of brain here. It doesn't seem like that would go too far."

Joel looked over at Mike, a bit impatient. "By 14 weeks gestation the fetus has already developed millions of cerebral neurons. On average it adds about several thousand per minute until birth."

"What?" Mike exclaimed, "Run that by me again. You mean per week or something don't you?"

"No Mike...I said per minute."

Then Joel pointed his flashlight at the other fetuses, "In the time it's taken me to explain it, all these guys have just added another twenty thou' each."

Mike shook his head in disbelief, so Joel continued his explanation.

"Actually it all finally levels off at birth...at around 100 billion neurons or so. It even sheds extra brain cells at birth."

Mike was perplexed, "Hey pal wait a second. Are you telling me that we don't grow any more brain cells after birth?"

"Not entirely, Mike. There are some residual stem cells that can repair damaged neurons. We lose about 20 grams of brain matter a year after about age 20 or so. So, these little buggers do what no other born human being can do. What you see there is probably the most concentrated human cranial matter on this earth. Packed with loads of stem cells, precursors, and progenitors. There's a gold mine of donor material in there."

Mike was puzzled. "How can that be? It's about a hundredth of my brain size."

"Confusing isn't it," Joel replied, adding. "Actually, your mature brain bulk is mostly interconnections. You know, axons, synapses, dendrites. That's the only part of the brain that develops later in life, after you're born, 'til you're a young adult. Maybe continues 'til death."

Mike interrupted, "But..."

"But nothing Mike," Joel interjected, "Enough on the neurological lesson. We've already been here too long."

Mike moved to another specimen tube, and hesitantly peered inside. . Mike described aloud what he was seeing and Joel responded that the specimen will be dead by sunrise. Mike felt helpless and frustrated. "Isn't there anything we can do?"

Joel answered impatiently, "Mike its just tissue once the brain is gone. There's nothing left there to save. Come here with your camera. I want you to photograph some formulas and schematics."

Joel was fascinated by the biotechnical advances he was seeing in the lab, and wanted to learn as much as possible on how they were doing it. No matter how corrupt in its use, science is science.

Joel remarked, "You know this same technology, if properly applied could reduce the morbidity rate in premature births. Save a lot of infant lives."

Mike remark sarcastically, "Apparently, there's not as much profit in that." Mike dropped the discussion, not wanting to start a deeper morality argument in the middle of their intrigue. He mechanically went back about the immediate business at hand.

He noted two specimens in fairly good shape, numbers UH0744 and NH0633. "Hey Joel these two fellows look pretty good. What do you make of it?"

Joel came over and peered through the hatch with a clinical eye, and looked at Mike mockingly, "First, these two guys are two girls buddy." Then he explained, "See the wound in the abdomen. That's where the liver is. They're doing superblood extraction on these two – the stuff I told you about yesterday. They'll drain her for a couple weeks"

Mike hesitantly looked in again briefly and just said, "Superblood. Uh-huh." Then, he put the flashlight to his watch, "Man, we've been in here for almost a 20 minutes, lets' clean up and blow!"

"OK, OK. Just let me finish with the files."

Mike added, "Whatever you do, don't take anything."

Joel noticed one draw on a file cabinet marked 'Job 901'. He opened it and illuminated it with his flashlight. Inside were several references to a 'Project Greenhouse' that neither had ever heard of.

Mike glanced out the window at the darkened parking lot, and noticed the latched casement windows, commenting, "You know Joel, I think this place must get stinky at times – needs fresh air.""

Suddenly Mike let out an excited whisper,"Oh, shit! There's a security vehicle coming across the lot. Let's get moving Joel." He doused his flashlight and put his hand on Joel's flashlight to deflect it towards the floor.

Joel objected saying, "No. No. This is some interesting material. Listen!"

"Enough!" Mike exclaimed, and nudged a reluctant Joel aside, then grabbed the open draw handle and added, "I know this Job 901. Been bangin' it with time card charges for years. Nobody ever asks what you do on it. Like a bottomless black budget."

Mike slammed closed the 'Project Greenhouse' cabinet draw and said, "We'll talk about it when we're out of this hellhole. This place is giving me the heebee -geebees"

The two perpetrators emerged from the lab with their eyes squinting from the bright office lights. They pushed out their cart loaded with camera, battery pack, and oscilloscope, disposing of their latex gloves in a nearby waste container. After locking up, they proceeded to Joel's downstairs lab by the service elevator. On the first floor, they stopped to covertly observe the security guard entering the building from the parking lot and walking down the hall. He was heading for the main elevator.

Mike quipped, "I wonder if that guard saw our flashlights in the R&D lab?" Then, he pulled the memory card from the camera and placed it in his shirt pocket, then put the camera in Joel's briefcase. They pushed the equipment cart into a corner of Joel's processing department, and donned lab coats. The pair made a hasty dash down the stairs to the rental car while the guard made his upstairs rounds. Driving slowly they passed the gatehouse with a smiling wave to the guard. Mike tensed to resist flooring the accelerator. The guard waved back, but did not recognize them, since he worked the night shift. Strauss's consulting professionals people routinely showed up at night. The lazy guard returned to his newspaper.

Mike headed back to Joel's house to drop him off. There was silence between them until Mike finally started the conversation. "You know Joel, this whole issue of fetal life. Do you ever question just when a fetus becomes human?" Mike tried to clarify his question, "I mean, those guys look pretty human to me. How do you handle dissecting these creatures? They could be future scientists, artists, teachers - maybe just simple loving people."

Joel interrupted with a hiss, "Or psychopathic murderers, child molesters, embezzlers, or rapists."

Mike asked, "Is that how you rationalize it?"

"Yeah. It's just something we have to do - a necessary evil. It's a matter of balancing things out. More like a tradeoff. If you let all these people that nobody wants into the world, you have an even bigger moral issue to solve. Starvation, neglect, abuse, foster care, suffering. That's not a life either. We help humanity with what is essentially discarded tissue."

"OK. I see your point, Joel," Mike responded indignantly, "So we just nuke all those millions of starving people in Africa? They don't have any hope anyway either."

Joel was becoming irritated by Mike's sudden altruism over a dead issue, and was too stressed at the moment to tolerate someone questioning his own ethics. "Mike, enough debate! You believe what you want, and I'll do the same!"

"So what did you see in that 'Project Greenhouse' file?"

Joel stared out at the street lights flickering by, still trying to reconcile the scientific value of what he'd seen and the trauma inflicted on those organisms. "Maybe the beginning of the end." he finally answered. He wouldn't elaborate, as he stared out the window into space adding, "I think I know how Oppenheimer felt when he stared face to face with the atomic bomb for the first time."

Mike was perplexed and said, "Hey man, no riddles. I've seen enough bio-science for a lifetime. What gives?"

An impatient Joel turned and said, "They've figured out how to make fetal specimens... like cookies from the oven. They're harvesting the 2 million eggs that each female specimen carries."

"You mean those fetuses were man-made?"

"No!" Joel solemnly replied. Not cloning - anyway, not yet". Head bowed, he shook his head. "This whole R&D revival thing is more ambitious than I ever imagined though."

Mike interjected sarcastically, "Yeah, like a Steven King novel."

It wasn't long before they arrived at Joel's house in Upper Saddle River. It was a well-to-do neighborhood of one-acre estates. Mike pulled into the long driveway and stopped with his lights illuminating the doors on the three-car garage. He turned in his seat, placing his arm on the center console and said, "Well partner, where do we go from here? Confront

Strauss with the evidence?"

Joel frowned and answered in a slightly irritated tone. "What, and lose all this," pointing to his expansive house. Exiting the car he protested,"No, no way. I think the media should handle this. Once this debacle is exposed, they'll push Strauss out, shut down the lab, and we'll get back to properly processing cadaver tissue again."

Mike was disappointed in Joel's plan. What he saw tonight changed his usual ambivalent feeling on human fetuses to a sense of dispair. He also was having serious doubts about what was human life and what was not. The whole experience seemed to blur the dividing line between human baby and fetus. Mike felt argumentative and demanded, "I thought you were gonna go after these guys yourself. That they broke their Hippocratic Oath, and all that dedication stuff.

"Anyway, give me the camera so I can return it to the cabinet."

Joel reached into his briefcase, leaned in, and passed the camera over, "Look Mike, I'll handle this my way. We have to be pragmatic. I have a family and a livelihood to protect. Uncovering criminal behavior is what the media does best. I have a reporter friend down in Washington at the Capital Post. They'll eat this story up, and put the brakes to this whole thing." Joel unlatched the door and stepped out, but leaned back in to add, "Remember, we're not the Department of Justice. We don't do the prosecuting. So, mums the word."

Mike didn't share Joel's faith in the media. He knew those newspapers were political hacks first before anything else. They wouldn't know the truth if it licked them in the face. "We'll try it your way... except make sure you stay anonymous to those reporter friends and their editors, See if they publish anything without the photos. The pics will tell Lifespan the story came from inside."

"I don't think they'll react to the story as credible unless they know it's from an inside source," Joel responded.

Mike felt uncomfortable about this and told Joel, "If these newspaper people double cross you and tell Lifespan they have an inside spy, the first person they'll come after is me. Then from me to you. If you're gonna do this, be anonymous. Maybe insure the leak is from one of the government consultant cronies that Strauss feeds money to. Like at the NIH (National Institutes of Health). That'll cover us in case your newspaper heroes suddenly become stoolies."

"Oh, wait," Mike added, as he grabbed Joel's arm. Wait 8 days. The CCTV surveillance cameras overwrite themselves every 7 days on Sunday nights. That will give us two overwrites – just to be sure."

"You do have a point Mike. It can't hurt to be too cautious."

They exchanged 'Good Nights' and Mike left for home. Neither realized the firestorm they will create.

Driving on the interstate alone, Mike had a mix of feelings; shame, disgust, pity, and ultimately anger. He knew that while he slept in bed tonight, newly formed beings were being snuffed out in silent secrecy. It reminded him of the kind of human tragedies that seem to happen in this world and are accepted on a regular basis - Syria, Ethiopia, Cambodia, Somalia, Bosnia, the Nazi and Communist concentration camps. Places where people lose their value as a human, simply becoming dried flesh on skeletal limbs. Dying in total obscurity without identity, on a scale beyond comprehension. *Whoever really gave a shit*, he thought. It seemed to him that society had a way to tolerating this stuff, as long as nobody rubbed their nose in it. In the end, the butchers never seem to pay for their crimes anyway. *So where was the loving God? Where was justice?*

The ride home in the dark gave him more time to reflect on Joel's rationalization of the larger issue of termination and decoupling. He recalled Joel's remark that it's a necessary evil that just has to be tolerated. That you sacrifice the good for the greater good, and avoid the subsequent suffering by all. Something , that even he, as a combat pilot veteran had always tacitly accepted. Except, now he had witnessed exactly what was being destroyed. Now he couldn't hide behind the veil of ignorance.

Mike arrived home about 10 PM, grateful to see his two sons lounging peacefully in front of the TV. Just being in a normal house with two healthy sons seemed like an awful lot right now. He went into the living room, poured a scotch and soda, and collapsed into an easy chair. Zoot curled up on the floor with his rear snuggled up against Mike's feet. In his doggie manner, Zoot just exuded his welcoming, unconditional, sympathetic companionship.

His son, Matthew, peaked into the room, only dimly lit from the light in the adjoining room, and said cautiously, "Another bad day, Dad?"

"Yeah, Matt, but nothing I can't handle," he sighed.

Matt wanted to show some commiseration and felt bad that at times like these his mother was not around to help his father through -whatever was tormenting him. His father never discussed business at home with them, wanting to be protective, and wanting them to enjoy their youth and innocence while it lasted.

"Well, Dad, if you ever need someone to talk to, we'll listen." Then Matt grinned, "We know a lot more things than you think. Maybe give you a different perspective."

Mike replied softly, "Thanks for the offer pal, but right now I'd just as well be left alone." Then after a pause added, "And I want to sit down with you one day to find out what you think you know that I don't know!"

Matt returned to the TV room disappointed that he couldn't reach his father.

Mike lit his pipe in the dark and watched the smoke drift upwards.

From what he had seen tonight, he wondered what made an individual human life any more significant that an acorn scattered on the ground. He pondered on what kind of society was being created for his sons to live in. He felt immersed in a decaying world culture where zealous self-interest had become the supreme virtue. Now the ultimate selfish prize was within the grasp of that culture...eternal life for the chosen few at the expense of the unprotected souls of the future.

So it won't be a nuclear war that destroys humanity, he thought. *No, its gonna be more subtle than that. It is gonna take more time... more suffering... on a scale beyond comprehension.*

He never felt like an anachronism, except now he felt out of sync with the world. Old values, old virtues... old fart.

More than ever, Mike was glad his days with Lifespan Corporation were numbered. Carlos was right. Big money or not, he wasn't going to be part of it. He already was "sandbagged" into building the equipment carts to torment those fetal specimens in the first place.

In a while Mike got up from his chair, rousted the boys from the TV room, kissed and hugged each one, and sent them to bed. Then he loaded the evidence from the company camera onto his home laptop, erased the memory card, and retired too.

Lying in bed, he clasped his hands behind his head on the pillow, and stared into the darkness above. His thoughts became more introspective, remembering his wife Laura's termination some 20 years earlier. It happened shortly after they were married. At the time they hardly hesitated much about having it done. They weren't ready financially. Laura had to work to help save for a house. It was so easy then, everybody wanted to help you get rid of it. Just another of life's little inconveniences. Happy faces all. He surmised, Maybe that's what we all wanted to believe. That way there's no guilt to live with. He reflected, *Anyway, back then I could separate every issue into black and white. Then there was no reason to deal with the 'in betweens'.*

He and Laura rarely discussed that event in their lives, and never revealed it to anyone, not even their parents. At times Mike thought that his wife was taken away from him as punishment because of that episode in his life - assuming God was a God of vengeance.

His mind recalled all those PBS documentaries on human development - images in tremendous detail and resolution. Though it was never real. It was never really human - more like CGI generated. After today, Mike had glimpsed a fetus close up and alive in its own world. A hundred documentaries could never convey the feeling of seeing that image, alive - in the flesh. He wondered that if a woman's womb was transparent to the outside world, like plexiglas, and one could see the developing life as it grows, would we be so quick to quench it?

126

Mike snickered to himself, *Here I am at middle age. Instead of getting more set in my ways, I'm thinking like a regular activist, challenging the establishment culture debating what's human life and what's not. I'm supposed to get entrenched in the accepted values, be a defender of the establishment, not a political heretic.*

He rolled over in bed and curled up for solace with his pillow. His dog, Zoot, wandered in through the darkness, slowly hoisting his bulk onto the bed, his tired back legs straining to boost his bony rear. Something he was never allowed to do when Laura was alive. Sniffing and walking in a circle on the bedspread, his paws alternately crushed Mike's legs with his enormous weight in the process. Finally, he settled down, curled against Mike's back. Mike turned his head and asked, "What happened boy? Did Matthew throw you out of his bed?"

Zoot ignored the insult, lowered his head, and rested his chin on his shaggy paws. He exhaled what seemed like a sigh from his big black runny nose.

Mike turned back and fluffed his pillow one last time saying,
"Zoot, you don't know how lucky you are. You only have to contend with nature. I have to contend with <u>human</u> nature!"

Lying there by himself, it felt like the sum of his friendships added up to two good sons and one loyal and agreeable old dog.

He felt melancholy thinking about his kids growing up in this hardened world without the tender influence of a real mother at home.

Would they ever experience or even value the total devotion of a woman to a child... or to a man? he pondered, *or is that gone forever too?*

He forced himself to think of something pleasant to get to sleep. His date with Phylis... what might be. What it would feel like to touch a soft woman again... to win a woman's heart.

He focused on the memory of Phylis's gentle face. Eventually, his tortured mind felt peace and sleep.

CHAPTER 12
Get ready, 'cause here I come

That same evening a blissful Phylis felt that her Sunday date at the car show with Mike required a new outfit, so she finished dinner with the kids and visited her favorite discount clothing store.. A pair of black slacks caught her eye and seemed appropriate for a day of walking at the convention. A pale pink silk blouse had also caught her eye with a pleasing embroidery of flowers running vertically along the button seam. She tried them on in front of the store mirror. Its tapered waist made her feel smooth, sleek ... and feminine. The blouse went prefect with her new slacks and black flats.

* * * * * * *

Phylis awoke on Saturday morning with a renewed feeling of optimism. She still had to do her early morning routine of making breakfast for the kids, except today didn't feel like the usual drudgery. After cleaning up the dishes, she went into her bedroom, and put on her new outfit. Staring into the full length mirror there was a magic feeling inside her bosom, a combination of excitement and trepidation. Her mind wandered, and she asked herself, R*eally, who was his new man in her life? How would he impact her mundane routine of life with her family? He definitely was someone special. Someone who doesn't come along too often.* Then concluded, *Oh well, one step at a time.*

* * * * * *

Mike woke up Saturday with Zoot's big black nose on his pillow three inches from his face - quite a different perspective. He did sleep, and awoke not feeling really rested with a slight headache. He still had to face the realization that last nights' visit to the R&D Lab was no nightmare, that this was reality.

Mike looked in the bathroom mirror and rubbed the stubborn bristles of his morning beard. *Now I know why ignorance is bliss*, he felt, and ruminated to himself, *all those years of human fetuses being used by his company, and personally, all the money he made out of it was at some poor creature's demise. All the clever political correctness or rationalization in the world didn't change that cruel fact.*

He debated whether to call off his Sunday date with Phylis. Eventually, he figured, the lid on this whole thing would blow soon and then it would be somebody else's problem. His friend, Joel, was wealthy, with plenty of influential contacts in the media and personal prestige in the medical profession.

Mike decided to relieve his distress by postponing a telephone call to him until Monday morning - after his date. Force the whole thing out of his head for the weekend until he was back at work. The first distraction would involve a tune-up on his old '65 Ford Galaxy sedan. That would occupy the morning and an afternoon detailing his car inside and out to make it presentable for his date with Phylis tomorrow.

CHAPTER 13

Phylis was grateful that she still had a living mother and father to come over on Sunday morning to watch her children. They had helped her through her divorce, and always seem to be there when she needed them. Besides, the kids loved their company, enjoying playing even simple card games like *Go Fish* which their uncouth grandfather renamed *Go Fart.*

As the 9AM. pick-up time approached for her date with Mike, Phylis wondered if she was doing the right thing. She would not dare reveal to her mother that she met her date through a dating website. Anyway, she asked around the company about Michael. Apparently, the ladies had a higher opinion than the men did – the male opinions were skewed by a bit of envy. Besides, she knew her way around Manhattan, and could take the railroad home if necessary.

Mike pulled up the driveway in a shiny white sedan with a black vinyl top. Phylis peeked through the front window curtain of her Cape style home, and didn't recognize the make of the car as it pulled up the driveway. It had a chrome bumper, so just she assumed it had to be old.

Mike stepped out, looking a bit rugged, dressed in his brown leather jacket, khaki pants and brown boots. *He looks like 'Indiana Jones'*, she mused to herself.

When he knocked on the door, Phylis made a bee-line for her bedroom. In the meantime, he was received by her father, and introduced himself to her parents and in the living room. Phylis's children chose to stay in the kitchen and sneak looks at Mike from a distance. Mike made small talk about his classic car with her father. Her mother came to Phylis' back bedroom. She leaned in and whispered with disdain, "He's Italian!"

Phylis was immediately defensive and hissed, "What of it!" and her mother immediately retreated. Phylis grabbed her pocketbook and short black leather coat. She came out to the living room, greeted Mike, and told her parents she would be home by early evening.

Mike sensed a little interplay with her parents, saying a cordial goodbye to them. He grinned and leaned over to wave goodbye to the kids peeking out of the kitchen doorway. They ducked back when they realized he had seen them.

Mike took her arm to lead Phylis down the driveway, and commented that from what little he saw of her kids, they seemed nicely behaved. He also noted that her house was neat and orderly. He liked that in a woman.

Phylis was amused by his male comments and just smiled tolerantly. Mike opened the passenger side door of his car. She waved through the windshield to her children at the front window as Mike backed out.

She asked Mike, "Is this your other car?"

"Yeah. It's a Galaxy 500, 1965."

Teasing she added, "Do you own any cars that aren't at least 70 years old?"

"I only buy cars that I can fix myself," he replied with manly pride.

Inside the car it felt like being transported back to Phylis' teenage years. The interior was done in black vinyl, metal and chrome trim. It looked a bit gaudy compared to today's flat finished plastics. And, the front bench seat appeared expansive compared to the bucket seats and center console of the foreign models she drove.

She commented on the lack of safety features, "No airbags, no shoulder harness."

Mike pointed to the hood, and laughed.. "We've got ten feet of ladder frame steel and 390 cubic inches of iron between us and everybody else. That means everybody else needs the airbag."

After a while, Phylis found herself sliding to the middle of the bench seat, close to Mike - as she recalled from dates in her teen years. Mike appreciated her closeness, slipped his arm around her, and both felt comfortable with the arrangement.

Mike drove one handed at a steady, quick pace in the light Sunday morning traffic. With the large steering wheel, he had skillful command of the car, as it moved almost gracefully around slower vehicles, always anticipating the other driver's moves. Phylis talked about her family and her divorce, hoping that Mike would open up and tell her more about his own past. All she could get was that his wife died 5 years ago and he had two teenage sons at home. He even had difficulty recalling their exact ages.

Just like a man, she thought.

Mike entered Manhattan through the Midtown Tunnel and decided on driving across town on 34th Street since it was a 4 lane, two-way street. He explained to Phylis that the other one-way crosstown streets were inevitably blocked by double-parked delivery trucks.

As it turned out, 34th Street traffic was also backed up by construction, buses, and (you guessed it) double parked delivery trucks. Phylis noticed Mike's demeanor turn from even-tempered to slightly anxious. They were now stopped dead at the Lexington Avenue intersection. Buses were unable to get to the curb because of the construction and stopped in the street to discharge their passengers.

Mike rolled down his window, and crept slowly over the double yellow line to peek ahead. Abruptly he turned to Phylis, ordering, "Slide over and buckle your seatbelt!"

Phylis quickly obliged, thinking she might have offended him or something. With no opposing traffic for the next block, he accelerated and crossed the yellow line into the empty opposing traffic lanes. The car rose on all four wheels as the V8 engine's huge torque lifted the front end. There was an embarrassing chirp of rubber, as the car lurched forward and Phylis was pushed back into her seat. It made her cringe, grabbing the armrest, as if she was falling off the back of a motorcycle.

With no oncoming traffic, in a few seconds, they shot past all the stalled traffic and darted back onto his side of the street. By the next intersection, he rapidly slowed down, and continued down a now traffic-free road at an even pace.

Phylis' heart was pounding, she felt like part of a '*Fast and Furious*' movie. Finally, she caught her breath and reprimanded Mike. "Don't you ever do that again, with me in your car!" she bellowed. "A woman doesn't dream of getting killed on her first date!"

"Sorry Hon. My instincts said I could do it safely, and I've got a car that never lets me down."

In a few more blocks, he nonchalantly announced, "Well we're here," casually pulling into a parking lot across from the auto show. He sensed Phylis's disdain, by her keeping her distance from him.

"I'm really sorry Phylis," he pleaded, "the street was clear on the opposite side and I figured I could safely pass that mess." Mike tried to look sincere, but Phylis could tell he probably enjoyed the whole episode.

Mike took his parking receipt, and they walked to the curb to cross 9th Avenue. Mike pointed back up the street, saying, "You know we'd still be back there."

Phylis, for her part could care less, now wondering how reckless this guy could get.

The traffic signal began to blink 'Don't Walk' in their direction as they crossed. Mike ignored it and grabbed Phylis' hand to follow him across. "Follow me!" Mike yelled, pulling her forward, as they broke into a full trot across six lanes of one-way traffic.

Phylis reached the curb just as the light turned green and the waiting cars lurched forward behind her heel.

On the sidewalk, she ripped her hand from Mike's grasp and leaned heavily on a lamppost to catch her breadth. They were breathing loud gasps, facing each other on the sidewalk. He was leaning over, resting his hands on his knees, smiling. "I knew you could make it. I noticed you have a nice set of legs."

A wheezing Phylis was initially upset, ready to berate him again, and then found herself suddenly laughing with him. Maybe, it was the exhilaration of beating out danger together - something exciting for a change.

An apologetic Mike offered his hand out to her and said, "Sorry hon. Bad start. Come on, I'll buy you a cup a coffee, and we can relax a bit...catch our breath.... Split a Danish?" With no immediate options, a frazzled Phylis accepted his hand and the invite, saying glibly, "You've got two strikes against you now."

They found a raised terrace overlooking the main exhibit hall and relaxed there for a while, sipping their drinks and enjoying the air conditioning. After the ride to the show, it felt calming to gaze down at the mass of humanity scurrying about below. Phylis was still not certain about a second date, and she would play it by ear the rest of the day. However, one more scare and he would be history.

Mike sensed he had pushed things too far, and sought to make amends.

"Look, what looks risky to you, may not be for me. I know my limitations. Sometimes they are beyond what's doable for most people. Believe me, I would never take a risk that would harm you....ever... sorry, sorry, sorry."

Later, on the show floor, walking hand–in–hand, Mike took her from carmaker to carmaker, explaining hybrids, plugin hybrids, and all electric models. Each touting outrageous mileage.

"Wave of the future," Mike said.

"Then why don't you have one?"

"Purchase price, and high cost of electricity in New York."

"I thought the government gives you tax breaks for it," she replied.

"Dealers just bump the car price up the same amount as the tax credit."

It was fascinating to see how every truck, SUV, and sports car had some electric drive component now.

As they meandered around the exhibit floor, Mike would comment on how much horsepower these electric vehicles had - 400, 600, 1000 horsepower.

Phylis could not reconcile these figures with the touted 'Green Energy' creed, as the supposed reason for electric vehicles to begin with.

Still, she enjoyed the magical ambiance of flashy, colorful cars, gleaming from the reflections of ceiling lights. Mike would keep interrupting her relaxed browsing by compelling her to sit in all the convertible floor models, regardless of make. Phylis felt self-conscious and timid, and Mike managed to get her into every convertible and took pictures with her cell phone. In time, she really enjoyed the look and uninhibited feel of a convertible. He kept trying to convince her that she would look great in a convertible. Once, he even gave her a backhanded compliment. "These cars were created for displaying good lookin' women, and right now you're one of the best lookin' in this place."

"OK then, "Buy me one?" she kidded.

"That will take a few more dates," he laughed.

Except for his occasional sideways leering at the female models by some manufacturer's cars, Mike was entertaining company. What Phylis did not know was that each time she bent over to look at a car; Mike was checking her out from behind too. Mike enjoyed trying to observe the lines of her bikini cut panties through her thin smooth black slacks.

After 2 hours of walking on three levels, they were both pooped, and Mike suggested they leave to get something to eat. Phylis agreed, as long as she was the one leading them across 9th street. This time, no more running 'Don't Walk' signs.

* * * * * * *

The car ride out of the city was less frenetic, and Phylis eventually felt comfortable enough again to slide over close to him on the bench seat. Once reaching Queens, they exited the expressway, stopping at an old German restaurant Mike frequented with business associates. The place had a pleasant, dark ambiance in the European tradition. The patrons were mostly gray-haired older people. There were pictures on the walls of famous racehorses and jockeys from Belmont Racetrack not far away. Mike picked a small table in the bar section of the restaurant.

After they were seated, Mike talked about his kids and how well they made do without a mother in the house. Knowing him now, Phylis just remarked, "I can imagine."

After drinks came, they ordered the house special, cold roast beef sandwiches on pumpernickel bread. She got around to asking about the version of the Lifespan fence incident that was on TV. Mike just answered, "Well, you know, in the media, you really can't figure out who are the real heroes and who are the villains. We did what any decent people should do. I used my military training. There are still some good people at the company that helped."

Phylis broached a rumor she had heard a rumor about his demotion.

Mike did not seem too upset. "I don't supervise Facilities anymore."

"You OK with that?"

"Yeah," he smirked. "No more clearing backed up toilet and computers that don't boot."

He did not seem to want to talk about it any further, and out of nowhere, got philosophical about what constitutes life and what does not. Phylis could not understand what suddenly brought that up. The normally upbeat Mike became somewhat subdued for a while in the dim light of the restaurant bar. Maybe she touched a raw nerve. She could not know that he was still haunted by the images of specimens mutilated in the R&D lab.

Leaning forward with his elbows on the table, and with a tired expression, he said, "Do you ever have doubts about what we're doing at Lifespan? I mean, this whole decoupling business?"

Phylis replied, "Not originally, not when the whole thing started. Except recently, strange stuff has been happening out there. I've been wondering why I'm staying in this occupation. I mean, if the money justifies the means we're using to get it. There's strange things going on at the plant. I'm not sure what that is about. We're taking specimens with their placentas now."

Hearing her placenta comment, Mike had a disturbing vision of the R&D lab. He collected himself and just said a perfunctory, "Really?" while adding things up in his mind, not giving anything away.

She continued. "And it starts to give you the creeps. If I could afford it, I would go back to getting a no stress job, and being home for my family every night. Then, the hell with all these shenanigans. "

He felt some consolation knowing that another person was having similar misgivings. Fortunately, there was still another person in this world who could appreciate a home centered environment too.

Mike thought to himself, *If she only knew what these guys at Lifespan were really up to!*

Phylis sensed that Mike needed some feminine compassion, and slipped her hand across the table. He gently grasped her hand and brought her fingertips to his lips. With a kiss in the mellow candle light, even his tired eyes seem serene when he gazed into her bright eyes. Nothing needed to be said. It was a tender moment beyond words that Phylis sensed he appreciated - more so than Phylis could imagine.

Their sandwiches came and broke the compassionate mood. Phylis divided their single side order of French fries and onion rigs onto their two plates. As small a gesture as it was, Mike had not felt that kind of feminine care by a woman in a long time – feeling important to someone. He mentioned with a grin, "You don't feel subservient, doing that for me?"

Phylis looked up a bit surprised by his remark, "Oh nonsense. I just enjoy taking care of people. Once I'm out of that feminist office environment, I let my natural female instinct show. That's all I know... or care about."

Mike took a large bite out of his sandwich that filled his mouth and jowls, and mumbled, while pointing his fork. "You know nowadays, some career women would look down on you for that – not man-like behavior." Mike chugged down some beer, while gauging her reaction.

As Phylis watched this masculine display of gorging himself, she thought sarcastically, *how charming. Sure. Of course. We career women really want to look like that when we eat too.*

Phylis just rolled her eyes upward, while watching this unabashed male. "So, how do women fit in your male world?"

Mike shrugged his shoulders. "Lately, there has been no fit outside of the office females...err, I mean professional relationships."

A smiling Phylis sat there thinking, *I think I know why*.

"Been on my own for a while now – maybe too long. With that posting on the date site, I finally realized the something was missing - needed to be found. He hesitated a moment, and look her square in the eye. "Maybe someone like you."

Mike slid his hand across the table to gentlty touch her smooth, soft hand again. He gave Phylis a heartfelt look. "If I ever forget what a wonderful woman you are, I don't deserve another chance."

It wasn't exactly the poetic compliment she wanted to hear, but it sounded sincere, anyway.

* * * * * * *

By the time they arrived back at her house it was early evening. Mike pulled into her driveway, ran around the car to open her door, and escorted her up to the stoop to her front door. Against the darkness, the reflected lights from the house windows sparkled in their eyes. A kiss seemed an appropriate way to end their first real date, and Phylis had decided she would let him do it.

Mike moved closer to her and said "I had a real good time with you, young lady."

"She grinned and squinted as she replied. "Except that driving part."

"Yeah, except that," he grinned.

They smiled and stared into each other's eyes. Mike gently placed his hand behind her in the small of her arched back, and pulled her closer. She could smell the beer on his breath and a faint smell of 'Aqua Velva' aftershave and perspiration. She lifted her chin lightly and closed her eyes waiting for his lips to touch hers.

Instead, Mike tenderly kissed her forehead and said goodnight. A startled Phylis opened her eyes and looked down in astonishment to see him merrily bounding down the steps to his car.

She was disappointed. Usually she had to fight the guy off on the first date This guy kissed her like she was his little sister. He didn't even mention another date before disappearing.

Mike backed his car out of the driveway into the street. He stopped, rolled down the window and yelled, "I'll call you at work."

Then he gunned his engine, chirped the tires and quickly disappeared down the road. Phylis hardly had time to wave.

In spite of spending a lively day together, now it felt like he blew in and blew out of her life in a flash. It left her wondering if she gave the right signals to be kissed.

She shrugged her shoulders with a sigh, and turned to enter her house. Her family greeted her all excited. They wanted to know whatever

Phylis would share, anxious to know if she was going to see him again.

After his quick departure, she really couldn't say anything with much certainty.

Anyway, it was a breathtaking date, that is for sure.

CHAPTER 14
Lifespan smells a rat

Mike cruised into work early Monday morning,, with the satisfied feeling that he knew something Lifespan Corporation didn't. Upon arriving in his office, he was still feeling upbeat from his last date with Phylis, and returned the company camera with the blank memory card to the department cabinet. Then he called Joel Rosen to make sure he was still 'in' on their caper.

"Hey Joel, how was your weekend?"

Joel answered, "Kinda dull," and promptly hung up.

Mike slowly put the receiver down, his earlier enthusiasm now diminished somewhat. He hoped Joel would sit tight for a week, before speculating any further.

* * * * * *

Over a week later, it was Tuesday at corporate headquarters. Max Brewster was in his office unusually early. Assembled in his fifth floor suite were Jane Savage, Norm Stark, Chief Counsel and Eve West. Max paced alongside his picture window overlooking New York Harbor. He was agitated and eventually groaned, "Son of a Bitch! Some greedy bastard is always trying to screw me."

Norm and Jane were mystified by Max's agitated demeanor. They were called to this hasty meeting not knowing what it was all about.

Eve asked in a supportive tone, "Why don't you share this problem with us. We can't help you if we don't know."

Max turned to look out the window with his back to her. He waved his hand saying, "No. Wait. Wait until Strauss arrives. I want you all to hear this at the same time."

Norm and Jane gave each other a puzzled look and remained standing. Eve was still vexed, and paced nervously. She was not accustomed to impromptu meetings without knowing the inside track ahead of time. She fumbled through her purse for a cigarette and nervously lit it, then puffed madly for a while. Eventually, she settled down spreading her posterior against the edge of the credenza.

Strauss finally entered the office, and reluctantly sat down without a greeting, much less acknowledging anybody's presence in the room. His longtime acquaintance with Max made him somewhat cavalier in demeanor. They met several years earlier at the annual Methuselah longevity convention in Reno, Nevada. The convention was a semi-informal group of scientists and business investors that were acting as a clearinghouse for numerous theories, experiments, and developments aimed at extending the average productive lifespan of the human species.

The conventioneers also recognized this as a ground floor business opportunity in the burgeoning biomedical industry. If Americans would spend $100 billion a year on cosmetics just to look younger, what would they spend to actually live longer!

Max had been an ardent enthusiast of different techniques and theories of life extension, and he made it a point to meet every researcher in attendance. If there was going to be a way to extended a person's life, then it was going to be his life extended first - not somebody else.

Max had already tried many of the conventional life extension gimmicks, consuming megadoses of anti-oxidant supplements like beta-carotene and vitamins C and E. Then there was the low calorie starvation technique that worked so well with in experiments doubling the lifetime of mice. Alas, that required too much anguish and character to be sustained by an executive with a busy schedule like himself.

Who wants to live forever as a mouse, Max thought.

With the more contemporary and exciting discoveries being made lately, especially from DNA research, it seemed a certainty that it was only a matter of time before somebody struck life extension gold. The subject of eternal life was now less a quagmire of illusionary potions. Once considered the domain of quacks, research into longevity was now firmly within the grasp of real scientists and venture capitalists.

Strauss had delivered a paper based on some novel research he'd done under several NIH (National Institutes of Health) grants. Strauss's treatises dealt with tapping the potential contained in the human fetus. He demonstrated an in-depth knowledge of the precursors and stem cell components of the developing fetus. These are the triggers that direct the developing fetus' body differentiation into the specialized cells of the organs, nerves, immune and blood system, and endocrine system. These precursors, if injected locally into an adult did remarkable things. Like re-growth of damage arteries in the heart muscle, or regeneration of broken spinal columns, or as a substitute for bone marrow transplants. Nothing short of amazing, begging the question on everyone's mind; How did he isolate these precursors? His sketchy reports on his experiments were reported in medical journals. However, no details beyond trial results was ever actually published. Hence, never duplicated independently by other

137

researchers.

At cocktail parties during the conferences, he rarely contributed anything intelligent to the technical discussions. Some researchers wondered amongst themselves where he even got the expertise to do the complex work he had already accomplished.

Nevertheless, Dr. Strauss was receiving a steady stream of government NIH grants, and his work displayed a progressively advanced knowledge of the human fetus. Strauss was on a roll and no one seemed to know how he did it. Or even want to stop him. The tide of public and political opinion was with him. After all, he was Hernando De Soto leading them to the fountain of youth!

The test trials of Strauss's miracle concoctions showed improved patient results for Alzheimer's and Parkinson's disease. The anecdotal side effects were also of particular importance in his study group. It seemed that the some older males had their gray hair turn back to its original color. Sixty year old women had the same hair effect, and some also began to menstruate again. Age spots (liver spots) on the skin began to disappear. One patient with false teeth began to grow a new set of teeth! Another woman grew 2 inches in height. All the subjects exhibited measurable improvements in skin tone and muscle and bone mass along with increased hand/eye coordination. It was obvious that something in his medicinal formula was having a more widespread biomedical effect.

Many aging government and political employees in the health administrations were intrigued by these developments. Many had a family history of mental diseases, and they were not about to suffer this regressive tragedy like the commoners in the voting public. Strauss was their savior. These bureaucrats would bring to bear the resources of the wealthiest government in the world to make his discoveries available exclusively to them.

Max had a great deal of admiration for Strauss. As Max would often say, "At least he was converting all this scientific mumbo-jumbo into something I can sell!"

He also heard one of Strauss's convention speeches when Strauss boasted, "If my extractions can extend a human life 30 more years, then the intervening advances during that time, will allow that person an indefinite lifespan. In fact, the aging process could even be reversed!"

It was all Max needed to hear, and the two were having breakfast, lunch and dinner from then on. Max wined and dined Strauss until he finally struck a deal, offering him a substantial equity position in a new start-up company named Lifespan Corporation. Strauss could be Chief Scientist and Vice President of R&D. He could hire many of these 'superior' conference researchers to work for him. Then, by making them 'defacto' partners in the deal, Strauss could insure continuing his work without government regulatory interference or scientific oversight.

Max used his Washington connections in the NIH to insure Strauss would have all the research grant money he could blow in the near term. Max used his DC Post influence to increase pressure on Congress and the White House to liberalize fetal tissue extraction regulations. Finally, he organized an investment syndicate to obtain an exclusive license from the State governments to begin large-scale production of fetal donor extracts.

To maintain absolute control, Max provided the first-tier capital of Lifespan, from his own money. Something he had never done before - actually using his own money.

Second-tier financing from his venture capital syndicate was more than enough to launch the corporation. Third-tier financing for land, building construction and capital equipment came later from several banks who fell over their moneybags trying to loan the new bio-company money. This was Bio-Tech! The magic of science and money.

Later, Max resisted pressure to take the company public with an IPO on Wall Street. This guaranteed him unequivocal freedom to manipulate the company to his own personal ends.

Thereafter, Max and Strauss stopped attending the Methuselah conferences.

* * * * * * *

With Dr.Strauss finally present, the group in Max's office represented the inner circle at Lifespan Corporation. Strauss finally recognized everyone's presence by asking a question in a curt tone, "Well, Mister Brewster why the urgent meeting?"

Max walked behind his own leather chair and braced himself on the back giving a nasty look to Dr. Strauss. In a very serious tone he addressed the group.

"Some of you here have heard that we at Lifespan Corporation have some very important and confidential projects going on in R&D. It's the reason I maintain such a high degree of security. These programs are our Company's future. And it is in everyone's interest in this room to insure the protection of that future."

The group looked at each other seeking some signal of where Max was going with this speech. Apparently, nobody knew, and out of respect or fear, nobody asked.

Max paused for effect and walked around his desk to lean his broad posterior on the desk front edge to be closer to his audience. "It grieves me to report to you that I have received information that an informant is in our midst. One of our consulting scientists, who accepts a paycheck from my company… has tried to sell us out!"

The inner circle reacted with shock both real and feigned. Norm

Stark was less startled than the rest, always waiting for independent confirmation, so he asked, "How accurate is your information? When did you receive it?"

Max chuckled and waved his hands in front, "No, no, no. My sources are confidential and at the highest levels. And besides, I can't tell you all I know, at least not yet."

He turned to face Jane. She tried to maintain her outer composure. Except, as Chief Security Officer, this problem fell squarely in her domain. On the inside she was in shear panic. As Max stared at her forming his thoughts, she mentally searched the employee files for a likely sacrifice – *Santino*!

"Jane," Max said in a low tone, "I want you to focus an investigation into all the research consultants we have on staff, full and part time." Jane was pleasantly surprised, no longer feeling in the hot seat for employees. Jane responded enthusiastically, "I'll get right on it Mister Brewster." *Thinking to* herself, *Now, I finally get the drones!*

Max turned around to look at Dr. Straus

Dr. Strauss immediately protested. "Wait a minute! Those are my people. Who says it's one of my consultants."

Max turned to confront Dr. Strauss. "The information I received points to one of your people, Peter."

"What information? From who?" Dr. Strauss craned his scrawny neck, and vehemently protested, sliding to the edge of his seat. He looked around as if to gain sympathy from his associates.

Max glanced at Jane, and sent her on her way. Then he politely requested that Eve depart also. He was going to have a private conversation with Strauss and Norm alone. Eve gave a look like daggers at Max, as she reluctantly but gracefully retired from the office.

When they were alone Norm asked Max where he got his 'G2' intelligence, and if the 'Greenhouse' project was ever mentioned. Max indicated it was the chief editor of the Capitol Post that contacted him, and thankfully, no one mentioned 'Greenhouse' yet. The leak would stop there. Norm looked relieved and said, "Thank God for that. That would really spell disaster for our California venture."

Max continued his explanation that a Lifespan consultant with information on our re-animation program contacted one of the Capitol Post reporters. Ergo, it had to be one of Strauss' R&D people.

Strauss refused to accept it, that one of his well-paid cohort could betray him. "Max, my people are the ones that greased the skids to get emergency approvals for all our therapies and drug treatments. Nobody gets emergency approvals in 3 months."

Max was unfazed, and an intense argument continued. Their meeting broke up on a sour note with bitterness on both sides. Thereafter, a repressed animosity would continue between the two that would fester as events unfolded.

* * * * * *

After laying low for over a week, Mike met Joel in the cafeteria. They picked a secluded corner table far from everyone else. Joel shook his head in dismay. "I hate to disappoint you Mike, but the *Capital Post* won't touch this story."

Mike was distraught after waiting a week. "How so? It's the story of the decade."

"Yeah, that's exactly why," Joel answered. "Last night, the senior editors told my reporter contact to back off, that Lifespan Corporation is a sacred cow. In fact, they pressed my friend hard for the source. Fortunately, he covered for me and said it was an anonymous NIH consultant." Joel leaned forward with a serious look. "The reporters said they were never under so much pressure to reveal a source. The backlash from the paper's management was like nothing they had seen before. I think we're finished Mike. I don't know what we can do from here on. The story's dead…maybe we're dead."

Mike sat dejected with his legs crossed and played with his shoelaces. He glanced out the window nearby, his engineering mind wrestling with this set back. After a few minutes, Mike leaned over and whispered, "Should we try the *Brooklyn Daily News*?"

Joel made a frowning face. "Geez, are you not getting it? You didn't learn anything from that *Capital Post* fiasco? Joel 's face contorted in anger, "Besides *Brooklyn Daily* is a scandal sheet."

When Mike mentioned the company telephones were bugged, that was the last straw for Joel, and only pushed him further away. Joel warned, "You know, I think we're in over our heads. I'm not so sure anymore," adding empathically, "Whistle blowers are never heroes. Don't mention that break-in again."

A dejected Mike left their meeting to return to his office. On his way back, he realized that Lifespan Corporate would probably soon know that somebody was the snitch. Luckily, the CCTV tapes would have been overwritten by now.

Later in the afternoon, he toyed with calling the *Brooklyn Daily New* s, but then abandoned the idea. He thought it too dangerous until he sees the fallout from the *Capitol Post*.

Mike sat at his desk watching people leave, as the building slowly emptied out for the day. He weighed his options, which at this point were zero.

Maybe write my congressman? He thought, *Ha! He's already on the treatment list for Lifespan therapeutics!*

Mike spent the next two days looking for suspicious signs that Lifespan Corporate might be aware of the newspaper contacts Joel made. The answer began to take shape in the form of a procurement requisition from Dr. Strauss himself.

The requisition called for ordering new digital security locks, the expensive, programmable kind that you need a digital code number to open. That had to be more than coincidence.

Then he received purchase request from Jane Savage requesting the purchase of Quantity 3, $5,500 drones. It seemed to him that Jane forgot he is not in charge of Facilities anymore. More importantly, the approval signatures from the top execs made this high priority with management.

The drone order made Mike think, *If it's so important to them, why don't I buy an extra controller for this model drone? See what makes it tick?*

With Al Greene away, he processed the requisitions and ordered the lock and the drones on their company account. Then, on his iphone, went over to Amazon to order the same controller with his personnel credit card.

Afterwards he decided to walk across the parking lot to see what Joel might have heard. Along the way, Harry, the gate guard, slowed down in a security patrol vehicle. Harry stopped and rolled down the window to say, "Hi, Mike. So what's new?"

"I dunno Harry. I think we're going into the digital lock business."

Harry beckoned with his hand for Mike to come closer to the driver side window, and glanced around the parking lot with a nervous look. Mike leaned on the door frame and moved closer. Harry whispered, "Something's up Mike. Jane's been berating the Department for two days now. Says we have to tighten up security with these part-time scientists that come in and out of R&D. We have a guard stationed full-time in the R&D Lab during working g hours now. He searches everybody's briefcase going in and going out."

Mike did his best to appear ignorant and asked, "Why the bru-ha?"

"Jane didn't volunteer too much," he rasped, "but it's obvious someone is trying to steal the company's trade secrets....anyway that's what I think."

Mike grimaced and nodded, "Heavy stuff Harry. Think you'll catch'em?"

"Naw it's too risky now. Whoever it is will probably go to ground for now." He paused for a moment to remember, "Although Jane called in the telephone people. That means they'll be recording our phone calls through our PBX." Then Harry chuckled, "Maybe they'll bug your phone, Mike!"

Mike laughed too, and waved as Harry pulled away. He didn't need to finish his trip to the other building. He confirmed Lifespan Corporate had been alerted. It was also apparent that they swallowed the "consultant spy" story. *A good omen*, Mike surmised.

Upon returning to his office, he found Jane Savage talking to his Admin, Nancy. She turned to Mike as he approached and said, "Well, where were you?"

Mike gave an icy stare, ignored her question, and said sarcastically, "Well, Janie, good morning to you too."

"It's Miz Savage to you. Jerk."

Mike walked past her, asked Nancy for any messages and walked into his office. Jane followed in a huff. Mike sat down at his desk seemingly disregarding her presence, as she waited impatiently for an answer. He fiddled with his terminal mouse just staring at his monitor until Jane's patience was spent.

"Santino!" she shouted.

He looked up, placed his mouse aside, and said, "Uh, you're still here. Have a seat - we haven't chatted for a while."

"No time Santino. I just want the keys to the R&D Lab."

Mike looked up still fiddling with the mouse again while staring at his monitor and quipped, "Don't got."

"What do ya mean, don't got?" an impatient Jane barked."

"I'm not in charge of Facilities anymore. Remember? No Facilities, no keys. Go see Al Greene that's his responsibility now."

Jane snapped back, "He's up in Boston on a symposium. I want them now!"

Mike looked at her directly. "I don't have time to play lost and found for you. Go talk to his Admin. Al confiscated them after your big meeting. Someone over there may remember where they put them.... I certainly don't."

He could tell Jane was reaching her limit as she unconsciously rubbed her hand on the holstered side arm on her belt. Mike wondered how many times she would have liked to use that weapon on him.

Jane finally gave a curt reply, "OK have it you're way. So, when Mister Greene returns, he'll hear about this!"

She turned abruptly and stamped out.

Mike did a singsong under his breath, "sticks and stones may break my bones...", and resumed sorting through his Email.

* * * * * * *

Mike spent the rest of the morning somewhat dejected. He had hoped that newspaper would jump on this Lifespan story, and now it was a dead-end.

It was comforting to think about Phylis, while all this was going on, but he also felt a bit guilty not seeing her. At the same time, it was as if he was being unfaithful to the memory of his decreased wife Laura. He mourned for his wife a long time now. Unfortunately, her memory was not enough help in facing this living world.

He also felt some regret for not revealing to Phylis what he was doing on the side with the R&D lab. Except, he still could not trust her yet, and could not put her job at risk to boot.

After a while he decided to call Phylis in the other building, but missed her twice, leaving a voicemail message. She finally called him back, and Mike invited her to go sailing on Saturday.

With some help with directions, she would meet him at the dock in Centerport Harbor at 10 AM. Maybe he would tell her about the R&D lab then. On Friday afternoon Mike took a ride down to the "Blarney Stone" for a pastrami on rye sandwich and a cool Yuengling beer."

On the way, he picked up a few 'burner' cell phones, now that he knew Lifespan's phones are going to be tapped.

CHAPTER 15
Doink!

In the past week Phylis had become doubtful if their relationship was still viable. But his invitation to go sailing on Saturday morning might rekindle their affair. With good weather forecast, it would be a perfect day to be out on the water. This date would determine if there really was a future with this new man.

With characteristic efficiency, she called her parents the night before, and gave the kids breakfast and. At 9AM her mother and father arrived to watch the kids. An excited Phylis took the opportunity to change into an appropriate outfit for her sea adventure with Mike.

* * * * * * *

Arriving at the marina, Phylis left her car at the harbor parking lot and could just make out her new romantic interest down at the dock below. Mike appeared to be busy doing whatever sailors do, making preparations on the deck of his 26 foot sailboat. As she made her way along the floating gangway, her legs felt like coiled springs as the floating dock bounced clumsily underfoot. Getting closer, she noted some fancy lettering painted on the stern of his boat that spelled, '*Mare Nostrum*'. *Latin name*, she thought to herself, *I wonder what it means?*

The pre-occupied Mike finally glanced up towards the dock, to acknowledge Phylis' approach and take in her features. A horizontal red striped T-shirt and loose white shorts flattered a trim figure. She looked winsome, and at a distance appeared even younger than her age.

As she arrived alongside he quipped, "Well don't you look like the first mate."

Phylis smiled and saluted, "Aye aye, cap'n!"

Mike reached out to help her step over the safety lines into the cockpit.

"Easy does it," he said, grasping her thin waist and lifting her light frame gently on board.

Mike proceeded to give her a quick familiarization with the boat and then cast off the bow and stern lines. Thereafter he started the outboard engine, and motored away from the dock into the boat channel. Phylis stored her gear and some sandwiches she made below deck, finding the interior accommodations somewhat cramped and confining.

Outside, Mike explained the working of the various boat sheets (lines) since Phylis had never been on a sailboat before.

She felt compelled to speak, uncomfortable in her ignorance of these things. "My husband once had a powerboat for a few years, but it became a real bore. He' would load it with gas and liquor, drive too fast, and then anchor in some inlet with his friends. They would carry on for hours getting drunk, play cards, and I would get sunburned.

"Yeah, I know the type, Phylis," Mike nodded. "For them, being on the water is just another excuse to eat and booze. The sea is just like a giant watery parking lot, where you can drive aimlessly in any direction."

They exited the channel into the open sound. At the tiller, Mike had Phylis turn into the wind as he hoisted the jib and then the mainsail. Then he walked to the stern, shut the outboard off, and tilted it up out of the water.

He rejoined her in the cockpit and showed her how to come off the wind to fill the sails, giving a casual warning to her about the swinging boom overhead. The boat suddenly healed as it bit into the wind. Phylis, at the tiller, was initially startled, but pleasantly surprised by the sudden surge and the sharp spanking grip of the wind in the sails. She remarked, "Gee this is really nice. We're moving smoothly without that irritating roar of the engine anymore. "She relaxed and smiled. "I could really get used to this."

Sitting next to Mike at the tiller, he gave her a pleasant if not humorous sailing lesson. Phylis found his close proximity next to her stimulating, almost arousing. Occasionally, when his hand would adjust the sails, his arm would brush her side, and her skin would get tingly. His aftershave mixed with the fresh salt air and light perspiration and gave him a very appealing male scent.

Eventually, with the gentle rhythm of wind and motion, Phylis settled back against Mike. He kept one hand around her and one on the

145

tiller. They talked about their childhoods and what they dreamed about becoming when they grew up. And, how things turned out so different from their expectations. Mike's answer to that was typically simple. "We weren't born into wealth." He paused to gaze out over the sparkling water. "So, we become pawns of fate, our future modified by how much talent and guts we have to offset the disadvantage at birth."

Time passed easily as they slowly moved out into Long Island Sound. With a cool breeze in her hair, Phylis was hardly aware of the shoreline receding farther and farther behind. The boat seem to dance over the gentle waves. Mike would hold her in one arm until the regular interruption of changing tack, re-trimming sails, and moving to the opposite cockpit bench. To Phylis, sailing was anything but boring, and she enjoyed being held by his secure grasp. With the steady bobbing and rhythmic swaying of the boat, and Mike's grip, it almost felt, in a way, like they were dancing together.

Phylis continued her questioning. "You've been sailing long?"

"About 3 years", he answered as he stared ahead, "I was looking for some project I could do in solitude after my wife died. Sort of lose myself in it. So, I bought this used rig real cheap, and worked all winter restoring it. And... well, here we are."

Phylis turned to stare in his eyes. At times, she felt his mind was somewhere else. That he was carrying a burden untold. Maybe it was his wife's memory. Still, her intuitive nature guessed that although there was an undercurrent separating them, she was still interested in him. Enough to want to know what that secret might be and face it.

Mike interrupted her thoughts saying, "You know we could use more canvas on the jib. Make a bit more speed."

He'd now decided he was going to impress her with how fast he could make his boat go.

Mike instructed Phylis to turn into the wind effectively stopping the sailboat, and freeing the sails. Mike pulled the jib sheet loose from the winch as he stepped forward towards the bow to change sails. Phylis kept her eye on the tassels at the top of the mast. She had some difficulty keeping them pointing to the stern to maintain the heading into the wind.

Mike stowed the 100 Genoa and secured the much larger 150 Genoa to the forestay, returned to the mast halyard and hoisted the jib. Phylis admired how confidently he worked, how comfortable he was with anything he tried.

Above the din of flapping sails, Mike turned and yelled for her to grab the jib sheet (rope) and wrap it around the starboard winch. As he walked back to the cockpit along the gunwale, Phylis leaned across the tiller to reach the line.

The tiller all too easily slid away. The boat quickly came into the wind, and the flapping mainsail instantly filled with a snapping jerk as the full force of the wind pushed into it. Suddenly, it seemed as though all hell broke loose. The main boom swiftly whipped around to catch Mike unaware. It crashed into his forehead with a loud 'doink' sound, like an aluminum bat hitting a softball. The impact hurled him head first over the lifeline and into the sea. Phylis lost her footing and also fell backward in the cockpit as the boat heaved under the wind.

Pulling herself up to her knees, she gasped as she watched Mike disappear beneath the dark surface of the water, leaving only a circular trail of fine white bubbles on the aqua green surface from his splash. Her eyes searched alongside the stern, trying to find his form or some air bubbles to mark his position.

Suddenly alone in the drifting boat, the sea, it all changed from tranquil to onerous. She desperately scanned the horizon for help, looking for another boat... anybody. Everything was so far away. Few boaters were on the water this early in the spring season.

One minute this solitude on the sea was a delight. Now the isolation was downright frightening. In the excitement, she spotted a large sailboat a good distance away and waved Mike's jacket, but apparently it was to no avail.

By now, the untethered end of the jib sail spilled overboard into the sea. The main sail fluttered furiously overhead, its boom jittering to and fro. Thankfully, the boat was dead in the water.

The turbulent beating sound of the flapping mainsail, and rattling serenade of the halyards frantically beating on the mast only added to Phylis's mounting terror. She felt alone in a vessel that was suddenly very unfamiliar, maybe even hostile as far as she was concerned.

Initially, she feared for Mike's life. With the enveloping solitude and helplessness, she began to fear for her own life.

* * * * * * *

Mike awoke from the momentary blackness somewhere else. He was still woozy as he stared upward at the shaft of light that pierced the murky water. An object appeared to gently float across the tunnel of light. It began to tumble and descend ominously towards him. Still delusional, he recalled his hospital visit with Mary Lou, the girl that hung on the Lifespan fence. For a moment, he wondered if he was dead, and her premonition of his drowning was coming true.

Precious seconds seem to pass as minutes. His rattled thinking was not too keen at this point and he questioned himself, *Am I crossing over to the world of the dead?* Mike squinted his eyes as that object drew closer. He instinctively reached out to bat it away, only to realize that the ghostly

147

object turned out to be something far less than mystical.

It was his sneaker!

Instantaneously, with that realization, all his senses collapsed in on him, the head pain, the biting cold, the exploding feeling of his depleted lungs. He wasn't on some journey to Nirvana. *You stupid ass Santino*, was all he could think. *You're drowning!*

Instinctively, he scrambled for the rippling surface. Breaking through the turbulent waves, it felt like his lungs would leap out of his throat to engulf the cold air above. Quickly he turned to scan the horizon for his boat. It was a good 10 yards upwind, its stern towards him. He could make out Phylis scrambling on deck looking for him, and concern for her well-being soon outweighed his own shock and fatigue. Mustering all his remaining strength he began to yell and wave. Now, all he could think about was getting to his frightened friend.

Phylis finally sighted him bobbing between waves, and leaned on the stern. She strained to hear, but still could not quite make out what he was yelling in the distance.

Mike began to feel his hands and feet going numb in the 50 degree water. He struggled to swim. The pain in his head was excruciating, making him wonder why his limbs were so numb, but his head wasn't. A modified breast-stroke proved effective in keeping his tormented head consistently above the bitterly cold water.

Phylis found a life preserver and line on the cabin wall, As Mike's writhe figure slowly approached, she leaned over the stern pulpit to throw it towards him. Mike signaled for her to hold it until he was very near and then when he was closer, waved for her to toss it. At least she'd be throwing with the wind.

Despite her best efforts her toss only went out about 10 feet from the stern.

Mike was exhausted now, and barely reached the preserver. As he snagged it with one weary arm, Phylis grasped the lifeline and dragged him aft alongside the outboard where a stepladder was overhung. Mike was so weak and cold that his soaking body felt like it weighed a ton. Phylis clawed at his disheveled wet clothes to haul him in from the stern. Mike told her to stop wasting time and get a boat hook and gaff him in by the belt.

"What! Are you crazy?" she yelled, "You're not a fish!" and pulled with all her strength.

Finally, Mike rolled into the cockpit and flopped onto the floor like a hooked flounder. His complexion was blue and a large lump on his forehead was punctuated by a one-inch gash across it. Surprisingly, there was little blood. Apparently, the skin capillaries were constricted and cleansed by the frigid salty water.

Mike just layed there, exhausted by the ordeal, his numb fingers could not undo his drenched clothes. Phylis clambered below for towels, blankets, and the First Aid Kit. She quickly returned topside to remove his clothing down to his underwear.

Mike's own fear and panic subsided as he gave himself to her implicit expert care. Phylis's feminine voice and consoling manner had a soothing effect on him, as she methodically stripped his wet clothes. Even his pounding headache subsided somewhat.

For the moment, Phylis forgot her own fear and concentrated on Mike's condition. She dried his face, and dried and pressed the skin around his gash together. Then placed steri-strips across the cut to keep it closed. Finally, she wrapped his head in gauze to hold it all tight.

In the midst of all this excitement, she took a moment to observe the hair growing upwards from his groin to fan out across his stomach and chest. Soaked from the water, its form reminded her of a fern. She had not been with a man for a while, and she found it appealing to look at his firm and lightly haired body. Several scars were also evident on his legs, arms and abdomen. There were two curious looking marks on his right side. Two circular mottled areas about 1/2 inch in diameter and 2 inches apart. With a guy like this, she wondered if they were gunshot wounds.

Mike began to shiver uncontrollably, so Phylis leaned over him, her tank top bellowed out below her, revealing her breasts gently supported by a light pink lace bra. Mike could not resist staring at the lovely view. The light freckles on her chest disappeared into the smooth pale skin of her cleavage. It looked warm and inviting in there to him. Mike looked at her straight in the eyes, and drew her lips close to his. Phylis felt his admiring eyes and did not resist. She lay on top of him to give whatever warmth she could generate

They kissed lightly at first, then more passionately. The desperate situation on the boat faded into the background. It was an odd sensation for Phylis, his cold outer lips and warm moist tongue. It was also a surprise to feel the bulge of his manhood rising beneath her, as she straddled his still quaking body.

She pushed herself up slightly and giggled, "Michael! Shame on you! How can you think of that at a time like this?"

Mike didn't seem worried about their predicament. He pulled himself up by his elbows to brace his shoulders on the cabin wall and said, "Hey, I find you appealing, pointing toward his groin. So does Wild Willy there. In fact, I think he likes you a lot."

There came a shout that interrupted their little romantic interlude, "Hello! Can I be of assistance?"

Phylis quickly sprang to her feet, feeling somewhat embarrassed, with the front of her shirt and pants soaked in all the private places. An expensive looking 35-foot sailing ketch was coming alongside.

They had not seen her waving for help earlier, but even at long distance, the loose blowing sails were a dead giveaway of a boat in trouble. It just took a while to start their engine and slowly maneuver their way over.

The large ketch came alongside, slowing down under inboard power. Phylis tried to arrange her clothes, and yelled that her friend was injured. An older teenager jumped aboard. He helped Phylis get Mike below and wrapped in blankets. Then the teenager went forward on deck and slowly retrieved the jib from the water. Inside the cabin, Phylis made an icepack out of a hand towel and ice from their beer cooler.

Mike was not appreciative of being 'rescued' - not in the middle of kissing Phylis. He could have made love to her right on the spot. Once he had made it back to the boat, the issue of a safe return to harbor was never in doubt. In his mind, he could have eventually returned home by sail or outboard.

Phylis returned to the cockpit outside, and in a few minutes, the young boy had them under sail, heading back to the harbor. The boy's father followed in his ketch off the port side, sailing in tandem. The young man was very pleasant and sailed expertly. They talked quietly in the cockpit and Phylis relayed how the accident had happened when she lost control of the tiller, and how grateful she was for their rescue.

As they entered the harbor channel, Mike, still woozy, slowly rose from the cabin casting off his blanket. He was fatigued looking with damp disheveled hair. From below, he had heard Phylis laughing with the young man. The boy had that relaxed and charming air you inherit along with wealth. Mike resented this rich kid's intrusion into his time with Phylis. He' had seen these rich hot shots, cut and run over in the Middle East when things got dicey. Mike interrupted in a curt tone, "OK son, you can rejoin your father now. We can take it from here."

The young man was caught off guard and said politely, "It's no problem sir. We anchor here too. I can take you all the way in to your slip."

Phylis interrupted, "Michael, it's only a few more minutes. Stay down and rest!"

Mike remained standing, braced against the cabin door. His pride outweighing his good judgment or his appearance. Phylis admonished him, sensing some macho stuff going on here. "Sit down! There's nothing to prove here."

She placed her hands against Mike's chest. It seemed to have a calming effect on him, and finally, he sat down opposite them in the cockpit, morose, and holding the icepack to his head. A silent tension descended over the group, as they proceeded through the last section of the harbor channel. Phylis noticed that he was missing one sneaker, and queried, "Where's your other sneaker?"

Mike sarcastically replied, "At the bottom of Long Island Sound. Adding flippantly, it's a toxic dump site now."

Arriving at the dock, the kind young man tied Mike's boat to the slip. He had already dropped the sails, stowing the jib in the forward locker and lashed up the mainsail.

He offered Phylis a ride home. She appreciated the offer, and declined in order to take Mike to the hospital emergency room for stitches. Mike was still chaffing from having his romantic interlude with Phylis interrupted. Looking unappreciative and gave a flat sounding, "Thanks sonny."

Mike immediately went below in the cabin to change clothes and gather his things in silence. Meanwhile, Phylis thanked the young man and his father again, and apologized for Mike's rudeness. Phylis leaned into the cabin saying, "Michael, you could have sounded more appreciative. He was only trying to help."

Mike said nothing in reply, so Phylis reiterated, "You know, if we don't get stitches on that soon, it won't heal properly."

Mike replied in a curt tone, "Thank you, but I'll take care of myself." Then added, "This was supposed to be a day for just you and me."

Phylis at first didn't understand his hostility. She thought that maybe he was agitated from a concussion. Then it hit her. Why the change in mood? Why the hostility? She surmised, *He's actually jealous! He didn't like my talking to a younger man!*

A subdued Mike climbed out of the cabin and locked it up. Phylis was disappointed by his childish behavior and remarked, "You know Michael, you put my life at risk today, and I did damn good helping out on that boat. You have no right to treat me this way."

Mike's cold silence continued as they left the dock and made their way to the parking lot. He limped across the lot's pebbles on his only sneaker.

Phylis tried to assist him, but he brushed her away. She felt terrible. She finally felt herself starting to care for him. Finally building a relationship, making a connection. Now having to deal with this.

Looking at the large bloodstain soaking through his bandage, she tried again to show her genuine feminine concern. "Michael, at least let me redress the wound."

He waved her away. His childish pride was hurt.

Mike stopped at her car in the parking lot and stared intently. You could see the pain in his face, as he opened the door for her. Mike mellowed a bit. "I'm sorry. You see, I always get myself out of a jam. I would have gotten you home safely. We didn't need help from anybody."

Phylis almost cried, but managed to control her hurt. She sat silently in her car with watery eyes. Mike began to close the door and said, "Maybe I just care too much for you," and closed the door. She rolled down the window and shouted, "Go ahead and sulk Michael! You don't need a woman, you need a nanny!"

Reluctantly, she slowly drove away, glancing at Mike's image through the rear view mirror. In spite of her anger, she still felt sorry for him, bandaged head and all. She watched him gingerly limp half-barefoot across the parking lot to his own car. On the way home, she listened to the song 'Harden My Heart' on the car radio, and fought back the tears. She knew she had done her best, and Michael was being an ass and totally unfair.

"Michael, you stupid jerk!" she exclaimed out loud, pounding the steering wheel in frustration. Still, she worried about him like the caring woman she was. *Will he go to the hospital? Suppose he passes out in the car from a concussion?*

Her heart felt heavy, and she asked herself how he could make her feel so great one minute and so miserable the next? All within an hour!

On the other hand, she recalled that in all the tension in the cockpit, Mike never asked about, or blamed her for mishandling the tiller that sent him crashing overboard

When she got home, she wanted to call him. Her good sense made her stop. She went to sleep wondering why he seemed to push her away, and again questioned if their relationship had any future.

* * * * * *

Back at the harbor, Mike slumped into the seat of his Mustang, and quickly pulled away. The total exhaustion finally cooled him off. His Goodyear 'Gatorbacks' dug into the parking lot surface spraying pebbles to the rear. The pounding headache returned, and sore muscles ached as painful reminders of the day's events. He listened to a Mike and the Mechanics song on the radio entitled, 'All I Need Is a Miracle', and easily related to the verse;

> ...I thought I was being cool.
> Yeah, I thought I was being strong.
> But it's always the same old story.
> You never know what you got 'til it's gone...

Listening to the lyrics, it didn't take long to feel like a total idiot, and he surmised that he had a chance to have a wonderful woman for a friend and blew it. "JACKASS!" he growled out loud, and thought about how careless he had always been with Laura's feelings too. *Only then, I never had the chance to say I'm sorry when it mattered.*

Arriving home, his first goal was to take a hot shower and get rid of the wet chill he felt down to his core. His son Brian met him at the door, noted Mike's head wound and joked, "Whoa dad! You're dating one tough dudette."

Mike replied angrily, "That's the last time you call her that way! She's not one of your little tarts. This one's got class and a whole lot of courage to boot!"

"OK OK, dad," Brian answered defensively, "I didn't know you were serious about her."

Mike's stern gaze ended the conversation, and he retired to the bathroom. The hot shower made his head bleed more profusely so a quick decision about it became necessary when he towel dried himself.

After hearing their father's story, his sons offered to take him to the Emergency Room, but Mike was too bushed to drag himself to the hospital for the usual four-hour wait, so he dried off and put the towel around his waist. His sons, ever resourceful, were called in to assist in putting temporary stitches in his forehead to hold until Monday morning. Brian rummaged through the medicine cabinet for the Ambesol bottle, a topical pain reliever for gum sourness. Matthew found a curved needle in his mom's old sewing basket. Zoot, their dog, came in to lick up whatever hit the floor. It became a family effort!

They cleaned Mike's wound with peroxide, applied the anesthetic to the gash, and temporarily held the skin together with steri-strips. Then Mike sterilized some thread by wetting his fingers with alcohol and drew the thread between them. Using the bathroom mirror, he made two stitches about a quarter inch apart, and tied them with double knots. That seemed to stop the bleeding for now.

"What do you think guys?" Mike said with pride. "Is that stitching or what?"

The boys shared his feeling of accomplishment, and laughed.

Brian said, "Hey dad, you look like Frankenstein!"

Mike chased them out of the bathroom walking stiff-armed like a zombie still wearing a bath towel wrapped around his waist. Zoot barked excitedly until his keen nose detected the blood stained gauze in the waste basket. He couldn't resist pulling the debris out of the pail and spreading it on the floor for a really thorough sniff.

That night Mike debated calling Phylis to apologize for his poor display today, except he felt too foolish and embarrassed by his behavior already. He decided to wait until he thought of a way to do it without the risk of offending her again.

* * * * * *

At Church, the following morning Mike tried to collect his thoughts on how to handle Lifespan, and what his own moral obligation was to this whole fetus situation. Initially, what was a revenge campaign to get even for his demotion was evolving into something else. He wondered if it would have been smarter to just leave the whole thing alone for somebody more influential and powerful to take it on. But then, who in influence wasn't already in on all Lifespan therapeutics and corruption?

Mike missed his father's council at this point. Even having Laura around would help him sort this out and arrive at some course of action. He recalled his encounter with the kindly Father Tom at the fence demonstration at Lifespan a week earlier, and decided to arrange a visit to his parish at Infant Jesus.

During the mass, his daydreaming was interrupted by the priest's soliloquy. The Pastor spoke of Christ's healing and saving of souls, but that even Christ could not save everybody. The message was that even if you can only help one needy person out of many, it still counts in God's eyes.

The words made Mike think that maybe he couldn't change the past, the lives lost at Lifespan. Maybe he couldn't save all the fetal lives in the R&D Lab. But maybe, just maybe, he could save a few.

The wheels began to turn as Mike's next plan developed in his mind. Somehow the pent up stress from the past week abated... because now he had a developing plan!

At the conclusion of mass, Mike and his boys drove to the hospital Emergency Room. After waiting 3 hours, a Resident finally removed Mike's temporary stitches and added 4 new ones. While the doctor worked, Mike daydreamed about Mary Lou's dream premonition two weeks earlier. The one about his drowning. He wondered to himself if it was a coincidence, or did she really have a premonition that this would happen?

* * * * * *

They returned home and Mike finally telephoned Phylis. Initially, her tone did not sound too friendly - she hung up. In his shame, Mike debated within himself whether to even try to reverse the negative impression he' had thoughtlessly created - or even proceed with the relationship. Or just call it quits.

Unexpectedly, Phylis interrupted his thoughts with a concerned text: "Michael, I was worried about U last night. Did U take care of your head injury?"

He saw an opening, although a distant sounding one, and texted back: "Oh that. Yeah. I just got back from the hospital - 4 stitches,"

Phylis texted back and reprimanded him: U should of let me take U yesterday. U could have scaring." Then softened up a bit to text: "Did U have a concussion?"

154

Mike had her attention, and sensed a softening Phylis. He telephoned her again. This time she didn't hang up. Mike tried to sound as sincere as he could. "An inconsiderate dummy shouldn't make apologies over the phone.

There was an uncomfortable silence from Phylis while she was debating seeing him in person again. "Michael, that really was strike 3."

She let him wait.

The silence made Mike think he was loosing her. He spoke plaintively. "Hopefully we're talking about baseball here."

"I don't think so Michael." She answered with a smile he couldn't see.

Mike detected the subtle change in tone, which gave him hope. "Can I at least come over and argue with the umpire?"

Phylis relented with a witty remark. "OK, but no kicking dirt at the umpire's shoes, like the pros do." He had been a jerk at times…. but still a charming jerk.

"How about I pick you up in an hour? We'll take a walk in the Pond Park. If you don't want to see me after that, I'll be toast - disappear from your life."

Phylis hesitated while she deliberated some more. Her soft heart answered first. "OK but if I say that's it, then that's it."

Before she could change her mind, Mike quickly said, "See you in an hour." And hung up.

* * * * * *

Mike arrived at Phylis's in the late afternoon with two baby pink, long stem roses in hand.

Phylis answered the door, startled by his peace offering. "Two roses. Oh, how beautiful, Michael! Even a little 'babies breathe'."

Mike grinned from ear to ear thinking, *It's working!*

Then Phylis gave Mike a critical gaze asking, "So why only <u>two</u> roses?"

He smiled and replied, "Two dates and two screw ups!"

They left for an afternoon stroll in the park. It was late in the day and it seemed that they had the park to themselves. A pleasant orange sunlight sparkled through the tree-lined path, enhanced by a gentle summer breeze. They slowly walked side-by-side looking down, kicking an occasional stone.

Mike still had a large bandage on his head, which stirred compassion in Phylis again. Mike talked about his experiences flying Navy jets in the Middle East, and how that jaded his attitude towards politicians and military bureaucrats.

"We'd fly fighter cap over an attack package of Apache helicopters," he revealed, "And, when Iranian fighters approached at low level, they'd fire some rockets at our helicopters, and then cut and, run for the Iranian border. We would come down to attack, and they would be across the border before we could get to them. Couldn't touch them over there in Iran – you know, rules of engagement. We lost a few choppers, a few good men."

Phylis couldn't resist sarcastically interrupting, "You mean they actually let you fly an airplane!"

Mike smiled and said, "Actually the Navy didn't let me fly too long after that. But, that's another story. It could've been worse. If I went down over Iran, the State Department would've denied my existence, and I would still be rotting away over there as a POW."

"Any way," he added, "My flying career had an abrupt ending because I didn't play their game by the big brass's rules."

Much of Mike's later career was truncated by that same attitude.

"Now I'm doin' it to myself again at Lifespan," he added."Sometimes I think there's something wrong with me."

Phylis asked, "Why so?"

Mike laughed, "Because 9 times out of 10, nearly every senior executive or high level officer I ever worked for, was an incompetent asshole or a pathological liar! Can there be that many?"

Phylis nodded her head sympathetically. "I don't know Mike, but there must be a lot of 'em." Then humorously added, "We manage to fill the House of Representatives with a couple hundred every two years."

They laughed until Mike stopped along the tree-lined path and leaned his back against an oak tree. "That's why I never trust anybody with a badge, a title, or a uniform. I trust engineering. Technology is straight forward and mathematically predictable. It's not good, it's not evil - like fire. It depends on how you use it."

Phylis stood close, as Mike reached for her hand and drew her near. The setting sun's rays played though her auburn strands, as he stared into her bright green eyes. "I find it easy to talk to you," Mike confessed. "I'm so sorry. Except sorry is too short a word to describe how badly I treated you on so many levels. If I don't screw things up again, maybe we could even be good friends."

It was not exactly the romantic words she wanted to hear, or the soft kiss she would have allowed. Anyway, she felt she was finally getting him to open up and let her see his more serious side. It made her feel more comfortable and secure with him. Instinctively, she gently touched his bandaged forehead from the sailing accident, wanting to give feminine consolation. Somewhere under that bandage was probably a nice guy.

When Mike drove her home, it was a lovely pastel sunset. At her house, they slowly strolled down her cement walkway, and stopped to sit down on her front steps before saying goodbye. Phylis sat relaxed with her hands clasped between her knees

Mike felt a bit more confident now and cautiously sprang a question. "How'd ya like to go on that company sponsored spring dinner dance on the Circle Line boat?"

"Uh, with me of course," he added awkwardly.

"Well," she hesitated, "It certainly would be a more conventional date." Then added sarcastically, "And you won't be driving this boat. Right!"

Standing up to leave, Mike grinned and replied enthusiastically, "Great!" He reached out for her hand as she stood up to say goodbye. He was not feeling quite sure enough to try a kiss. Leaning towards her, he grinned mischievously and asked, "Want to know why I really got you two roses?"

Phylis was puzzled since he already answered that question earlier. She suspected he was up to something and warily asked, "OK. How come?"

"Yesterday, when you were kneeling over me on the boat. Your tank top dropped and revealed your breasts. I got one rose for each one of those puppies."

Phylis stood speechless, inadvertently looking down at her blouse. She didn't know whether to laugh or be offended, feeling a bit embarrassed by his directness. She took a playful swing at Mike, as he jumped backwards and quickly retreated down the walkway to his car.

As he backed out the driveway, she giggled and yelled, "Michael, you are incorrigible!"

Mike waved, threw a kiss, and sped down the block, disappearing around the corner. A pensive Phylis slowly meandered back up the stoop, *"No kiss goodbye? Puppies? How adolescent."*

CHAPTER 16
Plant paranoia

Mike returned to work with the optimistic feeling that his life was finally coming together. That his relationship with Phylis was something special - at least it lasted more than two dates. Moreover, he had managed to obtain her forgiveness and secure another date. Adding to his euphoria was his own decision to finally do something about his company's R&D mischief. Now the questions were how and when to do it.

However, before he did anything, it would certainly help to plant some more paranoia in the gullible minds of Lifespan corporate management. Create a smoke screen. Make them think some other company is after their precious trade secrets.

At lunch break he used his 'burner' cell phone to call his older brother Vincent.

Vincent was different than Mike, different in many ways. If fact they did not even physically resemble each other. Vince was a regional sales executive for a pharmaceutical company. Married and stable with two children, Vince was employed by the same company for more than twenty years - an achievement having less to do with doing a good job, than having lunch with his bosses on a regular basis. He was more sociable and charismatic than Mike, a major attribute in business, especially sales.

Vincent answered his office phone, not recognizing the number, to hear, "Hey Vin!"

Vincent shrugged to himself, *Oh no, it's little brother!*

Mike continued to speak through the silence at the other end. "I need to see you. Maybe ask a favor. Can we get together tonight after dinner?"

Vincent did not approve of Mike's cavalier ethic, and how it affected his own family's well being. Except it was still his brother, so he answered, "Okay Mikey. Do you need money or something?"

"Naw, just need you to make a sales call. You're good at that."

Vincent was puzzled, but he was content to wait and hear Mike's 'cockamamie' story later.

Mike hung up and popped the cell phone in his pocket, and exited his office, Nancy the department administrator inquired about his bandaged head wound. Mike answered with a smirk, "Cut it shaving."

"*On his forehead?*" she thought. "Yeah right." From the curt tone of the answer she knew enough not to pursue it any further.

****

Later, he went downstairs to the repair shop, where he came upon a faulty fetal processing cart from the R&D Lab. It was the same apparatus he had built and seen during his break-in of the lab - less the top fetal revival tube, and the missing bio-system. Mike glanced at the repair ticket. He called over his supervisor Phil. "Put it aside and we'll fix it later. It's a good excuse to order more spare parts."

Mike paused to ponder other possibilities. He could use that cart as an excuse to order more batteries for backup, and possibly cannibalize miscellaneous items off it. Joel had captured enough specs to duplicate the parts Mike did not build.

Phil responded, "Whatever." However, he paused noticing the

loose plastic tubing on top, and asked a potentially loaded question. "By the way, what do they use these connections on the top shelf for? Could help with the troubleshooting."

"Beats the hell outta me," he answered, adding humorously, "Maybe a new device to grow mushrooms."

Then it occurred to him that the PLC already had all the parameters to run the entire fetal cart programmed by the R&D scientists. Mike stopped Phil walking away. "Tell you what. Just check the PLC to make sure its working properly."

"OK boss."

I'll take care of ordering another set of spare parts," Mike assured him again..

* * * * * * *

Later, a quick trip down to Human Resources yielded two tickets for the company sponsored Managers boat ride this coming weekend. Mike was looking forward to a safer evening out on the water with Phylis.

Real romantic stuff; scotch, women and dancin', Mike inwardly reveled.

* * * * * * *

That night, using his own credit card and Amazon Prime account, Mike began to ordered parts to build a duplicate fetal revival cart in his basement. It amounted to over $15,000. Joel will have to give him any bio-equipment he missed.

Thereafter, he left and drove to his brother Vincent's house. Mike slowly explained the gruesome details of what he found in the Lifespan R&D lab, the living beings he seen so closely, the Lifespan secret plan called 'Greenhouse', and the strong reaction to the story by the Capitol Post

Vincent absorbed this incredible tale dumbfounded. As farfetched as it all sounded, he believed his brother. Mike was many things, but never a liar. All he could say was, "Well now I've heard everything. There's no limit to how low people can stoop to make a fast buck." Then he paused, "And that's a salesman speaking!"

The levity was welcome after Mike's somber story.

Vincent asked, "So what are you gonna do Mikey? This is big time stuff, powerful people. They'll put more than those stitches on your noggin'"

Mike sketched out his plan in the next 15 minutes. He still didn't have all the problem pieces solved. Complicating matters, there was a limited envelope before some of those very human fetuses expired. Mike felt it was time to get the paranoid Lifespan executives to focus on an outside competitor - deflect company suspicion after his break-in towards someone outside the company.

He asked Vincent to make a sales call on Joel Rosen's assistant department manager, Dr. Jeff Ellar. Jeff was a real company climber type, always waiting for that opportunity to get Dr. Rosen's job. Doing mostly nonproductive busy-work aimed solely at impressing top management. Never had an original thought. Never took any risks. He was the perfect errand boy to plant a seed at Lifespan.

Vincent went over to his rolodex file in the kitchen and rummaged through his business cards until he found a card from a Reichmans Microfilters executive he met at a medical products convention last year. They were a German company aggressively marketing in the U.S. Vincent could pretend to be their sales rep.

"This guy sells all kinds of filtering membranes," Vincent said. "I even have a bunch of product catalogs to go with it. Your Lifespan boy will be interested in a little sales call on this stuff."

Mike nodded, "Get him out to lunch and tell'em the story I gave you."

Vincent laughed and patted Mike's shoulder saying, "Mikey, I hope you know what you're doin."

Mike shook his brother's hand and smiled, "Well Vin, thanks. I'll leave it to you to write that answer on my tombstone!"

Vincent watched his brother drive away wondering if he had a death wish since Laura died. He shook his bowed head and thought, *But, then, he never did run with the pack.*

CHAPTER 17
keystrokes

By midweek Mike had arranged to meet Joel at lunch in the company cafeteria. It was a good place to look inconspicuous, and with all the employees busily going back and forth, their presence together would seem unremarkable.

Mike sensed Joel's anxiety. By this point, it seemed Joel wanted to get this all over with and continue on with his career. If his personal friends at the newspaper didn't want to touch this story, then neither did he. That would necessitate drawing Joel in a little at a time.

The time seemed right for Mike to pose an odd question. "If I could build one of those R&D fetal revival carts, is it possible to keep the fetus alive until full term?"

Joel frowned in response, as though the question was ridiculous. During his silence, as an inquisitive scientist, he paused to consider the unusual problem posed.

"Mike," he said half-mockingly, "First of all, nobody has tried to go full term... including Strauss. Second, you are going to need a lot of fresh blood in ever-increasing amounts to feed the fetus. Third, the PVC tube isn't big enough to hold a large placenta, let alone a full term baby's shear bulk."

Joel looked around the cafeteria, leaned forward, and spoke in a hushed tone, "And lastly, where the hell are you going to get the parts you need?"

Mike grinned, "I already ordered all the parts to build one in my basement. I just need you to figure out the parts for the bio interface."

Joel slid his chair back from the table. He had serious misgivings on what they had already done, and hissed, "Whoa! Count me out Mike. It's way too dangerous!"

Undeterred, Mike gestured with his palms held up, "Well, just look at the pictures and specs we got from the lab. Tell me what else I need to order for the lash-up. You know the bio-chem stuff. I also need to have instructions on how to operate and monitor things. That is all I ask. Call it consulting."

"We're on enough thin ice as it is; it's time to call it quits! Didn't you see how unhinged they got to our break in? I think some of your brains leaked out through those stitches on your forehead."

"Joel, you are a doctor. If you can't give me just a little more help, that baby is gonna die. It's still a patient."

Joel pondered the predicament and relented. "OK Mike. But that is the last of my involvement. I mean, even being seen with you could be dangerous."

Joel was not aware of just how dangerous.

Mike returned to his office realizing that Joel's brave words at the beginning of this affair were quickly losing their verve. If a return visit to the R&D lab was in Mike's plans, Joel sure was not going to be part of that. Still, he felt that it was still a worthwhile meeting. At least now, he would get past his mechanical and electrical limitations of the fetal cart design.

* * * * * * *

Arriving back at his office desk, Mike found a FedEx shipment on his desk. It was Strauss' new digital lock for the R&D lab.

"Oh shit", he hissed, "There goes my access to the R&D lab."

Mike's set of duplicate keys to the lab just became obsolete.
And, with that, his whole plan. He took out the lock's programming instructions to take home and read. Maybe figure out how to beat it. Then decided to take the whole box home too.

Before leaving he made a call on his 'burner' to the *Brooklyn Daily* newspaper, thinking, *maybe I'm going to need them at some point to blow the lid off.* He reached the science reporters desk, and asked what he had to do to have them print a story. The reporter asked about the subject matter, and Mike replied, "Bio-technology."

The reporter replied, "First we need a synopsis, then supporting studies that can be vetted, plus any graphic materials."

"And then what? An uncertain Mike said.

"Well call you."

Mike hung up thinking, *Not yet....No. Not yet.*

* * * * * * *

Mike returned home to find a box from Amazon by his front door. It was his drone controller ordered with free shipping. He tossed it aside upon entering the house concluding, *Can't do anything with that thing until the drones arrive.* A while later he sat down to peruse the more important digital lock manual at home, Mike's son Matthew came over to see what his father was up to. Matt was an amateur techi-phile, and enjoyed programming things. Mike explained that the device was a digital lock and surrendered the instructions for Matt to read.

He told Matt, "I need to be able to defeat this thing, pal."

"Why dad?" he asked.

"Because I have to do something illegal to save some lives."

Matt was confused, and said, "I don't get it dad. You have to break a law to save people? Sounds stupid!"

Mike was uncertain whether to tell Matt anything further. "Let's just say you have to trust me on this one."

"OK dad. But, if it's that important to you, let me play with that lock mechanism."

Mike handed the digital lock to him saying, "Have fun," as Matt wandered back to his own smartphone.

Mike sat in his chair debating when to tell Phylis about what was going to happen at Lifespan. His feeling at the moment was that she would dump him if she knew. No single-parent woman with a family to support is going to want to be near the kind of risk he's taking. He just didn't want to lose her, but it seemed the longer he waited, the harder it eventually was going to be to tell her. He put the decision off until after the company dinner dance, and settled in his favorite chair to peruse the job recruitment websites. Right now he could use someone trustworthy to commiserate with. His father and mother had gone to their rest, and his brother Vincent wouldn't be sympathetic. Soon the good Father Tom came to mind.

Mike's thoughts were interrupted when Matt returned about a half hour later with a smirk of accomplishment on his face. "Piece a cake, dad!"

"OK, whatta ya got?"

Matt bubbled with enthusiasm, "It's got several options for setting the eight register alphabetical security code - a single universal code, and a separate code for each individual person."

"Yeah, go on," Mike said dubiously.

"Well, if I sequence the personal code option up to the last code ID at position 128, I can put in an access code for you."

Mike stopped to absorb the possibilities, rubbing the stubble on his chin. "You know, I think there's only about twenty people that access that lab. They'll never manually toggle that option out to the 128th entry."

Matt agreed, "Yeah, it's a pain in the ass to sequence this thing out that far. You gotta hit the same two function key 128 times to get there." Then he paused a moment to add, "So, let me put in your eight character password, dad."

It came to Mike in an instant. "How about L-I-F-E-S-P-A-N ?"

Matt manipulated the keys for several minutes, then exclaimed, "You are all set!"

Mike carefully put all the lock assembly items into there original plastic bags, and re-taped it closed with clear packaging tape.

* * * * * * *

The next day, as Mike sifted through his budget reports at the office, a call came from Strauss' Admin. She wanted to know if Mike's department had received the new lock. Mike answered in the affirmative, that it came in late in the afternoon, and assured its delivery to R&D this morning. Someone else in Facilities would do the installation. Mike no longer supervised that department after his demotion

He hung up and thought, *Well, let's hope whoever sets it up doesn't find Matt's back door.*

Later, Mike called Father Tom on his 'burner' to get directions to his parish for a meeting after work. He had some conflicting viewpoints that needed answering. Mike remembered the kindly priest from the incident on the security fence some days ago. As his ambivalence about his employer changed to malevolence, he needed to confide in someone. The next call was to Phylis to confirm their Saturday night date, and make final arrangements. He was gratified to hear that her voice still had a congenial tone...or did he detect maybe even a little enthusiasm? Phylis was momentarily puzzled by the calling phone number, but dismissed it as unimportant – now thinking more about wardrobes.

CHAPTER 18
A tough question

Mike pressed the door buzzer to the old brick building at Infant Jesus rectory in Newark. From the seedy surrounding neighborhood, he could tell this was a poor parish. After a few moments a slight, elderly woman peered suspiciously through the stained leaded glass door. Mike stooped down to announce his appointment with Father Thomas. The old woman, slightly hunched, nodded her head in acknowledgement and slowly opened the heavy wooden entrance door. Mike stepped into the vestibule while the aged woman slowly shuffled away to fetch Father Tom.

Looking around at the old fashioned house proved fascinating in itself. Beautiful turn of the century furniture, old style carpet runners, and detailed wood moldings throughout. Mike mused, *Laura could've appreciated this place. It's a step back into the golden age.* While waiting, Mike toyed with the idea that maybe this was the priest to perform a future Baptism on an, as yet, unnamed Lifespan specimen.

The next moment, Father Tom came into the foyer and asked him to come forward and join him. Mike was surprised to see the priest in a sports shirt and slacks, and commented, "Father, you're out of uniform."

Father laughed and replied good naturedly, "I can put my collar on if you like."

The laughter broke down any awkwardness to their introduction, and they shook hands. The good Father invited Mike to follow him outside through the back door of the rectory. "It's a bit stuffy in here this evening," he said.

The double French glass door opened to a small confined courtyard with a brick patio, dominated from above by a huge weeping willow tree. From the girth of its trunk Mike guessed its age at probably over 100 years old. Its shallow roots heaved rows of brick pavers into gentle meandering ridges. Just past the edge of the tree's protective shade, was a small, well maintained garden of flowers and vegetables. Then beyond that, there were the backs of dingy two story apartments on both sides, with laundry lines criss-crossing between them.

The priest led Mike to some wicker chairs beneath the old tree and said, "I'm so glad you came back to see me again. Sit here my son and we can talk."

Father Tom was a retired missionary before taking a parish position - probably in his early seventies. His build was slightly plump, with receding gray hair and a pale likeable face, almost grandfatherly in effect. It was easy to be honest with him; there was nothing judgmental in his demeanor.

"Nice compact little space you've got here," Mike started, "like an oasis from the madness outside," then tactlessly he added, "Who's your landscaper?"

Father smiled tolerantly, "Between the other deacons and our lay volunteers we manage to maintain it ourselves. There is really very little money coming into this congregation, you know." The priest gently slapped Mike's leg. "Now enough of that. Tell me, how I can help you my son?"

Mike was almost embarrassed by his own words, and decided to start in with his reason for being there. He requested absolute confidentiality, like in the confessional, to which Father Tom tacitly nodded agreement. Over the next half-hour, he explained the research at Lifespan, his own grisly discoveries, and the difficulty in sorting it all out.

The good Father listened intently, occasionally shifting uncomfortably in his chair as Mike proceeded with the description of butchered specimens. Once he interrupted, clearly agitated, pronouncing, "Murder never prospers in a society." He then asked, "Do you know why?"

Mike shrugged his shoulders, assuming the question was rhetorical.

Father bowed his head, answering, "Because when it does prosper in that society, then none dare call it murder!"

Mike hesitated a moment not wanting to reveal his plans to break into Lifespan again.

Father interrupted Mike' thoughts, and simply asked, "What is it that you need to know my son?"

It wasn't the first question Mike expected, but he abruptly answered, "Well Father... when is a human life a human life?"

Then abruptly added, "I mean, you know, from conception on."

Father Tom hesitated a moment as he contemplated the question, then, with stiffened legs he carefully stood up, and invited Mike to walk down a garden path, saying, "I've thought about that question myself for a long time now. It's not an easy one to answer."

He stopped again for a minute to look Mike squarely in the eye with bushy lifted eyebrows, "The answer depends on your system of values. In a way, a life's relevance is based on the values you bring to it."

Mike gave him a puzzled look.

The kindly priest smiled and clarified himself. "Whether or not you really believe in things - like God ...in a spirituality."

They resumed their stroll into the narrow garden paths, surrounded by hundreds of beautiful flowers in an endless variety of color and shape. Father plucked one flower from its stem and examined it in his palm saying, "I believe that God is represented in all living things, no matter how simple. And his people are like these flowers. Some more brilliant than others. Some more abundant. Some last longer. Ultimately, they all die. And when they do, this is what remains."

Father Tom reached into the pistil of the flower he was holding and produced some seeds. "This is what's important to God. The continuation of His life's purpose. The flowers will always come and go. They are not the end of purpose, just the connection between the past and the future. In His grand scheme even our lives, important as they are, are just a tiny link in a grand plan stretching throughout the course of infinite time."

Mike enjoyed the symbolic eloquence of the parable but didn't quite grasp the message's applicability, so he politely said, "I still don't understand."

"In the Old Testament, we are told that man is created in the image and likeness of God," he answered. "Well now, I don't believe that literally... not after 3000 years of biblical rewrites by imperfect man. However, I do believe in it figuratively."

The priest walked a few steps more into the flower garden and turned around with his arms outstretched to the flowers surrounding him. "God created all this, and us, and even the little creatures we don't see here. Then, isn't it all his image and likeness?"

Mike noticed a tiny beetle at his feet, scurrying across the path, and, smiling, pointed to it. "Him too Father?"

"Yes, even the ugly ones," Father laughingly replied. "But, how much more important to God are we? And when does our soul come into being?"

In a more serious tone, the clerical answered his own rhetorical question again. "God doesn't ask the question of when a human it is or isn't a human life based on its physical condition at any given moment in development. If a human life exists, then by definition, His presence is in there already. And as a human life, our spirit, our soul, must be there from conception onward too. At that point, from His divine perspective, the question of humanity is moot."

The kindly priest touched Mike's shoulder adding, "You know, it's funny you bring that question up today. The other night I watched a documentary about human artificial insemination on one of those science channels. It was about a fertility lab."

Mike interjected, "I didn't think you guys would condone that stuff."

"That doesn't mean we ignore reality."

Then the priest voice became more animated. "The doctors had a bunch of female eggs arranged on a dish in a grid under a microscope. Then they released male sperm among them. And, as those little swimmers swirled around - a sperm would occasionally penetrate an egg."

Father Tom's face brightened as he continued. "Well, in that instant of fertilization each egg would emit a bright circular flash of light!" Mike didn't quite believe the good priest. "Maybe it was some fluke of the camera."

No. It happened as each egg was penetrated in sequence."

Caught off guard, Mike could only say, "electro-chemical reaction?"

"Perhaps," the priest replied. "As a man of faith, I can only believe it as the 'spark of life'. So, for me, that answers your question of when the Spirit enters a human life."

Mike finally understood and commiserated. "I started to feel the same way about life too Father. I mean if we really do have souls, then I guess they have to be there from the beginning." Mike shrugged his shoulders, "Or, when else would that moment happen?" Then, dejectedly, he looked down and added, "Though, your beliefs won't hold up outside of this courtyard... or in the real world court of law."

The good Father stooped over to pick up a broken rock. In an angry tone he said, "See. It's cold, unchanging, unfeeling - just a material thing. There's no spirit there. No life. No God. This is the only kind of judgment supercilious man, or his worldly court, is fit to make with certainty about life and non-life."

He dropped the rock to the ground and regarded its dusty impact in the dirt. "I tell you this. As long as we have no respect for a defenseless human being in a mother's womb, then all this talk of human rights in this country is hypocritical hogwash. A deception. A ruse. This world will always be morally bankrupt for it."

Mike added, "I guess they'll always be a difference between what we are…. and what we say we are."

They slowly walked back to the chairs under the weeping willow tree to sit down while Father continued, "I fear for the future of mankind. This decoupling business. Fetal reclamation. More fancy words for murder."

The now uncomfortable Mike said, "I know. It seems every time some government wants to kill a bunch of people on a grand scale, they invent an innocuous sounding word for it."

The elderly priest nodded and continued, "And extending lives indefinitely. It may be the end of the only justice in this world." He leaned towards Mike and touched his arm. "In fact, I'll tell you a little true story.

"Once, a rich man with terminal cancer came to me, having lived all his life a material agnostic. He offered to make a substantial contribution to the church as some way of buying his way into paradise." Father hesitated and smiled, "It's the only time I ever meet rich people. When they're too sick to enjoy materialist things. Then, they assume they can buy eternal salvation."

"What did you tell him?"

"I went back to the teachings of Christ. I told him to give all his wealth to the needy. Not an organized charity that will name a hospital wing after him. No, not that. He should try to spend his remaining days in anonymity, personally searching out hard working individuals or families, and relieving just one torment in their miserable lives."

"What did he do?"

Father looked down and shook his head in dismay, "He had his brain cryogenically frozen, and left the balance of his estate to his children. Who, incidentally, fought over it in court like cats and dogs."

He clasped his hands and looked up into the tree, saying with a sigh, "Well, Michael, you've given me much to think about. This Lifespan company has to be stopped. Eternal life untempered by spirituality will lead to hedonism in the extreme. I fear our amoral society is regressing into self-interest at its worst."

Mike interjected, "Yeah, I know Father. This emphasis on oneself has become a real modern virtue. It seems to have eclipsed the virtue of taking care of each other."

Father Tom sighed in resignation, "Lifespan's therapeutics are an invitation for the wealthy and powerful to use the poor and defenseless as fodder for their own life extensions. To witness us reaching that point, sometimes I think, maybe, I've spent a life just preaching to the choir." Mike felt a bit sullen from the priest's remarks, but confident in the clerical's trustworthiness. He decided to tell the priest the rest of his plans steal a living fetus. At the conclusion of his story, Mike asked a question that was unusual for him. Until now, he always knew what he had to do and that was all the justification he ever needed. This time, for some reason, he needed some reassurance on this one.

"Father, if I take that fetus will I be guilty of something? I mean, you know, legally, technically ...it is their property."

Father Tom regarded him with a soft smile, "Kidnapping?" Then leaned over to pat Mike's hand. "No my son. No company, or woman for that matter, has the right to own another human life. I thought we put that one to bed with the 13th Amendment on slavery. The defenseless unborn are the children of God. His gift of life to give. His gift of life to take away."

The old priest stood up slowly on his stiff creaking legs and said, "If you've searched your heart about it, and still believe in what you must do... go forward." He looked down at Mike with sad wrinkled eyes and put his pale dry hand on Mike's shoulder. "Besides, how can any man be guilty of sin for saving another innocent human life from certain death?"

Mike thanked the priest for his council. It felt good to have a sympathetic ear, although the pressure of doing something immediate about the situation of Lifespan still seemed to fall right back upon himself alone.

"One last request Father," Mike said as Father Tom nodded. "You do Baptisms?"

"It is the one Sacrament I enjoy sharing the most. Welcoming the newborn to Christ."

As the conversation concluded, Mike cautioned the priest to keep their discussion secret until the newspapers revealed the story.

Father Tom, escorted Mike back to the front door, and clasped Mike's hand with both of his in a warm handshake, saying, "Bless you my son. Be like Michael the Archangel in your courage and determination."

He put his hand on Mike's forearm, adding, "You'll sense God's presence at the time things turn against you and you're sure all is lost. When you think you're done for. He will be your inspiration to innovate a solution. That's how God has always worked - through people."

Then his visage saddened and the old priest changed subjects. "You know. I really don't believe in the old adage, that evil prospers when good men fail to act. Evil is a more demanding force than that. Evil is actually triumphant when good men aren't willing to die in the war against injustice. You look back in history, all the martyrs, all the soldiers. There will always be tombstones on the path from evil to human justice."

Then his face took on a strange ashen, remote look. The now sullen elderly priest hesitated and looked down saying, "And there are many open graves still left to be filled." In deep contemplation, as if distracted from some portentous thought, he turned away.

Mike walked down the steps to his car parked at the curb. He stopped and looked back at the old brick building bathed in the fading pastel orange sunset, watching the sun glint of the stained glass windows. Mike felt a bit spooked and wondered, *This tombstone stuff. Was he talking about him or me...or what?*

In the darkening dusk, he had this vague melancholy feeling that he wasn't going to see that priest again. The same ominous sensation he had when he saw his own sick father alive for the last time.

CHAPTER 19
Oh, those sneaky Germans

Vince Santino fulfilled his promise to his younger brother to pose as a Reichmann executive, and contacted Dr. Jeff Ellar, Joel Rosen's subordinate. Ostensibly, to sell him some Reichmen Corporation micro filters. After some difficulty he arranged an 11:30 AM appointment with the ambitious doctor. This would allow Vince to segue his visit into a luncheon meeting.

Vince showed up at Lifespan, catalogs in hand, and signed in at the front desk for a visitor's badge, using the business card of the German salesman. He noted the security guard stationed in the lobby and humorously asked him, "You guys doin' work for the Defense Department?"

The guard didn't smile.

An Admin came to the lobby to escort Vince inside to Dr. Ellar's office. They greeted in his office, and sat down by his desk, Vince did his salesman schtick to a mildly interested subject, who was looking at processing yield reports on his terminal monitor. Vince was hardly disturbed by the lack of attention; he'd sold to doctors before. So, he went right into the routine his brother Mike had instructed.

"You know doctor; our corporation is going to be your competition soon."

The statement caught the insensitive doctor's attention, and he abruptly looked up. "Really!"

"Yeah, they're tooling up back in Germany. Got a building in Munich and a dedicated lab facility bigger than this Lifespan operation you have here. No expense is being spared. Very hush-hush."

Vincent hesitated to gauge Ellar's interest, and decided to drop the hook by mentioning casually, "Yeah, they've got all the equipment and facilities, but now they need top notch staff. I heard the executive director's spot is still open."

Dr. Ellar became intrigued, finally ignoring his terminal screen, and began to bite at the bait. He asked, "What kind of background or experience are they looking for?"

Vincent delayed his answer to build up a little suspense, and then faked surprise.

"Geez, you know you're probably the exact guy they're looking for!"

Ellar was flattered, but only thought of saying, "Relocating to Germany, that's a big change."

Vincent slipped him the Reichmen Corporation vice president's business card and suggested, "Why don't we continue this discussion over lunch outside. We can talk more privately."

The doctor looked at the card, and realized Vince was an executive of Reichmens. With that added credibility, he stood up to put on his sports jacket, and told his Admin that they would be back after lunch.

Vincent continued to work on the doctor during the car ride, convincing him that Reichmen Corporation was really, seriously interested in him for a top-level position in the company.

Vincent took Ellar to the best restaurant around, the Hermitage. It was a mansion converted into small private dining rooms, each with its own fireplace. By the end of lunch Ellar was convinced that Reichmen Corporation had a serious job offer for him.

Vincent flattered him with comparisons to Dr. Strauss, and how Joel Rosen was probably holding him back from realizing his full potential. Apparently, all of Vincent's schmaltz worked, because Ellar wound up giving him a litany of demands including a 5 year contract, moving expenses, travel expenses once a month back to the U.S.A., a Mercedes sedan, stock options. You name it and Dr. Ellar asked for it.

Vincent took notes and began to enjoy this little game. The guy was getting more and more pumped up over this fictitious position. So he decided as an 'officer' of the company, to make Ellar a formal job offer, and grant his demands in principle.

The doctor's tone shifted from elation to trepidation.

"I, uh... I'll have to discuss this with my family before I, uh... can give you a definite answer on this."

Vincent sipped his Bloody Mary and replied seriously, "Well, of course. I understand totally. You talk it over at home and I'll call you next week for your decision. But, remember Reichmen has you at the top of their list of candidates. You can be top dog in that Munich facility."

During the ride back in the car, Dr. Ellar popped a question that Vincent wasn't prepared for. "This whole meeting seems so unusual. How come you didn't contact me through a head hunter?"

Vincent hesitated to answer. He thought Ellar's ego would blind him from asking that question. "Well, uh... actually, we did use an executive recruiter. He gave us three candidates from Lifespan; Dr. Strauss, Dr. Rosen, and yourself. We ruled out Strauss since he was a principal in the Lifespan Corporation. And Rosen seemed to lack the drive and ambition, and, as you know, is getting on in years."

Vincent decided to lay it on real thick now, "For what Reichmen needs in Munich you're considered the best candidate." Then Vincent smiled, "We needed a cover story to approach you in confidence to personally convince you to say yes!"

Ellar seemed impressed enough, and spent the rest of their ride back to Lifespan asking questions about the cost of living in Munich and income tax consequences of living overseas. Vince dropped him off back at Lifespan, and drove off premises and called Mike's burner phone to tell Mike his mission was accomplished.

Dr. Ellar returned to his office and immediately called his wife to try the offer out on her. She went through the roof. Told him he was crazy to go to Germany. Her grandparents barely escaped from there in 1938. I'd rather die than return to that country!" she shrieked

That was the end of that! Ellar backed off and returned to his work routine in the Processing Department. He never could handle his wife, being almost afraid of her. If he couldn't accept the position, maybe he could use this offer to his advantage at Lifespan. He was beginning to do just what Mike Santino anticipated.

Rather than inform his immediate supervisor, Ellar walked over to R&D to see Dr. Strauss. He would endear himself to Strauss by informing him that Reichmen Corporation just tried to recruit him, and that as a dedicated employee of Lifespan, he had flatly rejected the offer. In the end,

Strauss was grateful for his loyalty, and indicated he would pass this incident of competitive treachery up to top management. Lifespan was on notice that Reichmen was becoming a direct competitive threat. The seeds for more corporate paranoia were now planted.

* * * * * * * * *

After working hours, Mike was in his office inspecting the three new drones just delivered. These black quad rotor type copters were as sinister looking as sinister could get. They looked like spiders with 4 extended jointed legs and a video camera suspended from their belly. He pulled one out of its packaging and sat it down on his desk. Its extended legs folded slowly inward to squat on the desk top. "Spoooky!" Mike whispered to himself. *"Let's get this bad boy home."*

Later that evening, after dinner at home, Mike showed his boys the black drone from Lifespan. "Oh cool Dad!" Matt exclaimed. Brian jumped into the conversation with, "Can we try it out?" Mike turned over the instructions in the packing box with a warning not to damage the packaging, and fly it in the yard. Then he asked Matt to see if he could control it with the controller he purchased from Amazon, and tie the camera app into his smart phone. Mike left the room to quietly relax in the family room and watch TV.

Within 15 minutes, the drone silently flew a few inches in front of Mike's nose, its 4 black spindly legs hanging bent inward. "So, I guess you guys figured it out." he chuckled, while watching Matt maneuver the drone around the room with Mike's Amazon controller. His son manipulated the camera towards his father. Brian came over to show his father his face on the smart phone.

"So, how'd ya do it," Mike enquired.

Matt answered, "This is a high end drone, GPS, cameras, and all. Can fly preprogrammed flight paths, and it can service multiple controllers at the same time." Matt landed the black thing on Mike's lap, and showed him a button o the side of the body that you press to bind a transmitting controller to the unit's receiver. "So, you turn the drone on, press this button until it blinks," Matt explained, "And then turn on your controller's transmitter. It automatically binds it to the drone's receiver."

Mike was amazed at how easy it was done "Now he had to go back to Lifespan to bind his Amazon controller's transmitter to the other drone receivers in his office.

Mike asked, "Sounds easy. So how do 'I' fly one of these things?" What followed was a lengthy flying lesson in the family room. Mike's main interest though was being able to stop the drone in its tracks and hover in place."

Matt showed his father how to set auto-hover mode, and then release it from the controller. Fifteen minutes later Mike finally managed to fly it.

Brian whispered to Matt, "Some fighter pilot, huh."

CHAPTER 20
Rock the boat baby

Phylis brushed her hair back, as she sat in front of the bathroom vanity mirror debating whether she would wear it up. Her hands expertly gathered the auburn strands together and placed a large white silk bow behind.

Standing up in front of a full-length mirror, she used her hands to smooth out her dress from waist to hips. Viewing herself with her black formal dress and exposed bare shoulder lent a feeling of sensuality to the night. She had not been out in formal dress ware for ages. In the midst of her nervous anticipation, daughter Kristy barged in to announce the arrival of her grandparent babysitters.

Mike Santino was due in another 15 minutes, and her anxiety about their relationship was growing. Each new step she took with him meant leaving her secure and predictable past behind. Each new encounter was leading to an odd combination of romance and risk. Mike was a boyishly attractive male, but so far, he'd only managed to scare her half to death on their previous dates.

Conversely, when she was with him, there was also that assuring feeling of security from his very male presence. It was like the confidence one senses from walking a 120 pound German Shepherd on a short leash. At the same time, having the trepidation of loosing control of this bridled power, should that wild animal be unexpectedly provoked the wrong way.

Phylis stood up and smiled in front of the mirror, sliding her hands down her hips, smoothing any wrinkles. Smiling, she wondered about what kind of dog leash would go with her black outfit.

* * * * * * *

A little later, Mike arrived in his '65 Ford all polished and gleaming. After he briefly chatted with her grandparents, Phylis kissed the kids goodbye, and cheerfully added, "Don't wait up!"

Mike thought she looked stunning and said so.

The ride to the Circle Line Dock in Manhattan was uneventful. On arrival, they pulled into a reserved parking lot near the pier that was already just about full with cars. The sun had set and the tour boats were lit with party lights gleaming from the cabin above. Indirect lighting flushed down the sides of the boat's white hull so it had that elegant look of a cruise ship, only on a smaller scale.

As the crowd of Lifespan employee couples approached the gangways from all directions, excited chatter could be heard. All were definitely impressed by the boats. Phylis stopped to ask Mike, "which one is ours?"

"The bigger one. It's for managers and above."

At the gangway, Mike could not resist adding, "That makes it the ship of fools."

Phylis frowned and chided him. "Come on Michael. We're here to have a good time."

They boarded and followed directions below deck for the cocktail hour. Moving through the crowd, Mike seemed to know a lot more Lifespan people than Phylis.

Mike leaned over and explained, "When you're responsible for maintenance in a company, sooner or later something breaks down, and eventually you meet everybody." He grinned and added, "Then, sooner or later everyone has a complaint about how you fixed it."

Phylis eventually found Katie, escorted by some big dumbbell that looked like Joey Buttafucco. Apparently this guy owned a health gym his father had given him to mismanage. Phylis could tell Mike didn't like this character; the guy was rich by birth. He gave Phylis a gentle nudge to move on to another couple.

Mike was on the lookout for other Lifespan managers. He had another agenda to attend to. In each succeeding conversation, while Lifespan managers sang the praises of Lifespan Corporation, Mike would intone the same remark.

"I hear they're sellin' the company. Brewster and company are cashin' in the chips."

This stunned most listeners and Mike's remarks were met with a combination of annoyance and resentment. After all, the company had gone through such a great expense for this lavish dinner/dance. They'd never sell this wonderful family-oriented company!

After two or three of these conversations, Phylis became concerned, finally pulling Mike aside.

"What are you doing Michael? This is hardly the time or the place to spread rumors."

Mike smiled and patted her hand. "I'm just stirring the pot, hon. I happen to know that they suspended ETC's (Estimates to Complete) this quarter on all budgets in-house."

Phylis frowned, "I don't get it. What does that have to do with anything?"

Mike replied, "ETC's are financial budget analyses. When you sell a corporation, you're legally obligated to disclose the true financial condition of the company at the time of sale... to the best of your knowledge of course. If there's no recent financial information in writing, the executives can lie their asses off. Overstate sales, understate costs and liabilities, and then jack up the company selling price."

She smiled, "Sounds a lot like what they call plausible denial."

Mike put his large hand over her graceful bare shoulder and asked quizzically, "Were you ever a politician?"

They laughed and felt the engines stir below decks signaling departure. For a better view, he invited Phylis topside. They made there way on deck to the outside railing that overlooked the dock. The boat was able to do its own maneuvering using side thrusters, fore and aft. Engineer that he was, Mike leaned over the railing to observe the foaming action in the water below. Phylis yelled 'Watch out!' at Mike, as his glass of scotch and soda spilled its ice cubes and contents overboard.

Smiling, she shook her head and said, "Michael, you are an accident waiting to happen."

He looked back up, grinned, and casually leaned with his back against the railing. With elbows resting on the top rail, he said, may as well get rid of this too," and inconspicuously dropped the empty glass over his shoulder to the water below.

Phylis just shook her head.

Mike eased his now free arm around her as the boat glided away from the harbor. They stood at the railing with Mike cuddling her from behind, while he pointed out different points of interest among the glowing buildings in the distance. The water was fairly calm and the beautiful reflections of the skyscrapers glittered on the water in between ship and shore. Mike moved along side her to silently gaze at Phylis for a while, admiring the reflected points of light, as they seemed to dance in her eyes. The sparkling light even added a lustrous sheen to her black silk dress. It gave her such a radiance that he was compelled to whisper, "Jewel of the Nile," in her delicate ear.

Phylis giggled not quite understanding the reason for his comment. "Sounds better than 'Jewel of the Hudson River'," she kidded back.

He gently touched the side of her face with the back of his fingers and explained, "I've got too much callous on my fingers. Can't appreciate how smooth your skin is unless I use the back side of 'em now."

Phylis accepted his awkward admiration gracefully, and grasped his large hand from her face. She felt chilled by the evening breeze on the bow, so she moved his hand around her waist again, and they moved slowly back inside.

Later in the evening they sat for a buffet dinner with some of Phylis' department friends. Mike was not invited to sit at the director's table after his demotion for obvious reasons. He noticed Dr. Jeff Ellar at the open bar and could not resist going over to antagonize him. Mike stood up, and asked if anyone needed a drink, then excused himself from the table.

He strolled up behind Ellar, saying hello, and engaged him in casual conversation. Mike eventually asked if he had his resume out looking for a job. The doctor was startled and thought defensively, *How would Santino know that he was being recruited by Reichmen?*

Jeff played dumb and asked, "I don't understand Mike. What do you mean?"

Mike looked around and stooped closer, whispering, "I heard a rumor that they're selling the company to the Germans, but first there's a big layoff coming."

Satisfied with his little needle, Mike picked up his drink and returned to his table to watch Ellar zip across the room and speak nervously to his wife.

While Phylis made conversation with the other couples at the table, Mike surveyed the crowded scene around him. He took particular note of the dais table on an elevated platform against the back wall. It was where the executives were prominently displayed for all to see. On a table below them was a large ice sculpture of each letter in the corporate name, LIFESPAN. Next to that was a smaller glistening orb of ice that looked like the corporate logo - the curious 'yin –yang' knockoff. Mike excused himself to go over and check it out more closely. Cocktail in hand, he slowly and discreetly approached. It became clear what it represented. Within it was a modernistic ice sculpture interpretation of a specimen in the womb. Several people nearby wondered how the sculptor managed to get one piece of ice inside the other, like a ship in a bottle. It did not seem to matter to anyone what was modeled inside.

For Mike it had a decidedly different effect. It reminded him of the horror secretly going on in R&D. Mike was miffed and looked sideways down the table where Sterno cans were keeping the food warm. He waited until no one was near and then he casually slid one Sterno, close to the ice sculpture. Innocently, he ambled away.

Just as he returned to his table, the younger John Lombardo, VP of Finance, was standing behind the seated Phylis, holding her seat back, leaning over her. Using his usual flattering spiel, he was complimenting her on how radiant she looked tonight, and her achievements in obtaining specimens. Her slender, graceful neck turned slightly to hear his voice.

Mike had no use for this guy. It was always just rumors until Mike drove by Lombardo's Subaru SUV parked at a local motel during lunch break. From his office window, he saw Lombardo return to his reserved

176

spot, and walk nonchalant, followed shortly by one of his 'hot'accountant girls.

Mike remained standing next to the smiling John, slowly brooding as John tried to charm Phylis, oblivious to the ominous man standing next to him. Mike held himself back waiting for Phylis to brush him off, until Lombardo placed his hand on her bare shoulder. Mike reacted immediately, and politely and calmly whispered, "I think your wife is looking for you John-boy"

John ignored the comment, and continued his dialogue with Phylis, while touching her shoulder. In an instant, Mike grabbed the offending hand and twisted it behind Lombardo's back. John grunted as Mike pulled John's other arm in a vice-like grip behind. Initially, this move was unnoticed by the other couples noisily chatting with each other at the table. Mike hissed menacingly into John's ear, "Why don't you take your wife on one of your lunch breaks at the motel?"

John's eyes raised in shock. He thought he had been so careful.

Phylis sensed the commotion behind, stood up, and threw her napkin on the table saying, "I think that's enough Michael!"

Mike released his grip immediately, as John loosened his tie, straighten his jacket, and wheezed, "Mister Brewster will hear of this Santino. Then we'll see what becomes of you."

"Why wait John-boy? Meet me on deck now, *stronzo*."

Phylis intervened, firmly placing her hand on Mike's arm, "Michael! I came here for a pleasant night out. Not for some macho-man exhibition. Enough!"

Lombardo back peddled away still straightening his tie. Looking back at a safe distance, he turned and crossed the dance floor back to the Executive table. Phylis looked at Mike with disgust.

He tried to explain, "He cheats on his family. Everybody knows it. If he's false to his family, he breaks the trust in his marriage. That makes him a deceitful liar. Besides, I didn't like the way he put his sticky fingers on your bare skin."

"If I felt offended, I would have removed his hand myself, thank you," she replied. "But that doesn't give you the right to start a fight."

"What fight? The guy drives a Subaru. Who buys a car that they advertise 'with love'? Phylis could not understand his rationalization that a car make reflected the character of the owner, and just gave up the discussion, "Can we just sit down now and salvage the rest of the evening?" The other seated employees went back to their chatter, occasionally looking her way. Phylis assumed their hushed conversation was about them. A few seat s away, Katie apparently enjoyed the spectacle, and gave her a smiling glance and a thumbs up.

Shortly, dinner was served, and the formalities of eating gave things a chance to settle down between the two of them. Later on, the DJ started the dance music with ' the classic swing song, *In the Mood*. Mike took off his jacket and asked her if she would dance with him. She hesitantly accepted, as he led her to the dance floor. In the crowd of dancers, Phylis twirled and spun following Mike's lead doing 'Swing'. After a while, as the dance floor became too crowded, he broke off that dance routine and started jumping around her in free style. She laughed as she tried to follow his steps, but for the most part, they changed at random. After a while, she could not tell what he was doing. Whatever it was, he managed to stay in rhythm with the music.

When the song was over, Mike was panting and returned to put his arm around her waist awaiting the next number. Between breaths, he told her he was sorry for the incident with Lombardo, for the profanity, and said, "I don't know. His hand on your bare shoulder...I overreacted...I understand you are not my property... I thought he was taking advantage."

Phylis's reaction was unreadable, because the incident reminded her of her own cheating husband, and that mollified her initial anger.

Mike was thirsty and returned to their dining table to gulp down the last of his scotch and soda. Phylis blandly accepted his apology, but deep down inside her the female instinct felt a little good too. After all, she actually had a man willing to fight for her honor. That was another thing that had never happened to her before.

For the rest of the evening Mike was a free spirit with the music and Phylis enjoyed his strong lead into Hustle moves'. Besides, she was having fun! By now, the incident with Lombardo was forgotten.

A few slow songs were sprinkled in between, allowing Mike to get some coffee and dilute the buzz from drinking. When they danced a slow *Rhumba*, he held her close and erect. There was a difference in style, not the traditionally stiff-back posture. His wide shoulders would dip slightly from side to side, a gentle motion that swayed her from the waist. It was a pleasant, added dimension to the slow dance rhythm.

When Phylis took a break for the ladies room, Mike headed for the men's room. Except he stopped to put a request in with the DJ. When Phylis returned, Mike greeted her and led her outside for fresh air on the dimly lit stern fantail deck.

While they stood alone under the starry night sky, Mike's song request was announced on the public address as a dedication to a Miz Phylis Daye. She was a bit shocked and embarrassed.

Mike said, "I thought if we were going to see more of each other, we should have our own song."

Phylis waited in delighted suspense to see what Mike chose for them.

Meanwhile, at the executive dias, Eve West heard the dedication and was upset that her date, Max, the goddamn boss of this whole fucking affair, didn't request anything special for her.

The beginning piano strings of '*Set the Night to Music*' started slowly followed by the vocals.

"How delightful Michael! I love Roberta Flack!" she said.

Mike put both his arms around her, and she felt completely enveloped in his strong embrace. By this point in the night Mike had lost the liquor buzz.

Mike slowly danced and methodically maneuvered her along the deck to a more secluded spot near a large, 2-foot wide, white ventilation funnel curving vertically up and forward. He danced her behind it until they were in its dark shadow and out of everyone's sight.

Then he stopped dancing and pressed against her, gently pinning her back to the ship's warm ventilator. His hands drifted down her waist to her buttocks, drawing her so tight that even a tissue paper wouldn't fit between their bodies. He kissed her lips separately top and bottom. While the one hand held her tight, he ran his other hand along her side to a breast. His gentle caresses didn't manhandle her, so she really didn't feel the slightest need to stop him. Her lover appeared as a dark outline against the nighttime stars and city lights in the distance behind him.

The slow music continued in the background:
'With your heart beating next to mine,
Perfect love in perfect time.
Watch the world,... just drift away.'

Her hands traced the edges of his broad shoulders and toned biceps. His scent was a combination of liquor, sweat, and aftershave. The low rumble of the ship engines pulsated against her back, adding a complementary dimension to their contact beyond the music alone. Her heart stirred, and she almost felt like some romantic character in a movie.

Their song ended as the boat approached the dock, and an announcement on the loud speaker broke the romantic mood.

It was stated that there would be some speeches and award presentations by the company president, Max Brewster, before disembarking.

Phylis reluctantly let go of her partner's embrace, and the couple, now looking diffident, returned to the party. Mike stood at the cabin door behind Phylis with his arms loosely around her waist. Inside the lighted stateroom, Max stood at a podium up front, above the now indistinct lump of partially melted ice sculpture (complements of Santino's makeshift sterno burner).

Max started his speech as everyone quieted down. "My fellow employees. I want to congratulate your hard work and dedication to

Lifespan Corporation. It's what makes it possible to have a wonderful time like tonight. Then he paused for effect and said in a more solemn tone, "But, I have to say that some people among us are not as loyal and dedicated as others, and we must be ever vigilant against those who would undermine our progress."

The managers in the audience looked around in bewilderment at each other, not sure of Max's target or purpose.

Max continued after a pause. "I assure you, though, our company has tremendous leading edge scientific and engineering expertise in our industry. We are the pioneers. And our latest research activities will insure that we will maintain that competitive edge!

At this next pause, Max received a round of applause. Mike leaned against the side of Phylis' face and whispered, "We won't be getting any awards tonight. Let's blow this place and that blowhard. I want to be alone with you."

Phylis turned around and smiled saying, "Just let me get my bag."

It was 12 AM when they reached Mike's car in the parking lot, and Phylis felt free to stay out all night. Her children were safe at home with their grandparents sleeping overnight. Mike suggested they drive to his secluded sailboat in Northport Harbor on Long Island. Phylis recognized the implications of the invitation, except by now, caution was thrown to the wind.

On the way, Phylis passed the time leaning on Mike's shoulder with his arm around her in the front seat. They exchanged an occasional tender kiss, as 'oldies' Motown music played on the radio. Mike sang along with the Temptation's song, "The Way You Do the Things You Do", while Phylis giggled, "Not too bad for an engineer."

When they arrived at the deserted harbor, the dock was dimly lit, quiet and secluded. A cool low mist enveloped the silent, barely visible boats, as they left the car behind. If she were by herself she would have felt fear – but not tonight. Not with the promise of romance. Walking on the dock in the eerie stillness, she could hear her high heels click on the wood planking below her feet.

Reaching his boat, Mike jumped into the dark cockpit and connected a power line to the dockside electric.

Recalling last time on the boat, Phylis quipped kiddingly, "Watch you head this tme."

They laughed as he unlocked the cabin hatch and turned on a small light inside. The golden glow felt welcomed as it pushed back the surrounding darkness. Removing her high heels, Phylis stepped over the lifelines with his assistance and watched his simple but charming preparations below deck. Phylis leaned down, and carefully entered the cabin, sat down on the entrance ladder and quietly waited at the hatch opening. With her high heeled shoes dangling from her finger tips she continued to observe her man busily preparing the cabin for romance.

Mike was engrossed in his preparations, busily folding up the galley table, and turning down the main birth. Phylis smiled in amusement as he sprayed deodorizer in the tiny head and closed the door tightly. Extra cushions were brought in from the forward berth, and then all the loose items in the main cabin were thrown back into the bow compartment. Mike fluffed up the cushions, and pulled all the window curtains closed. Then he put a disk in the DVD player with some old soft romantic music by the Johnny Mathis. Finally, he turned to her with a sense of manly pride and bowed, saying in his best Parisian accent, "Voilá ! Madam, toot-suite, she is ready!"

Phylis could not resist making fun of him and said, "You'll never get a job house cleaning."

Continuing in his French accent he answered, "Oh! Allurs! Non, non madam. He held up his index finger for emphasis and teased, "Is zee womanz work – No?"

Phylis feigned a frown, then laughed, "Michael, you are definitely not domesticated."

He helped her down from the ladder and locked the cabin hatch behind. Out went the light. They were alone in the cramped quiet of his ship with just the hushed sounds of their own breathing and romantic music. Faint light filter through the window curtains from a dock light some distance away. Mike gently grasped her waist and drew her to him. In the dim golden light he leaned down to nibble on her bare shoulder, and tenderly kissed his way up her neck to her waiting lips. Phylis thought about the dark mist outside that now seemed to provide a perfect blanket of privacy for two hidden lovers. Mike slowly and methodically, worked her garments to the floor.

They made love quietly and passionately in a way neither had experienced in a long time. The solitude in the isolated and gently bobbing boat made it feel like they were the only two people left in the world.

Phylis observed Mike's kind eyes as he methodically explored every part of her soft yielding body with his mouth. It felt like he was devouring her with his senses, as if he were figuratively breathing each part of her essence into himself. She seemed to gush passion like succulent fruit, awakening erogenous zones long forgotten. Her body became a fountain of heated tropical moisture that enveloped her and her lover.

As the sensual climax ebbed somewhat, she felt a little self-conscious about her middle-aged wrinkles and tummy sag that were the ravages of time and child rearing. When Mike sensed any uneasiness, he would just look up into her eyes and smile. In a reassuring serious tone he whispered, "A thing of beauty is a joy forever." Then he grinned, straddling

181

her from above with his knees. In his best Negro accent, he said," And yo is one fine mama pojama!"

It made Phylis laugh out loud. Thereafter, she forgot any more inhibitions, and enjoyed the moment together. Though at one point, Phylis became aware of the boat rocking in rhythm with the motion of their lovemaking. She wondered how this might look to some stranger outside. She visualized the top of the mast swinging back and forth as if telegraphing their intimate rhythms to the world. She mentioned it to Mike. Confidently he replied, "No problem," and leaned over to the crank mechanism on the boat floor to lower the swing keel. Then he added, "That'll dampen this baby down a bit."

After a while, they lay nude next to each other, sweating, and exhausted. It seemed there were no mysteries between them. Phylis examined Mike's body and its numerous scars. She perused the wound on Mike's forehead recalling when Mike was knocked overboard. Looking further downward, she inquired, "OK my 'Used Male'. How'd you get this odd two- hole scar over here," pointing to his side.

Mike looked down at his old wound and said, "The old metal Football spikes, heel pair. Got stomped on, playing ball in my college days."

Phylis winced as she ran her finger tips over the roughed and mottled surface. "How painful."

Mike replied, "Not really. Believe it or not, you hardly feel this stuff in the heat of the game."

They chatted some more, interrupted by occasional kisses and gentle embraces. Mike held her hand to his face and kissed her soft palm. She starred at him in silence.

Phylis had a thousand questions for this man she hardly knew, but could hardly resist.

"What does this boat's name mean, *Mare Nostrum*?" she casually inquired.

"It's Latin for '*Our Sea*'", he responded. "It's what the ancient Romans named the Mediterranean. It's what I call Long Island Sound."

"So, now you own Long Island Sound?" she giggled.

"Actually no," he quipped, "only the parts that touch my boat."

* * * * * *

It was getting late when they decided to end the evening before the sun came up. They would require all day Sunday to recuperate before the work grind on Monday again. Mike drove her home around 4 AM. Phylis was now in the habit of sitting in the middle of the front bench seat of his car and snuggling against him. Mike drove relaxed on the empty roads,

182

with his left hand on the steering wheel and his right arm around Phylis.
Neither wore their seat belts anymore.

CHAPTER 21
Somebody is having a baby!

A sleepy Phylis awoke late the next morning with her hair undone, feeling fatigued and sore. Stretching her arms and legs under the sheets, it felt as though she'd made love to 15 men the night before. Braced against her side was the rolled up beach towel, that she used to create the impression of the missing partner in bed. As she daydreamed under the covers, she could sense her affections for Michael solidifying into that elusive quality of love - the deeper kind, more like devotion. The fact was, the feeling went beyond just the passion of the night before. It was that special closeness of two people that can make the most mundane of activities something wonderful. Like simply walking hand in hand, or gazing at a sunset together until twilight. Just like people described in the website postings she had ridiculed when she found Michaels.

Oh, there were times when Mike seemed inconsiderate or even indifferent. Except, when he stared into her eyes, she could feel him bonding her image to his heart. It felt good to be loved again too. Still, she had so many poor relationships with other men since her divorce that she was afraid to trust any man after just one night of lust. Phylis fluffed up one of her pillows, and wrapped her arms around it. She did not have to dream about being hugged back anymore. No longer needed a rolled up beach towel for company in bed.

* * * * * * *

Mike debated calling Phylis all morning, not knowing whether he should tell her about the R&D lab or not. A lovely woman like her deserved honesty - at a minimum. On the other hand, the revelation could cost him their relationship.

After more soul searching, he decided she had a right to know, and have a chance to protect herself and her job. If she called it quits after that, then maybe it wasn't meant to be anyway. He knew he had strong feelings for her, but he also was determined to see this R&D nightmare through, even if it cost the second love of a lifetime. That love required both truth and trust

* * * * * * *

Kristy answered the house phone that afternoon, and excitedly called her mother to announce Mike on the phone. Phylis grabbed the phone as Kristy giggled, "It's your 'boyyyyfriend'."

Mike relayed his sentiments of their night together and told her he had something secret to tell her about himself. He wanted to see her in person and be up-front about it.

Phylis slumped with disappointment, thinking that the 'morning after' brush-off' was coming, now that she already went to bed with him. She tried to protect her self-esteem with a question. "Mike, if you're married or there's some other woman, just tell me on the phone and that'll be it."

Mike laughed, "Oh, no. No, it's nothing like that. That's would be easy. Let me pick you up later and we'll take a walk on the beach. Then I'll explain."

Phylis was wary of Mike now. She couldn't tell if he was committed to their relationship or not. Or, what he was about with all this 'secret' stuff. Still, one more meeting was a small price to pay to find out.

* * * * * * *

An unusually subdued Mike picked her up around 6 PM and then drove them to the beach. He made mostly small talk about the Lifespan boat party the night before. Phylis did not detect any coldness, but she remained skeptical anyway. Mike took sly glimpses of her bare legs in shorts. Phylis noted his stares and concluded to herself, *Italian men being Italian.*

After parking the car, they made their way quietly to the water's edge. The couple removed their shoes and walked barefoot in the wet sand, just out of reach of the small breakers.

Mike looked down towards Phylis' ankles, and complimented her on having nicely formed ankles and feet, as a way to bridge an awkward moment.

Phylis chuckled sarcastically, "Is that supposed to charm a girl off her feet?"

At that moment Mike abruptly stopped to face her, dropped his shoes, and put his arms on her shoulders for emphasis. He said seriously, "Phylis, what would you think about a baby entering our lives?"

Phylis was dumbfounded and had some difficulty answering, finally just blurting out, "What the _?"

She brushed Mike's arms away and quickly rattled off her answer. "We aren't married...I hardly know you...We don't even live together...And, I'm too old for that stuff!"

Mike began to laugh, "Oh. No, no. That came out wrong. I meant

184

that I'm gonna have the baby."

Phylis' face twisted in confusion, squinting one eye.

Mike desperately tried to clarify himself, "Err.. I.. uh, mean somebody else's baby."

Phylis's heart sank as she said, "Another woman's???" and began to turn away from Mike.

Mike gently grabbed her arm, and tried to straighten out his explanation. "Well yeah, I mean no… not really"

Phylis was utterly confused and disappointed. This is what she always feared about men. She tugged at Mike's grasp, and teary-eyed said, "Just take me home."

Mike's hand slipped along her arm, and hung onto her hand, "No, no. It's not my baby we're talking about!" Geez, I should have thought this through a little better." He reached down to pick up a pretty colored seashell nearby and offered it to her as a peace offering. "Hear me out a minute!"

A disheartened Phylis accepted the peace offering and finally relented. Subdued, she waited to here Mike's story. It took over a half-hour to recount all the things that happened at Lifespan recently, and the revived fetuses he discovered in the R&D lab. During that time they slowly strolled a long way down the beach, their footsteps leaving a meandering path in the soft wet sand.

Phylis listened intently while staring down at her feet, occasionally asking a question to clarify a person or specimen involved. She was beginning to have this uncomfortable feeling of knowing that indirectly she was part of the tragic story being revealed. Worse yet, she recognized that some of those lab specimen numbers he mentioned were obtained by her. It was even more personally distressing that a newspaper knows about it, and might go public. *How does she face her family? Her children?*

Phylis tried to rationalize some justification for this and said, "What about all the people we save with our drugs? You stop Lifespan and they start dying."

Mike was unequivocal in his response. "I don't know any society where there is a justification to take a life to save a life."

"What life? How do you know what a specimen is in the womb...if anything?"

"I was there," Mike explained. "With a dozen lives I've seen what's 'in there' - know they have real life. You don't know. I saw it with my own eyes."

The conversation drifted off, while the two walked separately each trying to understand the implications of this tragic story. After a half-mile or so, twilight was upon them. It seemed appropriate to turn around and head back down the beach to the parking lot. The enveloping darkness turned the ocean into a more murky and ominous scene, a metaphor of Mike's story.

Phylis recalled Mike's earlier confused statements about having a baby and commented, "Well Michael, that's some depressing and scary story. Except, what does this have to do with me?"

Mike stopped walking, saying, "A relationship can't have secrets." He looked directly into Phylis' inquisitive eyes, and this one has to be a parting of the ways."

Phylis stood still. She could not believe she was hearing this and exclaimed, "But why? You already told me the secret, and I can live with it."

"Because of the next secret……. I'm going to steal a fetus and raise the kid in my basement."

Phylis was dumfounded. "Michael, you' can not be serious! What do you know about keeping a fetus alive?"

"I'm damn serious," he confidently replied, "and I have Joel Rosen to coach me on the bio-tech details."

Phylis, head down, just kept shaking her head sideways in a negative way. By now, they'd returned to the car, and Mike sat Phylis down in the front seat. He stood outside leaning on the open door and looked down saying, "Which leads us back to us."

Mike bent down and gently took her hand, caressing her fingers. "You mean a lot to me. I probably should have told you what I was doing sooner. I guess I just didn't want to lose you. In the beginning of this whole story, I thought other people were going to carry the ball." Mike shrugged his shoulders and looked off into the dark. "Now it's down to just'me and my conscience. But…."

"But what?"

Mike continued, "I can't put you and your children and your job at risk any more by associating with me. Maybe afterward. Later. After the smoke clears, we can try it again."

Phylis listened carefully while scanning his face and eyes for sincerity. She appreciated his concern, but felt he was being presumptuous about her feelings. She let him continue.

"Whenever this story eventually goes public, we could all loose our jobs. There's gonna be a lot of powerful and unhappy people. And if I get caught they'll be coming straight at me. So, I have to distance myself from anybody I care about."

Phylis pushed him away, and got out of the car She stood up to face Mike. "You know I haven't had much time to sort this out...everything you told me tonight. Still, I think it's my decision on how much risk I take." Then she smiled adding, "And judging by our first few dates I think I've proven I'm willing to take a lot of risks for somebody I really care about."

She placed her hand gently on his cheek, as she intently examined

186

his blue eyes. "I can't just forget about you until some undefined moment in time. You can't expect somebody to temporarily suspend their feelings to when it's more convenient." Smiling with her eyes becoming tearful, she said softly. "Michael, I think about you every time I'm alone now."

Gently but firmly she placed her soft hand behind Mike's neck and drew him to her. They kissed and hugged tenderly, alone in the dark vacant parking lot. For the moment caution took a back seat to emotion, as two people shared a small moment of affection under a starlit night.

On the drive home they didn't make much conversation, and Phylis used the time to emotionally cool off and weigh the situation. She didn't know what to do. She thought about trying to talk Mike out of his wild plans, and, by now, she knew how almost self-destructively relentless he could be. Then, for some reason, Maria Alvarez and her specimen came to mind. It finally dawned on her what Maria was trying to tell her weeks ago under anesthesia before her decoupling.

"Take care of my lamb," Phylis whispered into the dark silence of the car.

Mike, slightly startled, looked over at Phylis. "What Phyl?"

"Oh... nothing Michael. Just a stray thought," she replied. Unpleasant memories of that incident came back to her. The decoupling business did not feel right back then. She knew that woman should never have been involved in this whole decoupling business. Phylis knew that Maria might have kept that baby and loved it, if she didn't do such a hard sell job on her.

Phylis was beginning to feel that she owed this woman and her baby something. That since if that baby was still alive at Lifespan, she had an obligation now. A second chance to set things right. She made her decision as Mike pulled his car into her driveway and parked.

"Michael, I want to help," she said in resolute tone. "Whether we remain together or not, this situation is going to take its course, and you're going to go ahead, regardless. I know this sounds crazy, but I feel like you'll need protection and help, and I want to be that person that's there for you."

After such a short relationship, Mike did not think Phylis would crawl that far out on a limb for him. He had increasing respect for her character and intelligence, and realized how much she really cared for him. Much as he feared for her security, in his loneliness it was awful tempting to have her support.

He put his arm around her as they gazed out the windshield into the darkness. Then he kissed her tenderly on her cheek, and hugged her. He whispered in her silky ear, "OK, hon but I still want you to keep a low profile on this."

Phylis turned to face him and made a request. "When you go back to the R&D lab, I want you to try to save specimen UH0744. It really means something special to me."

"Why?"

Phylis hesitated for a moment, and cleared her throat. "Because I think I made a real mistake when I decoupled it from its mother," she answered regretfully.

"Oh," Mike said sympathetically, "I understand." After a pause, he changed the subject adding, "I will keep you in the loop at a distance. It's really up to just me and Joel."

They sat huddled in the car for a few more minutes until her daughter Kristy looked out from the lighted front window and noticed Mike's car in the driveway. Staring at her daughter's image, Phylis thought about what she would have missed, if, when she was pregnant with Kristy, someone had convinced her to decouple her own daughter back then. She hesitated to think about how easily she gave up her own specimen to Lifespan so many years ago.

"Time to say goodnight, Michael," Phylis sadly announced.

"Yeah, I know," he answered regretfully. "And, I am so, so sorry for not telling you at the beginning." They separated and Mike sat back to stretch some stiffness from his limbs. He handed her another burner cell phone, saying," Use this from now on. Lifespan is bugging the phones"

A startled Phylis reacted, "Now this really is serious."

Leaning over they gently kissed one last time. Leaving his embrace, Mike watched Phylis' attractive silhouette until she reached the front door. Then, he backed up into the street, and waved goodbye. His tires gave a brief sharp chirp, like a gunshot in the night. It would remind Phylis of how, like a spent bullet, some decisions could become so irreversible.

CHAPTER 22
Scouting the opposition

Mike went home to sketch out the plan. It had to address four major areas of concern. First, planting a number of misleading clues to put the dopey security people on the wrong track. Second, arrange a foolproof method of entering and escaping the Lifespan compound with a live fetus. Third, equipment to keep the fetus alive and sustain it for the next several weeks. Fourth, a team of people who could be trusted to execute the plan.

* * * * * * *

Early the next day Mike returned to work at 7AM, long before the 8

AM employee start time. He entered his office with the drone and controller in a large plastic shopping bag. He turned the other drones on one by one to bind his Amazon controller transmitter to each of them. He carefully replaced each drone with its own controller into its original packaging. At 8 AM he told his administrator that he was driving across the parking lot to delivering some equipment over to the Security department.

Mike pulled up to the corporate building, entered the main entrance, showed his badge to the guard, and let him inspect the box with the drones. Then he proceeded to the Security Office containing all the CCTV monitoring equipment. Buzzing through the locked door, he was immediately greeted by Security Director Jane Savage.

"OK Santino, whatta ya got in the box?"

Mike tilted the open box towards her. Jane's face lit up with a smile, then turned sour when her gaze returned to Mike. "It's about time," she scoffed, and ordered an underling to take the box.

Mike took the opportunity to stall the conversation while perusing the monitoring screens. It seems all the building security cameras were pointed in a fixed direction especially the one at the back of the R&D building. "Nice setup you got here, Janie."

She took a step back, spread her legs slightly, and took what Mike jokingly called 'her combat stance' with him "Don't you have some engineering work to do?" she demanded.

Mike stalled a few seconds to scan the monitors again, "I take it that was a thank you?" he replied.

"The exit door is over there," Jane replied, pointing to the entrance door.

"Prego," Mike said in Italian, and then pivoted out the door, thinking, *Mission accomplished.*

* * * * * * * *

By noontime it was time to do a little scouting mission. He took a luncheon stroll around the R&D building following the cement pathway that surrounded each building. He noted that the back of every building was finished in Cinder blocks – no windows. He remembered it was for insulation reasons, and to hide the cremation activity. He stopped briefly, remaining unobserved, underneath the fixed cameras at each corner, all pointing towards the perimeter security fence. He checked the main gate guard shack around the corner to insure he could not be observed from there.

Continuing to look like a casual stroll, he reached the back of the building containing the small loading dock. There was one security camera pointing downward towards the dock and the two company panel trucks parked there. As a one time Facility manager, he knew where all the ladders and maintenance tools were in this building He rummaged through a closet and found a 5-foot step-ladder and screw driver. Underneath the loading dock camera, and out of view, he adjusted CCTV camera to point farther afield for his future shenanigans.

Returning to his own office, another purchase order for PRCB blood was on his desk. This time he had called up the blood bank vendor and negotiated to get some free units beyond what was requested by Strauss's purchase order. *Gonna need these extras later for my basement.*

Later, after working hours, Mike rolled an equipment cart over to the R&D lab, and made his way upstairs to the Lab. The new digital lock was installed, and the security guards had returned to their normal posts. Mike felt safe to enter the area again. He strolled around the outside offices with his cart to make sure anybody working late wouldn't observe him. One technician remained, who Mike greeted, and made some small talk before he left. With the technician's departure, Mike returned the door lock. It was time to see if his son Matthew's hacking job on the lock was still there.

He nervously looked up and down the cubicles again to make sure the coast remained clear. Slowly he re-entered his ID and then the eight character password, L-I-F-E-S-P-A-N. The green light came on immediately, and a turn on the door lever had it open.

Mike was debating whether to enter, when he heard footsteps down the hall. Gently, he clicked the door closed, wiped the handle, and moved on with his cart. It was a feeling of elation to know that he could get back into that lab. He had one less excuse not to go through with this. If fate allowed this fluke of luck to get back into the R&D room, then there was no turning back on what he had to do. No excuse of an insurmountable obstacle. The door for action was figuratively and underline literally/underline open.

Mike was returning to his office, but before heading back, he pilfered a few more blood PRCBs plasma bags from refrigerated storage to take home for his stockpile in the basement refrigerator Joel had told him it was going to take a lot of that stuff to keep a fetus alive for weeks. With the bags hidden in a cardboard box he left the building.

On the way home, he stopped at Home Depot for some metal 'S' hooks for his Sunday's night's caper. Once home he placed the blood pouches in his fridge, and had Brian drive him to a rental car lot. He picked up a grey 'plain Jane' Toyota Corolla, and drove it home behind Brian. His son was a bit perplexed by all this mystery.

Mike had been receiving parts piece by piece to build a life support cart. It was actually easy since he had all the schematics from his office. It was time to show his sons the fetal cart parts in the basement. They volunteered to do the build-up under instructions from their father. With their auto restoration work, they had already demonstrated their electromechanical skills to their father. He finished his directions, emphatically stating, "Absolutely…I mean absolutely, no one can know about this. No schoolmates, no relatives, no girlfriends No one down here except Dr. Rosen, Phylis and me."

He still needed to know how to connect all the tubes and connectors to the monitor the fetal blood chamber and support equipment.

The dialysis machine, and pulmonary oxygenator with interface parts were ordered from Joel's input, along with oxy tank and dialysate cartridges.

It was over $25,000. He had reached his credit card limit.

From here on in, things were going to get really hectic.

CHAPTER 23
Arborvitaes and 'S' hooks

The next morning Mike contacted Joel for another luncheon meeting, and this time they met away from Lifespan. Mike waited for Joel at the Blarney Stone bar and grill, and was encouraged that his friend had even agreed to come. Especially, considering his hostility at their last meeting, when Joel told him his plan was insane. However, since then, Joel did supply his list of the monitoring equipment and how to hook it up, which Mike ordered with Amazon Prime

Joel arrived and slipped into the booth where Mike was seated. In the next few minutes, the plan was described in more detail, once again indicating that he was adamant about stealing a fetus and keep it alive in his basement.

Joel sat back and reacted immediately, "You are one crazy son ova bitch! Even if this plan of yours works, the odds of success to bring the fetus to full gestation is maybe one in ten,"

Mike argued back, "Yeah. But so what? If I don't, the odds of anything surviving that lab are zero. I mean Lifespan, has been incinerating 20 to 24 week old fetuses for months." Then Mike shared the secret Carlos had revealed weeks before. Joel was noticeably moved, and became more attentive.

"And once I break this story," Mike heaved a sigh,"They'll kill off every shred of evidence immediately. Then, all that will be left are ashes in the incinerator, and some uncorroborated photographs sent in by some anonymous nobody."

Reflecting on Mike's words Joel recalled his conversation with Strauss about the fetal tissue coming into Joel's processing lab lately. "I confronted him about the mature nature of those body parts. He said it was a new process. So I asked about what studies were done. You know, clinical trials, quality parameters, FDA approvals."

"So, what did he say?"

"He just blew me off and said, "Continue processing the material." It made me realize that he was operating unchecked. No accountability. No professional scrutiny. Operating open loop. He has to be stopped."

Mike saw an opportunity to push Joel over the edge. "If we're able to keep one revived specimen alive, the world won't be able to forget his chicanery in a couple of days."

The clinical part of Joel's mind was piqued by Mike's last remark. He reasoned, "There's some real breakthrough science involved here... living preemies could be saved with much better outcomes."

"Damn right!" Mike exclaimed, "And, hey, maybe you could become the MD that did it."

Mike passed him a burner cell phone, saying, "Use this from now on."

"Man, Mike, you are serious."

"No, they're wire-tapping."

Mike was in high spirits with increasing confidence. He felt that with Joel's bio-technical help they could not fail. However, he still had not told Joel what else he would be required to do.

* * * * * * *

That evening Mike stayed late at Lifespan to begin laying the foundation for the outside break-in diversion. After dark, he walked furtively to the side of the deserted R&D building until he was under the side window of the second floor lab, out of view of the CCTV camera. No employees were in the building. He drove two holes into the soft moist garden bed mulch using a six-inch long 2x3 piece of wood. The holes were about 18 inches apart and parallel to the building wall, about 4 feet away to look like ladder imprints. He proceeded to trample the surrounding evergreen bushes, breaking several branches and leaving plenty of indistinct footprints in the mulch. When he finished, it looked like an army of people had been there with a ladder.

Suddenly, something dark caught his eye passing through the floodlights at the main gate entrance. "Oh shit!" Mike hissed out loud, as a drone began sweeping along the security fence. He shrunk back in amongst the bushes, noting the insectile hum as it cruised along the fence across from him. "Damn!" he whispered,"They got'em operational already."

With the bogus clues planted, Mike returned to the building front door and timed the passing of the drone at the front gate. Looking at his watch it looked like it took 3 minutes for the drone to sweep one circuit around the compound perimeter on a programmed GPS track. He crossed the parking lot to his office to pick up heavy-duty wire cutters and an adjustable clamp. He went downstairs to the rental car, and drove out the main gate. From the surrounding streets, outside the compound fence perimeter, he found a secluded spot along the chainlink fence. There was a spot where Lifespan planted dozens of 10-foot arborvitaes packed against each other to hide the crematorium beyond. Across the street were some warehouses that worked 9 to 5 during the day.

Carefully, with his lights extinguished, he backed his car up onto the grass lawn towards the bushes. Then he retraced the tire tracks back into the street, leaving nice discernible groves in the turf for the security people to discover. With the car parked, he took his briefcase of tools and drone controller, and squeezed between the bushes waiting for the drone to pass. It silently whizzed by and Mike checked his watch. *I got 3 minutes.*

He kneeled into the narrow space between the fence and the foliage. At a vertical support post he quickly installed 'S' hooks across the chain link starting about halfway up the post and downward every 6 inches to the ground. Checking his watch he slumped back into the foliage as the black drone buzzed past again. When the coast cleared he began using his wire cutters to methodically shear the chain links between the 'S' hooks. Each cut transferred the tension from the mesh to the hooks. After some more 'cat and mouse' games with the drone's passing he reached the bottom of the fence post. In about 20 minutes work, he had created a 4-foot seam, hidden from view by the fence post, closed by the 'S' hooks. Later this week, the S hooks could be easily removed to provide a quick entrance to Lifespan, and the exposed fence breach would eventually be another false clue for security to hang their hat on. Before leaving, he pulled out his Amazon drone controller to try one more thing. As the drone passed he commanded it to hover in place. It stopped and hummed in place, and then he let it continue.

Mike packed his tools in the dark, and cautiously peeked out from the bushes. Into the deserted street he moved swiftly, jumping back into his rental car. He sat for a moment, took a deep breath, and looked around one more time, and pulled slowly away. Farther down the block, he put his headlights back on.

He returned the Toyota rental car, and had Brian pick him up and take him home.

CHAPTER 24
The revival cart

The next morning Mike was down in his lab conversing with his model shop supervisor, Phil..

"How'd you make out with the PLC on that inoperative cart?" Mike inquired.

"Checked out OK," Phil said. "Problem is somewhere else. Phil was still curious and took advantage of a pause in the conversation and pointed to the empty top tray and loose tubes, asking again, "There could've been something else hooked into this thing. I could do a better job if I knew..."

Mike cut him off and with a smile and wav said, "Company proprietary." Then he bent down to look at the bottom tray, and quickly changed subjects. "Well, as long as we have it down here, R&D wants it upgraded with more holdup time." Pointing to the UPS (uninterruptible power supply) on the lower tray he asked, "Can you give me 5 hour's worth of hold-up power on the whole cart of equipment?"

"How many watts drawn?"

Mike answered. "400 watts average"

Phil rubbed his chin. "I see there's a 30 watt hot plate up top for heating something. Figure on 2000 watt-hours with 2500 for surge." He leaned down to inspect the space taken by the existing battery.

"Yeah, there's enough room down here if I replace the battery entirely."

Phil paused and frowned, "Can't they just use a long extension cord?"

Mike only gave a sly grin, and said, "Whatever soup R&D is cookin' in this cart, it's going to be moved between buildings back and forth for processing reasons. Whatever the chemistry inside, it could spoil if power drops out."

Mike was becoming adept at dealing in half-truths - the consummate liar.

Phil had some battery packs in stock that he could stitch together and give him 5 hours worth of back-up electricity and a 30-minute reserve cushion.

After a brief technical discussion, Mike curtly directed, "Do the mod, then and put it aside for now."

Phil, although perturbed, accepted his boss's unusually cryptic behavior, attributing it to some hush-hush, top-down corporate directive.

After working hours, Mike went down to the empty model shop, and plugged a programming connector into the fetal cart PLC. He ran a diagnostic program on a portable test set. After several test routines, it checked out fine. Fortunately, whatever changes made to run and monitor the biometrics would already be programmed in.

He removed it to install in his basement fetal cart build-up.

* * * * * * *

At home in the evening, Mike pulled up with a rented dark gray Ford Transit van with high roof- the one he would use to carry their cart and the fetus out of Lifespan.

He went down stairs to join his two sons who had finished the cart build. There had been some minor glitches, but it was a proven design, and problems easily resolved. He installed the stolen PLC, but could not run all its programs for the machine and dialysis unit without some fluid medium available up top. He called Joel on his burner phone to fill him in on there progress, and say they were ready.

He agreed to come over for the final stage. From what he had seen and studied in Lifespan R&D lab, he sized a small glass chamber to duplicate the space at the top of fetal tube above the placenta. It had the same sealed hoses and connectors as he had seen in the R&D lab. Everyone stared in tense anticipation after Joel arrived and filled the enclosure with the blood plasma Mike had stolen from R&D. With all the clear plastic tubes purged of air, and indicator lights green, it was time for the moment of truth.

The group gathered nervously around the cart as Mike connected regular AC power and flipped the power switch. With a whir and some bubble noises the unit, blood began to circulate through plastic tubes and Joel's glass chamber.

The elated group cheered and hugged, realizing that in a short time a living human being would benefit from their labor.

Joel hooked up a tablet with an app to the monitor, adjusting the parameters for temperature, pressure and flow rate. He made some adjustments to optimize flow.

"Hold on folks," Mike interrupted. "It has to run on battery Backup too."

The group turned silent and turned their attention to Mike, the atmosphere in the basement grew silently tense again. Mike had his back to the cart as he pulled the AC power cord.....Nothing changed. Within a millisecond delay, the cart continued to run from the UPS battery.

Mike said, "Voila!"

Brian exclaimed, "Whew! Kinda exciting to know a living thing is gonna benefit from what we built."

When Joel was ready to leave, Mike showed him the Transit van parked at the curb, and said, "One more thing."

Joel figured out what was coming and held his palms out, "No,No,No,No. I'm done here., Mike"

"Man Joel," Mike pleaded. "Imagine this. I manage to get out with the tube, and there's some difficulty. I don't know everything about making adjustments to the cart on the fly. You're the doctor. There could be changes since we last saw the fetus. The baby could die by the time I figure anything out. It's only going to have several minutes to live."

Joel was just staring down, hands in his pocket, and shaking his head in the negative.

Mike continued his plea. "All you have to do is stay in the van, wait until I return. You do not have to enter Lifespan. Just wait for me. Then I drop you at your car in the shopping center down the road. You go home. I go home."

Joel was still non-committal.

Mike added, "If you can't help then I'll have to ask Phylis."

"She's not a doctor."

"It's all I got, man."

Joel still wavered, and thought about the possibility of exogenesis –

Life outside the womb. Once this story broke in public, he could publish a number of papers in all the prestigious medical journals.

Mike pressed his argument. "Just give me 30 minutes. If I'm not out you drive away, and go back to your car.

Joel finally relented. "I hope we know what we're doing."

Later, he phoned Phylis on her burner phone to update her on their success. In spite of his confidence, Phylis was still apprehensive about Mike's safety, and the unknown consequences if he and Joel were caught. She was equally convinced that he would do this break-in with or without her. However, by her active involvement, she could stay close and look out for him part of the way on this caper.

"I may still need you at some point," he said

Undeniable now. It was all too apparent, that just seeing him again was becoming an end in itself. By this time, she was hopelessly captured by some kind of emotional gravity well called Michael Santino.

CHAPTER 25
Going down to the wire

Mike drove over to Joel's building to review the plan with Joel. Mike stepped into his office and enthusiastically said, "Come to a decision yet, pal?"

Joel was still uneasy and with a fretful look said, "I checked the R&D security guard schedule. He's out at 9 PM and back in at 7 AM"

"Good! Great!" Mike replied.

Joel just shook his head, "Man if my wife ever found out she'd kill me."

"I think she's the least of our worries."

Joel added, "Of course you realize Brewster and Strauss are gonna be pissed as hell when they see what we did."

With his usual crude humor, Mike said, "Yeah, so let them piss on each other's leg until their shoes fill up."

Joel did not smile at his pun, shaking his head. "A lot of stuff can still go wrong."

"That's why I need you, Doctor."

In spite of Joel's reservations, Mike was confident in his plan. Still gung-ho, because he was going to spite management. Right now, baby saving was a second priority. He drove back to his office to let his administrator, Nancy, know he was visiting a vendor tomorrow morning and would be back around noontime.

At workdays end he drove home, and got his two sons to side-load the heavy cart into his Transit van that night. With batteries, it was over 300 pounds.

* * * * * * *

Mike spent the evening explaining to his astonished sons what was about to happen. They sat outside together on the wood deck that Mike had built himself with their help. The boys were fascinated by his plan, and asked many questions, mostly about the fetus itself. They seemed more excited than anything else, and did not really sense the gravity or consequences of Mike's plans. He explained what their responsibilities would be to pitch in and maintain this living being in the basement. Regular daily maintenance that would occupy a lot of their time while he was at work. A lot of sacrifices would have to be made. In the end Matthew just wanted to know if their new guest was going to be a boy or a girl. Brian wanted to know whether they were going to keep the baby if it survived to full term.

Mike didn't have any answers to those possibilities yet. For now, he just instructed them to maintain absolute secrecy. No family, no friends were to know or see anything at all.

Phylis stopped by briefly to wish him success. She was still wary of leaving him alone. "Are you still sure you boys can handle this yourselves?"

Mike scratched his head. "As long as I still have you." Shortly, he led her back to her car in the driveway out front, and gave her a goodbye peck on the cheek as she sat inside. With the door still open, Phylis grabbed him by the collar and drew him inside. A startled Mike fell on the steering wheel and into her lap. Phylis grabbed him by the neck and drew him to her. She leaned down her lustrous hair blocking Mike's vision. He received a long, hard, passionate kiss.

Mike fell out of the car onto the grass. Phylis closed the car door and rolled down the window. "Now that's how you kiss a woman goodbye," she yelled.

As she slowly pulled away, she whispered a prayer. "God speed you, Michael Santino."

CHAPTER 26
Forever young

As instructed, a groggy-eyed Joel told his wife there was an emergency at the plant, and drove to Mike's house at 3 AM in the chilly, damp night air. His car lights partially illuminated the truck in the dark driveway. Mike was kneeling, dressed in a dark gray hoodie, doing something in the back of the van. Joel parked in the street, and walked up the driveway, speaking low, "Mike, what the hell are you up to?"

Without looking at him, Mike whispered, "Expired out-of-state commercial license plates."

"Where'd you get them?

"Junk yard in Newark - 100 bucks....just in case someone spots the van."

Mike finished and it was time to hit the road. Once inside the van, they gave the fetal cart a last checkout, including backup battery charge, and lie down straps.

"Kinda cramped in here Mike, Joel complained.

"Yeah, didn't realize how much space this cart would take up."

There was an unspoken air of urgent business, as they backed out of the driveway. In back, was Mike's old military duffel bag filled with every tool he could possibly need.

****

Phylis could not sleep. Although she wasn't actually going into Lifespan with the two of them, she did feel fear. She recalled Mike saying whatever happens, you are out of this. No matter what happens, you just show up at work like you usually do. When she arrives at work, she was to wait for his text code phrase that he and Joel were safe. The code phrase was, 'your library book is in', and she will know that they were home and the fetus was alive."

Still, it's not that easy to sit waiting on the sideline while someone you care about is in extreme danger. *How do I sleep? What am I supposed to think about all night? What to make for breakfast?*

****

At 4 AM Mike and Joel navigated the van through the industrial park avoiding the street in front of the main gate, arriving in the misty darkness at Lifespan Headquarters. Slowing down by the curb on the desolate side street, Mike dowsed the headlights, and moved forward enough for the arborvitae bushes to conceal them from the guard shack, CCTV, and drones.

Mike quipped from the passenger side, "Vell. Douctur, dis is dee place."

Joel had to admit that he had an odd way of relieving tension.

Mike grinned, as he rummaged through his duffel bag to retrieve some seeded bread sticks. "Want one?"

"Seriously now," Joel frowned, "how can you even think of food? My stomach is in knots."

Mike's tone became less frivolous, while he munched on his snack. "OK, let's talk serious stuff. "How much time do I have between disconnecting the fetus and getting it installed on our fetal cart?"

Joel answered dubiously. "Hard to say. The fetus has to be maintained at body temperature. That residual blood supply in the tube should sustain it for a while. Considering urea build up and oxygen deterioration, I'd guess 15 - 25 minutes."

"That's kind of tight."

"You could say that," Joel replied. "And that includes the time it takes us to reconnect it to our cart, hook up the tubes and monitoring equipment.

In the meantime, Mike managed to find some more de-stressing humor by smearing a wide line of blackface on the space over his upper lip and on then on his eyebrows. With a 4-inch long breadstick hanging out of his mouth, he turned to face Joel, who said, "Groucho Marx, right?"

Mike smiled. "You bet your life!"

Joel just shook his head. He could not believe he was mixed up with this harebrained engineer.

Mike continued to apply blackface on the rest of his face. He opened the door and glanced both ways to see if the coast was still clear. It did not lift Joel's confidence, when Mike managed to bang his head on the roof sill as he exited

"Owwww," he moaned and said, "I'll call you on the burner phone when I'm on my way back....ugh"

Joel was left to wait the tension-filled minutes, alone in the confining van, worried that some random police patrol car might pass by and look.

At 4:15AM, with his duffel bag in hand, Mike stooped and moved swiftly following the messy tire tracks he made on his last visit. He reached the evergreens and slipped through to the fence post dimly lit by parking lot lights 100 yards away. Crouching down, he located where the "S" hooks that were previously installed across the cut fence links. He pulled his compression tool from the duffel bag, and immediately stopped when he heard the whirring hum of an approaching drone. He disappeared into the darkness between the bushes.

When it passed, Mike moved quickly with methodical skill, putting the compression tool across the seam and compressing the chain links together. The loosened "S" fell to the ground as Mike collected them in his pocket. With the released tension of the last few hooks, the fence seam sprang open. Before the next drone pass, he peeled the chain link section towards him and to the side, leaving a 4-foot high triangular opening along the pole. He slipped through the opening, and folded it back in place. Using the compression tool, he reinstalled two S hooks to close the gap temporarily. It took about one minute.

Satisfied that the seam was not too noticeable in the dark, he left the compression tool in the high grass by the fence, and moved quickly to the shelter of the crematorium building. In less than a minute, Mike watched a drone move along the fence. "Man, that was close!" Mike sighed with relief

Fortunately, for him, the crematorium area in back was not lit for obvious reasons. That afforded the opportunity to run along the darkened walkway to the rear of the R&D building. With his dark hood over his head, he skirted the building sidewall, avoiding the rear security camera's view. The loading dock CCTV camera was still pointing beyond from the last time Mike was there. As expected the lazy, Security people had not gotten around to readjusting it. Standing beneath it, he put on his surgical gloves and fiddled with the duplicate keys until he found the one marked 'shipping and receiving' and opened the door. Huffing and puffing, he made his way upstairs to the R&D lab. Just a few ceiling lights were on to save energy and the office cubicles were dark and empty. He happily surmised, *still no CCTV. Love those pedantic consultant objections.*

Mike opened the outer office entrance door with his master key, and scanned the dimly lighted office areas to either side. He checked his watch, and saw that at a brisk walk, it took 7 minutes to get from the fence to the R&D lab. He quickly approached the digital lock to the fetal specimen lab hoping they did not do a reset that would regularly wipe out all the passwords.

Mike was very careful, and in spite of his large fingers, methodically punched in his password. He held his breath. Finally, after what seemed like eternity, it turned green and the LCD display spelled out 'AUTHORIZED". The door lock clicked opened. "BINGO!" Mike exclaimed, as he slipped in posthaste with the duffel bag.

The room was as dark and foreboding as the last time, with the only hint of activity coming from the whir of the mini dialysis and respirator pumps. The same air of detached evil still lingered. In the peripheral darkness, each red LED light was like the devil's eyes starring back at him.

His red flashlight skipped around the crowded room. "There must be two dozen carts in here now," he whispered to himself as he bumped into a cart.

Mike rapidly moved from cart to cart closely examining them for the specimen number Phylis had given him. He did not dare look inside at the fetuses themselves anymore – he had already seen enough of that. "There you are he said in a hushed tone, "Specimen UH0744 - the one Phylis wanted."

Mike approached the tube and opened the hatch to look inside. The fetus squirmed and eyes blinked in the bright light, and Mike whispered at the 8-inch long fetus, "Still alive. Jeez, you really managed to develop since we last met... and...and whoa, you're a girl!"

Mike closed the hatch, and moved over to the file cabinets to see if he could get any more data on the 'Greenhouse' project. "Geez," he hissed, "they moved a lot of file cabinets out of here. The rest have padlocks now."

Moving on, he still had some more bogus clues to leave, as he approached the outside windowpanes with his tool bag.

Mike took out a large crowbar out and engaged it to the latch mechanism. After a drone passed some 700 yards away, he gradually applied pressure until the latch popped with a sharp crack. The latch clanged to the floor, along with shards of glass from the bottom window frame. It was a better result than Mike he expected. This will reinforce the idea of an outside break-in.

As the cool humid night air drifted in, he kept watch for a drone, or any security guard reaction from the distant main gate that may have heard the noise. With the coast clear, he reached down into the duffel bag to retrieve a wood block, and leaned out the window opening to make several scratches on the outside wall below the sill about 18 inches apart. Combined with the two holes in the garden bed below, Lifespan security will be convinced a ladder was there, and the culprits broke in from outside.

Mike checked his watch and it was 4:35 already – time to get a move on. The first hint of dawn was an hour away. It was time to proceed with the most precarious step of exchanging the fetal tube between here and the van.

He returned to UH0744, keeping an eye on the fetal pulse monitor. It stayed around 130 to beats per minute - on the low side as Joel had predicted.

In any event, Mike shutdown the cart, and disconnected the blood supply tubes, clamping them off to preserve the fluid. Then, disconnected the single multi-pin electrical connector that ran the monitor and control PLC. He started the stopwatch timer function on his watch. From his duffle bag, he retrieved a large canvas firewood carrier with a layer of soft styrofoam padding, for insulation. With the canvas on the floor, he gently he lifted the plastic fetal cylinder, just barely feeling the weight of the bobbing individual within. Mike started his stopwatch while carefully positioning the tube on the canvas sling, he lifted it by the straps with the hatch facing up as Joel had instructed.

Mike left the lab with the duffle bag on his left shoulder, and the canvas carrier straps in his right hand. Stopping briefly with his foot in the doorway he looked back. It was one last look at the remaining fetal carts left behind, and caused him a pause to consider that in a few days all those fetuses would be dead. *All these souls*, he thought, *All their autobiographies, never to be written.*

Leaving all these lives behind to certain death, gave him a guilty feeling. Something akin to what the lone surviving soldier feels after a combat engagement where all his buddies die.

He hefted his duffle bag off his shoulder and sighed sadly, "Jesus, take them to your merciful heart," and made a sign of the cross with his free left hand. He called Joel on the burner phone to say he was on his way, and start the fetal cart in the van to pre-heat the tube cradle.

With the duffle bag back on his shoulder, he quickly exited the building. In the darkness, legs partially bent to relieve any bouncing motion on the canvas sling, he reached the perceived safety of the crematorium. His heart was pounding as he glanced down at his illuminated stopwatch. 8 minutes had passed.

Mike waited for the drone to pass on its regular journey, and stopped it with his remote as it passed by 50 yards away. He reached the perceived safety of the fence, picked up the compression tool and opened the fence. Making his way through on his knees, he slid the canvas bound tube onto the grass beyond. The forewarned Joel was waiting between the evergreens and retrieved the fetal tube. "OK Joel, take it while I tidy up the fence."

Mike slipped back trough the bushes, pulled his duffel bag through, and using his compression tool, put some S hooks back on the fence. Finally, he sent the drone on its way.

Inside the Transit van, Joel was already frantically making connections to the fetal tube now cradled on the top of the cart. With his flashlight darting around, Joel connected the tablet with the app to display vital signs. Immediately, the beep,beep,beep alarm sounded. A winded Mike opened the rear van doors just as Joel was shouting, "Heartbeat is down to 120 – blood pressure is dropping. Mike checked his watch – 15 minutes. Once inside, he gripped a flashlight in his teeth, and helped with purging the fluid tubes of any air with blood from a plasma bag. In the rush, some accidentally spilled on the floor of the van.

With all fluid connections made, the cart backup power was turned on, and all the support equipment whirred to life.

They nervously waited….Life or death?

Joel exclaimed, "Blood pressure is still dropping, pulse down to 100. They looked at each other puzzled, the cart system should be having an effect by now

A frantic Joel opened the hatch to physically check the fetus, and shouted, "The specimens entangled in its umbilical cord! You must have bounced it around too much." Joel had brought his own medical bag, and reached into it for a forceps. "Mike come over here and hold the hatch, and give me some light."

Working through the limitations of the access hatch, Joel managed to gently untangle the fetus, and prevent strangulation.

Mike checked the tablet display and enthusiastically shouted, "heartbeats climbing – 110…120…130…"

Both sweating, exhausted men rested their backs on the cold metal wall of the van. Mike wheezed, "That was close."

Joel answered, "Yeah. Give it 5 minutes to stabilize and we can make tracks out of here."

A quilted shipping blanket was placed over the cart, while Mike checked the cart tie-downs. He turned to Joel and smirked, "You know... depending on your beliefs... are we either kidnappers or just plain thieves?"

Mike drove the van slowly down the deserted road a bit and finally put his lights on. He turned onto the main drag that led to the to the empty shopping center parking lot, where Joel's car was parked.

Joel stopped as he exited the van and quipped, "Are you gonna wear that blackface all the way home?"

Mike laughed. In all the excitement, he forgot to remove it. He reached for a towel in his duffel bag.

****

Occasionally glancing in the rear view mirror to see if anyone was following, Mike solely rolled down the street, heading for the expressway and Long Island.

Now he knew that smug feeling that corporate executives have when they know something no one else knows. This time, He had the 'inside' information everyone else did not. Now the shoe was on the other foot. Now it was Mike's turn to play 'I've Got a Secret' with Lifespan corporate management

Turning on the Sirius radio, he flipped channels until he stumbled upon the 80s Rod Stewart song '*Forever Young*'. Turning up the volume, he felt good enough to sing along to his tiny human cargo behind.

'...May the good Lord be with you down every road you roam.

And sunshine and happiness surround you when you're far from home...'

Saving somebody's life proved to be an exhilarating high. He was saving a baby girl at that. Mike drove unusually cautious and slow, periodically adjusting the inside rearview mirror repeatedly to observe the blanket covered apparatus lashed to the inside wall. It was still amazing to think that a little human life was busy developing underneath, with no idea of what Mike was doing around it. Or how tenuous its existence had become.

Mike felt a joy like he had never felt before - something mysteriously wonderful. Something that transcends time and space. He thought to himself, *now I know how pregnant women feel.*

CHAPTER 27
Joy ride

Although Mike had driven with extra caution, the springy truck suspension seemed to translate even the slightest road imperfection into a bump. At times, with all the shakes and rattles, it felt like he was hauling a Conestoga wagon full of pots and pans across the Great Plains. Mike could only assume the little tyke in back was getting quite a jostling around. He tried to drive slowly, but he was also fighting time - time until the carryover batteries ran out. He had no idea just how much vibration his tiny cargo could handle, much less what its reaction to all this might be. For all he knew she might look like a fruit cocktail by the time he arrived home. Then there was that other possible umbilical cord strangulation possibility that played on his conscience.

* * * * * * *

The jolt from outside her tiny enclosure made Specimen UH0744 feel as though she was temporarily in free fall. The 21 week-old being would instinctively reach out with her hands, in the classic Moro response, a relic handed down from her early bipedal ancestors - the primitive reaction of grasping for the phantom tree limb.

However, in some respects the gentle bouncing was almost welcome. She never noticed the absence of rhythmic motion over the past weeks in Lifespan captivity. Strangely, the new sensation felt quite good, quite natural.

Then again, sometimes, the truck motion inside the confines of her tubular womb got downright violent, and caused her to begin swaying and rotating in a number of unwanted directions. And when the roller coaster effect became too much for her, she simply braced herself across the 4 inch inner diameter of the tube using her head and feet. With her back against the silicone gel bed, the stability of her liquid inner world was somewhat restored. In fact, she could almost enjoy the ride. When the swaying settled down, she began to suck her thumb to hasten that serene feeling of security. Specimen UH0744 eventually adapted to the road vibrations and continued to go about her own intrinsic business.

At this point in her development, most of the cortical neurons of her brain were already developed, but the critical interconnections were yet to be made. That would happen after birth. Right now, her brain was like a huge sponge tightly compressed inside a fist. Only after birth would a figurative hand open, releasing her mind to expand dramatically with axons, dendrites and synapses. These were the interconnections capable of absorbing the wonders of the outside world, transforming sight, sound and smell into mental webs of images, recording her life's events within the nebulous phenomena we call memory.

Basically, in her fluid world she went about very simple and predictable behavior. Mostly preoccupied with defining self, the beginnings of the human ego, determining where her body stops and the outside world begins. Often a touch of her hand to her face or a grasp of the pulsating umbilical cord would help in this orientation. Guidance in solving this puzzle would be limited by her own perspective and personal touch, until after birth, when her mother would provide the loving caress of a real human being.

Emotions were limited to irritation, pain, and tranquility. With poor eyesight and no sense of smell, her brain concentrated on the only senses usable in the womb; touch, sound, taste. Of course, breathing in the amniotic-like fluid added a bit of confusion to this whole defining and sorting process. *Was this fluid part of me or not part of me?* She might wonder. There definitely seem to be a relationship between urinating and the salty aftertaste she received.

However, from the standpoint of sound, there was still something missing in her prenatal surroundings, something that made her feel isolated. She could hear her own heartbeat, but no other. It made her more anxious than normal, but she could not reason why.

The daily superblood extractions by Lifespan had taken their toll on her minuscule body, and retarded her growth substantially. Still only about 5 inches long, her organs and physical features were now well developed, except her total weight was low. Normally, the remaining developmental challenge was simply to bulk up and grow for 16 more weeks. Except for specimen UH0744, her destiny was considerably more perilous. More like; was she actually going to live at all???

* * * * * * * *

At 7AM Mike called ahead to his boys waiting at home. He had them stay home from school to help unload the blanketed fetal cart and carry it downstairs. The hold-up batteries added an additional 75 pounds of weight to an already heavy load. His sons met him in the driveway, and the two unloaded the rolling cart from the panel truck. It became quite a cumbersome undertaking to keep it level while ascending into the house and then descending the stairs into the basement. Fortunately, the muscular Brian took the bottom lead position and they kept the precious cargo level. Both pestered their father to see what was inside.

Once downstairs, Mike grabbed an AC line cord to switch the electrical supply from battery to house current. Mike looked at the boys, and with a deep breath, he plugged it in. The power converter instantly switched over.

Mike plugged in the tablet to monitor all functions – thankfully no alarms. Mike opened the tube hatch to see a little being resting comfortably. He let the boys take a quick peep at their exquisite guest and buttoned up the hatch.

"Looks weird," Matt said.

"Hard to believe that's a little girl," Brian added.

"You'll see boys….when she grows up."

Mike turned his attention to briefing the boys on the care and feeding of their new friend. A small refrigerator nearby contained packed blood plasma bottles that Mike had been skimming from Lifespan, and would have to be consumed on an almost bi-daily basis. There was an oxygen bottle, and a dialystate tube that needed periodic recharge. The tube temperature had to stay at exactly 98.6 Fahrenheit.

At 8AM, with everything stabilized and reading to spec, Mike went upstairs with his burner phone to call Phylis at her office at Lifespan with the agreed upon cryptic message for success.

"Hello. Phylis Daye, please," he said dryly.

Phylis immediately recognized the voice, but stayed cool and answered, "Yes, this is she."

Mike continued in his monotone voice, "Good Morning. This is the Valley Stream library. The book you reserved is in, and we will hold it for you for 3 days."

She remembered Mike's warning on the phones being tapped, and fought to contain her excitement, replying casually, "Thank you very much" and hung up.

Phylis felt a combination of incredible relief followed by amazement, thinking, *Son of a gun! They really did pull it off!*

For her, it was the end of danger, not realizing that this adventure was not over, that it was really just beginning.

****

After breakfast, Mike cleaned the van, flushing out the spilled blood and dried out the floor with his leaf blower. He replaced the bogus license plates with the originals before returning it to the Rental company. From there, Brian drove him home, and by 10:30AM Mike was visiting a power supply vendor in New Jersey as part of his cover story.

****

On his way back to Lifespan, Mike called Joel at his Lifespan office on their burner phones to see how he was holding up. You could tell he was yawning, as he said he was doing all right, He had seen a flurry of corporate security activity upstairs early in the morning, but things were quieting down Mike briefed him on the basement setup of the fetal support equipment lash-up. A still apprehensive Joel agreed to be on call if any emergency arose, and to check on the fetus' health every few days. And with that medical care and attention, Specimen 0744 quickly went from 'specimen' to 'patient'.

Mike returned to his building before noon, and Nancy, his administrator, asked how his trip to the vendor went as Mike entered his office. "Good, "merrily answering. "There gonna replace the equipment under warranty."

"You missed some commotion over in the R&D building today. Some kind of burglary."

"Really? What did they steal?"

Nancy responded, "Don't really know. The Security people passed through all the buildings today."

"What'd they want here?"

"Just warning all employees to look out for any suspicious outsiders without badges."

"Oh well," Mike innocently replied. "If you see anybody suspicious let me know right away. Be safe. Don't approach them."

Nancy felt appreciative for his concern.

So far the ruse of an outside threat was working

CHAPTER 28
Surfin' and Sumo Wrestling

Kristy answered the house phone, yelling across the house, "Mom it's for you!" She couldn't miss the opportunity to tease her mother, saying, "It's that man again!"

Phylis walked briskly to take the phone as Kristy gave one of her knowing smiles. Mike sounded in high spirits and proudly exclaimed, "It's unbelievable! I really have this little human being alive in my basement. I want you to see her. She's perfectly formed... and healthy, so far."

Phylis hesitated, thinking that his enthusiasm sounded almost like a newborn's father. Except for her part, she had mixed emotions about facing this unseen and distant life. No doubt, she was happy about a life being saved, and there was still this nagging guilt to deal with. After all, she felt a part of the organizational machine that had extinguished that being's existence to begin with - and many more. And somewhere, out there, was the real mother, Maria, still far removed from her daughter.

After a pause, she answered his invitation, "Michael, I need more time. I don't know if I'm up to this."

Mike was too exuberant to detect her misgivings and said, "Hey, okay. You think about it. In the meantime, how about goin' to the beach with me on Sunday?"

"The beach?" she said with surprise. "Well, yes..I guess.'
Then added, "Uh, who's going to watch the baby...Er, I mean the fetus?"

"No problem," he replied, "It runs with a PLC (programmable logic controller) for baby sitting duty twenty-four seven. It monitors everything." Then he quickly added, "Pick you up at 9AM," and hung up before Phylis could say another word.

* * * * * * *

Sunday morning Phylis rushed around the house, looking for her one-piece bathing suit. It slowly occurred to her that the beach wasn't exactly the ideal place for a middle-aged woman to appear her most appealing. Her daughter, Kristy, acted as prospector and critic for the accessory items Phylis evaluated for her beach outfit.

Mike showed up in their driveway as Phylis was putting on eyeliner. Kristy came bounding in to announce, "Mom he's here ...and he has a surfboard on his roof!"

Phylis just groaned to herself, "Oh, no. What kind of beach are we going too?"

Grandpa, who was babysitter today, went outside to make small talk with Mike.

In a short while, Phylis came out of the house with a basket lunch and a folding chair. Mike walked up to her and kissed her affectionately, saying, "Hmm. Don't you look 25 years old!"

Phylis accepted the compliment with a gracious smile and said, "You know, I might've believed you, if you said, maybe, 35 years old."

Mike took the beach gear from her and loaded the trunk as she stared at the old beat up surfboard on the roof rack. It was obviously discolored where cracks in the fiberglass had allowed water to seep into the styrofoam underneath. The waxed side was filthy with embedded sand. Pointing to it, she asked, "How old is that thing?"

"About 40 years," he said.

Phylis just nodded acknowledgement, and waved goodbye to her kids and grandparents thinking, *What am I doing?*

On the ride to the beach, Mike was still as enthusiastic and animated as yesterday about his recovered fetus, talking about how well his sons were handling it. He was also worried about the possibility of some illness developing. After a while he finally talked about other things.

At the beach they parked in the lot, and carried their paraphernalia to the water's edge. Phylis looked around to see mostly teenagers and fairly young people scattered around on their blankets with surfboards nearby. For some reason she wound up carrying the lunch, blanket and chair, while Mike just carried his surfboard and walked up ahead.

Her senior surfer found a secluded spot away from the crowd and waited for a puffing Phylis to catch up. Then, he spread out the blanket, and put on an old Yankee hat and explaining, "Gotta keep the bald spot covered now." Then methodically he pulled up his 'shorty' wet suit, picked up his board, and pecked her on the cheek goodbye.

Phylis was abruptly left alone to get some sun and read a book she had the foresight to bring. Sitting down on her beach chair, she applied 50spf sun block and watched Michael paddle out through the breakers. Somehow, he managed to keep that cap on his head. Pivoting around, he took his place among the line of younger surfers in the deep water, and it appeared from his head and arm gestures that he already knew some of them.

When a wave set came, Mike would always wait for the others to take off in a crowd on the first two waves. He'd wait and ride the third one alone. Phylis found him to have a fairly graceful and easy riding style, something akin to a strong ballet dancer. So much different then the frenetic up and down zigzagging of his younger companions. She tried to watch him longer, but after a half-hour of squinting through sunglasses at the sparkling sea, she became a bit bored and opened her book. The sound of the surf, salt air, and cool breeze made for a relaxed reading atmosphere.

A while later, her meditation was suddenly interrupted by a sharp, crack-like sound that drew her attention immediately to the ocean. It was just in time to see two surfboards in the air come floating back down into the foamy remnants of a wave. Then two figures in black wetsuits surfaced from the froth and began walking towards the boards being carried up to the beach. Their arms were waving towards each other, apparently exchanging harsh words, while waist deep in water. Then Phylis realized one of those people was Mike. In no time, she jumped up from her blanket and ran down the beach to intervene.

Phylis charged into the foaming water just in time to hear Mike's insult, to the boy "You know with that feminine earring and pony tail, you look awful cute when you're angry. I don't know whether to spank you or kiss you."

She grabbed his arm from behind, and yelled, "Michael! Enough! This boy is just a young kid. Let's go back!" Standing knee deep in the surf, Mike turned his attention to the shoreline and his beached surfboard.

Suddenly, a large wave unexpectedly broke inshore behind them, and the foaming surge knocked them down, tossing them and his surfboard further up onto sand.

The young kids began to laugh among themselves, as the elder couple lay strewn on their behinds in the bubbling froth. Phylis was drenched head to toe, and felt a load of discomfiting sand in her bathing suit bottom as the water receded. In the receding foam, she looked down at herself and made a frowning grimace. "YUK!"

Mike picked her up, and retrieved his surfboard and his now soggy old Yankee hat. On their way back to the blanket, Phylis just stared at him in irritated amusement. "Michael, you are some date, getting baited by a kid. How'd you ever survive into your forties? "

"I guess there was always the right woman around to fish me out of trouble," he said sheepishly.

They grabbed towels, and Mike took off his wet suit. Settled down, Phylis unpacked lunch, and the pair sat cross-legged on the blanket facing each other. Phylis' hair hung in loose wet strings in front of her face and over her soft white cleavage.

"You look sexy like that," a satiated Mike said, with his mouth full of food.

She asked in frustration, "Michael, why is it, when I feel a mess, you think I'm attractive?"

"I dunno," he pointed as he chewed, "Maybe that's how I imagine you in the shower."

"Huh?"

With a crooked smile he said, "I'd love you wet or dry." Then added, "Look, I'm sorry for getting you soaked. Sometimes, I get in the middle of some stuff and I don't know when to quit." With a naughty grin he said, "How about coming to my place to shower and clean up?"

Phylis was wary of the hint and his twinkling eyes that accompanied the invitation. "OK, Michael. But no hanky-panky."

"Sure," he said all too agreeably, "No is no and yes is yes."

In a few minutes they packed up to return to his empty house. On the drive home, Mike appropriately played some *Beach Boys* music, and the gentle rhythm of *Warmth of the Sun* served to lend a healing atmosphere to the day's hectic events. Mike's boys were gone for a day of dirt biking. So, when they arrived at his plain 3-bedroom ranch, only Mike's dog, Zoot, greeted them with a wagging tail and a good sniff. Soon he was settled down, and curled in his favorite spot on the ceramic tiled foyer.

Mike guided her around his 'house of auto parts and surf boards' directing her to the bathroom and shower. On the way, Phylis looked around, and while passing the kitchen she noticed a large, outdoor trashcan holding one of those huge black leaf bags, and surmised to herself, *So this is how men store garbage when there's no woman to watch what they are doing.* While she showered, he went in the basement to check on the fetus 0744.

In a short time Phylis emerged from the shower, feeling refreshed and clean of all the sand and seaweed trapped in her bathing suit and hair. While she towel dried, Mike knocked on the door and peeked in with his eyes closed, purportedly to take his shower. Instead, he stopped and opened his blue eyes to study her body under the terrycloth. Phylis sensed that unmistakable look of desire and admiring lust as he approached her. In a moment ,Mike grasped her in his muscular arms and kissed her gently at first, then passionately. In no time, her arms returned his embrace and the bath towel slipped to the floor.

Somehow, their trip to the beach had now turned into a giddy shower together, and energetic lovemaking on the plush bathroom carpet afterwards. Mike seemed to roll all over the floor with her. First on top, then sideways, then on the bottom. Hands caressing and squeezing her everywhere. At one point a giggling Phylis asked, "Are we making love or Sumo wrestling?"

A half-hour later, Mike made fresh coffee. They sat together, on his wood deck behind the house eating crumb cake and chatting about the difficulties of single parenthood. Zoot laid down unobtrusively nearby, in hopeful anticipation of any discarded morsels. Phylis was relaxed with her hair in a towel. Eventually, Mike got around to asking her about going downstairs to visit the fetus.

"Seriously Michael, I still don't know if I'm ready for that."

Mike sensed her misgivings and walked around behind her chair, placing his hands on her bare shoulders. "You know, guilt is a tough thing to deal with by yourself. You're not alone on this one," he said sympathetically. "Remember, I was one of the 'bright boys' who built those fetal life support carts. I even designed and constructed those refrigerated fetal transport cases you procurement people use."

He gently messaged her neck, adding, "I have as much culpability in this tragedy as you." He leaned over and gently kissed her bare neck with warm lips. "So, take some guilt off your slender shoulders and put it on mine."

Phylis took his hand and looked up. "Thanks Michael, it's nice to have someone to confide in. You understand then?"

Mike moved a little closer, "Let me tell you a little story." He looked into her eyes and continued, "When Laura passed away, she made me promise to take the boys to church every Sunday ...me included. I never appreciated the significance of it until recently. Coincidently, it's the only time all week that I really spend any time examining my own conscience."

Phylis listened attentively, although not knowing where he was going with this.

Mike stared down at the deck and hesitated, still a little embarrassed about sounding religious, and sharing his inner most thoughts, and Phylis encouraged him to continue. So he added, "Well, I thought about what we'd been doing at Lifespan all these years, the thousands of fetuses we've taken, and remembered what Christ taught us about human imperfection. That it doesn't matter what mistakes you've made in your life. If you are truly sorry for them and straighten yourself out, God forgives."

Phylis nodded agreement, "As I recall he even forgave tax collectors." She quipped, "Now that's forgiveness!"

He smiled at her pun and looked back up at Phylis, "I think you see the same evil I see, and you want to set things right things. You still have a heart and a conscience."

Phylis stood and turned to caress his face with her long, smooth fingertips. She kissed him on his cheek, responding, "In spite of the short time we've been together, I think I know you Michael. You honestly believe in what you do. And I believe in you. Although, sometimes, the things you do scare the living hell out of me.

"I trust that you love me too, and that's what counts most for me. So, if you're committed to me, I'll face whatever we've done together, and help make it right."

Phylis looked skyward adding with a little misgiving, "Heaven knows what I'm getting into here."

Mike sealed their mutual empathy with a long gentle kiss.

* * * * * * * *

A while later, Mike led Phylis to the basement door, noting that he kept the lights off downstairs because of the fetuses eye sensitivity. As Phylis apprehensively descended the staircase, she was impressed by all the complicated equipment surrounding the fetal cart. "You really understand all this technology, Michael?"

"Real high tech stuff, huh?" Mike sneered self-mockingly, while the two approached the apparatus. "Joel is the guy with the all the bio-tech."

They both donned surgical masks to reduce the chance of infecting the fetus, and Mike carefully opened the access hatch of the fetal tube. With a dim lamp, Phylis leaned over closely with him, expecting to be grossed out somewhat. Instead, she was delighted to see a little miniature person floating unperturbed, knees drawn up and hands moving around in slow motion. "So frail", she said. It reminded her of someone sleeping in peaceful weightless on the space shuttle. The harder she stared the more detail appeared. Fingernails, eyelashes, lips, toes, ears. Fragile. Everything human.

"She's a beautiful in a way, Michael," she whispered, "but oh so delicate. So astonishing."

Mike answered with a hint of pride, "Give her a chance and she'll come back and grow up as strong as the next kid."

"How old is she?"

"I'm not sure," Mike said, "Because she's so underweight, Doc Joel thinks about 22 to 24 weeks. You have the records on this one, don't you?"

Phylis looked away and gave a weak reply, "I'm afraid so." Thoughts of the real mother, Maria, entered her conscience.

Leaning on his elbows and looking down at the little fetus with an admiring gaze, Mike added, "I've grown attached to her already. And ...I've decided to dump that specimen business and call her *Amnion* for now."

Phylis gave him a puzzled look and said, "Amnion?"

"Well yeah," he answered defensively, "it's the word for the placenta membrane. I think it's a derivative of the Greek word that means 'little lamb' or something. You know specimen name UH0744 never seem to fit her, now that I know her better. It sounds crazy, but, I still feel she's kinda of a real person, but ...at the same time....not all there yet."

In a flash Phylis was struck by the eerie 'lamb' coincidence. Maria Alvarez's slurred departing words several weeks ago in the hospital hauntingly returned. "Take care of my lamb," Phylis murmured, still pondering the strange coincidence.

Mike just looked at her quizzically again, distracted while checking the data on his computer monitor.

Still hunched over the baby, she looked at Mike more convinced than ever that he had done the right thing. And somehow, now that the fetus had a name, it was more human. It was a person. This was the same kind of life she called 'baby' in her own womb. She turned away, pulled down her surgical mask, and kissed her lover.

On the drive back to her house, Mike explained the basic operation of the fetal cart, and how he would manage taking care of Amnion. He also reviewed the limitations outlined by Joel, as the baby gets older and outgrows the tubular artificial 'womb'. Advanced as this technology was, no one had used it yet to try and actually bring a baby to full term.

Phylis' mind was now more preoccupied with her own problem of dealing with how she was going to continue doing her job at Lifespan, now that she'd seen a live 'specimen' in the flesh. How could she recruit another client? How does she keep going there to work? The prospect of loosing her job and lucrative salary over this was both depressing and at the same time seemingly inevitable.

She turned to Mike in an apprehensive tone saying, "You know there's going to be hell to pay over what we've done."

CHAPTER 29
Mad Max hits the roof

Seated behind his office desk, Lifespan CEO Max sporadically fidgeted, seated in his favorite plush leather chair. Although silent, his annoyance was quite apparent as he surveyed the executives in his office, and chomped off the end of his cigar. The constantly ringing desk phone would interrupt the chilly mood every few minutes, although he had his Admins intercept calls outside. It seemed like every line was lit. Max knew why they were calling. Word got out through his Strauss's consultants that a re-animation project fetus was stolen.

Jane Savage, head of security, was just concluding her briefing on the R&D Lab break-in earlier this morning. "So it looks like an outside job, probably industrial espionage," she said confidently. "It appears that they broke into the second floor lab from an exterior window and escaped from our facility through a hole cut in the chain link fence near the crematorium."

Max, now growing increasingly impatient, could not contain his wrath any longer. "You mean some competitor just comes into my company and helps himself to our proprietary technology, and nobody sees anything?"

Jane nervously responded, "Well, I think they had insider

information from someone."

"Who'?" Max demanded. "A second break-in in 2 weeks. And so far I've heard nothing out of you!"

Jane answered, "Sir, a lot of people have knowledge of the R&D labs operations. Those person or persons have not made any additional attempts to enter the R&D lab from inside. Until now, nothing new has surfaced".

The phone began ringing again. It agitated Max enough to throw the handset on the floor. He slammed down his fist on his desk, and stood up to walk around his desk to point his accusing finger at Jane, "Listen, if you want to stay in this company's employ, you better wrap this place up tighter then a drum!"

Jane tried to explain, "We've already added more guards, employee searches, new locks, drones..."

Max exploded, "Apparently that wasn't enough, was it?"

"But..." Jane pleaded as her eye's began to tear and her redden nose began to sniffle.

"No butts," Max warned. "I want more flood lights on the fence perimeter. Attack dogs on the premises at all times. And...uh,.. and get some private detectives to find the inside leak!"

He stomped back around his desk to sit down and added, "No more excuses". Then he waved her dismissal, "Now move your caboose out of here, and take care of it this time!"

Eve stood up feeling the need to intercede on behalf of another career woman under attack. "Max, Jane's not getting much cooperation from some of your managers. They appear to resent her for being a woman, and won't confide in her. Besides that, she hasn't been allowed direct access to the R&D lab to gather evidence."

Max surprised her with his curt answer. "You still don't need access! And no more female excuses. If she starts sniveling in front of them, what kind of signal do you think that sends. I gave her the responsibility, and she's got to produce like everybody else around here ...man or woman!"

Eve felt cut down a notch by his rude remarks. As a woman in business, she was always accustomed to receiving special treatment.

Jane departed feeling embarrassed and unappreciated. Until today, she was never on the receiving end of Max's criticism, and always had the cushion of someone's protection from a higher level. Now upset, she was determined more than ever to find the bastards who put her job in jeopardy.

Norm Stark waited for Jane's exit and commented, "You know Max, attack dogs can be unpredictable. It's risky... mixing them in with our own employees. Our female employees might get especially nervous."

"Screw the employees," Max retorted. "Did they prevent this

tragedy from happening to my company? Not one has come forward to deliver the names of our enemies. Even after that boat trip I shelled out for."

Norm shook his head in dismay, "OK, you're the boss."

Then, as he stood up to leave, he advised, "Also, let's not go outside the company too fast with this incident. If we bring in detectives then word of this breach may leak to our prospective buyers, the Japs or the Brits."

With Norm's mellow consul, Max had finally cooled down. There was money at stake. "Okay, okay." he relented. "Tell Jane to only conduct a quiet investigation in-house. We've already got plenty of ex-cops on the security payroll to use anyway."

Returning to his desk, the ever resourceful Max lit up with a smile and blurted out, "Wait a minute…. I have an idea! …Norm. How many terminations do they do in those old communist countries?

"Substantial compared to us," he replied. "So, what has this got to do with anything?"

"Newpapers, politicians, Right-to-lifer assholes," Max answered. "This situation will eventually get worse. Possibly dry up out domestic supply of specimens. So, give me some numbers."

Norm looked down at his iphone search. "Well, they do about 10 million a year in China, about 3 million plus in Russia, maybe a million in the smaller Eastern Block."

"Great!" Max declared. "If we could capture 5 to 10 percent of that market, we could import them here!'

Norm was dubious. "Exporting from those countries is easy – for cash. Max, I don't know how easy import is on our end - bio hazard material."

"Well find out."

Norm pondered the problem. "It might be easier to deal with the Russians. They're always looking for quick American cash, and they do a lot of illegal terminations anyway. Still, it's on the U.S. side that it's going to get sticky."

With Maxes blessing, Norm left to begin making foreign embassy contacts and locating indigenous trading companies.

Max now turned his attention to the subdued Dr. Strauss, and queried, "If we ship by air, how long will the specimens stay fresh? Can we use the existing transport equipment?"

The reply was cold with disdain. "You seem to have all the answers Max." The doctor was still annoyed that his professional associates were Maxes prime suspects. At the moment, however, Strauss was more consumed by his own professional vanity - a piece of his secret technology was already in the hands of some competing scientist in another company. Right now, he could care less about maintaining extract production schedules.

Max continued his diatribe. "Strauss, how much of our proprietary technology is out there?"

"Enough," he replied. "They now have a sample of the cellulose mucous membrane that we synthesized to attach the placenta. That's the key to it all – and also, our synthetic amniotic fluid. Straus perked up a bit adding, "Although they don't have our proprietary processing methods to manufacture them." Strauss slapped his hands on his knees, stood up, and left, leaving Max fuming.

Max finally reconnected his telephone jack and his Admin buzzed him immediately on the intercom. She said nervously, "It's the Governor's office, Mister Brewster - The Chief of Staff."

For a moment Max stared at the instrument's blinking extension light begging his attention. He hesitated knowing the prestige and power that Lifespan's magic elixir commanded. Then, picked up the telephone receiver.

For the most part, Lifespan would handle this latest crisis in the typical corporate reaction mode. They would be bogged down spending so much time reporting and analyzing outside inputs, that initially, they could never take the offensive. That would change as time went on. With Lifespan's lawyers, the money, and the clout of their political and liberal media connections, time would always be on their side.

CHAPTER 30
Tickling a crocodile's nose

By mid-week Mike was feeling confident that no suspicions were being cast towards himself or Joel. So, after ditching his old burner phone, he bought another one, and decided to turn up the heat on the Lifespan's executives. – see if he can get them to make a mistake. He settled on resuming contact with he young science reporter at the *Brooklyn Daily News*. At lunch break he made the call from a nearby shopping center while parked in his car. He chose the shopping center knowing that government intelligence agencies could triangulate a cell phone location, even though they couldn't identify the caller. There was no telling how long Lifespan's reach was within the Justice Department or the news media – including the *Brooklyn Daily*.

The science reporter was intrigued by Mike's description of the doings at Lifespan Corporation, but remained skeptical. Mike identified himself as a Lifespan consultant, and agreed to send him proof from the R&D lab, including documents and photos by postal mail. Mike finished off saying, "Don't call me. I'll call you."

Mike figured if they don't bite, or they're on Lifespan's side, there's no sense in pursuing this avenue anymore.

After a few days, Mike went to a different shopping center and called to see if they got his envelope. This time there was more enthusiasm in the reporter's voice. He said that they were delaying release of the story until the weekend. The digging they did into Max Brewster and Dr. Strauss' background was proving to be as interesting as Mike's story on Lifespan. Mike was curious about this development but the reporter said he would tell Mike more if Mike would reciprocate by revealing his identity. Mike adroitly declined.

The reporter added that they even had their medical experts examine the photos for technical authenticity. Except there was one big question. How do they know these pictures were taken at Lifespan? How do they verify that the pictures didn't originate in some other bio lab?

Mike hesitated while his analytically trained mind evaluated the problem posed. It finally dawned on him, and he explained. "Look at the photos you have again of the fetal cart NH0633. Magnify the area around the respirator and dialysis equipment."

"Yeah, we can do that. What are we supposed to look for?"

Mike exclaimed, "Calibration stickers. All equipment at Lifespan carries a yearly inspection stamp. It has the corporate logo and company serial number and date."

"Great! We'll check on that input right away," was the reporter's appreciative reply.

Then he launched into a list of questions he wanted answered. Filling in backgrounds on the various executives at Lifespan Corporation to aid in their story research. The only kicker in all this is that they wanted corroborating evidence, maybe another consultant or Lifespan employee to confirm the story. Mike would not offer anybody, promising to get back to the reporter on that issue. He was disappointed by this latest development. All the while those tortured fetuses that were slowly dying while he bungled his way through this. The time it was taking, the degree of difficulty in making something happen. It felt like their lives were grains of sand slowly seeping from his hand's grasp. Finally it hit him. The confirming information could come from the fetuses themselves! He remembered his conversation with Phylis about the new directive to take the placenta and fetus together. The specimen numbers identify the extracting hospital and the fetus case there. Mike finished his beer and telephoned the *Brooklyn Daily*.

"Hello Teddy? I have something that may help confirm things," Mike explained.

"Go ahead, shoot, I'm all ears and no story line."

Mike started "You know how those pictures I sent you show fetuses with their placentas intact."

"Yeah, go on."

"Well," Mike continued, "in the extraction hospital records you can look up the cases where they took the placenta and fetus."

"So?"

"So?" Mike quipped, "So, you can confirm that they're taking the fetus intact, where it went, and tie in to the specimen numbers."

"Interesting," the reporter said. Then there was a pause of silence as he digested Mike's input, and talked to someone nearby. Sounding more eager he continued, "I'm pretty sure we can get someone on the hospital staff inside to access those records, but I need specifics."

Mike briefly forgot where to get those case numbers from, then he recalled, "Look at the photos. At least one or two of the regeneration equipment shots have a specimen number on them. I'll check the rest of my photos and call you later with any other numbers I find."

"Fine," the reporter said and hung up.

Mike was juiced up again. Wheels were finally turning. Progress was being made at last.

* * * * * * *

The next day he called the reporter on his burner from a Home Depot parking lot. The reporter was still excited, though his editor wanted to squeeze more out of this informer.

"This story is a steam roller in here now."

Mike began to feel panicky and said, "Look, once you break the story, Lifespan will destroy all the physical evidence! All the specimens go up in smoke!"

The reporter was undaunted. "That's not my problem right now. We've got our job to do now, come hell or high water. I have to tell you, we will sell an additional 30% of advertising space for a Sunday special addition on this. Our advertisers will expect a blockbuster headline for their money."

Mike shook his head. Everyone, it seemed, had a way of converting this tragedy into profit. It wasn't that he was naive about the business world. It was just that he needed to know that someplace, somewhere, that in this nightmare world, there were still decent people left. People that could help one another without an angle to it. - without making a fast buck.

The reporter interrupted his thoughts, "Hey, You still there?"

Mike was having second thoughts now.

* * * * * * *

Mike spent Sunday morning breakfast with Phylis at a neighborhood diner. They sat in a booth where he briefed her on the *Brooklyn Daily* article he expected to come out.

She did not handle it well. "Michael. What have you done! "She said out loud. "You should have spoken to me and Joel before taking this public."

"Why?"

"Because we're all at risk – not just you!"

Mike sheepishly replied, "Keep it down, Hon. I figure it would put Lifespan in damage control mode instead of hunting for leaks."

An irritated Phylis stopped speaking to Mike for the rest of the meal.

Finishing up she said, "I thought we were a team. Now, just take me home."

Mike paid the bill at the counter and noticed a pile of newspapers and the headline he instigated.

He dropped Phylis off without her goodbye, and realized that 'impulsive Mike' probably lost this woman's trust, and worse yet, lost her love.

Returning home, he visited the little being living in his basement. He instinctively checked the cart readouts to make sure everything was within tolerances. Then he opened the hatch and peered inside to visit Amnion. With all the physical features of a human being Mike did not realize how attached he could get to something so extraordinary in appearance. It gave him comfort to just stare at this little girl that depended on him for survival – his girl.

* * * * * * * *

Early on Monday morning Mike was comfortably slouched behind his desk at Lifespan, immersed in department emails. He checked his burner phone log and found Joel, requesting an immediate meeting. Mike knew Joel was pissed too. It seemed wise to avoid a confrontation, and Mike resisted walking around the other Lifespan offices, keeping a low profile today. Nancy, his Admin, came in and excitedly asked, "Did you hear the rumor that the *Brooklyn Daily News* had done some kind of headline story about Lifespan?"

Mike looked up, feigning confusion, "What? Over the weekend?"

"Yeah, yes," Nancy replied. "In Sunday's edition." There's supposed to be a photo of a specimen on the front page."

Mike continued to pretend bewilderment. "Did the company announce a breakthrough in research? Are we getting an award?"

"No Mike," the frustrated young Admin whined. Impatient, she easily accepted that Mike knew less than her about all this and said, "When I find out more I'll let you know, Mike." Then she left.

Mike sat back in his chair for a moment as the gravity of the situation sank in – how he betrayed his best friends, Phylis and Joel. He knew they would have stopped him. The whole idea of going public with the story, all the people involved nationally, the power centers from Wall Street to the Capital now protecting their turf. It felt a lot more serious now - less of a game. More like going down to the riverbank, and tickling a sleeping crocodile's nose with a feather to see what it might do.

He stared out his window to observe small groups of disorganized demonstrators starting to gather at the front gate, stirring vivid memories of Mary Lou O'Reilly being strangled on that same fence weeks ago. He still felt the story needed to get out. He knew Joel and Phylis would object. Until now, the possible repercussions of his actions to his close friend's safety never really entered his mind. *Reckless fool!* he thought of himself. *Selfish fool.*

Soon New Jersey State troopers arrived, cleared the demonstrators, and some news cameramen. They blocked off all roads around the Lifespan campus. As the day progressed, the sky turned overcast. The dark clouds lent a portentous atmosphere to the developing crisis at Lifespan headquarters. Fortunately, the police presence kept a lid on things.

Still peering outside his office window, Mike observed increasing numbers of private security vehicles periodically splitting the crowd at the roadblocks and entering through main gate. It started him wondering how one thousand employees were going to get out of here in one piece, if those demonstrators became a mob. His first concern was to dial Phyllis to make sure she was clear of the plant. Katie picked up instead, explaining that Phylis was out on the road today recruiting potential specimen donors. Mike breathed a little sigh of relief.

At 1 PM word finally came down from corporate to close the facility down and send all employees home at 2 PM. They were told to call in tomorrow to confirm if the plant would be open. Mike did not wait. He dismissed his department immediately and stayed on alone until 2 PM himself.

Fortunately, everyone's departure from the plant went smoothly with confrontations limited to just some shouting, but no violence. Once the parking lot emptied, Mike departed too. As he crossed to his car, he noticed the parking spaces in front of the R&D building, was now vacant. Except, the spots reserved for Strauss' consultants, were already being filled by the expensive foreign cars of his research cohorts.

Mike regrettably concluded, *They'll be killing the rest of the fetuses tonight.*

221

He entered his car and rode past the scattered demonstrators on the way out. It occurred to him that there was something he could do, and parked at an Interstate Rest Stop. He called the *Brooklyn Daily News* reporter on his burner phone. "Here's something more for your story," he said bitterly to the reporter. "If you want more evidence on these clowns, watch for the crematorium to be running full blast tonight."

The reporter answered smugly, "We already have it covered. We have infrared cameras on the roof of the building right across the street, with a drone infrared camera ready to launch. From what I understand, we're looking right down Lifespan's throat. We even have a camera in the bushes back by the incinerator."

Mike was somewhat surprised, admitting, "You fellas really out did yourselves."

"You don't know the half of it," the reporter replied confidently. "And wait 'till you read what's coming in tomorrow's article about these guys you work for!"

"Like what?" Mike asked.

"You' wanted to be the mystery man….Now, you'll have to wait for our mystery."

* * * * * * *

Despite the plant closing, the scene inside corporate headquarters was one of chaos. Eve West, as head of corporate public relations, was deluged in telephone calls and Emails. Having been left in complete ignorance of the R&D project, she was totally unprepared to defend the company. TV stations, newspapers, patients, tied up all the incoming telephone lines. Eve's instructions to her administrative assistants was to give a polite 'No comment at this time' to any inquiry until she had more information from Max. Still, the cat was out of the bag.

* * * * * * *

CEO Max sat sulking in his comfortable leather chair, his Slinky toy bouncing from palm to palm. Dr. Strauss was sitting staring back across his desk. He thought of hiding the toy to spite Max. The newspaper revelations had already reached his ears. "Another fine mess your scientist prima donnas got this company into, Peter," he complained.

"Wait a minute Max," Strauss interjected, "You knew what we were doing! You signed off on all the project approvals and budgets!"

Max replied, "Yeah, but that was before I knew that one of those bastard consultants of yours would sell us out!"

Strauss fidgeted in his chair, his patience at an end. He stood up and pounded his fist on Max's desk and shouting, "I've had enough of your bullshit innuendos! Nobody in this company has come up with one shred of evidence that my people have been involved in anything! So far, my lab has been broken into twice, compliments of your crummy <u>In</u>security Department. Last week the thieves came in right under their noses!"

Max sat back in his chair, seemingly oblivious to the criticism, and said nothing in reply.

Strauss turned to leave cantankerously adding, "It was obvious last week that these incidents are being perpetrated by outside competitors, not by my associates!"

"Oh really?" Max answered. "And how'd you reach that conclusion?".

"Well, just last week one of my people, Dr. Ellar, over in Extractions, was recruited by Reichmen Corporation. They claimed they were setting up a competing extraction lab over there. They tried to pirate Ellar away, right inside our building."

"So what did Ellar say?" Max fumed, now more attentive.

"He's loyal. He flatly rejected the offer immediately, and came to report it to me. Now, that's what I call loyalty."

The paranoid Max remembered that Reichmen had expressed an interest in acquiring Lifespan, and began to think that, maybe, these Germans might be trying the cheaper alternative of stealing his technology instead of buying it.

Strauss continued, "And I also heard that some California outfit is poaching soliciting specimens in our territory."

Max stood up from his chair to approach Strauss with a patronizing smile, and adopted a more conciliatory demeanor. It was apparent now that maybe Strauss had some points. Max never trusted the Germans anyway. Besides, he still needed Strauss as his technical workhorse to help build his other future business at Extentech in California. And Strauss' anti-aging treatments were obviously making Max look younger and feel better.

"Easy Peter," Max said in a conciliatory tone, "You right, I'm sorry. I've been jumping to conclusions."

Then he put his hand on Strauss' shoulder as a pacifying gesture. "Sit down for a minute. Please. Let's make some sense out of this. Come up with a plan."

Strauss returned to his chair believing that his point was made. They conversed for a while, discussing their options and the effect of shutting down R&D operations temporarily until the negative publicity blew over. Strauss indicated that, technically, they 'have already learned everything they needed to continue the specimen revival operations at any other lab location. Max took the opportunity to ask him again if he could design a long duration transport case to bring fetuses across from overseas. Strauss was still non-committal, always keeping his technical commitments to a minimum.

Before they adjourned the meeting, Max had one last direction to give. "Before you dispose of all your specimens, I want every last drop of superblood drained, and every last tissue extracted, and put in storage for my personal use."

Max always likes to hedge his bets. If this situation really got out of hand, and production shut down, he would take the extracts to sustain his own person not Max. The discussion adjourned, and Strauss departed to carry out his orders. Max returned to his desk and favorite toy Slinky. The metal clinking pacified his initial stress. Time to summon Norm Stark. Time to get legal inputs and begin damage control.

* * * * * * *

Norm joined Max about a half hour later. He just finished reading the morning addition of the *Brooklyn Daily News* and had phoned the chief editor to see if he could learn anything about its source. He also called an attorney who occasionally represented the *News* during union negotiations for a possible contact to act as their snoop inside the newspaper. Maybe threaten a strike at the newspaper.

Norm sat down on the couch in his usual confident and placid demeanor. "Well, Max. There's good news and bad news."

"Let's get the bad over with first," Max answered dejectedly.

"From my conversations with the *Brooklyn News* people, it appears the informant behind this story is still unknown to even them... and prefers to remain anonymous - a 'deep throat'. It's going to be tough to track him, or them, down."

Max took advantage of a pause in his attorney's analysis to say, "So, what's the good news?"

"The good news is that without an identifiable witness, the story becomes hearsay. We may be able to get away with just denying it all until it blows over – like the Clintons. And, the informant probably won't dare to come forward. He or she knows they are dead meat if they do."

"Damn right on that one!" Max interjected, thinking of his mob connections.

A flustered Eve West entered Max's office interrupting their conversation. She was overwhelmed with phone calls all day and stormed over to his desk demanding, "Why wasn't I kept informed on this R&D breach? How can you expect me to protect us when I'm kept in the dark?"

Max clearly resented her uninvited entry and quickly moved to put her in her place. Pointing his finger at the door, he barked, "Next time you come in here when I'm in a private conference, you go through my Admins first!"

Eve was surprised by his gruff formality. She was accustomed to informal access to her boss... and lover.

Max continued his harangue, "And if I thought you needed to know more I would have told you. Now, get out there and prepare a strong denial of any wrongdoing! Tell them that the visual evidence may have been created using CGI by a rogue A.I. Also, remember to put emphasis on all the fine treatments this firm has historically provided to the aged and sick! Roll out some pitiful recipients in front of the TV cameras – maybe some kids too."

Eve stood there for a moment confused by Max's display, feeling her prestige and intimate relationship somehow diminished. Obviously, she was not his bedroom confidant anymore. For the first time, she even felt an insecurity to their personal relationship. For the first time in her career, she was actually worried about her job.

It was also now apparent that Max's physical appearance was changing too. He looked younger, with a fuller hairline, tighter facial muscles, and clearer eyes - almost a different person. During intimate relations, she was aware of his fetal drug treatments from the needle marks on his arms.

Eve tried to apologize, not understanding what she could have possibly done to earn his sudden indifference. She turned for some support from Norm seated to her right. "I'm just trying to be more effective in protecting the company's interests."

Norm just shrugged his shoulders and added, "And put in a statement that all our activities are conducted under a legitimate license from the State." Then gave her a dismissive wave to the door.

What Eve could not know was that Max's desire for self-preservation and protection of his fortune overrode any business, or personal obligations. In a crisis, that inner circle of influential associates at Lifespan would quickly shrink from a circle to a single point ...him. Worse yet, with his younger constitution, Eve was just getting too old for him - it was just that simple. It was time to spin ha story again about decoupling saving lives with her big TV network contacts.

With Eve's departure, Max had an idea. "Why don't we call our goomba, Tony LaRocca," he announced, "the guy up in Peekskill State Prison. He owes me a favor."

Norm queried, "For what?"

"For those free extract treatments we've been sending him for over three years. With enough money, he'll get the answers I need on who the stoolie is at Lifespan. Shut these traitors down, - I mean permanently down."

Norm nodded, "Yes, they do know how to get results."

"Oh, and one more thing, Norm. I have some information from Strauss that the Germans were in here trying a little sneaky personnel recruiting. Contact our international brokers. I want to know if these people are secretly building a competing facility over there."

His attorney answered, "So, you think they're interest in buying us, isn''t on the up 'n up?"

"Norm, don't we always 'do diligence' when it comes to money?"

* * * * * * * *

Dr. Strauss waited until after 6 PM, when all the Lifespan employees were cleared out, to conduct his little clandestine meeting. He stood at the front of the R&D conference room with a dozen of his most trusted colleagues and consultants from the FDA, NIH, and CDC. No one sat down. Instead, they gathered around the outer perimeter of the conference table or leaned on the wall, drinking complimentary coffee, munching on donuts or bagels. It was a relaxed mood, even allowing time to discuss mutual fund investments.

However, Strauss let it be known that there was a great deal of work to be done today. He had hand picked these doctors. They all were partners in one termination clinic or another, received grant money from NIH and Planned Parenthood, and had equity positions at Lifespan. Consequently, their loyalties to the company and its research were rock solid.

Dr. Strauss was solemn as he opened the discussion saying, "We have to move swiftly and confidentially to conclude our research at this lab. The public is not ready to acknowledge our achievements here, and the media will make a mockery of our science. My assistant, Rachel Stone, will assign you to your separate work areas and we will proceed with decommissioning the lab and reclaiming the specimen materials. Remember, we want to preserve and reclaim as much usable tissue as possible before these specimens are disposed of."

A question came from one of the doctors, "When will we be able to resume our research?"

"I can't make any guarantees, but it should all blow over in about a month," Strauss answered.

Then he added, "I'll see if I can keep you on the payroll in the meantime."

The statement reinforced Strauss' status among his peers, and obviously pleased his audience. The meeting concluded with the air of team spirit that people seemed to get from sharing a common goal.

Strauss went straight to the R&D lab with his assistant, Rachel. She had a lucrative position at Lifespan, and enjoyed the proximity to a renowned scientist like Dr. Strauss. She was young and intentionally single so as not to be distracted from her career objectives by a husband or children. Her divorced professional mother never encouraged those undignified feminine leanings. They were just a sign of weakness, and limited one's career potential.

They entered the room alone, and she immediately began preparing sterile hypodermic needles with huge doses of sodium chloride. Surgical masks were worn to preclude any chance of contaminating the specimen extracts during the procedure. Strauss opened each fetal tube, inspected the contents against his case file folder, and decided which extract potentials were most important for each. Rachel dutifully recorded his conclusions for each specimen number.

The task was remarkable efficient from here on. Rachel passed the hypodermic to Strauss. He leaned over the open fetal tube hatch and pushed the needle into the squirming specimen's thorax. Convulsions erupted for a minute or so, then blood pressure and heartbeat fell off precipitously. In less than 3 minutes it was all over.

Strauss nodded confidently and commented to Sarah, "In a little over an hour we'll be done with the whole batch."

She removed the connecting life support tubes and electrical monitors, and taped on the dissection instructions for the consulting scientist assigned. In the meantime, his research colleagues relaxed outside in the canteen and exchanged stories of their Ivy League college days.

By evening all the specimens had their blood drained, and cortical, muscle and bone tissues removed for processing. All materials were stored in the extract refrigeration units located in Dr. Rosen's department.

After nightfall and the surrounding area became peaceful again, the empty specimen carts were rolled between buildings for storage in a locked section of the warehouse.

The incinerator was fueled and pre-heated for the night's disposal of discarded remains. Alone, Strauss dragged the boxes of material out of the extraction building on a flatbed dolly and down the dimly lit path to the crematorium. Once there, he hastily began stoking the gas-fired oven with boxes, one by one. Even with the tall brick chimneystack dispersing the exhaust up 50 feet, the pungent smell of burning human flesh was unmistakable in the still night air. Nevertheless, he worked diligently and routinely. The doctor remained too distracted to suspect that all his clandestine activities were being filmed from the dense pine bushes and silently above by a Daily News drone with an infrared camera. From their vantage point, his sinister activities did not appear routine at all.

CHAPTER 31
Following the evidence trail

A Few days later Lifespan head security guard Sgt.Harry Sullivan walked across the empty R&D laboratory room, now completely devoid of the specimen revival equipment. The first thing that hit him was the strong odor of disinfectant. Even the file cabinets were gone, evident from the wax outlines on the floor tiles. He stopped to peruse the broken latch where the break-in happened last week. For now, someone had sealed the window with cardboard and duct tape along the edges. Behind him, his boss, Jane Savage, paced around the vacant room, intent on explaining her theory about how all this happened. She was enlisting his help and his police informants in determining who was behind it, and who inside Lifespan might have been involved.

Harry continued his own casual investigation, half-listening to Jane's harangue, and peeled the cardboard tape away from the window to glance to the garden bed below. He observed some wood like scratches on the outside window ledge. Jane continued to ramble on in the background. Harry's concentration was on the evidence at hand. He turned and surmised to himself, *Cleaned spotless like a covered up murder scene.*

He felt quite at home under the circumstances. Several years before Joining Lifespan as the Captain of Guards, he had been a Lieutenant in charge of burglary investigations in the Newark PD. That seasoned experience told him that this crime scene contained more clues than meets the eye. He listened politely as Jane paced the floor, her high heels clicking away on the shiny tiles. The gist of her remarks was now focused on tightening security and searching for clues to identify some external perpetrator.

When she was done with her discourse, Harry asked some simple questions, starting with, "From the newspaper accounts, it says a fetus was alive in here. Is that true?"

The ever evasive Jane answered impatiently, "Right now the company denies any wrong doing. It is all SFX – video special effects out there. For the time being you can assume some proprietary equipment was taken." Then she mockingly added, "Besides, it's not so important about what was taken. It's who took it."

Harry relaxed and leaned back on the windowsill, crossing his arms, comfortably convinced that his boss was no detective. He knew that when you look for a crime suspect, motive could provide a significant lead to the perpetrator's identity. With her one-sided approach to conversation, he did not bother to share that simple knowledge.

Then Harry commented, "This place looks awful empty and clean.

Was maintenance in here recently? Where's all the equipment? This was a crime scene. Where is Forensics? There could have been clues on the latch, windowsill, floor, that point to other possibilities."

Jane was rapidly becoming testy from his remarks. She wanted answers, not more questions. Her conclusions on the window break-in, the discovered breach in the security fence, were already reported to corporate, and there was no going back to present other conflicting theories. She barked, "What's the difference Harry? What's been moved out wasn't the equipment that was stolen!"

Harry was amused by her overly simplistic corporate mind and said, "We could have dusted for finger prints, or something other residual evidence left behind."

"It's too late for that. Anyway, everybody that worked in the lab had their hands on that stuff."

"So, what about the prints of the person or persons that maybe didn't work here?"

She answered contemptuously, "Forget about it. Strauss ordered that equipment disassembled a day ago."

Harry turned and looked again at the broken latch and down at the bushes below. Then he said, "And you're convinced the perpetrators came through here?"

"Yes! Obviously... of course."

"Anybody swept or cleaned this place since?"

"No! They just moved equipment out," she curtly replied.

Jane left, apparently fed up with what she felt were Harry's irrelevant questions. Harry looked around the room one last time, picked up a yardstick lying in the corner, and then examined the digital lock on his way out.

Fingering the keypad, he grumbled to himself, *Goddamn computer wonder shit. Now even the hackers can become crooks.*

He took the elevator downstairs and walked around the outside of the building, along the grass to the garden bed below the lab. The two ladder holes were still clearly defined in the ground. He placed his hand in the soft humus soil. It stuck to his hands. It stuck to his shoes. So much so, that he had to use the grass like a rug to wipe it off.

Squatting down by the ladder holes he placed his yardstick inside, lined up with the vertical side of the hole closest to the building. Although the hole was six feet from the building, the yardstick pointed straight in the air.

As he rubbed the stubble of his chin it became apparent that the whole's sides did not angle towards the building, and their straight-up vertical sides meant that this 'ladder' could never have leaned towards the building.

Harry slowly stood up and walked over to the first floor window sill, below the broken lab window. He inspected it closely for fragments of the garden bed soil or broken glass. He found none. He concluded that if someone with dirty shoes was on a ladder above, some of this garden debris would have dropped off as they climbed the rungs. There should also be a collection of this same stuff on the second floor window sill above too. Harry surmised that no one could have entered from the outside without leaving some of this telltale dirt or broken glass behind. Conclusion - inside job.

Before acting on his assessment, he returned to the empty R&D lab one last time. He looked at the digital lock with disdain once more, thinking, *A clue to who did this is probably hidden in this piece of tech gizmo.* Then he re-entered the lab and walked over to the counter to examine the broken latch. From there he went back to the window and noted the scratches on the window frame were on the inside, not the outside, and the frame hadn't been bent as if from an outside crowbar.

The conclusion was inescapable. There never was an outside break-in.

Harry glanced down one more time at the garden bed below and thought, *Clever inside guys. The ones who thought this one up.*

Initially, he was going to present his findings to Jane, but then had second thoughts. In his earlier career days, he would have informed his superiors with his insights. However, he was a lot savvier about the politics of the world. He'd come to realize that his superiors and the criminals were two fingers on the same hand ...and a dirty one at that.

Harry was retired on a nice police lieutenant pension now. There was no more reason to 'kiss up'. No more reason to cover up things, or share in the usual precinct payoffs. Now, he had the financial independence to live by his conscience alone. Nor did he desire to make Jane look any smarter. His job was secure whether he helped on this case or not. Besides, there was no rush. He would wait and read more about this Lifespan organization in the newspapers, then decide what to do.

CHAPTER 32
What goes around comes around

Doctor Strauss arrived at his office early, around 7:30 AM, carrying the morning addition of the *Brooklyn Daily News*. This time, the front page had a dark obscure photograph of a man throwing boxes into the Lifespan incinerator. Apparently, there was a magnified photo of a small hand sticking out of one of the boxes. Although he wasn't specifically identified in the article, Strauss recognized it as himself immediately.

What disturbed him most, though, was the news story appearing further inside, on page 3 - about his family. Someone had done a deep search into his past, all the way back to his grandfather in Germany. Then, halfway through the article was the real shocker. The writer had connected his grandfather's real surname, Straussenheim, to an experimenter at a Nazi death camp during World War II.

Strauss put the paper down and cursed it. "Bastards!" he groused under his breath. *After all these years*, he thought, *they couldn't just leave it dead and buried.*

In the solitude of his office, the doctor began to reflect back on the last days of his grandfather's medical career. When he had a lucrative general practice in Westbury, New York, and that grand three-story English Tudor home in Garden City. He remembered its huge dark attic upstairs framed by hewn oak timbers. The place always appeared mysterious to him as a boy, especially the huge black steamer trunk stored up there in a remote corner. The house became his parents after grandfather died

He trunk always intrigued him with its brass reinforcements and its old transportation stickers documenting travels through four countries; Germany, Argentina, Cuba, and finally America. Many times he fiddled with the huge padlock on its brass hinge, trying every key in the house to coach it open, always to no avail. Once he even tried lifting it. The trunk was so heavy it would not budge an inch. His childhood imagination had it filled with all sorts of gold jewelry and antiques - the family fortune from Germany.

When asked about its contents, his mother and father would get ambiguous and react with unexpected anger, bordering on hostility. With the strong reprimands and threats of punishment, he learned not to ask anymore. After a while, as he went on to college and medical school, it was almost as though the trunk didn't exist anymore.

Years later, after Peter graduated medical school, his father became terminally ill with pancreatic cancer. Eventually he was hospitalized and then the end came swiftly. Before he died, he gave Peter the key to the trunk in the attic, and explained its contents.

There was 300 pounds of paper inside. All of the clinical and scientific records of the research he had done in Germany during World War II. He wanted to pass it on to his son for posterity, saying, "One day, in a more enlightened environment, his work may be considered for its real contribution to science and humanity."

Some months passed before Peter had the ambition to open that trunk, and finally he did. Its contents were initially shocking though still intriguing, bringing back vague memories of his earliest childhood. There was a pungent odor in the trunk. The same smell he sensed the other night at the Lifespan crematorium. The trunk documents confirmed that his grandfather worked in a government lab next to one of the concentration camps. The inspiration for his grandfather's work, oddly enough, came from an American, Dr. Davenport Hooker.

Apparently, shortly before the war, Dr. Hooker had conducted a series of tests on living human fetuses, poking and prodding them to test their reaction to stimuli. Somehow, he kept them alive outside the womb for a short period of time. Soon, they all died in the course of his experiments.

Peter's grandfather had a theory that the fetus contained material that could speed up the healing process of German soldiers wounded in combat. Perhaps allow for the regeneration of amputated limbs. The plan was to use the fetuses from female POWs to generate an inexhaustible inventory of these extracts and spare parts.

In order to isolate the regenerative chemicals in the fetus, he would have to isolate the early fetal organs before they mature. With the technological limitations of the time, and the uncertain location of these organs in an immature fetus, his father came up with a simple solution.

His grandfather had each woman from the prison camps impregnated with a prisoner's sperm at one-week intervals. Then, from those that became pregnant, he surgically removed their fetuses starting at 36 weeks and worked backwards through all these pregnancies, all the way to a 4 weeks gestation fetus.

Dissecting these specimens at each development stage gave his grandfather a map of every organ's time of formation and pointed to the location of its earliest appearance and to all the important stem cells, precursors, and hormonal activity.

In the medical notes, there was no mention of what happened to all these women afterwards. His grandfather only retained responsibility for the fetal specimens themselves. His work went on for four years, finally reaching a dead end because he could not purify the extracted tissues with the technology available at the time. When the war ended, and the war crime trials were imminent, the elder Straussenheim realized that some of the collaborating P.O.W. doctors on this project might use him as scapegoat for their involvement in these experiments. With help from a colleague in South America, he escaped to Argentina under a new name.

Peter found his grandfather's work fascinating, and speculated that not only could you cure disease with these fetal extracts, but also you could potentially reverse the aging process. This research gave Peter the initial technical credibility on fetal anatomy to win several NIH grants from the federal government. From there on, success bred success in his career.

The doctor's reminisces ended with the intruding ring of the desk telephone. Looking down again at the newspaper in his lap, the cruel reality of the *Daily News* article only belittled those fond memories. It painted his grandfather as some kind of Nazi monster, a death camp tyrant. At this point in his life Strauss was in no mood to begin a lengthy defense of something that happened over 90 years ago, and could not be changed anyway.

His assistant, Rachel, walked in to interrupt his thoughts and tersely said, "Mister Brewster just called. He wants to see you at 9 AM. He says it's urgent." There was a look on her face he had never seen before - one of suppressed disgust. Strauss was not surprised and responded with a dejected, "OK," as she turned and departed. Now he wondered how his colleagues at NIH and other employees at Lifespan would regard him with this new development.

At this point, the Internet Bloggers and Streamers picked up the story - the situation began to spin out of control.

* * * * * * *

Max also finished reading the morning edition of the *Brooklyn Daily*, and threw it in the garbage can, thinking, *These bastards do a better job of investigating than the FBI.* Already one of the Board directors had called, wanting to know who checked out Strauss's credentials. The director threatened to call an emergency board meeting to find out how, and by whom, Strauss was hired.

Max knew the answer to that question and paced in front of his office windows trying to resolve his predicament. There were several Jewish members on the board, except Strauss was his ticket to youth and eternal life. At the same time Strauss was becoming a political liability. Max began to think of how to replace him when the time was right.

The buzz of his Admin's intercom interrupted his thoughts to announce Strauss' arrival.

Max started in as soon as the doctor entered the office. "You've seen today's headline, Peter Straussenheim? How much of this is true?"

Strauss answered defensively, "Is this just the liberal version of McCarthyism here - guilt by genetic association."

"These women your father experimented on, what were their nationalities?"

Strauss found the question inconsequential, "What's the difference? The names were all Polish sounding, "It's not significant anyway."

Max exploded, "Not significant! We have Jewish people on the Board of Directors, that's what!"

Strauss became infuriated too. "You know, every time people bring up this holocaust, it's like the only ones that suffered were Jewish. About 46 million other people were slaughtered on both sides in that war."

"No, no," Max waved his hands in the air, "This was different. This was a program aimed at one nationality. Systematic genocide. No military objective involved, just killing people for their religious beliefs. And, your grandfather, probably took living fetuses from Jewish women too!"

"Max," Strauss interrupted sarcastically, "That's essentially what we've been doing here at Lifespan. We accept specimens from all nationalities. Now, all of a sudden you have ethical problems with that?"

"I don't have a problem," Max retorted, "We paid for them!" You have the problem! This company has been dragged into a controversial issue because of you're grandfather's sordid past."

Strauss remained defensive, "His work was the basis for the technology that started Lifespan in the first place. It's where I got my start in specimen rejuvenation technology."

Max remained incensed, "I can't believe you can accept the terrible things your grandfather was involved in."

"You know Max," Strauss said, "You built an entire business doing the same thing. Where's the moral dilemma here?"

Strauss sat down on the couch and seemed almost relaxed. The doctor deliberately needled Max. "There were lots of collaborators back then...maybe some of their grandchildren are on your board of directors."

"I don't believe any of that," Max said indignantly, "There's never been anything publicized about such a thing."

"You think it would be?" Strauss replied as he stood up, ready to leave, adding, "This is so ridiculous. I mean, I wasn't even there. My father wasn't there either!"

Max stopped listening. He had heard enough. At this point, Strauss was just another business liability. And so, when the time came, he would sacrifice him to the media mob. Standing up from his chair, he dismissed Strauss saying, "I don't know how to address this issue. It's morally repugnant and an embarrassment to the company."

A disgusted Strauss shook his head while leaving, and stopped to say one last comment. "The answer you should give the papers is this; My grandfather experimented on expired fetuses only. It was innocent fetal research. Whatever tragedy befell the women was somebody else's responsibility, somebody else's decision. It was just out of his control at the time."

Then he quietly left the office.

Max sat down at his desk, his eyes transfixed on his telephone. He felt his world collapsing in on him, and decided from Strauss's remarks, probably untrustworthy to boot. He took his Slinky out and tossed it back and forth, clinking, palm to palm, for a few minutes. Finally, he sat back and gazed at the ceiling. It occurred to him that there must be other scientists around, ones that can pick up Strauss' work and carry it forward.

With all these consultants I pay, there has to be a qualified replacement, Max told himself. He called the Director at NIH, a fellow he knew fairly well. Perhaps, it was time to begin an informal search now.

CHAPTER 33
Lifespan plan B

Timidly, the Lifespan custodian, Carlos Rivera, knocked on Mike's open office door. He hadn't spoken to Mike since that emotionally charged meeting weeks ago - the one about disposing of dissected fetuses.

"Hey pal, c'mon in," Mike said, still seated relaxed at his desk. "So, how do you like workin' for Al Greene now?"

Carlos came in and answered solemnly. "I don't work for hem no more Mikey."

Mike was puzzled by his unexpected answer and asked, "How so?"

"I leave today," he said more explicitly. "El Diablo, he run dis place." Then Carlos slowly made the sign of the cross on his chest and sat down across from Mike, looked up saying, "Perdoname por favor Jesus."

Leaning a bit forward the old custodian whispered, "I told you dey was doin' bad things in dat building. Now you know. Now da world know. You should get atta here too, Mikey."

"Don't worry," Mike facetiously assured, "Soon we'll all be out of work here." Then, in a more solemn tone added, "Let's just hope the bad guys pay their dues first."

Carlos rose and extended his calloused hand across the desk to shake one last time. Mike grasped his hand with some sense of admiration for an older guy with a set of principles. "What are you going to do for a job? If you need a good reference you know you can count on mine."

"I dunno yet," he said, "But no matter how much money dey pay me here," then pointing to his temple. "I hava to live widda my conshunce." He put his hand on his chest adding, "My hearta, ita just ain't in dis no more."

"Via con Dios mi amigo", he added as he backed out of Mike's office.

Mike waved goodbye to a friend. A good person he would probably never see again. Then he sat back down in his chair to quietly contemplate this little conversation. He clasped his hands together, leaning forward with bent elbows on the desk, and rested his chin on his intertwined fingers. There were only two other people out of almost a thousand Lifespan employees that had actually quit after learning what the company was up to. In fact, it wasn't surprising that most of his coworkers didn't see any major problem with the company reviving fetuses. After all, there was the reality to this conundrum - no fetuses - no job.

.

* * * * * * * *

A reduced work week was instituted, triggering more rumors that Lifespan Corporation was about to go belly up. The demonstrators were now continually picketing the company headquarters, blocking access to specimen extraction hospitals, and generally harassing referring physicians. Fetal specimens began to dry up as doctors became reluctant to refer women, and amazingly, pregnant women were actually having second thoughts about their decouplings.

By burner phones, Mike had contacted a still distant Phylis and Joel to prepare for the worst by recommending they withdraw their company 401K accounts and transfer to an outside personal IRA. Mike told them that Lifespan would raid the 401 money when they finally ran out of cash. Neither answered, although he hoped they would now take his untrustworthy advice. Both were still peeved that impetuous Mike had not involved them in the *Brooklyn News* release. Thoughts about quitting were on both there minds.

In Mike's case, he wanted to stay on at Lifespan as long as possible. It gave him access to vital blood and spare parts to support the cart and insure Amnion's development in his basement.

* * * * * * *

Phylis met procurement specialist and friend, Katie, in the Lifespan company cafeteria. There were widespread rumors flying around the company grapevine of an impending layoff, a big one.

They sat down at a table with their ice teas, and Katie asked anxiously, "You getting any leads on specimens? I'm down to only one every other week."

Phylis feigned concern, "Oh isn't it terrible? I struck out entirely. I mean, there's nothing out there."

Katie glanced to both sides and spoke in a hushed tone, "Yeah, and if things don't turn around Lifespan's not gonna need many procurement agents anymore either." Then she leaned back in her chair, "You're lucky Phylis, you have seniority."

A nosy Katie eventually inquired about her dating Mike Santino. However, Phylis wanted to play down the relationship and discouraged any further association with Mike. "I haven't heard from him for a while," she lamented. Then shrugged her shoulder, "You know, nowadays, some men should come with warning labels stuck on their foreheads."

Phylis decided to share some misgivings with Katie about Lifespan's business of using revived fetuses. "Katie, let me ask you something. Do you think the fetus is a human being?"

Katie was surprised by the question, abruptly answering anyway. "Of course not!"

"You sound pretty sure of that," Phylis tactfully replied.

"That's not even the right question," Katie said adamantly.

"Really?"

"Yeah the important question is; does a woman have a right to put her career ahead of having to raise these unwanted kids?" Katie confidently sat back in her chair and said emphatically, "That is the real question. Right! "

Phylis didn't answer. She always thought of Katie as a sort of free spirit. Now she just thought of her as a self-centered nihilist.

"Right????" Katie again demanded agreement.

Until this moment, Phylis felt that Katie was a good friend. Now, suddenly, this huge gulf just opened between them. A division that was not apparent until now - until the issue of fetal life was raised.

Katie continued to stare at Phylis, demanding agreement, repeating, "Right?"

Phylis felt uncomfortable under Katie's assertive, almost paranoid countenance, and excused herself to return to her office.

Back in her department she passed by Jerry Klein's office door. He looked up and called her in, requesting that she close the door behind.

"Sit down Phylis," he calmly requested.

"I called you in because you're my best procuring agent. "I have to tell you," as he waved his hands around, "All this stuff going on is going to kill the business."

Phylis interjected, "Katie and I were just discussing the fall off in case load."

"Yeah. Exactly. So you know that a personnel cutback has got to come."

Phylis started to suspect that Jerry was building her up for a pink slip, terminating her job at Lifespan. She anxiously implored, "Jerry could you just tell me what this is all leading to? Please."

"Oh, I'm sorry Phylis. I didn't mean to imply..."

Then he reached into his business card Roledex on top his desk and pulled out three cards. "You've been a conscientious employee and a big help to me, and it's too bad there isn't much opportunity left here." Jerry offered the cards to her across the desk. "I know the people in these medical equipment companies. There always looking for sales people in the metropolitan area. Mention my name and they'll give you the extra consideration you need to get hooked up."

Phylis was grateful and didn't know what to say, commenting, "Uh, you mean I can look for another job while I'm still employed here?"

"You bet kiddo...but hurry up." Then he leaned forward and added in a hushed tone, "By the way, don't mention this to anyone else. The truth is, I don't see us getting specimens from the U.S. anymore."

Phylis was pleasantly surprised to be given the opportunity to arrange her departure from Lifespan on her own terms, and was indebted to Jerry for his consideration. She walked around the desk to give him a hug.

Jerry stood up to accept her gratitude and said, "I hope this works. You're a nice lady who should be far away from this mess we're in. You can count on a paycheck until you're hooked up."

Phylis turned for the door, stopping to ask, "What about you? What will you do?"

He chuckled, "I have a feeling they'll still need my services one way or another. Thanks for asking." Then he walked over to the window and pointed down to the processing lab. "Someone still has to manage getting in the supply."

Jerry sat back down behind his desk and began making phone calls. Phylis left feeling astounded that someone in this company could be as thoughtful as Jerry. It was also apparent that Katie and all the other procuring agents were going to be out on the street soon.

Phylis left the office with some bitterness towards Michael. This fiasco he started is costing her a career, and probably loss of income. She reminisced about the fun they had, and her high hopes for a loving, stable relationship.

All gone now. Alone again. All Michael's fault.

* * * * * * *

Max met with his top executives in the walnut paneled Board Room for a crisis control planning meeting. The discussion was actually led by Chief Counsel Norm Stark who opened the meeting with a brief recap of the current media and legal scenario. "You all know we have some major problems here. Some are addressable through litigation, and some just need political attention." As usual, he exuded an air of corporate invincibility. "It's all manageable, as long as everyone keeps their mouths shut and we stick together."

Norm held up some documents, one by one. "There is a suit filed against us by 'Operation Rescue'." He threw the document on the table with disdain. "Then, another negligence suit by a woman injured on our fence perimeter." It too was tossed on top of the other case folders with a measured amount of professional contempt. "And, a class action suit by patients not receiving our drug treatments anymore. Norm just kept tossing folders. "And another one from our own bank creditors seeking immediate repayment of substantial long term loans." They were all heaved onto the pile, eventually sliding off to one side.

While Norm paused, Al Greene quipped, "And it won't be long before our vendors start shipping cash up front - C.O.D."

Nobody laughed. Al cringed at his poorly chosen words, when Max looked at him critically, communicating his displeasure in words unsaid.

Norm continued his briefing unperturbed. "That's the judicial side, which we are prepared to handle with our in house legal staff – and, as required, some outside help. Beyond this there is the media, and special interest groups..."

Max interrupted with an extemporaneous quip, "Wait a minute! Why aren't we suing somebody? How come everybody is suing me!"

Norm turned to answer. The bombastic Max didn't give him a chance. "Norm, I pay a huge legal staff payroll, a whole floor of people. Your job is to confound, confuse, frustrate, and intimidate my enemies!"

Norm retorted, "If you consulted Legal before we launched these R&D programs we could have avoided this whole issue to begin with!"

Max regained control of himself. There was no sense in attacking Norm in front of others, and relented. "Enough said! Let's get on with the meeting."

Norm didn't appreciate Max's display of self-serving indignation, considering it almost infantile. However, deep down inside, he was comforted by one obvious fact about his own legal profession - that regardless of who wins or looses in litigation, the lawyers never go to jail or pay fines, only their clients do. Then he humorously thought to himself, *Max better watch out before he becomes one of those 'clients'.*

Norm finished his discussion, and the meeting moved on to other business matters. Eve West made a concise presentation on handling the media, and instructed, "Avoid the press. If they catch you in public, say 'No comment'."

She then outlined the counter-attack Lifespan was going to launch with the cooperation of two large New York TV networks, along with support from the *Capital Post* and *Manhattan Times* newspapers.

Eve added confidently, "Be assured that Lifespan has many supporters – the people that count. We are going to use the media to resurrect the old abortion issue. Zero in on the women's right to chose, *Roe versus Wade*, all the usual activist demonstrations. Then for added measure, we're going to parade some pathetic old people in front of the camera whose lives were saved by our treatments."

Eve paused to look at a cool and remote Max. He didn't seem to be as supportive as usual, not reinforcing her position. Nevertheless, she cautiously continued. "We're working through our political contacts in Washington. There's still support for our products in the HEW, and in Congress. But, we're hearing some opposition coming from the Social Security Administration." Eve smiled, "They think our life extending drugs are going to bankrupt them." Then she smiled, "As if they won't go under anyway."

Max interjected, "We know some pretty dogmatic women's rights lobbies in DC. Why not sic them on those Social Security administrators?"

Inwardly Eve resented what appeared to a sexist remark, and tactfully replied, "Yes, they do have a vested interest in our success."

Max grew tired of all this discussion, and rose from his chair to take over the meeting in his usual blunt style. "The bottom line of all this trouble is that we have to cut staff immediately. I want a 60% reduction in staff by next week. Al Greene reports just a few weeks of work-in-process and then we're out of specimen inventory."

It dropped like a bomb. The executives in the room knew things were bad, but this was an immediate drastic cut. Their first reaction was fear that such a deep reduction might include executives too.

Max continued in a business like fashion. "Human Resources have been authorized to work overtime and the weekend to get the paperwork ready. Tomorrow night you submit your cut list to Dean Reynolds in Human Resources. He'll submit them to me for final approval."

Max watched the executives murmur nervously amongst themselves. He loved to plant insecurity among his subordinates. It gave him absolute control over them.

Max interrupted their muttering, and held up his hand for quiet. "Listen. The news isn't all bad. Norm has something to add."

Norm rose back up to speak, and looked at Max with a grin, "I have to give Max credit for that entrepreneurial inspiration again. We have just sourced a deal with a Russian trading company to supply us with all the specimens we need to continue our business. They only cost a fifth of what we been paying domestically, except it's going to take 8 weeks before they arrive."

Max turned to Strauss. "You R&D people have to figure out how to get them over here in a viable condition." Norm's words were greeted with a sigh of relief and smiles by everyone.

Strauss stood up, and finally spoke out. "Until now we used fresh fetal cadavers to culture our drugs. My new R&D program with live specimen tissue resulted in improved yields and greater purity. I don't know how useful weeks old tissue would be in terms of culture yield.

Max dismissed the doctor. "Well, your people need to figure that out."

Max remained upbeat. "So you can tell our employees that this is more like an 8 week furlough, not a layoff." Max grunted a chuckle, "Maybe some of them can use up accrued vacation time." The usual compulsory nervous laughter followed from his underlings.

Everyone felt secure again and as the meeting concluded, leaving with a renewed feeling of strength and confidence in Max and his ability to handle any crisis.

Al Greene left with Dr. Strauss to plan the development of and extended duration specimen transport case. The two men set a tentative meeting date, and departed. On his way back to his building, Al decided to invite the always innovative Mike to attend as part of the design team.

CHAPTER 34
What's in a name?

Mike missed the medical confidence that Joel could provide, and the companionship of Phylis - he blew those bridges. For Mike and his sons, life at home with Amnion settled into a regular routine; changing blood supply, cleaning the dialysis machine, checking the oxygenator. Her gentle presence was almost like having a third child, baby, in the family. Mysterious but accepted nonetheless. Mike would routinely go downstairs every morning and check on this new family member before leaving for work, and the boys would look in on her after school. After a while, they even began to feel guilty about leaving her alone all day and then again when they slept. An arrangement was finally developed to visit her both morning and night after dinner. Like quality time together as 'family'. They even got some books out of the library to understand what they were looking at.

Still, it bothered them that she was still being left home alone for long periods of time during the day, so Mike decided to provide a more natural companion. At a local baby store he found DVD software that could duplicate the actual rhythmic internal whooshing noise of a mother's heartbeat. With his usual engineering ingenuity, Mike attached a miniature speaker to the plastic tubular fetal chamber, and plugged that into his laptop audio output.

Sometimes, when Amnion became particularly fidgety, he played the recording. It actually worked! In no time it could soothe her into serenity again. From then on, he rigged the device to play the 'creation concerto' (as he called it), day and every night when Amnion was alone for long periods. His little girl would never feel alone again.

Mike kept a logbook on Amnion's development to record her vital signs in the tube and surrounding events in the Lifespan saga, along with some periodic photographs. He felt that he might show them to her sometime in the future after she was 'born'. It would be a memento of a turbulent time in her life that she would never remember herself. Something, whose meaning, would gain importance when she was much older in life.

Matthew and Brian, being teenagers, were surprisingly responsible in making entries in the log and generally keeping tabs on the little evolving life. She was their 'little sister'. It was difficult to keep this wondrous being a secret, and tempting to tell the kids at school about this unique guest in their basement. Mike made it clear that her tenuous life would be dangerously jeopardized by even the slightest notoriety.

Evenings passed with Amnion's 'family', as Mike and his sons sat on stools, surgical masks in place, watching her occasional antics. In the dim red light, they all spoke softly to her, hoping she would somehow remember their voices later on when she was born. Initially, their words of encouragement would cause her to turn her closed eyes towards them, just like any human, Amnion seemed to tire of the same sound if repeated too often. Ultimately, though, their affectionate words had no more effect than any other parent's words to an invisible fetus.

It was fascinating to see how her sporadic movements of only a week or two earlier had slowed down into a graceful, more coordinated and fluid motion. Mike explained to his sons how Amnion's movements were influenced by her existence in an all-fluid world. At times, those slow motions were reminiscent of Tai Chi. The motions were frequent and surprisingly varied, involving her head, limbs and back. Amnion already shared many of the mannerisms of a newborn; yawning, sucking, general jaw movements, swallowing fluid and stretching. These were the movements a pregnant woman would naturally feel. Occasionally, Amnion would actually 'breath, but not through her nose. They were still sealed by a mucous plug. She would make gasping motions with her mouth as her lungs filled with the surrounding fluid as breathing practice. Even Jacque Cousteau would have been impressed with her water world antics.

Mike never ceased to be amazed at how coordinated she really was. Nothing like the seemingly mindless motions he observed on the outside of his wife's womb when pregnant with the boys. His gut feeling was that somewhere behind that tranquil and expressionless countenance a human brain was developing a human mind.

Once when Amnion had an attack of hiccups, it made him anxious to do something for her. He went upstairs and found a cotton-tipped applicator. Returning downstairs he sterilized it in alcohol. Carefully he inserted it through the open hatch of the fetal tube, and gently stroked her delicate cheek. Surprisingly, her hand came over to her cheek, as if to brush away an annoying fly. This incident led engineer Mike and the boys to 'experiment' further with Amnion's sense of touch, since it had became frustrating for them to merely sit and observe her. They even began to feel that natural human desire to hold her in their arms.

There in front of them, was a living mind, albeit a simple one, and that intrigued them no end. From time to time, they used the cotton applicator to tickle her feet and palms, as they seemed highly sensitive. They touched her nose and lips as well as her ears. Amnion tolerated these unintentional annoyances to a point. After a few episodes, it became apparent that their probing was not welcome or humorous. During the next few sessions, Amnion would rotate her posterior towards the access hatch as they opened it and point her rump to all parties. Mike began to get the message that their curious intrusions were not particularly entertaining to this little girl. It occurred to him that this developing child was a lot smarter, and warranted considerably more dignity than his foolings around would presuppose. He grew to respect her very human sensibilities, and resigned himself to be more sympathetic to her need for privacy.

At first, Mike's early observations of her rudimentary movements seemed to be an early mimic of movements that would occur after birth. Later, he concluded that her patterns were really an adaptation to living in the liquid environment of the womb, and what he was observing was nature's perfect accommodation to the existing environment. That same dexterity would not be noticeable after birth. As an infant, weighed down by gravity, she would hardly be able to move at all. As a baby, it would be some months before she could even turn on her side by herself.

During their observation time, Amnion could become quite animated pedaling with her legs as if riding an imaginary bicycle. She'd orient herself along the fetal tube's diameter and slowly pedal her feet against the curved inner wall until a complete somersault was accomplished. Mike's boys were impressed by this athletic show, thinking she was doing this to show off. Mike explained that her tiny developing brain was actually stimulating this movement to begin increasing her muscle coordination and balance, and aid circulatory development. It also kept her from sticking to any surface when lying there too long.

She also did a flex extension trick by first bending her head backwards and to one side, and then the rest of her body would rotate to that side along her lengthwise axis. These antics concerned Mike at times because he feared she might strangle herself with her twisted umbilical cord.

In later observations, Amnion would also exhibit characteristics related to life outside the womb. Of all these exercises the breathing was the one that disturbed Mike the most. Since her lungs were not fully developed, she wasn't really breathing in the sense that adults breathe air. In her liquid environment she was simply rehearsing the muscle coordination for the first breath that will take her from the womb into the outside world beyond.

When she did this exercise, her mouth would open and appear to slowly gasp a few times. Then stop, perhaps not resuming for quite some time. When Mike observed this behavior, he began to feel quite anxious during those long pauses. It was incomprehensible how she did not suffocate without doing what we do 24 hours a day, 7 days a week. Nature was in control here, allowing just enough, no more, no less, to keep this life alive.

These and many more little encounters bonded Mike and his sons to the wondrous little girl in a tube. Unknown to them Amnion, lacking a real mother, was also instinctively attaching herself to their voices and personalities too.

Eventually, it seemed so obvious to them, that Amnion had as much claim to life as any other human being.

CHAPTER 35
Paying the devil's due

Father Tom had been outside the Lifespan compound periodically since the first flurry of demonstrations after the *Brooklyn Daily News* exposé appeared. At twilight he led a small group of parishioners in a candle light prayer vigil. It was a fairly peaceful protest whose prayers were only interrupted by an occasional hymn from their gathering books. Lamentably, there were also a half-dozen other undisciplined radical groups from fringe organizations mixed-in and around his parishioners. This time, no police were available to handle that somewhat more rowdy group. The police force had been stretched thin to cover multiple protest demonstrations at City Hall, termination clinics, and participating extraction hospitals. Only one squad car would be dispatched - too late. The only media present was from a Fox5 Cable News team.

An approaching rainstorm made it prematurely dark as evening descended. The sunset was devoid of its usual rosy brilliance. Fingers of wispy advancing ashen clouds quickly smothered the twilight. Behind the Lifespan security fence, three black Lifespan drones took station on the other side of the fence, 50 feet apart. They hovered above, stationary, legs dangling half inward, like black widows observing prey. Since Lifespan's guard/operators had pistol licenses, they were able to weaponize the drones with a new feature. Slung below, a 380-auto pistol hung next to the camera. Its muzzle moved from side to side in sync with the camera. In this threatening air of gloom, the radical protesters converged on the corner of the Lifespan property where the corporate billboard and Yin-Yang emblem was prominently displayed - about 20 feet within the chain link security fencing. Some of the demonstrators had water balloons under their coats filled with lamb's blood. Encouraged by a media presence, they proceeded to hurl these balloons over the fence at the sign. A few hit their mark. Huge, dripping crimson red splashes now scarred the billboard.

Only a single network was still covering the Lifespan story. The other stations censored any further coverage of Lifespan. The Fox News team was quick to notice this unfolding drama, and ran over to illuminate the corporate sign with bright camera lights. The dripping effect of the blood stains formed a gruesome metaphor for what Lifespan Corporation was really about, and now that image was being beamed all over America.

Max had been outside his office building, near the main gate, when the commotion started at the corner of his property. He was immediately incensed at the distant desecration of his company's sacred symbol. Worse yet, the affront was being telecast on national TV. "Jesus Christ!" he muttered in frustration, "If it was a New York TV station, at least I could kill the video with a phone call."

Now angered, he ordered, "Get the dogs outside in front of the fence. Push those bastards back, and clean up that mess immediately!... and get rid of those Goddamn cameramen!"

From his main gate station, Lifespan security Sergeant Harry saw Max's personal security men bringing their four dark brown Doberman attack dogs towards him.

"Hey! Whoa! Where are you going with those big mutts?" he screamed defiantly.

"None of your business, flatfoot!" came the reply.

Harry remained undaunted and stepped in their path. "We've already got real cops on the way. They don't need you to handle this!"

"It's private property between the fence and the curb. We can do what we want along there," was the answer, and Harry was pushed out of the way, but he still followed some distance behind.

As everyone watched, the four Dobermans and their handlers moved outside the gate and turned along the grass parallel to the fence, still on Lifespan property. The mongrel group, side by side, strained against their thick leather leashes, looking like the fierce chariot horses from 'Ben Hur'. In a moment they were almost at the corner.

For a while, demonstrators, women and children shouted epithets at the threatening dogs. Father Tom came forward and tried to control the situation, despite his followers being a small group in this sea of indignant protesters.

The verbal screaming and taunting noticeably upset the dogs. They began to bark and snare, brandishing their huge gleaming white canines like small daggers. Saliva began to drip in sticky foaming globs from their curled muzzles. The irate animals pulled at their short leashes, and began rising in the air on their powerful hind legs, hack coughing from the chain collar's grip on their constrained throats. As their heads swung from side to side, the strings of gooey saliva were flung in the air from gaping jaws. Each time a dog came down on his front paws, its claws would scratch tenaciously at the turf for traction. The handlers began to lean back harder to restrain their animal's building aggression against the screaming tormentors.

With Max shouting commands to the handlers from his walkie-talkie radio, the canine group began to advance more deliberately on the demonstrators. The Doberman's back leg muscles bulged taught under their short glistening fur, straining to attack their noisy antagonists. By now, anger turned to fear in the protesters as women and children scurried to the rear of the crowd and everyone began to back peddle in unison. Even the Cable TV crew quickly withdrew and panned the action from the safety across the street.

Father Tom did not budge from the curb, and wound up alone between the two opposing groups. He was perhaps only 15 feet from the approaching dogs that were now rasping under their choker collars.

Gazing at the line of gnashing teeth, for some reason he thought, *The Four Horsemen of the Apocalypse.*

Then he raised up his palms and said, "Stop the madness. Take them back inside. You think these people deserve to have their flesh ripped apart over this?"

Pointing to the blood stained corporate sign he added, "Do you understand what this company does for a living?"

"Don't know Padre. Don't care!" one guard shouted back. "We get paid to protect private property. And you're on it!"

Father Tom knelt down at the curb in the path between the snarling attack dogs and the crowd at the corner in a gesture of passive resistance. Floodlights from the news cameras illuminated his solitary form in the enveloping darkness like a spotlight on an actor on a dark stage. Clutching his Rosary, he began the Lord's Prayer in a slow and deep voice. The dog handlers slowed their advance, temporarily stymied by his actions. For a moment it appeared that an awful nasty confrontation was being peacefully defused.

It became a surreal scene, as the contenders were momentarily split apart. On one edge of the camera spotlight, the darkness concealed a crowd of faceless frightened voices. On the other edge, four pairs of twin red dots moved erratically, reflections in the dog's eyes from the news camera lamps. Each iridescent pair accompanied by an equally intimidating set of front incisors framed by huge canine teeth that gleamed pearl white against the shadows.

Occasionally an insult was shouted, or a threat, daring the handlers to advance. Mixed in, other voices called for calm, and an end to this lunacy. Then, suddenly, one water balloons of lamb's blood were lobbed at the security guards from somewhere in the unruly multitude. One landed in front of the dogs.

The salty fragrance of the hunt was in the air. Black nostrils flared to inhale the scent. The die was caste. Instinct ruled. Dogs transformed into predators. The vulnerable Father Tom, the prey.

A second balloon descended on a handler, who impulsively raised his hands in defense, inadvertently allowing his dog's leash to uncoil. The enraged dog immediately yanked himself free and charged forward. All hell broke loose. People screamed in panic, scattering in every direction from the beastly threat. The Doberman went galloping undistracted, directly at the kneeling Father Tom. In an instant he leapt on the quarry with paws extended, viciously slamming into his side. Father raised his arm for protection, but the impact bowled the old cleric over sideways. The dog tumbled over him and fell on its side. It struggled violently to regain its footing, squirming and scratching sideways at the pavement for traction, its head twisted backwards, never taking its bulging eyes off the targeted victim. At once, it arose again and sprang back on the stunned Father Tom who was rising on his hands and knees after the fall to the cement curb. The dog impulsively sank its huge canines into the back of the good father's neck, and thrashed the Father's head from side to side.

The handler ran to retrieve the uncontrolled canine, as the other handlers fought for control of the remaining dogs. Reaching the animal, he desperately tried to pull the savage dog off the priest. Another picketer came forward, and tried beating the dog with his protest sign. The two men scuffled with each other. Women were crying, as the dog remained undeterred from maintaining its primordial death grip. Each blow delivered to its body by other spectators only caused it to react more territorially, violently shaking the priests head from side to side, now looking as if he were an old rag doll. In precious seconds, life was being ripped and squeezed out of the suffocating Father Tom.

Sergeant Harry had watched the melee some distance behind the dog handlers as the dog got loose. When the dog charged the priest, he broke into a full trot only seconds behind the others. The scene was almost a blur as he watched the useless activities of the men trying to dislodge the dog.

Then drawing his 9 mm revolver from its bouncing holster, he screamed, "Everybody get back! Get down!"

As the crowd retreated and dove for cover, Harry ran up to the enraged dog, put the gun to its chest and fired. There was the flash and that unmistakable sharp crack of gunfire. Then an ungodly howl and splash of blood into the air. The Doberman was knocked 3 feet sideways and rolled down to the ground. Harry leaped over the inert cleric's body and rushed to follow the dog's collapse to the street. With his pistol thrust forward, he quickly sent another round crashing into its skull with a thud.

For a moment, there was only an eerie quiet.....The dead dog...The dead priest...The lingering smell of gunpowder...The dank evening air....

Then, slowly, the muffled sobs of women. Some were still shielding their children on the grass from the bloody scene, others stood up to gaze in frozen silence. Each was filled with either absolute astonishment or shock. The news camera team across the street kept their video running through the entire episode, and they too stood silent, just looking at each other in disgust. Shaking their heads, one commented sadly, "What a waste of a life". Then they put down their video camera, and turned off the flood light.

Even the other three remaining Dobermans were stunned into submission by the gunfire. They ceased their aggressive actions and laid down in the wet grass, their cropped ears still pointing to attention. The frenzy was now over.. The deed was done, the hunt was over.

Attempts by the parishioners to resuscitate Father Tom were in vain. His carotid artery was severed and his windpipe crushed and punctured in several places. Harry tried mouth to mouth, but the precious air breathed in, simply sputtered and gurgle out the massive wound in the cleric's throat. There was nothing left to do except gather around him, and pray for his already departed spirit.

A heavy drizzle started, as if to mourn the night's tragedy. In Father Tom's crimson stained hands, still clutched tightly, were the rosary beads and cross his mother had given him 40 years ago when he was ordained as a priest.

In the subdued stillness, some woman started softly singing the clerics favorite hymnal, *Here I Am Lord*. Others joined in, singing along from the wet leaflets used during the demonstration.

The misting drizzle developed into a soaking rain that seemed to cleanse the priest's body of the crimson stains of violence and carried them away. His blood became a slowly meandering rivulet moving among the gutter's sand and grit. It was joined with the dog's blood dripping into the street nearby. Their blood merged into a stream, as if good and evil must have a final embrace in the destructive ritual of death.

In this circle of his parishioners, Father Tom had individually fulfilled his faith and realized his premonition. On a dirty street. In a brutal ending beneath the Lifespan corporate sign. He had joined the legacy of religious martyrs that stretched back some 2000 years.

The tragedy put an end to the protester's vehemence. Speaking amongst themselves in choked hushed tones, there was a feeling that all of them shared some blame in this tragedy. Even some of the Lifespan security personnel were visibly shaken, Harry included. When the ambulance carried away the body, the soaked protesters quietly dispersed and went home.

The police patrol car finally arrived too late to do anything, but call for an ambulance.

Inside the corporate compound Max mumbled under his breath, "Just what we need, another freakin martyr!"

From his immortal perspective it was inconceivable to Max how anyone could sacrifice his or her life for any cause – there was always tomorrow. He shrugged as he entered his limousine and grunted, "Serves the meddling bastard right."

In the darkness, his limousine clandestinely transported him back from the front gate to the safety of his metallic and smoked glass office building.

Harry looked back at the entrance gate and noted the limo's fading red taillights in the distant drizzle, realizing it was Max Brewster slithering off. He reflected on Brewster's callous behavior, disappointed that his chief exec did not even try to help. Any questions about sharing his conclusions about the R&D lab break-in being an inside job were resolved.

Right then, he swore to himself, *I'll be damned if I'll help Jane or him. Right now, whoever is this company's enemy, is my friend.*

* * * * * * *

At 8 PM that same evening, Mike was home in his basement, mask on, observing Amnion through a new clear plexiglass hatch he had installed earlier. When visiting her, he kept the lighting dim using special red lights, and with all the electronic and computer equipment, the basement looked like the interior of a nuclear submarine. He was interrupted by his son Matthew, who appeared at the top of the stairway, all excited about something.

"Hey dad! There was a news flash on TV. Something about somebody killed or badly injured over at Lifespan tonight."

Mike pulled down his mask, looked up and shouted. "What was the name of the person, Matt?"

"I didn't catch it Dad."

Mike's first thought was that Max Brewster had finally been shot by a demonstrator. "About time", he joked to himself. He hurried to finish checking Amnion's life support cart instrumentation, and covered the hatch with a dark cloth. Briskly, he ascended the stairs to the family room, and switched the TV from the Yankee game to the Fox news network. It took about 15 minutes for them to get around to local news again.

Then the television commentator announced, "It's been another day of protests and deadly confrontation at the Lifespan Corporate headquarters as demonstrators clashed with security personnel. This time it ended in tragedy for one protester, a Catholic priest from Infant Jesus parish."

The visual images that accompanied the commentary showed the advancing attack dogs, the bloody corporate sign, and the dead priest's shrouded body being loaded into the ambulance. The TV station thought the actual attack too graphic for viewers.

Mike stood silent in front of the tube. His heart sank. Filling with emotion, his throat began to constrict, and eyes moistened. His nose began to run. In his innermost thoughts he lamented, *Merciful Jesus, take him to your heart.*

Matthew heard his father quietly sniffle, and observed the reaction on his father's face. It was unsettling to see his father really cry. It was a truly rare sight. Something not seen since his mother's death.

The boy simply reacted with honest commiseration, "Dad. You know this man?" pointing to the TV.

Mike wiped his eyes with his sleeve, choked on his words saying, "In a way....I only met him twice. He was a sweet guy... a gentle person. I really liked him. I wanted him to be the one to Baptize Amnion when she's born."

Matthew didn't know how to react, and just stood close to his father in front of the television. Then an interview with corporate spokeswoman, Eve West, began. She calmly explained, "The priest's death was an accident caused by demonstrators acting like an uncontrolled mob. It' is just further evidence of conspiratorial activity designed to destroy a woman's right to choice, and deny sick people's right to Lifespan's healing treatments."

Mike quipped, "She's full of crap. The lying bitch is full of shit!"

Matthew was a bit shocked by his father's words. He had heard worse language at school, but never from his father's lips in the house.

"You know that lady too, Dad?"

Mike didn't pay attention to his son's question. He was too deep in his own thoughts and grief. He needed to be alone, and said, "Look pal, I need a little time to sort this out. I'm gonna go downstairs and get some more work done."

Mike left Matthew to watch his Yankee game, and went back downstairs to continue securing Amnion's environment. It was clear that he needed Phylis's companionship more than ever. He missed her so badly. He screwed up that relationship big time. He did not know if he could ever put things right with her or Joel. He felt the weight of so many people suffering for his decision. He sought a distraction, a justification for his actions. An escape from his lonely guilt - Amnion

Since Amnion's arrival, a dehumidifier was installed, and an air filtering system was working to combat atmospheric spores and such from the basement dampness. Walking over to the shiny circular plastic tube, Mike felt the compulsion to talk to the silent entity within. So, he switched the special red lights on, and rolled his lab stool over to the life support cart to sit down. Placing his hand on the shiny warm cylinder, he gently removed the black cloth cover over the plexiglas observation hatch, and moving close, looked down at the entity floating within. Mask on, he softly touched the smooth acrylic glass with his finger, he felt the urge to hold her in his hand.

Regarding her features, Mike noted that her facial cheeks were still sunken, and face still diminutive, which only accentuated the orbit of the still developing cranium. Mike remarked, "You know, Amnion, I use to talk to my sons when they were in Laura's womb. I use to think they were really listening to my 'pearls of wisdom'. I wish there was some way I could reach you too."

Amnion eyes remained sealed shut for now. Occasional a limb would jerk as though in a dream. For all external appearances, she seemed oblivious to Mike's lament, and he felt the futility of the one-way conversation.

"Well kid, I think we're all gonna be in big trouble before this is over. Someday, when you're older, remind me to tell you the whole story. There are some fine people with tremendous courage that will be forgotten and disappear into obscurity before this is all over. They were all a part of your still being alive today."

Amnion's smooth brow wrinkled slightly and Mike could discern the trace of eyebrows squeezing towards each other.

He chuckled with that sense of humor sometimes needed to relieve stress, *Either she disagrees with me or she's passing gas!.*

What Mike could not know was that Amnion, with no other stimulus, was beginning to imprint his muffled voice into her rudimentary memory. From her isolated perspective he was, in effect, becoming her 'mother'. Mike covered the hatch and sat alone in the dim red light, with only the swishing noise of a mother's heartbeat. His feelings about Father Tom's violent demise were a jumble of sorrow, guilt and desire for revenge. Mike wrestled with his own scruples. Mike remembered Father Tom complimenting him on having the quality of conscience. That same thought mechanism was making it more difficult for Mike to maintain his position in this battle, leading him into what seemed a paradox of contradictions. What started out as a prank, stupid spite, became a mission of mercy to save tiny humans. Now the downside was developing. Sick people were loosing their Lifespan therapeutic drugs, employees were being laid off, and innocent men like Father Tom were dying.

When Mike embarked on all these revelations about Lifespan R&D, it never occurred to him that anyone would be at risk besides Joel and himself. It never seemed a life and death issue beyond the fetuses themselves. As things developed, it seemed to Mike, that the burden for the fight and its consequences should rest solely on him alone. A burden he would, and have to, willingly handle alone. Now someone else paid that full measure of sacrifice. Mike just wasn't prepared for this business of being responsible for anyone else.

He resolved his deliberations with the conclusion that this was not too much different then going to war. Once you decide to fight, be prepared for the collateral damage.

Mike looked down again at the life he saved in that tube, heart fluttering, and weighed the possibility of giving up her life so someone else could live to a ripe old age. The emotional implications immediately resolved his confusion and re-crystallized his mission. In Mike's opinion, if this world is going to build its foundation on killing these fetuses, then this society wasn't worth saving!

He resolved that he would never doubt his goal again.

Then he recalled the words of Mary Lou O'Reilly, the woman injured on the Lifespan fence, and her earlier visions. Her statements on people sacrificing for the good and the ultimate price can be a person's life. Soon, he remembered Father Tom's reminder that evil only triumphs when good men are not willing to make the supreme sacrifice. In some ways their words were beginning to appear almost prophetic now.

CHAPTER 36
Change the conversation

In the early morning hours, the big shiny black limousine rolled smoothly up the curved driveway of crushed red stone in front of Max Brewster's mansion to pick him up The house itself was a large white two story colonial with four faux pillars in front, actually made of PVC plastic. It had a portico at the front entrance whose roof served as a balcony. There was an over abundance of black wrought iron railings along the balcony and porch below. Even the windows were trimmed with wrought iron gates that covered the bottom half of the window. It appeared so ornate that it almost reminded one of an old hotel building on Bourbon Street in New Orleans. Or better yet, a whorehouse. Max lived here in this gaudy expanse alone. He did have a family here years ago, but they separated and moved to Fort Lauderdale. Other than occasional late alimony notices, he rarely heard from them - nor did he really care too.

Work was his life - the company shareholders his family. Max kept his passion reserved for material things. Things that could be seen as assets to be envied by others. Things that could be converted into the only real common denominator - money. From that sprang equity, profit, possessions. From money to power, power to influence, influence to a choice of limitless sex partners.

In spite of this perspective, in his own unique way, Max did believe in the concept of heaven and hell. Not really in the spiritual sense, more with an earthly bent. His concept proved much more amusing. It had to be played out in the world of the living. He and his investor partners would acquire heavenly reward through corporate acquisitions, then, they would create hell on earth for everyone else.

Max came out of his house dressed in an $2200 tailored suit and tie, and entered the back door of the waiting limo for his trip to work. Unknown to either the public or Lifespan employees, he'd hired a security company to furnish him with a bullet-proof, anti-terrorist transportation vehicle to get back and forth to work now.

With the tragic death of Father Tom, some people were actually holding Max personally responsible, although he could not fathom why. If they should be mad at anyone, it should be Strauss. Threatening phone calls came into Lifespan at least three times a day. Not the kind of attention an immortal needed - and still enjoy his health.

The rejuvenating therapy that Strauss was administering to Max was not only making him feel good, he looked younger. The success of these drugs made Max realize that his biggest threats to immortality now came from only three directions - contracting some fatal bacteria or viral diseases, death by accident, or murder. Max had addressed the last two threats and was still working on how to protect him from the risk of infection.

Each day, for security reasons, the limo took a different route to Lifespan headquarters. On this particular morning, the vehicle was stopped at a traffic light. Max happened to glance out the car window to observe a nearby newsstand.

"Pull over Steve!" Max suddenly ordered his chauffeur. "And get me a copy of that *Brooklyn Daily News.*"

Steve dutifully obeyed, parked the limo and went out to the stand. Purchasing a paper, he glanced at the headline. He shook his head and returned to the limo. Once inside, he handed the folded paper to Max through the heavily tinted window.

Steve commented, "It ain't good news Sir," and resumed the drive to work.

Inside, Max cursed, "God damn it!" as he read the headline.

It seemed lately that the *Daily News* was presenting one explosive

253

exposé after another about Lifespan. No sooner did Max figure out a way to handle one headline, then the *News* seemed to come up with another. This time their investigation had uncovered Max's indictment several years ago for fraud in a defense industry company he was involved with. As he read the copy it became obvious that the article was well researched and revealed a lot of the 'clever' corporate shenanigans he had used to cheat the government. From the detailed account, it almost appeared as if someone was feeding the *Daily News* their leads. Someone close to him. *Character assassins!* Max grumbled to himself, as he tossed the newspaper on the empty seat beside him.

By this time, his vehicle was approaching Company headquarters, and the big black sedan slowed down at the corner of Technology Drive, the place where Father Tom had died. An arrangement of white and red carnations were carefully laid on the curbside, marking the exact spot where the priest had fallen just a few days earlier. A monument no one dared disturb. Nearby a few picketers stood idly with signs, and noticed the fancy limo's approach. Max leaned forward and smugly peered from the dark tinted side window. He passed them by, secure in the knowledge that he could see them, but they could not see him.

From angry faces muffled shouts of "Murderer! License to Kill!" faintly reached his ear. Ignoring the insults, he casually sat back in his seat and its perceived safety. When, suddenly, he heard a cracking sound behind him. It startled him enough to make him jump forward and turn around to look out the small back window.

There were eggshell fragments sliding down the outside window suspended in the transparent gop of the egg white. Max stared at the mess over his shoulder, calmly concluding an egg had been tossed at his car. He perceived a small solid object was in the middle of the yellow goo, attached to something that looked like a wiggly string. Max moved closer to the glass, only to observe a chicken embryo slowly sliding down the window in front of him.

It startled him and he recoiled, muttering, "Disgusting!"

The chauffeur cringed as he observed his agitated boss through the rear view mirror.

"What's the matter Sir?" he carefully inquired.

Max spun around and sat back in his seat sulking and mumbling, "These people are outrageous!" He pointed his thumb to the back, "When you drop me off, clean that mess off."

When the limo reached his building, Max didn't wait for the driver to come around as usual and open his door. Instead, he bolted out himself, hardly waiting for the vehicle to come complete stop. The metaphor of the chicken embryo wasn't lost on Max, and the message rankled him to no end. Outside his office, an even more infuriated Max, stormed past his secretaries and immediately ordered, "Get Norm Stark to join me for a conference... Right now!"

Then he stomped into his office and slammed the door behind him.

Norm arrived 5 minutes later and grunted, "Good morning," to his boss, now brooding in his leather chair.

"Norm, did you see today's headline ?"

"If I don't, someone always manages to give me a copy."

"I want to sue the bastards. And if we can't do that, I'll buy the fucking paper and then fire them all!"

Norm understood Max's frustration and commented reassuringly, "No double jeopardy here. Relax you can't be tried again for the same crime twice. Besides, I reviewed the article's content. It may be pretty accurate and factual. However, there are still no grounds for new litigation."

"So, Norm, what do we do about it?"

"Nothing. It's just another arrow without a tip. We'll let it bounce off us like the Clintons always did, and we continue with our business."

Norm paused and walked around Max's desk to pat him on the shoulder, and added, "In a few days it'll pass over. We'll issue a statement that our company and its executives have not been involved in government contracting for a long time now. And, you've already paid your debt to society."

Max still had some concern and said, "Yeah, but all I paid was a $10,000 fine and three months of stupid community service at a senior center."

"Not to worry. It's what the courts say that counts, not some news reporter's muck raking opinion. And, you know who owns the judges."

Max chuckled and finally began to settle down. Between the *Brooklyn Daily News* report and the chicken embryo incident this morning, his usual invulnerability had been shaken. Still, he had absolute confidence in Norm's legal skills and his excellent track record of protecting him.

"Yeah. Let's get back to our business," Max confidently remarked. "What's the latest on potential bidders for the company?"

Norm walked back to the couch and sat down to relax. "Well, no one is going to touch us now with the negative publicity as such. I spoke to representatives of the Japs and the Chinks. If we can come out of this situation and still do our specimen reclamation, then they'd still be interested in making an offer."

Max queried, "The Germans, what about them trying to pirate our people?"

Norm shrugged his shoulders. "Max, I talked to several executives over there right up to the Chairman of the Board. They deny everything, although they did admit to the possibility of obtaining their own license from their governments."

Max interrupted, "See! They're lying. Sneaky bastards. They are going to build their own facility."

"Max, I think it's premature to draw that conclusion yet. Besides it still would round out the bidding field for Lifespan if we keep them involved."

"I still don't trust 'em," Max countered, and then changed the subject.

"Incidentally, what's the status of the lawsuits?"

"I think we'll settle the personal loss ones out of court," Norm answered. "It might cost our insurance carriers a few million, but they're the least of our worries. And I've been assured that the State and Feds aren't working on any criminal indictments. So, that's covered."

Norm leaned forward and clasped his hands between his knees. "The one we need to be careful with is the Operation Rescue suit. They're actually suing the company for the wrongful death of resuscitated fetuses. That's where your personal exposure is greatest."

An enraged Max sat up and his keen ear took note of that last phrase. "Personal exposure! For what?"

Norm stood up to walk across the room to the window. He gave a soothing hand gesture with his palms outward, and calmly explained, "I know it sounds outrageous, but beyond this lawsuit, it could lead to pressure for criminal charges. It doesn't matter how frivolous their position, wrongful death is still a very serious charge."

Max swung his chair towards the window to face Norm directly and asked, "Norm, what's my exposure?"

"They're requesting affidavits of you and all your executives and directors. It's a good strategy when you have a weak case. The fear they generate in the subordinates usually gets someone to crack and turn States Evidence against the rest."

Max became increasingly concerned by Norm's worst case scenario. Living in prison forever or lethal injection was not his idea of how to spend immortality. Max voice quivered slightly saying, "Norm... you've got a way out of this... right?"

Norm turned, sat on the windowsill, and folded his arms comfortably answering, "They'd have to indict the Supreme Court before they could get you."

"So what's the plan?" Max asked eagerly.

"Simple Max. Simple," he smiled. "First, a fetus is not a human life protected by the Constitution. You remember Roe vs. Wade, and the last court decisions."

Max nodded.

"Second, the photograph in the paper will be explained as small scale experiments begun under regulatory changes started back five years ago that allowed research experimentation on fetuses."

"Third, we changed the goal of the resuscitation operation to a life saving one. Actually, we were inventing a new technology to save premature infants!"

"Hot shit!" Max exclaimed with glee. "So now we're saving infant lives. I love it!"

"Yes. Strauss just has to write a couple of internal memorandums to cover a different kind of research program. Back date them, and that'll close the case on the *Daily News* story too."

Max was in awe of Norm. He managed a totally dismal series of events and turned it into a positive. Max walked over to pat Norm on the back and gleefully remarked, "So, now I'm a hero. Right?" And, feeling magnanimous, he added, "I've got this lock on immortality. How'd you like a piece."

"Yeah, actually I could go for a 'piece'."

They laughed, and decided to celebrate later with lunch, drinks, and meet some sexy young women.

CHAPTER 37
The 'prodigal friend'

Attorney Richard Farmers arrived home from work a good deal later than he really wanted. A dinner meeting with the other Board of Directors of Metropolitan Bank was more of an exercise in plain 'bored-dumb' than business. His wife, Evon, met her tired husband in the parlor and delivered a warm moist kiss to his dry lips. Her sympathetic hug made him feel that the long hours at the office were all worthwhile for the abundance they afforded his family. Before he could finish removing his tie and suit Evon took charge and said, "I've got it sugar. You just make yourself comfortable."

Richard stared at her figure as she walked down the hall to the coat closet with his tie and suit. She was a tall woman, light skinned. Originally from Bermuda, a mix of English and African heritage, had given her face and figure a sculptured look. He felt lucky to have won her attention in spite of some unsolicited grumbling from his colored friends. There was always this implication that as an African American, she wasn't 'black enough' for him to pursue a politically orientated career.

His reverie was interrupted by Evon calling out from in the closet, "On the telephone table hon... your mail."

Richard reluctantly walked over and scooped up the stack of letters with some disdain. Nowadays, so much 'junk' mail came from brokerages, credit card companies, and insurance agents. Sometimes it felt like he was on every telemarketing mailing list in the country. The constant bombardment made him astute enough to guess the missive's come-on simply by looking at the envelope. Richard took the pile of letters into his study, and plopped down in his favorite old chair to relax. Evon brought in a glass of Chianti. As he examined the letters in his lap, a lone reading lamp bathed the room in a soft light that gave a pleasant deep amber aura to the room. The obvious solicitations found their way into his small brass wastebasket nearby. Eventually he stopped when he reached a hand addressed letter - rare in today's computer age. It was not a peel off label or a laser print job. It even had a hand written return address on the top corner, with an awful familiar sender's name. The lawyer slowly tapped the letter's edge on his forehead as he searched his distant memory.

"Mike Santino?" he murmured, "Why does that ring a bell?"

Then long forgotten memories of Mike streamed back to flood his consciousness and pique his curiosity. Now more intrigued, he grabbed his reading glasses from the table and unsealed the letter.

At the same time his teenage son and daughter came in to kiss him good night, and then, just as quickly, wandered off to bed. Evon strolled in with her glass of wine, drolly asking, "Anything interesting old man?"

Then she playfully rattled his reading glasses on the bridge of his broad nose, and sat down on a loveseat opposite him.

Richard stared at her with a fitful far-away look, as though his mind was a thousand miles distant. After 25 years of marriage, Evon could sense his moods. "What's the matter snookums?"

He didn't answer right away, simply looking at her over his glasses with that benevolent appreciative grin she'd come to love since they met 30 years ago.

Holding the open letter in the air he said in slight disbelief, "This is from a fellow I knew from Fordham in my college days."

Then starring at the page he shook his head, "Mike Santino. He played football with me. Even roomed together in our senior year."

Evon looked puzzled, thinking that she pretty much knew all of Richards's old friends and family, even the ones before they first met. So she asked quizzically, "That name doesn't ring a bell. You never mentioned him before?"

"Well," Richard smiled, "did you ever hear of a love-hate relationship?"

"Yes... So?"

"Well that's Mike Santino."

Evon became more interested in the letter now and asked, "What does he want?"

"He wants to meet me for lunch next week." Then looking down at the letter again Richard added, "It seems he works over at that Lifespan Corporation, over in New Jersey."

Evon instantly recognized the company name saying, "Oh dear, the one that's in the newspapers. The one embroiled in those supposed experiments or something on human fetuses."

Richard nodded in the affirmative.

She took a sip on her wine, and glanced over the rim, "So are you going to see him?"

Richard shrugged his shoulders in uncertainty. Evon sought to ascertain the reason for his reluctance, "Well, why not? Isn't he an old friend." When Richard didn't answer, she added, "Is it the controversy over his company?"

Richard seemed to discourage any further questions by answering, "It's a long story."

His wife put down her wine glass and shifted her position in the loveseat to recline with her arm clutching a sofa pillow. Smiling she said, "Well honey. I've got all night." Evon loved any kind of 'real people' stories, and snuggled up comfortably with her legs curled up.

Richard let out a sigh of resignation, seeing his wife was ready to probe this undisclosed part of his life. "OK, here goes," he said. "I first met Mike at football practice in my junior year. He was a lightweight kid of average height. Definitely out of place with the rest of us big boys. He played free safety on the second string defense. He really wasn't tall enough or fast enough to go toe to toe with those big wide receivers on offense – a regular 'Rudy-Rudy'."

A smiling Evon interrupted, "You played on the first string. Didn't you dear?"

Her interruption broke his train of thought. "Uh, yes. But anyway, we scrimmaged the second string the practice squad of expendables during the week before each Saturday game. Anyway, I remember watching one play where this small kid put his head straight into the thigh pad of a 250 pound fullback. Must have whacked the little guy back 10 feet. Knocked him out cold, right through the helmet and all."

Evon cringed sympathetically, "Oh, that must have hurt!"

"The kid was back in uniform a week later. This concussion protocol thing wasn't an issue those days. By the end of the next week his arm was badly crushed on a fumble recovery."

"Sounds almost suicidal, Hon."

"Yeah, I know. I spoke to the coach about playing him. He said the kid had heart, wanted to play football more than anything in the world. Besides, he had a nose for the ball. What he lacked in size and strength he made up for with smart play and aggressiveness. Eventually, this kid got another concussion in practice. Some of us players were actually concerned about accidentally killing him, and we talked to the coach again. He eventually agreed to only use him on passing downs and special teams."

Evon gave Richard a confused look. She was not an avid football fan. He sensed it and tried to explain. "Special teams, Evon. Kickoffs, punts, pass plays - that sort of thing."

Not totally following this and not wishing to slow down her husband's story, she gave a half serious nod and said, "Oh yes, those plays."

"Anyway, I remember one game when we played Bucknell for the big Homecoming weekend. We had a lot of injuries that day, so Santino was being used as a replacement on passing downs at free safety."

Richard leaned forward as the memories became more enjoyable to remember.

"It was third down and long yardage. We were ahead by a field goal. I was playing outside line backer on defense and Santino was somewhere behind me. When the ball was hiked, it looked like an end sweep to my side. The big tight end hit me and I brushed him off to the inside, reading the outside motion of the tailback."

Richard's voice became more animated as he vividly relived the moment. Evon patiently listened. "Well, I got faked out. The quarterback shot a quick look-in pass to that tight end, and I only saw open field in front of him. Then, as I turned in pursuit, I see Santino come up like and arrow from deep pass coverage and hit this big guy's legs. The impact knocked Santino backwards, but he managed to hold onto one of the tight end's ankles. The big kid must've dragged Santino 6 feet before he stopped in frustration and stuck his other foot's spikes right into Santino's side. I was running full tilt towards them, and I could see Mike's face inside his helmet. It was contorted in pain. Still Mike held on until I came up and hit this big white kid square in the shoulder. He fumbled and we recovered the ball - won the game."

Evon said good naturedly, "Sounds like the ending to one of those feel good movies."

"Almost," Richard replied.

"Except when I looked down at Mike, he was bleeding profusely through his jersey on his left side - puncture wounds from those old metal spikes we wore. When he struggled to his feet and limped towards our bench, the blood on his jersey seemed to enrage everyone. Our bench emptied out onto the field, and the biggest brawl in the school's history happened."

Richard looked up with an almost childish pride, "I even popped a few guys myself."

"Charming," Evon sarcastically remarked, "And in front of a homecoming crowd, too!"

"Yeah!" Richard added, obviously enjoying the recollection. "In fact the student government and faculty tried to force the school to drop the football program all together after that."

"But Richard, how could they do that after one mindless incident?"

"Sweetness, remember this was 30 years ago when all those old hippie professors were trying to make wimps out of everyone."

Evon sat back and smiled, "Well, you boys should have a lot to talk about over lunch." Then she added in jest, "Maybe you two can beat up the restaurant waiter after desert."

Richard's did not pick up on her jest. His face turned doubtful. She noticed the change right away and asked him what was wrong.

Richard explained, "In the summer before my senior year, my roommate was caught dealing LSD. He had to do prison time and I was forced at the last minute to dorm with someone else. Now coincidentally, Mike Santino's South American roommate was called home to Venezuela when that kid's father died."

Evon couldn't hide a smirk and said, "Let me guess... integrated roommates - right?"

Richard nodded in the affirmative. "Lord help us. We were the first black and white roommates in school history. It doesn't sound like much now, but it was a big deal then. It wasn't a storybook situation. Neither of us hit it off initially, and there was this huge racial gulf between us. Santino didn't care for blacks, and I didn't particularly care for whites at the time. We really lived under an undeclared and uneasy truce."

Richard sat back and crossed his arms, "Mike used to annoy me with his disparaging comments about blacks. Like; You people keep changing your nationality. Negroes, Afros, Blacks, People of Color, Chocolates. Like you never figure out that you should just call yourselves Americans."

Richard looked down smiling and shook his head. "The odd thing though was that he didn't think of himself as Italian-American. He didn't dig this ethnic pride stuff. Said he was a 3rd generation American, period. He was born here, and would die here. Didn't know squat about Italy. And he thought blacks should regard themselves the same way too."

"You couldn't exchange roommates or something?" Evon inquired.

"No. Those were the days when everybody was in college with all that government aid money paid for every warm body. The dormitories were packed. You couldn't change anything once the semester started."

"I tell you Evon, one thing about this guy Santino. He put those prejudices aside when it came down to specific people - individuals. Eventually that meant me too."

Richard seemed to change topics when he popped a question. "You remember my black friend Henry Parsons?"

"The one that became a country doctor?" Evon asked.

"Same guy," Richard said, and continued his little story. "Well, engineer Mike went out of his way to tutor my friend Henry through Calculus. He was failing badly. None of us brothers really had a talent for it. As an Engineering major, Mike loved math and volunteered to help him. Spent dozens of nights and Saturdays with Henry to get him through. That was more than any of my white liberal friends were ever willing to do. I asked him about it, and in his usual sardonic reply, Mike said, "I'm a technical evangelist! I'm going to convert Henry into an Engineering major.""

Richard clapped his hands together and exclaimed, "Henry managed a 'B' and was accepted to medical school."

"So, when did you last see this Mike guy?" Evon said.

Richard paused to scratch his head for a moment, "Believe it or not, I was invited over his house for Italian dinners on several Sundays before graduation."

Evon laughed, "So you'll tolerate a bigot for a free meal."

Richard grinned while patting his stomach, "Ah, the compromises one must sometimes make for fine cuisine." In the end we actually did become good friends."

Richard paused and became more serious as he tested his memory. "He didn't come to graduation and I lost track of him when I went on to Law school. About 4 years afterward I joined Senator Wilson as an aid up in Albany. It was then that I heard about some Long Island kid that was a fighter pilot for the Navy. He was up on court martial charges, and the kid's father wrote to the Senator for help."

Evon paused then interjected. "And I presume the pilot was Santino?"

"Yes," Richard said. "He was smack in the middle of bombing missions over in the Middle East."

Evon was delighted and sat up in her chair. She had little contact with people actually fighting in that war, and found this story becoming more interesting.

"Tell me what happened."

"Apparently on his own initiative he attacked an Iranian jet fleeing into Iranian airspace after downing one of our helicopters. Chased the SOB all the way to an Iranian airbase. Shot the guy down 200 feet over their airbase runway. Then tried to high tail it back to his carrier ."

"Then what?"

SAM's." he remarked.

Again Evon asked,"What?"

"Surface to Air Missiles, muffin. He lost his F18 over the Gulf. Bailed out, and was eventually rescued."

"Oh."

"It was quite an embarrassment to our government. Very hush-

hush. We even had to quietly apologize to the Iranian Government – had to pay for their aircraft and the damaged runway."

Evon stood up and exclaimed, "Well, didn't that Iranian pilot start the fight?"

"Sure," a tired Richard replied.

"Now doesn't that sound stupid," Evon added.

Richard just nodded his head in agreement.

Evon asked with concern, "So, what happened to this Mike Santino?"

"The Senator intervened and the Navy arranged an honorable discharge under the condition that Santino keep the incident confidential, remain silent, and not contest his separation from the Service."

"Too bad for him…politics."

"Yeah, he got a raw deal... and that's the last I ever heard of him."

Evon walked over to sit on the cushioned arm of her husband's chair. She slipped her hand around his neck and kissed his cheek. Richard beamed from his wife's attention and squeezed her so that she fell against his chest into his lap.

They laughed and Richard stole a kiss. A sultry Evon pushed him away and changed the subject, "It's only a lunch. See the man!"

Richard replied, "I just hope he doesn't want to borrow money."

They laughed and sauntered arm in arm into the family room to catch the late night news on TV before retiring to bed.

CHAPTER 38
The reluctant lawyer

Mike entered the immense office building on Madison Avenue and 54th street in Manhattan for his appointment with Richard Farmers. The structure was a turn of the century granite edifice whose huge and intimidating lobby exuded the opulence of an earlier era of American business tycoons. Everywhere there were Italian marble columns, frescos on the ceiling, brass fittings and gold leaf trim. The interior failed to intimidate Mike. On the contrary, to him it was just an inventory of collectible knickknacks. He thought the only reason somebody hadn't stolen all this stuff inside, was that you would need a power chisel and a dump truck to cart it away.

After checking in with the security guard, Mike ascended rapidly in the elevator to the 19th floor. He arrived at a richly appointed walnut paneled lobby with paintings hung of various deceased partners in the law firm. Gazing at these chubby old men, Mike wondered if anyone ever tried to paint mustaches on their faces.

Outside Richard Farmers's office were several neatly attired middle-aged women in business suits and skirts. Mike couldn't help but contrast this formal extravagance to his meager office when he was a Vice President in a defense company. His office was probably as big as this guy's coat closet. As he reflected on that office, he remembered that he had to reprimand his assigned Admin wearing blue jeans and a Mickey Mouse sweatshirt to work.

Mike finally meandered over to the receptionist and announced his arrival. She indicated that Richard was still in a meeting, and for Mike to make himself comfortable. In the meantime, Mike did some mental arithmetic figuring out square footage and the monthly upkeep costs of this law firm. The answer was definitely in astronomical figures.

After a while Richard finally came out of his office to greet Mike. He was taller than Mike remembered him, and a bit heavier too. Richard's voice was very deep and smooth, aloof but cordial.

They shook hands and exchanged nervous pleasantries. "Mike said, "Got the full beard now, eh?"

Richard messaged his beard, and invited him to lunch. He guided Mike to the elevator inquiring if he cared for Italian Cuisine. Mike laughed, "How could I say no."

Walking through the building's main lobby several people waved to Richard. Outside, on the crowded sidewalk, several more people greeted the pair saying, "Hi Dick!" It seemed as if everyone in New York knew Richard Farmers. As they strolled down the blocks and crossed some busy city intersections, they exchanged personal information about their families. Richard expressed his condolences regarding Mike's loss of his wife, Laura, and Mike thanked him and didn't dwell on it.

At the exclusive Italian restaurant everyone greeted them with a 'Hello Mister Farmers or a 'Hi Dick'.

Mike commented, "You know Richie it sounds strange to hear people call you 'Dick'. We called you Richie back in school."

"Times change, Mike," Richard answered. Then he added, "When we were on the football team, we used to call you 'Crash'."

Mike laughed as those college football memories returned.

Once seated, there was a brief uncomfortable silence until their drinks came. In spite of the friendly atmosphere, there still seemed to be this distance between them - A gulf of 30 years and financial status that seemed difficult to bridge.

Mike restarted the conversation with a question. "So Richie, how did you get from pre-law at Fordham to Madison Avenue?"

In responding, Richard was unexpectedly candid, attributing his success to a series of political contacts made by his association with the

Republican Party. Back then, he was one of only a few educated blacks politically active in their realm, and who scored the highest grade on the NY bar exam. Working on Senator Wilson's re-election campaign, he was noticed being interviewed on a local T.V. station. Once he was mentored by the Senator, the opportunities to advance just seemed to find him.

Mike admired Richie's modesty. He had met so many egotistical executive people that attribute their success solely to themselves. He concluded that Richie was a smart person all right, and it was obvious he kept his triumphs in perspective - didn't flaunt it at those of lesser achievement. It was no wonder so many people genuinely liked him.

Richard interrupted Mike's thoughts with a question, "So what about you Mike? How did your life turn out?"

"Not as interesting as yours pal." My first mentor was Uncle Sam. He gave me a free education in ROTC and a seven-year commitment, and with my Mechanical Engineering degree. Got sent directly from boot camp to OCS (Officers Candidate School). Three months later I was in flight school. Imagine putting a helmet on my head again and giving me 20 tons of fighter plane to cruise around in!"

Richard chuckled, "Yeah man! I can see 'Crash' conserving bullets so you could ram some unsuspecting enemy pilot with the whole plane!"

"Yeah," he laughed, "I did some damage."

Richard turned a bit more serious and said, "So how did you find flying in the Middle East?"

Mike wrinkled his brow, a bit perplexed. "How'd you know about that?"

Richard related how Senator Wilson had intervened in Mike's court martial case with the Joints Chiefs of Staff in Washington. "They were going to fry your bacon, man!"

Pleasantly surprised, Mike leaned back in his chair and said, "I always wondered why the Navy brass suddenly backed off. I guess I owe you one." Then with an innocent look added, "I settled down after that. Came home to Laura in the States, got a job as an aerospace engineer. Then marriage, a house, kids." Mike let out a sigh saying, "A very conventional career working my way up from the bottom based on merit to a VP."

Richard nodded in agreement, saying, "It takes a life time doing it that way. It's who you know, to get there quicker." After an awkward pause in the conversation, Richard asked, "Then how'd you get hooked up with that Lifespan Corporation?"

Mike leaned back in his chair trying to suppress the bitter memories of laying off all those people in his defense business. "When the aerospace business went bye-bye, I was eventually laid off too. After several months, I managed to land a management position at Lifespan because of my background in automated test equipment. Actually, I think it was just a fluke. You know, right place, right time."

Richard's order of macaroni and peas arrived, as well as, Mike's veal parmigiana. It allowed for a break in the conversation, and Mike looked around the restaurant. The tables were fairly spread out, not like the places he would be jammed into for lunch. Patrons spoke in hushed tones, maintaining an air of exclusivity and privacy.

Mike thought, *Jeez, is this place gonna be expensive.*

Richard restarted the discussion as he leaned over his entree. "So what's the real story over there at Lifespan? I heard that they pulled some real media muscle to censor and debunk all those negative articles in the *Brooklyn Daily.*"

Mike stopped eating and took a sip of his `Corona Light'. He debated whether to tell Richie the whole truth. It was apparent that his old friend was well connected, maybe all the way back to Lifespan. There was also the potential risk of scaring him off. Mike decided to roll the dice anyway.

"What you see and read in the papers is actually the truth. They take fetuses, revive them, and then extract the life out of them for three or four weeks. The crematorium smoke is their epitaph."

Richard's face contorted into a grimace. This was not exactly luncheon conversation. After gulping his white wine he said, "How can you work there?"

Mike decided to chance it and figuratively 'roll the dice'. "It won't be for long....since I'm the whistle blower. I'm the guy who gave the story to the papers."

Richard was caught off guard by these revelations, and unintentionally dropped his fork. His world was always carefully choreographed. People were thoroughly vetted before a meeting. You always knew the outcome before anyone else. And, above all, you never took risks. Richard debated whether to conclude this re-union right away, and distance himself from a person who might be considered a felon.

Mike sensed Richie's discomfort, but was intent on putting Richie on the spot. "So," he continued, "They have another more advanced project called 'Greenhouse' to fertilize human eggs *in vitro*, clone them, and grow human fetuses in secrecy. Create their own herd of human extraction clones."

Richard wiped his mouth with his napkin and interrupted. "Mike I think I've heard enough. You know how crazy you sound."

Mike answered sarcastically, "You're the lawyer Richie. You know you can't judge someone's mental faculties, unless you have a psychiatric expert."

The meeting turned awkward, and Richard started to look around the restaurant to see if anyone was paying attention to his companion. He had not been in a touchy situation like this before, and tried to sound prudent. "They have a pretty big legal staff over there. Isn't Norm Stark their Chief Counsel?"

"Yeah. So?"

He cautioned Mike, "That's high powered. You really should seek professional help."

At this point Mike didn't know if he meant a psychiatrist or an attorney.

Richard glanced nervously at his smartphone saying, "I have a 1:30 meeting," and summoned the waiter for the check. Mike offered to split the bill. Richard refused. He avoided Mike's eyes as the conversation wandered into a less derisive discussion of the weather.

On the sidewalk outside Richard shook Mike's hand to wish him well. It certainly made sense not to be seen on a public street with him again.

Mike held his hand firmly but didn't let go. "I need your help Richie," he said. "I need a lawyer to fight these Lifespan executives, and end the horror. Before this nightmare really becomes our children's future."

Mike's eyes engaged Richard's with sincerity, and determination.

Richard was sympathetic, but feared getting involved in such a sordid mess, and tried to withdraw his hand from Mike's grip. "You know Mike, you can't sue a corporation just because they're being unethical. You have to prove a law was broken, damages to injured party, business or personal,... or at least psychological distress. Do you have that?"

Mike looked down at the curb, knowing that the only injured party alive that was a testament to Lifespan's operations, was growing in his basement. He dared not reveal that knowledge. Lord, he had already scared Richard enough. So he replied, "Can't you just sue them for what they're doing in general?"

"No Mikey," the attorney explained impatiently, "That's what Operation Rescue tried in court a week or two ago. You see how poorly that progressed with the judge."

Mike was still adamant. "Richie, I don't think you see how much is at stake."

Richard continued to nervously glance around the sidewalk for any witnesses to this meeting and wanted some excuse to flee. So, he relented somewhat and said, "Look, I'll see what can be done. Write me a little summary of the facts surrounding all this and I'll review it. Maybe find someone to take your case."

Mike released his grip on his tall classmate, patted his shoulder and said, "Thanks pal. And, if you don't have the stomach for this I'll understand too."

Richard left his old friend at the curb, feeling apprehensive and imposed upon by a troublemaker that should have stayed forgotten 30 years ago.

Mike left feeling depressed that he did a lousy job of trying to recruit Richie's help. This first meeting did not go in the direction he hoped it would. He had his shot, and did not do a convincing enough sales job. It never seemed appropriate to bring up Amnion, as compelling as her situation was. Richie was too well connected, and it wasn't clear to Mike that he could be trusted with that knowledge yet.

Mike returned to the parking garage still disappointed in himself. Once again, it was time to retreat and regroup in this private war with Lifespan.

What's more, will Richie betray his trust and reveal Mike as the mole?

* * * * * * *

When Richard returned to his office suite, he was still disturbed by his luncheon with Mike. It was not that Mike was particularly convincing in his plea for help. It was just that his mind kept dwelling on those unborn fetuses Mike spoke about, all this decoupling, fetal derivatives, embryo farms. How Lifespan's technology would shape the future into self-entitlement at the extreme – a future his children would grow up in. An old quotation came to mind that went something like, 'When you destroy someone's culture, their customs, their religion, you better be damn sure you replace it with something of value.' And this Lifespan culture reduced mortal value to an all-time low – eternal wealth.

After his 1:30 meeting concluded, Richard summoned two of his company's best young paralegals, Brenda Schuster and Greg Stevens to his office. They were pursuing their own Law degrees in night school.

When they arrived, he announced a special assignment. "I want you two to look into a special problem that I need some visibility into." He turned to Brenda. "First, I want you to research everything you can on Lifespan Corporation. Focus on their special organ donor license from New Jersey. I want to know exactly what they are authorized to do and not do. Then go back through the last several weeks newspapers and determine just how closely they have adhered to their license. And, if they exceeded it, where?"

Brenda enjoyed the sound of this assignment. It was something in the media, a current event for a change - not another dull merger and acquisition. "I think I should start with the New Jersey recent legislation on RTL and decoupling."

Richard nodded in the affirmative. Then he turned to Greg and issued separate instructions. "Second, I want you to start piecing together that old abortion-fetal life issue. Start with Roe v Wade and recent rulings. Give me a synopsis of each court's ruling in these matters. See if you can find any 'bright line' test used by the Courts to determine when a fetus becomes a human being."

Both paralegals greeted these strange assignments with enthusiasm and curiosity. Their routine duties usually involved some minute technical detail of corporate finances - balance sheets, a return on assets employed, or the like.

Brenda asked, "Mister Farmers, will we be taking on a criminal proceeding or something?"

Richard ginned and slowly shook his head from side to side. "No, no. This is just some background research for an associate down the street."

Brenda looked at Greg and shrugged her shoulders. Richard added, "Keep this little investigation quiet. It's personal. I'm doing this 'pro bono' for an old friend down there. So, don't discuss this around the office, you know what a 'hot potato' issue this is. And only report your progress directly to me."

After Brenda and Greg departed, Richard turned in his chair to gaze across at the city skyline. It took a lot of 'yes sirs' to sit where he was today and look down on everybody else. It took a lot of friendships and influence peddlers to secure his position... and compromises with his conscience.

Oddly, at middle–age something was beginning to kindle inside. Maybe an indignation that only a minority person could comprehend better than others. Perhaps it was the idea of fighting against conventional wisdom on something. Restoring dignity to a group of innocent people that could hardly defend themselves.

He had not felt this kind of fervor since working on racial discrimination suits as a high-spirited junior attorney right out of college. Still, there was no mistaking that whatever the cause, a fire was building inside his belly.

CHAPTER 39
Amnion 'on the ropes'

Joel and Mike sat on stools next to each other, hunched over in his basement, deep in concentration. Mike passed him another burner phone, which Joel accepted without comment.

Joel had just finished conducting his first weekly checkup on Amnion. They stared expressionless at her fetal support tube, contemplating the ever more serious issue of her long-term survival. There was still a coldness in their relationship since Mike contacted the *Brooklyn Daily News* on his own. Still, Joel felt a professional obligation to Amnion as a patient that trumped sour feelings towards Mike.

He also knew that Mike still had not patched things up with Phylis either.

Joel decided the time was appropriate to tell Mike of his latest decision, and broke the silence, "I'm leaving Lifespan Mike. I thought you should hear it from me before it percolates through the company `grapevine'."

The sudden pronouncement interrupted Mike's deliberations. Caught off guard he could only think to ask, "When????"

"Two weeks from last Wednesday."

Mike sat in silence for a moment trying to comprehend what this meant to Amnion's situation. He queried Joel, "Where...Why?"

"My cousin is a surgeon over at New York University hospital. They have a teaching position open for a pathologist. The time is right for me. I've had enough of Lifespan and that Neo-Nazi Strauss. I just can't work with those kinds of people anymore."

Joel paused and sighed, "My new position is less money and less glamorous, but I told my wife I could spend more time with the family. So, yeah, I'm still upset about you contacting the *Brooklyn News*. Anyway, in the long run, it worked out pretty good for me.""

Mike couldn't help feeling somewhat abandoned by Joel in the middle of all this turmoil and hoarsely replied, "Well...I guess I wish you well Joel."

In the middle of his despair, Mike felt a tinge of envy. Doctors always seem to be able to change jobs and locations so fluidly. Like any setback is no problem.

Then he refocused, and pointed to Amnion saying, "Unfortunately, Joel, I have to be pragmatic and ask, What about her?"

Joel smirked, sensing Mike's apprehension and patted Mike's knee, "Hey, she's still <u>my patient</u>. Of course I'll help as long as you need me."

Mike felt an enormous surge of relief, although he felt ultimately responsible for Amnion. Except the biological knowledge to give her a chance at life was well beyond him. He would be lost without Joel.

Joel reviewed the monitoring data, finished his examination through the hatch, and said, "She needs to bulk up some more. Weight is still on the low side." Closing the tube hatch, he rolled his chair back from the fetal cart. He methodically removed his mask and surgical gloves, and walked over to the basement sink to lean against it. Mike spun on his stool to follow his friend's movement across the dingy basement.

Joel spoke in a more solemn tone, "We need to talk about this situation here Mike, and then make plans for the near future."

Mike sat attentively, anxious for further explanation.

Joel resumed. "Assuming we can get Amnion past 26 weeks in this fetal tube. Hopefully, she'll have lungs mature enough to survive in the extra uterine environment."

Mike felt positive and optimistic by his friend's commentary.

"But," Joel emphasized, "A big but!...When that happens she's going to need intensive care in a real state-of-the-art neonatal ICU."

"So?" Mike said.

"So, how about $150,000 in hospital bills. Whose insurance is going to cover that?"

"Good question," Mike conceded, "I never thought about it. In fact, now that you mention it, we're not going to be able to just role this cart into the delivery room without someone asking questions - a hell of a lot of questions!"

"You've got that right!" Joel said as he finished washing and drying his hands. Then pointing his finger at Mike, he added, "You take care of getting the bill paid." And pointing at himself, saying,"I'll figure out how to get her in."

The two went upstairs to the kitchen for a cup of coffee. Joel sat down at the table to recap his clinical assessment of Amnion. "There are still a few things we have to address here. She has a low antibody count. If she weighs more than a pound, I'd be surprised." Then he sipped his coffee and added, "And, there's that other problem we discussed last week with the undersized placenta."

Mike interrupted, "Yeah. How can I forget?"

The doctor explained. "I have something that may work." Joel leaned forward on his elbows and continued. "Strauss has a special stash of fetal superblood extract in one of my refrigeration units. If we mix that in with the PRCBs plasma on the machine side it just might give us the margin we need to get through the next few weeks."

"Fetal blood to supercharge fetal blood!" Mike exclaimed.

Joel interrupted his euphoria. "Whoa, Mike!" he intoned, "There's still more problems."

"Like what?"

"What's your blood type Mike?"

"O positive. Why?"

"Good! That's the same as Amnion. We're also going to need fresh blood, not PRCBs from here on in. We need to stimulate her immune system with antibodies and antihistamines - like her mother's blood would give her. Otherwise, she won't have much resistance to infection when she's extra uterine."

Mike immediately volunteered his own blood, as well as his sons, even though it would require a pint a week from each. Furthermore, the residual stock of packed blood plasma Mike had stolen from Lifespan's abandoned R&D project was running low.

"There is one more problem, Mikey. You have to wait 56 days between donations. You need a lot of donors."

Mike did not have an answer for that issue. They concluded their meeting and Joel departed, promising to keep regular tabs on Amnion and return regularly to take blood donations from Mike's family. Even donate a pint himself. Mike remained upbeat. As long as he was able to do something for Amnion, as long as there was a plan, there was always hope. He would bleed himself dry for her.

A while later he had an idea on how to pay for Amnion's hospital stay. That evening he called a distant Phylis and arranged to meet his reluctant lover for lunch at the Blarney Stone Bar and Grill.

Unknown to Phylis, once again, she was being drawn into one of Mike's outlandish plans."

* * * * * * *

Far away, in a Tudor style home, in an upscale neighborhood far different from Mike's, Richard Farmers was relaxing. He sat at the kitchen table after a delicious home cooked diner, sipping a warm and soothing cup of coffee. His wife, Evon, was just finishing rinsing the pots and pans after loading the dishwasher. Once the machine was cycling she sat down across the table from Richard and relaxed with her own cup of tea. The humm of the dishwasher added a soothing atmosphere to the room.

It had been a few days since Richard's luncheon with Mike and he had not had the opportunity to discuss the substance of that meeting with Evon. He recapped the encounter for his curious wife, including Mike's request that Richard take on Lifespan Corporation in a civil suit. Evon listened without comment although her suspicions were being aroused and her reaction was building. Richard casually said, "I had some of my people review this Lifespan organization, and the whole issue of fetal life. It really does need to be revisited."

Evon reacted to the his statement with a good deal more emotion than expected. "What! Have you lost your mind? It's none of our business. You saw how ineffectual the media blitz was defending that company."

Richard was caught off guard by her heated remarks. "Listen Muffin. I haven't committed to do anything yet!"

Evon was vehement. "Yet? Like it's even conceivable for you to play criminal lawyer?"

Evon pressed her opinion further. "You're a successful corporate lawyer. You haven't pleaded a case since you worked as a public defender 25 years ago. They'd eat you alive in a courtroom today."

Richard was a bit resentful now. Evon hit a nerve. Every lawyer prides himself on being able to argue a case in front of a jury. It is like a film actor proving himself to his profession by acting on the live stage.

Evon could sense that her dynamic husband really was seriously contemplating something and continued her harangue. "Honey, everything about your career has come, because you've learned to accommodate the people that control this country. You gave us, your family a comfortable life. Why jump on a high horse now and be some kind of Don Quixote?"

"Evon," he answered sternly, "I spent my life, a good life, playing by the rules. Sure, I could cruise through middle age like my partners. Be like any good rich white boy!"

It was obvious that Evon's prodding was perturbing her husband. She decided to tone down her remarks. There was no sense in arguing over something that Richard was not sure he was going to do anyway - and then risk his disaffection. Maybe drive him the wrong way.

She tried to soften her position somewhat and reached for her husband's hand across the table. "Richard honey, I didn't mean to be demeaning or insinuate that you lacked the ability. If you pursue something like this, it will destroy your career. You'll be sucked into that old abortion quagmire. You'll be ostracized by your law firm and your clients. Our children will be stigmatized at school - even our country club will bar us."

Evon stood up and swiveled around the table to be closer to her husband, "We live in a different age of the politically correct. If you take on Lifespan, you have to take on fetal life. You take on fetal life and you're taking on that old abortion issue. You take on abortion and you take on all those politically-connected career women. Besides, do you think over 10 million women want to hear that maybe they were misinformed? Resurface 80 years of that ugly history?"

"Well I'm not here to pass judgment on the past. I can only change perceptions for the future," Richard dryly answered.

"Pass the cup, honey," she implored. "Let Mike Santino fight his own battles."

Richard pulled his hand from hers, "It's everyone's battle," he asserted. "The more I think about it, this decoupling and fetal life issue is like a festering sore in the side of this country. It divides us. It bleeds any respect for the human spirit right out of our souls. There's never any resolution.

"All this science I hardly understand. I'll tell you this, as they keep peeling away the mysteries of human life. As they reduce it to chemical reactions, equations - electrical impulses. They 'will strip it down to where there is no humanity left. Then, any horror against any unprotected life is justifiable."

He turned away in agitation to stare at the window over the kitchen sink.

It seemed the more Evon spoke, the farther she drove Richard in the other direction. For a while, he just stood there sipping his coffee and staring out the window. She walked over to the sink and leaned her back against the counter top to put her curvaceous figure in his view again.

She spoke softly, "Richard, do you remember the Republican Committee dinner last year? They were talking about making you the first elected black Governor of New York.- maybe the first real black President in the entire country!"

Richard maintained that cool detachment and even temper, noted for in difficult situations. He turned and leaned his back on the sink counter next to her. "I know Muffin. I sometimes dreamed of holding a high office one day. Get into a position to do some real good." Then he said sarcastically, "Make Mom and Dad real proud. Set an example for African-American kids everywhere. Right?"

He put his coffee cup down and turned to face his wife and hold her gently by her shoulders to emphasize his sincerity, "I have to get there as my own man with my own values intact. Not just another clever chameleon. If I wanted power that bad, I could have accepted those other political appointment offers years ago."

Evon admired her husband's ability to stand for principle, it was one of the reasons she loved him in the first place. She also realized the impracticality in placing faith in such grandiose philosophy that was beyond their own relationship. Finally, in frustration she commented, "I wish I never encouraged you to meet this Santino person."

Richard took her last comment badly. "Evon!" he said brusquely, "I think that's enough discussion for tonight," and he abruptly departed away from her with a terse remark, "I'll be in my study... alone!"

Evon was left in the kitchen to ponder her situation. She was not comfortable appearing as a nagging wife, but Richard had a history of trying to stay above the politics. And those same political forces had shaped his success. True, he did pass up a lot of political appointments, not wishing to owe anybody anything. Although, it seemed that the more he turned offers down, the more they wanted him.

Still, it was clear to everyone that he was being groomed for an influential spot one day. This would be the end of that political support, and her aspirations for him
....Forever.

* * * * * * *

Richard relaxed again in his study in the soothing light of his reading lamp. He thought back to the tumultuous events in the sixties; Vietnam, civil rights, free love, hippies. Then the southern politicians from Lyndon Johnson on down, stacking the Supreme Court with 'good ol' boys'.

Richard recalled his thesis research on the Supreme Court of the late sixties/early seventies, and the transition from Chief Justice Warren to Chief Justice Burger. He titled that paper, *Rationalizing the Constitution: Ignore What You Don't Like.*

The one case he remembered most vividly was Roe vs Wade. It arrived in Chief Justice Warren Burger's court with the sympathetic ear of several justices. Effectively, the court was stacked in favor of decoupling - something you would expect in a small town kangaroo court.

Richard always knew Roe v Wade was the most obtuse legal presentation ever made to the court. He recalled the amateurish oral presentations by representatives on both sides of the issue that added nothing to the understanding of the real issue of life and death. In a highly unusual process, the Supreme Court even restored the case to their calendar a year later for re-argument. And then, the Court did not even solicit additional commentary from the opposing attorneys. The court itself really struggled with this one on its own. Most of the decisive analysis was done by the judges, not the litigants.

Imagine, he thought, *Five constitutional amendments cited as arguments for abortion. As if in 1783, the framers of the constitution were worried about abortion rights in every other amendment!*

Recently the Supreme Court threw the whole bucket of worms back to the individuals States - kicked the can down the road. They ignored the fundamental question of when Human Rights become Civil Rights. It was one of those irksome travesties of justice that festers just beneath the public conscience. It seemed to him that nobody really wanted to surface the issue anymore. Or face the personal consequences of knowing more about fetal life. It was so much easier to hide oneself in feigned ignorance.

Richard lit his pipe and blew a smoke ring into the air that gently floated away to slowly dissipate into an ever widening circle. Staring at its tenuous existence, he thought, at the moment, that his daydream of undoing all this historical legal precedent had about as much substance. After all, the Supreme Court was becoming, figuratively, as infallible as the Pope.

CHAPTER 40
Will you marry me?

Phylis reluctantly made her way through the noisy crowded bar, knowing Mike would be waiting somewhere on the other side of the gorilla sized men jammed around the bar. His old Mustang was in the parking lot, so he definitely was in there. She methodically jostled her way through the boisterous patrons, feeling like cork in an angry sea. She already was in a bad mood as she approached Mike's favorite small table in the back - all the time wondering if this would be their last encounter.

Mike finally noticed her and stood up from his table to wave. Phylis acknowledged his signal with a frown and a nod, and elbowed her way forward trying to avoid being doused with beer. Mike tried to greet her arrival with a peck on the cheeks, but was quickly rebuffed.

"God," she said above the noisy din, "and you actually like to come here?"

Mike leaned across the table as she sat down. He shouted, "It's the most private place I know. You could shout `I have a bomb' and no one would hear you."

Phylis ordered her white wine from a young buxom waitress in a tight pub T-shirt, noticing how Mike's subtle glance made a quick measurement of the departing waitress's twin endowments.

"You can eat with her if you like," Phylis commented with disdain.

Mike gave that boyish innocent look with his head slightly bowed, eyes peeking out below his eyebrows. His only reply was a shrug of the shoulders and the lame excuse, "Male instinct?"

Giving him a stern look, Phylis moved on to another topic, informing him,"Well, thanks to you Michael I lost my job, and have to go on interviews again after 5 good earning years."

Mike just stared at her. Then, both leaned back while their order of tuna salad sandwiches, fries, and onion rings arrived with the buxom waitress. Mike, wisely kept his eyes focused on the silverware.

Phylis still took over organizing the table and splitting the side orders between them. Mike sat back and enjoyed that missing feminine kindheartedness again.

"I have something more serious to ask you Phyl," he started to say.

Phylis interrupted him, "Did you hear me? I'm going to lose my job because of your *Brooklyn News* stunt." With all the background noise, Mike leaned a bit more forward across the table, as she bit into her sandwich.

Ignoring her lament, Mike announced succinctly, "Will you marry me?"

Phylis was stunned by a proposal in a bar, with the smell of onion rings. She sat back and stopped chewing her food, and almost choked, patting her chest. With her career in turmoil, and this tenuous relationship, she never expected that question - not now, not ever. Swallowing hard to get the food down her throat, she reached for the white wine to wash it down. Mike leaned on his elbows, rested his chin on his clasped fingers, and continued to stare intently into her eyes awaiting a reply.

"You've got some nerve, you idiot! I came here expecting a sincere apology from you after that *Daily News* business. Maybe a bit of groveling too!" Her face became flushed and her eyes reddened. She debated getting up and throwing her napkin in his face. Finally regaining her composure she exclaimed, "Why now? Why here? You think a tuna salad sandwich makes up for everything!" This was not the way Phylis's `Cinderella' affair with him was supposed to turn out. A proposal in some noisy bar filled with drunks.

When she began to stand up, Mike gently touched her sleeve. "Wait…wait, just give a chance to explain.

Phylis slowly sat back down saying, "Michael, I don't know if I can still love you, but right now I do know I really don't like you!"

"Can't really blame you for that Phyl, Mike said with sincerity. "I know Joel's upset too. It's just I've spent so many years on my own now. I'm used to acting impulsively without input from anyone else. I'm not offering any excuses Honey. I screwed up with you. I betrayed your trust. You can't love someone without trust. Maybe some day you can see your way clear to give me another shot."

Phylis listened but remained stoic. Deep down inside he still loved this rash guy. "Well, what's this marriage thing about anyway?"

A sheepish Mike began to brief her about Amnion in his basement, her need for fresh blood, and the necessity for neonatal hospital care in a few weeks. One way or another, his little girl was going to be 'born' soon. And, there was this medical insurance consequence.

"So, she needs a mother now," he said, "a legal mother."

Phylis pushed back from the table, and began to understand, asking, "Why me?"

"Maybe you don't trust me. But, I sure trust you implicitly," Mike replied. Then his countenance became very genuine, "I don't know if this will only make you angrier, but I still love you,….and Amnion needs you too."

That simple statement, 'I love you', was one that Phylis always knew she wanted to hear straight from his lips for quite some time. But, no, not this way. Not a marriage of convenience.

"Well I think I've heard just enough, Michael." You know, it's not like we're two kids again, starting out with nothing."

A pragmatic Phylis began to weigh the consequences of staying involved with Mike. Her kids, assets, mortgage, and career were a lot of variables to weigh compared to when she took a marriage vow 20 years ago. Phylis looked around, as if for support from a bellowing bar crowd unaware of her predicament. Suppose she said no? Where would Mike go? What might he feel compelled to do?

Mike interrupted her silence by adding with a cheeky grin, "If the answer is still no, I'll marry that bitch, Jane Savage."

The statement made them both laugh, and it helped to dissipate some of the tension building between them.

Mike said, "Get a lawyer. Write up any kind of pre-nuptial agreement you want. Protect your assets, set up all kinds of conditions. I don't care." He paused for effect and concluded, "For my part I'll go into this unconditionally."

Mike was flying into a marriage like the kamikaze pilot he invariably was.

Phylis contemplated her next statement carefully, "Michael I think my decision really hinges on only one question," she paused then added, "and it's not whether you really love me or not."

Mike was a bit surprised and disappointed by her statement, and let her finish.

"The question is," Phylis continued, "are you doing this for us or for Amnion?"

Mike sensed that his answer would be the difference between a yes or a no from her. He felt hemmed in. Before replying, he called over the waitress to pay his bill as a delaying tactic. Meanwhile, he thought of the right response. He knew he loved her, and she him. Contrary to *Hallmark* movies, love was not always enough to carry the day.

Mike invited Phylis to leave, while she patiently waited for his response. Once outside, away from the noise, Mike searched with his eyes for somewhere private to talk. His gaze settled on an unoccupied old, red antique English telephone booth on the sidewalk outside the pub. Grabbing her hand, he led an unsuspecting Phylis toward it.

Phylis trailed behind skipping along on her tiptoes and protesting, "Michael! Where are we going now?"

Mike entered the bright red booth, pulled her inside, and closed the antique glass framed door behind them. In the tight confines of the booth Phylis was squeezed tight against his chest. His arms embracing the small of her back, their noses barely an inch apart. His face, his eyes expressed an overwhelming look of genuine honesty and admiration. "Phylis," he whispered softly, "I think I loved you from the first time I saw you sitting at your terminal at Lifespan. If my life wasn't so complicated right now, we could take as much time as you need to feel comfortable about me again. Do this thing right. Have a real wedding."

Phylis felt herself getting a bit aroused by the feel of his body pressed hard against her again. The smell of beer on his breath only seemed to accentuate his masculine scent. Her eyes frantically scanned Mike's facial features searching for the true feelings beyond the words.

Mike kissed her lips tenderly, cradling her head gently in his fingertips. Then he spoke softly with a tinge of desperation, "Right now I have a little girl that needs me. I'm the only friend she has in this world that stands between her and oblivion. That obligation is forcing me to put you, the one I really love, in one helluva awkward position."

He kissed her gently again on the forehead and whispered, "Somehow, someday, when this Lifespan is behind us, I'll make it up to you. Once Amnion is born, it will be just us two again."

Phylis deeply understood his predicament and found herself beginning to cry. There was no escaping the fact that everything in their relationship inevitably included that fetus - Maria's baby. Mike's eyes began to well up in tears, too. They kissed and hugged each other in that tiny, cramped phone booth. Outside, passersby looked on incredulously.

Phylis was doing things she would have never dreamed of just a few weeks ago. It was crazy. This singular man in her life seemed to turn everything upside down, inside out, and 180 degrees from everyone else's perspective.

How could she entertain a marriage proposal in the din of a noisy bar? Then have a romantic interlude in an antique telephone booth from *Doctor Who*.

Had she lost her mind too???

CHAPTER 41
Getting into the NICU

Joel stopped by Mike's house with the last of the stolen blood supply from Lifespan. It was another evening down in Mike's basement. Joel was wrapping a thick rubber band around Mike's arm in preparation for drawing blood. Mike's sons stood by waiting for their turn, as a pale Mike reclined on a folding table brought down for the occasion. He tried to act courageous as the needle punctured his arm. Turning away in a grimace he grunted satirically, "Don't be surprised if it comes out as tomato sauce."

With the rubber band released, blood immediately rushed down the clear plastic tube to the waiting bag.

"Keep exercising your fist tough guy," Joel kidded, "it'll be over before you know it."

Mike grumbled, "Okay, but you're next ...then I get to put the needle in you!"

They all laughed together in the basement. Mike could not help occasionally glancing at Amnion's fetal tube. Everyone could feel that a hidden person was waiting for this gift of life, only another human being could provide.

"Won't be long now," Joel said as he regarded the PVC tube, "She's responding to the blood transfusions and superblood mix. I've also arranged with an obstetrician, Dr. Samuelson, to handle her. He has privileges at University Hospital."

Mike's face turned from pale to anxious as he propped himself up from the table. How do you know he can be trusted?"

Joel smiled, "He's 'old school' ...nearing retirement. Never was inclined to do terminations anyway. Very trustworthy. Well respected. And, he knows <u>everybody</u> in the hospital. Besides, we need help. You can't expect us to pull this whole thing off ourselves."

"Why can't we just pop her out and show up in the emergency room? They would have to take her," Mike insisted.

"It's not that simple buddy. University has an excellent tertiary neonatal facility. Takes in preemies from a 20-mile radius. You'd have to get through triage, and that's where they determine which infants get the most benefit from neonatal ICU."

"So?" Mike pronounced.

"So, you go on a waiting list to get in, and if Amnion doesn't meet the 500 gram weight minimum, (17.6 oz.), or has too many anomalies, they won't treat her." Joel raised his finger in the air for emphasis, "BUT... with Samuelson as her obstetrician, no one will question her immediate admission."

Mike had little choice but to accept his friend's judgment on this one. "OK, so what's the plan? What do I have to do now?"

Joel gently pushed him back down onto the table and said, "Well, first your 'new wife' has to call his office and set up an appointment to come in and register as his patient. Let the office staff knows she is six months pregnant, and fill out all the insurance forms. Then we have to arrange for her to call his answering service one night after office hours with an emergency delivery. Then he'll meet Phylis at his office. You bring the fetal cart, and Dr. Samuelson will take care of the rest."

Brian interrupted, "Geez, that sounds easy."

Mike chimed in too, "Yeah! Why not get Phylis and Amnion to the hospital directly? He can't deliver her in his office - there's no facilities."

Joel answered, "There's more details. We can go into that later."

Mike wasn't sure he liked the plan. He did not know Dr. Samuelson and he still did not know how Amnion was going to get to the neonatal unit in the hospital. "I don't know Joel. It seems to me she'd be better of getting straight to the hospital first."

Joel was a little irritated at Mike's persistent doubt, and answered, "Look Mike, if we bring Phylis and Amnion to the hospital together, everybody from admissions to maternity is going to get involved. Is Phylis going to fake a Caesarean section to the residents and nurses when they try o admit her too? No way! We have to keep the 'mother' at a distance, and Doc Samuelson will figure that part out too."

Mike finally acknowledged his ignorance of things medical, and nodded his acquiescence.

Joel dropped the discussion and returned to Mike's side to shut off the blood transfusion apparatus. He commented humorously, "This poor girl is going to smell like spaghetti sauce when she's delivered."

Mike chuckled, "And after a dose of you, she'll come out looking like a shriveled knish!"

They all took their turns giving blood, refrigerated some, and loaded the rest into Amnion's blood bank. Joel left for home, and Mike and the boys returned upstairs with their bandaged arms, and eat some therapeutic pasta.

* * * * * * *

Later on that night, Mike called Phylis to arrange their trip to town hall for the marriage license. A cautious Phylis, first had him sign a pre-nup agreement, notarized at her bank, maintaining separation of assets and children.

"Getting any cold feet," Mike queried.

"Not yet," she replied, "What about you?"

CHAPTER 42
Adios Eve

Eve West sat across from Max in his comfortable Lifespan office suite, but it was not that familiar anymore. That close feeling of intimacy only a few weeks ago had evaporated. As things at Lifespan continued to unravel, Eve desperately wanted to ingratiate herself to him again. However, Max's libido was on to younger pastures. He had a new consort from the Accounting Department that was at least 20 years her junior.

Stealing a glance at his face, she could not help but notice how well he looked, almost younger than her now. In fact, he actually needed a haircut for a change. And in spite of all the turmoil lately, he didn't look the least fatigued. Eve decided to try apologizing again. "Max, I'm really sorry for interrupting you with Dr. Strauss last week. I didn't realize ..."

Max cut her off with a wave of his hand and decided to appear magnanimous. "It wasn't that big a deal after all. Consider it forgotten."

Eve sheepishly nodded in appreciation, while at the same time wondering what softened him up.

Her boss continued his dialogue, almost bragging, "Well, at that meeting, I was just in the middle of telling Strauss to get rid of all those old specimens in the R&D lab that were givin' us all that negative press. Unfortunately, he was caught on camera at the crematorium. But, there's no physical evidence left of what they did."

Max leaned backward in his chair, "Regrettably, that leaves us with

281

no inventory." He looked down and shook his head, "And, no specimens in process - a real shit situation."

Eve was still at a loss to understand why he was relating all this information to her.

Then he sprung the news. "Eve, I want you to take an important assignment."

Suddenly it was music to her ears. If she could not secure her position in the corporation the old way, then she could prove her worth again as a dedicated corporate officer.

"Quite honestly Max," she replied, "after all that anti-decoupling nonsense quieted down, I'm really ready for a challenge."

"Good!" He exclaimed, "Then pack you bags for Bangkok!"

Eve was caught completely off guard by his pronouncement. She didn't know how to react and stuttered, "I ah... I don't have a passport".

Max dismissed her misgivings with a chuckle. "Not to worry. My limo will drive you into Manhattan and you can get one in three days."

It was obvious that the answer he expected to this offer was an enthusiastic 'Yes!' Ignoring her delayed response, Max followed up with an explanation of her assignment. The Russian specimens did not work out. She was to be his 'point person' in Bangkok making sure the first Asian specimen shipment comes off without a hitch.

Those responsibilities included shipping out the new long range transport carriers, and then on a return flight with specimens, clearing U.S.Customs. She would fly wth the goods on a connecting charter cargo jet to New Jersey's Teterboro Executive airport. After that, insure safe arrival of the shipment at Lifespan.

Beyond the obvious production implications, Eve realized the symbolic importance of this situation. It was the rebirth of Lifespan from the ashes of its dwindling domestic specimen business. Thankfully, she was the key person that was going to pull it off.

Max assured her that whatever support she needed from the U.S. would be available from Lifespan, and to be ready to leave by next weekend. He stood up and walked around his desk over to her. In a formal gesture, still keeping her at a distance, he shook her hand and wished her good luck. Eve left the office with a positive feeling that even though Max no longer had romantic feelings towards her, he had arranged an important assignment for her. And, at least her lucrative career at Lifespan was secure.

Upon Eve's departure Max called Norm Stark to inform him that Eve West would be expediting the first shipment for Lifespan. Norm's comment was, "That's a real no-win assignment. Less than a 50/50 chance of success on the first try."

Max acknowledged his estimation, "Things are quieting down

around here. She's a good expeditor, knows how to get things done. Besides, she needs to get away from me, and get accustomed to being on her own."

Norm didn't share Max's enthusiasm. He had some feelings of kinship for Eve after working with her over the years. She could get things done all right. Sadly, working with the Asians was a different matter altogether. It's an environment where invoking Max's name to get action would amount to nothing, and they had a customs bureaucracy that functioned entirely on bribery and intimidation. Norm also knew that Bangkok was a pretty tough town. Over there, sex was the biggest business going, and exploiting women, even little girls were a regular part of their culture. In a society with so little regard for women, Eve was going to find it tough going compared to the U.S.

Later on, for his own peace of mind, Norm called Eve to caution her to the dangers overseas. He recommended a full-time bodyguard anytime she was in public, and reminded her there was no equal opportunity laws over there, no submissive men, no Uncle Sam.

* * * * * * * *

Later in the day, Max met with his Marketing V.P., Bob Fisher, to discuss the final arrangements of importing specimens, and instructed him to meet with Eve to go over the details of her new assignment.

Max then changed the direction of the conversation asking, "What do you know about fetal stockpiles? I remember reading about it a few years back after the Congress legalized fetal experiments."

Bob Fisher, hesitated answering as he tried to anticipate where Max might be heading with the issue. His mind quickly reviewed what Lifespan's competitors were up to, and made sure he had not missed anything. His reply was cautious, "Max, I know our competitors in Chicago and Atlanta have established some warehouse regional refrigeration facilities to stockpile specimens for their market entry later this year. My sources indicate only a few hundred currently in inventory. They are all beyond their expiration date."

Max shook his head in disagreement. "No, not them. Aren't there some other research institutions or something with an inventory?"

Bob finally understood. "Oh, those. Yes, in Detroit. A couple thousand are there."

"So why don't we make them an offer? Buy a few thousand," Max suggested.

"That may not be wise Max," Bob replied cautiously, "They're all in formaldehyde solution. We couldn't reclaim anything from such contaminated tissue. Some specimens are many years old."

Max frowned with disappointed, "Too bad. I mean, hey, it's a domestic source." Max leaned back in his chair staring at the ceiling in deep thought, finally saying, "How about Planned Parenthood? They were selling fetuses under the counter for years."

"Naw, Max", Fisher answered. "The crooks were caught too many times, and those administrators took early retirement to avoid prosecution."

Bob Fisher departed the office realizing how little Max actually knew about the technology used in the Company, and how important fresh specimens were to the reclamation process. For now, he was just glad he gave the right answers to Max's asinine suggestions.

CHAPTER 43
Reasonable doubt

R ichard Farmer sat in his office late in the evening after everyone had left. He stayed behind with Greg and Brenda' to review their investigation into Lifespan and fetal life.

Greg commented, "As far as case law is concerned, everything for the last 60 plus years has been based on the original Roe vs. Wade high court ruling."

Richard asked, "Then did you spend anytime actually reading through that ruling?"

"Yes!" Greg said, starting to display a bit of youthful excitement. "It is the most convoluted legal argument I've ever read. Judge Blackmun wrote the majority opinion in a rambling 4000 word opinion. Much of the rationalization was based on the toleration of abortion in ancient Greek and Roman cultures. They spend all sorts of time examining the ancient term 'quickening' in past law as a basis for fetal viability – I mean who cares what the ancient Greeks or the Romans thought about human birth. I mean what did they know about medical science?"

An astonished Brenda excitedly interrupted, "You mean the judges used the morals of cultures that condoned slavery and murder of people for entertainment as the basis for how a human fetus should be treated?"

"Incredibly, yeah,"Greg answered pointing his pile of reference books, "I want you to hear this part of the majority opinion, by Justice Blackmun, since it specifically addresses the question of what is a human life."

Greg rifled through some case history books until he found the one with the book marker. Flipping rapidly to the designated page, he stood up and began to read the justice's opinion while pacing the floor to an interested Richard and Brenda.

'All this ...persuades us that the word 'person' as used in the

14th amendment does not include the unborn.... We need not resolve the difficult question of when life begins. When those trained in there respective disciplines of medicine, philosophy, and theology are unable to arrive at any consensus, the judiciary, at this point in the development of man's knowledge, is not in a position to speculate as to the answer.'

Richard appreciated the significance instantly and pointed out, "In their zeal to apply some social fad, it appears the erudite justices ignored their own words and one of the fundamental concepts underlying our entire judicial system."

Brenda didn't appreciate the point immediately and leaned back in her chair saying, "I really don't see it."

Greg chimed in, "Haven't you ever served on jury duty - in a criminal case?"

Brenda felt a bit awkward, looking down as she answered, "Well... actually I've only been called once and got a postponement. Never heard from them again."

Richard grinned and said, "You should know the point anyway." Then he stood up and walked around the desk to sit facing his juniors. "When a jury is instructed by the judge before a trial, he asks every potential juror the same basic question; Do you understand the concept of guilt beyond a reasonable doubt?"

Greg could not contain his enthusiasm and interrupted, "And here the court admits that bonafide experts can't agree on whether a living fetus is a human being or not at any point in gestation, casting serious reasonable doubt on the question of humanity. Then, in face of the conflicting opinions of experts, and their own admitted doubts, they take it upon themselves to conclude fetuses are not human lives in need of protection! All the human fetuses of the country were instantly sentenced to death in spite of reasonable doubt regarding their basic humanity."

Brenda was a bit embarrassed for not seeing that simple point sooner, and offered an alternative, albeit technical, viewpoint. "Maybe the court felt that a fetus is like an alien and although alive, is not a citizen by virtue of not being born in the U.S. - like a foreign national would be."

Richard stood up and pointed his finger skyward saying, "Ah but!". Then he paced around the room and continued. "If an illegal alien enters this country, can we kill him without due process? After all, he's not protected under our constitution. He was not 'born' here."

"Of course not," Brenda replied.

"Exactly!" Richard said pointing to her. "Under the 14th amendment that 'not born here person' is entitled to due process by the government.

That is because of the concept of intrinsic value. The alien only needs to be human to be given that protection. And, I haven't heard one medical expert dispute the genetic humanity of a fetus. Whether you are a comatose patient on a respirator, or a corpse for that matter, you have an intrinsic human value that should be protected by law."

Leaning back on his desk, Richard lectured in the even tone of a college professor. "Conversely, each human fetus aborted never gets due process of law. Never is its intrinsic value acknowledged. They just disappear one day behind and operating room door. The Supreme Court essentially declared that its primitive existence did not deserve institutional protection, its mortality sufficiently unimportant that its rights are subordinate to any interest of a woman or a doctor or and individual State Legislature."

Greg joined in again like the enthusiastic law student he always was. "And, let me read you their own words from the earlier 1970 decision *In re Winship*. Here the government requires all states in criminal cases to 'provide proof beyond a reasonable doubt', saying it was one of the 'essentials of due process and fair treatment'."

Richard patted him on the shoulder then spent a few moments of silent contemplation. Richard eventually changed subjects and asked Brenda to report on her review of Lifespan Corporation's exclusive State license.

She looked down and stabbed her pen at her tablet responding, "The executives have the usual checkered past of shady but legal chicanery in their business involvements. Mostly 'gray area' deals. In addition, the information on their past businesses in the latest newspaper accounts appears to be surprisingly accurate. As far as the corporation itself, their FDA exclusive decoupling license runs out in another year. Although their underlying technology is still a secret. Some industry observers on Wall Street believe the company has become overly bureaucratic and too inefficient to compete once their exclusive license expires."

Brenda looked up animatedly, "There's one more piece of third party ruminations on Wall Street, that there may be foreign suitors looking to acquire their company and technology. It's probably going to be the current executive's bailout vehicle."

Richard thanked her for the brief and concise report, and then asked, "But what about their recent actions under the license? Are they legal?"

Brenda smiled saying, "Actually, no." She flipped her notebook pages and searched until she reached a reference tab. "Under the license, they're only entitled to decouple and process fetal cadavers. The recent activity in the papers, admitted recently in the Operation Rescue court complaint, is that they also took placentas."

Greg injected, "So what?"

"So" she continued, "The placenta is considered medically, as a separate organ! They violated the license by extracting and processing additional human organs."

Richard patted Brenda on the shoulder and complimented her, "Good work!"

Brenda continued, " State law does not allow 'valuable consideration' or direct payment to women donors. However, the legislators circumvented that restriction by a loophole in a subsection. And I quote, " …valuable consideration … does not include reasonable payments associated with the transportation, extraction, implantation, processing, preservation, quality control, or storage of human fetal tissue."

Greg chimed in, "And let us not forget their unlicensed revival technology."

"Well," Richard said, "this is all a lot to chew on…good work."

He finally concluded the late night meeting, instructing his paralegals to keep this information absolutely to themselves for now.

"Put it on the 'back burner'", he instructed, "and we'll let it simmer for a while."

A somewhat disappointed and dejected young pair packed up their notes in their briefcase and reluctantly went home. For their part, they were already juiced up enough to push a case like this through litigation.

Regrettably, what they did not yet have, was a plaintiff.

Richard called for the limousine to meet him downstairs for the long trip to his quiet abode in Westchester. He was tired after a long day, and still wasn't sure what to do with these new findings. The limo ride would give him a chance to unwind, and dwell on all this in dark seclusion. He thought about these narcissistic Lifespan scientists. The bureaucratic NIH and FDA supposedly maintained oversight. It reminded him of the infamous Tuskegee Syphilis Study - the one that started in 1932. The one where the government studied a group of illiterate Negro men in Alabama with advanced syphilis. The study did not involve new treatments or disease management. Just document the progress of the disease and do the autopsies.

By 1940, a cure had already been found in penicillin. The only problem was that the government scientists withheld the drug from their impoverished test subjects. Instead, the medical investigators gave them a hot bowl of soup on exam day and a $50 death benefit. All the while the good doctors continued the study - continued collecting a lucrative fee from their grant salaries.

And so, it lingered on for another thirty years. Terrible pain and suffering to a group of poor African-Americans whose only sin was their disease and being a poor black. Only in 1972 when someone in the press exposed it, did the government finally conclude the study.

All because some researchers felt the end justified the means. All because a group of innocent human beings where redefined by some researchers as 'test subjects' and lost their humanity to the cause of science. All because the research was so important. So important, that after 40 years of torment, nothing was ever added to the understanding of the disease from the study.

Richard gave a deep sigh, and sadly told himself, *And these people should be trusted to work in secret with a newly developing life?*

* * * * * * *

That same evening, 'newlyweds' Mike and Phylis were in the obstetrician's office waiting room. Phylis sat with pen in hand filling in the patient's insurance form data. Mike sat next to her, as she leaned over to whisper, "I can't believe I'm doing this."

Mike gently patted the small cushion on her abdomen strapped under her blouse and teased. "Man you look ready to pop." He chuckled. "And that that wonderful glow of an expectant mother."

Phylis discreetly delivered an elbow into Mike's ribs. Then returned the finished forms to the receptionist and sat down again to wait a long half-hour. Meanwhile, Mike socialized with the receptionist, leaning through the sliding glass window.

The receptionist was a friendly middle aged woman who complemented him."It's so nice to see a husband accompany his wife for one of these visits."

Not wanting to miss an opportunity to playfully fool somebody, he whispered, "Actually, we had to get married right away."

The receptionist's eyebrows rose, and while her face tried not to reveal any adverse reaction, she was obviously disturbed about two mature middle aged adults not taking proper precautions. Mike returned to the seated and unsuspecting Phylis who was busy reading a woman's magazine. Finally, they were called into Dr. Samuelson's office for a consultation.

Mike liked the elderly doctor right away. He was totally unassuming and had a compassion for people that shown easily through his tired eyes. No compensation would be required.

Over the next half-hour he explained the details of how Amnion would be delivered and transported to the hospital. He spoke slowly, stopping several times to ask for questions from the couple. His manner reminded Mike of the good Father Tom – now gone forever. With a cautious air, he emphasized how risky this delivery would be for Amnion, listing the myriad of complications involved in premature birth. He also warned about the potential for considerable suffering by the baby, or even death, as she struggles to develop outside the womb. And, how difficult it may be for the 'parents' to witness all this.

As a physician, the elderly doctor was also naturally curious to actually see the amazing fetal cart Amnion lived in. It was arranged for him to meet Joel at Mike's house one night to show him the unit, and work out exactly how they were going to safely remove her from that tube.

Before they departed, Mike shook the doctor's hand, and thanked him for his support. Dr. Samuelson replied, "I took an oath 50 years ago never to lift my knife against another human life. How could I do anything less?"

The 'odd couple' left the office, and Mike still felt a bit unsettled by the description of life in a neonatal unit. He remarked to Phylis, "And I thought her life was tough being stuck in that tube in the R&D lab."

Once in the car, Phylis popped the pillow out from under her blouse, and gave a sigh of relief that this part of the ruse was finally over.

Mike commented as he drove, "I find it wonderfully ironic that Lifespan's insurance is going to pay to keep Amnion alive considering they were the ones who tried to kill her."

Phylis added a coincidence only she was privy to. "Not only that, Amnion is going to be delivered at University Hospital."

Mike gave a quizzical look, as she explained further, "It's the same hospital that decoupled her in the first place."

With that revelation, Mike perked right up. With a big grin, he said, "Alright!" slapping his hand on the steering wheel. "Man! That's my kind of divine justice!"

CHAPTER 44
Persistence

Mike realized he was running out of time. Amnion would be delivered in another week or two, and the whole phenomena of her preservation in the life support cart would become an implausible occurrence to those who had not witnessed it in person. At this point, he felt he had no choice but to take a chance on that old friendship.

Mike was persistent in his phone calls to Richard Farmer. As a busy executive, Richard was definitely hard to reach, and Mike left both a morning and afternoon message with his Administrator. With no response and in desperation, the last message Mike left said 'Urgent!'.

Late in the day, just before 5 PM, Richard's legal assistant called to say that her boss was tied up in a board meeting until late that night, and inquired as to what the emergency specifically was. Mike could not reveal the nature of the message to her, indicating that it truly was life and death. He asked that Richard call him tonight at his home number.

* * * * * * *

Richard read his Assistant's message that evening at his office, half-believing it, and wondering if Mike had finally gone off the deep end. In any event, he reluctantly dialed the number, feeling he owed it to Mike to at least return the call.

Matthew answered and called his father to the phone. After some superficial and awkward greetings, Richard asked about the nature of Mike's 'life and death' problem.

Mike was apprehensive and said, "You know the story in the paper about my company, Lifespan?" He paused; feeling like his long kept secret would explode inside him and finally blurted out, "Well, I have one of those live fetuses in a cart in my basement! I stole it, and now the child is ready to be born!"

Richard was speechless in stunned disbelief. Initially, his legal mind did not know how many crimes had actually been committed, or if this was just a pun in poor taste. "You want to play that by me again Mikey," he dubiously suggested.

"No kidding Richie," Mike exclaimed. "I never mentioned it to you at our luncheon. Couldn't take the chance. Except time is running out. She is going to be born!"

Richard was still trying to play catch up to these wild revelations and retreated to a few basic questions. "How long have you had it? How are you keeping it alive? Who's the mother?" Finally he asked a more pointed question, "Why do you need me?"

Mike had calmed down by now and responded to his questions one by one, slowly revealing the story of Amnion's decoupling and removal from Lifespan.

"I think she needs a lawyer now," Mike said in conclusion.

Then, he invited Richard to visit the little girl and see for himself.

After Mike's literate and detailed explanation, Richard began to entertain the notion that his wild old friend really did have a living fetus in his possession. There were also those Lifespan stories in the newspapers a few weeks ago to corroborate the possibility. He was so intrigued by Mike's account that he agreed to visit Amnion the following night, and see this mysterious entity for himself. As he hung up the phone, the significance of Mike's precious evidence sank in, and the complex web of a lawsuit began to weave itself together in Richard's legal mind, *we have an injured party!*

He called his wife, Evon, to let her know he was on his way home, and thought surreptitiously, *Man, if she only knew what I was up to!*

CHAPTER 45
We have a lawyer!

The following evening, Mike led Richard's tall form down the darkened staircase. Each wooden step creaked and groaned with age, as their weight tested its strength. Mike's weakened condition was apparent, as he held tight grip on the railing, and descended with an ungainly stride to the bottom. The bi-weekly blood donations to Amnion were literally draining his strength away.

"Watch your noggin'," Mike warned, as Richard ducked slightly to clear a low header beam at the bottom of the staircase.

Mike looked back and added with his usual crude humor, "If you still wore that college afro, your hair would be scraping splinters off this ceiling."

Richard smiled politely taking no offense and surmised to himself, *Some people never change, do they?*

Actually, his attention was focused on the array of fancy electronic equipment gathered around the fetal support cart. It was totally out of place, in contrast with the dingy unfinished basement and its wooden joist ceiling and stark cement floor. An old oil burner on the far side reminded Richard of the unfinished basement of the small modest house where he grew up. It seemed ages ago both in time and affluence.

Richard pointed to the support equipment and commented, "Very impressive."

They donned masks as Mike adjusted the lighting and they approached the cart.

The hatch was flipped open and the two leaned over the opening.

Richard stared for a full 3 minutes and simply whispered, "Incredible!. Impossible."

With a proud father's voice Mike added, "Isn't she beautiful!"

After a few minutes of awe-struck observation the hatch was closed and the two men sat on the lab stools, listening to the soft maternal whooshing sounds of the "mother's heartbeat" generated by the audio player on the computer hookup. Mike answered some general technical questions from Richard, and explained how the maze of tubes and wiring made the whole life support system work.

Over the next half-hour Mike revealed Lifespan's next project "Greenhouse" to grow and harvest fetuses directly from embryos like wheat in a field. Extract biological materials from the living fetuses – cut the middle woman out of it. Richard was touched by Mike's sincerity and found he had similar misgivings about where all this technology was leading the human race.

Mike explained, "When I started into this, I just wanted to embarrass Lifespan – get even. As time went on I decided to save this little girl."

Then Mike stood up for emphasis "Now I want to shut their whole stinking operation down." He pointed to Amnion's cart adding emphatically, "I want the world to learn what I've learned about human life ...insignificant as it may appear to most."

"Well Mike, this is certainly the strangest legal situation I've ever encountered," Richard said with consternation. "I think you're forgetting the legal actions already taken against Lifespan."

"So what?" Mike demanded as he began to nervously pace back and forth.

Richard answered discouragingly, "With all the revelations, neither the State of New Jersey or the Feds took criminal action against the company. That means they still have considerable political clout in high places. Even that civil suit by Operation Rescue fizzled with the help of an unsympathetic, politically appointed judge." Richard swiveled on his stool to follow Mike's erratic movement.

Richard noticed Mike's weakened constitution, and asked, "You all right buddy?"

"Too many blood donations. Richie"

They sat down in front of the computer terminal. Mike was undeterred by Richard's arguments, and was beginning to feel his old friend really may not be up to it.

A frustrated Mike impatiently asked, "Enough diplomacy, Richie! Just give me the name of another lawyer who's got the balls to duke it out with these corporate clowns."

Richard could have taken offense by Mike's rudeness, but he evaluated Mike's fatigued face and demeanor, knowing that his tired friend must be under a lot of strain. In fact, Richard had been making up his mind to take the case a while ago. Now it was more important to know how strongly Mike felt about litigating this thing. From his point of view, it was the client's existence that would be the linchpin to any litigation on an issue as volatile and controversial as this case could become. Furthermore, Lifespan Corporation was not going to lie down and rollover in court. They would use all their political clout and media blackouts to suppress this case and intimidate the plaintiff.

Mike turned and busied himself with the tablet keys, entering monitoring parameters, trying to fill the awkward moment of silence while Richard evaluated the situation. Richard sat and stared for a while at the fetal tube. Finally, it dawned on the attorney what this whole case was about – civil rights. The rights of the last group of unprotected human beings in America. He stood up and walked over to his old roommate, placing his hand on Mike's shoulder. "You don't need another attorney, you've got me!"

"How much?" Mike brusquely asked.

"How's Pro bono sound, Mikey?"

Mike's beleaguered face perked. "Put it there, Pal!" bumping fists with his old friend.

Richard walked back over the Amnion's cart and touched the tube's warm plastic surface, cautioning, "Of course you realize how important it is that this girl survives her birth?"

He pivoted to face Mike again adding, "No baby. No client. No case."

Mike's physical appearance looked gaunt as he said emphatically, "she will survive even if it <u>kills me!</u>"

"It could get all of us killed," Richard replied facetiously, adding, "Then we'll all be looking like you!".

In the dingy unassuming basement, they grasped each other's hands in a gesture that would ultimately seal the fate of Amnion's life, change Richard's career trajectory irrevocably, and delivering the vindication Mike wanted so desperately.

CHAPTER 46
The 'delivery'

Late one evening, in Dr. Samuelson's private office, Mike, Joel, and Phylis gathered for what would be the most bizarre medical experience of their lives. For a while, they just stood huddled together in the small examining room, carefully inspecting Amnion's unusual life support cart. It was time for Amnion to be "born".

To the elderly doctor it was as if a flying saucer had just landed in his examining room with some awesome new technology.

"I can't tell you how much suffering by mother and child could be avoided if this was used for more ethical purposes," he said while shaking his head. "The premature births I could have saved."

Mike answered cynically,"If someone puts a healthy price tag on those ethical purposes, then you'll get your invention."

Mike interrupted the philosophical atmosphere and returned to the business at hand by slipping a large plumber's pipe cutter jaw around one end of the PVC tube. Joel joined in, lifting that end clear of the cart.

Inside a startled Amnion slid down to the opposite end, slamming against her placenta.

Mike began to rotate the tool and tighten the cutting wheels simultaneously. It easily chewed through the soft plastic as it rotated around and around the cylinder. In just a few minutes, Amnion would be free of her canister, and begin life outside the 'womb'. Beneath, Phylis held an orange Home Depot bucket.

The exertion, combined with the anxiety, caused beads of sweat to appear on Mike's forehead. Tension filled the small room as the moment approached when Amnion would either breathe air or die in front of their eyes. Phylis assisted placing surgical masks on everyone while Dr. Samuelson prepared to deliver another life into the world. It was decided to leave the life support cart running until the umbilical cord was cut.

Fluid began to dribble from the pipe cutter seam, signally the time to stop cutting and break the tube end off. To ease the tension, Mike commented with usual crude humor, "Anyway, her water broke like a normal delivery."

There was some nervous laughter, as four anxious people staring intently at the same subject.

"Everybody ready," Mike said haltingly, "here she goes!"

The end cracked off and the saline solution spilled into the waiting bucket. The silicone gel bed came out in clumped globs that plopped in the bucket, splashing saline all over. Joel gently tilted the tube to slope downward towards the now open end and Dr. Samuelson's experienced grasp.

Amnion's scrawny legs poked out first, but paradoxically, a slight tug couldn't free her from the tube.

"She's stuck!" Samuelson exclaimed immediately.

In near panic Mike and Joel converged on the open end, bending over, almost banging heads. Phylis felt helpless.

"What's the problem," Mike declared excitedly, while Joel leaned down with a flashlight to examine the tube close up and gently pull on Amnion's tiny limbs.

"Umbilical cord's rapped around under her arms!" Joel responded, "I can't tell from here!"

Samuelson immediately ordered, "Pick up the tube and slide her back in!"

Joel moved back to the other extreme of the tube and opened the access hatch at that end. Inside, he could see Amnion was slightly bent and mushed against the placenta end of the tube with her umbilical cord wrapped tightly around her chest. Joel recognized that Amnion was being crushed just when she needed most to breath. Her little body began to writhe with signs of distress and her face began to take on a bluish tinge.

Joel's first reaction was to untangle the cord. The hatch opening was prohibitively small and Amnion took up most of the space inside. Covered in vernix, she proved to be too oily and elusive to grasp.

Mike looked anxiously over his shoulder saying, "C'mon Joel!

We're outta time! Do something!"

Samuelson yelled authoritatively, "Cut the damn cord! We'll untangle her outside."

Joel put his hand in the hatch, and promptly slipped in a small clamp over the cord, then, reached in with a scalpel to cut the tiny lifeline. Once free, Amnion was quickly sliding back down the tube into Samuelson's hand. Joel deftly undid the umbilical from the little tyke. Finally she was outside - a tiny, squirming, wrinkled little entity of a pound and a half. Hardly representative of the species that could send men to other planets, or weave intricate musical symphonies, or reproduce her own kind.

Her face lacked the plump fatty cheeks of a full term baby, so her eye sockets looked overly prominent. With her fine covering of lanugo hair, spindly legs and furrowed brow, Mike honestly thought she looked like a monkey.

At a foot long even her diminutive size was no more substantial than a telephone receiver. Mike was surprised and said, "Man, she looked a lot bigger inside the tube."

Joel suctioned her bronchial and tracheal passages. Then, Samuelson began patting her back with his palm to stimulate breathing.

Mike watched these proceedings in terror, waiting to here the sound of a newborn cry. He even forgot to shut the fetal cart life support system off. It softly whirred and pumped in the background, unaware its mission was over. He finally blurted out, "Why isn't she crying?"

Amnion was then transferred to a table with a heating lamp and pre heated terry-cloth towels quickly provided by Phylis.

Dr. Samuelson answered Mike's question, with self-assured confidence. "Preemies rarely cry." The doctor gently continued suctioning the mucous from her esophagus and nasal passages, then rolled her over to firmly pat her back again stimulating respiration. There was no outward sign of panic or lack of confidence in Dr. Samuelson's methodical actions. His proven lifetime of skill and adroit hand movements were an inspiration to all in the room.

Finally, Amnion responded to their prompting.   First with intermittent grasps and then shallow steady shallow breaths. Phylis placed an oxygen mask on the towel next to her and gently blew life giving sustenance into her small drawn face.

Samuelson commanded, "Take over here Joel," handing off the manual aspirator, "I'll call the prenatal emergency unit now."

Mike, now feeling relieved, looked over Joel's shoulder and quipped, "I told you she'd come out looking like a knish."

Joel gave a nervous smile.

After a minute Samuelson returned to announce, "They'll be here shortly".

Then he brought a small scale over to Amnion and weighed her. It was as if he were handling a potato, the way he moved her around.

His head shook as he said with dismay, "630 grams." Turning to Mike he asked, "Are you sure she's 29 weeks. This is right near the absolute minimum survival weight."

He did some engineering calculations in his head. *650 grams = about one and a half pounds – not much.*

Phylis chimed in, "I'm sure," hesitantly explaining to the group around her. "I knew the mother and her gestation period."

Joel added, "The birth weights low because of the limitations of the artificial womb. I did medicate her with dexamethasone to speed up lung development of surfactant bubbles. I also supplemented the PRCBs plasma solution with folic acid and other vitamins."

"Good," Samuelson said, "Because she has to master breathing first. If her lungs can't handle the air, everything else is meaningless."

Looking at Mike and Phylis, he added in a grave tone, "Look, I'm sorry, but I have to be honest with you. At this point, she probably has a 50 percent chance of survival. If she lasts two days without serious complications, it improves to 60-40. It's really a day-to-day thing."

To an apprehensive Mike it sounded like her problems were not over. They were just beginning.

* * * * * * *

Next, it was time to get ready for the hospital's ambulance. The fetal cart was finally shut down and hefted into to the Transit rental van parked behind the doctor's office. Although the cart had not been designed to save lives, it proved to be a marvelous piece of technology - for once put to good use.

A large examining table with sheets was brought in to the cramped 'delivery room'. The time had come to make it appear to the arriving EMT's that Phylis was the exhausted post-partum mother. She donned a surgical gown, slipping in her shallow tummy pillow, and climbed onto the table. It was embarrassing enough to do this without make-up, and Mike did not help with wetting her hair and thoughtless suggestion, "Mess up your hair Phylis. You'll really have to look a wreck."

* * * * * * *

The EMT's from University Hospital arrived in their special neonatal support ambulance. It contained a portable version of the life support augmentation equipment existing in the intensive care unit in the hospital, including a mobile incubator.

Dr. Samuelson led the technicians in through the front entrance reception area and into the rear examining room. They immediately located Amnion swathed in terry cloth, and evaluated her responsiveness. An I.V. was started and some additional suction of her tracheal passage was done. Monitoring electrodes were taped to her body and an oxygen mask tied to her tiny face. A blood sample was drawn for blood chemistry and analysis to determine if any genetic complications might be lurking. Her squinting eyes were treated with silver nitrate.

Mike winced as he watched from behind the EMTs. All this sticking and prodding of his frail little girl was hard to watch. Except, these people looked so expert at what they were doing, he decided it was best not to interfere.

In the next minutes, Amnion was placed in the portable transport incubator to be whisked away to the hospital neonatal ICU. She was now 20 minutes 'old', and her life would be a miracle as each hour passed.

Before leaving, the supervising technician pointed to Phylis reclining under some soiled sheets and placenta blood on the examination table. "Dr. Samuelson, how about the mother? Shouldn't we admit her also?"

Dr. Samuelson grinned confidently and guided the technician away from Phylis. He whispered, "Confidentially, she's a bit high strung, and requested that I keep her under my care at my private clinic for tonight. I have my nurse practitioner on the way. Her situation is quite stable, so there's no concern. In fact, I have another ambulance coming to take her there shortly." He put his arm around the tech's shoulder, as he guided him to the door. Then he smiled and added with a wink of the eye to Mike, "Then, tomorrow, we'll transfer her to University."

The explanation was accepted quite easily. Samuelson's reputation didn't invite doubt or suspicion. The technician went ahead, finished filling out some paperwork, and eventually asked for the child's name. Dr. Samuelson answered carelessly, "Her name is Am...err." But cut his answer short. He
corrected himself saying, "Err... I mean Amy Santino."

The technician laughed off the apparent hesitation, "Yeah Doc. I know it's been a long night for all of us," and continued with his paperwork.

Mike accompanied the incubated Amnion to the ambulance as she was loaded in, and the doors slammed closed in his face. The red color of the flashing lights of the vehicle danced across his face in the dark as it pulled away. Then the ambulance disappeared around the corner, and it became distinctly dark and peaceful. He felt an unexpected emotion of letdown as tears formed in his eyes. He listened to the distant siren fading into the night carrying his little girl.

In a short time, Phylis came outside to join him, and intuitively felt his loss. It was just like the post-partum letdown mothers sometimes feel. She placed her arms around him and pressed her cheek to his chest. She looked up sympathetically to kiss his sullen face.

"It's OK 'mister softy'," Phylis said reassuringly, "Amnion's with people who know what they're doing. Certainly more than we ever knew."

Mike looked down at her and brushed her wet stringy hair back from her damp face. "I know. You heard Samuelson. He's not giving her odds better than 50-50."

Still, it bothered Mike - the first time separation. She had never been out of his care so far away. Now it was totally out of his hands.

Joel bounded out, stepped behind them, and put his arms around Mike and Phylis. He was upbeat and cheerful saying, "Come on mom and dad. Lighten up. We just delivered the first human baby from an artificial womb!"

Mike and Phylis managed a smile at the sudden intrusion, and gradually broke their embrace. They all walked around the back of the building to load the fetal support cart back into the rental van, while Joel babbled in excitement. A bottle of champagne remained on the van floor, unopened. It was originally brought to celebrate Amnion's delivery. For some reason, Mike could not bring himself to pop it. It just did not feel like a celebration – more like the start of another ordeal.

He was doubly fatigued from the emotional intensity of the evening and the loss of several pints of blood during the past few weeks. Phylis volunteered to drive him home that night, and climbed into the driver's seat. In the dark Mike began to recline in the passenger seat for some welcome rest when Phylis interrupted him.

Fumbling in the unfamiliar and dimly lit van, she asked Mike for the whereabouts of the headlight switch - then the location of the ignition switch, and the rear view mirror control - then to explain the operation of the seatback mechanism.

Mike patiently answered one question after another, with their locations and operations, and couldn't help teasing, "Why is it that women can never enter an unfamiliar car, and figure out where everything is? Guys do it all the time like duck soup."

Phylis was miffed at the chauvinistic remark and scornfully replied, "Why is it that dopey male engineers, who design these things, hide the same damn control in a 10 different places in every damn different model!"

"Good point kid. I don't know." Then added with a slight dig in rebuttal, "We do it so all the women in the world can barrage us with complaints when we're trying to get some sleep!"

Phylis hit Mike affectionately on the arm, as he feigned to defend himself, and said, "Michael, next time you fake the pregnancy."

Phylis shook her head in dismay at his typical male attitude, clipped on her seatbelt (with no further instruction from her male counterpart), and put the car in gear to pull away. Mike contently went back to nodding off.

During the drive home, Phylis occasionally glanced at this man's sleeping form next to her. He radiated this masculine air of confidence even in his sleep. For a person she had only known for a few months, it already felt like they had spent a lifetime of emotion and experiences together. She had finally found a real man.

In spite of the sometimes embarrassing involvement in his escapades, there was a special feeling she felt after tonight. Tonight, as a team, a man and a woman, husband and wife, they had been instrumental in delivering a human being - the life of a little girl. A life that would have passed away unnoticed and unaccounted for just 3 month's earlier. It was pleasing to discover that her natural nurturing instinct was still alive even at middle age. She even daydreamed of one day holding Amnion in her arms as a real fully developed baby. Tapping her finger on those tiny pursed lips, and seeing her eyes light up in amusement. She thought of gentle Maria Alvarez, Amnion's real mother. How wonderful it could be to reunite them again. She wondered what Maria would feel now... if she knew.

Phylis had no idea that this was not the end of the story. Once again impetuous Mike never discussed the planned lawsuit against Lifespan that he and Richie Farmers were about to undertake.

* * * * * * * *

The next morning Mike awoke still groggy and fatigued. As if by habit, he went down stairs to check on Amnion. From the stairway in the dim morning light, the hollow tube and life support cart were now vacant of life. The surrounding monitoring electronics, inert and silent. No LED lights telegraphing status. No CRT monitor screen to read and check vital signs. No DVD playing the whooshing sound of mother's heartbeat. Just a dingy basement. The only sound, the whirring whine of an old oil burner.

It was hard to believe that this dark place was home to an emerging human life. And almost as ludicrous, was his yearning for that old routine. As hectic as it had been down here, as much as the ordeal physically and emotional drained him, he missed taking care of her. But, he realized that she was now in better hands than his. Still, he missed his daughter Amnion.

After a few more minutes of contemplation trying to cope with sudden feelings of separation, he trudged upstairs. Time had come to start thinking about disassembling the cart and returning some of this equipment 'borrowed' from Lifespan. It was also the moment to call Richie and finally announce that Amnion was successfully delivered - alive! It was time to launch the legal battle with Lifespan and engage the special interest establishment.

CHAPTER 47
Let your fingers do the walking

For a change it was a tranquil morning at Lifespan headquarters. The Lifespan story was finally fading from the headlines, like any other story in today's media attention span.

Weeks of hectic work by the staff had finally set up the Asian specimen deal. Max sat relaxed in his office suite, ensconced in his snug leather chair, with his big feet up on the desk. He cradled the Wall Street Journal in his lap. Outside his office, the administrative staff was busy with the morning ritual of sifting through the mountains of mail that found its way to Max every day.

The desk phone rang, and was intercepted by one of his secretaries, who buzzed the intercom to announce, "Norm Stark on line two."

After the usual greetings Norm's voice grew quite serious, "Max, I have bad news from Bangkok."

Max reacted immediately, "What? Is it my specimens Is it? Those chinks backed out on our deal."

Norm tried to interrupt but Max was adamant about finishing his diatribe, "The crooked bastards want more money. Right?"

"I'm afraid it's not that, Max," Norm managed to interject. "I've been contacted by the U.S. embassy over there. It seems Eve West has disappeared."

Max hardly hesitated to answer, "What do you mean, <u>disappeared</u>?"

Norm's tone continued to sadden, "She hasn't been seen at the hotel for three days - missed all her business appointments."

Max sat silent on the other end. His mind was speculating on what schahnigans Eve might be up to. From his egocentric perspective, he assumed she was plotting something against him.

After a brief silence, Max queried, "What about the specimen shipment?"

"I think the first lot is ready to go tomorrow. Do you think we should risk shipping them without our own representative shepherding it?"

Max quickly jumped to the conclusion that Eve was doing this disappearing act maliciously just to jeopardize the shipment - to spite him for dumping her. He curtly replied, "Let it come in. We have no inventory, can't afford any further delays!"

Norm tried to intervene, "Max, I think we should wait until we can send..."

"No more delays!" Max barked, "You know how much it's costing us everyday to burn overhead waiting for something to process"

As a lawyer Norm felt comfortable to disregard a business decision, and, instead, said with urgency in his voice, "So, what about Eve? What should we do?"

"Nothing!" was his response, "She'll probably turn up in a few days."

Norm hung up, disappointed in Max's insensitive attitude, and decided to do something on his own recognizance. He recalled warning Eve about traveling over there as a woman alone. Now she was God knows where. For his own peace of mind, he decided to contact the Bangkok police directly and put up substantial reward money for action and answers.

Max sat hunched forward at his desk, still agitated by the phone call. All he could think was that this little bitch was trying to sabotage his plan to salvage his business. A drink from his liquor cabinet seemed appropriate for his agitated mood, and after a while, it did finally sedate his earlier emotions. He sat down and grabbed his southing Slinky out of the draw, and cradled it palm to palm. Carefully, he debated about who should cover the specimen shipment. The solitude did not last.

Suddenly, the quiet seclusion of his office was pierced by the screams of his secretarial staff outside. In thoughtless reaction, put down his toy and dashed for his office door to investigate. His suspicious character gripped him as he neared the door. At the threshold, he stopped and cautiously opened the door, just a crack, and peered into the reception area. The women outside were standing behind their desks staring in horror at a small plastic bag lying on the plush carpeted floor. A thick, open telephone directory was also lying on the floor nearby.

With all the negative publicity, Max had this increasing paranoia about assassination interfering with his immortality. He had arranged for the office women to systematically go through all his mail first. It was a sensible precaution to take with all these maniac demonstrators terrorizing legitimate businesses. After all, the potential did exist for a letter bomb to arrive at his address one day. It never crossed his mind, nor did he inform his secretaries of the potential dangers that this opening his mail could entail. He reasoned that sooner or later they were going to die anyway, so what is the difference.

One of his young clerical aids aid, hurried towards him in a dither. With her hands on her cheeks she exclaimed, "Mister Brewster! Mister Brewster! I...I just opened the box to take out the book! It just slipped from my hands." Beverly, his senior administrator, chimed in and pointed a trembling finger to the bag on the floor, "It just fell out!"

Realizing he was in no imminent danger, Max finally came out of his office to comfort her. He benevolently patted her on the shoulder. "Easy Bev, calm down now," he reassuringly said.

Then he walked over and bent down over the translucent plastic ziplock bag saying reassuringly, "Let's see what this is all about here."

His face cringed as he distinguished two adult human fingers inside the package, each severed at the knuckle. From a distance Beverly pointed her twitching finger at the telephone book nearby and said, "There, in there. The bag just fell out of the pages."

Max walked over to the yellow pages telephone book and picked it up off the floor. Inside he immediately noticed a 6 by 4 inch square had been cut out of the middle of several hundred inside pages. It essentially formed a hidden compartment inside the closed book. Max turned to Beverly asking, "Did anything else come inside with this?"

Beverly tried to compose herself, but could not help glancing at the bag of fingers still resting on the floor. After a pause, she replied, "Oh...uh, yes Mister Brewster."

Then she retrieved a small sealed envelope addressed to him, and handed it over. Max took it and read the return address, which simply said 'Tony the Tiger'. Max slapped his hand with the letter, as he instantly knew this was the work of his underworld connection, Anthony (Tony the Tiger) LaRocca.

Max moved swiftly now, to gingerly picked up the gruesome bag of fingers and place them out of sight back inside the telephone book. He headed for the privacy of his office, but before disappearing, he turned around to face his secretarial staff with a stern expression. "Do not, do not, mention this to anyone," he admonished them. "It's just one of those Pro-life pranksters trying to intimidate us and get our name in the papers again. Forget you ever saw this. I'll contact security and the proper authorities. They'll know what to do."

As he retreated to his office with the phone book, the staff just looked at each other stupefied. It seemed the police or somebody in the government should be called immediately. Obviously, those were human fingers. They belonged to some real person.

Sitting down at his desk Max put down the telephone book and its grisly contents. He opened the envelope and read a hand printed note that read;

> *"Want to find somebody fast?*
> *Just let your fingers do the walking.*
> *Try the yellow pages.*
> *This info comes to you compliments of the Capitol Post reporter*
> *who identified the 'anonymous' informer after a persuasive*

discussion, e.g. took two discussions. See page 609 for your informer. Your next wish is our command."

Tony the Tiger
(getting younger every day!)

Max chuckled to himself that these gangsters did have a way of getting results.

He was both amused and impressed by this display of ruthlessness and power. It was tempting to be part of an organization that could do these brazen acts without fear of the law or the media.

He also marveled at the power of his longevity elixir. Controlling the power of the underworld was even better than manipulating the politicians in Washington.

Max reached over his desk and slid the delivered telephone book onto his desk blotter. He delicately put the bag of fingers in his side desk draw and turned to page 609 as instructed in the letter. Scanning the directory, he came to the R's and a name with yellow highlight over it – Rosen, Joel.

Max was stunned and grumbled, "Doctor Joel Rosen. Son of a bitch!" He swiveled around in his chair to look out the window. "I would've never guessed."

Now he had his inside traitor. So, what to do about it? Max's thoughts revolved around how much this unfaithful employee had cost him. How this elitist professional, this traitor on his payroll, was going to jeopardize his immortality. Then, to his disappointment, he recalled that not long ago, this stoolie had resigned from the company! How would he get even with this doctor when he was already out of his grasp at Lifespan?

The answer to that problem was as obvious as the letter from Mister LaRocca in his hand. Max realized he had the big time syndicate clout to take care of this squealer in his own time and in his own way. Maybe even start with a few fingers again.

CHAPTER 48
Where the hell am I?

She found the loud voices around her disquieting, but somewhat familiar in their blurred mumble. Human, but still unreadable. None of them resembled the maternal voice that could instinctively deliver peace and security in her mind, and lend some badly needed psychological support. Amnion did not know why her mother's voice and heartbeat was not nearby

303

anymore, especially in this strange, new world of light and air. Nevertheless, she continued to expect her appearance soon – as nature intended

Alas, that anxiety would drift and ebb through unmeasured time, dissipated by her long periods of comforting deep sleep. The fact was, that she wasn't mentally developed enough to ponder any question in depth. Like any baby there were still no great human insights, nor any thoughts much beyond her immediate self, just simple basic inner feelings. Life was still more instinctive, some tutelage passed to her in the human DNA. However, it fell short in preparing her to handle this newfound extra uterine world of pain and noise.

That irritation included the protective cotton balls taped over each of her eyes. They were there to protect them from the light of the incubator heat lamps. Vision-wise, it was of no real consequence to her since the iris was not fully developed. She had been in the dark all her life ...both literally and figuratively. Clues to this contentious world of neonatal intensive care would have to come from her other senses.

And come they did, starting with gravity. She did not move much lying on her back or side, legs spread apart. It felt like her own body was crushing her back, even forcing her lungs to struggle to inflate. It took all her strength to move just her arm and hand to suck her thumb. No more fancy flips and gentle tumbles, cushioned on all sides by the moist caress of the amniotic fluid. More so, her feeble limbs were no match for this strange force resisting her every move, constantly tugging at her delicate frame. If only she could just curl up in the fetal position for a while, it would be so much more comforting.

Then, there was the incessant external background noise, the sound of the neonatal ICU; other babies crying, boisterous attending physicians, fumbling residents, the calming melody of nurses coaxing babies to live. What a far cry from the predictable serenity of the womb.

Sporadic non-human noises also proliferated; high pitched machine whines, elastic snapping, gurgling suctioning tubes, paper diaper tape being ripped, soft rock music. From her perspective there really was no sense to any of it. It would confuse and interfere with her developing brain. Eventually, over time, she did manage to start associating one thing with another. It was a different world of sorts - her new world. Too tired and too preoccupied to do anything about it.

Occasionally, the dull routine was suddenly interrupted by the screech of a fetal monitor alarm as some other baby stopped breathing. In fact, even Amnion's own fetal alarm would be set off now and then. It hardly startled her as she was already fading off to the blackness of death, only to be revived by something pounding on her back, jarring her back to consciousness. A nurse cooing encouragement for her to live another day. It was almost as though life and death ebbed and flowed in a regular routine, like the rippling remnants of waves washing up on a moonlit shore, each replaced by the ensuing one. Each wave never progresses beyond the sea's fringe, as her life seemed to hang in the balance at exactly the same point.

Existence was also the daily flood of new physical and environmental inputs. Far different from the constancy of the serene unchanging fluid world of the womb. Air entered her lungs with a cool tingling sensation now. Her skin felt tight and dry. The heat lamp kept one side warm but left her backside cool, unlike the all-encompassing constant temperature fluid she had grown accustomed to in the fetal tube. Confusing to say the least. Uncomfortable to no end.

Then there were all these foreign tubes and needles sticking into her everywhere, that would probably drive a sane person crazy. Fortunately, her level of awareness and conscience development was sufficiently low enough to somehow tolerate all this torment.

It was a cruel metaphor to be entering life hooked up to all this medical support and monitoring equipment. Starting in the same way many sick and feeble people wind up leaving this world. She was a child in purgatory, fallen from the heavenly peace of the womb into a cruel inhospitable hell on earth. Caught somewhere between the womb and the existence of a fully developed baby. And, as always, pondering the continual question of 'where is mother'.

If Amnion could speak, she probably would scream, *OK then. Enough! Where the hell am I ????.*

CHAPTER 49
Try to keep you pants on

At University Hospital Mike tried to make sense of the hospital gown, cap, mask, and booties handed him by the neonatal nurses. All he heard from the nurse's instructions was to change and put these hospital garments on. He took the instructions literally. He was both distracted and excited to finally get inside neonatal and see his little girl close up again. Finding an empty utility closet, the distracted Mike took off his shoes to put the booties on, and removed his pants and shirt. Carefully he stood up and tied the gown on, modestly overlapping the opening in front.

A NICU (neonatal intensive care unit) nurse came down the hall just as Mike exited the cramped closet. She took one look at him, his underwear showing and hairy legs sticking out below his gown, and began laughing in amusement. Mike assumed it was the blue cap, booties, and mask that made him appear funny. She called another nurse over, and they covered their mouths in muffled giggling. Mike turned around assuming something happened behind him. With nobody there, he glanced down at himself to fathom the apparent joke. The confused look on his face compelled one nurse to finally explain, "the gown sir...it goes <u>over</u> your clothes...and you have it on backwards."

Mike tried to look nonchalant, like he knew that all the time. The other nurse giggled and admonished him, "and the booties go over your shoes, not your socks!"

"Yeah, he answered appreciatively, "I thought they were a bit oversized."

"Let me see if I can help you," she said, as she thoughtfully pulled the elastic cap down to cover his ears and directed him back to the closet for alterations. She couldn't help adding, "And don't forget to put your pants back on, Mister Santino."

Mike felt like the perfect fool. He imagined the nurses at the front desk having a good laugh all night over this one - at his expense.

Mike finally made his entrance again, this time properly attired, but feeling dressed like 'Bozo the Clown'. Upon reaching the NICU this time, he peered through the plexiglass window at the crowd of a dozen or so babies scattered about the room. Each one lay on its own incubator cart with zillions of tubes and wires stuck all over its body. Most laid motionless, a disturbing sight for such young life.

A pleasant looking, middle-aged nurse, named Sandy Hart came over, introduced herself, and regarded this new father with a critical eye. He had already been tested for Hepatitis, and other disease markers. The nurse politely led Mike to the NICU entry door. Warm and humid ambience enveloped him as the door opened. Mike pulled up his surgical mask and was led to Amnion's special bed. To say the least, he was shocked by the tiny child's gaunt appearance. Not pink and chunky with rosy cheeks as he imagined. Instead, there was not much of an improvement from her appearance right after her delivery. Amnion was dark and sullen with veins visible on her head and abdomen. Her shrunken face was contorted into what appeared to be a frown. Her thin wrinkled abdomen led to scrawny limbs tinged blue and dusty yellow. This scrawny vision below reminded him more of a baby chimpanzee than a human being.

She lay there helpless, naked and inert with her legs spread apart. In the stillness, the fetal monitor was the only clue that life existed there at all. Her arms were aside her head, held with clenched fists. Electrodes were taped here, there, - everywhere. Cotton was taped over her eyes and an intravenous line was stuck into a vein in her forehead. A ventilating tube was inserted through her nose and down into her lungs. She had skin so thin that the shadows of her internal organs were almost perceptible within.

Mike had to question himself, as to whether all he had done was fair to this child. Whether all that suffering would pan out.

Mike stepped back and whispered politely to the nurse, with a mix of concern and indignation, "She's naked."

"All the babies are kept that way," nurse Hart calmly explained. "We keep them warm with the heat lamps. We also need access to get at all the monitoring leads and to provide hourly care."

"I want Amy covered with something...something soft," he quietly insisted.

Nurse Hart was skilled in handling argumentative parents and replied unequivocally, "I'm afraid it's not procedure, Mister Santino. It will take more time to keep covering and uncovering Amy when we medicate her."

Mike looked around at all the naked babies aware that they were all treated the same. "I still want her covered," he reiterated with a hiss. "She has a right to her dignity too. They all may be babies, but they're still people with feelings – as rudimentary as they are."

"I'm sorry," she answered with finality, "our neonatologist sets the procedural rules in here. You'll have to speak to him."

"Well, where is he?"

"He's on shift at 7 AM tomorrow morning."

"Then I'll take it up with him," Mike concluded.

The nurse nodded amicably, and explained to Mike that these intrusive methods were a standard and necessary routine with a child this premature and of such a low birth weight.

Mike listened with only half an ear, as he returned to Amnion's side and leaned closer towards her while inquiring of the nurse, "Is she in pain."

Before the nurse could answer, the seemingly inert Amnion suddenly snapped her tiny head towards Mike. If she actually could see, she would be staring directly at him.

The nurse was puzzled by the child's response and said, "They usually only respond to their mother's voice like that."

Mike smiled saying, "You don't know the half of it."

He made the most of Amnion's attention now and put his gloved pinky in her tiny palm. She gripped his finger purposefully and kicked her legs. Mike leaned over and cooed baby talk to her, reveling in the ability to prompt a reaction from a mere touch. He was communicating with her...even at this elemental level.

Nurse Hart began to lose her wariness of Mike, at first impressed, and then delighted. She knew that babies who feel loved and wanted had the lowest mortality rates, and the best outcomes. This one now showed encouraging signs of awareness and affection.

Before long, Mike's brief visiting time was up, and he left the neonatal room to linger for a while and watch through the plexiglass window from outside. Behind him nurse Hart removed her mask, leaned against the wall and said, "Amy's a fighter, that girl, I can tell. Some that we get, give up right away, like it was never meant to be. Some have genetic defects that are impossible to overcome. Then, there are those who won't be denied their destiny. We see all that in here."

A teary-eyed Mike turned to face her, "How do you do this everyday?" he asked incredulously. Then realizing he may have offended her by his bluntness, he tried to apologize.

Nurse Hart raised her hand dismissing his apology. "It's not easy. But it is rewarding, when some of these children actually make it. You see them years later as real little people with personalities, with families... with a future."

Mike added, "What about the ones that don't make it."

She compassionately gazed back at the nursery through the plexiglass and spoke with a sullen voice, "We give all of them their best shot at life and everything possible to give them a fighting chance at life - no matter how sick or damaged. We lose a lot, but take comfort in those we save. The rest is in the hands of the Almighty."

Mike admired her character, and could sense a motherly, loving woman beneath the formality and hospital uniform. It was the first of many intimate chats he would have with Nurse Hart.

Upon his departure, she commented reassuringly, "You've got a good obstetrician with Dr. Samuelson. If any complications should develop, he'll make the right recommendations along with her neonatologist."

Mike was comforted by her remark, and thanked her as he prepared to change and leave. He lingered outside the neonatal room to gazed one last time at Amnion and mused,

A feeble spirit in limbo,
at the fringes of survival.
If she died tonight,
would anyone grieve but me ?

Nurse Hart observed his departure and recalled how few fathers ever even showed up to see these preemie fetuses. Nobody wants to get attached until they are sure their child will live. Equally strange, was this fetus's strong attachment to him....surprising. There was something wonderfully different about this man's connection to his child. Like the motherly bond with a child, at birth.

Of course, there also a special air about this little girl of his. She had that certain magnetic aura that made you want to help her too.

As far as having Mike Santino, the doting father around, Nurse Hart humorously concluded to herself, *Only time would tell if he was going to be helpful... or a royal pain in the ass.*

CHAPTER 50
Bangkok arrives

D r. Jeff Ellar paced the floor of his new office in the pharmaceutical production building of Lifespan. His wish for promotion was finally fulfilled when Joel Rosen abruptly resigned, and Dr. Strauss immediately appointed him to be Head of the Processing Department. Unfortunately for Ellar, this was a hell of a time to take over processing operations. With specimen inventory now approaching zero, Jeff's minimum staff was rapidly running out of work. After the Russian disaster, the fetal shipments from Bangkok were absolutely essential to keeping product moving and cash flowing into Lifespan.

An earlier call to Marketing confirmed that this first batch had cleared customs at Hawaii yesterday, and was at Lifespan. Returning to his office, Ellar nervously shuffled some papers at his desk, as Mike's boss, Al Greene entered.

"What's the latest ETA, Jeff?" he asked.

Ellar looked up, then apprehensively checked his watch and replied, "I understand the shipment is already here."

Al was obviously agitated. "It took three days to get here. It's about time we see something delivered."

His boss then shifted gears and changed topics, "What's the work-in-process picture? I need a billings forecast to close the month."

Jeff nervously rifled through some computer printouts and clumsily checked his smartphone. He did not have the foggiest idea of where his department was on shipping since Joel left and blurted out last month's figure, "About $4 million."

"Not too bad," Al commented, "that's about what we did last month." Then he sat down and asked, "What about next month?"

Ellar had guessed with the first figure, so he guessed at the second number too. We'll roll off pretty dramatically without fresh specimens, but I think we can get another $4 million out the door."

Al didn't know what a false sense of security he was given with those numbers. Especially since he was passing them up the corporate chain.

Just then, a lab tech came in and interrupted, "Dr. Ellar, there's an awful strange odor out here." Covering her nose and looking out the door she added, "It's really repulsive."

No sooner did she say that, when the two also caught a whiff of the pungent stench. Both men immediately left the office to trace the offensive stink. All over the building people were making faces and holding handkerchiefs to their mouths and noses. Ellar and Greene followed the scent trail to the back warehouse receiving dock. Piled in the main aisle were several pallets loaded with fetal shipping containers.

The Bangkok fetal shipment had arrived! And just in the nick of time.

Al Greene became incensed as Lifespan workers tried to lay plastic over the reeking pile of boxes. Others were busy re-opening the overhead doors on the loading dock to let fresh air in.

Al's worst nightmare just became a reality.

Ellar had a devastated look, as it was obvious that rotting tissue from the Bangkok shipment was the odor culprit. He could only remark, "Well there goes next month's billing forecast."

Al grabbed a wall phone to call Mike Santino over to the scene, along with other key engineering managers.

In the other building Mike sat at his desk with the telephone in his ear and a huge grin on his face. Listening to Al's lament, it was so tempting to tell him and his bio-med engineers, I told you so!. In spite of Al's urgent plea, Mike walked leisurely across the parking lot to the other Lifespan building – he already heard about the smell.

When he arrived, Al was already conducting an impromptu meeting in the warehouse with other directors and department heads. The smell was nauseating.

"What the hell happened?" Al demanded of his audience.

The Marketing VP, Bob Fisher, volunteered an explanation, "Apparently, the cargo jet had electrical problems at the refueling stop in Honolulu. They lost several hours on the ground with no power. Ambient cargo temperatures went from a cool 45 degrees Fahrenheit probably reached over 120 degrees."

"Why didn't we know, Bob? Who was supposed to track this shipment?" Al demanded.

"Eve West."

"Well, where is she?"

"Damned if I know Al. You can ask Brewster."

Al shook his bowed head and glanced at Mike with a look that seemed to acknowledge Mike's warning about the cooling limitations of the transport containers.

Mike noticed some technicians in masks beginning to unload the pallets. He immediately yelled, "Hey! Stop!"

Ellar intervened, "It's OK. They're my techs doing the unloading. We have to see if some of the specimens are salvageable."

Mike warned, "You open that pile of garbage in here and you risk contaminating the entire ventilation system, and the clean rooms."

Al interceded immediately, barking orders, "Get a forklift and open the cases outside on the back lawn!"

"And close the doors," Mike warned.

Mike mused to himself, *Yeah, Then throw gasoline on the whole pile and torch it.*

* * * * * * * *

Max sat slumped in his office chair, its leather material seemingly losing some of it soft luster. With the Bangkok shipment ruined, rumors were running rampant throughout the company that Lifespan was on the verge of total collapse. On the couch in his office sat a subdued Norm Stark, shoulders slumped forward. Even he was really down after receiving the bad news of the airborne shipping delays. Even more affected than usual. He knew Maxes decision to ship without an escort was downright foolish to begin with.

"It's those fuckin' engineers again!" Max railed. "I tell you, we get rid of Al Greene and some of his cronies, and that'll solve half our problems."

Norm continued his briefing, as Max fumed. "Not only did the transport cases fail to cool the specimens over the extended shipping time, but some of the specimen's themselves were up to 36 weeks gestation. Totally useless."

"The chink bastard shipped anything they could fit in the box." Max complained. "No sense of quality control over there."

The unusually dejected Norm interrupted, "There's more bad news Max." Then he paused to collect his thoughts, "I found out what happened to Eve."

Max's attention perked up. He blamed her and Al Greene for this fiasco, and was anxious to meat out punishment. OK, what gives?" he said.

Norm's face saddened, "She's been kidnapped."

"What?"

"Kidnapped, Max," he repeated.

"How?

Norm explained what he'd found out from the Bangkok police. "Apparently she was last seen being picked up in front of her hotel by a Taxi company named 'Green Dragon'. And, as you can guess, it turns out there is no such taxi company in Bangkok."

"So", Sam said.

"The local police said it was the typical method for capturing white women over there. Then they sell them as sex slaves for wealthy drug warlords up north in the mountains."

Maxes mind had this image of Eve on her back, stubbornly explaining women's rights to a primitive tribal chief. The thought made him feel like laughing at Eve's dilemma, but he suppressed his humorous

311

thoughts so as not to offend Norm. Max easily feigned concern and asked, "What can we do to get her back?"

Norm shrugged, "I'm afraid very little. White women, especially attractive ones like Eve, are at a premium over there. Worth more than gold or money." Norm let out a big sigh. "Maybe we can try hiring a private investigator. I expect it could still take months to locate her."

Max replied, "Unfortunately in our financial straits, we can't afford that kind of luxury any more. You know what's happening here now. We just can't afford it."

Norm knew Max was bullshitting him. Lifespan had enough money in reserves to choke a horse. Just a short while ago, Norm had arrived in Max's office dismayed. Now he was leaving angry and resentful.

Nevertheless, Norm was still determined to save Eve from her captors.

CHAPTER 51
Bare ass naked

Phylis busied herself aboard *"Mare Nostrum'* in the cabin galley preparing a lunch, consisting of a tossed salad and coldcuts. Mike secured the anchor line outside with a strong pull. A warm, sultry August breeze crossed through the sailboat cabin and caressed her bare arms and legs with its moist salty air. This was their first, real time alone since Mike saved Amnion from Lifespan. With all the hectic activity over the past several weeks there had been little time for solitude away from the kids, and just each other.

Mike picked a deserted cove for their anchorage, near a small curved spit of sandy beach just outside the harbor entrance. Beyond the beach, a thirty-foot dirt sand cliff topped with scrub bushes hid the horizon and civilization beyond. Lying at anchor about 30 yards offshore the boat rested alone on a placid bay.

It also was a weekday, most everyone else was at work. All things combined, Mike had managed to find a private place that finally afforded a needed respite from all the turmoil surrounding them.

From the cockpit, Mike bounded down the narrow steps to join Phylis in the tight confines of the dark cabin. She was busy tearing some lettuce and cutting tomatoes for a fresh salad.

"This sure beats sailing across the Sound, huh?" he volunteered.

Phylis turned with a doubtful grin, remembering having to rescue Mike back on that bitter cold trip in April, months ago. She answered humorously, "We're not on dry land yet. If I give you enough time, who knows what you'll get me into."

Mike brushed off the remark and glided up behind her to gently wrap his hairy tanned arms around her waist, softly kissing her delicate neck. His body pressed against her posterior as his strong hands slowly began to roam about her shapely form.

Phylis tried to ignore his amorous male advances as she mixed the salad and giggled. "You want to eat today...or spend the day feeling me up?"

"Both," he softly moaned more serious now, proceeding to sensually nibble at her bare neck and tanned freckled shoulders.

Phylis smelled his Aqua Velva aftershave mixed with a manly scent of perspiration. It suddenly began to feel very warm inside the cabin, and uncomfortably confining in her one-piece swimsuit. Mike gently turned her around to face him, giving her a look as if he would devour her with his lust. In a firm embrace he kissed her long and hard, almost taking her breath away. Her arms dangled lose as she dropped her tomato knife into the metal sink behind. Before she could respond, he had her swimsuit undone down to her waist, and fell to his knees, caressing her bare breasts with his mouth and hands. Her limbs felt weak, and her hands sought to brace herself against the galley counter top behind. Looking down at him, and all she could think to express was a soft moan, "Ooh, Michael."

Soon they were in the snug confines of the forward cabin making passionate love in the heat of the summer afternoon. Phylis was reclined on the berth, looking up through the square deck hatch open above. White puffy summer clouds slowly passed by in a royal blue sky. She forgot about her children, the mortgage payments, the Lifespan fiasco - even Amnion.

For the moment she could be free to feel life's pleasures for herself and her man. Free to sense passions that she'd never dreamed were possible again.

Mike made love to every inch of her body, making her feel as secure and voluptuous as a 20 year old. Throughout this erotic lovemaking, his lips regularly returned to hers, as if to reassure that he knew who he was with.

Her lover was like a bear on honey, and the stimulating sensations compelled her at times to gasp for air. She watched all this activity through limped eyes, caressing his powerful shoulders arms and hands as they went about their instinctive ritual of releasing succulent pleasure from a woman's yielding body.

After a while, the eruption of passion was complete, and the two lovers lay on their backs, separated on the V berth of the bow, drenched in sweat. Now the warm breeze did little to cool their exhausted spent bodies. Mike joked, "We should light a cigarette like in the movies now. Shouldn't we?"

Phylis gave a thin smile, and fanned her face with her hand, "I think we've already generated enough smoke for one day!"

Mike decided to take a quick dip before eating lunch and walked over to the cabin door to peek out and make sure no one was around the cove. Before Phylis could say something, he bolted outside - bare ass naked. Then he jumped off the stern with a yell, "Geronimo!"

He called back for her to join him. She would - but not before donning her bathing suit.

Mike complained from the water that he was already nude and she was being a prude in her swimsuit. An astute Phylis just retorted, "There's a difference."

"Like what?"

She leaned down over on the stern safety line and snickered, "The difference... my dear naked man... Is that nobody wants to <u>see you</u> in the nude."

Then she laughed heartily, leaned over the stern and, splashed him with water, as he dove below, his white bare bottom was still visible in the murky water. She paused for a moment to muse to herself. *If the Hindus are right, in the next life he'd come back as a sea otter.*

Phylis carefully slipped down the side of the boat and they frolicked together in the refreshing coolness of the bay.

* * * * * *

After toweling drying and getting Mike to put his bathing suit back on, they sat in the cabin for lunch. Phylis served up the delicious meal of salad and cold cuts. She sipped wine cooler. Mike slurped down a Corona. Then, he proceeded to devour everything else on the table.

Mike baited Phylis with the seemingly innocent comment. "Food tastes much better," he quipped, "... prepared by a woman."

"You just like being waited on, Michael, because you're lazy." Phylis retorted as she wiped up crumbs from the table.

He grasped her wrist before she could return to the sink, and looked up at her with that confident male grin she'd come to know. Mike appreciated that his comment didn't start a discussion on equal rights, and said in a solemn tone, "Don't ever believe that I don't love you or appreciate what you've done for me. No matter what happens between us in the future, no matter what I fail to do or fail to say, you will always have a special place in my heart. That's something that will never change until I die."

He surprised her by pulling her close and kissing the open palms of her dishpan hands. Phylis looked down and simply murmured softly, "My sweetheart," and pressed his head to her chest. It was comforting to hear those endearing words from him. Frustratingly, he always had a way of making their love affair sound so tenuous, as if it was only renewable on a weekly basis.

She tried to put aside the lingering apprehension for the moment, not really knowing what further challenges to their relationship might remain.

CHAPTER 52
Wabbits

Richard regarded his spouse's irritated countenance in the comfortable confines of his dimly lit study. Across from him, Evon sat rigid on the loveseat, her arms folded and legs tucked underneath. Until now, their whole marriage had been a steady series of open discussions on what career moves her husband had made to advance himself in a liberal society. Richard valued her counsel and her usual thoughtful perspective, never doubting that her motivation always was to look out for his best interests.

This time it was different. He had broken that collective decision-making tradition within their marriage - taking on Lifespan without her input - broken a trust. From Evon's perspective, there was no well-connected mentor giving Richard the usual advanced inside-track information on how this one would play out. This time the politically savy decision was to back away and let someone else do it. This time, every force in American politics would be lined up against her husband, not with him. Now everything they had accomplished over a lifetime was on the line. Evon was clearly upset as her husband related his decision to represent some fetus named, of all things, Amnion.

"Richard, I can't believe you!" she said in a high-pitched voice, "you're really going to throw away your 30 year career on some crazy lawsuit. This Amnion thing. What are you going to prove?"

"I'm going to prove that a tiny human life has a right to play out its existence. That American business has no place dealing in living human flesh - at any stage. And that when society begins to label one defenseless group or another as something less than human, that society needs fixing."

Richard pressed his point more personally, "You haven't been exposed to discrimination to appreciate that."

Evon was really vexed. "What? So now the darker we are," referring to Richard's complexion, "the more we can appreciate discrimination?"

She still could not accept this high-minded philosophy and shifted the discussion to the immediate family. "Then what about us? What about our children? The house? Their educations? Our friends??"

"I believe we have a net worth of $30 million, Muffin."

"Fine! Now you expect us to just live our lives out, selling everything we own," Evon retorted.

"You're being ridiculous. I think I've met my obligation to provide for my family," He answered dryly. "Now I'll do what I want to do. What I have to do."

Richard added nonchalantly, "and besides, Evon, the kids already know."

Evon sat there, mouth agape, surprised and now miffed even more.

Richard sat back and folded his newspaper. "I spoke to the children at length upstairs. - last night. They know the story and they're willing to accept the pro-life stigma associated with this case."

Leaning forward and smiling, he tried to make a consoling gesture by tapping her leg with the newspaper. "Come on honey. Realistically. I mean, we have enough money to send them to college 10 times over."

Evon brushed the newspaper away. She was still stunned that even her children were consulted before her. She could not believe her two children's reaction - that they could be so apparently unselfish. She always viewed them as nice but spoiled kids.

For a while, there was a detached silence between them, as Richard read the paper and Evon her magazine. Shortly, Richard broke the silence with an invitation, "How about coming over to University Hospital one night and meeting my client, the child Amnion?"

Evon looked up over her reading glasses and grumbled, "You've got to be kidding!" Then she stared down at her magazine and thought about it some more. A figurative truce was declared when she reluctantly grumbled, "We'll see Richard. We'll just have to see."

* * * * * * *

Mike followed the directions through and old industrial neighborhood to a ramshackle building in College Point. He pulled into a crumbling asphalt parking lot and parked his dull gray Mustang in the visitor's section. It seemed such an unlikely place to meet Richie. He really expected to meet their legal team in some fancy skyscraper in Manhattan.

Mike left the car and checked in with a guard at a guard shack. The cheerless guard checked his ID and ushered him in. The place appeared to be a private security systems company, more like a warehouse, complete with armored trucks and all. On the second floor, he re-checked his written directions for the correct room number, while he meandered past old offices that look like they had not been painted in a hundred years. Farther down the hall, he found the right one. Upon entering, he was met by Richard Farmer, who introduced him to paralegals Brenda and Greg.

"This is it people. This is the team that will be filing the suit," Richard announced to all.

Mike was at first disappointed, then skeptical. He asked himself whether these young people could have the legal backgrounds necessary to challenge a behemoth like Lifespan's lawyers. He remarked sarcastically, "We're a little light on lawyers here, aren't we?"

"Mikey," Richard laughed, "If you hired my firm, one of the biggest in Manhattan, how many lawyers do you think we'd assign to a case?" Richard pointed to himself and the paralegals counting, 1-2-3. Then added, "Except you wouldn't get to hand pick the best of the bunch." Richard pointed towards Brenda with a manila folder in hand. "That girl is a forensic accounting whiz. If there's anything wrong with Lifespan's books, she'll ferret it out."

Mike looked at the young woman and couldn't resist a pun. "So you flush all their ledger toilets until you see which one backs up?"

Brenda gave a polite smile at his crudeness, and turned to stare incredulously towards the ceiling.

Richard cheerfully continued, "And Greg here can dig out historical case law precedents on any argument you pick. Find all the ones that agree with you, and undermine the ones that do not. These professionals are working at half pay – no question about dedication."

Mike conceded Richard's credibility behind the introductions and nodded agreement, differing to his friend's experienced judgment. Thereafter, Richard sat down at the conference table to explain why he picked this meeting location and the strategy to be followed in working the case. Apparently, his brother-in-law owns the security company they were in, and donated them 200 square feet of office space as the staging area and focal point for their casework. It had four desks with networked computers, secure wireless Internet access, a fax, burner cell phones, copy machine, file cabinets, and a conference table. It was also across the street from a 24 hour-a-day delicatessen. In addition, as a security facility, it is guarded 24 hours a day. A private spot to meet and work safely. A perfect place to protect files and records.

"Madison Avenue it ain't," Richard joked, "but we have all the tools we need to get the job done. And, you have to understand, Mikey… that these people we're facing will stoop to anything to undermine our case – legal or illegal."

Mike's first assignment was to tell his story to the paralegals, who took copious notes. He outlined the Lifespan corporate organization and personnel for possible written depositions and the departments and files that would be best to search during the document discovery phase.

At the conclusion of the meeting, Richard addressed Mike. "You have contacts in the *Brooklyn Daily News*?"

"Sure. Why?"

"Good," Richard said, "Then, your job will be to get media focused on presenting our point of view when the mud starts to fly."

"OK. I'll do my best," Mike replied, knowing the *Brooklyn Daily* reporter would still probably resent Mike for not revealing his identity.

"And for God's sake," Richard cautioned the group, "stay away from the termination issue zealots. Don't allow any contact with either side. No comments or interviews. We have our own agenda here – one fetus, one company."

The meeting broke up with more assignments made. A timetable was established for their complaint to be filed in State Court by next week. Richard indicated he would pull some strings to get a particular old judge he knew to try this case. The person he had in mind was nearing retirement and would at least insure an impartial trial.

Richard eyes rose upward, as he quipped, "God help us. This case is going to take some explaining before any judge or jury"

* * * * * * *

That evening, Mike and Phylis sat in an office at University Hospital awaiting the arrival of Amnion's neonatologist, Dr. Shahdrey Shahdere. The NICU nurse had indicated that Amy had some problems and tests that they should be aware of, and a consultation was in order.

Phylis was fidgety in her chair, quite nervous about appearing before a doctor as wife, much less a post-partum mother. Mike tried to calm her, saying, "I'll jump into any conversation if it gets sticky."

The doctor entered and politely introduced himself. He was a young pleasant looking Indian, short with a thin build. Mike was at first put off by his being a foreigner. On the other hand, Phylis liked him right away. He had kind eyes. Even Mike, after a few intelligent remarks by the doctor in perfect English, began to feel more comfortable with him.

Dr. Shahdere gave them a run down of Amy's health status, stating in a relaxed tone, "There were some complications that required testing. Amy's had another episode of apnea, uh, cessation of breathing, so I ordered a CAT scan to make sure there was no evidence of intraventricular hemorrhage in the cranial areas."

Mike and Phylis's faces betrayed their underlying anxiety coupled with confusion, so the doctor stopped to simplify the discussion. "Bleeding in the head," he added.

Then the doctor sat down behind his desk and continued. "It's not unusual in a preemie as young as your daughter. The bleeding appears to be very slight, not unusual in a baby this immature. We are monitoring it closely with ultrasound ... as a precaution."

While Phylis and Mike digested this new information the doctor startled her by asking, "Are you lactating, Mrs. Santino? We really need it for an infant this underdeveloped. If you can express breast milk, we can refrigerate it and feed it to your baby in a few weeks. "

Phylis hesitated, "I'm afraid I can't," she answered looking desperately at Mike for help.

"Oh yeah," Mike interjected, looking at Phylis for what seemed an awfully long time. Then he spoke up, "Dr. Samuelson said her blood test showed some signs of serum hepatitis from an infection many years ago. So he gave her something to dry her up."

Phylis was both impressed and relieved by Mike's quick thinking.

Dr.Shahdere gave a serious, "Umm," and scribbled some notes on his pad. "Then it's best we don't use yours anyway. I'll work on the donor breast milk issue tomorrow. So today, we will have to test the baby for that hepatitis - might even warrant isolation."

"Jeez, I hope not Doctor," Mike added, realizing his little lie would result in more unpleasant testing of his little girl.

The doctor paused, and then resumed his recap of Amy's early condition. "Last week's bout with jaundice is almost over with a declining bilirubin count - almost normal now. Doctor Rosen, I think you know him, was helpful in avoiding any serious intervention on that one."

The doctor closed his notepad and asked the couple if there were any further concerns or questions. Phylis was getting up to leave when Mike tugged her arm to remain seated. He told the doctor, "Yes, there's one last thing. I want my daughter covered with something, so she's not lying naked all day."

The doctor did not expect that, and tried to dismiss the question with a normal procedural answer, and that it was inconvenient for the hourly care given each child and would add to the expense of running the neonatal unit.

Mike remained undeterred but now agitated. "Hey, what does it take? An extra 2 seconds to remove some covering and put it back? These kids have dignity too. They know when there naked and exposed."

Phylis felt embarrassed by Mike's impolite manner, and feared another one of Mike's ugly confrontations developing She apologized to the now slighted doctor and tugged on Mike, who was now standing across the desk from the doctor.

Dr. Shahdere stood up. His reaction surprisingly very calm and non-confrontational, while still standing his ground. For some reason his posture seemed to pacify Mike.

The cooled off Mike explained, "Look doc, I know my daughter has some feelings right now, simple as they might be. She's been in a warm protected world for a long time. Now she's alone. Out in a place that's loud, cold, and alien. She needs to sense something protective."

"Like what, Mister Santino?"

"Like this," Mike answered as he reached for his jacket pocket, and unfolded a soft flannel burping towel.

Phylis couldn't help smiling at the white flannel printed with a scattering of tiny figures of plump gray rabbits. Each cartoon character had an oversized bulbous bright pink nose as they munched on huge orange carrots. Phylis reached over to examine the cloth. In the corner, in small print it said "Wabbits".

Doctor Shahdere looked at the towel and also began to smile, then they all laughed.

"OK," the doctor relented, "It requires sterilization." Adding chidingly, "So, when it gets soiled, Santino, you will kindly wash it clean each time?"

Mike held up the burp towel happily agreed and quipped, "Err, what's up Doc!"

With the confrontation avoided, a pleasantly relieved Phylis left with 'Mister Bugs Bunny' to join Amnion upstairs.

* * * * * * *

Dressed in protective gear, Mike and Phylis stood over Amnion. He was now able to pick her up and cuddled her, as he wanted to do for so many weeks. Even with the facemasks, Mike's shit-faced grin of satisfaction was still evident, as if proving to the world that he knew this child better than anyone else. Slowly, Phylis had begun to get concerned with this behavior - more and more possessive. He was starting to act as if this little baby was actually his daughter. Phylis, although sympathetic, was not as attached by virtue of not seeing Amnion everyday in her basement.

After their visiting time was over, Mike joined Phylis in the corridor outside neonatal, removing his sterile gown, mask, and booties. He asked for her reaction, and Phylis related both her enjoyment and distress. Brief as the visit were, the sight of all those tubes and monitoring leads attached to Amnion's body made her wince in empathy. Phylis didn't smile and broached the subject of his relationship with Amnion. "You know Michael. Sooner or latter this child has to be returned to her natural mother."

Mike waved his hand to immediately dismiss the thought, saying, "No way! That lady gave my kid up for dead a long time ago. We brought her back from the grave."

Phylis thought about the real mother, the gentle Maria Alvarez and argued, "Michael, this isn't like a 'rescue dog'. How do you know her real mother would not love her too? Maybe she couldn't afford another child, maybe ....."

An irrational Mike cut her off, "The hell with the mother. I put my career on the line for this kid. **My blood** was in that tube with her. I'm just as much a mother now too."

Phylis was afraid of this. Mike had put so much of himself into this child, that it was becoming impossible to reason with him, to separate judgment from emotion.

"I knew the mother, Michael. She's a good person. If she knew her daughter was alive, I know she would cherish and care for her. Probably love her even more than you."

"Apparently, a few months of gestation didn't show any motherly instinct," an unsympathetic Mike answered with disdain.

Phylis was a bit insulted by his remark. "Sometimes, Michael, you can really be a selfish and unfeeling jerk. So judgmental."

With Maria's caring visage in her mind, Phylis continued her tirade, "You know, sometimes women get caught in between choices where they can't win either way. Where society says do this, or do that. And you're wrong, no matter which choice you make."

"Well in a few days it won't matter anyway," he said

"Why?"

"Because we're filing a lawsuit against Lifespan, and Amnion is the plaintiff," he said dryly, "and we'll be the parents!"

Phylis was dumbfounded. Up until now, she thought that this ordeal was nearing its conclusion. That, hopefully, Amnion would pull through this and be returned, eventually, to Maria. Then she and Michael could disappear back into their own private romantic world.

Caught off guard again, she protested, "Are you nuts? You never consulted me again. Do you realize what you're up against? You think anyone can stop Lifespan and those people behind it?"

"Yeah," pointing to his chest, "**Me!**"

"And what happens when the entrenched woman's organizations in the country feel threatened and jump all over you."

Mike smirked, "As long as they're all naked when they do it, I don't care."

She did not find his macho humor entertaining at all and said abruptly, "Just take me home. I think we are done for good."

It was a silent ride home from the hospital. Phylis felt betrayed again, and as if her fledgling romance was becoming bogged down in some useless crusade for social justice. The idea of being in the spotlight of media attacks or having to testify in a public courtroom made her shudder with dread. It would be weeks before a trial would be over, and she wondered what would be left of their personal relationship after that kind of ordeal. What's more, they were already legally married!

Mike pulled into her dark driveway and leaned over to kiss her goodnight, but Phylis exited in a huff, and slammed the car door behind. She walked up her sidewalk and didn't even pause to gauge his reaction. Mike opened his door and stood with one foot on the pavement while resting his arms on the roof. He shouted in agitation, "Nobody wants to go the extra round anymore. Finish the fight." He shook his head saying, "That's not me. This thing isn't over until I say it is."

She looked back and shouted back, "Well, it's me or your court case mister 'Man of La Mancha'!"

Mike barked back, "Don't make me chose. Not between you and my daughter's rights. Don't do that to me." He crossed his arms sideways like and umpire calling her out at home plate, bellowing, "No deal!" He jumped back in his car, and hit the accelerator. The tires squealed in reverse. The car bounced backwards down the driveway into the street, scraping its bottom on the pavement. Sparks flew. His tires chirped as he shot forward down the block.

"Great," Phylis remarked. He left her feeling somehow incomplete - that their argument accomplished nothing. She stared down in the dark at her dragging feet, not feeling the same sense of conviction about fighting this fetal thing the way Michael did. Reluctantly, lonely, she ascended her front stoop, faintly illuminated by soft light of the living room window and thought to herself, *How would I explain this to my parents? My children? That I have another screwed up relationship. That we split up over a fetus we stole from my company and grew in my fiancée's basement. That I faked a pregnancy. I mean, how would anyone believe this?*

In the distance, the screech of Mike's tires departing from the corner stop sign, interrupted her deliberations.

She turned to see his Mustang taillights in the distance disappear down the street, noting his typical unruly male display. *Well, one thing about that man. He's consistent ...consistently unpredictable.*

CHAPTER 53
Lifespan Plan C

CEO Max sat in his office suite barking into his phone. "We need cash flow, John. Real money, right now!" he complained. "You tell Dean over in personnel, that everyone we temporarily furloughed for a month. Well, now they're furloughed indefinitely."

On the other end of the line, John Lombardo, his timid finance executive, was already aware of how bad their current situation was. He had no clue about fixing it.

Max continued to bark, "And we need to halve again the remaining staff in each department ...but, leave Security alone for now."

John was still wondering why Dr.Ellar never raised a flag over in the Processing Department that they were going off the cliff so soon, and, that his production inventory was so low. Of course, if John had simply left his executive tower and walked over to the Processing building, the emptiness would have been all too obvious. By now, his managing by fictional numbers on a spreadsheet had left him blissfully ignorant.

The bewildered John tactfully inquired of his boss, "Jeez Max, what's the game plan? How long until we see positive cash flow in?"

Max deflected the question he had no answer for, instead ordering, "John, just do as I instruct. And stop payment on all invoices...except utilities. Put all your staff to work on receivables. Give our customers a 5% discount for net 10."

Now John understood how serious this was. Max never gave a discount to anybody for anything. "Okay sir," he dutifully replied. Shortly, he added a question on the earlier layoffs Max had directed. "How about the research staff? Are we going to hit all departments across the board?"

Max had to stop and think on that one. He was not sure how to handle Dr. Strauss yet. He might need some of those people on the staff of his secret fledgling company, Extentech, in California. Max lit his cigar and concluded the phone conversation saying, "I'll get back to you on that one. In the meantime get the rest of the cuts done."

Then Max remembered one more important thing, "And by the way, how much money is in the 401K account at Security National Funds."

The confused executive replied, "I think about $20 million."

Max answered confidently, "Good!" Then he added almost nonchalant, "Begin taking out about 500 grand every week. In the meantime no distributions or transfers to employees."

The young executive was stupefied, and stumbled out his reply. "Max... It's not our money. It's an employee trust fund. I mean..."

His boss abruptly cut him off. "John, didn't the company match contributions? Half that money was ours to begin with. What did they do to save our company? Call it a loan, we'll pay it back. Don't worry my boy."

John knew the government didn't insure those accounts. He also knew he could legally hold onto that money indefinitely. Maybe there was enough time to pay it back?

While John dwelled on the implications Max casually continued, "And, ah, I'd like you to hold onto your, ah… accounting staff until further notice."

John understood the subtle meaning immediately, knowing his bosses latest affairs was with some of the girls in his office. He could easily empathize with Max on this one – also having some side action of his own.

Finished with Lombardo, Max dismissed him and sat back in his leather chair thinking of ways to raise cash. He took out his comforting Slinky toy and bounced the metal coils from palm to palm. The tinkling felt so relaxing again.

He knew the company was going under, and the only way to get maximum benefit to himself and his investors was to reduce everything to the liquid commodity - currency. In the near future, he would accomplish the covert task of moving the cash out of the company's control, where his investors could not filch it.

After a while, his business sense realized that the most valuable thing he owned was not really the company assets after all - it was the technology.

His secret project, 'Greenhouse', was close to fruition. Soon he would be able to grow millions of his own specimen's in the lab. No more women intermediaries. Enough to supply a hundred Lifespan Corporations. Then he could operate in the background of the flourishing biomed industry. No government oversight. No rules ...except the ones he made. Maybe do the whole market by cloning eggs off just one female specimen.

In his enthusiasm, he phoned Norm Stark over in Legal. Max wanted to float this phenomenal idea he had. "Listen Norm, I want you to look into something with Marketing. It looks like selling the company at this point isn't going to give us a fair return on our investment. See if we can franchise our decoupling revival technology to several of the 'Big Pharma' companies. We'll keep the Greenhouse tech, Then, it won't matter if Lifespan is viable or not."

However, right now, Norm was less than enthusiastic to new business ideas, and changed the subject, leaning closer to the phone. "Max I think we should get together immediately and discuss a new lawsuit just delivered against us."

"Later Norm," Max interrupted barking into the phone, "I don't want to feel negative waves while I'm being creative. Listen. I'm talkin' about franchising hundreds of companies. All across America! Europe! A trillion dollar business! We could become the McDonalds of specimen processing!"

Norm would have none of Max's inane entrepreneurial bullshit and replied impatiently, "Max! I have to see you now. About this new lawsuit. Now!"

"Okay, Okay. Come on up to my office, and we can talk about the franchise some more."

Norm looked at the phone receiver in disbelief. Where was Max's mind? Growling into the disconnected phone he said, "This is something like Nero playing his fiddle while Rome burns to the ground."

Then Norm slammed the receiver down in frustration.

* * * * * * *

Norm walked in the executive office, greeted by a still effervescent Max, who was practicing golf with his putter on the office carpeting.

"Sit," Max invited, pointing with his putter. "Sit and relax over there on the chair."

Norm, thinking Max would look more suitable in a Roman toga now, sat down on the edge of his seat, while Max waltzed over twirling his putter like a baton. Max cheerfully collapsed into the nearby loveseat, lighting a cigar, and indulged Norm. "OK, what have we got here?"

Norm passed the lawsuit over to him, and coolly announced, "We're being sued by one of our specimens – something called Amnion."

At first Max smiled, thinking this was some kind of crudely funny lawyer joke. Norm's face remained stone cold serious. Max slumped uncomfortably forward in his seat, and looked at the summons - in astonishment. So far, the impact of Norm's statement had yet to sink in.

He flipped a few pages into the suit and mocked the charges, slapping the paper with each pronouncement.

"Deprivation of life?   Ha!"

"Aggravated assault?   Sheeet!"

"Conspiracy? Come off it!"

"Violating our State license?   Bullshit!"

"Destruction of evidence. Double shite!"

Then with disdain, he threw the document onto the cocktail table, and stood up, demanding, "Who the fuck is this, Norm? And who the fuck do they think they're dealing with here?"

"I don't know yet," he replied. "However, I do know their lawyer, Richard Farmer. He is a senior corporate lawyer from the big law firm in Manhattan, *Burnham, Farmers & Peck*. Lots of political connections in New York. And he's a Black no less! It beats the heck out of me why he's even involved in a civil case like this."

"So much for the schvartze from New York," Max grumbled. "Now, who the fuck is this plaintiff Amnion?"

"Don't have the answer to that one yet either."

Max was clearly vexed and finally unloaded his rage on Norm. "Then what the fuck do you know?!!"

Norm was fed up with this nasty verbal barrage, and answered bluntly. "What I do know is that you, Strauss and Lombardo are personally cited along with the company. If they pierce the corporate veil, you are, personally, in big time trouble."

Norm stood up unruffled, leaned over the cocktail table, and calmly collected the lawsuit papers. He walked to the office door and turned around defiantly, "Max, one last word." Norm pointed the lawsuit papers at Max for emphasis. "Take your verbal abuse out on someone else. I don't have to listen to your brand of shit anymore. I'll let you know more after we go before the judge on Monday."

Before Norm left, he turned around at the doorway. "Oh, and one more thing Max. The thing that scares me the most about this one."

Having been put in his place, a more subdued Max inquired, "What's that?"

"They're not suing us for a lot of money. Just legal and medical expenses. Like they're on some kind of 'high horse' mission from God."

"So?"

"That makes them even more dangerous." Then he calmly walked out, leaving Max speechless and alone.

Max retired behind his desk to his soft leather chair, and pulled out his Slinky toy to console himself. It seemed that again, he was a victim of all these lawsuit crazy people. Like small dogs constantly yapping and nipping at his pants cuff. He spun in his chair to stare out the window at the R&D building across the mostly empty parking lot, soothingly stretching the Slinky from hand to floor and back like a yo-yo. This Amnion business continued to eat at him until it dawned on him, "Son of a bitch! It's got to be the one stolen months ago ...out of my R&D lab!"

It wasn't long before the name Dr. Rosen also came to his mind, and Max snapped his fingers, surmising, *He was the cocksucker behind this from the beginning ...The inside man!* Max's blood pressure rose in proportion to his desire for revenge.

Then he remembered all those laid off ex-Lifespan employees out there. Some of them might be disgruntled enough to come forward and testify against his company, and become more turncoat stoolies. Some of Strauss's consultants might get charged and plea-bargain. Max decided to act of his own volition, without Norm's counsel. Norm and everyone else did not need to know this decision. This punishment had to be more than a missing finger - settled quickly and violently for public consumption.

Max swung back to his desk to place a phone call to his intermediary contact with Anthony LaRocca. At his fingertips, Max had the ultimate power over the underworld. So why not use it? Frustrating his plan, it turned out that this guy Rosen had already escaped his clutches at Lifespan. With this pending lawsuit a harsh and ruthless example had to be made for everyone ...and more importantly, every ex-employee. He had to show that even Rosen could be reached, even beyond Lifespan.

CHAPTER 54
Opening arguments

The opposing attorneys, Norm Stark and Richard Farmer, stood in the courtroom before Judge Solomon Burger's bench for pretrial hearings.

The judge was an elderly man with thinning white hair and pale wrinkled complexion that contrasted with his dark robes and thick, old-fashioned black framed glasses. The hearing was not publicly announced.

Norm approached the bench as he adjusted his tie and pulled in his stomach to button his pin-striped suit. Briefly, he glanced with contempt at Richard and then spoke in a firm tone, "Your Honor, the defendant, Lifespan Corporation, moves to have this case dismissed immediately."

Then looking sternly at Richard, "We have a right to know our accuser. Norm then put his hands in air each with two fingers symbolizing quotation marks, "And why this mysterious 'Amnion' moniker?"

Richard answered, "This is our 'Jane Roe'. You know from…"

The judge interrupted in reply to Norm, "This court reserves the right to protect the safety an identity of an underage minor," the judge retorted. "And I have issued a Gag Order for the balance of this trial, as well as, an additional order to prevent disclosure of the Plaintiff's real identity and whereabouts until this proceeding is concluded. Furthermore, all hospital staff are subject to same, until disclosed in open court."

Norm turned towards his Defense table and let out a muted, Harrumph."

Then turned around to face the judge again."We still move for dismissal."

"On what other grounds counselor?" the judge inquired.

"Simply put, Your Honor. The Plaintiff was not a 'person' under constitutional law at the time of the cited allegations."

"How so, counselor?"

"From what we can gather, this 'Amnion', was not a human being as defined under 60 years of litigated termination case law. It was just a fetal cadaver donated by the birth mother. Plainly a tissue specimen like any other organ of the woman's body, and therefore not entitled to specific protection under the law."

Richard interrupted in retort. "Your Honor, case law uses viability outside the womb as an argument for constitutional protection. My client has existed, live, outside the womb since she was at 14 weeks gestation - at the beginning of the attacks. "

Norm interrupted, "Yes, but you are talking about artificial life support. The specimen in question was not 'viable' on its own."

The old judge looked down at some photos of Amnion in her old life support cart and now surrounded by apparatus in the neonatal NICU.

Then he looked down from the bench at Norm below." I have carefully reviewed the medical background of the Plaintiff. At the present time, she is being kept alive with a respirator and incubator, and would no doubt expire without intervention by the medical community. So, your same issue of non-viability could be made for all neonatal premies, when good medical practice insures heroic efforts to maintain their lives."

The old judge motioned for Norm to come closer to his bench. Leaning forward over the bench and looking down sternly, showing Norm her picture, "You wouldn't have a problem with disconnecting her from life support right now. Would you???"

Norm sensed the hostility in the judge's tone. He had to be careful about answering that loaded question. He feigned a conciliatory tone and said, "Why no. No, of course not. We are not interested in intervening in a hospital's medical decisions."

The judge leaned back in his chair to add, "Well, I didn't think you could answer that one." The Judge scathingly continued, "Her living existence outside the womb constitutes a living human being as much as any other premature infant. Maybe less developed than some. Maybe more helpless than others. Unable to speak for herself. But, in whose interests, this court **can, and will** assert an interest."

Placing the photos down carefully, the judge leaned slightly forward to look Norm square in the eye. "Mister Stark, these proceedings involve alleged serious harm to the Plaintiff during the extra uterine time period. Motion by Defendant denied!" banging his gavel for emphasis

Richard had a slight smirk on his face. This time he was pulling the strings.

Norm started right in, "Your Honor. Please. Wait. So, how can we ascertain that this specimen has anything to do with Lifespan?" We need to know who this Amnion creature is?"

Richard interrupted, "Your Honor. The Plaintiff is unable to be present because of the serious state of her health, and is on life support equipment. We have already provided court appointed officers access to my client as well as documentation that traces her suffering directly from her decoupling at University Hospital to Lifespan Corporation.

"In addition we, request that since the birth mother gave up rights to her fetus, her right to privacy should still be protected, and her birth mother should remain anonymous and protected through these proceedings."

The judge agreed. "The birth mother's identity is part of the Gag Order."

Richard turned to Norm, and said, "Any objection? Norm gave a wave of dismissal. "None your Honor."

With that established, Richard paused, and made another motion, "May we proceed discussing subpoenas for the discovery phase of this litigation, and set a date for jury selection."

The judge smiled at Richard and said, "I like attorneys who don't dilly-dally. Give me your list and we'll get on with this." The judge solicited comments from Norm and scheduled a meeting between counselors in 5 days to check progress on the case by both sides.

Norm was a bit stunned. He was not orchestrating this one, and this judge was not entertaining any of his usual stalling maneuvers. He tried to think of a State Supreme Court judge that might exert some control over this old geezer on the bench.

*   *   *   *   *   *   *

Mike used his burner phone to contact the *Brooklyn Daily News* reporter, who immediately recognized Mike's voice, even after a 2-month hiatus. He was not particularly friendly, because with out Mike's identity the story had played itself out in the media. Mike did not particularly feel the need to apologize for that one, especially since the newspaper gleaned a pot full of advertising money out of a free story.

Mike baited him, "Well you can feel resentful or you can listen to an even bigger follow-up story."

There was a hesitation then the reply, "Yeah. Like what?"

"Like I stole one of those live fetuses from Lifespan. And she's been delivered as a baby."

There was silence on the other end as the reporter tried to determine if this was a crackpot on the other end, or one hell of a story. In a skeptical tone he said, "Interesting stuff - if it were really true"

"It gets better," Mike continued. "The child is suing Lifespan for assault and deprivation of life."

The reporter could not believe his ears and said, "Now I know you're not bullshitting me. I really don't have time for this kind of malarkey."

Mike wasn't surprised by the reaction and suggested, "Tell you what. You call up the Manhattan District Courthouse Clerk's office, and ask for the docket of 'Amnion vs Lifespan,' docket number 940214. Right now, you can have an exclusive story. Check it out, and I'll call you in two days to see if you're still not interested."

"What's this going to cost," the reporter asked.

"Whatta ya mean?"

"How much money for the exclusive on it? If what you have is as controversial as you say, it's big stuff. Could be worth big money," the reporter concluded.

Mike paused a moment. It was awful tempting to cash in on this. Then he thought of Mary Lou slashed to pieces on the Lifespan fence.

Father Tom, torn apart in the gutter. Amnion doing all the suffering right now in neonatal. He gave the only answer he conscience could allow. "You may think I'm a fool. But, this story was paid for by the suffering of a lot of people. You just promise to give our side of the story. And, when the political backlash comes, I want your guarantee that our side still gets to be heard too."

The reporter was not used to dealing with people of character who did not have a price. He found it hard to believe anymore, that people could really do things out of concern for others. Mike's request was the kind of out-of-fashion nobility that disappeared back in the last century. The reporter felt moved to give an honest commitment. "You're making this too easy, mystery man. If the story checks out, I'll have our chief editor personally make the guarantee."

"Then the story is yours," Mike simply replied, noting that, "Nothing hits the media until our court case is filed. And you also have to allow us to use any of your video coverage of Lifespan as evidence."

"Okay," the cautious reporter answered. "If it is for real." He did not see any problem with releasing what was already publicly broadcast, since a court order could do that anyway.

As the conversation ended, the reporter inquired, "By the way. Are you ever gonna tell me who you are?"

Mike chuckled, "When you and your editors commit to cover this. Then you'll find out."

CHAPTER 55
Consequences

In neonatal, Mike listened to Nurse Hart explain the latest in a series of complications with Amy. Although Amy's weight had not gone down precipitously anymore, it seemed like one grievous event after another. Mike's visits had become a blur of conversations and consultations with different specialists in the obtuse language of medicine. EKG's, EEG's, CAT scans, ultrasound, intravenous alimination. To Mike, it was like learning the names of all the lines and fittings on an old sailing ship.

The two stood together over Amy, who was now resting on her side with her thumb knuckle in her tiny mouth, and in the other lilliputian hand clutching the silken edging of her blanket. It was the same soft flannel cloth Mike insisted she have.

Her eyes were closed. Mike could discern her pupils moving under her delicately thin, veined eyelids. Apparently, she was dreaming peacefully in REM sleep. Someone had put a sign on her crib telling the world, 'Amy loves Wabbits', referring to the name of her burp rag. Mike could only assume that's what she was dreaming of.

The neonatal staff had become accustomed to Mike's recurrent presence in the unit, and it earned him a certain amount of freedom and extra consideration. They accepted him simply as a friendly, caring, trustworthy father, whose presence always perked Amy up.

In the evening quiet of ICU, with his scrub suit and mask on, Mike looked around at the other sick babies. After so much time he'd come to know many of them and their individual struggles. Some were suffering through drug withdrawal from uncaring mothers, others had congenital defects that parents find embarrassing. One fetus, a boy named Robert was born without a brain. Anencephaly they called it. The child looked like a healthy baby. Mike would occasionally stare at him in passing. The boy's eyes would follow his motion, and for all appearances he could be thinking, *'Do I know you'*, as far as Mike could reckon.

Spooky, he thought.

Another infant, Stephanie, had some kind of disease where her skin would peel off at the slightest touch. Even the skin layers of her mouth and lips sloughed off. She was a mass of bleeding sores exacerbated by the constant re-attachment of monitoring instruments and tubes. The staff kept her on massive doses of painkiller and pumped up with antibiotics. It hurt Mike's heart just to look at her, and made him question whether termination would have been the kinder choice for this girl. Except, here she was. Somehow hanging on for her dear life in some catatonic state. Entitled to life by the simple state of just being.

Tough beginning for a tough little girl, he empathized.

For the most part, though, Mike rarely saw the parents of these waifs. Nurse Hart had explained that the parents didn't want to become attached too early to these waifs, and then suffer more grief later if the child didn't pull through. Others, the welfare ones, just didn't give a damn one way or the other. It was Medicaid's problem. Mike's succinct opinion on those parents was typical Mike. If they represented today's humanity, then he would rather live with the apes.

So it was a surreal environment, this neonatal. The nurses were the surrogate mothers to transitory orphans. Any shred of human affection received by these infants was delivered by them. They were the cheerleaders and the protectors.

On the other hand, the specialists were the dispassionate purveyors and dispensers of treatment. Always running in and out. Mostly out. Time was money.

Mike occasionally overheard some sobering deliberations among the staff when an infant was on its death throes, and they were continually grappling with the ultimate question of artificially sustain life. When to withhold new treatment? When to stop extraordinary measures? When is the quality of life, a lost cause? How much influence should the parents have on the decision?

At times their deliberations sounded more like a conversation between attorneys. Some of the specialists were, legitimately, more concerned with being sued than losing a patient.

Another sign of our times, Mike would surmise to himself.

To Mike, there seem to be an odd contradiction working here. Had these preemies still been in the womb they could be terminated at the sole discretion of the mother – no questions asked. Move the preemie six inches, out of the womb, and it was a legally protected human and all concerned participants had to be consulted. The legal status determined by a few inches, in or out of the womb.

Luckily, there were doctors like Shahdere and Samuelson. Mike admired their compassion for the infants as real patients, and their respect and fair treatment of the nurses. That unified team atmosphere gave Mike the confidence to weigh their recommendations and allow them to make the almost daily decisions on Amnion's therapy.

Nurse Hart interrupted Mike's daydreaming saying, "These things are never easy Mister Santino."

Mike turned around to face the nurse again, as she efficiently cleaned some greenish brown excrement from between Amy's legs, "Amy's problems are typical of a preemie, and manageable."

"Yeah," Mike grimaced, trying not to look at the soiled wipe, or acknowledge the smell.

"By the way," she carefully inquired. "We had a court order, and a visit by a group of peculiar 'relatives' - lawyers I think. Took some pictures. Is there a lawsuit involved here???"

"Yes, but it doesn't involve your unit, your doctors, or your hospital. Just trust me on that."

Nurse Hart made a frown and said, "I hope it doesn't interfere with Amy's care."

"Believe me Sandy, this NICU is considered the safest place in the world for her right now."

At the end of his visiting time, Mike and Nurse Hart left the NICU and stopped in the hall to remove their scrubs. He was tempted to confide in her about who Amy really was and how she really got here. It seemed unfair to be running this ruse around her. She had been so honest and straightforward with him. However, Richie had not given the OK yet to go public, so it would have to wait for another time.

Mike finally left, and down the hall, he ran into Joel at the end of his shift. His friend was genuinely buoyant.

"I'm so glad I made the change," Joel related. "I'm teaching how to save lives now. Not capitalizing on their demise."

They jumped on the next available empty elevator down. On the way, Joel mentioned the rumors he'd heard that the 'Greenhouse' project was still going full speed at Lifespan.

"I think they have this new mucous compound, to bind the embryos to a transfer membrane," Mike explained.

"Really," Joel said, "And what will they come up with next?"

"Can you give me some way of keeping the embryos from attaching to the membrane," Mike implored. "Something subtle. Something they won't be able to troubleshoot easily?"

Joel silently contemplated the question until they exited the hospital and reached the doctor's reserved parking lot. From his medical background, the only solutions came from his knowledge of contraception.

"I can only think of one thing off the top of my head," Joel volunteered. "There is a synthetic hormone, progestin. It thickens the mucous of the uterus. Makes it impossible for the embryo to attach. If you could get this into the blood supply, it might have the same effect on their mucous formulation."

Mike agreed that it might work, and he did have access to the Lifespan blood PRBC plasma supply. "Can you get me some of this progestin stuff?"

Joel took out his prescription pad and wrote one out.

"How about temperature?" Mike asked. "I can screw up the calibration in the microprocessor. Would that work?"

"Maybe," Joel said, "If you can raise it 4 degrees or so, that may be enough to disturb the cell division process, and not be obvious to observers."

It was all the information Mike needed to start devising a sabotage plan of his own.

* * * * * * *

The following morning, Mike was back at work in Lifespan attending another engineering meeting. Since his old boss, Al Greene had been laid off, there was another reorganization and Mike now reported directly to Dr. Strauss. He missed Al. At least he was a guy you could argue technical merit with. Not a dogmatic 'do-it-my-way' dictator like Strauss.

The bio-engineering staff had come up with a new design for specimen maturation. A large rectangular design with PRCBs flowing along the bottom chamber and a large horizontal cellulose membrane stretched above it that separated the dialysized blood from an amniotic solution chamber.

333

Strauss explained in a series of chemical structure diagrams about how they had synthesized a new mucous material to add to the membrane. Mike listened attentively. He would have to talk to Joel again to explain all that bio-stuff one more time and check that the progestin hormone is really going to react with this new material.

This was 'Project Greenhouse'. This was the tank farm where they would 'plant' embryos side by side, like stalks in a cornfield. Grow them by the hundreds. Worse more, with hundreds of tanks, grow them by the tens of thousands.

In spite of all the publicity, all the financial difficulties in the company, the lawsuits, the negative publicity, this project was in a 'balls out', go mode. In fact, it was the only work running in the company. By now, only a hundred or so loyal people were left on the payroll. A last ditch effort to use what was left of 'other people's' money.

Mike studiously recorded all the design engineer's specifications for fabrication of the first prototype. He would be responsible for fabricating the stainless steel chambers and the microprocessor controls. It was made clear to him that his job with Lifespan depended on the success of this hardware - hardly a threat under the circumstances. Mike already had a departure date in mind.

Mike took a keen interest in the writing the microprocessor software control portion of the system. He could add some bugs in this part of the unit and bury some subtle bugga-boos in the feedback loop. It would be his parting shot at Lifespan.

On his way back to the office, he passed the high-resolution color copier. Fingering his security badge hanging from his shirt pocket, it occurred to him that it was only a matter of time before he would be laid off, a new identity might come in handy. Memories of working in the defense industry and all those layoffs years ago returned. Surrendering his badge would be the first event of his departure. If he ever needed to get back into Lifespan, a valid ID would be the only way in. Looking around the hallway to make sure there were no eyewitnesses to this little exercise, he made his way to the copier. In a moment, he had two exceptionally clear copies of his face and badge ID.

Mike snickered to himself, *The more sophisticated all this security gets, the easier it is to beat it.*

* * * * * * * *

Later in the day, Mike called the reporter at the *Brooklyn Daily*. This time there was no hesitancy on the reporter's part. He'd checked out Mike's story. Now his paper really wanted it.

As agreed, Mike finally revealed his name to the reporter, and they began to develop a friendly rapport that would carry them through the coming weeks of public turmoil. He still wanted his name to remain anonymous to the public for now.

It was decided that the *Brooklyn Daily News* would be able to break the exclusive story the morning of the trial date with a lead-time of 3 days for them to do their research and fact checking.

CHAPTER 56
This old heart of mine

Phylis sat alone and downhearted at a table near the window in the University Hospital cafeteria. Lingering thoughts of Michael drifted into her mind amid her dull daily routine. The new job was nowhere near as interesting as Lifespan was. In spite of all the terrible things they did there, it was still exciting to have made so much money. Unfortunately, the salary of her new job was highly dependent on earning smaller sales commissions.

She slowly nursed a cup of hot tea while awaiting a PA announcement that Dr. Petersen was out of surgery. Her appointment with him was already held up a half-hour, and he still had not emerged from the operating room yet. The unforeseen delay was giving her too much time to dwell on her own more personal feelings about Michael.

Adding to the misery, was the receipt of a subpoena to give a statement to a bunch of lawyers and probably appear in court. She dreaded the thought of giving testimony in public. What's more, having her new employer find out about her involvement in all this Lifespan turmoil might cost her job. She was still on 2-month probationary employment.

After putting it all out of her mind, Michael's face just seemed to pop right back in her head again. He had not called in over a week. Much as she wanted to, she was not about to initiate the first contact. After their argument in her driveway, it wasn't clear anymore how much he really loved her anyway. And, with his prolonged absence, the test of time was not looking too promising either. It felt like she was losing out to his crazy obsession of bringing Lifespan to justice. Now it just seemed that Michael had breezed in and out of her life, spun her around, and left. Just as the passion peaked.

The thought of dating someone else passed her mind. The idea of going online again did not seem too appealing. She would always wind up comparing them to Michael. In addition, Katie wasn't her dating sidekick anymore. She smiled as she reflected on Michael. *He sure knew how to push my buttons. That is for sure.*

In spite of the frustration in dealing with him, she missed that rare child like personality. A real man who was comfortably secure in his masculine stubbornness. Willing to sacrifice everything for anything he believed in. Unfortunately, it seemed that sacrifice now included her.

Resting her chin on her folded hands, her gaze fell on the Rejuvenation Center across the parking lot. Construction had stopped. It seemed like she was sitting in the same place months ago when she worked for Lifespan and recalled that emotional scene before Maria Alvarez's decoupling.

Still, it was amazing to think about it. Right now, that same specimen was alive four floors above her in the main building. A living little girl, struggling for her life. The recollection of that extraction resurrected the same uncomfortable misgivings she had felt back then. Moreover, there were all those risks and actions she had taken since. All because she believed that a man really loved her.

She let out a disappointing sigh, *Well, here I am —back to struggling.*

So now, a month later, an income less than half of what it was back then. A new job selling high tech A.I.virtual imaging headgear to coddled and condescending surgeons.

Until last week, the past three months felt so happy and secure, feeling so sure she was doing the right things with the right man. Then, all of a sudden the future had evolved into a litigation and this sudden abandonment by him. Phylis started to feel used, and then the memory of Michael's passionate embrace seemed too real to have been just an illusion. The caring way he looked at her with those eyelashes after the passion. The intimate conversations and laughter. If that was not love, then maybe there was no such thing as love left in this world.

Her melancholy deliberations were finally interrupted by the blaring PA announcement that Dr. Petersen was out of surgery. Phylis grabbed her demonstration instrument case and pocketbook to head for his office. It was time to get down to business again.

* * * * * * *

The meeting with Dr. Petersen went fairly well for Phylis. He was impressed enough with the virtual imaging equipment, and she handled all his technical questions. The only problem was that the hospital had frozen the capital budget for the balance of the year. Apparently, the fiasco at Lifespan had put a big crimp in the hospital's plans for that Rejuvenation Center's cash flow. It all boiled down to one simple conclusion for Phylis - No Sale!

She left his office before lunch, thinking about her afternoon appointment at an ambulatory surgery center across town. Out of the blue, something made her stop. Amnion came to mind again.

The little girl was still upstairs. Phylis wondered how the struggling infant was doing these past two weeks. Her curiosity was aroused sufficiently to take the elevator up. Since it was midday, there would also be no chance of an awkward scene - running into Mike up there.

* * * * * * *

Phylis arrived at neonatal a bit nervous, and inquired at the nurse's station about her 'daughter' Amy. She was the 'mother' absent for two weeks now, and did not know how the staff would react to her sudden appearance. Nurse Hart approached her with a sympathetic smile and commented, "Misses Santino, it's nice to see you've recovered. We all heard about your relapse. Got your figure back too."

Phylis initially thought to herself, *Recovered from what?* And played along with the conversation until she could figure out what was going on. Phylis stood silent and nodded agreeably, concerned about what crazy things Mike must have said.

Nurse Hart continued in her friendly tone, "Your husband has really done a nice job of filling in for you. He's here 4 or 5 times a week. He's been very effective at doing 'kangaroo care' - a good father already."

This caused Phylis to warily ask, "Say that again please?"

"What?"

"......that 'kangaroo' thing."

"Oh," Nurse Hart explained, "It's what we call skin to skin touching. It aids the fetuses healing process."

Phylis was amused, thinking about her romantic memories of lovemaking. "Yes, you could say that he does have the touch."

Nurse Hart then led Phylis over to the sterilized gowns assuming Phylis wanted to pay Amy a visit. As they dressed, Nurse Hart continued to talk, "Your husband told me about the sacrifices you made to bring Amy into this world. He seemed pretty down in the dumps the past two weeks over it. Said it was unfair to do this to you."

Phylis looked up incredulously, as she snapped her elastic cap on and tucked in her hair, "Oh really?"

"Yes, it must have been some sacrifice to give up your career, and take all these pregnancy risks at middle age. Your husband can't say enough good things about you. He said you are a rare woman. I think he really missed you during your hospital recovery."

Phylis smiled, leaning over to put on her booties. "He's been a talkative little bugger, hasn't he?"

They laughed as they slipped on masks and entered the ICU.

337

Arriving at Amnion's cart, Mike's Wabbits flannel bib partially covered a myriad of tubes and electrodes attached to her chafed and tortured skin. The sleeping babe's face appeared as a somewhat contorted frown, her mind lost somewhere in the catatonic state of formation.

Phylis remarked pitifully, "She still looks so undernourished."

"You have to understand that your daughter is not like a full term baby that bulks up rapidly," the nurse explained. "So, she's developing slowly as if still in the womb. Nature doesn't care that she's extrauterine now."

Phylis gently touched Amnion's dainty wrinkled palm and instinctively the tiny fingers firmly grasped her pinky. Phylis gently stroked the infant's bare forehead with its mesh of fine bluish veins. Then Amnion's eyes slowly opened, and the two jet-black liquid eyes searched for her mother. She weakly tried to pull Phylis' gloved finger to her mouth to suckle. Phylis felt an instinctive motherly bonding to this helpless human form, and thought again about her real mother Maria. She gently picked up the fetus and held her to her breast whispering, "Such a long way to go," and leaned over to kiss the baby's pallid head through her mask.

Nurse Hart observed Phylis with a trained eye. She could tell the caring mothers from the phony ones. "Don't you worry, Misses Santino," she reassured, "I keep my eye on your daughter. Amy's a little sweetheart, and she's going to make it out of here."

After a few more minutes, there was an alarm buzzer and a crowd of doctors and nurses came running into the room. Phylis and the nurse had to leave abruptly, as the medical staff gathered around another preemie in distress. Each staff member worked with skilled precision as a team, with hardly a word spoken between them. The disturbance was played down by Nurse Hart, "Don't worry. We handle these emergencies almost every day."

Once outside they took off the sterilized gowns and such. Phylis stared anxiously back through the plexiglas window as another distressed baby in apnea started breathing again. With a sigh of relief, she removed the elastic cap, now feeling the need to comb out her hair. The empathetic nurse directed her to the ladies room.

"Take care," Nurse Hart said. "Your husband was really concerned about you and Amy. He deserves a big hug for that." Then she waved and disappeared behind the nurse's station.

Phylis began to accept Mike's close attachment to Amnion, and her own 'backseat' role right now. That maybe it wasn't entirely fair or unselfish to make him chose between her and Amnion's desperate situation. There truly was a certain priority to things – and Amnion deserved that priority right now.

She also came to understand that, somehow, he still cared for her too - even though he had not called. It made her reconsider the possibility that maybe their relationship was not over for good.

Driving in her car to a Surgery-Center appointment the 'oldies' radio station played an old Motown favorite by the Isley Brothers, *'This Old Heart of Mine'*.

She asked herself, *How come the more Michael breaks my heart, the more I want to love him?*

CHAPTER 57
The princess and the frog

Mike sat at his office desk, staring at his terminal screen, now blank except for the screen saver. His Lifespan account deleted. The department was devoid of people. – all ready laid off, except for him and a few techs. There was just the surrounding quiet. The only discernible sound was the soothing hum of the computer electronics and HVAC cooling fans. The eerie silence and vacant offices were a ghostly witness to the twilight of Lifespan Corporation. The few 'borrowed' pieces of equipment for Amnion's fetal cart were already returned.

Mike gingerly ran his finger over the keyboard without depressing them, feeling the ripple effect of the dimpled tops. Today he had no command to spring its awesome computational power into instantaneous action. Now it was just another surplus terminal loaded with expensive application programs with no data to enter and no human to serve. So, as a result, no idea of what to do with itself.

A short time ago, Mike had just been spitefully notified by telephone that he too was laid off, - his five plus years with Lifespan suddenly a memory. Someone would be down shortly to collect his badge and Department keys. Apparently, his new boss, Dr. Strauss, was off at a NIH conference, and left this dirty detail for a clerk in Human Resources.

Mike was honestly impressed. It was fast work on Lifespan's part. For a change, the bureaucracy actually did something efficiently fast. Mike had just finished the first 'Greenhouse' prototype unit for growing embryos in culture. Bio-Engineering took the software source code for the microprocessor controller just yesterday. It felt comforting to know that he had managed to sabotage everything before his departure. A simple value change of a resistor in the CPU motherboard would screw up the temperature calibration for a while. In addition, their plasma bank was already contaminated with the inhibiting hormone from Joel.

There wasn't much left to do now. His office was already cleaned out of personal effects, and all the files needed for the lawsuit had been secretly copied long ago. He stood up and took one last look from his office window. The empty parking lot below, a mute testimony of his interference with Lifespan's grand plan. Standing with his hands in his pocket, he leaned closer to the window and gazed to the far left. There, beyond the corporate sign, was the corner where Father Tom expired. To the right, the fence where Mary Lou hung upside down.

He reflected on his own participation in building all their processing equipment. This business monstrosity called Lifespan. He was part of that debacle too. It was on odd mixture of both satisfaction and regret that muddled his conflicting emotions.

Not very good memories, honey, he told himself as if talking to his deceased wife Laura. *Not much to be proud of after spending 5 years of my career here.*

From behind, a voice interrupted his gloomy mood. "I've waited a long time to show you the door Santino."

Mike pivoted to see a grinning Jane Savage, Head of Security, leaning relaxed on his doorframe - arms folded defiantly.

Mike was surprised by his old nemesis, but smiled and said, "You do look lovely today, Janie."

Jane was startled by his unexpected compliment, until Mike added, "It must be because you're firing people."

At least the sarcastic remark was the familiar Mike that Jane had come to despise.

Mike sat down behind his desk, folding his hands and putting his feet up on the bare desk. In this relaxed pose, he leaned back in his chair, staring up at Jane with a shit-faced grin.

Jane moved her svelte figure into the office and sauntered gracefully around looking at all the empty shelves and occasionally opening an empty file draw. "So Santino. Where do you go from here?"

"I think it's the unemployment office next," Mike said dryly.

"It won't be the same place without you, you know," she said in an almost accommodating tone, as she slowly circled around him like a shark.

"How's that?" Mike inquired.

Jane gave a leer of her own. Almost a seductive one. "No one to steal Lifespan's specimens anymore," she slyly replied.

Mike laughed and pointed to himself, "Moi?"

Jane became more direct and belligerent, "Come off it Mike. Don't play footsie with me. I always suspected you. You're the only prick in this company with the balls to pull it off."

Mike chuckled, "I'm flattered. I take that you have proof?"

"Well, not yet buster." she replied, as she moved around to his side of the desk, and leaned her torso on the edge of the desk facing down at him.

Mike spent the next moment of silence, observing the outline of her round hips and tapered thighs beneath her pants, and blouse pulled tight against her breasts.'

The inner male in him mused, *Now that's what I call distracting.*

It made Mike's mind drift off again about what she'd be like in bed. *Probably a real wild cat*, he thought.

Jane was aware of Mike's glance, and it gave her a certain sense of power over the situation. She became more contentious saying, "Do you realize the damage you've done to this company? All the jobs you've cost people. The money lost."

Her tone woke Mike out of the relaxed male stupor he was in, and he slid his feet off the desk. "Do you realize you're a part of wholesale murder?" Mike shot back, and gestured towards the R&D labs, "Fetal human lives by the thousands." He got up out of his chair and pointed out the window, "Father Tom at the corner."

The light banter turned sour as Mike threw off his badge and slammed his office keys down on the desk for emphasis.

Jane became defensive, and slowly walked over to the window. "I did not order the dogs. And I did not order the dog handlers that evening."

"It was on your watch, Jane," Mike barked as he swiveled in his seat to face her directly. "You're head of security. You could have protested. You could have at least tried to head it off. Instead you kissed up to 'Mad Max' with obedient nods like all his other lap dogs."

Jane's passive mood abruptly turned aggressive by his verbal attack. She ordered Mike out of the building immediately.

Instead, Mike spun around in his chair, and leaned back with his hands clasped behind his head. "Now Janie, suppose I don't?"

Her hand slipped down to the gun holster at her side and flipped the flap open. It revealed her underlying insecurity with Mike. A deep-seated hatred of male dominance, and betrayed her otherwise authoritative facade.

"I can get more people up here," she said, "if I need them."

Mike replied in confident contempt. "Why don't you get more shoulder pads for your jacket there? Maybe that will intimidate me more," He read her inner feminine uncertainty like an open book.

Jane hesitated, not sure of how far Mike was trying to take this confrontation. One thing was certain, if it became physical, it was not going to be her alone escorting him out of the building – not without a bullet in him. She relaxed for an instant, and moved her hand from the holster to the handheld radio on her belt to call for back-up.

In a few minutes, three sizable security-contractor types joined her, and Mike was escorted outside to his car in the empty parking lot. Jane held his arm as Mike opened his car door to get in. The other guards stepped back, thumbs in their belts. Suddenly, Mike grabbed Jane and twisted her gun hand behind her back, embracing her. He planted a slobbering kiss on her lips, as the startled woman yielded a few steps back.

H quickly jumped in the car, and looked back through the open door, imitating Bugs Bunny's voice saying, " Err, what's up doc?"

The other guards laughed, recalling how Bugs Bunny would always kiss the hunter, Elmer Fudd, at the end of the cartoon.

Mike sped off in his old Mustang, spraying sand and pebbles behind, leaving Jane totally off-balance. She went to wipe the kiss from her lips, but something about his kiss made her stop half-way.

She watched Mike's car fish tail around a corner and speed out the gate, leaving a swirling trail of dust like a jet exhaust to mark his departure. Jane went to wipe off his kiss, but a pleasant tingle made her stop. For just that instant, she was simply a woman kissed by one helluva audacious man. She turned away and thought, *I just might miss that son-of-a bitch.*

* * * * * * *

That evening Phylis answered her door to find a flower delivery boy handing her a plant wrapped in wax paper. Phylis tipped the boy and turned into the house to see who it was from.

Pulling the wrappings aside revealed a miniature bonsai planted nestled in a planter in the backside of a cute green ceramic frog. She held it up in her hands, smiling at the two big yellow eyes that looked cross eyed at a little brown fly perched on its snout. The frog's shiny pink tongue curled below its pouting mouth ready to strike.

Her attention reverted to the wrapping paper; anxiously searching for a greeting card stapled somewhere. She found an envelope with a hand-scribbled message on a card. It said:

The prince has been a real toad lately.
He needs the forgiving kiss of a princess lady.
To be placed on the tip of his ugly nose,
And maybe, again, be the love that she chose.
~Your Used Male

Phylis beamed, feeling Mike's handiwork - his awkward way of getting back in her good graces. An attempt to make amends for his long absence.

Digging further into the envelope, a small memory stick was also enclosed. She could not guess what was on it. He always said song words sound stupid if you actually said them to someone. It had a label with 'Forgive' written on it. On the way to the kitchen, she popped it into her stereo player USB port, and cheerfully took the frog planter to the kitchen. The song on the stick was, *Just Once in My Life'* - a song by the Righteous Brothers.

The stirring melody from the stereo filled her heart with emotion. Latent feelings for Michael that were always there, always ready to resurface.

There's a lot of things I want, a lot of things that I'd like to be.
But girl, I don't foresee a rags-to-riches story for me.
There's just one little dream I've got to make come true;
There's just one round I've gotta win, I can't be a loser with you .

When she reached the sink, she added some water to the dry soil of the planter with feminine care, replacing it on her windowsill above the sink. She smiled at its funny grin and bulging eyeballs. She quipped to herself, "Pretty good likeness Michael."

Then, in the privacy of the kitchen Phylis impulsively leaned over, and following his poetic instructions, kissed the ceramic frog's broad snout.

CHAPTER 58
Clear and present danger

Norm Stark sat in his office at Lifespan reading from different department reports on the steady flow of documents being requested and copied from Lifespan during the discovery process of Amnion's civil suit. It seemed as if their legal people always knew exactly where to look for all Lifespan's dirt. They named specific meetings, job numbers, people's names, dates. So thorough, that every employee depositioned even had their security badge photocopied to prove their identity. It was not the usual shotgun approach to the discovery phase of a litigation. These requests for documents were much more exact, like well aimed rifle shots.

The chief counsel leaned back in his chair and figured, *Someone on the inside here has to be guiding these people.*

The telephone rang and broke his train of thought. Max called to find out the results of the one-million dollar Lifespan offer to settle the civil suit out of court.

"No go," Norm answered. "This lawyer Farmers thinks he's a prize fighter, says he wants to go the distance. He keeps talking about fundamental rights."

"More money," Max replied, "He's bluffing. He wants more money."

"I don't think so Max."

"Why?"

"He's suing us for only a quarter million dollar trust for this Amnion kid. Why continue a suit and not get more?"

Max was perplexed. In his experience, everything in life had a price. It was just a matter of finding out how high.

"Up the offer," Max insisted, "then we'll see about all this fundamental rights bullshit."

Norm gave a reluctant 'OK'. Norm had already talked to this Richard Farmers fellow. Enough to know that his opponent had that rare and dangerous trait - character. Norm had a bad feeling all along, that this was going to be a court fight to the death. The only comforting thought in this messy case was that, historically, the fetus has never been granted human status or protection by the courts. Norm had over 70 years of legal precedent on his side and a lot of politically influential people who wanted the fetus to stay just that way – meaningless.

His deliberations were interrupted by a telegram brought in by his administrative aid. It was from Bangkok. And, it was good news for a change.

The private investigator he hired, had located Eve West in a northern province of Thailand. The telegram requested that he wire more ransom money to buy her release and arrange for transportation back to the U.S.

Norm excitedly phoned Max to get approval for the funds. He had already wired $ 15,000 on his own authority. Regrettably, it was going to take another $50,000 to get her back.

"What? Are you mashugana?" was the answer from Max. "We have umpteen lawsuits, no cash coming in, and most of our staff layed off. I mean. Hey. We could use that money for the out-of- court settlement!"

Norm interrupted, "We sent her over there. We're responsible!"

Max would have none of it. "You get these Amnion people off us. Then we'll see if there's money left to pay Eve's ransom."

"Max, fifty K is peanuts compared to what we're still spending in R&D alone."

"Take it out of your Legal department budget if you feel that strongly about it," Max ranted. "Get rid of one paralegal's salary," he arrogantly suggested, and hung up.

Norm was pissed as hell. Whatever Eve's faults, she was still a human being and a loyal employee. Besides, there was no out-of-court settlement in the offing anyway.

He looked at his discretionary travel budget. That would pay her airfare back to the U.S. He telephoned John Lombardo in Finance. For sure, John could be intimidated into releasing additional funds for pre-trial expenses.

* * * * * * * *

In the hallway at University Hospital, Joel appeared very anxious while standing next to Mike. Mike attributed Joel's fidgety demeanor to the revelation he was about to make to the hospital staff. Stationed outside the neonatal unit they were joined by Dr. Shahdere and Nurse Hart. It was time to reveal who Amy really was, and the civil law suit of *Amnion vs Lifespan*.

Nurse Hart was first to react saying, "So you're not the real father?"

Mike answered unequivocally, "Biologically no. In point of fact yes. I raised her in a Lifespan fetal revival cart."

Nurse Hart felt a bit betrayed, but understood his motivations, adding, "So, the newspapers were correct, why and all these mysterious 'relatives' have been passing through here lately."

Dr. Shahdere's reaction was more philosophical, "It was only a matter of time before our technology reached this point. And already we have a tragedy."

Joining them, a little late for this meeting was a young David Whitman, administrative head of the neonatal unit. He strolled in as though his presence suddenly legitimized the meeting, immediately apologizing, "Sorry folks. Pressing business. You know how budget meetings can drag on infinitum. Can never get rid of enough fat."

Mike did not like this person's condescending tone from the start, thinking, and another *Ivy League graduate who probably never had an original thought in his career.* He wondered how many asses this guy kissed to get his high paying do-nothing administrative job.

David leaned over to view the preemies through the plexiglas, commenting, "These little ETs cost a bundle. You should see how much they……"

Mike stopped him short. "Excuse me. What did you call them?"

David was a bit startled. "Call them?"

"Yeah."

Then he nervously laughed. "Oh, you know, extraterrestrials." David was the only one smiling at his pun. "Not very appealing. You know. Big heads., little bodies ..."

Mike interrupted the conversation by closing the distance between them, his indignation slowly building. "I guess that makes you an EBA."

David was bewildered, "EBA?"

"Yeah Dave. Extra Big Asshole ...all uppercase."

Joel knew Mike long enough to know where this confrontation was heading and positioned himself between the two.

In his smugness, the administrator did not fathom what triggered this sudden hostility and his callously continued, "We spend over a quarter

345

million per preemie here. In fact, it's our loss leader."

Mike continued to close the space between them. "Save your Harvard business school vernacular for your administrative cronies. This isn't assets and liabilities here. These are people! Life and death people." Then Mike forcibly drove Joel into him. Dave stumbled and slammed back against the observation window. The loud thud made everyone stop what they were doing inside neonatal. Joel was squeezed in between, as Mike reached over to grab David's expensive *Pierre Cardin* tie, pulling it taut.

"Just think," Mike barked, "If they got rid of your prissy ass job and the exorbitant salary, the neonatal unit would probably make a profit... get new equipment."

David struggled to regain his tie and breath, as Joel managed to push Mike back a foot or two. Dave promptly straightened his disheveled $2000 silk suit, as he glanced at the observing staff. They were obviously enjoying this spectacle at his expense.

He asserted his indignation, "I think you're mistaken sir. This is my hospital. And you are no longer welcome in it."

Mike pressed against Joel's restraint. "First of all buddy, it isn't your hospital...and here is a Gag Order from the court buddy, and slapped it against his chest. No one is to know that Amy Santino was in fact the plaintiff Amnion. And no one can have access to Amy except the medical staff, and legal guardians, Phylis and myself. You or your hospital fucks this up and I'm coming for Y-O-U."

Dr. Shahdere intervened to cool things down. "Perhaps we should go to my office, and finish our discussions in there."

Nurse Hart secretly enjoyed the verbal pummeling Whitman received, grabbed Mike's arm, and urged, "Mister Santino we can take care of all the details ourselves," and waved for Dave to find the nearest exit.

David had no problem retreating. To him it was just another irate customer passing through his domain. In a few weeks this Santino and his preemie would be out of the hospital anyway – one way or the other. The patients come and go. The hospital administrator's public sector job is always there.

Mike cooled off in Dr. Shahdere's office, returning to review the expected events as the trial unfolds.

When the meeting concluded, Joel accompanied Mike out of the hospital and out to the doctor's parking lot. Mike filled him in on the details of how he had undermined the Greenhouse project at Lifespan. As they stood talking in the dark next to Joel's car, Joel suddenly became very serious and abruptly changed subjects. "Mike, I gotta tell to you," he suddenly blurted out, "Man, I'm scared."

"Hey," Mike assured, "It's a public trial. Don't worry. With Richard calling the signals in the courtroom we'll be alright."

Joel's demeanor looked more fearful than nervous. "No Mike. No, it's not that. Not that at all."

"Then what?"

"Remember that reporter friend of mine at the *Capitol Post*?"

"Yeah. So?"

"He's not there anymore. I mean he didn't quit or get fired or go on vacation. I mean he's disappeared without a trace."

Mike was not particularly disturbed and quipped, "Maybe he moved to another newpaper."

"No Mike. Seriously. There's more. There was news article yesterday. That an unidentified reporter was found drowned in Chesapeake Bay."

For the first time in their conversations tonight, Mike could appreciate Joel's anxiety, "Now that sounds like a hell of a coincidence. Doesn't it?"

Mike's next gut reaction was immediate. Wondering whether there was any threat to Amnion's life.

Joel interrupted his thoughts, "This is going to sound paranoid, but I picked up a pistol at a gun show in Pennsylvania."

"What?"

"I noticed a black Mercedes limo in my neighborhood, this past week, and nobody is getting married on my street." Then added with nervous humor, "And it's too early for the senior prom."

Mike nodded with a concerned "Hmm…"

Joel added with even more alarm. "I noticed the same car in the parking lot here - last night."

Joel's suspicions were too unsubstantiated to go to the police. At the same time, in Mike's mind, this was too probable not to be taken seriously. "Look Joel," Mike offered, "I'll see Richard on Saturday. He'll know what to do if this is Lifespan muscle. Just sit tight," Mike added with emphasis, "Be careful with that gun!"

They both departed the hospital lot, and Mike could tell his friend was genuinely frightened. The conversation made Mike much more wary about the sinister forces he was dealing with. If Joel was in real danger, then they were all threatened. Even his own boys ...Phylis too.

CHAPTER 59
Here we go again

Amelancholy Phylis leaned down to finish loading the dishes in the washer, the usual tiresome after-dinner drudgery. Scrapping the partially eaten fragments of food off the kid's plates made her wonder why she still bothered to cook hot dinners for her children to begin with.

The seasonal sun was beginning to set later now, and projected its fading dusky orange light through the kitchen window. By now, the kids were busy getting ready for another semester. It all seemed to remind her of another summer season gone with little prospect for a bright future.

On the windowsill, Mike's frog planter still grinned at the fly on its nose, reminding her of the happier moments with him. So, where were her lover's interests now?

Lately, she was financially struggling just to keep up with bills and property tax increases. The kids would be going to college soon, adding to her money woes. It wasn't apparent how she was going to swing all this at once, Now that her salary was not what it was at Lifespan. It felt almost embarrassing to be thinking of trying to get financial aid from a college. Fortunately, she heeded Mike's advice and moved her Lifespan 401K into a personal IRA - $400,000. After that, she heard from Katie that Lifespan pillaged the employee 401s.

The house phone rang and interrupted her thoughts. As usual, her daughter Kristy rushed off to answer it. From down the hallway the child yelled at the top of her lungs, "Mom! It's that 'man' again."

Surprised, Phylis froze in the kitchen, face flushed by her inner excitement. She half-stooped over the garbage can, not quite believing her ears. Somehow, just the sound of his name could resurrect the exciting sensual attraction to him. On the other hand, her sensible side was still upset with his recent neglect of her.

It felt awkward to be caught in the middle of all this kitchen mess. Phylis nervously pulled off her rubber gloves and straighten out her hair on the way to the phone - as if Michael could see her disheveled appearance over the telephone.

Kristy smiled knowingly and nodded her head, as she handed the receiver to her mother.

"Hi Phyl, miss you. Did you get the planter? " Mike said with friendly cheer.

Phylis, a bit flustered, tried to sound more subdued, and sarcastically replied, "Uh...yes, uh yeah Kermit." referring to the Sesame Street character.

After that reply, Mike sensed her hurt and tried to sound remorseful. "Well, I've been busy. You know.... with the trial and all."

"Yes, I know," she answered dryly, "I have my subpoena in hand." Her reply tried not to betray any hint of emotion. She wanted him to know her sorrow without having to say it.

Mike changed tack. "I finally got kicked out of Lifespan. Fired. It's all over for me too."

"Do you have another job to go to?" Phylis expressed with some concern.

"Actually...no." he admitted. "I got so busy with the case and screwing up their last project at Lifespan, there just wasn't time for anything else." Sheepishly he added, "Unfortunately, not even for you."

Phylis accepted his remark as the beings of an apology, but asked, "How are you going to live?"

"I don't know yet," he said. "I pulled out my 401K out after I mentioned it to you. Got 90 days to decide if I need it before rolling it over."

"Transferred mine out to an IRA," Phylis answered, "So, thanks for that he heads up."

"Good. So, you're clear of them," Mike answered, then abruptly changed subjects. "Anyway, I wanted to tell you how much I missed you." He paused, hoping for some words in return to make it easier to continue.

With Phylis's stone silence, he plaintively asked, "Just let me see you one more time. These kind of apology things never come off sounding genuine on the phone."

Phylis remained distant, but thinking about that complement he made to Nurse Hart about her, when she visited Amnion a few days ago.

"There's something big missing in my life," he added to bridge the silence between them.

She mulled it over in her head, then finally relented. "Okay Kermit. It doesn't mean we're a couple again. I can't take this 'on– off' relationship anymore. "

His voice perked up immediately, "How 'bout I pick you up on Saturday. Ever see a Yankee game?"

"No…Well…yes…,but…"

"Great! Pick you up at 12 noon."

How romantic, she sardonically pondered to herself.

Somehow, to her, being together with thirty thousand screaming baseball fans, didn't seem conducive to repairing a romantic relationship. She hung up the phone and asked herself, *What ever happened to a dozen roses, you stupid frog?*

CHAPTER 60
Go Yankees!

Phylis found herself surrounded, more like engulfed, by tens of thousands of screaming Yankee fans. She could not remember of ever being to a live baseball game, and this one certainly was exhilarating - especially the fans.

The score was tied in the bottom of the eighth inning, and the outcome was anybody's guess. Adding to the excitement was their opponent - their perennial rival Boston Red Sox. In middle September of the season both teams were tied for first place in the Eastern Division. Now every remaining game was crucial for each team.

At this point in the game, Phylis was probably the only one still seated, feeling almost buried in a valley by the screaming fans standing on their seats around and above her. A smiling Mike looked down and pulled her up to stand on her seat, holding her waist. Then, turning back to the field he facetiously yelled, "Go Yanquis!" in a Hispanic accent.

He returned his attention to Phylis smiling from above, with his arm around her hips and his head leaning on her breast. She looked down and gazed into those excited and sincere blue eyes. *Like an excited little boy,* she felt

Looking up, Mike basked under her sweet gaze saying in a joyful tone,"It don't get any better than this"

Phylis was about to ask, *Get better than what?* Too bad the intimate moment was drowned out by the crowd. Every pitch was greeted with stamping feet, screams, groans, arms waving. Now, even Phylis began to feel the surging force in a sea of human fervor. This whole world was reduced to a grass field and a small dirt spot at home plate. The stadium vibrated with sounds, bodies in motion, people united at this moment in a common cause. It was controlled violence just this side of a riot. The smell of spilled beer permeated the air.

Phylis was not much of a baseball fan, but still found herself suddenly carried along the tide of frenzied enthusiasm. She began to yell too.

"Give'm the heater!" she screamed, surprised at her own ferocity.

A smiling Mike looked up and calmly explained, "You scream that when the Yankees are pitching."

Phylis felt a bit embarrassed by her botched attempt at a cheer. Mike hugged her with delight anyway. Undaunted, she composed herself and then correctly and enthusiastically screamed, "Belt it outta the park!"

Mike laughed and nodded his approval, giving her the thumbs up sign.

* * * * * * * *

With the game over, Mike walked briskly through the exiting crowd, squeezing Phylis' hand, as she strained to keep up on her toes. Hundreds of excited smiling fans passed in a blur as they surged and maneuvered between cars in the parking lot. Even outside the stadium, you could still feel the crowd's euphoria. The Yankees had won today's match-up in dramatic fashion with a home run in the bottom of the ninth.

Leaving the stadium grounds, the couple crossed into a seedy Bronx neighborhood, a few blocks from the stadium. Mike had parked here on the street to avoid the parking lot traffic jam. Fortunately, it was still daylight, and Mike's old '65 Ford was not of interest to local car thieves anyway.

He unlocked her side first and Phylis anxiously jumped in. As they pulled away, she felt a certain feeling of relief in the apparent safety of the locked car. Mike quickly found the expressway and they were on their way home.

Phylis eventually snuggled up to Mike in the front bench seat, exhausted from all the fresh air and excitement of the game. Her throat was dry and hoarse from all that cheering. Mike put his free arm around her, and they just drove quietly for several miles in the moderate outflowing traffic.

It was a secure and peaceful feeling. The kids were safe at home with grandma and grandpa, and her outing to the game turned out to be a more entertaining date than she expected.

Mike drove with his usual flair, darting in and out of lanes, smoothly passing slower traffic. Exchanging only occasional small talk, Mike eventually suggested a return to his favorite German restaurant for a beer and a cold roast beef sandwich on pumpernickel. Phylis remember the place from their first hair raising date to the New York auto show.

Arriving at the old restaurant, the sky became overcast and threatening with intermittent spritzing of raindrops. Mike noted how lucky it was to get the ballgame over before it started to rain. Once inside the restaurant bar, they found a small round table in a secluded corner of the bar area. A friendly old waitress came over and took their order. With the darkened room and flickering candle light on the table, Phylis took the opportunity to have a more intimate conversation about the future - their future.

"Michael," she began by stretching her slender arms across the red checkered tablecloth and holding his stubby finger tips. "What are you going to do when this trial is over? I mean how will you live?"

He leaned forward and sipped his beer, the candlelight flickering in his tired eyes. "Actually with the trial and all the excitement I haven't really had time to worry about it. I have 5 weeks severance pay," he volunteered, "...and some savings."

"Not much in today's world of middle age unemployment," she added.

Mike nodded in agreement. "Still, I'll find something." Then he sat back and grinned. "Something that doesn't involve bio-chemical technology ...and none of this medical stuff either."

Phylis felt sympathetic and looked into his eyes, "Well, I'm here for you Michael. For whatever that's worth."

Mike brightened up immediately, "Well then, that's everything in the world to me."

He gazed at her kind green eyes and pretty face, illuminated by the amber candlelight that softened her features. He moved his chair around the table to sit right next to her. Tenderly he touched her delicate chin with his fingers. She responded to his attention, stretching forward, and closing her eyes as he planted a soft kiss on her lips.

Phylis stayed peacefully motionless and sighed, "I wish this was all over. I wish we could just live together alone. Someplace far away. Live somewhere in peace."

Mike answered, "Sometimes life is like this. You do the right things, and you're only reward is having everybody else watching passively, as you dig yourself out of the hole you created."

Their meal and sandwiches came. Mike clicked her drinking glass and changed the subject, "Hey, the hell with tomorrow. We're still together tonight. Besides, the Yankees won!"

After an hour or so, it was dark outside and the rain began to fall steadily.

Mike paid the bill and asked, "You want to go home?"

"I don't know," she said coyly. "What do you want to do?"

"Find a private place to park and talk," he offered with a hint of mischief in his eyes.

They left the restaurant and drove in the rain to a dimly lit street near her home, lined with huge old maple trees. The dense foliage of the leaves choked off most of the light from the street lamps, allowing only small islands of light to punctuate the dark ground every 100 feet or so. Mike parked in between, in the shadows by a vacant garage. Then turned off the motor, and flipped on the radio to an 'oldies' station. Phylis initially felt a little insecure in this secluded parking spot. However, the locked doors and Mike's presence seemed enough to forget about any dangers from the world outside.

The rain beaded and streamed down on the windshield, as streaks of light from a distance street lamp randomly found their way through the rustling leaves. The dimpled raindrops on the glass, cast faint speckled shadows on their faces.

Alone in the dark, Mike turned to embrace her on the bench seat. In their seclusion, it felt like the entire world was reduced to only two people again.

"I missed you a lot," he whispered into her silken ear.

Phylis answered his embrace, hugging him and kissing his cheek, sighing, "Oh, Michael."

She ran her hands over his broad shoulders and reached for the back of his neck to kiss him fully on the lips. His scent was a combination of perspiration, beer, and aftershave, like all outdoors. Very manly. Very enticing.   Even the old car interior, with its big steering wheel, bench seat, and chrome trim throughout, made her begin to feel the passionate abandon of a teenager again.

The car windows were now almost completely fogged up. Mike leaned over the dashboard and with his breath blew condensation on the last clear spot. On the radio, the old song, "Hello Stranger", sung by Barbara Lewis began. It seemed so appropriate.

"It seems like a mighty long time..."

Phylis nodded seductively in agreement, as Michael gently slid her down on the seat. She shimmied down along the back cushion until her head touched the armrest. Mike straddled her and interrupted things to reach into the back seat and produce a small pillow to support her head.

Phylis playfully surmised, *Hmmm...always plans ahead..*

Then he hung down over her like a hungry wolf over its prey. His kisses came more quickly now. All over her face, neck, and down her blouse. His hands squeezed and probed her body through her clothes while his mouth nibbled and gently bit. It was only a matter of time until his hands found their way to the smooth moist skin underneath. Phylis didn't resist.

Although, for a second, she asked herself what a middle-aged woman is doing lying in a parked car. In the middle of the night. On a public street. About to have her clothes methodically removed.

Thankfully, the fogged windows and rain outside gave her a sense of privacy sufficient to dispel her momentary apprehension.

It seemed only a moment had passed before her unbuttoned blouse and unzipped pants exposed her lacy underthings. Mike lay aside her on the front bench seat gazing and admiring her femininity. His appreciative gaze only made her feel more desirable and less inhibited.

They made love in the cramped confines of his front seat, in the dark to the pattering sound of the raindrops dripping from the tree canopy on the roof. With all that passion released in the confined space, the humidity was almost stifling.

Suddenly, Phylis noticed a dull red glare on the roof headliner. "What's that Michael?" she inquired with alarmed panic as she looked up and past him. "Is that a car behind us?"

"What's what?" was his confused reply.

"The red light reflection on the headliner there."

Phylis became self-conscious immediately, now looking for her clothes.

Mike turned to look up over his shoulder. He briefly caught a glimpse of the red glare out the back window. Then, it disappeared abruptly. A confused Mike looked down at an apprehensive Phylis. After a moment, he smiled. Then laughed.

"What's so funny Michael?" she said indignantly.

"Watch."

The red glare on the headliner flashed on an off.

It finally dawned on her that Michael's legs had been down on the floorboard on the driver's side of the car. His foot was occasionally pumping the brake pedal at times during the rhythm of lovemaking, turning the brake lights on and off.

Then she had this humiliating thought. "Michael! Were you touching that pedal the whole time we were making love?"

"I don't know," he snickered, "I really wasn't feeling my feet at the time."

Unabashed Mike tried to continue with lovemaking, but a now self-conscious Phylis pushed Michael away and sat up to straighten out her disheveled clothes. A shirtless Michael sat back at the driver's seat with one knee tucked up against the steering wheel He chuckled some more.

"Do you realize that all the people in this neighborhood could tell what we were doing!" she hissed in embarrassment, now feeling a more urgency 'to get her clothes back on. "You blinked it out in Morse code."

Mike could care less about some strangers. "So what did they really see?" he replied.

Phylis quipped satirically, "You men! Sometimes I think you'd do it on the sidewalk ...if it wasn't against the law."

A grinning Michael just shrugged his shoulders and nodded in agreement, as he put on his shirt and zipped up his fly.

CHAPTER 61
Opening round

R ichard Farmer's tall, imposing figure rose slowly from the Plaintiff's table. Amnion was still not present in the courtroom next to him because of her poor health. Instead, propped up on the Plaintiff's table was a 12x18 inch enlarged color photograph of her in the neonatal ICU.

The jury selection process, *voir dire*, had been completed a day earlier. Norm made a silly attempt to pack the jury with wealthy jurors who had been receiving Lifespan treatments. Richard was smart enough to use Lifespan's own client list to include that juror question in the screening process, and eliminate them.

Behind Richard, the room was packed with spectators. Mike had arranged for the single a *Brooklyn Daily* reporter to share his observations with other media, Judge Burger sternly limited him to a paper notepad and no electronics, and in addition, only a sketch artist was permitted in the courtroom. The thick atmosphere was so intense that any gesture by either litigant would automatically cause a low undertone to permeate the room. On the way into the courtroom, Mike suspiciously eyed several drones jockeying for position in the sky above. He knew how dangerous they could be

The fact was, that the trial was already being held in the media forum. With all the reporters outside, it was a struggle for the trial participants just to get up the courthouse in the morning. In reaction to all this sensationalism, the astute judge had barred cameras from the courtroom to keep the trial being conducted in the media. Too many times, he had seen what a farce the media's presence could make out of the most serious of trials. He was not going to let that happen here. He also sequestered the jury for their protection.

Adding to the jostling chaos outside, protestors from both sides of the termination and decoupling issue filled the streets below. Several drones jockeyed for position above in violation of a "no fly zone". Security became a major concern, as the antagonists waged a running battle of shouts and signs from opposite sidewalks - a marked contrast to the slow drama unfolding inside. The signs they carried were indicative of how polarizing the issue had become. At one extreme the signs said, 'Decoupling is abortion' and "all human life is sacred'. At the other extreme the signs said, "Women have a right to sell their fetuses' and 'God save termination'. Unfortunately, the focus of media attention had moved from the front entrance of Lifespan headquarters to the front entrance of the courthouse. On top of that, white, black and orange media drones filled the sky above dogging for position like the demonstrators below. Unlike most people, Mike found them somewhat threatening. With his military experience he knew that any one of them could be armed with and RPG missile.

****

In the hushed courtroom, Richard approached the jury box for his opening remarks. Confidently, he held two oak frame pictures at his side. Everyone in the court room was curious as to what was on them.

Even before Richard spoke, one could sense his natural warmth and sincerity. The same magnetic personality that, up till now, won him friends all over the city.

"People of the jury," he started in a relaxed tone sounding more like a family counselor than a lawyer does. "The case that we will plead today against the corporation known as Lifespan is really about life and death - whether my client had fundamental rights from the very earliest stages of her humanity. Moreover, whether human life has an intrinsic value that transcends all other considerations. So, I ask you, should any organization, or government for that matter, has the singular right to manipulate that

355

precious human life for profit."

He was holding two beautifully framed documents, that he placed on the jury box railing to face the jurors. Slowly, Richard began again. "These were hanging on my office wall. They were a present from my parents when I graduated law school over 25 years ago." Richard leaned over the top of each frame as though he were reading them. "They are the Declaration of Independence and the Bill of Rights...perhaps something we need to revisit in this trial"

Richard face took on a nostalgic countenance as he said, "My parents didn't get past high school, but they loved to read. And they really admired the words in these two documents."

Richard smiled, "My father was a car mechanic. Even so, he always seemed to be smarter than I was. He said, that when I become a 'big time lawyer', never forget what our Christian founding fathers were really trying to achieve. In addition, to remember how long it took for those rights and protections to be granted to minorities, women, and underage working children. I introduce these two documents as Plaintiff exhibit A"

Lifespan chief counsel, Norm Stark, sprang from his seat, "Objection Your Honor!" he bellowed. "The very law of the land can't be admitted as evidence to laymen jurors. They are not qualified attorneys. It is ridiculous."

Richard contained his delight. He baited Lifespan's counsel to object to the foundation of the law of the land, and, on top of that, insult the juror's intelligence.

And Lifespan did it.

Richard gave a curious stare at Norm. "Does the Defense have a problem with the self-evident part where, 'all men are created equal'? Or, maybe the jury isn't capable of understanding our Bill of Rights without guidance from some very clever lawyers?"

An irritated Judge Burger overruled Norm. "The Plaintiff has leeway in his opening remarks." And nodded for Richard to continue.

Richard pointed to the Declaration of Independence first. "This is where he said the rights of people are rooted. Not in a king. Not in any form of government. But in the Almighty ...the Creator...That law should flow from those ethical, not legal, underpinnings.

"I would like to take a moment o focus on one key phase, 'All men are created equal'. So I ask you, you the jurors. At what point were you created equal? Sounds like a simple enough question." Richard turned to point at Amnions picture. "Put yourself in that little girl's position. At what point was she created equal.... and then entitled to protection."

Richard paused to let the jurors ponder the question.

Justice Burger interrupted Richard, looking down from the bench, "Counselor, where is this going?"

"Your Honor, I believe the defendants will drag out a litany of litigious case history and witnesses to confuse the jury on the issue of human life and who is protected under our Constitution. I want the jury to have access to what the Constitution actually says, not a series of interpretations from other litigations. The jurors are intelligent people. Let them read it for themselves."

An agitated Norm began to stand up again. Judge Burger motioned him down with a flourish of the hand. "I can see nothing improper about restating the rights of the people to the jury." Brenda quickly handed out copies of the documents to each juror."

Norm' rolled his eyes in disgust.

Richard continued. "Each of you here today, bears the tremendous and unenviable burden of sorting through some very gruesome and contradictory evidence." He paused, then added contemptuously, "To be made even more confusing by supposedly 'expert' opinion."

Richard's voice rose slightly as he accusingly pointed to Max Brewster seated at his table. "The question is simply this; Did Lifespan exceed it's authority from the government by collecting fetal cadavers and then…reviving them? More importantly, does Lifespan Corporation have the right to process living human beings into pharmaceuticals? Government license or not?"

Norm rose and angrily objected again. "The 'human' status of a fetus specimen has not been legally established!"

The Judge admonished Richard, "Mister Framers your statement is conjecture at this time."

"Legally human? He answered. "I invite you attention to the picture of the human life at the Plaintiff table. Well, your Honor, that child is at the essence of this trial."

The judge mulled it over. He was a pro-decoupling supporter, but now he was confronted by a living fetal life in the flesh. It left him uneasy, maybe doubtful. Still, he said, "Objection Sustained, until I hear more evidence."

Norm let out a triumphant, "harrumph," and sat down.

Richard walked over to regard Amnion's pitiful neonatal picture on the Plaintiff's table. "This case will be more than an 'us versus them' contest. I hope it is going to be an enlightening trip through both science and our sense of values. The culture of what we are now, and what we should be as Americans."

Richard picked up Amnion's picture and began his return to the jury box, carefully insuring that her pitiful picture faced the jury. "Some cringed and squirmed in their seats at the sight of this scrawny effigy stuck with tubes and needles." This child is still too weak to appear before you," he said. "Even if she could, she couldn't speak to defend herself." Richard hesitated for a moment, and looked at the picture himself. He added, "So, if she could speak, what would she ask of you?"

After another grave pause, he walked across the courtroom to face the Lifespan table, "Her developing life has been interrupted so traumatically by her revival by these people, such that she is still suffering months of complications." Richard bowed his head for emphasis, and sighed sadly. "Perhaps she will never lead a normal life."

Richard took a silent moment, returning to the Plaintiff table to place Amnion's picture back on the plaintiff table stand He slowly walked to the jury box."

An impatient Judge Burger interrupted Richard. "Mister Farmers, please conclude your opening remarks."

"A moment of your indulgence, your Honor." Richard said, and returned to the jurors leaning forward with both hands on the jury box railing for emphasis, looking at each juror's face with unmistakable sincerity. The kind of look you cannot fake. "The plaintiff will show Amnion's perilous journey from decoupling in University Hospital to Lifespan's secret R&D revival lab. From her rescue by Mister Santino, to his basement using Lifespan's revival cart equipment. To her delivery in a doctor's office, and finally, as you see her today, in the hospital NICU."

A deep, eloquent voice intoned, "In the end. After all the testimony. After dozens of witnesses and arguments. You the jury, will have to interpret the facts. In the next few weeks, you will decide the destiny of one little girl named, for now, as Amnion." He paused for dramatic effect adding wistfully, "...then perhaps seal the fate of millions more like her."

With dramatic silence, Richard returned to stand behind the Plaintiff table. In a courtroom hushed by the strength of his dramatic oratory, Richard silently adjusted Amnion's picture back on the Plaintiff's table

After a few moments, Norm rotund figure stood up for his opening remarks. He buttoned the lapels of his custom tailored pinstriped suit, and turned to Richard in a mocking bow, saying sarcastically, "Thank you for your 'Sermon on the Mount'."

About one in ten people chuckled at his pun. However, the jury remained stoically silent.

Norm's approach to the jury was more legally polished and business-like, though almost condescending. "You are all aware that the medical community has a program for organ donation. Whereby, a deceased human being voluntarily gives up his or her organs to help another human being suffering from a life threatening disease. Norm paused with a slight smirk towards Richard, and continued. Well, we at Lifespan Corporation have a similar program whereby a donor gives up a fetal cadaver in a decoupling procedure. Lifespan then makes use of what would be discarded tissue, cultures and processes it, creating lifesaving drugs for very ill people. Wonder drugs that many of you or your families may benefit from in the future, or maybe even save your own lives."

Norm gave a smiling leer at Richard. "Lifespan is good science, not some social justice crusade. Moreover, this is a court of law. And your job, as jurors, is to weigh the evidence presented in accordance with the law - as it is already written!"

Norm spoke in a belittling tone, "The Plaintiff counsel infers that there's something wrong with our laws." Then he chuckled, "As if we should have juries making up the laws as they go along. That would be ...would be...simply chaos!"

The Lifespan attorney sauntered over to Richard's table and looked down at Amnion's picture. To him it was fortuitous that Amnion was not here in the flesh. A live baby would only generate more emotional sympathy for the plaintiff's case. He then turned to face the jury again while pointing his pen at the picture. "Ladies and gentlemen. Any suffering his specimen is experiencing was caused by individuals outside of Lifespan's control," pointing to Mike at the plaintiff's table. "This thief and his co-conspirators. Any suffering to this specimen was brought on and prolonged by them."

Raising his voice, Norm boomed, "Furthermore, we at Lifespan will prove, beyond a shadow of doubt, that the charges brought against it by the Plaintiff are unsubstantiated by law. That Lifespan has been peacefully pursuing its legitimate business interests of harvesting cadaver specimen organs under a State and FDA license with official NIH oversight. And finally, that much of what is presented as supposed evidence is mostly irrelevant or conjecture on the Plaintiff's part."

Norm gave Richard a triumphant grin, as he waltzed back to face the jury, and concluded, "Remember that the opening remarks by the Plaintiff's attorney are neither evidence nor testimony. Just a reactionary's war against progress and medical science. Norm walked by Richard on the way to the defense table, and scoffed. "The status of the fetal specimen has been adjudicated in case after case for over 80 years, including our very own Supreme Court. It has no legal status in both New York and New Jersey even up until birth. What we have here, are a few zealots trying to use this case to further the radical pro-life political agenda."

Norm concluded, "And I ask you simply. Does this jury really want to be part of a political movement to deny a woman's right to decoupling, and deny your access to life saving drugs?"

The courtroom let out a hushed tone of whispered agreement.

Not bad, Richard thought, *"Make it personal, but the lunch break will lessen the impact.*

* * * * * * * *

That afternoon Richard called his first witness, John Lombardo. Mike Santino had provided background that this Lifespan executive was the weakest link in the chain. Mike's reasoning was typical Mike, "He cheats on his wife. A lady's man usually has no real balls."

Richard and the jury noticed John's hand withdraw from the bible at swearing in, choosing to swear in as an agnostic without the bible. It would be how all Lifespan executives would swear in. Richard took his time approaching the witness stand, using the delaying tactic used in football to make an opposing field goal kicker nervous. It was easier to just let the young executive's own apprehension wear him down. On the way to the witness stand, Richard glanced at the next page of his interview notes on his tablet. There was a video clip of the original Mickey Mouse film called *'Steamboat Willy'* whistling and bouncing along behind the steering helm. *Mikey Mikey. So, this is what you think of Lombardo.* Mike had added tidbits to Richard's notes with his opinion of witnesses.

Finally, Richard faced John and gently inquired, "Mister Lombardo. Would you tell the jury your title and position at Lifespan Corporation?

"Uh," he hesitated, "Vice President and Chief Financial Officer."

"Hmm, impressive" Richard mumbled, "And for how long in this capacity?"

"Five years," John said with a touch of smug pride.

Richard looked down to enter something on his tablet computer. The activity proved to be quite distracting to John who lifted his head to try to peer over the top of the pad.

"And what was your position before that?" Richard continued.

"I was in the financial department of a major food processing company."

"No," Richard followed up, "I mean your specific job title."

John fidgeted in his seat, continuously glancing in Norm's direction at the Defense table. He was desperate for any cues on how to answer. Richard nonchalantly placed his body between the two to block his view. In John's nervous attempt to see around Richard, he almost leaned out of his chair.

"Mister Lombardo, we're all waiting."

"I don't exactly remember," was his evasive response.

"Then, let me refresh your memory on that," Richard said, as he looked down at his tablet. "You were a junior bookkeeper, according to that company's records."

John felt like his life's secrets were somehow captured in that electronic gizmo in Richard's hand, and wondered if his extra marital affairs were somehow in that machine too.

360

"Well, uh. Yes. I guess," he reluctantly replied.

Richard shook his head, "Now that's remarkable. Overnight from bookkeeping clerk to Chief Financial Officer of a $500 million corporation."

Richard turned to the jury with a look of astonishment, "How'd you manage that?"

John was completely flustered, tugging on an ear lobe, his Adam's apple visibly bouncing up and down on his neck.

Norm jumped up to raise an objection. "The question is irrelevant! The witness's career is not on trial here. Let's stick to the trial issue at hand."

Judge Burger looked down at Richard for a rebuttal.

Richard replied, "Your Honor. The witness's position at Lifespan is at the financial center of Lifespan, and those financial records have a bearing on this case. His credibility to act as a responsible financial officer has to be established."

The Justice overruled a disappointed Norm this time.

Richard continued the grilling. "Mister Lombardo. Is it not true that at the time you were hired at Lifespan, your father was a substantial investing partner of mister Max Brewster, President and Chairman of Lifespan?"

John tried to keep his composure, tugging at his collar, leaning in his seat to see Norm for queues. Then, answered in a quivering tone, "I, uh, don't remember." By now, the jury had the true message.

Richard paused to keypunch something on his tablet. "Let's move on," he said, adding, "I have the financial performance data for the months in which your organization started to revive human fetuses."

"Objection Your Honor," Norm interrupted. "The statement is conjecture. This revival business remains to be proven."

"Sustained," the judge acknowledged, "re-phrase your question Mister Farmers or move on," he directed.

"Yes, Your Honor." Richard conceded and asked it a different way, "Going back 12 months, Lifespan's monthly pharmaceutical shipments and profitability continued to increase dramatically, while your specimen acquisition costs dropped precipitously. How do you explain that?"

"We probably worked down our inventory and work-in-process," John answered confidently.

Richard looked down at his tablet. "Amazing," he said. "According to these records provided by your company, your inventories and WIP actually went up for 12 months straight, as well as shipments out the door. Where did all this extra fetal bio-material come from Mister Lombardo?"

"Objection Your Honor, Calls for speculation." Norm said. "The witness is not an expert on the company's production processes."

Richard spoke to the judge while also turning toward the jury and quipped, "Well, he's not a financial expert, and now the company attorney says he doesn't understand how his business produces its products either."

The jury laughed, and the Judge banged his gavel for order. Norm stood up again. "Objection. Argumentative."

The judge responded, "Sustained," and admonished Farmers. "No more sarcasms please."

"Sorry your Honor."

In the meantime, John did not know what to say, and looked desperately at Norm for some guidance. Richard resumed the attack, "I have the records of all the R&D work orders budgeted and tracked by your Finance department."

He held up a work order for Job 901, or 'Project Greenhouse'. "Are you familiar with this one? ...Job 901."

John squinted at the document; his face flushed, and stammered with uncertainty, "Well, I guess so."

"It has a blank for the job description. All the other R&D jobs have a description. This one doesn't. Why?"

John tried to buy time by reaching to examine the document more closely. After a few nervous breaths, blinking excessively, he whispered, "I don't know."

Richard said, "You don't know? Your R&D department charged $20 million to this Job 901 account every year for four years, and you, the chief financial officer, do not know what they were doing with your company's money? You didn't find that suspicious?"

John had reached his breaking point, and tried to defend himself, whimpering with trembling lips, "The job was a company secret." He grabbed the witness box wood railing and craned his neck around Richard for some coaching from Norm, then looked across to the judge, "Nobody knew what they were doing over there. Nobody was allowed to ask." Still unsure what to say next, he blurted out, "All I know is that they were making drugs to cure disease." Then he looked over at the jury for sympathy, whose constituents were more amused by his attempts to peek at Norm around Richard."

In disgust, Norm's face dropped, and buried the heel of his palm in his forehead. All John had to say was, *I don't remember*, just like he was coached.

Richard made his point and quickly said, "No further questions for now, Your Honor. Right to re-call the witness."

Norm did not bother to cross-examine. He just wanted the bumbling idiot off the stand as quickly as possible, not being sure what John might accidentally blurt out next in his near panic.

Richard called his next witness, Carlos Rivera. The gentle Hispanic took his oath on the bible at the witness stand and sat down nervously.

To calm him down a bit, Richard started with some simple basic questions regarding his past employment and duties at Lifespan.

Richard asked, "What did you see, that made you leave Lifespan?"

Carlos bowed his head and spoke softly in broken English. "Dey do things dere. Things I don't like."

"Like what?"

"Exzperimen. On da baby."

Norm rose and loudly objected, "Witness has no medical credentials to speculate on what he saw!"

Judge Burger spoke, "Overuled. The witness is not being asked for a medical opinion – just what he observed."

Richard continued, "Can you describe what you mean a little more specifically, Mister Rivera?"

Carlos paused and looked at the judge with fear in his eyes. Justice Burger encouraged him to continue. "I take da wasta from da R a D room, and burn in da furnace. Dey come in boxes." He motioned with his hands to draw a small rectangle in space. "about dis big."

"Are these wastes identified with any markings?" Richard continued.

"Yeah. Dey have a job numba tag. Si. 901. I mark it down in a book and da specmen numba, and den burn da boxes."

Richard began to dig in now, "About 12 months ago, what changes did you notice?"

"The boxes," he mentioned with his hands, "Dey got bigga."
Carlos stretched his hands apart adding, "Much bigga."

"Did you ever examine the contents of one of these larger containers, Mister Rivera?"

"Jesus hava mercy on me," he said, as he looked towards the jury with eyes filled with tearful remorse. "Dey had bebés in dere. Little people. The fingers, toes, eyes. Soma in pieces." Carlos' eyes welled up near tears as he continued. "Sometimes dey had a head split open, and a no brains left in dere."

Carlos looked at the judge and the jury, and then bowed his head towards the floor, wiping his eyes with his sleeve. The courtroom silence was deafening. His testimony made everyone in the room uneasy. Everyone of course, except the Lifespan representatives.

Richard grimaced as he continued the questions, "About how far along in gestation would you guess these human fetuses were? eighteen, maybe twenty weeks?"

Norm rose to object, "Calls for speculation. The witness is not an expert on fetal development. He does not have the clinical background to make such an assessment."

"Sustained," the judge ruled with displeasure

"Withdrawn." Richard said, not wanting to debate Norm's challenge. The damage was already done.

"One last question Mister Rivera," Richard added. "These larger boxes of destroyed human fetal tissues. What was the job number marked on them? What specimen numbers?"

Carlos looked back up with reddened eyes, "Afta a while, dey got no more specimen numbas. Just jobba 9 - 0 - 1."

Richard put emphasis on the number as he turned to the jury. "The same 20 million dollar secret job number 901 that CFO Lombardo claimed to have no description.

Richard ended with, "No further questions of this witness."

The gallery noise faded as Norm stood up to cross-examine. The attorney's tailored suit and Norm's executive swagger trigged a certain fear in Carlos. He slowly approached Carlos like a roaming shark, and asked curtly, "Did you tell anyone at Lifespan about this? Did you alert your supervisor of this alleged 'bizarre' activity?"

Carlos, still wary, had no trust of the courts to protect him. And he would not reveal his discussion with Mike Santino either. He just shook his head and answered a hushed, "No."

Norm continued his barrage, "Did you open up all the large boxes you testified about?"

"What? You loco gringo?" Carlos looked up and blurted out. "You see dis una vez, you never wanna look again!"

"So you couldn't tell if what you saw might have been just an isolated experiment."

Carlos shrugged his shoulders and gave a sheepish, "Si."

Norm was feeling a little better now about debunking Carlos' testimony and began his rap-up questioning. "You quit shortly after this?" Norm said, "and never discussed this again? Even with the authorities?"

Carlos felt guilty enough already for not going to the authorities, and surprised Norm with his answer. "No. No, I do not. I'm afraid."

Norm smiled smugly and remarked, "Perhaps you were afraid you made this all up."

Before Richard could object, the impassioned Carlos responded loudly and unexpectedly to the insinuation, "I'ma frade for my life! For my familia." Then he bolted up onto his feet and grabbed the railing in front of him. Lifting a quivering hand, the little man pointed his finger at the Lifespan executives seated behind the defendant table, and exclaimed, "Dis

364

Lifaspan. Esto es la casa del diablo!" Carlos leaned over the railing, shaking his fist now, bearing his teeth. "All you company gringos. *Usted se quemará en el infierno* for what you do!"

Norm was stunned, and threw up his arms in frustration. "Your Honor, I request these wild statements be stricken from the record!"

Judge Burger answered, "Basis?"

Norm replied, "I don't know. He's speaking a foreign language half the time. Obviously, he is a hostile witness. The witness is not a medical expert."

"Objection Sustained. The jury will disregard witness's outburst."

It was clear from Carlos's incendiary statements, that the witness had inadvertently undone Norm's thread of questions. Undoubtedly, the jury would only remember Carlos's simple fear and sympathize with him.

Norm spun around and shook his head in disgust. "Witness excused."

Richard and his staff suppressed a smile – damage had already been done to Lifespan's Defense.

* * * * * * * *

Court recessed for the day of dramatic testimony. News reporters jammed the steps outside at the building's main entrance. It was chaotic spectacle outside, with protesting special interest groups each vying for camera time. Both sides to this trial were drawn up according to the political lines of battle over fetal life. On the one side, women's activists, wealthy professional women's groups, Planned Parenthood, government welfare agencies, and the ACLU supporting Lifespan. On the other side, operation rescue organizers, Catholic clergy, and working class mothers protesting against Lifespan.

Most politicians stayed on the fence over this one and played it cagey. From what they knew of the evidence, and the executives involved, the outcome was just too close to call. Moreover, you never knew how far this case could erupt into the broader abortion issue - an issue all would prefer buried.

CHAPTER 62
The parable of the acorn

Richard started the next day in court holding a small clear plexiglas cube, filled with potting soil. He stood up and addressed the court saying, "Your Honor, I would like to address the jury before I call my next witness."

Norm objected, "You already had your chance to address the jury during opening remarks!"

"Sustained."

Richard acquiesced and moved on to other matters. "In that case, Your Honor, I call Dr. Davidson, horticulturist at State University."

"Then proceed Mister Farmers," the Judge intoned.

Richard walked over to Professor Davidson, and held up the cube of soil in his hand. "I have here a piece of mother earth. And, I thought it might be instructive to the jury during this trial to explore something about creation and life."

Norm stood up and barked, "Relevance Your Honor?"

The judge looked at Richard. "Mister Farmers???"

"The question is: At what point have you destroyed a living organism, Your Honor. I am introducing an analogy."

The judge was intrigued. "Then proceed. Defense overruled."

Richard reached into his pants pocket and retrieved a brown acorn, which he held aloft between his thumb and index fingers. "This humble acorn may be able to teach us something about nature and ourselves." He waved the kernel around in the air so all could see. "A professor from Texas A&M sent it to me." Handing it to the professor, Richard asked, "Do you recognize this professor Davidson. "

He examined it and stated, "Of course. It belongs to the genus *Quercus* ...an oak tree."

"Thank you."

The jury's attention was fixed on this little developing parable being played out in front of them. Richard inserted his finger into the dampened humus dirt to make a hole, retrieved the acorn from the witness, and placed the acorn in about 2 inches deep, sliding along one clear wall, and then covered it with loose soil. He walked over to a south facing window, next to the jury box, and gently placed the cube on its sunny sill the acorn side visible from the courtroom.

Norm stood up, "Objection your Honor. This trial is turning into theater."

"Mister Farmers? Where is this going?"

"Your indulgence your Honor. "Only one last question of this witness your Honor. This demonstration will be germane to testimony given by expert witnesses about the question of when life starts. We expect the Defense to introduce this issue later in the case."

He returned to the professor, and pointed to the window. "At what point in the germinating process do you kill that oak tree?"

The professor shrugged his shoulders, answering, "I would say once the acorn germinates. The shell breaks open in the humus soil, and forms a root and a stalk."

"So it's still unseen in mother earth."

The professor agreed. "Exactly."

"Norm objected again. "Your Honor, Mister Farmers is testing the limits of this Court's patience! The counselor is testifying again."

"Sorry your Honor. Question withdrawn. Witness dismissed."

The jurors turned to observe the window, and looked at each other somewhat amused and intrigued by the demonstration. Richard hoped they got the point.

Norm vehemently objected, "Your Honor. This is ridiculous. This has nothing to do with this trial!"

Justice Burger still intrigued by Richards's presentation and decreed, "I will rule on the objection based on additional expert evidence provided by the Plaintiff."

Norm stood dumbfounded, looking back at his staff, muttering,"Bizarre, just bizarre," as the judge waved him to sit down.

The little tree will haunt Norm's case.

* * * * * * * *

Richard went on to call to the stand, Dr. Petersen from University Hospital, where Amnion was decoupled. He would establish the trail from Amnion's decoupling as specimen UH0744 to the Lifespan lab, and the procedures Lifespan had instituted to retrieve the fetus and placenta as a unit.

Once past the medical credentials questions, Richard began to pursue the main point of the testimony. "Doctor," he said, "In your medical opinion. Is the placenta a separate organ from the fetus?"

"Yes," he answered assuredly. "A fact, I think most of my colleagues would agree on."

Richard rapidly fired the next question. "Then how did you go about enlarging the scope of your decoupling extraction operations taking out essentially a separate placenta organ in addition to the fetus?"

Petersen still felt secure and replied, "I received an email from Dr. Strauss of Lifespan Corporation, specifying the extraction of both."

"And what other criteria were specified in that directive?"

The confident doctor was beginning to show some signs of discomfort, aware of the newspaper accounts of what probably happened to these human fetal lives afterwards. He cleared his throat and answered, "They," stopping to clear his throat, "Ahem, meaning Lifespan, wanted both the specimen and placenta intact as a unit. They were very insistent that this be done without risking damage to the specimen or placenta."

"Did you follow these procedures in the extraction of fetal specimen 0744?"

"Yes I did. In fact, I can still remember it as a particularly difficult one."

Richard waited a few seconds to let the testimony, so far, sink in with the jury.

"And what about the woman's uterus," Richard enjoined. "What ramifications did this new placenta extraction procedure have on the woman?" Richard demanded.

The wary doctor fidgeted in his chair, hesitating a moment. "It would usually result in increased erosion of the uterus lining, while excising and cauterizing a circular area about the size of a half dollar."

The gallery behind Richard let out a collective low moan.

Dr. Petersen began to feel like he was being painted as a butcher, and added nervously. "We used best medical practice precautions. Rarely had a bleeder."

Richard left the witness to Norm's cross-examination.

Norm stood up and tried to restore the doctor's sagging image by asking, "Did anyone tell you, or for that matter did any directive from Lifespan say that these specimens were going to be revived?"

"No. No one. The objective of this new procedure was simply to obtain more material for blood extraction of stem cells and purification."

"Right," Norm agreed, and added, "Did any employees from Lifespan assist in extracting any specimens from the donor's wombs."

Petersen was annoyed at this obvious attempt by Lifespan to distance itself from the decoupling, and dump it all on the hospital. He hesitated, then responded, "Well, no. But..."

Norm cut him short. He was more interested now in introducing his 'smoking gun' issue to blow the case wide open. He quickly asked, "Specimen UH0744 on your medical records. Is she this Amnion plaintiff?"

"I'm not sure," Petersen said.

"Why aren't you sure?"

"Well, I recall that specimen being a <u>male</u>, just as the written records indicate."

Norm waved a medical form in the air, "Here is the actual hospital record for this specimen. The jury is advised that it indicates 'male' as the sex. Not female!"

Norm turned with a broad grin, and howled to the jury. "So, now we don't really know where this <u>female</u> specimen, 'Amnion', came from!"

He pointed to the Amnion's picture, "We don't even know if this

Plaintiff specimen was ever involved with Lifespan to begin with. Who knows where it came from?"

He pivoted back towards Judge Burger and loudly announced, "This case should be dismissed! The Plaintiff is bogus."

The room reverberated in whispered speculation, causing Judge Burger to bang his gavel several times with calls to order.

Richard sat there rubbing his beard, dumbfounded. He was not prepared for this revelation. His whole case was based on tying specimen 0744 to Lifespan and Amnion to specimen 0744. He swung around on his chair to look at his paralegals for input.

"Where's the DNA lab report? The DNA match?"

They shrugged their shoulders in ignorance too. Somebody forgot to follow up on it.

"What about the FBI guy?"

Unfortunately, all Richard got from his assistants was a vacant look.

Richard quickly motioned for a recess to address this new revelation.

"24 hours," the judge ordered, and dismissed the courtroom.

Norm sat comfortably with legs stretched out below his desk, hands clasped together on his belly. With the smug look of final victory on his face, he casually turned to whisper to an aid, "That should do it!"

Mike came up swiftly from the spectator stand to huddle with Richard and his paralegals. It was a disheartening development, and it put a damper on everyone's spirits. However, Richard remained outwardly optimistic and suggested they meet later in the College Point office, get organized, and try to sort it all out.

* * * * * * *

After the courtroom emptied, Richard packed his briefcase in the vacant silence of the court. The spectators had already bolted out with news of the trial's dramatic ending. Richard was left quietly alone, except for the chatter of distant conversations in the hallway outside. Norm had stumbled on a small point that could do major damage to his case. The hospital records on Amnion's sex were surely wrong, but they were a written hospital document - it was tough evidence to fight.

Richard sighed and picked up his briefcase, strolling over to the windowsill where the planted acorn rested comfortably in its small patch of earth. In the empty room, he wondered if that tree's life would ever see the light of day in this courtroom. Then from behind a woman's voice with a Jamaican accent called, "Pardon me Mister Farmers."

Richard turned to see Nurse Ozzie Smith in the solitude of the empty courtroom.

"Oh, I'm sorry to have you come here today," he said with sincerity, "and never get your call to testify".

"On the contrary, "she replied in her slight Jamaican accent, "I'm glad I did come."

She walked over to the window and picked up the planted acorn cube, examining its four sides. "Sometimes we all need a lesson on the value of life. No matter how insignificant it appears at the time."

Then she explained how she had attended the extraction of specimen 0744 and had subsequently opened the 'egg' after the extraction. That she, in fact, had seen that the inanimate specimen inside – and, it was a female.

Richard felt like the heavens had opened and delivered him from disaster. All he could say was a loud grateful, "Well, hallelujah!"

He hugged the startled witness. Then he looked upward, hands outstretched, and trumpeted out loud like a Baptist minister, "Lord Almighty. Thank you!"

CHAPTER 63
Touché

The following day's trial opened with a motion from Norm for an immediate dismissal, based on the apparent discrepancy between the sexes of Amnion and the hospital record for specimen UH0744.

Judge Burger looked to Richard for his rejoinder.

Richard waisted no time. "If it would please the court, the Plaintiff can produce evidence to the contrary regarding the sex of specimen UH0744."

Norm yelled, "Wait. The written evidence is undisputable."

"I want to see more evidence," the judge said. "Proceed Mister Farmers.".

It was Norm's turn to be shocked, as Richard called Nurse Norm Smith.

Nurse Smith gave her testimony under Richard's careful questioning, and then was turned her over to Norm for cross-examination.

"Well, Nurse Smith," Norm bellowed, "Are you an expert on fetal anatomy?"

"No. I am not."

"Then how do we know you aren't mistaken in what you saw? That this immature specimen's reproductive organs might not have been easily distinguishable?"

The nurse was a bit annoyed by this discrediting tactic and replied, "I can tell a male from a female. Do you need a PhD for that?"

The jury giggled, but Norm persisted unfazed, "Really though. I understand it's difficult to see these sex organ details on a specimen at this maturation stage."

Ozzie was confidently relaxed when she answered defiantly, "That's why the surgeon, Dr. Petersen, was mistaken. He only viewed her through an arthroscopic scope during a complicated hemorrhaging incident. I saw her outside the womb, cleaned of blood. I had that little girl over there, no bigger than my thumb," pointing to Amnion. "In my hand. In the flesh."

Some jurors nodded and the audience gasped.

Norm turned to the jury in conclusion, "Still it's only your word against doctor Petersen and, I might add, the hospital's written records."

"Its more than that," the nurse piped up from behind Norm.

"What's that?" he pivoted back to inquire.

"There's a video tape of the operation."

"What!" a surprised Norm exclaimed.

"Dr. Petersen had the procedure taped to train other surgeons in this new Lifespan technique of removing the placenta intact."

Norm was suddenly caught off guard again. With this new development, it was time to break off the attack - regroup. Disgusted, he began to walk away from the witness saying, "No more questions Your Honor."

Nurse Smith looked up at the Judge and reached into her purse. Holding a memory stick in the air she announced, "I have the copy here. I mean, if you're really interested in seeing the truth of the matter."

"Objection your Honor," Norm barked. "Defense was not given this evidence in advance. It is inadmissible."

Richard rose from the table. "Plaintiff could not provide this evidence in advance, since it arose during the witness's testimony."

Norm walked away, shaking his head, and sat down at his table – frustrated as hell. He buried his face in his palms, and looked down. It was then he noticed that the neurotic Max had brought his Slinky toy, and was cradling it between his legs under the table. Norm gave an angry hiss, "Put that goddamned thing away....and leave it in your office!"

Richard arose and walked over to Ozzie to retrieve the evidence, and excuse the witness with a grateful, "Thank you."

He turned to the bailiff and said, "Please enter this as Plaintiff exhibit 'D'. We'll arrange for the jury and Defense to view it later....that is, if they're really interested in viewing the real facts." Richard returned to his table and said, "Now, Your Honor, may we proceed with this litigation?"

Norm suddenly shot up. He got an idea for another angle and objected again. "This testimony aside, we still don't know that the Plaintiff in this video, wherever she is, is in fact specimen 0744. All that's been demonstrated is that they are both female."

The judge looked impatiently at Richard for his rejoinder.

Greg tugged at Richard's sleeve, pointing to a man in the gallery, and whispered, "Our boy's here."

Richard turned to verify the witness's identity, and breathed a sigh of relief. Then he addressed the court, "Your Honor. I believe this next witness will clarify the Plaintiff's identity once and for all."

"By all means counselor," the judge decreed.

"Plaintiff calls Special Agent Ronald Spence."

The conservatively dressed man came down the aisle with a group of large charts under his arm. With his crew cut, it was clear that this agent was a disciplined, no-nonsense personality. Paralegal Greg arranged a large flat panel TV on a small table alongside the witness stand. During the delay to connect power cords, Norm looked on passively, while preparing his cross-examination. After swearing-in and identifying himself as chief forensic technician for an FBI forensic lab, Richard began questioning his witness.

"Mister Spence, How does government law enforcement distinguish between one unique individual and another?

"One proven method is by comparison of DNA. Like fingerprints, no two are alike."

Richard continued his line of questioning. "You received a blood sample from the plaintiff Amnion?"

"Yes, I did. It was taken and hand carried down to our regional lab in Washington by a retired judge named Allen Roche, the custodian of evidence appointed by the court."

Richard added for clarity, "along with the DNA records secured from University Hospital on Specimen 0744."

"That is correct."

"And what did you do with these blood samples?" asked Richard.

"We ran the usual tests for blood type and other chemical constituents focusing on the PGM (Phosphoglucomutase) and EsD (Esterase D) enzymes."

"And what did you find?"

"The blood workup of the plaintiff Amnion matched the Lifespan record of results for specimen UH0744."

The FBI agent leaned forward and gave the bailiff a memory stick to plug into the TV. With a remote control, he called up a .jpg file containing some charts. He flipped up a columnar bar chart and began to explain the test when Norm immediately stood up. "That's not totally conclusive. Those tests only have a 95% probability of correctness. Not beyond reasonable doubt."

The judge leaned forward and asked, "Mister Farmers?"

"I can clarify." Then, Richard turned and gave Norm a look of annoyance, returning to the witness, "Did you do any further tests?"

"Yes, we did a DNA fingerprint analysis." The witness called up another file. It presented three columns of horizontal bars. The agent explained, "We ran a more precise PCR test using the DNA from a ruptured white blood cell. The same test Lifespan used in screening its fetuses for DNA abnormalities. It's a lot more involved than the PGM. That's why we're a little late in getting results ready for this trial."

Spence leaned forward and explained the chart, "The separation bands represent different molecular weights of various protein structures in the DNA. This first column is the mother's blood sample, the second is Amnion's and the third is specimen UH0744."

The agent followed the row of lines across the columns. "Note that these several bars line up exactly between Amnion and the hospital fetus UH0744, but not the mother's DNA. In her case we only see these three major bar matches."

"Why is that?" Richard inquired.

"Because the mother's blood is not the baby's blood. And, shortly after conception, the fetuses DNA is now a distinct combination of the father's and the mother's DNA."

Richard turned to face Norm, and asked the witness, "What's the reliability of this test?"

"99.99999% accurate," the agent said, "That's a probable error less than one in a million."

Norm turned his attention to frown at Max.

Richard decided to go a little farther with this testimony. "That makes the human fetal life kind of a unique individual within the mother's womb. Doesn't it? Not just another organ of the mother."

Norm objected, "Asking a conclusion from the witness."

Richard answered, "You keep raising the issue of a women's right to privacy, and the lack of humanity in the fetus. This Federal government agency distinguishes human beings based on their DNA structure. When my fetal client was assaulted in your lab, she had her own unique DNA too. Not a specimen as you keep calling her. She was a distinct human being!"

The judge allowed the question to stand, and cautioned Richard again about straying too far from the issue at hand. The witness and his charts were excused.

Norm lodged a motion with the judge to introduce his own DNA experts later in the trial. With no contradictory testimony on hand to debunk a certified lab's results, especially one run by the FBI, Norm excused the witness subject to recall.

At this point in the case, Judge Burger returned to Norm's earlier motion for dismissal and finally ruled, Defense motion for dismissal denied, and banged his gavel. Thereafter, he recessed the Court for the customary 2-

hour lunch.

As usual, Max, Norm, and their entourage headed for their limo in the downstairs garage. They had a reservation at an exclusive French restaurant nearby. Richard, Mike, and the paralegals headed to a Jewish deli across the street from the courthouse. Pastrami on rye and a coke was more like their taste in fine cuisine.

* * * * * * *

Later in the day, when court reconvened, Richard followed the judge's prompting to get back on the track of addressing the issue at hand - that Lifespan exceed their State donor license when they began taking placentas.

Richard called Dr. Sterling Roberts of the government NIH. Roberts was one of those career researchers living on the government gravy train, and looked, typically, like a college professor - mid fifties, salt and pepper beard , thinning hair. Thin build from spending most of his self-indulgent life jogging and eating vegan cuisine. He had every intention of spending a long time collecting on his lucrative government pension.

Richard glanced down at his tablet. A cartoon of Daffy Duck appeared when he entered the doctor's name. It said, *You are despicable!* Richard smiled and glanced back at Mike, realizing his old friend must have gotten into the software with a graphics clip art package again.

After the swearing in and usual background credentials questions, Richard became more specific. "You' are the science administrator on this fetal experimentation area for the NIH. Did you have oversight responsibility for Lifespan Corporation's operations?"

"Yes," the witness replied with a hint of smugness.

"Did you or the NIH ever audit Lifespan for compliance to their State license?"

The doctor gave a bewildered look, as if to comment, what for?

Richard persisted. "Did you ever check to see if they were processing fetuses over 12 weeks gestation?"

"Well, not to my knowledge," he hesitantly replied.

Richard shook his head in obvious disappointment, "Our taxes at work." Then followed up quickly, "Well, I'll get right down to the heart of the matter doctor,"

Richard said firmly, "Under the decoupling license, did Lifespan have any authority to extract placentas?"

Dr. Roberts hesitated a moment. He was mainly concerned with his own job security and pension at NIH, and the possibility of being ridiculed for failing to take action against Lifespan. His reply was carefully worded, but betrayed a certain air of controlled hostility.

"While the special donor program does not specifically allow taking the placenta, it does not specifically prohibit it either."

Richard sensed he was dealing with a clever PhD, and realized he'd have to get this witness irritated to undo him. He simply asked, "Do you also believe the placenta to be a separate organ from the fetus?"

A slightly more uncertain Sterling answered, "Well, uh. Yes. Yes, I guess so."

"Good of you to agree with the rest of the medical community," a sarcastic Richard replied.

"Now let's suppose, under the decoupling extraction license, Lifespan Corporation decided to take out a woman's uterus with the fetus? From your reply that's not prohibited by State license either."

"Objection Your Honor!" Norm screamed. "That's a hypothetical question!

"Sustained," the Judge acknowledged. "Withdraw the question counsel."

Richard acquiesced. "Your Honor. I will rephrase."

He returned to confront the learned witness with, "What organs can be extracted from a woman under the State decoupling license, and what organs can't be extracted?"

Dr. Roberts becoming annoyed at being maneuvered into giving the answer that Richard pressed him to deliver. He became evasive. "I can't say. Beyond the fetal specimen, I don't know."

"I understand you personally authored the medical wording of the State Special Donor License," Richard reminded him, as he turned to face the jury with his eyebrows raised in suspicion. "What was your intent then? What limits did you want set in doing this?"

"Objection," Norm cried. "Badgering the witness. He cannot answer for the whole of government's intent in issuing this license."

Richard looked back at the judge and replied, "I didn't ask the witness for the government's opinion. I asked for his opinion!"

"Overruled," the agitated Judge said, "and pay closer attention to the questions, Mister Stark!"

The audience and jurors smiled at the slight reprimand. A disgusted Norm plopped back into his seat at the Defense table. Norm sat down and leaned down to rub his forehead.

Richard returned to examining Roberts. "So what was your intent, Dr. Roberts? What's your limit on extracting organs during these operations?"

The doctor hesitated, still not wishing to give Richard the answer he wanted, and finally said dryly. "I really never gave it any thought. I would suppose that other medical regulations would restrict the limits during operative cases."

A tenacious Richard would not let him off the hook. "Once again doctor, what do you think? Where do you think the limits should be?"

The doctor didn't respond, and Richard turned to the jury shaking his head in obvious disdain, "Non-responsive your Honor. This is a federal government official responsible for monitoring Lifespan's compliance to its State decoupling license." Then he looked back at the contemptuous witness, "And he doesn't know where to place limits on their behavior. He doesn't even know what he himself believes. God protect us all from this public bureaucrat."

Judge Burger interrupted, giving Richard a stern look. "Mister Framers! No more proselytizing!"

"Forgive me Your Honor. Comment withdrawn."

Turning to face the witness again, Richard looked down at his tablet and fingered the touch screen. The irritated witness leaned slightly forward as if to glimpse what the attorney was looking at. A vexed Dr. Roberts began to stutter something. Then Richard held up his palm for silence, and redirected his next volley of questions at the flustered doctor. Richard looked up and inquired, "Did you ever work for Lifespan?"

"No." he quickly replied, "I never worked directly for the company." He paused to gauge Richard's doubting demeanor and quickly modified his statement. "I mean....I mean not as an employee."

"I know," Richard added, "but did you ever receive any compensation from Lifespan? For consulting services rendered?"

"Well, uh, yes," he reluctantly replied.

"Dr. Roberts," Richard interrupted, "the company records show you receiving consulting compensation averaging about $90,000 per year. Richard caustically added, "Does that sound more familiar now?"

"Well, yes. Maybe."

"Good," Richard quickly acknowledged. "Add that to your $250,000 yearly government salary, and some might even say you are a rather wealthy fellow."

Norm objected, "This is absurd. The plaintiff is badgering the witness again!"

Richard faced the judge and rebutted, "I think the relevance will become clear with next question."

Judge Burger nodded approval and waved a hand to proceed.

Richard returned to the meat of his questioning. "You say you were compensated as a consultant there, yet you were in charge of overseeing their compliance to their government license." Richard turned with a grin to the jury, "Didn't that appear to you as a conflict of interest? A conflict of interest, to accept compensation from the company you supposed to be overseeing? "

The doctor tried to appear nonchalant in reply, "Well ...it isn't unusual for government researchers to work on their own time for private organizations."

"Can't argue that point doctor. Except I found six other NIH personnel on Lifespan's payroll. They were also responsible for monitoring Lifespan's compliance to their decoupling license."

Richard paused to let the message sink in with the jury. Then turned to continue his interrogation. "But let' us get back to you, doctor. Now what work were you involved in there as a consultant? What project?"

Dr. Roberts shifted in his seat, and hesitated again, trying to collect his thoughts. "I assisted in the investigation of *in-vitro* fertilization experiments on embryos."

"Human embryos?"

"Yes."

"To what end?"

The doctor wrinkled his brow and gave his interrogator a quizzical look.

Richard repeated his question, "What was the name of the project? What was its objective?"

The witness remained silent. The doctor knew full well what Lifespan was up to.

"Come on Mister Roberts. You spent 5 years on this project." Richard looked down at his computer tablet pad, "Received over a quarter million dollars in compensation from Lifespan Corporation, I believe."

The audience gasped at hearing the dollar figure.

Norm felt his witness slipping into perjury, and shot up howling, "Badgering the witness!"

"Objection overruled," the judge announced.

Doctor Roberts sought to minimize his role in all this by countering, "I can't speak for Lifespan Corporation, or its business objectives for their research. My investigative role was strictly in the area of thickening the mucous coating of the uterine lining to aid implantation."

"Now that sounds innocent enough, doctor," Richard smiled politely, "Implantation into what? A woman? A machine?"

The doctor didn't answer right away. His hesitation implied some other unspoken answer, and gave Richard another opportunity to remark, "Could it have been Project Greenhouse? The mysterious Job 901? Could it have been to artificially grow your own herd of human donors for slaughter?"

"Objection Your Honor!" Norm shot up, howling like a wounded animal. Calls for speculation."

The audience was in a dither with Richard's inflammatory remark, the noise building into a low rumble of whispers. Judge Burger pounded his gavel, and threatened to remove the audience if it didn't come to order.

Norm struggled to be heard above the background commotion and shouted, "He's calling for a conclusion from the witness!"

"Objection sustained," Justice Burger bellowed, still hammering his gavel.

The crowd finally quieted down with the arrival of more bailiffs, and the threat of removing some spectators. The judge admonished Richard, "Less conjecture Mister Farmers – please."

Richard acknowledged, "Question withdrawn Your Honor. May I proceed?"

With the judge's nod Richard returned to the now thoroughly unsettled witness, "Did you take the Hippocratic oath for your MD license, doctor?

"Yes, I did."

"Have you abided by that oath in all the things you've done professionally?"

An indignant Roberts replied smugly, "Of course I have."

"Then in keeping with that oath, have you abstained from whatever is deleterious and mischievous to human life? Have you never administered a deadly drug or participated in killing a live human fetal life?"

Norm objected again, and was immediately overruled by the judge who ordered, "The witness will answer the question."

"Of course not. I'm a pure researcher."

For the first, time the doctor showed signs of perspiration on his forehead and water in his eyes. Deep down inside a haunting memory came back of the night he assisted Dr. Strauss in the mass killing of the living fetuses some weeks ago in the Lifespan R&D lab. Back then it didn't seem so bad. Back when it was out of sight, out of the public eye – done and buried.

He looked to Norm for some kind of support or direction. All he could think about was self-preservation, protecting his cushy government job and pension.

Richard grew impatient and threatened, "We have other witnesses that can answer that question for you. Who did you terminate?"

After some continued delay by the witness, the annoyed judge prompted him for a reply.

Roberts looked across at Richard's stern demeanor and finally whimpered, "I uh... I uh, invoke the Fifth Amendment." Then he looked up at the judge for support, "Can't I?"

The judge unsympathetically explained, "Yes, if you believe you're testimony could lead to your prosecution for a criminal act."

Richard observed the disillusioned look on the jurist faces. As far as they were concerned, Dr. Roberts had already convicted himself. On his way back to the Plaintiff table Richard commented out loud with disdain,

"You've been under oath for this testimony, doctor. I wonder if you really know what it means to take an oath."

"Objection, Your Honor," Norm hollered, "Counsel is harassing the witness. This witness has broken no laws."

Richard was quick to reply in rebuttal, "We are simply trying to establish the character of the witness."

He turned to face Norm, "Criminals are people who are caught breaking the law. Then there are other criminals, who don't get caught."

Richard returned his gaze to the doctor. "Those without character. The ones that skirt the intent of the law, but manage to stay concealed in the murky gray area."

The judge acknowledged Norm's objection. "Sustained… and Mister Framers, you are clearly on thin ice in this Court. Jury will disregard his comments."

Richard apologized, and dismissed the witness.

Norm waved cross-examine. He wanted this witness forgotten as soon as possible.

* * * * * * *

At home, Richard was hunched over his desk at 11 o'clock in the evening with just a desk lamp to bathe a darkened room. The house was serene with the children already in bed on a school night. He had spent the night preparing for tomorrow's day in court.

Evon stood quietly behind her husband sitting in his dimly lit study, reflecting on the testimony she had heard from her seat in the courtroom gallery. It was now apparent why Richard was so adamant about fighting these ruthless people, both at Lifespan and in the government. Evon gently massaged his tense shoulders, and Richard turned wearily to look back at her compassionate face above his head. At the same time, his squinty eyes revealed both fatigue and appreciation.

His wife said, "I saw you in court today. I was proud of you. The way you handled those smart PhDs ...the other attorneys. I'm sorry I doubted your abilities."

"Yeah, but how are the kids holding up at school?" he inquired, "with their friends? Their teachers?"

"Actually, with the other kids quite well, hon – the teachers not so good. The trial is bringing this whole fetal life issue out of the closet. Making people face up to it and think. They even talk about it in private conversations now."

She kissed the bald spot atop his head and hugged him from behind. Richard reveled in his wife's embrace. There was nothing more soothing to him right now, than a gentle woman's sympathetic caresses.

"And I did miss your support honey bunch," he said, slowly swiveling in his chair to capture her on his lap. "In fact," he sighed, "I have just enough energy for one more thing."

Evon smiled at the mischievous twinkle in his eye, and playfully plunked his blunt nose. She coyly teased, "You naughty boy. If I let you make love to me, you won't be so nasty in court tomorrow."

Richard picked her up and placed her gently on the loveseat, and responded, "Soon my face will have that wonderful afterglow that the female jurors will love."

He proceeded to methodically unbutton her loose blouse and buried his face between her smooth warm breasts. Evon slid down to a more comfortable position on the loveseat, and delightfully enjoyed giving herself to her husband's passion.

When it was over, Evon lay in her man's fatigued embrace, their hearts still pounding and lungs grasping for air. Having satiated her husband's lust, she coyly commented on his performance, "My, but you did have some energy left after badgering all those witnesses."

Then she added provocatively, "And what are you going to expect if you win this case?"

Richard picked himself up and thought about it for just a second, finally answering, "How about gel beds and mirrors on the ceiling at the Hideaway Motel."

They quietly laughed as they picked up their clothes and headed upstairs to shower and sleep.

CHAPTER 64
Loss of a friend

Phylis fidgeted in her chair on the witness stand, her throat feeling dry and uncomfortable. Dressed in a ruffled white blouse and dark blue skirt and blazer, at least she looked professional enough, even attractive. A drink of water helped to sooth the itch in her larynx and relax her a little bit. Scanning the hundred or so faces in the courtroom, it was hard to believe that her involvement all started with answering Michael's 'Used Male' web posting. Except right now, her mind was preoccupied with how she would holdup under cross-examination.

A sympathetic Richard started her testimony off with softball questions about her early employment with Lifespan and the nature of her duties in the specimen procurement department. He queried her specifically about specimen UH0744, and then the commission records she kept on each specimen she delivered to the company. Phylis produced the memory stick from her office terminal containing the identification numbers of each specimen, including those that were extracted with placentas intact and sent to the R&D lab.

Norm sat on his chair uncomfortably surprised by the physical evidence represented by a memory module. Up until now, he had been assured by Strauss and Max that no written tracking records were kept on the R&D specimens. And based on those assurances he assumed that he could debunk the testimony of specimens going to the R&D lab by generating conflicting testimony between any witnesses. However, this memory module was written evidence of a number of specimens that were actually sent to the lab. Worse yet, it was a former Lifespan employee presenting it.

An annoyed Norm turned around and leaned over the railing to privately consult with Max in the spectator gallery. It was obvious that they were having a difference of opinion. Judge Burger noted the loud murmurs and banged his gavel saying, "Mister Stark! Silence! Do I have to treat you like school boys, and separate your seats?"

His reprimand brought a giggle from some in the audience and jury.

Richard released the witness to cross-examination, satisfied that he'd established the trail of Amnion from University hospital to Lifespan's R&D labs.

Then Norm stood up to cross examine the witness. If Phylis was going to be unnerved, this was the moment.

"Misses Santino," Norm said authoritatively, "this memory record was kept by you personally. Wasn't it?

"Yes."

"Did you ever tell anyone else of its existence? Your supervisor? A colleague?"

"N-no." Phylis stuttered nervously.

Norm thought he had something here, and followed the thread. "And why not? What were you trying to hide?"

"It has my commission salary record on it too," she answered, a bit indignantly. "I felt my commissions were personal. I didn't want my fellow employees to know my salary."

"So you could have made this whole list up yourself. At any time."

"No! They were recorded at the time they happened," Phylis adamantly retorted. "You can look at the last SAVE dates in the file directory."

"Well, anybody can manipulate these kinds of computer records."

Phylis answered, "You probably would know how to do that better than me. You're the corporate executive!"

The audience laughed at her answer, and Judge Burger banged his gavel for order.

Norm objected to the judge, "The witness will answer the questions, not make accusations."

The justice leaned over to Phylis and congenially advised her to endeavor to give simple yes or no answers. She politely nodded agreement to the judge.

A satisfied Norm felt he had made his point and began his concluding remarks. "So, you're the only one with access to this disk record, and the only one who seems to have made a record of all this alleged specimen activity?"

Phylis' eyes glanced downward and she paused for a moment. A gesture that psychologically cast doubt on her testimony. All of a sudden, it seemed crucial to recall something to corroborate her own records. Her anxious mind began to feel like it was racing with dizzying speed to come up with something.

Mike watched sympathetically from the gallery wishing he could do or say something to help her. Norm had taken some good evidence and managed to put his own dubious spin on it. Richard looked on passively, but thinking ahead of how to undo whatever came of Norm's manipulations.

Finally, Phylis looked up. She was more confident now, and spoke with an almost buoyant tone. "If you check Lifespan's Payroll Department records," she started, "you'll find a specimen by specimen accounting in the commissions earned records for everything I delivered and recorded here."

"Yes, but what proof that they went to the R&D lab?"

Phylis answered smartly. "After a few commission screw ups, a procedure was instituted by the Payroll Department where they entered a notation for those commissions that didn't go through normal receiving and went straight to the secretive R&D lab."

Norm was caught off balance again. As far as he knew, no one in Lifespan management had told him of such a procedure. Norm inquired, "Who authorized this?"

"I don't know. My boss at the time, Jerry Klein in Procurement, said he was told about it by the Finance department."

A disgusted Norm turned to look back at CFO John Lombardo seated in the gallery behind the Defense table for some clue to all this. The shrug of John's shoulders and his dopey look seemed to once again signify management's ignorance of their own operations.

Phylis volunteered from behind, "I'm sure you can check this out with the people who worked there. - in Finance."

Norm wasn't about to pursue this line any further without more analysis. So, he dismissed the witness.

Phylis remained seated and added earnestly, "I can give you other Lifespan employee names if you're really interested. I'm sure they'd be happy to confirm ..."

The exasperate attorney turned his back, angrily saying, "No more questions Your Honor." Then he simply dismissed her with a wave of his hand, and returned to his Defense table seat. Not very polite. Phylis could care less. She made her point.

While seated, a note was passed to Norm by one of his paralegals. It was a short telegram from his detective in Bangkok. Norm's gloominess disappeared abruptly, replaced by a smile of relief. Apparently, Eve had been recovered from the drug warlords up north, and was admitted to a hospital in Bangkok. He had no details yet. At least he knew she was alive and safe.

* * * * * * *

In the late afternoon, after court adjournment, Mike sat down and relaxed among the stacks of the Lifespan documents forcibly obtained during discovery phase of this litigation. Richard's makeshift College Point law office had become crammed to over-flowing with personal computers, tablets, DVDs cardboard boxes piled one atop the other, and file cabinets jammed with folders. Tables were piled with the evidence they had collectively sifted from the thousands of memos, faxes and accounting records of Lifespan. Mike and the legal crew had spent nights and weekends doing non-stop reading, discussing, copying, and feeding Richard with anything that added to the case. They even programmed Richard's tablet computer to guide him through the interrogation of witnesses.

After months of tireless effort there was barely space left in the room for the investigators themselves. It became so congested that from across the small room you could barely see the top of Mike's head seated among the clutter.

The team Richard assembled had collectively put in thousands of man-hours together. They had built a meritorious case distilled from a monumental mountain of facts and data.

From Mike's perspective, the really hard dog-work was over. It only remained for Richard to methodically deliver the evidence to the jury with pizzazz. So, he felt comfortably at ease among the stacks of paper, as though they were now his fortification against failure.

For Richard, nearby, today was not going to be easy or relaxing. There was tragic news that had to be revealed to an unsuspecting friend. He stood up from behind his desk and solemnly approached Mike saying, "Mike, I don't know how to say this easily. I don't know that I can entirely accept it myself." He took a deep breath and rasped, "Your friend...Dr. Joel Rosen is not going to testify."

"Cold feet?"

After a further pause to find some more soothing words, Richard could only add, "No...no... I'm afraid he's dead."

Mike thought his heart skipped a beat from the sudden shock. "When? How? " Was all he could muster for a reaction.

"Police say it was a suicide, Mike. I couldn't get much more detail than that."

Mike's eyes began to fill with tears. Deep down inside he knew a happy Joel too well, for too long, to accept that explanation. Mike had no details, but immediately, in his gut, he knew Joel was murdered. Too much of a coincidence, it happening right before he was to testify.

Mike felt guilt well before remorse or outrage. Guilt for being the one who encouraged him to get involved in all this.

He thought about Joel's wife and kids. *How would they remember their father? Like some nutcase that killed himself?*

Mike kept shaking his head, and choking on his attempts to speak. His head sort of slumped on his shoulders. He leaned forward, elbows on his knees, hands over his reddened face.

Richard left and came back with a glass of water, which Mike gratefully accepted. Then Mike drew a deep breath and exhaled in resignation, his nose running profusely. Richard found a tissue box and offered it to his friend.

"You know Richie," Mike sniffled, "we played softball together. Even won a softball league championship together."

Richard sat down on a table next to Mike and patted his shoulder. "Nothing like a winning season," he nostalgically replied in comradeship.

"I thought," Mike sobbed, "that once Joel was out of Lifespan, he was out of danger." Finally, Mike blew his nose, and, slowly, his composure began to come back.

It was then that Mike went on to explain the missing Capitol Post reporter, and the suspicious limo that dogged Joel this past week. "No one had any reason to just kill him," he contended. "The Lifespan cat's already out of the bag."

Richard weighed the gravity of Mike's accusation. He had been around New York long enough to know that anything can be arranged in this city for the right price. In this trial, they were playing for high stakes in a town that traded with unbridled violence and greed. For that culture, eternal life would be the ultimate trading commodity. Among the Lifespan executives and investors, it would be just cause to kill any number of people, including himself.

"This may appear insensitive, Mikey. Only, we have to discuss how to handle what was going to be Joel's testimony next week. All we have is his written affidavit to submit to the court."

"To hell with the case," Mike adamantly replied, "all I want to know is the name of the detective on Joel's case."

"At least that I can help you with," Richard replied sympathetically.

An agitated Mike continued, "Then I get Max Brewster myself. My way!"

"Hold on 'Crash'," Richard said, remembering Mike's football nickname. "Slow down here. You will get yourself a life sentence in Elmira and jeopardize this case."

Mike was as stubborn as usual, and demanded, "You think you're gonna catch that slippery dirtbag with all this courtroom mumbo-jumbo?"

Richard chided him, "Just give me a chance before you go 'Rambo' on us."

At this point he knew Mike needed some space to work off his emotions. Certainly, this was grounds for a delay in court. Richard could use the extra time to regroup and figure out what this all means.

"Mike, just keep your cool for a couple days. I'll get back to you on this….I promise."

They stood up and awkwardly hugged each other, ever so briefly. That show of emotion had to be brushed off by some manly fist bumps.

Then Richard changed subjects and asked, "By the way how is Amy doing?"

"Good days, bad days," Mike replied. "In fact she's scheduled to move out of NICU in a few days, once her bowels straighten out. They said something about necrotizing enterocolitis."

"What the hell is that???"

"She needs mother's milk to supply some kind of harmless bacteria that coats the intestinal wall – keeps the bad germs from getting a toehold. There's these lactating woman that come forward to supply breast milk at $4 bucks an ounce. Our insurance won't cover that. Claim they don't cover it in New Jersey where the insurance is issued. Go figure. So I pay out-of-pocket $50 a day. Anyway, I think my daughter is worth it."

"Good," Richard said hopefully. "I could use her presence in the courtroom soon."

After Mike departed, Richard began to have second thoughts about his friend and his deepening relationship with Amnion.. Phylis had already told him about Maria, the real mother. Her gentle words at Amnion's decoupling, 'Take care of my lamb' - and of Mike's possessiveness. It was obvious to Richard that once the little girl's identity became public, the natural mother would fight for custody. A battle Mike would probably lose, and maybe should lose. For the sake of his friend, Richard wasn't looking forward to that day.

CHAPTER 65
Lifespan unravels

A cursing Max stormed out of the Board of Directors meeting, stomped across the reception area, and then disappeared into his office with a slam of his door. Doors were also slammed shut in the Board Room. From the earlier shouts inside the meeting, the ad minis outside were aware that something was in the wind. It was apparent that Maxes presentation to the Board about further delays and more technical problems on Project Greenhouse went over like a bomb.

Alone in his office suite, the tyrannical CEO looked at his flushed red face in the mirror by the door. Wrinkles and crow's feet, were reforming around his eyes, and creases were now visible again above his mouth. The lack of specimen extract from Dr. Strauss was already allowing aging to resume at a rapid pace.

Gazing in the mirror, his fingers stretched his skin as if to regain the smoothness of youth. Running his hands through his hair collected a half dozen loose strands. He rolled up his sleeve to observe the needle tracks from the last injection treatments weeks ago. They did not disappear as fast as before. It was as if both his physical and financial well being were unraveling at the same time. 'Project Greenhouse' was more than just a financial imperative. His youthful life was on the line now, and it showed.

The problems within the artificial womb caused by Mike's sabotage of the instrumentation had worked. What's more, his bugs had still gone undetected by his project researchers. To explain the failures, Dr. Strauss had spoken at the board meeting, confidently theorizing that there was some genetic defect in the immature fertilized eggs that was causing them to detach from the mucous membrane. He said it would take another few weeks to complete a DNA screening test of samples to confirm this conclusion. He did not dare disclose that he and his technical team of NIH consultants were baffled.

Unfortunately, time and more delays were now a luxury that a cash-strapped Lifespan could hardly afford. At the board meeting, some Directors expressed doubt in the timeframes presented by Strauss to overcome further technical hurdles. Plus, there was another several million dollars in development costs to bring the technology to commercial production. Worse yet clinical trials could add years to a payback of their growing investment. Some members suggested liquidation.

At this point the investors were more interested in limiting their financial exposure and losses. Adding to the negative atmosphere was the ongoing litigations that were running up astronomical legal fees. At one point in the meeting, a Board member, representing the investment bank's interest, challenged Max's optimism on 'Greenhouse' by demanding that

Max put up another 10 million of his own cash before the board could consider funding the another million.

Max wasn't about to increase his exposure either. He still had his own long-term interest in the California company, Extentech. A little detail that these investor Board members knew nothing about. If his money was going anywhere, it was traveling west to Extentech.

For the first time in Max's business career, he'd heard suggestions from his contributing partners like; going Chapter 11, cutting losses, bailing out. His image as the savvy wheeler-dealer was crumbling. The usual verbal bravado of 'turning the corner', and 'attracting more capital' now fell on disbelieving ears.

By now, Max had almost 15 million dollars of his personal capital invested in Lifespan. It was the first time he'd ever risked any of his own money on putting a deal together. The prospect of bankruptcy and getting back 5 cents on the dollar was totally unacceptable.

Infuriated, he paced the floor in his office, grumbling, "Goddamn engineers! Fuckin' biochemists! Bullshitting PhD's!"

Norm soon knocked on the door and entered in time to hear the tail end of Max's tirade. Max looked up and added, "Friggin' lawyers too!"

Norm calmly brushed off the insult, and chalked it up to Max's usual obnoxious temper, and sat down to relax on the couch.

Max continued his lament. "I tell you Norm. That Strauss is trying to screw me. I told him off a month ago and now he's getting even. He's purposely screwing this project!"

Norm shrugged his shoulders, seeing this R&D issue in its proper perspective. The immediate legal and financial problems of Lifespan were of greater concern to him. In his mind, the technological future was a secondary consideration that would have to wait.

"Have a seat," he calmly suggested, "there's a change in the case you should be aware of."

Max suspended his tantrum and retreated to his comfortable leather chair behind his desk.

Norm said, "This lawyer Farmers has dropped you and Strauss from his lawsuit."

Before he could finish, a delighted Max interrupted, "Great! Good news for a change. The schvatza lawyer's losing his nerve!"

Norm relaxed, crossing his legs and sat back comfortably in his seat.

"Uh, not quite," he said. "You see, before, as defendants, you couldn't be called as witnesses and testify against yourselves. Dropping you and Peter as parties to the complaint allows him to subpoena you as witnesses in court. And, later, your testimony could expose you to perjury or a criminal suit by the feds."

Max's face dropped. Up until now, he could sit back and contemptuously complain about how poorly each witness did on the stand, immune from direct questioning himself. Protected by his corporate veil. Now he was going to get his turn in the barrel too.

Norm watched the color drain from Max's face.

"You gotta do something," Max implored, now leaning forward on his desk, "You've got to cut a deal. Settle this horse shit out of court. Get this mess behind us."

"I'll continue trying," Norm replied with some resignation. "However, we should plan for the worst." He tried to bolster Maxes spirit saying, "Keep in mind that I'll be with you for your written deposition. And we'll work out a method to coach you on the witness stand."

Max's wasn't really listening and his thoughts turned inward to his syndicate connection, 'Tony the Tiger'. If he could get Joel Rosen bumped off, then why not this Amnion thing? After all, breaking into a hospital and pulling some plug is easier than arranging a hit. With his clout, all it should take is a phone call to arrange it.

Satisfied with his plan, and assuming this meeting with his counsel was over, he rose and began to head for a lunch date with his new mistress, the young girl from Accounting. Norm stood up and interrupted his departure saying, "There is one bit of good news."

Max stopped immediately, desperate to hear something positive.

"Eve's on her way home next week!" Norm said enthusiastically.

There was a long silent pause as Max's face sagged, and he couldn't decide whether to escape or stay.

He finally feigned interest asking, "Oh how nice. How is she feeling after her ordeal?"

"Well, I'll tell you Max. For a woman who was gang raped for over a month – it's remarkable that she's alive. We had her in the hospital for three weeks recovering. Dysentery, gonorrhea. Even a broken wrist and nose. She lost about 30 pounds."

Max listened politely and dispassionately. He was already thinking ahead about her unexpected return. From his perspective, she was just going to be more excess baggage to carry around. With all his troubles lately, this was the last thing he needed to deal with.

"I think we should keep her away from work," he cleverly advised. "Get proper medical attention in one of those convalescing homes - lots of rest."

Max continued walking towards the door, implying the end of the discussion. Norm followed him out, content that Max didn't ask about how much it had cost Lifespan to get her back.

Then Max turned with a start, "Listen Norm, if this Amnion thing expired tomorrow what happens to the lawsuit?'

Norm became wary of the question. "Dead things can't sue anybody. I understand the Plaintiff is out of the NICU. Why the question? I hope you are not contemplating anything stupid!"

Max just smiled and glided out the door

* * * * * * *

The pudgy middle-aged NYPD Detective Sergeant sat at his old wooden desk, jelly donut in hand. His pock-marked face betrayed a youth of chronic acne problems that never altered his eating habits. Even his mottled face fit right in with the dingy surroundings.

He leaned forward and took such a huge bite out of his donut that some of the mushy strawberry filling squeezed out and dripped on the desk blotter below. Mouth full, he reached for his coffee cup across the desk, inadvertently dragging his tie through the sticky droppings.

Even Mike had to grimace at this spectacle of 'New York's Finest'. Worse yet, this clown's salary was pretty near his ...only Mike wasn't getting a guaranteed three-quarter salary pension starting at age 55 for the rest of his miserable life.

And this guy's desk. It was strewn with forms, carbon copies, mail trays, and an old black and white computer monitor left over from some old PC network. Mike's impression was that this beanbag still looked for clues with a magnifying glass. The dilapidated station house itself was an embodiment of the New York urban blight just outside the window. There was little here to instill any confidence in Mike - only the signs of political corruption and personal indifference.

The shabby detective put his donut down and found a napkin in his draw, proceeding to lick and wipe his tie clean. "So, you think this guy Rosen was murdered," he mumbled through the donut fragments, still remaining in his mouth.

Mike pressed his argument, in spite of the unprofessional demeanor of this public servant. "You tell me how he died, and I'll tell you how he was murdered."

The plump detective gave a shrewd smile and slouched back into his chair. He rocked slowly, forward and back, and clasped his hands over his protruding gut. With each pitch forward, he delivered another sentence in staccato fashion.

"Shot in the head -
In the hospital parking lot -
In his car -
Driver's side -
Gun registered to him in Pennsylvania."

Then he leaned forward, slapped his pudgy hands flat on the desk and added smugly, "Suicide! Any more questions?"

"Yeah. Which side of the head was he shot on?"

"Right side," he answered, holding his finger to his head. "Just behind the right ear."

Mike replied, "Joel was left handed."

"So what? Strange people off themselves in strange ways."

Mike continued, "What was the bullet trajectory?"

"Out his ear on the opposite side."

"Well," Mike insisted, "Don't you think it strange to blow your brains out from behind the ear? I mean, I couldn't imagine how to hold a gun behind my opposite ear and point it."

The sergeant laughed knowingly, and demonstrated with his left finger pointed to his ear. "Hold it upside down!"

Mike was getting increasingly frustrated by this rush to judgment of his friend's death. He asked, "Did you trace the bullet to his gun?"

"Nope. The bullet went out the window....God knows where."

Mike lamented, "And nobody heard or saw anything?"

"Nope."

"What about garage CCTV?"

"Broken that day."

The sergeant leaned forward and tried to commiserate with Mike. "Look buddy, let me tell you something, and save us both a lot of time. The word here, from the top down, is your pal was a suicide. So, there's not gonna be any more investigation."

He leaned back and folded his arms in a gesture of finality, "Sorry. That's it!"

Mike began to fume. This whole thing began to stink from the bottom to the top. Justice wasn't to be had when the big boys got involved.

Mike stood up and leaned across the desk to confront the detective. "This guy - my friend. He was going to testify against some real big time murderers. And you're not doin' jackshit to track down the killer."

The detective shrugged his shoulders and reached for the rest of his donut. Mike noticed his objective and quickly drove his fist down hard on the uneaten half of the jelly donut. Its smashed contents spewed out all over the desk and splattered the detectives shirt and tie with globs of crimson goo.

The detective bolted straight up in rage, and looked down at his shirt. "You asshole" he groaned. "You fuckin' asshole," he bellowed. "Get the fuck outta here!"

Mike left quickly without another word. If he needed evidence that Joel was assassinated under someone's orders, it was this interview.

While walking back to his Mustang, Mike became increasingly focused on Max Brewster, as the only suspect with the motive and the power to do his friend in. He was convinced more than ever, that with the trial and all the lawyering Richie Farmers could do, was not going to get Brewster. That even if Richie was successful, Max would never be held accountable for his murderous deeds.

He made up his mind that he would avenge his friend's death in his own time and at the right place. No one would know. Not Richie, not even Phylis. This deed would be between him, Brewster and the Almighty. Even if it meant going to hell, Mike would have the satisfaction of dragging Max down there with him. Maybe even get to beat the crap out of him for all eternity.

CHAPTER 66
Joel speaks from grave

Before court was called to order everyday, Richard had a habit of walking over to the windowsill with a small cup of water to tend to his planted acorn. It became a daily ritual that the jury would observe with quiet amusement. He would hold up the clear plastic cube and observed that the acorn buried within had split open. It had cracked open exposing the inner pulp that would feed the sapling. Below, it sprouted a thin scraggly brown root that plunged downward into the moist mother earth. A separate stalk, cream white and silky smooth, probed its way upwards through the coarse soil. Richard made an exaggerated observation of the plexiglass container to make sure the jury was paying attention.

A frustrated Norm observed these pre-session antics and scowled to Richard, "Counselor! Really ? Can we avoid these quaint horticulture lessons and get on with the relevant issues in this trial?" He plopped back down at his table in quiet consternation over this little distraction, impatient to get on with the subject matter at hand.

Richard calmly returned the clear cube to the windowsill, so the jury would see the germinating acorn as they left for the day.

****

The courtroom was called into session, and Judge Burger said, "Everyone please be seated." He then turned to Richard. "Ready to proceed Mr Farmers?"

"Your Honor, Richard said, "The Plaintiff would now like to enter the testimony of Dr. Joel Rosen."

Norm shifted in his seat to stare up and across at the tall black attorney. By now, it was common knowledge that the doctor had purportedly killed himself only a few days before.

391

Richard said, "In light of the witness's untimely death." He paused to glare, almost accusingly at Max seated next to Norm. Then continued, "I have requested a close friend and associate of his to read his pre-trial sworn statement into the record."

Richard turned towards the gallery and announced, "I call Michael Santino to the witness stand. Norm huddled in caucus with his other legal aides, vexed by this unusual turn of events. Max leaned over to whisper something in Norm's ear. Mike Santino took the stand while the Defense table hummed with panicked voices.

Richard approached the witness stand as Norm raised an objection, and came forward. "Permission to approach the bench?"

The judge waived them forward, and leaned forward to hear argument. Richard reached up and handed a copy of Joel's deposition to the judge.

Norm started first. "Your Honor, you can't delegate one witness's testimony to another. It becomes hearsay. Besides, how do I cross examine a dead witness?"

The judge looked to Richard for rebuttal, and Richard responded. "Your Honor, I am simply having a sworn deposition read verbatim into the record by that witness, who, for obvious reasons, is unable to complete his testimony himself. Mister Santino signed as a witness to the deposition, and was named as involved in the same subject matter. Therefore, as a deposition, it is not hearsay. The Defense attorneys were at this deposition meeting and did have an opportunity to cross-examine Doctor Rosen at that time. It is my intent to raise those same defense questions also during the reading of the deposition. Defense will get fair treatment before the jury."

Judge Burger sat back to digest this unusual approach. Norm still did not like it, and maintained his objection.

Finally, the judge addressed the jury. "This is highly unusual, but in light of the witness's untimely death and the serious nature of his testimony, I will allow his words to be read, as well as the words of the Defense attorneys present during the deposition process."

He turned to the two attorneys and said, "Objection overruled. Mister Farmers, Mister Santino. You will confine your words strictly to only those written in the sworn statement before me… and nothing added!"

Norm shook his head in disappointment and returned to a fuming Max, who leaned over and whispered in his ear, "I put the son-of-a-bitch six feet under and I still didn't get rid of him?"

Norm was shocked. For all of Maxes foibles he could not believe that his boss could actually orchestrate the doctor's death. He looked Max straight in the eyes, and concluded that it must be true. Someone else might have been repulsed by such a revelation, except Norm, was a professional lawyer. This was his client, right or wrong, and paid to provide the best defense money can buy.

On a personal level, Norm would not forget what Max did. Or, for that matter, abandoning Eve West in Asia.

Meanwhile, on the witness stand, the role-playing testimony had Richard playing the part of the two attorneys, and Mike his friend Joel. The presentation added a stage-like dimension to the words.

Mike began reading Joel's account of conversations with Dr. Strauss, his clinical and pathological conclusions of fetal material coming out of the R&D lab. The medical detail left some jurors squeamish. Later on, the spoken account of a break-in by Mike and Joel to rescue Amnion took on more drama than just written words could convey.

Judge Burger halted Mike at this point, to remind him that Joel's testimony could subject Mike to civil prosecution for breaking and entering the Lifespan labs. Mike responded undaunted, "I understand, Your Honor," and continued his reading.

After almost 30 minutes of this dramatized testimony, Dr. Joel Rosen had made his impact against Lifespan. Even after death.

* * * * * * * *

After the noon recess, Mike resumed the stand. On his way, he could feel the undercurrent of hate in the gallery. Depending on what media platform you followed, he was either a disgruntled employee, a thief, a con man – or all of the above.

Mike was sworn-in, hand on a bible, to give his own corroborating testimony, recounting his planning and execution of both Lifespan break-ins. He was careful to avoid mentioning Phylis' involvement in any of it. She watched from the gallery as he recklessly left himself wide open to criminal prosecution.

Mike discussed how he had kept Amnion alive in his basement with Joel's help. When he started to describe the Lifespan technology used, Norm vigorously objected to this testimony citing the need to protect Lifespan's technical know-how and trade secrets.

"We have pending patent applications on this whole area!" he cried.

Richard responded, "Their license to this technology is about to expire. In actuality, the seed technology is essentially the property of the federal government, who is not part of this litigation."

"Besides," he argued, "disclosure of the existence of an artificial womb is hardly a trade secret. Photographs of these devices and processes were disclosed in the newspapers some months ago, and as such, ate already in the public domain."

Judge Burger allowed Richard to proceed.

It would take another few days before Norm would get his shot at

393

cross examining Mike.

CHAPTER 67
A ghost appears

From his fifth floor office window, a melancholy Max stared down to survey the skeletal remains of what was once his little empire. The tinted smoked glass window concealed his image from outside view, like some wealthy passenger passing through in a dark limousine. Below, the few scattered contract security people on patrol in vacant parking lots and wandering drones epitomized the empty culmination of his investment. Even Jane Savage, his security director, was making too much money to retain. He had Norm handle her layoff just a few days ago.

Right now, he was dwelling on the syndicate's flat rejection of his request to assassinate Amnion. The surprising answer through intermediaries was curt and vaguely hostile, "We don't do babies. It violates our code of honor."

Honor among thieves? Max groused to himself.

Max felt disappointed and impotent, like his license to kill had been revoked. Not being able to control these people was a real blow to his ego, as the ultimate judge of everyone else. When he appealed directly to 'Tony the Tiger', he took the issue a step too far. The reply was almost derogatory. "We did the doctor, now we're even. You want it done? Do it yourself."

Max was so deluded by his sense of importance, that he pressed the issue further, unwisely threatening to cut off the life extending drugs to Boss LaRocca. By now, the mob already knew there were no more drugs coming out of his plant. Max forgot that he was dealing with people whose business was to know these things. He also disregarded the fact these gangsters would repay an insult in their own time.

Adding to Max's misery was the reluctance of his investing partners to continue their support. It was the last straw. Now it was time to move on - on to California with its new, favorable fetal decoupling laws, and a future at his other investment, Extentech Corporation. There, he could pursue his ambition again, restore his fortune and power, and resume his youth injection treatments.

The ring of the desk phone behind him interrupted his cheerless deliberations. He pressed the speaker button to hear the Main Gate security guard request permission to allow a woman named Eve West to enter. Max's face dropped. He hurriedly rushed to the outside window and looked down at the distant front gate.

"Shit" he accidentally mumbled in reaction.

The security guard overheard and asked, "What was that Sir?"

A thin woman was standing outside her car, next to the guard shack. She was staring straight up at his window. Even from behind the smoked glass he sensed she could see him.

Her appearance at Lifespan was truly a shock, and he wondered, *Geez. Wasn't she supposed to be in a convalescent hospice someplace?*

Also noticeably absent, was her bright red BMW convertible. Instead, her car looked like a plain black Ford, maybe an SUV or something. Max hesitated a reply, being caught totally off-balance by her sudden and unwelcome appearance. If there was a graceful way to avoid this meeting, it had escaped him. And, worse yet, she already knew he was in.

After a further prompting from the guard, Max gave a reluctant OK to let her enter. He watched with dread as her car drove up to the building. What he really wanted was to escape this confrontation. There were numerous explanations he would have to invent for not doing more to get her out of captivity. And, reasons for not visiting her in the hospital during her convalescence.

When she finally entered his office, Max was taken aback by her appearance. It was as if, overnight, she'd aged 30 years. Thin and gaunt faced, her trade mark bright red lipstick replaced by pallid lips. In fact, they actually looked a bit bluish. Her cheekbones seemed to jut out from beneath sunken black ringed eye sockets. In between, a swollen nose broadened at the ridge, a legacy of the beating she took at the hands of her captors. The once carefully coiffured and colored hair was replaced by darker hair pulled back into a simple bun. Gray strands noticeably mixed in.

As she approached Max, he didn't seem to be able to move forward. It was if his legs were cemented in place. Paralyzed - perhaps out of fear of incurring her wrath.

In flat heals and no tailored business suit, her size seemed even more diminished. Svelte curves replaced by protruding bone. The ravishing image of the powerful career woman was replaced by what looked like a bag lady with a broken nose.

There was no warmth in the room. No tender I miss you. Only two people in decay. People who used each other for different reasons. Both of whom were now sullen and disappointed with the results.

After a few awkward moments of silence, Max shuffled over, and finally asked how she was feeling, inviting her to sit on the couch next to the coffee table. He hesitantly put his arm around her shoulder, and guided her thin bony frame around the cocktail table. She brushed off his hand as she sat down. Her wasted form hardly depressed the cushion. Max sat next to her, and made some perfunctory small talk inquiries about how she was feeling and where she was staying.

"Do you have enough money?" he asked as he bent forward to rest his hand on her knee.

"I don't need money anymore Max," she sullenly replied, slapping his hand off her.

Max joked, "Come on. Who doesn't need money nowadays?"

"I have HIV-AT, Max," she answered abruptly, her somber eyes fixed on his.

Max unconsciously shifted a few inches away, as if it she were contagious, and turned briefly to avoid her stare. Moving to a seat further away, collecting himself, he asked, "Is that the new Asian strain I saw on TV?"

"The same."

Max swallowed hard and callously asked, "Is that the one, that, uh, kills you in a few months?"

"Yes. That's the one. The attenuated strain. The one that backfired as a vaccine and mutated after it was introduced."

"No cure then?" Max somberly asked.

"None," was the sullen reply.

Max was initially, briefly sympathetic, and then relieved at the same time. Their terminal relationship had now, in fact, become fatally terminal for Eve. Their time together was just another business relationship of convenience. Not meant to last forever anyway. In a few months he wouldn't have to deal with her or her hurt feelings.

Eve interrupted his thoughts and tactfully asked, "Is there anything you want to tell me? About us, about the intimacy we had."

In his mind she was already a write-off. Now a liability on his valuable immortal balance sheet. No longer a contributor to life's carnal pleasures. He side stepped the question with a canned corporate type answer, "If you need anything just call. Money? Doctors? Medicine? We'll get them for you."

Eve judiciously read the insincerity of the offer and answered politely, "Well, I do appreciate the money that the company put up to get me out and home."

"Never was a problem," he said, clearing his throat, and now sitting across from the coffee table.

In corporate fashion, Max took credit straightaway for her ransom, even though he opposed it all the way.

On the contrary, Eve was not deceived. Her contained anger began to rise to the surface. Immediately she stood up and replied with a hiss, "Save you lies for the next mistress, Max."

Looking up he gave an innocent look saying, "What? What?" to the change in her tone.

"What?" she rasped with a cold stare. "You could have called me in the Bangkok hospital. You could have visited me here. Found out where I was hospitalized. Maybe do half of what Norm did for me."

Max leaned forward, trying to touch her hand. Instantly, she recoiled.

"Eve," he implored, "I've had the fight of my life back here at Lifespan. Trying to save an entire company, thousands of jobs." He spoke as if he actually expected sympathy from her.

He paused with a sorrowful look on his face. "There just wasn't time."

Eve was not buying it. "Not even for a short text?" she countered. "Even your lawyer found the time to visit in the middle of the trial." She was no fool. She had always suspected he had lost interest in her. Obviously, the suffering she had endured on company assignment changed nothing after all. Before accepting the obvious, she had to hear it first hand ...from his own lips.

As she stared down his dispassionate face, somehow Max did not glow like the sun anymore. Now a sad little man. Didn't radiate the power and prestige that attracted her to him years ago. Now she was just another one of his discarded disciples, and Max, as remote as the dark side of the moon.

Looking away, she said indignantly, "Thank you for your precious time Max." Her diminutive form stood up, and carefully walked around the coffee table. Then caustically she added, "Don't stand up, you bastard I know the way out." There was still a hit of dignity in her manner. Still the poise and attitude of the executive holding her inner tender feminine emotions in check.

As she departed, Max stayed seated and crossed his legs, looking almost relaxed, with an arm outstretched on the seat back. He had little empathy for how she was feeling, smiled politely, and waved goodbye. To him, her tragedy was unfortunate. She should have been more careful after she accepted the Asian assignment. Norm warned her to be careful. Max still held her accountable for the Bangkok shipment fiasco. Now her story was no more significant to the grand scheme of things than an obituary column of a faceless mortal in the evening newspaper .

Max stood up and returned to his desk to retrieve his Slinky, thinking, *that was easier than I thought. At least this is one mess that's over for good.*

Except, Eve was not quite dead and cold .. and not through with Max yet.

CHAPTER 68
Amnion has her day

For a change, the long suffering Amnion felt quite content this day, snugly wrapped in the soft flannel burp towel 'Wabbits' that Mike had provided months ago the NICU. Lying in her infant seat, it felt cozy and secure. Her cheeks had finally filled out and muscle had been added to her once spindly legs. Tiny frothy bubbles formed at her lips, producing a moist tingly sensation that was at the same time both pleasurable and distracting.

From her perch on the Plaintiff table, she could listen to the garbled sounds and voices of a courtroom preparing to go into session. Although the words spoken were entirely unintelligible, she still knew they were uniquely human. It was the only sound similar to all those noises she left behind in the neonatal ICU.

Today, a great deal of public attention was focused on a girl named Amnion. It was the first live public appearance of the 'Plaintiff' in this sensational case. Everyone in the courtroom wanted a peak at the girl who survived death, who beat the odds, who was now taking on Corporate America. It was hard to imagine such a scrawny, simple life form could be at the center of such a politically complicated controversy.

Earlier in the morning, Amnion had been in the judge's chamber with University Hospital neonatologist physician Shadere, obstetrician Samuelson, and Richard Farmer. They were verifying her medical documentation under the gaze of a disgruntled Lifespan legal staff. Norm, in particular, was not looking forward to arguing his case against a live infant, in front of a sympathetic jury. He tried to get her barred from the courtroom with a phony concern about the child's health and safety.

Judge Burger was already distracted by the time Norm expressed his opposition. The judge was tickling the baby's toes as they wiggled inside her knitted booties. Richard smiled, as he watched Norm dejectedly wipe his fingers on his facial hairs with frustration. His Honor was now bent over the little tyke and cooing baby talk.

Again, the frustrated Norm made a motion for dismissal based on the fact that Mike and Phylis were not the real biological parents. Therefore, could not legitimately act on her behalf. The distracted judge looked up to remind Norm that they, Mike and Phylis, were appointed as Amnion's legal guardians by his court. However, he did add that he was still concerned about her return to her biological parents – still kept secret. It was a matter to be addressed when this proceeding was all over.

The judge's commentary was duly noted by Mike, who was normally sensitive to anything that jeopardized his future with Amnion. But, he held his tongue. That day in the future was a long way off. So, he ruminated to himself, *wasn't possession nine-tenths of the law anyway?*

* * * * * * * *

Later in the courtroom, Amnion reclined comfortably, feeling no threat from the surrounding audience, as if surrounded by a friendly tribe in her own cave. She was already capable of discerning any emotion attached to the voices. Even before any concept of language was grasped by her, the subtle vocal inflections of anger, happiness, fear, affection were all already quite familiar. In fact, everyone sounded altogether friendly and the extra attention actually felt reassuring if not overpowering. The familiar scent of her baby powder provided additional reassurance.

Surviving for several weeks in the neonatal unit had allowed her to associate repetitive vocal tones with events. For the present, hearing and smell were still the most trusted senses. At this point of cerebral development, those faculties were so much more acute than sight.

Amnion glanced around with wide eyes that appeared as two dark brown bottomless pools. Though her vision was still blurred, the shadowy movement of humans was perceivable around her. Not very disturbing, as long as the strangers kept their distance, and the maternal voice of mother remained nearby.

'Mother' being either nurse Sandy Hart or Mike Santino. Surprisingly, after so many weeks in neonatal, Amy easily accepted the possibility of two mothers simultaneously. After a time she responded equally to both. Her sentiment was very simple and humanly logical, *If one mother is good, then two mothers is even better.*

At the equivalent of a normal baby's first month of extrauterine life, Amnion's brain spent little time on what we know as human thoughts. Being out of the womb had surprisingly little beneficial effect on her intellectual development; some theorized it was a detrimental effect. Her brain was hardly different from the one normally in the womb. Nature made no adjustments for a premature birth. The pattern of development had to follow the normal and natural sequence of events, regardless of outside interference or stimulation.

There were no great human mathematical postulates or political theories being debated inside her cortex - or long term memories of today's events. Instead an interpretive protocol was building in layers within her brain, transforming the physical world into the virtual world of the human mind. Sort of establishing the broad generalities dictated by the senses. Over these background analogies and rules, the detailed experiences of her life would be superimposed.

Her mind would work on very general problems; light and dark, separating colors, distinguishing self from non-self, spatial relationships between objects, the motion of things, gauging sounds moving away or closer. Assimilating the rules of nature and within the limits of her immediate senses. Studying physics without the written formulas or textbooks for those things.

It would be many years before she could tackle more complex problems like separating circles from squares and triangles, mastering language, or writing. Even walking was years away. The beauty of her brain's development was the ability to build on concepts that are more general and fit specific experiences into those generalities. Each fit reinforcing the next, ultimately layering specifics over broad generality into a complex framework. Some of those perceptions would eventually create the mental illusions that sometimes fool us all, the rest of our lives.

Above all else, though. Above all other deliberations, she was always most concerned with discerning the temperament and location of her mother.

* * * * * * *

The courtroom was called into session as the judge's appearance was announced. Nurse Hart placed Amnion down on the seat next to her, behind the Plaintiff table. The large photograph that was used as a substitute for her lack of presence was placed against the wood railing behind the table. Mike scampered back to his seat in the gallery, to sit in the row close behind. Phylis nervously sat next to him and held his hand to lend moral support, as Mike was to be cross-examined today. With Mike's uninhibited temperament, she was more concerned about what he might say on the witness stand than what the Lifespan attorney had in mind.

Compounding things, it was getting increasingly difficult for Phylis to spend time away from her new job. Because of her recent hiring, she had to take time off with no pay. Moreover, at half her old salary, it was becoming costly to come to these trial proceedings. In a way it didn't really matter. She was with her man, and in this maelstrom with Michael to the end. One saving grace, was that Richard Farmers was able to arrange for her to use subpoenas as an excuse to take the time off from work.

Phylis' thoughts were interrupted by Richard Farmers introductory remarks. He formally introduced his client, Amnion, to the jury, who slightly stood to get a good peek at her.

Finally, Mike was called to the stand. He was still under oath from a few days ago, and waited patiently for Norm's approach.

Norm took his time, finishing with arranging some papers on his table. Norm's strategy was to attack Mike's character, and his employment record. Expose him for illegally breaking and entering, and theft of company property. He took a curved path past Amnion and the jury, giving Mike the impression of a shark sizing up its quarry. Mike was not the least bit intimidated. On the contrary, his guarded suspicion was more like a diver with a spear gun.

"Mister Santino," he began, "You've testified under oath that you broke into Lifespan premises on at least two occasions, and stole company property. Is that correct?"

"I'm an employee there," he replied and grinned. "With the all the overtime hours I've put in there, I wouldn't know when I'm breaking in and when I'm just working late again."

The gallery chuckled, and the judge called for silence.

Norm was clearly vexed by the response. "Don't try to avoid the issue. You broke into an area clearly marked for authorized personnel only. Yet, you entered like a thief in the night anyway."

Mike interrupted, "Who said Dr. Rosen and I weren't authorized?"

"Dr Strauss, that's who."

"Really?" Mike answered, "So where's the written list of who is and who isn't authorized?" He knew there was nothing in writing within the shoddy security procedures at Lifespan.

An agitated Norm also knew that, and looked at Strauss in the gallery with some disappointment. Then he returned his gaze to the witness. "Of course there's no written list. These things are normally handled verbally."

Richard raised an objection. "Your Honor, Mister Stark is simply badgering the witness. Mister Santino would have no way of knowing to whom Dr. Strauss did or did not give verbal authorizations to. For all we know, the deceased Dr. Rosen could have had a verbal authorization."

"Your Honor," Norm responded, "All I want this witness to answer is whether Dr, Strauss gave a verbal authorization for him to enter his lab."

Mike interrupted saying innocently, "Ohhh." Then added, "No he didn't."

A frustrated Norm exclaimed in a loud huff, "Well, thank you Mister Santino."

Richard sat down and Norm continued. "Mister Santino, you testified that you raised the plaintiff in your basement. Whose equipment did you use to do that?"

Mike answered casually, "Mostly my own. I had the Amazon Prime orders and credit card charges entered into the record….it was a lot of money."

Yes, but what else did you use?" Norm enquired.

Mike answered innocently, "and some items 'borrowed' from Lifespan."

"Borrowed?" Norm whined. "You mean stolen, don't you?"

"No. Loaned," Mike innocently replied.

"And how do you arrive at that interpretation?"

"Whatever equipment used in saving the little girl's life was returned in working condition after she was born. As equipment manager for the company, I was given discretion on its use."

This brought some giggles from the gallery, and a stern look at them from above the spectacles of Judge Burger.

Norm turned to the jury with a disbelieving face. "The witness has admitted to breaking and entering, stealing company property, and using proprietary company technology."

Then he turned to the judge, and loudly demanded. "All the evidence and testimony submitted by this witness is inadmissible. It was obtained illegally, and should be stricken from the record."

Richard stood up and objected. "Your Honor," he shouted, "It remains to be determined if Lifespan itself was engaged in criminal activity at the time that these events took place. If so, the witness's actions could be viewed in a totally different way. In which case he is afforded whistleblower status and protections."

Judge Burger briefly mulled over the arguments and leaned forward to address the Lifespan Defense table. "The possibility of felonious activity by Lifespan is part of the issue before us in this case." He gestured towards Amnion and continued, "However, more importantly, the Plaintiff's survival was predicated on the action this witness had to take to preserve her life. In matters of life and death, the state is hardly in a position to critique the exact methodology used when the result is a human life saved from certain destruction."

Glancing back at Norm the judge added, "Objection overruled. Defense counsel may proceed."

Norm exploded in rage, "What human life! It's not a human until it's born! We have 60 years of case law that says so."

The courtroom fell silent as a huffing Norm scanned the courtroom. All eyes were on the infant Amnion, whose gurgling sounds could now be heard in the silence. Nurse Smith played with Amnion's kicking feet clad in the knitted booties.

Norm had lost his audience. His technical point obscured by the unfathomable power of human empathy itself. In resignation, he dismissed the witness.

Mike returned to Phylis, seated in the gallery. She greeted him with a smile and a kiss on the cheek, saying, "You know, you just admitted to a quite a few felonies there."

Mike remarked off-handedly, "A lot of people suffered and died to get us here. Compared to that, if I got to do a little hard time, it's no big deal."

Phylis shook her head and smiled, knowing that this man would really do jail time if it came to that.

CHAPTER 69
The Amnion orb

Just before dinner, an exuberant Evon met her tired husband at the front door. "Honey! You'll never believe what came by UPS today."

Richard reluctantly listened, kissing her cheek and giving a slight embrace. The tired lawyer was just anxious to relieve himself of the weight of his bulging brief case. The stress and sheer work involved in the trial was finally beginning to physically wear him down.

"What is it, Peaches?" he asked impassively.

She scurried over to the telephone stand to a small opened box filled with styrofoam packing nodules. As she eagerly reached into the box, some of the packing 'peanuts' flew out and floated to the floor. Richard approach and stooped over to pick them up when Evon thrust the object in front of his nose.

While bent over, a startled Richard exclaimed, "I'll be damned."

With a twinge of back stiffness he stood up straight again to remark, "Now I've seen everything."

Square in his face was a crystalline orb filled with an amber fluid, about the size of and ostrich egg. Richard reached out to grasp its weighty form, and examine it more closely.

Within the glass was suspended a miniature porcelain figurine of a fetus sucking its infinitesimal thumb. Its ivory colored body was curled in the classic fetal position, with a thin umbilical chord spiraling upward. At the top, it was attached to a bright red multifaceted glass structure representing the placenta.

Evon pointed to the wood base. "See. They even have her name engraved on it,

"*Amnion at 14* ." Obviously, alluding to the weeks of gestation when Amnion was decoupled.

Although amazed by the artistry involved in this construction, Richard, the lawyer, was nonetheless perturbed. This was, after all, an unauthorized use of her name.

"We never commissioned this piece," the lawyer complained. "Who sent this?"

Evon returned to the shipping box and picked out an envelope. She replied, "Operation Rescue, I guess."

She handed it to him. The note greeted Richard and his family. It congratulated him on fighting the Lifespan case, and presented him with serial number one, the first piece of ten thousand copies of this limited addition sculpture. There was also a written commitment to give Amnion a significant share in the financial proceeds of this offering.

Operation Rescue had made several unsuccessful attempts to meet with Richard during the course of the trial. So they never had the chance to discuss the figurine. Richard had purposely avoided any formal communications with either side of the termination. Each side represented an extreme point of view, each with their own agenda. Up to this point, he wanted this case to be strictly between a fetus and a company. Besides, Mike had set up an online website to gather donations. There was tens of thousands of donations from $5 to $1000 dollars – so they were not cash-strapped yet.

Richard had another unspoken agenda, one that went beyond Amnion's ordeal or Lifespan. For him, this journey through the appeal process was inevitably going to end up in the United States Supreme Court.

He said to Even, Let's not get ahead of ourselves yet"

Even accepted his decision, and slid her arm around her husband's waist. Together they walked to the kitchen. Sitting down at the table they placed the glass piece between them, still mesmerized by its life-like intricacy.

Richard still remained miffed and distracted at what he interpreted as some organization capitalizing on Amnion's notoriety. Evon was less disturbed.

"You know," she volunteered, "I've looked at this object all afternoon. And it really does accurately depict what's developing in a woman's body."

She gently touched the object's polished glass surface with her fingertip. "It's not gross. In a way, it's almost beautiful."

Richard also found the image compelling, and his mind still dwelled on the issue of using Amnion's name on the orb. Finally, he concluded, we must return it. Right now, I'm not authorizing anything. I just don't have time."

Evon gingerly picked up the amber crystal orb and placed it on the windowsill to catch the late twilight. Leaning closer to it, the tiny face inside was incredibly detailed. Tiny nose, ears, eye buds, fingers and feet. Even toes. Initially so alien, so primitive. Now, almost hypnotically, it seemed to give the observer more of the feeling of peace and serenity than anything else. A friendly, purposeful entity, whose purity of innocence is suddenly revealed for what it is.

CHAPTER 70
Rhythm and Rhyme

Phylis laid a squirming Amnion down on the Plaintiff table while nurse Hart knelt down to dig through her diaper bag for a clean one. A brief 15 minute trial recess had been called to take care of this natural but still unexpected event. Phylis undid the soiled diaper and handed it off to the nurse, working with surprising skill.

It must be 15 years since I last did this on my own two, she thought as she wiped the baby's bottom clean.

Amnion stared up intently at Phylis's face as her two tiny hands tugged at Phylis's pinky. The smiling infant kicked and shuddered with delight at the freedom afford by her nakedness. Phylis looked at her and whispered with a grin, "You and Michael have a lot in common."

Nurse Hart glanced up from the floor and giggled, "Yeah. Men!"

Actually, Mike was absent from the trial today. All Phylis knew was that he was somewhere across town, tracking down some mysterious witness for Richard.

When Amnion was diapered and redressed, the court returned to session. Phylis decided to remain next to her since she started to fuss more than usual, and nurse Hart looked like she needed some help today.

Richard waited patiently at a safe distance, for all this smelly activity to be finished, then approach and patted Amnion's head and rose to call his next witness, Dr. Strauss.

The doctor came down the aisle looking serious and annoyed. As he passed Amnion, an overzealous woman's camera flash went off from the gallery right behind her. Somewhere deep in her little brain a fragment of memory somehow remained and made her remember. A painful recollection of her early life in the Lifespan R&D lab. The sudden flash of light when the hatch of her fetal tube was opened. The anticipation of being stuck with an extraction needle and stabbed with pain.

In an instant the sharp screech of a baby in distress shattered the courtroom silence. It was. as sudden and shrill as a dog's yelp when its paw is stepped on.

Phylis was so startled by the piercing cry that she thought the baby was injured somehow. Nurse Hart picked her up as Phylis joined her in looking for pinched skin or something stuck in her clothing. The two women offered motherly consolation. Instead, Amnion continued to wail. Judge Burger was at a loss to decide what to do about her. In exasperation, he ordered that the offending woman be ejected from the courtroom and had a bailiff confiscate her camera.

Nearby, Strauss stood frozen for the moment, looking down at the screeching babe. For some reason it just looked as if her cries were caused by his shadowy presence. And, unfortunately for Strauss, that's the way it appeared to the jury and everyone else.

Richard offered to remove the infant outside until she was calmed down. Norm and Max looked on with frustration and shook their heads in disgust. The nurse picked up the baby and hurriedly walked down the center aisle with a crying Amnion bawling over her shoulder. Phylis watched her depart, feeling a bit helpless and sad that she wasn't more of a comfort to the little girl. You could tell that some females in the jury were responding, at least psychologically, to the waif's distress

There was no one that could appreciate the terror instilled within this newly created child during her primordial past, or possibly know the secret and sinister routine that had been Lifespan specimen operations. What victim would bear witness to the mass murder? All the specimens were dead, save one. Even if they were alive, how would they give testimony? Only one human brain with some faint recollection was left. One whose ghastly memories that had faded into an obscure dark blanket of ambiguous fear.

Strauss stalked over to the witness stand totally pissed off at having to endure that entrance. It felt unwarranted and unseemly - insulting to a man of his scientific prestige.

Richard picked up his computer tablet and keyed in Strauss's name. A graphical presentation appeared on the display with a caricature of Dr. Frankenstein reviving the monster, and Strauss's name beneath. Richard shook his head as he looked down and smiled thinking, *Mike's been in the batch file again!*

After some preliminary background questions, Richard asked, "Did you take an oath never to raise a scalpel against a human fetus?"

An indignant Strauss replied, "No, I don't do terminations ...if that's what you're insinuating."

"Not at all doctor," Richard said as he turned to the jury and asked more directly. "Have you been involved in the revival of human fetal lives at Lifespan, and their subsequent termination?"

Strauss replied evasively in a calm serious tone, "I had a great deal of leading edge research going on at Lifespan over the past several years. I don't keep track of all these specimen projects."

"Specimens?" Richard snapped with indignation.

He paused, then angrily continued. "Well, fortunately, others did keep track of what went in and out of your lab. And we've heard their testimony." The determined lawyer leaned forward on the railing in front of the witness box. "But what about you? Your personal involvement doctor." Richard pointed his finger for emphasis, "Did you terminate any fetuses at Lifespan yourself?"

Norm stood up and objected, "Harassing the witness."

Judge Burger replied, "Overruled. The actions inside the defendant's labs is central to this case."

The doctor appeared more annoyed than afraid by this verbal

barrage. He shifted in his seat and avoided the question. "I have many people working for me, and little time to get involved in all those little details."

"A living human fetal life is a little detail? Can you just give me a simple yes or no on what you did?" Richard demanded.

Back at the defendant's table Max leaned forward on his elbows, anxious about how he would handle being interrogated when it was his turn to testify. Strauss looked at Norm, seeking some relief from these incessant questions. Norm discreetly held up five fingers from his hand resting on the table as a pre-arranged signal.

Strauss picked up on the message and smugly responded, "I afraid I'd have to invoke my Fifth Amendment rights on this one."

Richard gave a knowing smile. "I thought you would," and turned around to face the courtroom again. "So, in that case, we, the Plaintiff, submit the following photographs taken and published by the Daily News some months past. They show the good doctor incinerating the remains of human fetuses in the Lifespan incinerator. There is also an article regarding the seed technology that doctor Strauss brought to Lifespan – Nazi technology."

Amid a low rumbling of voices in the audience, Richard passed the photos and newspaper articles to the judge and jury, along with a copy for Norm. "We've had the image enhanced by Resolution Technology, a defense contractor for NSA (the National Security Agency), and an expert in this technique. You'll see someone who looks very much like the good doctor here."

Richard held one photo in the air and pointed, "Note the small human foot hanging from a box in the lower right."

Norm sprung up and objected. "This proves nothing! The company processes fetal cadavers under government license. This doesn't prove that the doctor killed them."

Judge Burger gestured to Richard for an explanation.

"Your Honor," Richard said, "we have eye witness testimony of the actual killing of these fetuses by this doctor on the same date, shortly before these photos were taken. Expert neonatologists have examined the fetal foot in this photo as from a 22 week-old human fetal life. Well beyond the limits for experimentation!"

Richard returned to Strauss. "You had an assistant help you that night. A Miss Rachel Stone, I believe." The lawyer leaned on the railing in front of the witness. "Now do you remember?"

"Sir, I work for Lifespan Corporation," was the reply. "Anything I did was under a federal government grant to do my research. I only did what I was instructed to do by higher authority."

Richard verbally barreled right into that answer. "So who gave you the orders to terminate the live fetuses? Who ordered their execution?"

An unrepentant Strauss sat rigid, eyes fixed on Max, across the silence of the room. Max avoided his accusing gaze and sat stone faced, looking straight ahead. The doctor was thinking about the bawling out he received from Max weeks ago, the accusations against his German father.

By now, everyone, including the jury, was assessing Maxes demeanor. Richard stepped from between these two shysters, and leaned back against the judge's bench. He could sense this unspoken testimony was better than actual words. That his jury was coming to the right conclusion, with or without an admission from the stonehearted Strauss. Each juror's face expressed the desire for an answer, maybe some sign of remorse from Max.

From the Defense table Norm spoke up. He had to break up the damaging atmosphere of innuendo that was forming. "Your Honor, 50 years of case law on fetal life invokes no constitutional rights to these specimens. Mister Farmer's allusions to some kind of murder taking place here are wildly irrational and unsupported by our legal system."

Richard responded, "The issue before us is not about case law. The issue is simply about when my client's early life should have been protected. And at that time, who was attempting to kill her."

Norm rebutted, "At the time this all allegedly took place, our company was operating legally with written, documented federal authorizations. And, with properly executed consent from the Plaintiff's biological mother to process her specimen."

Norm turned to the jury and waved his hand in the air. "The counsel is usurping that mother's decoupling right to chose, along with all women's rights everywhere."

Richard paused to let nurse Hart return up the aisle with Amnion laying on her forearm arm. The wide eyed infant was cradled on her stomach, looking around at her audience, apparently content again. When they were seated, Richard walked to the judge's bench. "We will excuse this witness for now, Your Honor, subject to recall. The Defense council has raised the issue of when we award a human his or her life, and who has the ultimate right to terminate it."

Richard returned his gaze to Norm and said, "So, I will call relevant witnesses to refute these arguments."

Norm waved his hand down at Richard as if to poo-poo his remarks, "No way Your Honor. The Plaintiff is broadening the scope of this case beyond the issue at hand. I thought this case was about one specimen, not the broader decoupling issue."

Judge Burger gestured the opposing attorneys forward for a side bar and they began to huddle over the bench with the judge. After some heated bickering in low voices, a short recess was ordered. They would discuss this new development and Richard's new witnesses in the judge's anteroom.

Max finally sat back, satisfied that nobody 'spilled the beans' and if Strauss was able to survive this ordeal, he could handle it too.

During this lull in the action, Phylis spoke quietly to the nurse, then sat back down next to the little tyke bubbling froth formula from her tiny pursed lips. She could not help feeling empathy for this appealing tough little girl. Still enduring without her real mother. Serene in the naiveté of ignorance. Having her early life argued in a world of contradictions, probably never to be resolved.

Phylis felt emotionally moved by what she'd heard and seen today, and stared for a while at the magnetic creature next to her. Technically, she was still a fetus. In the lull, while the attorneys met in the judge's chambers, Phylis took a pencil and pad from the table, feeling the need to speak for this child. She began to write a lyrical verse about the diminutive Amnion in the artificial womb. Over the course of an hour of cross-outs and erasures, she had the rhyme completed:

> *I lie here, as God intended to be,*
> *for better or worse, should not he judge me?*
>
> *A chance of nature was how I was created,*
> *but now that I'm here, should my life be debated?*
>
> *The right of living is my simple defense,*
> *to play out my time regardless of consequence.*
>
> *Perhaps a future of suffering, sorrow or pain,*
> *or the joy and comfort where love remains.*
>
> *But, whatever the reason of my earthly flight,*
> *I come from the Father to claim that right.*

* * * * * *

Mike showed up later and Phylis inquired about what he had been up to in the city. "Find your witness?" she asked.

"Yeah," he answered, "Mission accomplished." Then leaned forward to kiss her cheek, and tickle Amnion's toes, oblivious to the eyes of the people in the gallery.

"Which witness?" Phylis persisted.

Mike sat down next to her, and purposefully dodged the question by changing subjects. "How'd we do with Strauss on the witness stand?"

"OK, I guess," she replied, "he came off pretty deceitful. He took the Fifth on all the important questions."

Mike hunched over and looked down. He shook his head slowly from side to side with a hint of dismay. "It figures," he griped. He turned his head sideways and gave Phylis an odd look - a kind of expressionless face. He added, "We'll never get these guys on their home turf ...this courtroom. Even with a good lawyer like Richard there. You got to get these kinds of people outside the corporate veil. In the open. Take them down in the street."

Phylis didn't like the comment or the devilish grin now on Mike's face. "What do you mean?" she inquired, "What do you have in mind, Michael?"

Mike sat up and abruptly changed subjects to elude her suspicions, asking, "What cha got there," pointing to her tablet.

A somewhat flustered Phylis reluctantly showed passed him the pad. He read it silently and intently. Then he teased her with a parody of the rhyme, "Now I lay me down to sleep..."

"Michael!" she said defensively, "How could you."

Mike held up his hands apologetically, "No, I'm just kidding. I really like it." He read it again and added, "Tell you what. I'll get the *Brooklyn News* to run it in the paper. They like this human interest stuff."

Phylis felt embarrassed as she reached to retrieve the pad. Mike played hard to get with it, finally convincing her that he was serious about getting it published.

He asked, "Can you write more of this stuff?"

"I don't know," she shrugged, "I never felt the need to before."

* * * * * * *

That evening, after dinner, Phylis sat alone on the backyard deck thinking of all that had happened in the trial, and the pitiful little girl adrift in a sea of hypocrisy. She thought more and more about Amnion's mother Maria Alvarez, and her timid reluctance at her decoupling. Once again, poetry seemed act like a catharsis to bring out Phylis' feelings and put them to rest. Other thoughts came to mind; of watching Amnion in Mike' basement cart; delivering her from a plastic tube; the ordeal in Neonatal. She began to write additional verses as they flowed into her mind like drifting smoke from a dying ember. It was just something that had to come out. Almost like some thing that was always there.

By nightfall she was totally immersed in writing, and her daughter, Kristy, shouted with concern from the lighted kitchen window, "Mommy, it's getting late. It's dark. When are you coming inside?"

"Just a moment honey," a distracted Phylis replied, reading the last few lines of her creation in the twilight.

To move beyond my darkened confines,
and gaze at the world now by light defined.

Alive outside, on a day with the sky so blue,
white clouds, green leaves, shades of every hue.

Sweet air to breathe since my early birth,
of touch and scent - the things on earth.

The sound of children filling my ear,
of parents and loved ones soon drawing near.

To gaze in wonder at my own worldly visage,
now reflected, at last, in a smooth mirror's image.

But especially, I want to behold my mother,
whose meaning to me is like no other.

The face that is God and the universe for me,
whose vision means love, and allows me to be.

To sense the warmth of that gentle caress,
that calms me down and soothes my distress.

And nourish beneath her soft velvet bosom,
gaze up at those eyes, whose intent I must fathom.

It is nature's way that she decides my soul's fate,
that I die alone , or make heaven wait.

CHAPTER 71
The bald eagle

Outside the courthouse, there was the usual swirl of media press and demonstrations. Experts were on TV every day arguing for and against decoupling.

Inside, Richard methodically resumed his case by interrogating a federal government witness, a Dr. Tyler Forsythe, Deputy Director of the U.S. Fish and Wildlife Service. This puzzled the jury and spectators alike. It wasn't readily apparent as to what this person had to do with the case at hand - or anything else.

From the Defense table, Norm sat with a look of bored consternation, and leaned over the table. His face rested on his two clenched hands that stretched the loose skin of his cheek into folds that piled up around his eyes. Previous objections to these odd witnesses had been overruled by Judge Burger in his chambers the other day, and this just seemed like another exercise in judicial futility.

Richard asked some preliminary questions regarding Dr. Forsythe's duties and the Department's responsibility over the many wildlife refuges throughout the United States. Then he became more specific. "Your department has a number of animals and plants on the endangered species list?"

"Yes we do," the deputy answered, "About seven hundred species at this point, I believe"

Richard remarked facetiously, "No humans on the list yet?"

The doctor smiled, "Not yet."

"How about the Bald Eagle?"

The deputy hesitated an instant trying to understand where the counselor was leading him, finally answering, "Uh, yes. Haliaeetus leucocephalus. We have several sanctuaries established in the west and northwest. I think Alaska too."

"And what is the federal penalty for some person killing or injuring one of these creatures?"

The witness hesitated for a second, then answered, "Well under the Bald and Golden Eagle Protection Act, probably a maximum fine of $100,000 or one year imprisonment. More if it's a second conviction."

Richard then returned to his Plaintiff table and produced a medium size speckled bird egg from his brief case. Returning to the witness he inquired, "This simulated eagle egg , I borrowed from the New York Museum of Natural History. The curators of the American wildlife exhibit were kind enough to loan it."

Richard held the egg up with his thumb and index finger, and turned towards the jury. "If I happened upon an Eagle's nest in a tree, in one of your wildlife refuges. And, for some thoughtless reason, I stole a real egg from the nest and smashed it on the ground."

Richard paused for effect, then added, "What would be the penalty for my action? I mean, if I was caught doing this?"

"A $100,000 fine or 1 year in jail," the Deputy replied again with certainty.

"This would only be an embryo, sir," Richard protested. Holding the egg out in his open palm he added, "I don't see any wings...feathers." Then he smiled and weighed the egg in his hand. "Can't fly either."

"It doesn't matter to the government," Forsythe interrupted. "The damage to an egg obviously prevents the emerging eagle life from adding to the future bird population. Under the Endangered Species Act of 1973 it is illegal even to disturb its natural habitat."

"OK," Richard said, "So, the federal government essentially equates destroying an embryonic egg with destroying a fully developed eagle."

Norm stood up with a frustrated look. "Your Honor, Objection. Relevance? Where is this avian Zoology story going? I hardly see what all this has to do with this case, Your Honor?"

Judge Burger turned to Richard.

"Richard answered, "The relevance, Your Honor, is whether a human embryo, or a fetus for that matter is entitled to the same protection under law as a grown human being." Adding with a touch of sarcasm, "Hypocritically, the Federal government does not see the need to protect my client in all her development stages."

Richard turned to the jury saying, "Isn't it ironic. Of how much less value is a precious human embryo compared to a simple bird." Richard pointed to his client Amnion, "How much less was she worth 7 months ago?"

Then he looked at Norm, "Except, in the case of Lifespan Corporation, we already know the answer to that question."

The judge overruled Norm's objection. But, chastised Richard again for addressing the jury.

Norm and Max sulked in their seats, as the case took on a flavor for the dramatic. Richard walked over to the windowsill where his planted acorn had sprouted through the topsoil with two delicate branches supporting miniature yellow-green leaves that remained folded on top. Through the clear plexiglas, the original acorn was still visible below the surface. The split shell and inner pulp was still nourishing the root and stem.

Richard picked up the cube, and returned to the deputy director, still on the stand.

"One last question, Mister Forsythe," he said mischievously.

Richard thrust the potted plant forward at the apparently confused and wary witness. "In your opinion, as a representative of the federal government. Is this an oak tree or not?"

The government employee was not going to risk his job and pension over an oak sapling. "I, uh. I uh, am not an authority on plant life," he stuttered. "I mean it certainly doesn't look like a tree yet." As a political appointee, he hedged his response. "Then again, I, uh, am not a botanist either."

Norm interrupted, "Your Honor! Calls for speculation. The witness admits himself that he is hardly an expert on plant anatomy."

"Sustained. Jury will disregard his remarks."

Richard smiled, confident that the point had been made with the jury anyway. "I withdraw the question Your Honor. Witness is excused."

Richard returned the cube to the sunny windowsill.

* * * * * * *

Later in the day, when trial was recessed, Richard sat and relaxed in the solitude of the empty courtroom with Mike. A relaxed Mike leaned backwards on his chair against the railing, hands held on the table edge.

"I received a strange phone call yesterday at my home," Richard said cautiously. "Some gruff sinister sounding voice with a message."

"Ooh, mysterious," Mike kidded with a smile.

"No Mike. You could tell this guy meant business."

Mike now leaned forward on his chair. "Like what?"

"Before I answer, you promise not to do anything rash. No wild man stuff."

Mike raised his palms in the air, "Hey, like what?"

Richard hesitated a moment - still wondering if Mike should know this. Finally, he said softly, "Our friend Joel Rosen..."

"Yeah. Yeah. What?"

"This voice claimed that he was killed under a contract."

"By who?" Mike implored.

"He said that Max Brewster ordered the hit. Then just hung up."

Mike's form slumped as if the full weight of this revelation was resting on his shoulders.

"Son ova bitch!" Mike growled. "I knew it. The miserable son ova bitch!"

There was no joy in Mike's original suspicions finally being confirmed. There was only the recurring sadness of Joel's untimely end. And his courage in helping Amnion survive, and paying for it with his life. And ultimately, the knowledge that 'Mad Max' was getting away with murder again and again.

Richard could sense some of Mike's swelling rage, and reached over to pat his knee. "Hey Mikey. There's no proof that this call is legitimate. It could be just a crank call. I mean, why tell us at this point?"

"I don't know Richie."

"Well, don't make me sorry I told you," Richard pleaded. "You leave it up to me. I will get this swindler. You just give the courts and me some time. We'll get justice."

Mike looked down, now keeping himself surprisingly contained. Although, his thoughts were actually drifting off into another plan of action. He'd hardly heard Richie's cautions or words of consolation. Neither did he have the patience to watch the wheels of justice grind ever so slowly towards a probable plea bargain.

Richard was left uncertain by Mike's silence, and implored, "Promise me you won't take revenge. It will only screw up this case, and destroy any sympathy for Amnion."

"You're right Richie; Mike looked up with a devious grin, answering, "Let's just say that nature, the <u>physical kind</u>, will have to take its course."

Later, Richard went to see Judge Burger about receiving this anonymous threat. He revealed something that was also stated in the call, and concealed from the impulsive Mike – for good reason. "The caller also said," Keep an eye on that kid Amnion."

The judge, noticeably disturbed, ordered extra police protection of Amnion in the University Hospital Nursery, and to and from the court.

CHAPTER 72
Mortality - guaranteed

Early Saturday morning Mike rummaged through the storage boxes at their makeshift trial headquarters in College Point. Alone and with a singular purpose, he worked fervently until he found the cardboard box that was the beginning of his plan to end Max Brewster's reign on earth. It was the one containing depositions from the Lifespan R&D staff, including photocopies of their Lifespan security badges.

Mike told no one of his plan. Not Richard. Not his sons. Not even Phylis. However, if this secret scheme panned out, he was not going to drag anybody else down with him.

Mike knelt and sifted through the box, finally locating Dr. Sterling Roberts' folder, and lifted the security badge copy. The facial image was out of contrast. However, the bar code identification lines and QR code were quite clear. Mike returned to one of the desks, plucked a utility knife from a draw, and cut out the coded square and the doctor's name from the photocopy badge.

His own security badge, the one he made before leaving Lifespan, made an excellent facsimile for a genuine badge. With some clear cellophane tape, Dr. Robert's bar code identification and name were now, cleverly, on the badge with Mike's smiling face. Satisfied, he promptly left the office and drove off in his Mustang. There was a lot of ground to cover this day. At his next destination, the local business supply store, a plastic coating machine applied a suitable finish to his new makeshift Dr. Roberts security badge.

Nearby was an Avis rental office where he parked the Mustang and picked up his beige sedan. Once at home, he put on his handy junkyard plates on the rental. In a short time, he would be back with his old employer again.

* * * * * * *

It felt really odd to approach the main gate at Lifespan and not see Harry Sullivan's smiling mug peeking out. Weeks ago, the old internal security staff had been let go, probably a week before Mike was laid off. The place looked almost deserted now. Parking lots empty, bushes overgrown, even the sod grass looked like a wheat field.

A security guard from an outside agency was at the main gatehouse now. A weekend shift type, probably an off-duty cop, the brother-in-law of somebody in Lifespan management.

Mike stopped at the gate, rolled his window down, and nonchalantly passed his phony ID badge.

"Doctor Roberts, huh," the stolid guard grunted, as he leaned down to check Mike's face against the photo. He turned into the guard shack and pulled out a laser scanner to read the bar code.

Mike watched the red beam of light flicker across the badge. There was no beep or other sign that anything was wrong, so he figured he was home free. Mike accepted his badge back, when the guard looked at a paper log of some type.

"Wait a minute, doctor," he abruptly announced. "This car. It isn't registered in my book."

Mike had to think quick. He didn't have any idea what kind of car this Doctor Roberts really drove. So, he feigned annoyance and leaned out the window to demand, "Well, what vehicle do you have me down for?"

The guard replied, "A red BMW."

"Oh, the Beemer," Mike answered with a laugh. "It's in the repair shop. Takes forever. Damn thing costs a fortune to fix. Parts come from Germany. I had to use a dealer loaner today."

"Oh," the guard said as he copied the license plate on his keypad. "Next time buy American," he added with a smirk, and waived Mike in.

Mike looked through the rear view mirror and observed the guard disappear back into his booth.

He was in!

Parking in the spaces reserved for R&D seemed like a good idea. There were only two other cars parked there, a good sign that few people were working in the building today. The rest of the lot was deserted except for a half dozen other cars he assumed belonged to other security people.

Mike grabbed his briefcase, briskly hiked up the walkway, and took a quick look at the CCTV camera as he approached. He walked head down anyway as he entered the lobby of the processing building. Mike was not

416

too concerned about the cameras, since they overwrote the video every seven days. No one would be looking for that missing radium for some time.

Another security type greeted him at the front desk, and Mike confidently waved his badge, never breaking his steady stride. In another moment, he was through the inner lobby doors and on his way down the deserted hall to Joel Rosen's specimen processing department.

Mike had remembered Joel describing some radioactive tracer isotopes they used when creating 'designer' molecular markers during the processing of specimen extracts. The lead-lined storage closet was isolated in the back warehouse area of the building.

As he neared his destination, he nervously fingered the keys he had duplicated months ago trying to remember which one fit. It was still a gamble that these pass keys would still fit the locked office doors.

"Boo Ya!," Mike declared, one did work!

Arriving at the padlocked storage closet, it didn't take a person long to understand that this was dangerous territory. There were large, round yellow and black radioactive warning signs all over, and a heavy looking dull grey door. It took a dozen fidgety attempts to find the right key. Mike finally coerced the padlock opened.

He couldn't believe his luck. Apparently, the Lifespan bureaucracy had changed all the R&D locks on the second floor, and felt no need to do so on the first floor processing operations.

Warily looking down both ends of the hallway, Mike removed the lock and entered the room. It was tight quarters in there, just a small room about 4 feet wide by 5 feet long, dimly lit. Steel shelves covered each longitudinal cinderblock wall, imparting the feeling of a basement bomb shelter. A myriad of dull gray lead covered 'pigs' (storage cylinders) with all kinds of chemical labels were scattered about, marked with, *Danger Radioactive Material*. For some reason, the little round yellow and black radiation warning stickers reminded him of those nasty, stinging, Yellow Jacket bees.

Mike slowly read the labels and isotope names until he found one marked, "Radioactive Radium 226 - Danger! High Concentration." On the label was written the amounts and dates used, and the amount left of Radium . This particular container was hardly used, and he unscrewed the lid to find three sealed glass vials inside suspended in Styrofoam sleeves inside.

There's enough here to kill an elephant, he happily mused - m*aybe enough for Max to crap an atomic bomb and kill all of his cronies,*

Mike screwed the lid back on, opening his briefcase and careful placed the heavy radioactive radium container in, strapping it to the bottom.

In a moment, he was out of the gloomy closet, had reengaged the padlock, locked all the doors, and promptly made his way back to the lobby.

The anxious Mike flashed his badge as he passed the guard. The security man shouted, "Hey wait. Gotta check the briefcase."

Mike stopped in his tracks, then slowly turned around, returning to the guard desk. Now he had to do some fast talking as he propped the briefcase on the desk top.

"Oh shit!" Mike announced before opening his briefcase, "I forgot my damn cellphone. Good thing you stopped me."

Mike slapped the case closed again and quickly headed back down the hallway. "Be right back in a minute. Thanks for stopping me."

The confused guard could only think to say, "Uhh. Yeah. You're welcome."

Mike briskly walked back down the hall to some vacant office cubicles nearby. Slipping inside, he began to ponder his predicament. Within a minute or two the solution became apparent. He immediately took off his sport coat and loosened his belt. Next the latches on his briefcase were sprung and the lead container was removed. Nervously he shoved the cylinder down the back of his pants. A pull on his pant's belt held the container in place, tight against the base of his spine. With his sport coat back on, the loose material of the suit overlapped the small bulge in his back.

Back at the guard desk Mike returned, waving his cellphone, and popped open his briefcase. After a brief inspection, Mike started a conversation about the Giants football team. In the meantime, he backpedaled his way out, eventually out the entrance doorway. By now, the lead pig painfully dug into his tender posterior skin.

Once outside and back at his car, he gingerly backed into the driver' seat, and removed the annoying cylinder. Then he secured it back in the briefcase, and strapped the briefcase upright in the passenger seat. It crossed his mind that he might've given a dose of radiation to his spinal column, but it was too late to worry about that now.

With the radium safely stored away, Mike drove past the gatehouse stopping to have his badge scanned again. With a red blink of the laser he was cleared again and on his way.

Mike rubbed his sore back wondering if he really did do any permanent damage.

* * * * * * * *

After dropping off the rental car, Mike returned home early in the afternoon. He stopped at his mailbox on the street, filled with the usual handful of bills and junk mail. One missive caught his attention right away. It was from *Selective Heath Care*, the managed care insurance company covering Amnion's bills. Mike opened it, assuming it was some annoying detail or another, and was shocked to read;

Dear Mr. and Mrs. Santino,

We have recently been informed by your company that the patient, Amy Santino, is not an actual member of your immediate family.

Under terms of your policy, this company cannot consider further payment of the neonatal or postnatal costs currently billed by the service provider, University Hospital. We have informed the hospital and attending physicians under separate letter that we will not be liable for further expenses incurred by this patient.

It light of the above, all expenses paid to date for this patient were not considered legitimate charges under your health care policy. Our company expects reimbursement from you for the attached payments incurred and previously reimbursed by us during the past 3 months.

Please remit $195,229.57 to the above address within 30 days from the date of this notice. Your failure to provide prompt payment will result in possible legal consequences.

Yours truly,
Janice Deveroe
Collections Department

Mike couldn't believe it. *I'll be damned*, he thought. Lifespan obviously informed them of Amy's true identity.

Then he perused the computer printout of the billing submitted by the hospital, and looked at the cover letter again. The body of the letter was printed in CG Times font. His name, address, and Amy's name were added in Arial font.

"It's a friggin' computerized form letter!" he remarked out loud, slapping the paper to his palm. "And they couldn't even keep the fonts consistent."

It frosted him that they would send a form letter to impersonally collect what was obviously a life savings from somebody. No advanced calls. No human contact. Just tell the computer to ask for money.

The annoyed Mike parked his Mustang in the garage and carried the radioactive radium into a storage shed in his backyard.

He returned to the house still agitated, and finally called Richie on the burner phone to discuss what to do.

"I could contest the basis," Richard volunteered, "since the court has essentially made you and Phylis her legal guardians." Then he added, "It's up to you Mike."

Mike thought about it a while longer. "No Richie. I have a better idea."

"Like what?"

"Like out national coverage." I'll give this to my newspaper contact at the *Brooklyn Daily News*. Put these blood suckers in the public light. Get'em on *Fox News*."

"Well Mike, it sounds OK to me …if they'll do it."

Mike thanked Richie, then hung up and dialed the *Brooklyn Daily News* reporter.

The reporter was more than happy to print it. The editors enjoyed exposing big fat medical insurance corporations to public ridicule.

"In fact Mike," the reporter added, "Don't be surprised by the public reaction to this kind of an article."

Mike mailed a copy of the letter that day. In a few days, *Selective Healthcare* would have more national exposure than it ever dreamed of.

CHAPTER 73
Belated remorse

In spite of an entire day's worth of pre-trial coaching, a now aging Max Brewster remained nervous. He was tired from lack of fetal derivative injections and disgusted with this whole mess. It caused hin to unwittingly slouch in the witness stand. This was one situation where he couldn't put the fix in ahead of time. Couldn't control the questions to be asked …or the outcome. Couldn't pay somebody else to take the test for him. Could not have his Slinky toy for reassurance.

It had already become obvious to both Max and Norm that the tide of public and media opinion was beginning to rise against Lifespan. Regrettably, from the testimony and judge rulings so far, Norm was not too optimistic about the trial outcome either.

The defense of Lifespan was actually an inconsequential issue, compared to the protection of top management from any post trial fall-out. Personal interest, always an executive's prime motivator, was the paramount issue now. Damage control and isolation. All Maxes lawyers had to do was contain and deflect the liabilities solely at the already floundering Lifespan Corporation.

Maxes deliberations were abruptly interrupted by preliminary background questions from Richard Farmers - questions that were fairly easy to answer. He knew the tough ones were yet to come.

Richard paused now to look down at his computer tablet and to bring something up on its screen.

Max took advantage of the break in the action to survey the

courtroom. His gaze first fell on Norm, seated at the Defense table. Norm had tried to cover all possible questions and answers yesterday, and developed a system of hand signals that could be used to cryptically supply answers to Max during testimony on the stand. With Norm's surreptitious guidance, at least some comfort level could be had should Farmers' spring any unexpected questions.

Norm acknowledged Maxes apprehensive look with a confident nod of his head, even though he too was haunted by uncertainty with Maxes mental condition.

And there was always the Fifth Amendment. Max could always fall back on that to avoid any embarrassing questions. Today, he only had to survive a few minutes of public scrutiny. Afterwards he could disappear back into his own hidden world of making money. That place where he was the king in his own private court.

Over at the Plaintiff table, Max observed the diminutive Amnion in her infant seat. He still could not believe that one of his own specimens could survive processing and cause the financial destruction of his corporation. That one lousy specimen could screw up years of wheeling and dealing, a profitable future measured in the thousands of billions of dollars. It was mystifying how the courts, the courts he thought he controlled, allowed something that happened months earlier to get this far. *The kid didn't even have a brain at the time*! he reassured himself.

Maxes attention was eventually drawn to the surly character seated next to the little infant, Mike Santino. The man's intense eyes met his wandering glance immediately and stayed riveted onto him. Mike's jaw clenched and the rest of his body didn't move a muscle, as if his entire inner soul was focused on Max. It was an icy stare - the look of an Alpha male. Without his superior management title to dominate this individual, Max was forced to withdraw eye contact first. He sought to avoid that malevolent gaze by looking over at the jury. In the corner of his eye, Max could still sense the menacing eyes on him and the intense animosity projected by this guy. It felt uncomfortable enough for Max to hope that Richard would resume his interrogation again to take his mind off Mike's disturbing glare.

Max surveyed the gallery, wondering how many more traitors like Mike Santino were out there in the audience. Ungrateful employees he paid good salaries to. People that received a good living, courtesy of Lifespan Corporation. They all had real career opportunities with him.

Ingrates, he concluded, *all I wanted in return was a little loyalty.* Max never thought himself disloyal by trying to sell the company right out from under them.

Richard missed all this interplay while he was looking down at his tablet. The computer screen showed an animated video of 'Uncle Scrooge McDuck'. The greedy Disney cartoon character was sitting on a pile of gold coins and joyously throwing them in the air over his head. The picture was captioned underneath with, 'Mad Max McDuck'.

Mikey, Mikey, Mikey, Richard shook his head light-heartedly and thought to himself. *In the software again!* Then he pressed his pen on the touch screen to move onto other text data.

Richard looked up to begin his next inquiry. "Mister Brewster," he said, "From previous testimony, we are aware of Lifespan's government charter to extract pharmaceuticals from decoupled fetuses cadavers for various human therapeutics."

Max nodded passively in agreement.

"And you yourself, were the beneficiary of these treatments?" Richard suddenly asked unexpectedly.

Max was more than a bit surprised. No one outside of Strauss was supposed to know about that. He nervously glanced across the courtroom to Norm for some sort of guidance.

Norm shrugged his shoulders, since this was news to him too.

Max became tongue-tied trying to form an answer. "I... I, uh ...I'm not sure."

Richard shook his head from side to side, "Do we have to get you to roll up your sleeves? Count the needle injection marks?"

Max was stunned, thinking, *How could he know that?* Soon, a ghost would surface and solve his quandary.

Norm stood up and objected immediately. "Your Honor. Are we off on another hunting expedition? The Plaintiff is obviously trying to draw some kind of drug addiction connotation out of this. It's totally irrelevant!"

Richard wheeled to face Norm. "Your Honor, the Plaintiff is attempting to ascertain if Mister Brewster used his Chairman position at Lifespan to obtain special treatment. Please indulge me a moment more in establishing motive and a pattern of corruption."

Judge Burger gave an affirmative nod and said, "Overruled."

Richard continued his argument, returning his attention to Max. "You are aware that your company policy dictates that all patients must be put on a first-come waiting list? That your federal charter dictates that treatments are to be dispensed fairly and equitably sold to all the public?"

Max was still trying to figure out who spilled the beans on this. He didn't really hear the question.

Richard walked over to his paralegal, Greg, for a folder and said in a loud voice, "I have all the official computer lists of all the eligible names waiting patiently for Lifespan treatments for the past four years. Your name's not on any of these lists. Doesn't appear even once. Ever!"

Max sought Norm's hand signal for his unspoken guidance.

While Max hesitated, Richard was unrelenting. His voice boomed, "So, did you violate the federal regulations for fair treatment of all patients?

Did you, yourself, ignore your own company policy? Did you, in effect, put yourself as number one on that list for treatment?"

Behind Richard, Norm discreetly held up five fingers from his palm resting on the table.

Max blurted out, "The Fifth Amendment. That's it. I want to use it now!"

For the jury, it had the same effect as if he'd screamed, 'I'm guilty as charged'.

Richard paused to let the impact of the verbal exchange linger a bit. Then he looked at Max with a smirk and concluded, "Well that's certainly not what I call a firm denial."

It brought a low-level giggle from some in the audience.

Norm rose and bellowed, "Your Honor, argumentative. Counsel drawing a conclusion."

"Sustained. Jury disregard Mister Farmer's remark."

Max was agitated by the embarrassment at Richard's hands. Red faced, he suddenly turned to look up at the judge, shouting, "I demand to be excused. I don't have to take any more of this horse-shit!"

A shocked Judge Burger looked down and gave him a harsh stare. He had not been given demands by so crude a witness since he took the bench 30 years ago - and he was not going to set any precedent today. The judge leaned over, pointing his gavel at Max, and diplomatically replied, "Since you're so preoccupied by horse dung I can arrange for you to give your testimony on video ...from a horse stall at the Belmont stables!"

The audience and jury burst out in laughter at the unexpected admonishment. It was totally out of the judge's usually polite and formal character.

He banged his gavel for a return to order in the courtroom, and warned Max that another snide demand from him and he would be held in contempt of court, spend the balance of the trial in a jail cell. Max just sat back and crossed his arms, stewing in his own immortal juices.

Richard looked down at his tablet for his next flurry of questions, and delayed as he thought through his strategy. Max was unsettled, like prior Lifespan executives by Richard's tactic with the tablet. They all wanted to know what damaging data was programmed into that electronic gizmo.

Then, the attorney's verbal grilling resumed, first with commentary. "We've already have depositions and testimony from other employees and executives of Lifespan Corporation of an R&D project that revived human fetuses for extraction of biological materials. This same project included our Plaintiff, Amnion, known you as specimen UH0744." Richard closed the distance between himself and the witness, putting his face within two feet of Maxes, and asked abruptly, "Did you have personal knowledge of what was going on in the R&D lab? On this project 'Greenhouse'?"

Max looked Richard straight in the eye. For his response, he would have to rely on all the proven instincts that helped get him were he was today.

He lied.

"No I did not," he indignantly replied. "I delegated all details on R&D projects to my Chief Scientist, Dr. Peter Strauss."

"Come on," Richard ridiculed, as he turned to walk over to the jury, "This situation was in the newspapers. You mean everyone else in America knew about this but you, President and Chairman of the Board of Lifespan Corporation? It was only you, who didn't know anything?"

Max retorted, "Well, of course I became aware of this after it became public. And I took corrective action to oversee that such a matter couldn't happen again."

The last phrase of his denial was interpreted by the more astute jurors as a Freudian slip. Richard didn't miss that either and added, "Well, corrective action implies something previously existed that needed correcting."

The hard edged attorney returned to face Max directly once more. "Did your corrective action include ordering the death of dozens of living fetuses in the R&D lab? Was that your idea of preventing it from happening again? A quickie cover up? Destroy the evidence of human lives?"

Norm rose and objected strenuously. "Your Honor! Lack of foundation!... Badgering the witness! These accusations are still speculation on the part of Mister Farmers. Mister Brewster need not answer such unsubstantiated accusations."

Your Honor," Richard countered, "We've proven that Lifespan was spending ten of millions of dollars per year on these fetal experiments, and by testimony of its own employees was processing living human beings into drugs. Do we have to sit here and accept that the executive in charge didn't know where tens of millions of dollars per year were going?"

"Even if he did," Norm rebutted, "there's no law against terminating a fetus. It's just an organic specimen, not a human being." Norm raised his hands for emphasis, "Women terminate these things all the time. There's no crime in that."

Judge Burger, surprisingly animated, intervened, "The status of a fetus in our society is an important question. Certainly, it is an issue worthy of further review by the judicial system. However, the plaintiff was clearly alive, on her own at the time of the allegations, as corroborated by other Lifespan employees. Mister Farmers question is merely to find out if this executive was involved in terminating live fetuses, one of which was the plaintiff at the time. Then, obviously, he would also have been a threat to her life at the time."

The justice leaned over and directed Max to answer the question.

Max looked helplessly at Norm for some direction, hesitating through an agonizingly long period of silence.

"We're still waiting," the judge reminded him.

Max answered defensively, "I'm just a businessman." Panicky, he looked to the jury for some sign of sympathy, "Just trying to make a reasonable profit for my family."

"I'll bet you profit," Richard commented with contempt.

Norm interrupted again. "Your Honor. My client is protected by the 'corporate veil' from any wrong doing that may occur in the corporation. He is not on trial here, the corporation is. His decisions are made within the context and protections that corporate business law affords."

Richard argued, "What's your point Counselor? Mister Brewster is no longer named in our complaint?"

Judge Burger barked, "Overruled. Answer the question Mister Brewster ...and remember you are under a sworn oath of truthfulness."

During this interplay, Max did some fast figuring. Strauss was the only one who knew he gave the orders, and he'd already stonewalled this issue using the Fifth. No one would ever know the truth anyway.

He swallowed hard, and finally replied in a hoarse whisper, "I categorically, and unequivocally, did not order any such thing."

It had all the credibility and sincerity of OJ Simpson.

Richard's reaction surprised everyone. Instead of continuing his tongue-lashing, he shifted to a calmer tone. "OK, we have your sworn denial under oath subject to perjury. We have no further questions from the witness." He waved his hand as he turned away from Max. "Excused. Subject to recall."

Max stood up promptly. He was a bit stunned, and moved out of the witness stand without delay, almost trip coming off the platform. He told the 'big lie' and got away with it again!

Norm couldn't believe they were off the hook so easy.

Even the jury thought Richard had the witness on the ropes. Why did he not finish him off?

Noon recess was ordered, and the trial was adjourned until after lunch. Max was back at the defendant's table with his cohorts and body guards shaking hands and feeling a bit giddy. It was celebration time and lunch at a favorite downtown bistro. They kept exchanging forced laughter as some kind sign of bravado as they filed into the aisle to leave. Mike walked up alongside, and suddenly whispered into Maxes ear, "It ain't over yet, you dirt bag."

Max flinched, recoiling from the sudden insult and turned indignantly saying, "Get this bum outta my face!"

His armed bodyguards moved towards Mike, as Richard adroitly maneuvered in between the two, preventing an incident. He quickly shuffled Mike away to another exit, where Amnion and nurse Hart were waiting to have lunch together with him. Max was whisked away downstairs by his guards to his black SUV with heavy tinted windows waiting in the basement garage.

* * * * * * * *

As the afternoon court reconvened and the judge seated, Richard made a motion to add another witness to the proceeding.

"I believe this next witness, Your Honor," Richard explained, "will tie up some loose ends left by this morning's witness testimony."

"You may proceed, Mister Farmers."

A nervous Max sat up on the edge of his seat asking Norm, Who's this loose end?

Norm objected to this new witness. "No prior notice, Your Honor."

The Judge turned to Richard for rebuttal. "Your Honor, this witness is being called to shed light on statements made by Mister Brewster's testimony this morning.

Judge Burger stated, "Under those conditions you may proceed, and make sure this witnesses testimony has basis with the prior witness testimony."

"Thank you your Honor," Richard said. In a loud voice he called out, "The Plaintiff calls Eve West to the stand."

The corporate boys at the Defense table were flummoxed. Norm mumbled to them, "How did they find her?" Max whispered,"I thought she'd be dead already."

Eve made a grand entrance from the back door of the main aisle. Her subdued form was even more diminished than the gaunt form that visited Max just a week ago. A bailiff lent his hand to gingerly guide her down the aisle and through the bar gate. Her hair was pulled back in a simple bun, and her dress hung like an oversized potato sack on a scarecrow, her eyes sunken, with dark rings around them - like a raccoon. A form so ashen and wasted that it could be mistaken for a ghostly apparition.

She paused for a moment as she passed Max. He was unable to verbalize an utterance. He looked up from his seat with eyes begging for forgiveness. Hoping that somehow he could still control her the way he did a year earlier. Control her testimony. That she could sympathize with what he was going through in this trial. Provide the understanding he was incapable of giving.

By now, Eve was all out of empathy for anyone else after what she had been through. She was already past the point of accepting the

426

inevitability of her own premature death. There only remained to tidy up her affairs on earth before time ran out.

After her swearing in on the stand, Richard offered her a glass of water, which she gratefully accepted. After a sip, she coughed as she swallowed, and handed the glass back to Richard. She found the nerve to sarcastically quip, "Hurry up with your questions before I die right here on the stand."

Richard smiled graciously at this obviously tough woman. Even in her final days she, somehow, found some trace of human witticism.

Richard began his examination by establishing her position as Director of Corporate Communications within Lifespan Corporation's executive hierarchy, and her duties at the time when Amnion was a fetal specimen.

"During the period after the story about fetal revitalization was in the newspapers, what did Mister Brewster do? What did he say?"

Eve paused for a moment and looked directly across the courtroom. "He called several staff meetings to try and cover up what we were doing. I was told to create a smoke screen to feed to the media. Plant misleading information. Stir up the women's rights groups."

The courtroom remained absolutely hushed into silence. Eve's condition seemed to stifle her voice. Everyone in the courtroom wanted to hear her faint testimony and strained to discern every word. At the Defense table, Max leaned his elbows on the table and bowed his head, rubbing his hands over his face. Norm could not bring himself to rise up and challenge the testimony of an old friend on her way out. Especially, when it was the truth.

Richard zeroed in on the all-important question, "Who gave the order to destroy all the live human fetuses in the R&D lab after the story broke in the newspapers."

Eve looked down at her trembling shriveled hands for a moment, and then collected her energy to announce in a clear voice, "Max Brewster said to me that he gave the order himself to Dr. Strauss to kill everything in the lab ...to get rid of all the evidence. Burn all the fetuses."

Some in the audience gasped at the abrupt simplicity of destroying dozens of human lives from just a single man's word.

Richard turned to the jury and quietly remarked, "And some two dozen human being's early lives went up in smoke like Auschwitz." He walked back to Amnion's innocent form, and turned towards the jury."My Plaintiff could've been butchered there too - if she hadn't been rescued."

All eyes in the courtroom fell first on the innocent Amnion and then on Max Brewster. Max prodded his attorney to do something. Norm finally stood up, still trying to formulate an objection or something. Instead he requested, "Your Honor. Defense requests a recess to evaluate this new witness and her testimony."

An unsympathetic Judge Burger replied, "Your request will be granted at the conclusion of this witness testimony. You can hardly expect someone in her condition to be subject to the rigors of coming back and forth to this courtroom over several days time."

Richard resumed his examination of Eve. "You were also personally involved with the chairman, Mister Max Brewster,"

"Yes I was," she replied calmly, "In fact ...in fact, I was his mistress."

People in the gallery were actually leaning forward on their seats as the testimony became as juicy as some kind of sordid and weird soap opera.

"Were you intimate," Richard asked.

"We had sexual relations," an unabashed Eve volunteered.

"Then you were able to see every part of his skin?"

"Yes, I saw every ...every little thing."

The answer was interpreted as an off-handed pun of Maxes genitals, and caused some nervous laughter that abruptly subsided when the stern judge reached for his gavel.

Richard suppressed a smirk, and asked. "What other unusual things did you notice?"

"Well," she started, "he had these needle marks on his arms.
At first, he explained they were vitamin inoculations. Except, I noticed changes happening in his appearance."

"Like what?"

"His bald spot began to fill with new hair growth. His gray hair began to disappear. Wrinkles on his face began to fade."

"Remarkable," Richard sarcastically added. "Did you ask Mister Brewster about these changes?"

"Oh, I mentioned it to him. He always was evasive about it. Said the needle marks there were from weight loss injections. Finally though, one day, I cornered Dr. Strauss. He confided that he was giving Max, I mean Mister Brewster, specimen extract injections. Lots. Several times a week."

Richard turned to face the jury. "But both of these gentlemen have either denied or declined to admit what you're saying. It's your one word against theirs."

Eve looked composed and unemotional, speaking in a low even tone. "I realize that. However, my word is the truth." She looked up plaintively at the judge, and then turned to face the jury in the continuing silence of the courtroom. Her voice quivered slightly. "I'm going to die soon. As surely as the sun will set. In addition, up until recently, I've pursued my life and career for my own personal advantage. So...I think, before I leave this life, that I owe all those lives lost in Lifespan the truth of their demise. I bear witness to the truth. The truth is the only thing I can both take with me and leave behind."

With her gaunt face and pathetic physical image, it was almost as though she was already speaking from the grave. The full glossed red lips were now only a narrow pale slit. Her voice became raspy yet still intelligible in the hush of a hundred listening ears. "We did terrible things at Lifespan. We sacrificed the future generation. We killed innocent lives in a mad dash for profits with the excuse that we were saving lives."

A single delicate tear ran down Eve's cheek, as she looked down at the skeletal joints of her thin fingers. Richard tried to remain composed as she gave her last confession.

"You know," she added, "the government gave us the license to kill. Said these people were not human. Unscrupulous people were in control. The people who financed and orchestrated it. They are still sitting untouched and unremorseful in this courtroom. Right over there."

She pointed a thin bony, curved finger at Max, like the Grim Reaper..

There was a silent pause as all eyes fell again on Max. He nervously leaned over to Norm and whispered something in his ear. Norm listened without taking his gaze off Eve on the stand. He shook his head and seemed to object to whatever he heard. Max remained undaunted and poked Norm's shoulder with his elbow to carry out his wishes.

Finally, Norm reluctantly stood up. "Your Honor. Although the Defense is sympathetic to Miz West's grave condition, she really is a hostile witness. Her testimony has to be viewed in the context of a failed emotional relationship with Mister Brewster. It is extremely jaded by that situation, and really should be inadmissible as evidence in these proceedings. This is essentially a hostile witness."

Judge Burger responded, "Let me remind you that it is not your prerogative to determine which witness is truthful and who is not. That is why we have 12 jurors in attendance over there – glancing their way. Their mission will be to sift through this testimony and determine where the truth lies."

Norm had no desire to cross-examine her. Any brow beating of this witness would only antagonize an already sympathetic jury. "Waive cross." he concluded.

The judge turned to the witness, "You are excused if Defense counsel has no further questions."

"None your Honor.'

.

Richard helped Eve's wasted form down from the stand, and turned her over to the bailiff. She slowly shuffled towards the center aisle, her back arched forward, her head erect. Her body racked by disease, at the same time, feeling her soul cleansed. She stopped briefly to smile at Amnion, now comfortably drooling in her infant seat, unaware of Eve's farewell. Eve gently held the baby's pudgy hand for a moment.

Norm stood up from behind and touched Eve's elbow as she passed. He spoke in a low tone, "Eve. I'm so sorry. I never should have let you go over there." Eve patted his hand and gave him a serene look of forgiveness.

Behind Norm, a sulking Max, was not to be outdone by Norm when it came to being magnanimous. He shot his hand around Norm to shake Eve's hand in business fashion. Somehow he felt the necessity to forgive her for her testimony and said, "Hey, no hard feelings."

Eve stayed motionless, looking down at his outstretched hand, staring straight at him. It was a blank look of incredulity, from two dark eyes vacant of emotion. No hostility or feelings of remorse. Only a faraway expression. More like a person daydreaming. Or, maybe, a person gazing at nothing at all.

Max finally withdrew his awkwardly dangling hand and sat, staring down at the table in front of him. After that testimony, she was just another traitor to his generosity. Another ungrateful person who accepted his money and influence only to turn on him when he needed them most.

Eve turned and slowly exited the silent courtroom on her way to her own ultimate demise. To meet the inescapable and heartbreaking conclusion of her affliction alone.

The courtroom remained silent for several minutes.

CHAPTER 74
Roll out the clichés

Peacefully, Phylis relaxed alone in her bed, propped up by two plump pillows. She was reading a romantic novel before going to sleep - the quiet time afforded by children already tucked away in bed. Reading at night had become routine, probably one of the few single-people rituals that were actually pleasurable. Settled between her smooth Egyptian cotton sheets it felt like something of a luxury, a brief indulgence accorded by mere seclusion.

She was always on the bestseller waiting list at her library, sometimes waiting weeks for a good romance book. Only when Michael was actively courting her, she hardly felt the same need to read the latest novel. Real life was far too interesting. However, once again, Michael was too distracted and too remote right now. Now it was time for romance stories again. She managed to get to the library for a new book on her way home from work, anxious to start a new story in her life, as fictional as it might be.

For years now, Phylis' bed had become her private sanctuary from the outside work-a-day world and the hectic life of raising children alone. Many times she wondered what it would be like to share this very private place with Michael. Wondering how to give up the independent solitude, originally forced on her by circumstances, now a comfortable and routine way of life. As unfulfilling as this singular, peaceful habit could be, it was safely predictable - and always, more or less, under her control.

Could she tolerate the day to day, hour to hour contact with a man around the house again? More cooking, more cleaning, more ironing ...more pubic hair in the toilet and shower drain. More mess.

Phylis returned the book to the nightstand and turned off the table lamp, snuggling between her covers, imagining a life with Michael.

If he were here, a man's hairy arm would be around her, and a fresh kiss would be on her cheek. Creaking noises in the house would hardly feel threatening in the dark. Lovemaking could be a real thing again, not someone else's passionate affair in a book.

Schedules would have to be juggled, and kids sorted out. But now, broken things would finally get fixed, and tomorrow's problems would always be faced by the strength of a two person team.

Still Michael was a hard man to figure. Wild, uninhibited, unpredictable ...and stubborn. Phylis giggled to herself, now thinking almost like an animal trainer. *It would certainly be a genuine challenge to try and domesticate him.*

Phylis turned on her back, her reverie finally focused on Amnion's litigation and the situation surrounding it. She had not been able to attend the trial too regularly, and tried to keep informed of developments by texts to Michael. He had mentioned Max's testimony as a good day to come, only her new job did not allow taking days off with out good reason. Moreover, she had already taken quite few days without pay already, just to testify. It was frustrating, because from Michael's recent conversation, some awful interesting developments had taken place already, and she missed them. In a couple days, there might be an opportunity to spend some time there again with Michael in the afternoon session. She had a sales appointment at a neurosurgeon's office right down the block from the courthouse.

Phylis turned on her side and fluffed her pillow, feeling a bit envious of Michael's constant involvement in the trial.

She concluded to herself, *Well, one of us has to keep their job and make money.*

* * * * * * * *

The next morning's trial began with the same mob outside the

431

courtroom. Norm called a number of expert witnesses hired by Lifespan Corporation. Norm had given up fighting the issue of what actually happened in the R&D lab. Too much evidence was presented in the media videos and by ex-employees interviews to deny that charge any further. His best tactic was to accept those circumstances and then argue that nothing really unlawful had been committed anyway. Fetal specimens had no rights

If he could maintain that fetuses were not human beings, and therefore not entitled to protection under the Constitution, then at worst, the jury could only find Lifespan negligent in not following some government regulations. That is grounds for, at worst, a stiff fine. Not deprivation of life. Not personal liability. Not incarceration.

It was a simple strategy. A tactic rehearsed in his pre-emptive trial simulations played out at Lifespan over the years. Regardless of what they did at Lifespan, their argument was that everything was done to specimens, not people. With the right collection of experts, and historical abortion case history on their side, it was possible to win the case on technicalities. And, as his boss, Max, had said many times before, Lifespan had contributed to all these women's activist and special interest groups for 5 years. It was time to collect something in return.

Richard sat at his Plaintiff table, amazed at the list of experts Norm had assembled from his stable of groupie bureaucrats. He didn't know there were that many women's activist groups in the whole world, let alone Washington DC. It was easy to attract these people to the case. To them, any attempt to dignify a fetus with a semblance of humanity was an immediate threat to their lifestyle of multiple decouplings-- and self-serving careerism.

On the other hand, Richard Farmers had avoided any contact with activists from either side of the decoupling debate. Their political agendas had only served to polarize public sentiment in the past. With such outspoken sentiments, the termination issue had become an insoluble conflict like the struggle between the Jews and the Arabs. Neither side willing to compromise. Both believing their position with almost fanatical conviction. Richard wanted to keep that kind of debate out of the trial. He simply had a client whose life was threatened months ago by a bunch of profiteering pirates. Simply stated, had they succeeded with their plans, she would not be here today ...she would be dead.

* * * * * * * *

Norm introduced one influential, fashionably dressed female witness after another. All stern-faced well-paid government professionals. Each had one of those bureaucratic titles like: Director of such and such, Chief Administrator, or Legal Counsel. Richard let them trot out all their well-worn arguments against the human fetus. Tales of illegal terminations, rights to privacy arguments, equal rights, illegitimacy. They even dragged out a narcissistic, obese white haired woman on the stand. The one that acted as one of the front women lawyers to the Roe vs Wade court decision over 70 years ago. Apparently, after ruining 'Roes" life and abandoning her to her fate, she succeeded in milking the notoriety into one cushy government job after another.

Richard spoke softly in a contemptuous tone to Brenda. "Worse yet, they sandbagged the woman known as 'Roe'. That woman never got her abortion, had a baby, and, sadly, gave it up for adoption."

Greg overheard and whispered sighed sarcastically, "A legal 'hat trick'?"

Richard didn't challenge these witnesses. The jury has heard their acid spiel for 60 years.

* * * * * * *

As the day progressed, Judge Burger noted with curiosity that the Plaintiff's attorney had passed several opportunities at cross-examination. By the afternoon session, he asked the Plaintiff counsel table if they were ever going to cross examine <u>any</u> of these experts.

In response, Richard silently stepped around the table to walk by the jury and picked up his little potted oak tree, slowly examining its progress. Finally, he turned and said, "We seemed to have heard about all the ills of our society foisted on women by the 'affliction' of bearing new human life, and how the law trumps a human life. Richard put the sapling down on the windowsill. "Good thing they don't like oak trees," he added sarcastically.

Norm furiously objected, "Counsel is testifying again!"

"Sustained." The judge said, "Mister Framers you are out of order."

"Sorry your Honor."

Richard returned to his table standing alongside Amnion. "Whew, I'll tell you, I've never seen so many witnesses marching up and down the courtroom aisle with the same dogma. They could have slapped hands as they passed."

It brought some chuckles from those in the gallery, and angry stone cold stares from the female professionals in the audience.

:"Mister Farmers" the judge shouted. "Keep your personal opinions out of this courtroom! The jury will disregard all his statements."

"Sorry, your Honor"

"Then continue…but very very carefully"

Amnion looked up at Richard from her perch at the Plaintiff table, as if perplexed.

Richard continued, "Seriously Your Honor," he added, "Our rebuttal to all these experts will only involve only three more witnesses." We need to remember, what <u>this</u> case is about. About what was done to my client as a human fetus by Lifespan. Not to shrewdly use the law to condemn my fetal client the 'Original Sin' of creation."

Richard turned to face the executives crouched at the Lifespan table, placed himself next to Amnion. "If they were successful my client who is still a human fetal life, would not be here today…she would be dead."

Norm began to stand up to object again, but thought better not to draw attention to the little tyke next to Richard. He slumped back down in his chair.

CHAPTER 75
An odd witness

Phylis had arrived after lunch, annoyed to find the courthouse steps overwhelmed with pro-decoupling activists. With all the nationwide coverage of this trial, every paid activist was converging on this courthouse these days. Norm Stark had secretly arranged to have a public rally carefully staged in support of his Lifespan trial defense. He called in all Maxes favors with the establishment organizations. He had the media televise more and more pitiful human-interest medical cases saved by Lifespan therapeutics. Modifying public opinion had become another facet in modern trial strategy. It might influence the judge, it might influence the witnesses. If the jurors see the demonstrations on the way to the courthouse, it could affect them too.

With her subpoena to testify, Phylis was able to wedge past the guards and the pandemonium and buzz of drones outside. She made her way up to the second floor courtroom, locating Mike and Richard at the opposite end of the hallway. The judge had arranged security to bring Amnion through the guarded back door of the courthouse. They were at the courtroom entrance, Mike holding Amnion on arm, probably giving nurse Hart a breather.

From a distance Michael looked surprisingly comfortable with the baby in his arms, although his dark muscular arms seemed to make her small form look almost pearl like. He had a confident look about him today with his burp rag of 'Wabbits' on his shoulder. If he were standing in a shopping mall, one would assume he was the little girl's proud father. As Phylis walked down the hall, Mike played with the baby's dainty fingers. He leaned his head down, speaking something affectionate to her.

When Phylis arrived, Mike looked up and smiled, planting a quick kiss on her velvet cheek, and waved his free hand towards the courtroom door. The afternoon session was just starting. Phylis took advantage of the opportunity to hold Amnion, and carried the babe inside.

As they walked in, Mike leaned over and said, "Wait until you see our next witness."

In a few minutes the judge emerged and called the room into session. Norm had completed the testimony of his list of experts, concluding his examination with a statement to the jury. "We had all the proper contracts executed by the biological mother to process this specimen UH0744 at the time in question. Whether the specimen was alive or morbid tissue is of no legal consequence. At the time it had no rights of citizenship." He stared at Richard, his voice rising for emphasis, "It's still not a human being until it's born!"

Norm also sought one last time to undermine the rights of the custodial parents appointed by the court, and argued, "If the biological mother exercised her right to a decoupling, then who in this court has a legal right to interfere with that decision?" he bellowed. "And, interfering with the processing of her specimen UH0744 is a violation of her decision, and her constitutional right to privacy." Finally, Norm concluded, "The custodial parents appointed by this court are invalid."

Before Richard could respond, an irritated Judge Burger chastised the Lifespan attorney. "This ground was already covered earlier. The Plaintiff is the legal ward of the State of New York until ruled otherwise ...by me! The birth mother's identity will remain secret "

Norm sat down, satisfied that the objection was in the record. He' would use it as another reason for an eventual appeal.

Richard resumed his case by calling one Shirley Shudder to the witness stand. All eyes turned to the back of the courtroom at the sound of spiked heels clicked on the tile floor. Then all the male faces in the courtroom transformed from boredom to full gaping - including Mike.

This witness was quite an eyeful. A tall attractive mulatto woman with an orange, low cut tank top that accentuated an ample bosom, and a black skin-tight leather miniskirt outlining a curvaceous figure. With jet black teased hair, she appeared to be six feet tall.

Phylis elbowed Michael in the ribs to turn him around. "Stop drooling," she chided.

Norm pivoted in his seat at the Defense table to look back over his shoulder. He could not believe the eccentric people that his opposing attorney could drag up, thinking, He turned and whispered to Max, "Now Farmers will look like an idiot."

Max was less judgmental, and stood up slightly from his seat. He liked what he saw.

Shirley strutted up the aisle, as Norm's frumpy 'expert' witnesses in the gallery looked on with envious disdain. It didn't really bother this woman though. She was accustomed to being on center stage. The tall dark

435

woman took the witness stand and was sworn-in as her large orange hoop earrings dangled from each ear. Judge Burger also looked on somewhat perplexed.

Richard had to be cautious before starting his line of questions. He had to get this witness's testimony without allowing her to incriminate herself. A little pre-rehearsed dialogue was arranged to get past Shirley's real profession.

"Miss Shudder," the attorney said as he approached, "would you please tell this courtroom what you do for a living."

Shirley glanced up at the judge and carefully responded, "I guess you could say I'm a tailor of sorts."

"A tailor?" Richard asked, feigning surprise.

"I fix men's pants," she coyly replied.

The answer caused some snickers in the audience.

"Really?"

"I specialize in men's zippers," Shirley smiled. "When they, uh, you know ...get stuck."

Her innuendo triggered a burst of laughter from the gallery.

From the defendant's table Norm began to stand. Judge Burger beat him to it, slammed his gavel, and bellowed, "Mister Farmers! Where's this going? This is a courtroom not a vaudeville theater."

The judge continued to bang his gavel to dispel all the giggling and buzzing chatter. A threat to clear the courtroom finally settled everyone down.

An adamant Richard then started to explain. "Your Honor, this witness has pertinent testimony regarding the, so called, women's right to privacy that the defendant's attorney and his witnesses keep citing."

"I better hear something soon regarding that," the judge boomed. Then, he turned towards the jury. "I will rule on the admissibility of this testimony shortly. In the event it is inadmissible you will be expected to ignore it in your deliberations."

"Proceed counselor," he ordered, "but be careful with this court's patience."

Farmers nodded obediently and continued. "You live in an apartment in Manhattan?"

"Yes."

"By yourself, Miss Shudder?"

"Yes," the woman said, "but I get a lot of company ...you know ...boyfriends."

Richard nodded. "And, these, uh, friends, do they give you money?"

"Yes, there very appreciative," Shirley said with a smile, "Very."

Some men in the gallery couldn't help grinning ear to ear.

Phylis quickly tied together the witnesses' Manhattan address to

Mike's mysterious visit to the city last week. She frowned at Mike, "This is your handiwork, isn't it?"

Mike gave his usual 'who, moi?' look of innocence.

Phylis hissed in his ear, "You found a hooker. Of all people, you bring back a hooker to testify!"

Mike leaned over and answered, "Yeah. And I told her all about you and Amnion. She can't wait to meet you."

Phylis shunned Mike and his glib answer and just stared forward.

In the meantime Norm stood up and objected. "Your Honor, enough! What does this have to do with this case?"

Richard turned to the judge. "You'll see with the next question."

Judge Burger shook his head in frustration, and waved his fingers to proceed.

Richard asked the witness, "These 'boyfriends', the money, where did it all lead you?"

"Well," Shirley complained, "one of my busybody neighbors got uptight. Before I knew anything, I was arrested for prostitution."

She leaned forward in her seat for emphasis. "So, I got a good lawyer, and we fought the case."

"Based on what?"

"My zone of privacy, of course!" Shirley answered with an almost southern drawl. "What I do in <u>my house</u> with <u>my body</u> is my business ...not some honky governments."

Richard turned to address the jury and asked, "Then how did your attorney argue this case?"

"He told the judge about all these kinds of constitutional rights of privacy. Some legal stuff he got from some of those abortion case trials, I think. And he told the judge about contradictions in the law too."

"Like what Miss Shudder?"

"Like common law marriage. You know, when a women lives with a man for a long time. Gets free room and board. An allowance. Nice jewelry. You're being paid. I mean, hey, that's not a crime? And you're talking steady income – a lot more than I make."

Richard added, "Not only isn't it a crime, I think the woman is eventually entitled to half her boyfriend's stuff."

"Man, I'd settle for half of my boyfriends' loot," Shirley replied enthusiastically.

"Then, Miss Shudder, what was the outcome in your case?"

"Well," she whined, "The judge said my right to privacy had nothing to do with anything. Besides, I waved any privacy when I accepted the money, and allowed men to enter my body. Prostitution is against the law. Period."

"So," Richard added, "this inviolate right of a woman's privacy is a convenient argument when you want justify something… like making decoupling of fetuses legal."

Norm objected, "Argumentative! Counsel is trying to draw a conclusion from the witness!"

"Sustained", "Jury will disregard his statement."

"Sorry again, Your Honor. I was hoping that we could take a moment to review the Constitution and Bill of Rights for the word 'privacy'."

"Objection you Honor," "Plaintiff is cleverly addressing the jury again!"

Mister Framers, you are overstepping your privileges here."

The judge then turned to the jury. "Disregard his statement."

A disgusted Norm waved his right to cross examine. In his mind he wouldn't dignify such a low life, or justify any of her testimony with a rebuttal.

Richard sheepishly returned to his witness." You're excused Miss Shudder. Thank you for sharing your experience."

Shirley pulled down the hem of her leather miniskirt as she stood up, and then Richard helped her prance down from the stand.

A grinning Max leaned over to whisper in Norm's ear, "Just get her phone number."

Miss Shudder stopped for a moment at the Plaintiff table to see the little life Mike had told her about. She stooped slightly, and touched Amnion's stocking clad feet. The seductive woman turned to Mike and Phylis seated behind, and gave Mike a wink and a provocative smile.

An awkward Mike, sheepishly, gave a taciturn wave of the fingers on his knee as Phylis looked on. Then every man in the gallery intently watched Shirley, as she sauntered, head erect, down the courtroom aisle.

Richard's wife, Evon, gave her a husband a stern glare. He was gawking like everyone else.

The seated Phylis caustically asked Mike, "Did she 'fix' your pants too???"

* * * * * * *

After a brief recess Richard returned to the courtroom to resume his case with an odd witness. He rose from the Plaintiff table, turned, and called Jennifer McDonnell – a conspicuous contrast to his earlier witness. This slight young woman was more subdued, more serious - perhaps because of her one-time notoriety.

The name was, in fact, familiar to many in the audience. Miss McDonnell made headlines a few years ago as a surrogate mother. The young girl was artificially inseminated with embryos of a wealthy East

Hampton couple. In fact, the whole story had become a media sensation at the time.

After swearing in, Richard approached the witness and began his questioning. "Miss McDonnell. Are you married?"

"No. I'm divorced ...with, uh, no children."

Have you ever been pregnant?"

She paused to swallow and calmly replied, "Yes. About three years ago."

"Under what circumstance?"

"Well, I was working as a summer waitress in a restaurant in the Hamptons - out on Long Island. At that time, I became acquainted with these people that I waited on every night for dinner."

She interrupted her testimony to clear her throat.

"We became friendly, and eventually, they asked me if I wanted to make a lot of money. Like $50,000."

"And what did you have to do to earn that tidy sum?" Richard queried.

"Well, all they wanted me to do was carry their baby for them."

An undercurrent of hushed voices circulated in the gallery.

Norm stood up and objected, "Your Honor. Relevance?"

Richard stared angrily at Norm, "Your Honor, we've had to listen to a dozen of repetitious expert witnesses called by the Defense over several days on this privacy issue. I would like to have a chance to finish with just one last rebuttal witness!"

"Proceed," said the judge. "Let's see where this takes us."

"Richard leaned forward with interest, one hand on the railing. "Then what happened?" he inquired.

"I was implanted with an *in vitro* fertilized embryo from four of my client's eggs. The father, he wanted a boy. So, they destroyed the leftover female embryos. I received a down payment of $25,000 and free health insurance.

Some spectators in the gallery and jury bowed their heads in dismay at the thought of where modern science has taken society.

Richard continued, "And how did you feel about that?"

Norm objected, "Your Honor. Relevance? This trial should be over by now."

"Mister Farmers. Make your point with this witness," the impatient judge said.

"Thank you," Richard replied, "A few more questions." He returned to the witness. "Then please continue Miss McDonnell. What happened next?"

She looked down at her lap and tried to maintain her composure, finally saying, "After a while I started to feel I wouldn't be able to give up this growing life inside me that was part me. That I would be faced with a full grown baby being taken away from me at birth."

"Then what did you do?" Richard intoned.

Jennifer shifted in her seat, unconsciously pulling the hem of her skirt down. "At 12 weeks gestation I went to a Planned Parenthood termination clinic and terminated the gestational pregnancy. It was quick and easy. No questions asked."

There were rumblings in the gallery as some in the audience found the testimony increasingly disturbing. And others misunderstood this young woman's outlook as pitifully heartless.

"And what did the biological parents do when they found out?"

The witness looked up with reddened eyes. "They sued me for breach of contract. Accused me of murdering their child. Wanted their money back."

Richard turned to the audience. "Many of us are familiar with that case. Could you refresh our memories? Tell us what this couple's argument was?"

The witness sniffled, "They said I had a verbal contract with them to deliver their baby, even though I didn't sign anything."

"What was your defense?" Richard asked.

She looked at the jury, "My lawyer argued my right to privacy and surrogate rights. That what a woman does with her body is nobody's business."

"I know this is difficult," Richard said. "Hopefully you could remind us of the outcome of that litigation?"

Jennifer sorrowfully explained through tearful eyes, "The judge ruled that by accepting the money, I entered into an implicit contract. And, when I allowed the artificial insemination, I had allowed a foreign substance to be inserted in me. Between the two, I had effectively waived any 'right to privacy'."

"Interesting," Richard paused again and then asked, "And what about the deprivation of life issue?"

"The judge ruled against me," Jennifer quickly answered. "He said that their DNA represented a separate individual in my body, and was actually the property of this couple. I had to pay punitive damages for destroying their 'property'."

"How much?"

"They asked for a million dollars," she volunteered in a low voice. "But since I had no assets, we settled out of court by returning the $15,000 of the advance."

The young girl wiped her tears with a tissue from Richard. She continued. "It hardly made a difference though. I couldn't afford to pay either amount anyway."

"So what did this childless couple do?"

"I think they sued the termination clinic, the fertility clinic, the doctor who performed the termination, and all the insurance companies. Just about anybody they're lawyers could find."

"I am truly sorry to have put you through this," Richard said.

With swollen eyes the young Jennifer sniffled, "I can't change what I've done. I can only influence what happens in the future ...to other young women ...other mistakes."

Richard excused the witness, shaking his head, and turned once again to the jury. "I can't help but keep thinking that in all this litigation no one ever remembers the fetus was a human being.

Norm objected again.

"Objection sustained. The jury will ignore Mister Farmer' comments.

The judge called Richard over to the bench, leaned over and reprimanded Richard. "You a hairs breathe away from Contempt of Court. Hold any further opinions to summations."

A dejected Richard slowly retreated from the witness, and returned to the Plaintiff table. He silently looked down at Amnion, happily suckled her juice bottle, kicking the bottle with her toes. Nurse Hart tucked in her bib.

The courtroom remained in an enigmatic silence. There was this profound feeling in the room, as if everyone in our society had a collective share in this young girl's tragedy.

Richard turned to face the judge. "Witness excused."

Judge Burger interrupted the silence asking, "Defense?"

Norm saw no value in keeping a tearful, sympathetic witness in front of the jury, and waved a dismissive hand in the air. "Cross waved."

Thereafter the judge asked, "Plaintiff, do you have any further witnesses?"

Richard stood up and replied," Uh, yes Your Honor – just one last witness. I call Dr. Shahdrey Shahdere, Amnion's neonatologist."

Norm frowned and sat at the Defense table wondering how this new witness was had any bearing on the case.

After swearing in Dr. Shahdere took the stand. Richard breezed through some preliminary questions regarding his credentials and experience.

"You see a lot of babies and preemies, I presume, Doctor?"

Yes, somewhere over a thousand so far - anywhere from 24 weeks gestation to full term."

"So," Richard continued, "I would like your professional opinion of the psychological difference between a fetus and a newborn."

"Well, behaviorally speaking there's little difference between full term baby and a 32 week old fetus. New more sophisticated research indicates would imply that a fetus can feel, dream, and could probably enjoy Sesame Street if it could see." This brought a chuckle from some in the audience. He continued, "Biological development doesn't reach some magic break point at birth. Of course, for parents it is so because at birth they can finally see their progeny. Fetal development is a continuous process. Even after birth, a newborn isn't a totally functional human. There is no magic point to distinguish human life from non-human life."

"Objection Your Honor!" Norm howled as he bolted from his seat.

"Basis, Defense counsel?" Judge Burger requested.

"This witness has a built-in bias as one of Amnion's caregivers."

Richard rebutted, "The witness was not asked anything specific about Amnion herself. He is giving a general opinion."

The Judge mulled it over and responded, "Overruled, I see no prejudice in witness's remarks."

A frustrated Norm frowned and plopped down in his chair.

Richard returned his attention to the doctor. "Ah, one more thing. Is a fetus a woman's organ?"

"Well, no actually. Without protection a woman's body sees it as a foreign body and her immune system would kill it. That is why nature provides a woman with a uterus - sort of a protective buffer. The fetus can defend itself with its own separate organs such as the placenta, amniotic sack, and amniotic fluid."

Richard let that last statement hang in the air for a moment, then, excused the witness.

"Cross examination Mister Stark?" the judge asked.

"No Your Honor," we've already presented expert Defense witnesses to contradict this witnesses testimony."

CHAPTER 76
Summations

R ichard returned from lunch for end of trial summations. The Defense expected to open arguments first. This means there is no opportunity for their rebuttal during summation. This puts Norm at a real disadvantage. Namely, there is no opportunity to respond to the Plaintiff's arguments after he sums up next. Defense counsel is faced with the problem of trying to anticipate and neutralize his adversary's closing remarks before they take place

Norm had a clever plan to neutralize this dilemma. This tactic seeks to have the jurors place themselves in the position of Defense counsel and answer the questions and issues that will be raised in summation by the Plaintiff.

With an invite from the judge, the rotund Norm stands up. buttons his jacket closed and confidently walks slowly over to the Jurors.

"Ladies and gentlemen of the jury, I am not here to deny all wrongdoing on the part of Lifespan Corporation. "

Richard listened, perplexed by what seems like an admission of guilt.

Norm glances at Richard and continues, "Based on information provided to our management for the first time in this trial we have taken corrective actions to preclude some of these excesses from happening in the future. In fact many of Lifespan's employees involved in these violations of our license have already been terminated." "So, we are prepared to settle this portion of the complaint out of court" He glanced over at Richard to gage his reaction.

Richard returned a blank expression.

"However, and that's a big however, we believe the charge of assault, or deprivation of life, or conspiracy to commit fraud has not been established." Then, Norm turned to address the Defense table, and continued with a smirk, "In spite of all the eccentric characters that have been called as plaintiff's supposed witnesses."

Turning back to the jury Norm continued in an even tone, "We the Defense, have proven without any doubt that the plaintiff specimen was not a human being as defined by 60 years of litigation carried out by over a dozen national lawsuits. IT and I repeat IT had no legal status at the time in question. This history has been reinforced by our witnesses, medical experts, and government attorneys. The plaintiff's lawyer gives you personal opinions and amateurs as witnesses. Lifespan has given you case law and expert testimony."

Norm paused and scathingly addressed the jury," Your duty as jurors is to administer the law, not write it."

Norm had a head of steam rolling, as he pointed out the thousands of people saved by Lifespan drugs. Norm pressed each finger for emphasis, as he rattled off all the diseases either cured or reduced in severity. "Alzheimer's, diabetes, leukemia, heart disease, and osteoporosis - I could go on and on. Then he walked along the jury box railing fixing his eyes on each juror, saying,"Ailments that each of you in the jury may have or confront in your own future.... is your life not worth more than some biological tissue?"

Norm was feeling more confident as the jurors started to nervously look at each other. He was getting somewhere. "And remember, the specimens so dramatically shown on the plaintiff's videos were part of a research program to save neonatal lives – to develop a portable artificial

443

womb."

Norm abruptly turned to face the Plaintiff table and Amnion. "Just like the specimen over there."

Just then, Mike began to rise in his seat. Phylis grabbed his shoulder to stop him short. He hissed at Phylis, "He calls my baby girl a specimen one more time and I'll knock his teeth out." Richard turned around to silence Mike and place his hand on his arm. Turning back to the Judge he said, "Beg the Courts indulgence, your Honor."

Others in the courtroom did not hear what was said.

Norm hesitated, annoyed by the commotion, and continued unfazed. "No, jurors," the only real crime was committed by people like Mister Santino over there. A common thief, a person truly responsible for the suffering that specimen now endures."

It had not occurred to Norm that the derogatory term "specimen" so often used by him to describe Amnion was beginning to sound more like corporate arrogance than science.

Norm returned to face the jury again in a more conciliatory tone. "Now this will be my last chance to speak to you directly. Once I sit down, I can no longer respond to what the Plaintiff's lawyer says. So, I hope when he makes his arguments you will answer his charges for me. He puts on a pretty entertaining show, except this is not about entertainment it is about the rule of law. No matter what he says about my client, the supposed proof, or even me, I will not have a chance to answer. So I hope you remember all the wonderful investments in research that Lifespan Corporation has made, to take, what is, essentially, discarded tissue and turn it into pharmaceuticals for the ill."

Norm took a dramatic pause for effect,"To bring sick patients back to life." The courtroom remains silent for a few seconds to absorb Norm's brilliant summation. "Defense rests."

The jury's faces were unreadable. The audience in the gallery were nodding agreement.

Richard waited for Norm to be seated at the Defense table, looking down at his notes, seemingly unfazed by Norm's summation. He stood up and turned to the jurors and the audience, saying,"Geez, for a moment there I thought they were going to plead guilty to everything,"

This brought a low murmur of laughter in the audience, which Judge Burger promptly gaveled into silence. "Mister Farmers, Please!" the exasperated judge said."Move on with your summation."

With head sheepishly bowed, he replied. "Yes, Your Honor."

Richard approached the jury box. He had to undo some of Norm's thunder, and addressed them affably, "First, I agree with Attorney Stark on one thing - when he said please listen to my arguments, and then use the

Defense arguments to challenge the Plaintiff's arguments. So, I simply ask you to put yourself in Lifespan's management position and ask yourself; "Given the facts, would I have done what Lifespan did?"

He paused to let the weighty statement sink in, and resumed his arguments. Secondly, let me say that the Plaintiff, Amnion, does not intend to settle out of court. Plaintiff has already turned down generous offers even before we came to trial. The Plaintiff wants you, a jury of honest men and women, to decide her fate."

Richard waked slowly in front of the Judges bench, and spoke with pauses in between. "This morning Defense spoke about the weight of case law. Wistfully, he said, "Funny thing. ..This morning.... When I entered this building... I happen to glance at the top of this building's entrance portico. Do you know what it said in front? He paused a moment to let the question hang in the air..... "It said Department of Justice. It did not say Department of Case Law. If you believe the defense witnesses and defense arguments then the buildings façade needs a revision.

Instead remember when this case began and we started on this journey of discovery - the Bill of Rights, and the Declaration of Independence. Inalienable rights. Life, liberty, all men are created equal...Created. ....Was Amnion not created? Have you seen any of those rights for my client over there during her torturous imprisonment in Lifespan? Richard turned to the Plaintiff table and pointed,"Did that little girl over there receive any of those inalienable rights from God? Did she do anything to deserve the suffering?" Richard looked down shaking his head slowly.

We have established the path from Amnions decoupling at University Hospital, to Lifespan, to their top secret lab, to Mister Santino's basement, to the NICU, and finally to the little girl at the Plaintiff table over there.

At that instant, Amnion passed a noxious, gaseous bowel movement, sending Phylis scurrying out of the courtroom with the baby. The courtroom erupted in laughter as Judge Burger slammed his gavel. Richard turned to the judge, and just shrugged his shoulders, arms spread helplessly.

Judge Burger demanded, "No more outbursts from the Plaintiff."
That brought another round of laughter from his unintentional pun. Somewhat embarrassed, he waved his fingers in a flourish, directing Richard to finish his summation.

A smiling Richard took a minute to collect his thoughts again and let the audience settle down. He walked towards the Lifespan Defense team, and paused for a moment to look at Max slouched in his chair, the CEO looking very bored by the ordeal. "A world powered by science," Richard intoned. "An exclusive utopia driven by their personal interests - where what is technically possible automatically justifies the expense to achieve it. And in the end, when this promise of profits and immortality has triumphed human dignity, then all other reservations are swept aside."

Richard looked back towards the jury in a courtroom now devoid of the slightest noise, and in an even tone said, "They say they were developing a life saving portable artificial womb. So, I ask you from the testimony of their own employees, how many fetal lives did they supposedly save with this 'miracle' technology? ....NONE! ,,,,Zero percent! All they did do with this 'artificial womb' was to suck the life out of human beings and covered their crime by incinerating the survivors in a crematorium. That can hardly be seen as saving lives."

Richard walked over to the jurors. "In fact the only fetal life saved was Amnion, using the very equipment that they were unable to a save life with. Pointing towards the Plaintiff's table he added, "Engineer Mike Santino, another 'amateur' as they call us was able to use this same Lifespan equipment in his basement to safely sustain and deliver Amnion - 100 percent success!"

Swinging around he leaned on the jury railing with both arms spread, eyes locked on each juror. "Mister Santino had none of Lifespan's technical resources or high powered consultants – just the desire to SAVE life – not EXPLOIT it."

Richard paused to control a building anger in his presentation, while walking back over to the Lifespan Defense table. "Lastly, we've heard about all the wonderful things Lifespan has done with these fetal derivative drugs." Richard returned to the jury box. "I will ask you the same question he did." Richard walked slowly in front of the jurors to eye them one by one, while asking, "God forbid you ever get seriously ill. Which one of you would take a Lifespan drug knowing you would be putting that little girl over there and others like her to death?"

He let that sink in for a moment, while walking over to the Defense table. "Well... I have another answer to that question for Lifespan. Corporation." Richard leaned on the Defense table, staring sternly at Max, bending down in front of Maxes face. In a booming voice he bellowed, "DAMN IT! FIND ANOTHER WAY!"

The placid Norm was briefly shocked in his chair by the outburst. Recovering his composure, he boomed, "Objection your Honor. Badgering the Defendant!"

Judge Burger immediately interceded and banged his gavel. "No more outburst!" He bellowed, and ordered Richard to move away from the Defendant table. As Richard retreated, he added, "Mister Farmers...are we finished here????"

"Not quite your Honor" Richard walked over to the juror's panel one last time, scanning the jurors eyes, one by one. He addressed them as he strolled back and forth, "Mister Stark, in his summation, invited you to take the side of Lifespan management." He paused. "So, I have a hypothetical rhetorical question for you." Then surprisingly, said, "What if each of you, for the moment, assumed a position in Lifespan's corporate management."

Norm was wary of Richard's tactic, but would be powerless to intervene.

"So…. after all the testimony of Lifespan's actual employees of the horrors inside that organization, what would you do?"

He paused to let the idea germinate. "I know it sounds nonsensical. Doesn't it?" Richard retreated to the widowsill and composed himself. He picked up the nearby watering can, and quietly sprinkled his fledgling oak tree.

In a hushed tone, almost circumspect, Richard spoke his last unrehearsed remarks. "But, you the jury can act, figuratively, act like a responsible executive and stop the reckless behavior of a corrupt Lifespan management.

He returned to the Plaintiff table and stooped to look at Amnion, saying out loud. "Just because a lighted candle is so easily extinguished in the dark, doesn't mean it never was aflame….".

Richard turned to address Judge Berger. "Your Honor, Plaintiff rests"

The battle was over. The decision, now out of his control. It was all in the hands of twelve ordinary people.

Mike felt like he figuratively "hit it out of the park."

Judge Burger gave the jury instructions, and the Courtroom adjourned for jury deliberations.

CHAPTER 77
Waiting

Max stood in his Lifespan office this evening next to his massive antique wooden desk, the one he inherited from his father's old garment factory. In a few weeks this family heirloom from Germany would be three thousand miles west - in California.

In the darkness outside Maxes office building, it was foggy with a light drizzle falling. It only added to the dreary mood of depression within. Through the picture windows behind Max, there was no jewel-like flickering of city lights in the distance. Just the beading and trickles of water coursing in translucent veins down the windowpane. The floor to ceiling windows were black as the night, and seemed to suck the light out of that whole side of the room.

An agitated Max bit off the end of a cigar and spit it in the wastebasket, then lit the other end and continued packing his personal belongings in a cardboard transit box. He made sure his precious Slinky was safely packed away.

Norm quietly sat across the room on the couch, measuring Max's testy mood. It was everyone's unspoken assessment that they'd lost the case, time to cut losses and split. The jury had concluded its deliberations in just 6 hours. If Lifespan were to be vindicated, they would have asked for more information supplied by his expert witnesses. Instead, the sequestered jury requested clarifications from the judge of the charges against the corporation. That meant that tomorrow they would be in court to hear the inevitable bad news.

Max puffed and blew smoke from his cigar at a furious pace. After each desk draw was cleaned out, he slammed it shut with a loud whack. A series of burn marks dotted the floor where his ashes had carelessly fallen. At this point, why should he care? His office was already history.

"I want everything shredded Norm," Max announced. "Destroy it. Burn it in the incinerator."

"Do we really want to do that?"

"Why not?" Max grumbled.

Norm calmly explained, "If we're going to start up again with Extentech in California, we need to appeal this case. This trial represents a dangerous precedent. It could prevent us from using specimens anywhere. The public might want the government to shut this whole technology down."

Max finally sat down in his leather chair, still puffing madly away at his cigar, and blowing smoke into the stale air above. He leaned back to digest Norm's comments and started to relax a little. Max gazed upward following the smoke rising from his stogie and he asked, "So, what would be the basis for an appeal?"

"I think we can fight the jurisdictional angle. This trial was in New York. The specimen was revived and alive in New Jersey, that is, before this Santino guy scoffed it."

Max leaned forward and interrupted, pointing his cigar at Norm, "Don't mention that scum bag's name again!" Then he slumped back and took a long drag from his cigar. With smoke spewing from his mouth he quickly added, "I should've fired the bastard, the first time I heard his Ginny name."

Norm remained calm and professional, continuing his legal assessment. "The women's rights groups are already mad as hell about this case. This case could set the stage for some ridiculous regulations protecting fetal life. I'll use that threat to sway political and media opinion against this Farmers character - especially, down in Washington."

"Besides," he snickered, "we have a large clientele of powerful people that still want our drug products."

Satisfied with Norm's initial thoughts on an appeal, Max abruptly changed the subject. "What about the fines. How do we duck the quarter million bucks? The possible punitive damages?"

Norm confidently replied, "Don't worry, I have that covered too." Then he gave a hearty laugh that began to lift Maxes spirits too.

Max joked, "Hey after tomorrow we get on a jet and go to Hollywood, and meet all our movie star clients." Max sat back and waved his arms in the air, "Then we become celebrities too!"

Norm replied in rare humor, "After this, I'm going to Disney Land!" The two laughed even harder.

The loss of this case appeared to be like water on a ducks back. After all, they were rich and superior. They were the untouchables.

* * * * * * *

That same evening, Evon was at home at night with a somewhat subdued husband. In the dim golden light of the study, Richard sat across from her loveseat in his own chair, fingers tips pressed together in front of his nose.

Evon tried to be reassuring, "How ever this turns out honey, I'm proud of you. Your children are proud of you. You stood up for a little girl. You brought a tiny human fetus out of the closet. From here on it's no longer just some worthless thing. It has its humanity back. It's something of value again."

Richard was still despondent and Evon continued to try and buoy his spirits. "You are going to put that company Lifespan out of business. Maybe stopped that whole fetal processing business."

Richard interrupted, "Lifespan was like shooting fish in a barrel. I wanted to go farther with this case." He shook his head in disappointment. "Sure, I wanted to get some justice for Amnion. But, I wanted to accomplish more ...establish the intrinsic value of human life. Especially that unique custodial relationship between a mother and her fetus."

Evon stood up and walked over to Richard's desk. She came back with a stack of letters, and sat on his lap. Lot's of hate mail too. "I've been reading and answering the kinder letters that have been coming in since you started this case. There are thousands of them. People sent money for little Amnion. Fifty cents to a hundred dollars. These people said hundreds of thousands of prayers for us."

She shuffled through the pile in her hand, until she located one letter in particular. "Listen to this one," she implored.

Dear Mister Farmers,

449

...my boyfriend and I have followed your case. We stopped and thought about what we'd created, and how we felt about each other when we did the creating. I canceled my termination and, we're getting married, and we're going to tough it out. We're having a baby!

Richard glanced briefly at the letter, and reached up to pull Evon closer. He kissed her full lips and said, "I'm so glad I married you."

Evon stared down at his beaming face. No further words need be said between these two old lovers, for all times, all cultures.

* * * * * * * *

Mike spent the early evening looking for some divine inspiration to add a nugget of legitimacy to his lethal scheme. He would dare not share his plan to any earthly person – especially Phylis.

His quest led him across the Hudson River to Father Tom's small Infant Jesus parish in Newark, the one with hardly any parishioners left. He parked across the dark street and approached the old red brick building that had become an anachronism in these modern times. With the pastor Tom gone and low attendance, the church probably decided not to replace him and close it down for good. Mike surmised it would not be long before a condo or multi-car garage would be built at this location.

At the church front entrance, he was surprised that the big door was unlocked – considering the rundown neighborhood. Walking down the dimly lit main aisle, it was a bit spooky to be alone in a church at night. *Probably can't afford the electricity anymore*, he thought.

Without the back lighting of daylight, the beautiful stain glass windows were almost blackened. Their images almost indistinguishable. Even the somber sainted statues were covered in sheets awaiting the inevitable. In stark contrast, the brightly lit altar stood out with its focal point, the crucifixion, unchanged in its brilliance by the time of day. The altar was understandably devoid of the usual silver and gold accoutrements, explaining the unlocked church door. Still, it was a perfect setting for a 'last confession'.

Mike sat in a pew a few rows back from the altar, and thought about life and death, all the killing he accomplished long ago. About all the bombs he dropped in the Middle East on people with no faces, and the collateral damage to civilians.

Just targets - he never actually saw anybody on the ground during those raids. Mike tried to fathom this deep-seated feeling of regret. Perhaps it was the disappointment that with all that killing, it never solved anything.

Reflecting on that era, he concluded, *now our government says some of those cutthroats are our buddies.*

Mike's thoughts gradually returned to the here and now - Lifespan and his plans for Max Brewster. That regardless of the trial outcome, this corporate clown would walk free. Protected by the corporate veil. Free to start another corporation, another slick deal. He remembered Father Tom admonishing him to take some kind of action months ago at the Lifespan fence. Mike carried that ball all the way to the courtroom. But, the game was not over.

The goal was not really a matter of revenge. He was past all that get-even stuff. Nothing would bring back the lost fetal human lives, or for that matter, Father Tom and his buddy Joel. If anything, Mike's thoughts were plagued the revival lab break-in and the vision of tormented fetal babies, and beyond that, the tiny innocent babies of the future. Decoupled human victims, unaware of what atrocities were involved in this new rendering of an immortal society. Eternal life at the expense of the unprotected. Everyone in wealthy society a benefactor...thoughts drifting off...still feeling very much alone. No divine inspiration.

Unrelieved, Mike finally stood up and exited the pew, genuflecting on one knee and blessing himself with the sign of the cross. He stared one last time at the crucifixion above the altar. He froze in that instant. The statue's tortured face seemed as though Christ was looking right down at him in center aisle, demanding his attention.

"Forgive me Jesus," he whispered. With weary eyes Mike stared back at the statue's suffering effigy and empathetic face. For some reason he was drawn forward, and took a seat at the edge of a front pew. At some point in his meandering thoughts, a gentle spirit descended onto his mind. It felt like Father Tom's spirit was sitting right next to him with comforting hand on his shoulder. Mike turned toward this ethereal presence and whispered with a smile, "Funny, I thought you might still be hanging around here."

Feeling somewhat secure in Father Tom's presence, Mike resumed his deep contemplation, trying to commiserate with Jesus again.

I mean, even when you were here, you could not stop the powers that be on this earth. The powerful moneyed people, the politicians. And 2000 years later, even your words and sacrifice wasn't enough to undo these kind of people. They are still here, still doing the same crap.

Mike shrugged his shoulders, feeling the need to justify himself to Father Tom. *Look at it this way Father, I saved one innocent life, maybe many. So if I kill one evil person, it's a wash with the big guy. Right?*

Mike started to feel a certain lack of sympathy by the shadowy spirit, reminding him, *"Thou shall not murder."* He smiled at the image at the cross whispering, "Yeah, I know, You and Father Tom aren't buying all this either."

451

Mike bowed his head slightly and concluded his thoughts with Jesus. *You know about these things. You were here. When my time comes, try to put my sins in context. Try to square it for me with the Father.*

Mike searched his conscience for some sign of heavenly reassurance, or some consolation by Father Tom's spirit. None was forthcoming. The signs of a spiritual presence abruptly drifted away - leaving an empty nothingness.

Then again, he thought, how could God sanction his plans? It was, after all, premeditated killing - something he had already done, effectively, even expertly in the Middle East. A disappointed Mike stood up, blessed himself, and turned down the main aisle. After all, what did he expect for his cold-blooded plan in a house of God? Clemency? An Epiphany?

In the desolation of his departure, his footsteps echoed on the hard granite floor. He came to church looking for some kind of consolation. Some spirit that would say, 'Yeah, we're OK with this. You do mean well."

Instead, he left the church with a vacant feeling - no divine revelation or insights. Outside the church entrance, there was only the hard sound of the heavy oak door on its wrought iron hinges slamming behind him - his covenant with the Catholic Church and the Almighty abrogated. Michael was no longer in God's grace.

A lonely Mike drifted across the dark deserted street to his waiting Mustang, thinking, *Who was I kidding here anyway? You can't negotiate with God.*

* * * * * * * *

Far removed and alone at home in bed, Phylis closed the book on her lap, and removed her reading glasses. Mike had wanted to be by himself tonight, which left her wondering. She turned, clicked off the lamp on the night table, and slipped under her comforter. Lying alone in the dark, she remained anxious to hear the final trial decision one way or the other. Tomorrow might be the big day, and she had managed to get the time off from work to be there with Michael. Hopefully, this would end the distraction that was keeping him away from her. Tomorrow would be the culmination of all their sacrifices, and the beginning of an undisturbed lifetime with Michael.

Still Michael worried her. He remained a bit distant when she talked to him on the phone tonight. She could tell he knew something he wasn't telling. By now, she could read him well enough to know that he was up to something. It scared her. And she knew, with his kind of determination, he was capable of anything.

In her nighttime prayers she asked for God's protection for her rash but principled lover, and finished, *Dear Lord, he always means well.*

CHAPTER 78
Justice lost & justice found

At 8AM, the front of the courthouse steps was pandemonium, jammed with demonstrators of every special interest group in the country. An imminent jury decision was announced. The street in front was jammed with over a dozen media company panel trucks. Each one had its white van with a communication dish pointed skyward. It was the culmination of weeks of trial coverage. More drones hovered above.

At 9AM, trial participants arrived moving inside a 50-foot long NYPD police gauntlet. Heavy security screening was set up at the entrance to the courthouse. Mike took note of the assorted drones crowding the sky. He recalled Lifespan armed drones. Moreso, the videos from the Ukraine war demonstrated the devastating effect of FPV suicide drones as anti-personnel weapons. It never felt safe from threats anymore - on the ground or in the air above.

At 10AM, the courtroom was packed with spectators. The atmosphere
filled with the static electricity of anticipation, and as noisy as a high school cafeteria. It all came down to today. Phylis stood alongside Mike at the Plaintiff table, a napping Amnion passively nestled in Nurse Hart's loving arms. Richard was there with his two paralegals Brenda and Greg. This was jury decision day, and hushed conversations filled the air with a low hiss. Behind, in the first row of the gallery, were all the children of Richard, Phylis, and Mike. Also present in the gallery was Mary Lou O'Reilly, the woman hung on the Lifespan fence, and Joel Rosen's family too. Even hospital staff from neonatal came, including doctors Shahdere and Samuelson. All those who had a part in saving the little girl wanted to witness Lifespan's undoing. Adding to the air of anticipation was the media coverage. There was a sense that history was being made today.

Max stood across the aisle behind the Defense counselors table surrounded by his horde of lawyers and bodyguards. He would occasionally sense Mike's intense stare from across the room. Sandwiched between his cohorts he still felt safe but strangely uncomfortable. Like this guy could still reach him.

It was annoying that a non-person like Mike was even allowed to stare at his countenance, or even be in the same room. Max feigned interest in the proceedings to avoid any direct eye contact with Mike.

The courtroom was called to order as Judge Burger entered the courtroom from his chambers, adjusted his black robe, and took the bench.

The drone of voices in the room was promptly transformed into absolute silence, only punctuated by an occasional cough. The stern judge wasted no time and identified the case by docket number, made some preliminary remarks about potential outbursts during any verdict, and instructed all to be seated. Thereafter, he instructed that the jury be brought in.

In single file they shuffled in, stone-faced serious, and quietly seating themselves. The judge directed the Lifespan Defense table to rise and face the jury, then turned to the jury and asked in a resonant voice, "Have you reached a verdict on the charges, ladies and gentlemen of the jury?"

The Foreman stood up and answered, "Yes we have, Your Honor."

"And how did you vote on the first charge of Lifespan Corporation violating their government license?" the judge asked.

"The vote was unanimous, Your Honor."

"Then what is that verdict?"

"We find for the Plaintiff Amnion Your Honor." We conclude that Lifespan's fetal processing operations went beyond any real or implied government license, and violated both the law and decency of this society we are all a part of."

Norm leaned over to Max with a smirk, "No surprise there. We already admitted that."

The judge queried the jury again. "And the charge of conspiracy?"

"We find for the Plaintiff Your Honor. We also find Lifespan Corporation and its officers guilty of conspiracy to conceal these deeds through the premeditated murder of additional individual fetuses not named in this lawsuit."

This triggered a low undertone in the courtroom. In reaction Norm confidently patted Maxes nervous hand

"And the more serious charge of aggravated assault?"

The jury Foreman continued, "We find for the Plaintiff, Your Honor." There was the expected whispering in the courtroom as people leaned closer to each other.

Mike looked across the table at the Defendant's table. They seemed to be amused.

The judge continued to address the jury. "And, the most serious charge of deprivation of life?"

"We find for the Plaintiff Amnion, Your Honor. "He continued speaking. "Furthermore, the defendant, Lifespan Corporation, was negligent in the attack on the complainant…with depraved indifference to human life."

More gasps in the audience.

The jury Foreman cast a scornful glance at Max, who shifted slightly behind Norm at the Defendants table to seek invisibility.

The rising level of noise in the audience caused the judge to bang his gavel and demand silence.

The judge then asked for the jury's assessment of damages.

Then the foreman looked up from his notes. "We award compensatory damages in the Plaintiff Amnion's claim of $250,000."

The spectator crowd was mildly impressed until the foreman continued. "...and additional punitive damages of 50 million dollars."

Max nudged Norm, leaning over to whisper, "What? What? Now we're guilty of all the crimes in the world?"

Norm shook his head in dismay.

Mike kissed Phylis and Amnion, then hugged Richard. Everyone was ecstatic. Richard stood up, turned, and leaned over to kiss a proud Evon in the row behind him. Then he noticed the rest of the smiling audience. In an unusual outpouring of emotion, the audience began to clap. First a few hands, then the jury, then a crescendo of thunderous standing applause. Richard felt a little awkward by the spontaneous outburst, but waved his hands to acknowledge the people's appreciation.

Judge Burger pounded his gavel for a return to order.

"Mister Farmers," he yelled, "Counselor sit down! This isn't a rock concert!"

Richard reacted by bidding his audience to be seated and calm down

In a few moments order was restored. Everyone returned to their seats, Within all the celebration the jury Foreman remained standing. The mystified judged observed his odd behavior and asked, "Do you have something to add?"

"Well, Your Honor," he hesitantly replied.

"Yes, what is it?"

The Foremen cautiously continued. "I have a written statement prepared here. It is signed by all twelve members of the entire jury, as well as, the alternates. We'd like it read into the record."

Judge Burger paused to decide, rubbing his chin, and staring down at Richard who couldn't make anything of it. Then he answered, "This is highly irregular. After I read it, I'll rule on its admissibility"

The bailiff passed the document to the Judge.

It read: "*We, the jury, have sifted through some gruesome evidence in order to make a fair and just decision in this case. However, the deliberate actions of the executives and investors in Lifespan Corporation call to mind the basic issue of protecting human rights - humanity at its simplest and most defenseless. We have found the existing laws unable to deal with this new kind of corruption, this new evolution in the form of murder.*

"We therefore recommend that criminal proceedings be brought by the state against all individuals, corporate and government who

precipitated the killing of fetal life at Lifespan Corporation. Whether by participation or laxity in oversight. And, that the laws surrounding the protection of fetal life be revisited by the government of this country at the highest levels."

Judge Burger thought the comment too incendiary and too prejudicial to be read into the record. In any appeal, it could show bias on both the jury and him. "I will take it under advisement," he said," and as such it will remain unread and sealed for now."

The foreman bowed slightly and said, "Thank you Your Honor," and returned to his seat.

The courtroom remained silent, wondering what the Judge read.

Evon sat in the audience feeling satisfied that her husband's concern was born out in public by the jury.

Judge Burger moved on to the Defendant's table. "Counselor for the Defense Mister Stark."

Norm stood up, "Yes, Your Honor."

"You've heard the jury's decision?"

"Yes."

"Your client, Lifespan Corporation is directed by this court to recompense the Plaintiff Amnion with a cashiers check for $250,000 by 3 PM tomorrow. The balance of punitive damages will be paid by the end of this calendar month." Then banged his gavel thinking the case was closed, and began to stand up.

To his surprise Norm, remained standing as Max snickered in his seat. Then Norm cleared his throat before dropping the 'bomb'. "If it pleases the court, Your Honor, Lifespan will be unable to comply with the court's directive."

The surprised judge looked down over the rim of his glasses and inquired, "And why is that?"

Norm could not help grinning a bit as he replied, "Because, as of 9 AM today, Lifespan has already filed for bankruptcy in the courtroom downstairs, and will be is in receivership until sometime in the future."

A stunned crowd mumbled in disbelief. It was a rollercoaster of emotions for the audience, from apparent victory to a sudden defeat on a technicality.

Max never felt more invincible. He covered his mouth to hide the suppressed grin on his face..

The judge was furious. Everyone was surprised. Everyone but Mike. He knew these people. He's known them all his life. He could smell it coming. Call them politicians, executives, admirals, union officials, public advocates. Makes no difference. It was always the same sideshow, the same deceits. They were the moneyed people. The people that never pay for their own villainy and mistakes.

The agitated judge banged his gavel for silence. He leaned forward to address Norm, pointing his gavel, his voice booming. "You people may think you're real clever over there at Lifespan. But this court will not tolerate an obvious maneuver to disregard its directives to avoid a court ordered judgment." Mike took advantage of the confusion, and turned to Phylis to excuse himself from the room. He said he had an upset stomach. Phylis was too distracted by the interplay between the defendants and the judge to pay much heed to Mike's complaint. Unnoticed, Mike walked gingerly out of the courtroom to the vacant hallway outside. A soda machine was down at the far end, where he casually purchased a cup of coke, then boarded a nearby elevator down to the underground basement parking garage.

Mike appeared outside the cement-block elevator anteroom. He had previously surveyed the area where there was a rusted metal drainage grating at he curb, about 10 feet in front. This would be ground zero, a place where the cleanup crew will wash away the evidence and the danger to everyone else. Max and his armed bodyguards always used this exit to make their clandestine getaway in their black Chevy Suburban. As expected it was illegally parked near the elevator entrance. Mike s sloughed off the crushed ice from the top of the cup and dribbled out about another inch of coke. Casually he walked among the brown-stained concrete pillars and other parked cars to his Mustang. It was a dimly lit place with low hanging heating and plumbing pipes on the ceiling covered in dust and soot. Eerily quiet - especially so, after leaving the pandemonium of the courtroom above. Everyone was still upstairs to witness the courtroom action.

Mike cautiously looked around the dingy garage, then popped open his car trunk to find the briefcase containing the radium. It was time to mix his radioactive cocktail. He nervously extracted a vial of radium from its dull gray lead pig. Carefully he poured a deadly dosage into the cup of Coke, and placed the empty vial back in the sealed container. Mike placed the radioactive soda on the roof of a nearby car while closing the trunk lid. He walked to a nearby dumpster and threw the hermetically sealed lead pig into the dumpster, feeling it could no longer do harm to anyone. Eventually it would wind up at the bottom of the landfill or the bottom of the sea. Returning to the car he carefully picked up the deadly soda cup and returned to the drainage grating in front of the elevator. He quietly waited for fate take its course.

* * * * * * *

Upstairs, in the courtroom, a heated discussion was coming to an end, with Judge Burger threatening that the executives and investors of Lifespan would be held <u>personally</u> accountable for the fines levied. A

457

hearing would be held in two days to resolve it. Norm left the room still mumbling something about an appeal. Max and his entourage left hurriedly through a side door, avoiding reporters outside. Escorted by his armed bodyguards, they were the first to leave the courtroom. Quickly the group headed for the elevator and their waiting Suburban SUV in the basement.

Although money was not the essence of the reason for this trial, ducking the fine left Lifespan's opponents feeling cheated. Somehow, justice was not served.

In the noisy post-trial crowd outside the courtroom, Phylis left Richard and her kids to look for Michael down in the corridor near the men's room.

* * * * * * *

Down in the basement garage, outside the steel door, Mike listened for the elevator arrival. The bell dinged and he could hear muffled laughter and Max's boisterous voice. Quickly he cocked his arm to deliver the insult in less than a second. As the group emerged through the door, two bodyguards flanked Max, followed by Norm and another lawyer.

Mike waited for Max to reach the drainage grating, then lurched forward at the bunched-up group, launching the deadly liquid at Max. The first splash hit his chest, causing Max to yell. Then a second lunge splattered the remnant of the deadly coke square into his face and gaping mouth. Max jerked and twisted away immediately. Mike felt a crashing blow to the side of his face.

Stunned by the impact, the empty cup fell from his grasp. In his zeal to deliver the coke, Mike had left himself totally defenseless. Then a pounding push from behind drove him into the side of the Suburban parked nearby. He literally bounced off the car, sliding down to the pavement. Just as suddenly, someone jumped on his back, grabbed his arms, and pushed a knee into his spine. Mike's body crumpled as he was driven to the floor, his face smashing into the concrete with a thud. Dazed, face down on the ground, he tried to bring one hand around and protect his face. Then a foot stomped on his knuckles.

By now, it was pandemonium in the garage with Norm yelling to get Max the hell out of there, and the body guards kicking Mike's ribs and delivering punishing blows to his head. One guard drew his 9mm pistol. They'd assumed he'd thrown acid or some other caustic chemical on Max. Mike looked up through a red blur of a swelled partially blocked eye at the infuriated Max who was pre-occupied with wiping his face with borrowed handkerchiefs. Leaning against the front of the car, Max had an odd look on his face as he recognized the taste of coke in his mouth and on his mustache. There was even some coke in his nose. He felt instantly relieved that this

458

wasn't something more toxic.

From the ground, Mike spit blood and managed a labored hiss. "I'll see you in hell!"

An enraged and disheveled Max stopped cleaning himself, came over, and bent down with a sneer, "Well, my friend. You're gonna be awful lonely down there waiting for a long, long time."

Feeling more secure now, the immortal executive slowly leaned closer to Mike's fallen figure, and kicked his ribs. "Fuckin schmuck traitor," he groused.

Norm rushed forward, grabbing Max's arm and pulling him back causing Max to kick in the air. Norm shoved the bodyguards, yelling, "We could have sued him for assault!" He pushed a reluctant Max into the limo admonishing him. "Now you made him look like a martyr."

Mike felt the painful weight finally come off his back, as the heavyweight bodyguards stood up and left with the group. As a parting gesture, a bodyguard put one more shoe into Mike's rear end. Abruptly, there was the screech of tires as the Suburban flashed away. Mike groaned. In spite of his serious injuries and grogginess, he was more concerned about whether any of the radioactive coke had somehow spattered onto his own person or his family.

In another moment he passed out.

* * * * * * *

In no time, up on the second floor, there was a commotion down the hall with several court police at the elevator. Phylis never did find Mike and was becoming increasingly concerned about his whereabouts. She returned down the hall to a distraught looking Richard, who said s apparently someone, had been mugged down in the garage. Then he grabbed her shoulders and looked directly into her eyes, saying, "I think it's Mikey."

Her heart sunk as she immediately reacted with a woman's unbridled compassion. Avoiding the packed elevator' she raced to the back stairway down to the garage, stumbling, then peeling off her high heels. Arriving below, in stocking feet and breathless, she put her dress shoes back on. A crowd had gathered around someone on the ground by the elevator. Frantically pushing people aside, she found Mike lying on the cement floor in a pool of blood. His nose was swelled and faced puffed up like 'Rocky' in the 15th round. There was blood flowing freely out his mouth, nostrils, and torn ear. His shirt was soaking wet with blood to his waist, forming a huge crimson stain. With blood clotted in his mangled hair, it looked like his skull was fractured in.

Apparently his sons had already reached him and propped his head up so Matthew could cradle his father's head in his lap. They crouched, teary-eyed, while waiting for an ambulance. Mike looked up at the boys through the narrow slits of his swollen eyelids, struggling to speak. "Take the keys to the Mustang...", he gasped, "...get it home."

They nodded obediently without question. "Sure dad," they sniffled. Brian added, "But later. OK?"

In the midst of his pain, he managed a joke in a style so typical of Mike. With a rasping voice he slowly mimicked Rocky Balboa. "I think ...they broke ...my fuckin' nose."

It brought a forced smile to the boy's faces.

From amongst the surrounding onlookers, Phylis pushed through and came over to kneel down beside her pathetic lover. When Mike heard her voice it seemed to revitalize his sinking semi-conscious spirit. In response, he formed a weak grin, each tooth outlined in a ring of blood, his distended lip lacerated and limp. He touched her arm with a hand whose knuckles were open wounds of shredded flesh.

Richard pushed through the crowd and joined the group huddled around him. "Who did this to you buddy?" he asked, "Who's the miserable bastards that did all this?"

"Don't matter Richie," Mike choked, "It's all over now anyway ...it's done."

Richard gave a puzzled look to Phylis. Each assumed he was talking about the trial.

Lying below them, Mike was beginning to sense a pleasant cooling sensation that seemed to relax his entire body - as if preparing him for someplace else. The pain and soreness of his wounds miraculously began to ease. Shock was setting in, although he didn't realize it. His tired gaze returned to Phylis' anguished face. His limp finger tips brushed back her frazzled hair, to gaze at her reddened face. He touched a daggling cold crucifix that had come out of her blouse and whispered, almost in a sleepy daze, "Jesus, protect her ...my boys ...and my Amnion." After a pause he added, "And forgive me for what I've done."

Phylis couldn't understand why he was asking for forgiveness. She leaned forward and took his badly mauled hand, returning it against her soft cheek. "You're going to be fine Michael she sniffled. You hold on. I know God is here with us."

He managed a faint smile and whispered in delirium between labored breaths, "Uhh...set... the night... to music," referring to the company dinner cruise. The song from that first night they made love.

A kneeling Phylis, heartbroken, nose running, rocked back and forth on her knees. A torrent of tears washed over his limp hand. In grieving silence she gently kissed his mangled hand and surveyed his shattered body.

This was the man she'd been intimate with. The warm body that gave and received so much loving passion. The strong arms that could hold her so securely. The hands that animated his amusing conversations ...and aroused her most passionate feelings. Reckless and insensitive at times. A man that made her want to reveal the tender sensitivities of the real woman inside.

The ambulance siren could now be heard echoing loudly in the garage as it approached, red lights reflecting off the walls and ceiling. It interrupted any chance to say the personal things that needed to be said.

Then Mike's feeble hand dropped. His breathing becoming more irregular and labored. He grew more subdued. Very still. Like he was just surveying the faces of the family and friends immediately around him. Silently, through the narrow slits in his swollen eyes, he focused on each of his sons, finally resting his squinted eyes on a sobbing Phylis. Through the blurred veil of blood, her face seemed to shine with a halo - almost angelic to him ...like his deceased wife Laura.

A vague fading sensation enveloped him, induced somehow, by that secure feeling of being loved. A peaceful ambience from the satisfaction of a completed mission. The end of a bad time followed by good times to come. A time to pass the torch without regret.

His peripheral vision darkened and narrowed, all color changing to black and white He'd had his share, the good with the bad. The love of two beautiful women in his life. With a short sigh, his fatigued eyes closed, the last images capturing those he really loved.

And, now, finally, all the troubles and contradictions of the world were someone else's problem. Then there was a thud outside.

An explosive device detonated near the courthouse steps.

CHAPTER 79
Senseless

In all the excitement and confusion in the underground garage, a distraught and thoughtful Richard, volunteered to accompany the still comatose Mike into the hospital ambulance. He wanted to give Phylis an opportunity to make arrangements for the care of her own children before going to the hospital herself. Matthew also jumped in alongside his father's stretcher, leaving his brother Brian behind to get Mike's Mustang home.

An EMT rushed around to slam the doors shut, while a devastated Phylis watched silently from among the stunned onlookers. Then the orange and white emergency vehicle quickly pulled away with its flashing red lights reflecting off the dirty ceiling, parked cars, and disconcerted faces.

As it disappeared up the smoky exit ramp, the crowd began to dissipate immediately - the show was over. Phylis just stood there by herself for a moment, feeling numb. Her sweetheart was slipping from her grasp, and there was nothing much she could do about it. She folded her arms together, and pulled tight as if to strengthen a wounded heart heavy with sorrow. It was as if this couldn't really be happening. Staring down at her lover's blood spatter on her blouse, it was a grim reminder that this was no dream. And, glancing over to the place where Mike had fallen, the dark maroon blood stains congealed on the pavement was a profound sign of how serious this all was.

The departing ambulance siren echoed down into the garage exit ramp and stirred Phylis back to reality. Although totally frazzled by the tragic drama, she hurried up the stairs to the second floor courtroom to round up her own two siblings. Everything was happening so fast now, and it seemed there was hardly time to think straight. She called her parents to meet her at home and look after her teenagers, then called Mike's brother Vince. It was also obvious that Mike's boys would be on their own for a while too. She explained that situation to her parents and they immediately volunteered to feed Mike's sons and have them stay at her house until things were settled down.

More ambulances and police were outside. Some demonstrators were injured, but no fatalities. Phylis ignored the chaos, ushering her children to her car. Someone else would have to take care of those injured. She had only had her lover on her mind.

Eyes tearing and swollen with emotion, she drove the kids home, briefly trying to explain the sickening and confusing turn of events to them. Once home, Phylis hastily changed out of her blood spattered dress and showered. By this time, a driving headache replaced a queasy stomach, so she returned to the kitchen to gulp down some Excedrins with a glass of water. While staring out the window, her attention was drawn to Mike's gift of the frog planter, smiling across from the sill. It brought back pleasant memories of his awkward way of apologizing, and her premature belief that the tough times were over. With Mike's grievous injuries now, she wondered if memories might be the only thing left of the love they shared. Before departing for the hospital, impulsively, she leaned over the sink and kissed the frog's nose for luck.

Phylis continued to move through the house like a whirlwind, rushing to hug her family goodbye and then leaving for University Hospital's emergency trauma center. It was a nerve racking drive, not knowing what condition Michael would be in when she arrived there. Wiping her eyes, she resolved that she had to be prepared for the worst.

* * * * * * *

Mike's inert form spent the afternoon moving from the ER to X-ray to MRI and back to ER. Several specialists were already pouring over the pictures from those tests and discussing his case. As it turned out, the story behind his injuries was as much an interest to the staff as his vital signs. They had all followed the Lifespan trial with acute interest. Mike remained unaware of the swirl of activity around him, and his newfound celebrity status – some were fans, some were not.

When Phylis arrived at the hospital, a plastic surgeon was already called in to suture his lip and the gash in his cheekbone. She stopped at the ER Reception, and asked, "How is he?" she anxiously implored, "I'm his wife."

They let her see her husband lying on a gurney. Mike's swollen face was barely visible with all the gauze wrappings on his head. And with the busy trauma team packed all around him it was difficult to discern his condition, although Phylis keenly noted no discernible signs of movement.

A young ER doctor turned around and took her aside to apprise her of the situation. He spoke in a guarded low voice, "He has some superficial facial lacerations that we've already repaired - no discernible nerve damage." He has a concussion."

Richard arrived just in time to join Phylis and hear the doctor say, "We managed to get the torn ear reattached too." Richard winced in empathy.

Casually, the ER doctor pointed his thumb over his shoulder at Mike on the treatment table, "The surgeon is working right now on setting his broken nose. X-rays showed no evidence of internal cranial hemorrhaging or other organ damage, but he does have both a bruised rib and another one possibly fractured on the left side. MRI confirmed some serious head trauma, and there's some fluid build up that we're watching."

Phylis interrupted, "When will he be conscience? When can I talk to him?"

The doctor hesitated, becoming a bit more evasive. "We're going to move him to ICU for a while. We need to monitor fluid buildup in the brain tissues for possible drainage. If that goes well then we'll try to find him a room on the post op floor."

"OK so when can I speak to him?" she insisted.

The doctor became more serious, "Well... actually... right now, he appears to be comatose..."

That answer didn't sit well with either Phylis or Richard. She felt a bit wobbly from the news and clung to Richard's side for support. Images of other coma horror stories put fear in her heart.

"But when will he wake up? A day? A week? When?"

The ER doctor shrugged his shoulders. "Everybody is different. I really can't say." While Richard kept a slumped Phylis propped up, the doctor concluded, "We'll know a lot more in a few days."

"Look doctor," Richard interjected, "I have a private room for my buddy, and, whatever else this lady needs to be comfortable."

"That will have to be cleared with the Admissions Director, Mrs. Deever," he said with an implied warning.

"I've been there already," Richard said, "And all you people down here have to do is just call her for the room number when you ready to move him from ICU."

The young doctor lifted his eyebrows in disbelief. Getting a room in this hospital was always a monumental undertaking. What? A private room? "OK, I'll believe this when I see it," he cynically responded.

As he returned to his duties, he stopped and asked, "By the way. Your friend. Was he in a car accident?"

"No, not quite," Richard quipped with ironic humor, "but, you could say he took a beating in court."

* * * * * * *

Outside in the Emergency waiting room, Richard hugged Phylis goodbye, and left the hospital to begin tracking down those responsible for Mike's beating. He had already taken steps with the hospital director to prevent any media people from disturbing Mike or Phylis, leaving instructions to just give a statement that the Mike was in guarded condition.

What had been a day of triumph, had abruptly become a sober day of bitter disappointment. And, as for Richard, all the hard work leading up to this point was now made inconsequential by Lifespan's bankruptcy. Complicating matters, he still did not know entirely what had happened to his buddy, down in that garage, or who started it. All he was thinking about, was that whatever the reason for Mike's injuries, somebody was going to answer for it.

In a few monotonous hours, Phylis was joined in the waiting room by Mike's children, and together they played the interminable hospital ritual of keeping vigil. It was not long before, word got around the hospital of Mike's admission, and friendly staff stopped by to see how he was doing. First Dr. Shahdere and nurse Hart from neonatal, then Dr. Samuelson, who delivered Amnion. All reviewed his chart and provided the usual words of encouragement to Phylis. It did give her a measure of comfort to have inside hospital people following his progress, and insuring he received the best treatment. With these caring people around, at least he was in no danger from Lifespan anymore.

By the time Mike's brother Vince arrived, Mike had already been moved to ICU and Phylis was at his bed side with the boys. Matthew finally broke down and cried. Until now, Phylis hadn't much close contact with them. They knew little of the intense romantic relationship between

464

their father and her. Initially, casual acquaintances, they were now intimately bonded in this tragic vigil together.

Hesitantly, she offered her outstretched arms to the boy, and to her surprise, Matthew savored her embrace. It almost felt like fate had naturally dictated that she have a greater family now. With Mike's son in her arms it felt as if she was clinging to a small piece of her wounded lover.

A sort time later, Phylis was interrupted by a phone call at the nurse station nearby, and passed the distraught Matthew over to Vince. It was Richard on the phone.

He explained, "I received a call from Norm Stark, Lifespan's attorney. He wanted to explain what happened in the garage.

"Apparently, Mike threw a cup of soda at Max, and the bodyguards mistook it for acid. They over-reacted. Norm tried to stop it."

Phylis thought it odd that Mike would do that. She would have accepted that he tried to beat Max up, even to shoot him. All this just to throw some soda? It didn't make any sense. It was so stupid. So senseless.

Richard continued speaking, "He'd like to execute a release so neither of us sues the other party. He says he's very sorry, and they'll cover his medical expenses. They want to make a deal."

Phylis was bereft of sympathy for anyone connected with Lifespan, and asked, "What did you tell them?"

"I said, your being sorry is not going to bring him out of a coma, and hung up."

Miffed by Lifespan's attorney, Phylis put the nurse's desk phone back on the receiver, forgetting to say goodbye to Richard. Mike's behavior still left her disappointed and confused as always.

Returning to Mike's side, she found Matthew had finished his cry, and on the other side his dismayed brother Vince shaking his head.

"My brother," he muttered, "Sooner or later this had to happen. He always did push things to the extreme. Never thought about the consequences to his boys ...or Laura."

With that comment he related the story of Laura's accidental death, and how Mike had been driving when it happened. He concluded, "That's my brother, always the half-cocked pistol."

Phylis could have argued the point. Except she was now Michael's wife and Vince was family. After some further conversations with him, it became surprising, how different, two brothers could be.

* * * * * * *

By nightfall, Mike's vital signs in the ICU were stable enough for a private room on the surgical recovery floor. During all this time, Phylis had received numerous hospital visitors. Apparently, Michael made quite a few friends in the time he had spent over in neonatal with Amnion. However, noticeably absent were any administrative types. Phylis couldn't know that even with Mike unconscious, they wouldn't dare approach him. Word had gotten around of what Mike did to the NICU administrator back when Amnion was there.

Phylis finally sent Mike's reluctant boys home with Vincent, while she promised to stay the night and watch over their father. She kissed each one of them on the cheek, and promised to call them if there was any change in Michael's condition. On a scrap of paper she scribbled her cell phone number. "You call this number if you need anything," she insisted, then exchanged one last tearful hug with everyone before they departed. "I'll call with any news."

By now, her legs ached from being on her feet all day. With Michael unconscious, and her answering all the hushed questions in the ICU waiting room, it was almost like being the widow at a wake. The same physical and emotional drain, except there was no closure afforded by the certainty of death.

She called work to arrange a few days leave due to a family emergency. They would not mind since it would be unpaid anyway.

Late in the evening, alone in the downstairs hospital cafeteria, and in spite of a dry throat, she managed to eat a fruit salad. With the exception of the cashier, the cafeteria was now devoid of people or conversation. It was the same locale where she pondered Maria Alvarez's decoupling months ago. Her small round table was illuminated by a harsh spotlight that only accentuated the surrounding darkness of the unlit areas of the deserted place. This lonely solitude gave her a chance to reflect on how it had all started in this same hospital. The institution that can take a life and save a life - all on the same day.

It seemed incredulous to Phylis, that so much had happened in so little time. How unexpected. The way things can turn out. Amnion beginning her new life, Michael barely hanging on to his, Joel loosing his ...and Phylis in the middle, trying to hold together the broken pieces of what's left.

After eating a little bit, and not feeling really hungry, the forlorn woman went upstairs to visit Amnion who was back on the Pediatrics floor. Nurse Hart had left instructions with Phylis as to who to see at the nurse's station to get into the nursery.

Wandering down the unusually quiet hallway, at the nursery entrance, she was approached by an armed police officer appointed by the court to protect Amnion. He checked her identity before allowing her to proceed. She found Amnion in a semi-private room with another ailing infant. It was such a sad vision. One that a few unlucky parents see, let alone have to live through first hand. Their sick tiny forms reminded her of how fortunate she had been with her own children's health.

Amnion was peacefully asleep on her stomach, thumb stuck in her mouth. The tyke's crib was surrounded by four mobiles, and lined with at least a dozen stuffed animals. Little thoughtful signs of support from the hospital's nursing staff. She just dozed quietly, oblivious to the swirling controversy and lives sacrificed around her.

Phylis recalled Amnion's real mother, Maria. Her haunting last words before Amnion was decoupled. "So you're the little lamb", Phylis whispered.

Then she began to ask herself things. Did Maria somehow still sense the existence of this little life across the gulf of time and space? How will she react when the Judge Burger contacts her, and reveals Amnion as her child? Anger? Happiness? Both? Would she hold her responsible for keeping Amnion incognito? In a few days time all these questions would be answered.

Still staring at the tiny child in the dim light, with the other frail little baby, Phylis's motherly instinct could not be denied. As Amnion restlessly stirred, Phylis stooped down, gently picked up the tot, and cuddled her to her bosom. Tender emotions, only a woman can feel, filled her heart. The child, smelling fresh with baby powder, snuggled peacefully in her arms. A kind of sadness enveloped Phylis. A disappointment that she could no longer bear these newborn treasures - that she could no longer create a child with Michael.

Somehow, in a way, this was their child. At least in a figurative sense. The product of their labor together. In a way Amnion was now part of their handiwork.

* * * * * * * *

Later, Phylis returned to Michael's private room, where a security guard was seated outside per Richard's instructions. With the courthouse bombing there was no taking chances. He cleared her to enter Mike's room, where he was still comatose and hooked up to cardiac and respiratory monitors. In the empty silence of the room, his still body exhibited no awareness of her presence. She approached still feeling the need to speak to him and have him somehow know she was there. Leaning over, she brushed aside his IV tubing and kissed his bandaged forehead. Tenderly, she ran hers fingertips over his bearded cheek, and cocked her head a little to the side. "I love you Michael," she murmured with a tear. "I love you more than any man I've ever known."

Then she smiled, pulled back her hair, and whispered in his one good ear, "To me, you're even hunkier than Mel Gibson."

One of his bandaged fingers jerked. It almost felt as if he heard. It was hard to figure if that were true, or if she was just kidding herself.

The private moment was interrupted by an orderly, who came in to arrange the room for the night. He was friendly and sympathetic, helping her maneuver an extra bed set-up next to Michael's. Mike's dear friend, Richard, had thoughtfully used his pull to get hospital administration to allow Phylis the privilege of spending the night.

The kind orderly even produced a drinking cup and sleeping pill, along with a nightshirt that Phylis could use as pajamas. Before he left he said, almost reverently, "You people...you did the right thing.....just don't let anyone know I said that."

She thanked him for the courtesy and considerate words. It was reassuring to know that good people still exist in this unmerciful and politically correct world.

* * * * * * *

In the solitude of the dark hospital room, Phylis lie awake in bed staring up at the ceiling, wondering where this turmoil would all end. In spite of all the concerned visitors and their good wishes, it was, in the end, just her and Michael in this lonely predicament. No media fanfare, no accolades, no heroic ending. Just two people that tried to do good, suffered, and paid the price.

From time to time, a nurse would come in to check vitals and offer some kind words. Phylis could only nod with a vacuous expression, wiping sniffles from her nose. Even something as simple as sleep would be a welcome refuge now. If there was a compassionate God, this was when she needed Him most.

She turned her head back on the pillow to face her lover.

Next to her, Michael remained inert, with tubes in his nose and arm. Head, hands, chest, and ears all bandaged. His breathing shallow but consistent. The surrounding monitors only showing the steady rhythm of his sleep. In this uneventful tranquility, it reminded her of observing the helpless Amnion, when she had to survive on her own life support system.

Phylis regarded his swollen features, trying to imagine the pain Michael could be feeling, wondering where his mind may have drifted off to. Maybe it was just as well that he was unaware of his injuries. Then there was the issue of when and if he'd ever wake up. And if he did comeback, what would be left of him. Her earlier misgivings about marrying and sharing her life exclusively with him appeared so pitifully selfish now.

She reached across the narrow space between their beds and placed her hand gingerly on the skin of his swollen hand, as if to take a share in his pain. In her heart she wanted to believe that her love could transcend his physical afflictions. That if she could just love him strong enough, put her own life's energies into him, he would pull through.

Fatigued, the sleeping pill finally overtook her troubled mind, and she began to slip off to sleep with a hand still on his arm. Before completely succumbing to exhaustion, she prayed in a low voice, "Dear Jesus I love this man with all my heart and soul. He's my hero. If your message is love, then love him too ...and let all our love bring him back to me."

CHAPTER 80
Recovery

Mike's limped eyes blinked open as the early dawn light filtered through the green curtain of his hospital room. The nothingness of his blackout began to retreat as the startling bright sense of consciousness swiftly filled what had just been a dark, endless void.

His recovery wasn't like waking up from some dreamy sleep. It was more like a period of black non-thought having no time dimension with all the mental substance of a blank TV screen, and all the body senses on novocaine. Then, you are suddenly awake where you left off. Engineer Mike interpreted all this to be like his desktop PC when suddenly switched back on, his brain having to 'reboot' all the basic sensual connections before reacting to any outside stimulus.

While Mike's body stayed rigid, his eyes scanned the surroundings. The tubes, monitors and curtain obviously suggested a hospital environment. The bandage over his broken nose partially blocked his view. It began to remind him of why he was in a hospital to begin with. His first thought was to speculate about whether or not he was under arrest for assaulting Max.

Remembering that horrific beating by Max's body guards, he instinctively slid his good hand under the blanket to his crotch.

Thank God my balls are still attached!, he painfully grinned to himself with manly relief.

As his mind slowly came back up to speed, his next immediate concerns were what day it was, finding out how long he'd been knocked out, and how soon he could get out of the hospital. Unfortunately, in the midst of this returning consciousness also came the arrival of dull pains to remind him again of why he was here. Although reluctant, it was about time to assess the damage to his body in detail.

His hand moved slowly up to his bandaged face and mouth. He felt for his teeth, relieved to find them all in place. To him, the thought of dental work was more terrifying than death. The pressure of bandages taped around his rib cage immediately told him what that meant. His broken nose was a forgone conclusion. And the perception of muffled sounds explained the packing in his right ear. With a dry tongue he could vaguely feel the suture threads on his swollen lip. His mouth tasted stale and tongue felt like #200 grit sandpaper. He was weak and hungry too.

At this point, his sensations returned sufficiently to now sense the touch of a light hand on his shoulder. He turned his bandaged head slowly to see Phylis curled up on a cot against his bed, asleep.

Her presence instantly raised his spirits, realizing that this beautiful devoted woman could still care for him after he had done one stupid thing after another - especially this last stunt.

So, nothing else really mattered anymore. She was at his side, and he cherished the love of a beautiful devoted woman. It was her love that would make the rest of his life worthwhile. Her love, that would help him overcome his immediate pain, get past his injuries over the next few weeks, and face whatever recovery trials lie ahead.

He brought his other arm with IV attached across his chest to gently touch her hand. Phylis slowly stirred, her hair disheveled, and face wrinkled from the pillowcase creases. She opened her eyes to look at Mike's black and blue eyes staring out from deep in their swollen sockets. He managed a forced smile and facetiously said to her, "Well, now I know what you look like in the morning without makeup!"

Phylis just rolled her eyes. Still, it was a wondrous surprise, and her face instantly lit up in unbounded delight. All at once, she threw off her blanket and sprung up onto her knees in bed. Not saying a word she kissed his hand and bounced with joy, rocking from knee to knee. She laughed. She cried.

Apparently, Jesus was closer than she ever imagined. For a moment she paused - time to remember to thank Him in the privacy of her own mind.

Mike beckoned her closer amidst her revelry to say something. As she leaned down, he grinned against the constraint of his bandages, and asked in a low hoarse voice. "Did we have 'rough sex' or what?"

Phylis smiled and shook her head, "Idiot! Some things just don't change. Do they Michael?" and planted a kiss on his parched lips. His sutures pricked her lip, but it was no matter. She cheerfully skipped out of the room, like a schoolgirl, to tell the duty nurses of his miraculous recovery.

Phylis knew that this was the first day of the rest of their lives together. The day she wanted and waited for so very long.

* * * * * * *

Later on in the morning, after Mike was examined by his attending physician he was able to sit up slightly and eat a light breakfast. Phylis spoon fed him the soft food a little at a time, as Mike seemed to relish the attention. In between mouthfuls he tried to converse. His swollen face made speech difficult. Phylis leaned closer to try and understand his muffled diction.

Mike dryly murmured, "I'm doing Marlon Brando - the Godfather."

She laughed, "Silly boy." left and returned to his room with a copy of the *Brooklyn Daily News*. Smiling and occasionally kissing him, she sat down on the edge of his bed with an excited look on her face.

Holding the paper in front of Mike, and pointing to the headline she exclaimed, "Look, its all on the front page." *THIS TIME IT'S SUDDEN DEATH FOR LIFESPAN!*

Mike flashed a crooked smile at the headline. No one knew the irony of the headline and Max's condition except Mike.

"Oh, and look here Michael, there's also a picture of Max Brewster boarding his corporate jet at Newark. He looks a bit weak. Looks like he needed assistance to climb the aircraft folding door steps. Then, it says there's rumors circulated about Brewster restarting decoupling operations in a friendlier California."

Phylis excitedly leafed through the pages to find an article on page 3. "Here you are Michael! They wrote about you being beat up."

Mike quipped, "So, this is my 15 minutes of fame that Andy Warhol said everybody has in their life."

Phylis became more serious. She took the opportunity to ask Mike some more about it. "I still don't understand how you could do such a meaningless thoughtless act."

"It was carefully thought out, and it was meaningful," he rasped.

Phylis just looked back at him confused.

Mike paused knowing what he was about to tell her could risk loosing her love. He recalled his promised that there would not be secrets anymore in their relationship. "Mike said almost casually, "The coke, I poisoned the sonovabitch with the coke,"

"What? Why? How??"

"Because he killed a lot of people....including Joel. A priest. He tried to kill Amnion. Killed Joel and Father Tom…the other human fetuses. It's a long list."

Phylis took a moment to digest what Mike was saying. Somehow this sudden revelation changed her view of Michael. There was this malevolent side she had never truly faced before. *I'm in love with a premeditated killer?* crossed her mind.

Mike could see her revulsion and wavering affection. He looked at her through the bandages, saying apologetically, "I know what this makes me. God knows. But, the trial, it was never going to punish Brewster or

Strauss. It was going to punish that faceless corporation. I just can't see any real justice in that.

Mike reached over to touch her hand, but Phylis withdrew, head down, hands to her lap.

He tried to explain. "I killed people fighting in the Middle East. Eliminated evil people. Try to understand. This was just one more evil monster."

"How can I ever trust you again?"

"If I told you of my plan in advance, there was the risk of you being prosecuted for aiding and abetting. Besides, you would have tried to stop me."

"You bet I would have," she scowled.

Mike whispered through his scratchy throat, "I won't blame you if your feelings have changed. I broke your trust - broke your heart too many times. I never deserved you to begin with anyway."

Taking all this in, Phylis raised her head to look into Mike's sad eyes. Tears welled up in her eyes. She could not understand how she still loved this guy. "No more secrets Michael, no more secrets between us." She leaned over to embrace his broken body, and kissed his forehead.

"No more secrets," Mike promised.

....except, he still had one more.

They spent a quiet moment together, albeit subdued. The affectionate bond survived.

In the afternoon Phylis was still in the hospital at Mike's bedside, and rifled through the *Brooklyn Daily* for another article about Lifespan "Here," she said, "Look, here. The insurance company, *Selective Heath Care,* the one that wanted us to pay for Amnion's medical expenses."

"Read it for me," Mike spoke in a scratchy nasal tone.

"Well, they say that they re-evaluated their position on her medical expenses. They're going to continue to reimburse her medical expenses even after she's discharged from the hospital."

"How thoughtful," Mike sarcastically hissed, adding, "Amazing how a little media attention can give some people a conscience." Then, he became a bit more serious and asked, "Incidentally, how's my little girl?"

"Good, Michael," she replied. "I rocked her to sleep the other night."

"When can I see her?"

Phylis hesitated a moment, as if not wanting to reveal something and stuttered, "Uh, oh, maybe tomorrow."

It was Phylis's turn to keep a secret.

A distracted Mike accepted the answer without sensing something was amiss, and shifted his attention to the here and now. "So, when am I getting out of here? Did you speak to any of these witch doctors yet?"

Phylis put down the paper and stood up. "They say you have no serious internal injuries. Mostly just external wounds and bruised ribs that can heal at home. Maybe be out by tomorrow. You'll get some home care and physical therapy courtesy of that miserable insurance company."

"Great," Mike interrupted. "So, did you ask when we can have sex again?"

Phylis gave an understanding smile, ignoring his last remark and walked over to stroke his cheek and mention her more important reservations, "Whose going to take care of you there? I can't take anymore time off from work."

"I'll manage with my boys," Mike answered, "As long as I know you're somewhere out there. I'll have someone to watch over me."

* * * * * * *

When Mike's sons arrived at the hospital, they were elated at seeing their father awake and rational. This time both Matthew and Brian could not hold back the tears in their eyes. They took turns kissing his forehead, and holding his hands.

"We'll kick Brewster's ass, dad," Brian promised.

Matthew added, "Kick it all the way back to New Jersey."

Mike smiled saying, "Hold on. That won't be necessary for you guys. Trust me. He's already taken care of."

The boys looked at each other, bewildered.

Then he waived his bandaged hand, "Someday I'll explain it all."

The boys just figured their father wasn't totally with it yet. Matthew followed his older brother's lead and shrugged his shoulders too.

Mike quickly remembered. "That package in the trunk of the'Stang did you throw it I the trash?"

"Yeah. Dumped it a week ago."

Unknown to Mike, his sons were preparing their own surprise for him and his '68 Mustang. They'd finally arranged to bring the car, in its gray primer, to the paint shop. Soon it would sport a dazzling Dark Highland Green exterior finish like the 'Bullitt' Mustang. In a few days Mike would be sitting in his dream car.

* * * * * * * *

Mike received other visitors that day, including Mary Lou O'Reilly, the woman hung on the fence. It was an odd turn of events, as she regarded his form in bed instead of the other way around.

"So now, you're the one in bed," she kidded.

473

Mike didn't reply, and managed a strained grin.

Mary Lou recalled some of Mike's words when he visited her in the hospital months ago. She reiterated one of his blunt questions, and asked sarcastically, "Was it really worth it?"

"Yeah, Mary Lou," Mike admitted, "more than anyone will ever know."

Their conversation was interrupted by a nurse who administered Demerol pain medication. It a few minutes he became a bit punk and it was time to let him rest.

Phylis sent Mike's boys home to eat dinner with her parents at her house. Ever thoughtful, she also planned a visit to Mike's home to straighten up things and make sure there was food in the refrigerator for his expected return home in a few days. She would pick up his list of scripts at the pharmacy

CHAPTER 81
So this is goodbye

The next morning Richard Farmers showed up at the hospital with a folder of papers in hand. Only the comforting Phylis was still present in the room. He stood alongside Mike's bed, after Mike had just finished breakfast and was now well enough to sit up. Richard walked to the side of the bed and grasped Mike's hand firmly, holding it for a few seconds. At same time, a Phylis became suddenly subdued and drew closer to Mike from the other side of the bed.

From their collective behavior, Mike smelled something was up. *It's an ambush. Maybe I am going to jail after all*, he thought, but gave no sign of his suspicions. Instead, he said cheerfully, "Hey Richie, I never got the chance to congratulate you," he grinned through the bandages. "You really beat the bastards in court. We should call you 'Richard the Lawyer-Hearted' from now on."

Mike's old friend didn't react to the pun, and remained solemn while sitting on the edge of the bed. He talked for while about the trial and Mike's legal options after being assaulted by Maxes bodyguards, still not understanding why Mike wasn't particularly enthusiastic about pursuing Max in court. After a fashion Richard got around to the papers inside the folder on his lap. Phylis sat down on Mike's other bedside, getting closer and taking his hand. From her distraught look, Mike could sense that the suspicious ambush he felt earlier was about to be close.

Richard swallowed and cleared his throat before starting, placing the Manila folder in his lap, "Mikey, I have some custodial release papers from Judge Burger for you to sign."

Mike looked down on the forms in his lap and quickly scanned them. Then, he became glassy eyed and morose. Deep down inside, Mike had always realized the inevitably of losing Amnion, no matter how things turned out. He just didn't expect to face it today - so soon.

Phylis tearfully added, "I've already signed them. Amnion has to be with her own family now - with her real mother."

From his bruised eyes teardrops soaked the gauze bandages and ran down Mike's face. He would have to give up the little life he had fought so hard to preserve. Release the little girl that he, so profoundly, and so literally, grew to love. His mind drifted back in time to reflect on all the little private moments he'd spent with the acrobatic Amnion in his basement. Then there was her momentous 'birth'. And, the painful struggle to cling to life in neonatal. Ultimately, the fight to gain her own human dignity in the courts. The other lives lost along the way.

He tried to avoid his two companion's sympathetic stares by looking sideways out the window.

"I didn't beat anybody in all this," Mike sniffled. "I think I beat myself."

Even Richard became a bit misty eyed. He had not been that personally moved over anything since he could remember.

Mike continued to face the window and speak softly. "Maybe I always knew that this day would come - that I was kidding myself ...I just kept pushing it to the back of my mind."

Phylis came closer, touched his chin, and gently guided his bandaged face towards hers. She leaned forward to place herself inches from his sorry face. "Michael," she said with all the sincerity a woman can muster, "if I could give you our own daughter I would." Then gently kissed his bruised forehead.

She pulled slowly away and added, "It would be selfish to deny this infant her natural mother. I know this woman. She's a good full-time homemaker. I honestly believe she never really wanted to give up her baby to begin with."

Richard chimed in too. "It's time to let go of the fetus Amnion, Mikey. Time to realize that she is now a baby, a growing girl. Time to let her be a real person with a real first name and a real last name."

Mike looked down at his broken body lying in bed. The unsympathetic cruelty of reality was all too apparent. It was obvious that he wasn't going to be able to take care of a baby at home. He didn't even have a job at this point. He stared hopefully at Phylis for an instant, only to concede that she already had her own family responsibilities and had to work on top of that.

Deep in his heart he'd always believed that raising kids was a full-time job. After Amnion's struggle this far, she deserved at least a full-time mother and a real father. He would just have to trust Phylis's judgment on the suitability of the parents. Any other arrangement would be selfish on his part.

With his empathetic friends still patiently awaiting Mike's decision, he breathed a long sigh of resignation and said, "Hey, when was I ever good for anyone's health?"

Richard hesitantly offered a pen. A remorseful Mike reluctantly scribbled his name, and made a request. "Bring Amnion to me. I want the chance to see my little girl one last time."

Richard collected the forms back into the folder, and nodded in the affirmative saying, "Believe me, you did the right thing Mikey.

A tearful Phylis chimed in, "It may not feel too good right now. It may take a while. In the long run, we'll see, you did the right thing."

* * * * * * *

Phylis returned that afternoon with a fussy Amnion. As an infant, it was sometimes a mystery as to why she might be feeling irritable at any given time. Perhaps something in the child's formula was disagreeable. Who knows?

Nurse Hart accompanied them from the Pediatric floor.

"Finally getting some chubby cheeks!" Mike chuckled as he pointed a bandaged finger at the little girl's pudgy face.

"Finally," nurse Hart smiled with pride. "And some peach fuzz too!" she added, as she stroked the fine brown hair on Amnion's soft scalp.

Mike sat up painfully, requesting that the baby be put down on his lap on the bed in her infant seat, facing him. He asked for a few minutes alone with the tyke.

Phylis and the nurse retired into the corridor to discuss Amnion's discharge from the hospital.

Once alone, Mike looked at the tiny form that he had known since she was no bigger than his pinky. Once some mysterious entity growing in the basement life support cart. For a brief time, she was his alone, something of no consequence to anyone but him. He tried to imagine what kind of girl she would eventually grow up to be. Like a true parent, only superlatives entered his thoughts.

Amnion stared wide-eyed, scanning Mike's bandaged and swollen countenance, and could not recognize him immediately. She remained puzzled by the bandaged face. Eventually though, the tubes and instruments surrounding him proved more distracting, and her eyes darted around him from one object to another.

"How's my little pal?" Mike mumbled.

Amnion paused for a moment of reflection. After a while, she smiled with the pleasant recognition of his voice. Her deep brown eyes widened and returned to stare at his face, criss-crossed with tape. Finally, her little booty feet kicked in a kind of happy acknowledgement. Mike watched her little mouth drool with bubbles.

Would she go to college? the weary Mike speculated. *Get married. Have her own children ...Of course!* he told himself.

"Well," Mike continued with his monologue, "there's a lot of things we won't be doing together anymore."

Mike dreamed about the things he was going to miss. Her first birthday - the magical reflection of candlelight in her twinkling eyes. The excitement in her face at a park playground. Her first steps. The first day at school - the tears at the bus stop. Dance recitals. Little girl stuff.

"Hey," Mike sighed, "who am I kidding anyway. My chance for a daughter was over with Laura."

Mike tried to maintain Amnion's wandering attention. "You won't remember me kid," he intoned, "or the other people whose lives were lost in your creation."

Mike reached out his hand to touch the soft skin of Amnion's pudgy little calf. Then he paused and concluded, "I'll always remember you kid. I'll always remember being there when you struggled to take your first breath."

Amnion began squirming and stretching, now oblivious to Mike's concerns.

"Hey, your diaper too tight?" Mike kidded.

The babe didn't understand the pun and her face continued to grimace and turn a dark beet red. Her attention was getting more withdrawn from the outside world, and more preoccupied with whatever was bothering her insides.

Inevitably Amnion had reached her limit. Her irritable bowels gave her sufficient cause to let out a piercing wail.

Phylis and nurse Hart heard her cry and rushed back into the room, acting protective. With all the pandemonium, reality re-entered Mike's room, like a door being kicked in by Arnold Shwartzanegar.

Phylis picked the shrieking child out of the baby seat and made soothing sounds to comfort her. Nurse Hart looked sternly at Mike and asked kiddingly, "Did you scare this child?"

A defensive Mike shrugged and felt a bit embarrassed by it all. The two women continued to soothe Amnion, and stare accusingly at bad old Mike.

After a few moments the women finally decided to let him off the hook and smiled. Mike felt relieved that it was only a put-on, but Amnion's irritation continued to trouble him.

Phylis's motherly attention seemed to calm the little babe, and the babe finally wound up cradled, face down, over Phylis' forearm. It was a strange position, as it always worked for this child.

There was this tremendous feeling of relief in the room once peace was restored to the little girl. All seemed right with the world again.

The bandaged Mike asked that he be allowed to say goodbye. Phylis brought her over to his side, while he stared into Phylis's moist reddened eyes Mike planted a tender kiss on Amnion's tiny soft forehead. Desperately, he tried to breathe in that baby powder-newborn smell one last time, and said with a rough Humphrey Bogart imitation, "Here's looking at you kid."

Mike quickly filled with emotion again, and with a bit of clumsiness he tenderly patted her diapered bottom with his bandaged hand as Phylis drew her away.

Phylis observed Mike's gesture and could feel their bond tugging at his heart. She began to sniffle as she passed the baby over to the nurse. Nurse Hart tried not to look into the eyes of either Mike or Phylis lest she also would start to cry. She busied herself by gently placing Amnion back in her child seat and then spirited her away.

Phylis stayed behind to comfort a forlorn Michael. She sat down next to him and wiped his anguished face with a damp cloth, choking back her own tears. "I'm proud of you Michael," and kissed his brow.

CHAPTER 82
Redemption

A few days later, outside the courthouse, the city air was cool and fresh - a crisp hint that winter was not far away. For this secret proceeding, there were no more screaming activists outside on this clear and bright Sunday morning. No agitated strangers fighting amongst themselves trying to make a partisan point. No signs and placards to blot out the view of the brilliant orange and yellow treed park across the street. No politicians competing for media exposure. No violence. No police. No buzzing of black drones. No television cameras and satellite dishes. Nothing to demean or trivialize a human life. Only peace and quiet.

It was a wonderful day to be alive.

Inside the courthouse, Amnions dainty fingers clutched Maria's cotton blouse and seemed to be intrigued by the flickering glow of a plain gold crucifix dangling in the cleavage between her mother's silky-smooth breasts. Secure in her surroundings, she gazed up at a gentle oval face. Amnion was comfortable now, cradled snugly in the arms of a woman who seemed to radiate every human kindness. And the little girl knew, some how, some way, this was 'mommy'.

In such close proximity, Maria's facial features filled Amnion's entire field of vision, occupying her attention completely. Everything beyond was a meaningless blur, every other distant sound inconsequential. Maria's gentle words fell as softly as a snowflake on her little, willing audience - the exact meaning of the words inconsequential when compared to the subtle inflections of her mother's soothing voice. All emotion and caring is expressed simply without need of language translation. A warm smile brought instant reciprocation, instant love, instant gratification. The growing bond that can survive all the tragedies and separations society can devise. The enduring and uniquely human attachment that will last a lifetime.

A little girl was home. Home was any place this mother of hers happen to be. This was Amnions long sought security. Finally, her own sense of family. This is where she always belonged, and never knew. No understanding of where or why she had not always been there. Simple fulfillment.

From that innermost perspective, all Amnion ever really wanted out of life was to be loved and give love in return. And, now that tender world was hers to have.

Still, some pleasant memories of Mike and Nurse Hart as 'mother' lingered, now rapidly fading, as her brain constantly rewired itself. It was the here and now that she lived for. This woman, now the sole object of her innermost hopes and dreams.

* * * * * * * *

Inside, Judge Burger called the courtroom to order to begin this brief, clandestine hearing. He picked Sunday morning, because the courthouse building would be devoid of everyone except those involved in this proceeding. No workers, no police and no media. It was the moment he had been anxious to reach ever since the case of this baby, Amnion, had first reached his bench. The media had been hounding all the trial participants round the clock. So, everyone had to sneak out of their houses before 5 AM.

Gathered below his bench in a small semi-circle, stood a pleasant looking group of happy smiling faces. There was Evon and Richard Farmers, Mister and Mrs. Alvarez, Mike and Phylis, and, of course, Amion. She was dressed in a white dress with lace trim. And, probably by now, uncomfortable as all hell.

There was a formal atmosphere, the men dressed in jacket and tie, women in full dresses. Mike was up and about, still uncomfortable, as he tugged at his collar. He was bandaged over his nose, and his skin itched under his taped ribs. Phylis held his arm tightly and gingerly in case he needed support.

There was an excitement in the air. As if something monumental was about to happen.

In the festive atmosphere the judge looked up and quipped, "This must be a Christening."

The spectators in the gallery laughed, the normal formality of the courtroom taking on a more congenial manner. Most were either family, neonatal hospital workers, or friends. Many of their own children were in attendance

Richard came forward and presented all the properly executed adoption documents to the court clerk, who in turn presented them, with his approval, to the judge. Richard had also arranged a trust fund from all the online money contributed to the court fight in her name. He submitted that paperwork also.

Judge Burger took a moment to retrieve his spectacles and check the forms for proper signatures. After a few minutes he called the Alvarez couple forward and leaned over his bench top to address them. Maria looked up with Amnion nestled in her arms, her eyes filled with tearful joy. "The State of New York," he spoke loudly, "And, guardians have no further claim to this individual, and awards custody of the child Amnion a.k.a. Amy Santino, to the adoptive biological parents, the Alvarez family." Then paused and asked, "What will the child's legal name be?"

Maria looked to the side at Mike and Phylis standing there and announced, "My baby... daughter... my sweet little lamb. Her name will be Michelle Felicia Alvarez after the two people who cared enough about her to save her life."

The judge instructed the name be entered into the court record then stood up and leaned forward with a broad smile, "God bless you and your mother, little Michele." He sat back and removed his spectacles adding, "God bless all of you. I wish that all of you live long and healthy lives."

The old judge banged his gavel, "These proceedings are closed."

The gallery instantly lit up, cheering and applauding, as the small group around the judge's bench, shook hands and shared embraces. In the gallery children clapped and jumped up and down on their toes. Even Judge Burger came down and around from his bench to shake everyone's hands. A family member with a video camera was running around trying to record everything. Amnion's siblings came over to Maria to greet their new sister, Michele.

People who didn't know each other poured champagne and celebrated together. The young and the old, one generation in concert with the other.

That was part of what this was really all about - harmony in the respect for the sanctity of human life - at any age, in any condition. A battle had been fought and won for one simple life.

Amidst the celebration, Richard walked over to the windowsill where the oak tree seedling, the one he used during the trial, with broad leaves it was now flourishing at about a foot tall. He returned and presented the plant to Michele's father saying, "Plant this in a special place by your home. It will remind you of the strength Michele has shown these past months."

Mike wandered through the jubilant crowd towards Maria, the woman that up until now he'd always held in contempt for giving up her child in the first place. Seeing Amnion in her arms, he could still feel, deep down inside, that she was holding his little girl. He took in a deep breath of resignation and walked over.

Oddly enough though, he liked the woman immediately. She had that appealing quality of a devoted, compassionate woman. The special something missing from today's modern woman. Something lost from the generations of women before. The kind of lady you marry and cherish for the rest of your life. And her family seemed like honest, real people. The kind that worked hard, loved each other, and pulled together in hardship. The kind of people you never hear about - his kind of people.

Mike leaned over and kissed Maria's soft smooth cheek, looking at Amnion close up for, maybe, the last time. He presented her mother with a folder containing copies of photos he'd taken all through Amnion's gestation in his basement and then at University Hospital neonatal.

"I thought," he said, "that someday, you might need to fill in the gaps you missed."

Maria had no animosity towards Mike or Richard for keeping her baby's identity from her all this time. The little girl had received the best medical care and loving concern every child should have. From her religious perspective, God and these people had not only given her daughter a second chance, but also given Maria her own kind of second chance.

She kissed Mike back, grabbed his wrist, and asked him to stay close there for a moment. Maria turned around and whispered something in her husband's ear. Then her enthusiastic spouse stood up on a chair.

"Hey! Every one! Silencio!" he shouted and waved his hands above the noisy crowd.

The loud din in the courtroom quelled and her husband shouted, "I want to tell you all something." He glanced downward at Mike and Phylis standing together arm and arm, and pointed at them. "These are the Godparents of my daughter, Michelle. They are my friends. They are my family too!"

Mike and Phylis were pleasantly startled as everyone cheered and applauded. For the first time since taking Maria's fetus, Phylis felt the lifting of an ancient weight from her conscience. The haunting guilt of all she'd done while working for Lifespan was gone. She was redeemed. In a queer way, saving one simple human life seemed to make up for all the others lost.

For Mike's part, he was overjoyed. It meant this would not be his last time with Amnion. He would get to see his little girl grow up after all.

Although the Judge insured that no media would be present, there was one reporter allowed in on this celebration. The one from the *Brooklyn Daily News*, the one that helped Mike and Amnion's cause. Amid the frivolity, the reporter walked over to Mike and shook his hand, introducing himself. This was the first time the two had actually met in person.

"So," he said smiling, "you're the mystery man." Noting Mike's bandages he quipped, "Still a bit banged up too."

"Yeah, sometimes making news can be bad for your health," Mike grinned. Then he introduced the reporter to Maria, Phylis, and Michele.

The news reporter couldn't resist interviewing the natural mother. "You've been through quite a revelation, Mrs. Alvarez. First loosing your baby, and having it go through Lifespan. All these months being in someone else's possession." Then he asked his leading question. "Are you upset by that?"

The smiling Maria hesitated a second almost puzzled by the question. "I can only feel gratitude," and in a two-sentence reply, said, "Mi bebé, my lamb, was lost. Now she is found." The issue was really that simple to her.

The disappointed reporter scribbled in his notebook, "no animosity – no story." He excused himself and took Mike by the arm to a corner of the room. Mike didn't know what to make of this, staring back at Phylis, and went along.

"My editor," the reporter started with a hand on Mike's shoulder, "he wants an exclusive on your story."

Mike took the reporter's hand off his shoulder, and politely smiled. "It's not for sale."

The reporter put up his palms, "I know, I know. So, how does a hundred thousand dollars sound?"

"Sounds like a lot of money."

The reporter thought Mike's reticence might be a negotiation tactic, and replied, "I can go to 200 grand for an exclusive. But that's it!"

Mike laughed saying, "Save your breath."

"I don't understand Santino. We're talkin' big money here."

"I'll make it simple," Mike insisted. "It's not my story to sell."

Then Mike pointed at the baby across the room. "She did the suffering. She had the fear and pain. She did the fighting back from oblivion."

The reporter remained undeterred, "So, I should make my deal with the parents?"

"You know," Mike answered impatiently, "Every time somebody does something that makes news, you think they have to cash in on it."

"That's the common measure of everything these days, Mike. The public eats it up."

"I don't care. This is one tragic story that has a happy ending, even without everybody getting rich."

"How do you measure victory without a dollar figure?" the pragmatic reporter replied, alluding to Lifespan avoiding the court judgment.

Mike had learned by now, of the two-sided nature of the news media, and their ability to do tremendous good or tremendous harm - sometimes simultaneously. He decided to end the conversation with. "Why don't you just put a dollar figure on a human life yourself," he curtly answered and walked away from the frustrated reporter.

* * * * * * *

It took some time to move the crowd of well-wishers out of the courtroom. A Christening party was arranged for 2 weeks from now. A disappointed Mike originally had planned to have Amnion Baptized by Father Tom in the NICU. That opportunity passed with Father Tom's demise. So, a Christening date had been set 2 weeks from now. For the time being a baby shower party for Michelle Felicia Alvarez was arranged across town, that all would attend. In fact, so many people wanted to come; it was going to take a large catering hall to handle them all.

After the crowd left for the party, Mike, Phylis and Richard stayed behind, sitting outside in the bright morning sunshine at the top of the deserted courthouse steps overlooking the park and its autumn foliage. They spent a somber quiet moment remembering those who were not here to celebrate victory - Joel Rosen - Father Tom - all the human fetal lives that didn't make it out of Lifespan. All those little people in the lab that simply 'were' for a brief moment - never had the chance to breathe the same fresh air of today.

Mike asked Richard what he planned to do now. Now that his old law firm partners had voted him out of their partnership - too many of their wealthy clients were on Lifespan's side. The backlash of the lawsuit decision was horrendous.

Richard hesitated and looked down at his feet before answering. He remembered Mike's aversion to the legal system, and his conclusion that justice is never really served by it. Avoiding Mike's eyes he stared into the distance. "It ain't over Mikey."

"What do you mean, "Mike quipped.

"We won in a civil suit – monetary." Richard sadly replied. "Not a criminal suit. So no one is going to jail for a crime. And, I haven't heard of one government enforcement agency move against Lifespan or decoupling. Too many rich and influential people don't give a rat's ass about some obscure fetus, when their health and longevity are at risk. I expect Lifespan will appeal in State Appellate court with their liberal judges. We'll get overturned, and have to fight this all the way back up to the U.S.Supreme Court.

"Geez," Mike said, noticeably disappointed.

"Worse yet," Richard added, "The wealthy media has been attacking us nonstop on almost every channel. And, interestingly enough all the civil rights organizations are taking a backseat to the issue."

"What do we do?"

"Well, the Lifespan appeal will commence in a few weeks. We continue the fight. And, Max Brewster is somewhere out there, putting money together with his investor friends, trying to set up the next decoupling operation."

"Not for too much longer," quipped the enigmatic Mike.

No one other than Phylis could really understand what he meant, or placed any great significance to his statement.

Then Evon came out to join them and sidetracked the conversation. Mike, Phylis, and Richard stood up and shook hands, and everybody hugged each other.

Richard broke the silence, saying, "You know, I still can't believe you dragged me into this."

Mike smiled and answered, "Admit it. You dragged yourself in. Once you saw my little girl. Once you knew the truth of what was at stake."

They embraced one last time before departing. Still shaking hands Mike and Richard stared at each other for a moment. The years of two separate lives apart after college had melted away. For that instant they were just two Americans, united in the last great fight for human rights.

Richard embraced Phylis and said, "Bon Voyage".

As the couple turned to leave, Evon said, "You two should keep a low profile for a while. Get out of town. But, you make sure you come for dinner when you come back."

Mike and Phylis stood still and waved goodbye, watching their newfound friends walk down the steps and disappear around the corner.

To Phylis's chagrin, Mike sat back down on the cold granite steps again, overlooking the park across the street. Leaves rolled gently across the park lawn, making her think how many human lives literally just pass unnoticed in the wind. Blown away.

It was down to just the two of them alone again under a brilliant blue sky. Phylis didn't quite understand why they weren't leaving for the party too. Why Richard said 'bon voyage', like somebody was going on a boat trip. And then there was Evon's comment about dinner when they get back. *Back from where?* Phylis asked herself.

In a quandary, she dutifully sat down alongside her man, and put her arm under his arm. She leaned her head gently on his shoulder. The chaos of the world seemed distant now. Mike sat silent for a while, reflecting on all that happened. In reality, what he was actually doing, was speculating about Max Brewster's health. How this indispensable entrepreneur would soon be just another expendable dead person. Wondering how long it will take the radium to begin its poisoning effect. He also pondered how long it would take his legion of personal physicians to get him X-rayed. Their initial diagnosis would probably be side-tracked by his Lifespan drug treatments. Then he wondered, what would they make of Maxes illness, when his radiation lights up under X-ray - like a Christmas tree?

He'll probably try to buy up every organ transplant imaginable, Mike concluded to himself. These thoughts left Mike strangely unemotional, almost clinical about Maxes demise - the same detachment as Lifespan and its scientists felt about fetal lives. There was no anger left in Mike's heart, but there was the realization that for every selfish, unethical bum like Max, there were millions of others just like him. People that use the term 'business' to hide chicanery, and 'state license' as their justification to legally steal someone else's future. People in positions of wealth and power that continued to infect the human species. A tyranny against mankind itself. And, a disappointed Mike knew, he could never get them all.

Phylis drew closer and snuggled up to the subdued Mike, resting her cheek on his shoulder and putting her arm around his taped ribs. In the breezy silence of the courthouse steps there was almost a feeling of letdown. So much emotion happened today, after so many months of stress, and at times, near terror. What a price she had paid to have a man again, and what a wild one at that. Looking to the future, everything should be a 'piece of cake' now. Everything would be so predictable from here on - hopefully boringly repetitious.

While she daydreamed of that tranquil time, a gray limousine silently pulled up to the curb at the bottom of the courthouse stairs. Phylis hardly noticed it park below them.

She turned to her man and finally asked,"So, where do we go from here, Santino?"

He turned to look at the graceful feminine features of her face with a gleam in his eyes. "Well wifey. We've been married a few month's now..." Then he helped her up, and placed his bandaged hand under her chin. "...

and I haven't done anything for just you yet." Leaning slightly, he kissed her ever so softly on the lips. Phylis's face grimaced from the prickly stitch on his lips.

Slowly, they walked down the granite courthouse steps, while a well-dressed limousine driver came out of the car. He looked up at them with a smile and gave a little salute, then opened the rear passenger door.

A startled Phylis laughed, "We're going to the party in this?"

Mike stopped at the car door saying, "No. Not quite pal ...We're leaving for our honeymoon in this!"

Adding to the surprise, Mike and Phylis' children suddenly appeared out of a car that pulled up behind the limo. They all piled out, and ran over to kiss their parents goodbye.

Phylis was totally flabbergasted, and shouted in rapid fire, "Where are we going? Who's going to watch the kids? I'm not packed!"

Everyone laughed at her confusion. Her son, Mark, shouted out, "Don't worry mom it's all arranged. Here's your passports!"

Phylis hugged her children, still spewing out questions, "Where are we going Michael? How long?"

Mike was his usual inscrutable self and chuckled, "You'll find out.... when we get there."

"What about the party? People expect us there."

Her daughter Kristy answered, "They already know you're leaving!"

Phylis couldn't believe how everybody knew about this but her. How well kept this whole secret had been.

In the exhilaration of the moment, Mike ignored his injured ribs, stooped over, and swept her off her feet, holding her like a feather in his strong arms. Gritting teeth from his injuries, he carried her to the car doorway, leaned in, and placed her gently on the back seat with a kiss and a slight grunt.

"Don't say I never carried you over the threshold!" he said. Then he popped in a memory stick into the backseat USB port and turned up the volume. The jumping Motown sounds of Jackie Wilson singing 'Higher and higher' filled the back seat and street beyond.

> 'Now once I was lost and downhearted,
> Disappointment was my closest friend.
> When you came, trouble soon departed,
> And I've never seen his face again.'

Inside the car Phylis looked out at his grinning face still under some bandages, as he sang with the music. She could not help smiling and crying at the same time. He was still the hopeless romantic clown she fell in love with.

For just an instant she sat back in her seat, isolated from the rest of her family, behind the tinted glass of the limousine. She reflected on Mike's humorous website posting that started her on the road to so many new challenges. Maria's unsettling decoupling several months ago. Once just a numbered specimen, now a little girl with a mother, a family, a name ...a newborn life. How a few innocuous decisions made a short time ago, led to the unbelievable impact on so many lives. The changes in her own convictions - about so many things. And, finally, God help her, the future still seemed so uncertain. It left her wondering what adventures still awaited with this unpredictable man of her dreams.

www.ingramcontent.com/pod-product-compliance
Lightning Source LLC
Chambersburg PA
CBHW021212260626
47172CB00002B/390